To Katie

MW01534315

Flight into Fate

and

Flight into Destiny

Thanks for getting On Board

By

E. K. Barber

E. K. Barber

PUBLISH AMERICA

PublishAmerica
Baltimore

ISBN: 1-4241-6307-2
PUBLISHED BY PUBLISHAMERICA, LLLP
www.publishamerica.com
Baltimore

Printed in the United States of America

To Ken
Love at First Sight doesn't just happen in books!

Acknowledgments

Thanks to the readers who will recognize in the following pages their suggestions: Kim, Carol, Maureen, Marlane, Judy, Erin, Hazel, Michelle, JoAnne, Eric, John, and Terri. Initial edits were completed by Ms. Barb Estervig and Ms. Kristen Beach. A special thanks to Mary Kay Gottschalk and her own real life hero Bob, who did an extraordinary job!

Professor Elaine Estervig Beaubien(www.elainetrain.com) is an award winning educator, an experienced corporate trainer, an accomplished speaker, a published writer and a successful entrepreneur. She is a member of the tenured business faculty of Edgewood College and is CEO of Management Training Seminars. As a corporate trainer, her clients have been as diverse as Harley Davidson, the Peabody Hotel, St. Mary's Hospital, the State of Wisconsin, Bayer, and Rayovac. Having met all of her personal and professional goals, she semi-retired and moved into other areas of interest. Some would say Elaine completely jumped the track when shed her briefcase, PowerPoint presentations, and class notes and became...E. K. Barber, writer of romantic fiction. Writing under the pen name of E. K. Barber (www.ekbarber.com) to protect her polished, professional persona, Professor Elaine Estervig Beaubien continues to teach business and consult with corporate clients by day...and by night she sits tapping on her laptop. By day, marketing, supply and demand, leadership...and by night love, lust and intrigue. From the corporate boardroom and college classroom to the world of romance and suspense...from the pragmatic and practical to the provocative and romantic. Now that is a paradigm shift!

Flight into Fate

CHAPTER 1

"Fate dictates the meeting of hearts when that meeting is random and unexpected. Recognition pulls the individual souls to a shared journey. Love has them moving as one toward their combined destiny." Samantha Jayne

Deep underground in the Euro-Disney complex near Paris, two characters were suiting up for a very important assignment.

"Adventureland has better costumes," grumbled Aladdin a.k.a. Special Agent Alexander Springfield as he donned the vest and pantaloons that would transform him into the hero of the Disney classic.

"The meet is set up for Peter Pan's Flight. That's in Fantasyland." Special Agent Skyler Madison worked on getting into her own costume. They were a team and they were on assignment. They were also engaged and would, before the end of the year, become the department's only husband and wife team in the field.

"This sure is nothing like any fantasy I've ever had," said Alex frowning at the little gold vest. "If I were in Adventureland, I could be Indiana Jones…a heroic, manly intellectual. Instead, I look like a damn belly dancer."

Skye laughed as she glanced over and possessively took stock of his tall muscular body. A lot of it showed underneath the loose shirt and vest and she thought it made him look hot as hell. His magnificent blue eyes defied an Arab ancestry, but otherwise he looked like a very sexy desert chieftain.

"Being characters is great cover, Aladdin. We're perfectly disguised and can casually wander around forever without looking out of place. It's an ideal operational situation."

"I'm not going to wear those shoes." He scowled down at the slippers with the long rounded toes. "They look obscene."

"Actually they're called pigases, pigache in French. You have to wear them. They're regulation."

"How do you know these things?" Alex admired his partner and future wife's command of trivia, but sometimes it could be annoying. Not as annoying as the absurd slippers, but coming on strong.

"I read the regulations."

"No, I mean the name of these things?" He held up Aladdin's regulation footgear.

"They're shoes aren't they?" Skye shrugged and gave him her 'that should be obvious' look. "I know shoes."

"Oh, yeah. Right." And he shot back his 'get a life' look. "The things I do for my country."

"To make the world safe for Mickey Mouse and Golden Arches."

"Christ, I feel stupid," he said as he stomped on the shoes. Standing in front of the mirror, he struck his best Arabian macho man pose...arms crossed over his chest, his legs spread apart. He was six feet four inches of muscular manhood and no costume could diminish his incredible charisma. He was handsome in the extreme and his appreciative audience of one stopped to admire what she saw.

"Darling, you look exotic and gorgeous. *Vous êtes un beau diable.*" Skye moved easily from English to French. She spoke five languages fluently and could pick up most conversations in any European tongue. Her mother worked for the state department while she was growing up and they were often stationed in the great capitals of Europe.

"Translation please?" frowned Alex.

"Handsome devil." Skye winked one of her sparking brown eyes.

"Ah. Well I don't feel like a handsome devil," he said turning toward her. "And you better stick to English, darling. You know French makes me hot. Say one more word and I'll want a piece of your fairy tail."

"Control yourself. We're on duty. No hanky panky between characters."

"Hanky panky?" snorted Alex. "You sound like an inhibited temperate spinster with issues."

"We're inside the Disney grounds. Everything gets a PG rating."

"But this is France. They have different rules when it comes to hanky panky." He extended the words hanky panky, saying them in a low, seductive voice, making them sound decidedly less PG.

Laughing, Skye tested his control. "*Nous serons postérieurs dans Paris à notre hôtel bientôt assez.*"

Alex looked over at her intently, then slowly started toward her. "I told you to quit talking French at me, now suffer the consequences, wench."

Moving quickly, Skye put a table between them. "I'm not a wench, I'm a virgin."

When Alex raised his eyebrows, she smiled wickedly.

"All right, so that's a stretch, but that's why Jim called in his best. I can pull off any role." Skye deliberately adjusted the bodice of her costume to cover more of her luscious curves. "Besides, Monsieur Beaulac speaks French and you don't try to jump him."

"Monsieur Beaulac is bald, fifty pounds overweight and only has three workable teeth. And what did you just say to me? I didn't catch it."

"I said we would be back in our hotel room in Paris soon enough."

"Will you order room service in French? Then read from the guide book while we wait."

"Yes, now finish dressing."

Sighing, Alex went back to his small pile of costume accessories. Skye had to hold back a giggle when he picked up the little hat and frowned.

"And don't scowl. If you go out looking like that, you may scare the tourists."

"How come Barclay doesn't have to play dress up? He could be Goofy or Dopey without even a stretch."

Barclay was their high-tech genius who was a little light on personality.

"He'll be up in the listening station, taping everything and making sure all the surveillance equipment works."

"Do I have to wear this wig?" He poked at the black wig wondering why all the male Disney characters had hair like Elvis.

"You've worn disguises before."

"Not that made me look like a cartoon character."

"Darling, you *are* a cartoon character. Just feel fortunate you were too tall to be one of the seven dwarfs. Although I think you could have pulled off Grumpy well enough," she said under her breath.

"I heard that."

"You were meant to."

"Why couldn't I have been Prince Charming or something? You once said I looked like Prince Charming. Besides he goes with Cinderella, doesn't he?"

"I'm not Cinderella. I'm the young and innocent Snow White." Skye looked over at him and batted her eyes.

"Young and innocent," he snorted. "Not in your lifetime."

"And just what do you mean by that?" Skye looked at herself in the mirror as she applied the ruby red lipstick. The costume really did transform her appearance. Her honey colored hair was tucked into a black wig and her endless legs were surrounded by a long skirt. Nothing could disguise her succulent curves and stunning face, however. It wouldn't be easy for her to pull off a virginal Snow White when she looked more like an exotic goddess. She was, however, a master of deception, an accomplished role player.

"Now, darling. I'm only saying that you wouldn't have waited for your prince to come." Aladdin grinned and considered his beautiful fiancée and partner. Leaning casually against a high table in the center of the room, he watched her expertly transform her lovely lips into a luscious red smile. He loved watching her. Loved everything about her, actually. "You would have gone in and kicked your wicked stepmother's ass, slain the dragon, flattened the witch, organized the seven dwarfs to act as your backup and gone shopping for a new glass slipper."

Laughing, Skye rolled her eyes. "I can see I'm going to have to brief you on the Snow White caper. You're getting your fairy tales mixed up."

"Well, didn't she have a prince charming, too?" He grabbed her around her slim waist and pulled her to his nearly bare, well-sculpted chest. His intense blue eyes looked into her chocolate brown ones and held. She felt the connection, familiar but forever exciting. Her heart thrummed beneath the demure bodice of her costume.

"I could kiss you and end the spell or curse or whatever the hell plagued her," he said in his low, compelling voice.

Little shivers in the pit of her stomach added another few watts to the already heavy electrical charge vibrating through her. But then the dedicated, disciplined special agent kicked in and put the brakes on her racing hormones. Skye sighed with exaggerated regret and put her hand on his hard chest.

"Darling, you've already done that. Now, don't kiss me or I'll have to redo my lipstick. When Jim approved your strategy for us becoming a team, I'm sure he trusted you to keep the personal out of the professional." Smiling, she ran her finger down his torso where his open shirt revealed skin, going a little soft in the knees when she felt his response. "I'm going to need my legs for this operation and you're beginning to mess with their ability to operate effectively. We can play Snow White and Prince Charming later…when we're alone."

"I think I'd rather play James Bond and Pussy Galore later, if it's all the same to you." He looked into her beautiful brown eyes and saw she'd be ready and willing for anything later. It took all his discipline and training not to dive into the luscious lips that were only inches away from his. Knowing they were his and would be his for the rest of his life gave him patience and the extra bit of steel he needed to resist. "Seems to me every fairy tale ended in only one chaste kiss." He gave her a quick peck on the cheek. "I don't think I want the day to end like a fairy tale."

"Oh, I don't know. I rather like that 'Happily Ever After' bit."

"Doesn't this Aladdin character have a girl friend?"

"He does. A very exotic woman named Jasmine. It was love at first sight."

"And he was wearing this stupid costume?"

"I think you look completely erotic in it. Very sexy. I'm going to have to scrape the young French women off you." Her hands ran under his shirt and over his chest. Then she planted a ruby red kiss right over his heart like a Snow White brand. "I'd be more comfortable if you had Kevlar here instead of a bare chest." Her fingers unconsciously went to an old scar on his shoulder and a cloud flashed over her face.

"Are *you* vested?" he asked softly, taking her hands and kissing the tips of her fingers.

"*Touché monsieur,*" she sighed. "No, I'm not. There's tremendous security here. No one should be able to bring in a weapon."

"You know from personal experience that there are ways to breach security."

Skye nodded. She'd been involved in a hijacking earlier that year in which several men had brought guns onto her plane…through a very secure area.

"Let's finish suiting up."

Together they picked up their weapons, chambered a round, flicked on the safeties, and placed them in strategic locations on their bodies where they were both hidden and handy. Armed and ready for action.

Skye checked the clock. "Our marks could be entering at any time. I want to wander the park and get the feel of the place. We should be able to go anywhere, but let's stick pretty close to Peter Pan. I'm not quite sure where they'll enter and what their movements will be prior to the meet."

"Just so we don't have to go into the corridor of horrors," said Alex, straightening his shirt as he headed for the door.

"Excuse me?" Skye followed him out into the elaborate hallway system that lead to the outside and the world of fantasy.

"I'm afraid I have to confess a deep seeded phobia, born of a childhood trauma. I'll go anywhere in the park, but don't make me enter the scariest attraction here."

"Phantom Manor?" she asked, smiling. Sometimes her man was just so adorable.

"No," he said giving an exaggerated shudder that really did make him look like a cartoon character. "The *Small World* pavilion."

"What?" Her eyes danced with humor.

"Let me tell you, even the thought of going in there gives me the jitters. Play that horrible, insipid, repetitive music in my ear and I swear, I'll reveal all the secrets I've sworn to die for, sign over all of my assets, and willingly give you the keys to my truck."

"Good God, not your truck. Tell me." Now Skye was laughing. The thought of Alex being that freaked out about anything tickled her.

"When I was a kid, we got stuck in the damn ride in Disneyland. We only went into the torture chamber in the first place because Rita begged us to. We'd just rounded the corner into what we prayed was the last room and our little boat stopped. We were in there…trapped…no way out…for over an hour." Alex put his hand over his heart dramatically and went on with exaggerated horror.

"Everything was broken except the piped in music. That song. Over and over again, as those dolls spun around. Joy. Happiness. Smiles. Cheerfulness. We were all completely cockeyed by the time we got out…even Rita. I swear I couldn't get that tune out of my head for a month. It was on an endless loop…bouncing off the interior of my skull. We probably should have sought therapy right away. You know, worked through our deep seeded angst. Because from then on, Rita had a weapon. She'd torture us by singing the song whenever she wanted to drive us mad. Sometimes she'd just very quietly hum the tune in the back seat of our station wagon and when I slugged her, I got the punishment.

"Then there were times when she was being just plain bitchy, she'd place herself barely out of my reach and sing the song over and over again. Even Dad would sometimes lose his cool." Blake Springfield was the even-tempered one in the family. Although he was a very well known district attorney and a tiger in the courtroom, he was a fun loving, good-natured man at home. Alex's mother, Wyatt, was a Chicago police captain and much more volatile.

"Don't worry, darling. Our mission should all take place outdoors. I think you're safe from terror and insanity. Now, shall we test our transmitters before we go out?" Back to business. But with an interesting tidbit stored away in her brain. "Barclay? Are you there?"

"Here, Skye. Are you there?"

Skye looked over at Alex and smiled. Barclay was one of hers. Brilliant, but a few bars short of a symphony when it came to human interaction. "I don't know. It depends on where there is."

"Huh?"

"Never mind, Barclay. I'm here."

"Okay. Good. That's good. Is Alex there, too."

"Here, Barclay," responded Alex.

"Okay good. Should we do testing, testing, testing?"

"No, no, no," said Alex, tapping the earpiece where Barclay's voice was coming in loud and clear.

"I think we just did, Barclay," said Skye, giving Alex a little punch on the arm.

"Oh. Okay. Harriet always does testing, testing, testing."

"That's because Harriet is a brilliant technician, just like you," said Skye tactfully.

Also, Alex thought, a little low on the human interaction scale. Must be the geek gene. "You bringing her to the wedding?" he asked.

"I…ah…I haven't asked her yet."

"Do you want me to?" asked Alex, smiling. He really did like the little guy and he was one of Skye's favorites.

"Ask her to your wedding? Aren't you going with Skye?"

Alex laughed. "Was that a joke, Barclay?"

"Huh?"

"Never mind. I mean do you want me to ask her for you?"

"Gosh, Alex. Would you? You scare her sometimes, but maybe if you e-mail her for me, she'll be so impressed, she'll say yes."

"I scare her? How do I scare her?"

"Barclay," interrupted Skye. "Why don't *you* e-mail her? I think she's crazy about you and is only waiting for you to ask." Actually she was sure of it. Every time Harriet knew Barclay was in the building, she took off her thick glasses. She ran into walls, kept walking into the maintenance closet and thought Faye Brunswick was Skye, even though she was a full six inches shorter and twenty years older, but Skye knew signs of infatuation when she saw them. She was taking Harriet to get contact lenses the following week. Her treat.

"You think?"

"I know."

"Excuse me," interrupted Linda. Skye could hear her smiling. "Do you suppose we could get back to business?"

"Just testing the equipment," said Alex. "Hey Linda, am I a scary guy?"

"It depends."

"On what?"

"On what button Skye pushed, of course."

There was amusement and affection in her voice. She'd been with Skye since the two of them were rookies and worked with her in the field whenever Skye was Special Agent in Charge. She was also one of Skye's attendants for the wedding.

"Anyway, I'd say the equipment works. Just remember to turn it off if the two of you get, ah…well, you know…amorous. We don't want to fry the equipment…again."

"Ah, man. I kind of like that part," said Barclay.

"Now that *was* a joke," laughed Alex giving Skye a wink. Barclay sometimes peeked out of his shell. "Hang on Barclay. Don't start the recorder yet. I'm going to give Snow White a big smooch, then we're going out and get the big bad guys."

He produced the tube of ruby red lipstick he'd palmed from the cosmetic tray, presented it to Skye, then gathered her in for a final, breath-stealing kiss. She decided to return the favor and deepened it…looking for buttons to push. Alex smiled down at her when they parted and blew out a breath. Buttons found, pushed and activated. He gathered in some discipline with the promise of more later. She grinned, took the lipstick, and drew on her mouth again while Alex wiped the red from his.

"If the toes of these stupid shoes hadn't been curled up before, they would be now," he said, his eyes flashing her a message…later.

"Hey good one," said Barclay in his ear. "That was a joke, right?"

Maybe there was a seed of a personality in there after all, thought Alex. And if there was, it was due to Skye's influence and leadership. She'd chosen him out of several compu-geeks at the department, put him into field operations, and made him feel like a hero as well as a genius. He'd throw himself in front of a bus for Skye. Actually, he'd probably trip and the bus would miss, but the sentiment was there.

"Is our backup in place?"

"All here and ready to come into the action if needed."

Alex and the local liaison had placed a dozen or so operatives around the perimeter to be sure nothing or no one got through.

Prepared, covered and ready for action, Aladdin and Snow White went out into the sunshine of a beautiful late summer day.

They didn't try to stay together, although they were in constant radio contact. Families crowded around the beloved characters and asked for autographs. As Skye had predicted, the young French women in Fantasyland seemed incredibly dense and needed Aladdin's constant assistance in finding the attractions that were right in front of them. He'd smile brilliantly and dazzle them while Skye translated in his ear, along with some pithy comments about turning down his testosterone.

For her part, Skye, a.k.a. Snow White, attracted a great deal of attention. Children seemed to particularly love her. So graceful and lovely. Skye stood nearly six feet and made Snow White larger than life for the children surrounding her. Many had never seen such a tall, beautiful woman. And her smile could melt metal. The papas were pretty impressed as well.

Then she spotted them. Time for action. The waiting and watching were over.

"Aladdin," she said under her breath, casually changing direction and moving quickly, smiling and waving at the guests, but not stopping to chat. "Suspect Alpha is at the entrance of Peter Pan. He's looking left."

"I see him. I'm closer. I'll take him, you keep moving around and find Beta."

Turning, she nearly ran right into him. She smiled and in perfect French asked if she could help him.

He merely glanced at her, shaking his head and dismissing her immediately. "Damn foolishness," he said in Portuguese. "Idiot French people."

Skye smiled at him and moved out of his way. He didn't realize she also understood Portuguese. She didn't speak it well, but she could easily translate. Interesting. It wasn't a language one heard very often and the accent didn't really sound European. As she did with all random facts she encountered when working a case, she filed it away for later.

"Moving with Beta," she said, while smiling broadly at a family near the entrance of the Fantasyland Railroad Station. Her movements were causal. Completely unhurried and natural. She moved from family to family, her peripheral vision having Beta in view at all times.

And there it was. The meet. The culmination of weeks of work. Alpha and Beta were within an arm's length of each other. Skye felt the adrenalin pulse through her. The end of the op was in sight. All the intelligence, planning, tactical maneuvering, and equipment came together for this incredibly satisfying finale. It all happened as she'd predicted and her team was in place and ready for the final act.

Alpha nodded to Beta, who walked over to him. Beta carried a backpack; Alpha had a slim envelope. The envelope would contain the numbers of the Swiss Bank account, already traced and frozen by Barclay. The team knew that the backpack contained several very sophisticated, very tiny tracking devices for missiles that could be used in attacking targets with incredible accuracy. Only a few governments had access to them and it was illegal in the extreme to sell them to non-sanctioned governments and never to individuals. They'd been stolen from a secure location in Arizona. The department had been on the trail of the thief and caught a break when they uncovered the buyer.

Skye could see Alex out of the corner of her eye. Alpha and Beta were between them. No escape. And from their body language, they didn't suspect the surveillance.

"There's a Delta. Repeat a Delta." Skye heard Alex's voice in her ear. The unknown, unpredictable twist in the plot had just happened and they would need to adjust accordingly. They both had extensive field experience and Alex easily spotted the third person. Probably a lookout or an individual brought in to create a diversion if necessary. "She's in yellow…standing next to the concession. Holding a bottle of water. Looks too cloudy to be water. She's watching our man."

"I see her." Skye moved in and passed the woman in yellow, turning and smiling broadly at her. The woman frowned and looked away. Definitely a third person. She just wasn't getting into the spirit of the place. "Looks like an accelerant. Damn it. You take her. She could do some damage."

"Ready?"

"Say *Abbra Ka Dabbra* and make my day." Snow White, her ruby red lips transforming into a very wicked smile and no longer looking so virginal, glanced over at the tall Aladdin.

"*Abbra Ka Dabbra.*" Alex moved behind the woman with the bottle and quietly and quickly took her out with a hard chop to the side of the neck. As she slumped, Alex gabbed the bottle. Catching the woman, he looped his arm around her shoulders. Smooth, efficient, silent.

"Sick woman," he explained to a few startled onlookers. "Fainted. Excuse me, please. Coming through." He went immediately to the Cast Entrance where the French authorities were waiting with restraints.

Skye went up to Alpha, grabbed the backpack, hit the startled man in the face, and whirled him around, taking all the fight out him with a strategic hit to the solar plexus. She moved him toward Alex who was coming back to their location. The contents of the backpack were the most critical asset right now and Alex needed to secure it. The men were secondary, although they intended to take them in.

She turned to get the other man, saw him recover his wits, reverse his direction, and start running. It was a good sign as far as Skye was concerned. When they ran, it usually meant they weren't armed.

"I have a runner. Take this guy and the merchandise and seal off the exits. I'll pursue." She pushed the man and the backpack into Alex's waiting arms then started after the running man.

"Damn it," she cursed under her breath as her skirts tangled around her legs. Snow White never swore and she was aware of several families staring in her direction. Whoops, she thought. She ripped off the billowing skirts, revealing a form fitting black leotard beneath. Unencumbered, she was able to pick up the pace. This was going to be a foot race and a hand-to-hand take down…two things on Skye's personal hit parade.

Her quarry darted around people, strollers, characters, vendors, and strategically placed food carts. Damn, for being so large, the guy was quick. There were no straight-aways and the path was so congested that it was difficult to use her long legs to full advantage. She could hear people comment as she tore out after her man.

"Wow, way cool!"

"Look at Snow White take off. Like a super hero or something."

"I didn't know she had a secret identity."

"What a performance!"

"I've been here several times and have never seen this show. Awesome!"

Several checked their programs to see what they called this exciting new addition to Disney's live action entertainment.

Skye steadily gained on the man. People seemed to get out of her way more cooperatively and she was in better shape. Finally, she jumped over a small fence like an Olympic hurdler, hopped on top of a picnic table, and propelled herself into Beta. He went down with a whoosh and broke her fall.

The big man recovered quickly, however and used his superior size to push Skye off his back. He was fighting for his freedom and he knew it. It made him strong and vicious, but it was just the way Skye liked her adversaries. She chewed up strong and spit out vicious. She loved close hand-to-hand and was more than up to the task of subduing her target. Her black belt in Tae Kwon Do made her world class before she could drive and combat was as second nature to her as squinting against a bright sun.

She'd have rather played with him for a while, but they were in a public spot and a crowd was gathering. Assessing his position, his size, and his vulnerability, she took him out with a brilliant well-executed side kick, followed by a combination punch, spin, and kick to his face and chest. When he went down, she straddled him, flipped him over onto his stomach, grabbed his arms, and snapped restraints on his wrists. Like a rider hogtying a bull in a rodeo ring and just as quick. Her breath was coming a little more rapidly from her sprint, but there wasn't a hair out of place on her black haired wig, nor a smudge on her makeup. Aladdin came up behind her and helped drag the dazed and semi-conscious man to his feet.

"May I help you with that Snow White?"

"Why thank you Aladdin."

Alex grinned and looked around. "Take a pretty bow and let's get this dastardly evildoer to a less public spot," he said as the group of tourists who had gathered around them applauded, whistled, and snapped pictures.

"Thank goodness we're nearly unrecognizable in all of this costume and makeup."

"Yes and everyone here thinks it's part of the show. Snow White transforms into Snow Storm, reveals she can fly, and takes out the witch's idiot, misguided henchman." He looked at all the cameras. "Linda will send in the sweepers to take care of the permanent records."

As Skye and Alex took Beta to the nearest employee's entrance, three people discreetly passed through the crowd with very powerful magnetic devices. Several disappointed tourists would find significant blank spots on their family vacation video, and pictures would be strangely black and blank. There was a little regret that other photos would be lost as well, but agents needed to stay in the shadows. Skye and Alex's work was covert. They couldn't have their pictures pasted in family albums or sold to the press. Not that any of the crowded guests would ever guess they just witnessed something newsworthy.

Their backup team, disguised as store clerks and concessionaires, followed them in. There was a celebratory feeling running through the group as they walked through the hallways. Both Linda and Barclay added their congratulations to the several they heard over the earpieces. A perfect takedown. Except for the surprise addition of a third person, everything went without a hitch.

"Let's move them together and see how they interact," suggested Alex. He liked to mix it up a little to see if anything perked. The time to do it was just after a collar, when emotions were high and their bravado was still pumping them up. He put perps together in an informal setting before the real interrogations began. Their expectations of success would be dashed. In their initial shock, they might reveal something of importance before they understood their true predicament. Sometimes there would be a falling out and high temper could be very revealing. Of course, he and Skye would be listening in.

Alpha, Beta, and Delta all sat restrained on the floor with their backs against the wall. The bottle the woman carried was carefully placed in evidence. A quick field inspection revealed it was filled with a highly flammable liquid and would have done a lot of damage if ignited. It had a little wick and they found a lighter in the woman's pocket. Amateurish, but potentially a very effective and deadly diversion.

Alex made a show of leaving them to talk and went over to speak to the French liaison. Skye strategically placed a listening device in the jacket of the man she tackled. As adept as she was at picking pockets, she was equally skilled at putting something into one. Voices were coming in loud and clear into their earpieces.

"I think these three and the woman in the car outside the gates are probably it. I don't think we have a real refined group of terrorists here. Their meet was well planned and would have been seamlessly executed, but the bagman leaked all the way giving us the information we needed to stop them," said Alex.

Actually, the thief and traitor had a very sophisticated and well-hidden Internet network along with an extremely complicated ciphering code as double protection against outside detection. The Justice Department would never have found the trail or translated the messages once they did if it weren't for the department's even more sophisticated weapon…Skye's fourteen-year-old sister Sloane. Sloane was a card-carrying genius with an official IQ of 235, although everyone suspected she was just toying with the standard tests. She'd be finishing her Doctorate in Computer Science in the fall and as penance for hacking into some highly classified files the summer before, she'd been interning with the department.

A preliminary test of a new software package Sloane had developed to decipher encrypted messages using key words had uncovered the communications between the buyer and the seller. It was a stunning discovery. The test ended abruptly and the immediate universal installation of Sloane's package was authorized by the Director himself.

"Those two," Alex went on, indicating the buyer and his accomplice. "Appear to be driven by idealism. They'll be tougher to crack. They wanted the merchandise for something and it couldn't have been good." The components had been missing for months and there'd been a great deal of anxiety over where they would end up. Weapons systems had replaced drugs in the high-end contraband market.

Skye let Alex handle all the details of who would handle the interrogations, where they were to be and how information was to be shared among the various law enforcement agencies. Linda was going to be staying in Paris to coordinate the questioning and extradition.

Skye observed the prisoners from a distance…watching their body language. It was obvious that each thought the other had screwed up…or worse yet, set them up. The seller positioned himself away from the buyers. It became clear that the woman was with the buyer and that she was some kind of leader. She was furious over what she interpreted as either incompetence by her colleague or treachery by the seller. Her eyes demanded accountability. Someone was going to pay for this monumental screw up.

Good, thought Skye. Angry people liked to vent. Criminals and terrorists seldom disappointed her and these three were no exception. The seller said little, but the buyers, thinking they were alone, talked rapidly in low voices. She translated as she listened to the exchange.

Skye recognized the language and made a mental note to have the departmental translators send her a transcript of the taped conversation to double-check her interpretation. Portuguese. She shifted her brain to try and get every word but she got only phrases.

"*Fale só em português.*" "Speak only in Portuguese, translated Skye mentally. They ranted at each other for a while trying to assign blame. She pushed the earpiece further in...she wanted to be sure there wasn't another accomplice lurking on the complex or something else she should know about immediately. At first Skye was just listening. Interested. Then things heated up. Fast.

"*Que horas são.*" "What time is it?

"*Quase tempo. Outra hora.*" Almost time. Another hour.

"*Bem é escondido.*" "It's well hidden.

"*Será uma explosão glorioso.*" "It will be a glorious blast.

"*Eles nunca saberão.*" They will never know.

"*Seremos vitoriosos.*" We will be victorious.

"*O mundo saberá nosso nome.*" The world will know our name.

"*É um mundo pequeno.*" It's a small world.

"*Eles nao nos pararão.*" They will not stop us.

Skye straightened and walked rapidly over to where they sat. Needing a visual confirmation, she stared right at them and had her answer immediately. She saw it on their faces. In their eyes.

The woman smirked, glanced at the clock on the wall, and looked away. Waiting for something. Counting the minutes to a moral victory. When she looked back at Skye, she couldn't hold back the subtle look of triumph. Her eyes said she won. They won. Damn.

Skye's smile came slow and it was both victorious and insulting.

"The world may not stop you, but I will. I understand Portuguese, you pathetic screw-up." She spun around to go into action once again, but not before she saw the shock and fury on the faces of the terrorists. Not just purchasers of a dangerous weapon system, these assholes were bombers.

"Alex, Barclay, Linda," Skye called in a calm but urgent voice they all recognized. Alex spun around and watched her stride out of the room. Linda and Barclay simultaneously said "here" in her earpiece. They knew that tone and were immediately alerted.

"I think there's a boomer in Fantasyland. Linda, alert the security forces. We need to activate the evacuation plan. Everyone out of Fantasyland first. Barclay, get the Paris bomb squad here, then patch us into a direct line with them. Alex and I will try to locate it. According to our prisoners here, we have time. They said an hour. Everyone check your watches and mark the time. 1:45. We'll work it until 2:30, then evaluate ourselves."

Linda came over the earpiece. "Skye. Are you sure you translated the time correctly? Maybe you should be getting out of there now."

"I'm sure of the translation. Also, the prisoners were waiting, but the tension wasn't high enough yet. We have time."

Her first inclination was to run to the bomb, not away from it and Alex was right behind her. He didn't question her translation or her assessment.

"Where is it?" asked Alex as they hurried back toward the entrance to the park.

She looked up at Alex. She couldn't help it. A small smile pulled at her mouth. He read her look perfectly.

"No. Please."

"Yes, darling."

"Oh God," Alex moaned as they burst through the doors and jogged toward the building with the bomb. "Maybe we could just let the bomb do its job." When she frowned, he said, "okay, okay."

As they hurried through the park, they noticed the employees of Disney quietly and firmly beginning to get people away from the buildings and out of Fantasyland. Well-organized and well-executed evacuation protocol. Didn't surprise him a bit. Disney had a well-organized plan for everything.

As they approached the front of the building where people movers were unloading and the line was being directed to the exits, Alex took a deep breath and steeled himself. He needed to fortify his courage, build up his ability to withstand torture, raise his threshold for pain and torment. When he knew he had an extra layer of mental and emotional armor, he followed Skye into the darkened interior of the *It's a Small World* pavilion.

"Anything more specific?" Alex asked looking around at the spinning dolls from every country. "The ride was endless as I recall."

"No, but I have a hunch. They spoke Portuguese. There are several countries whose population speaks Portuguese. Angola, Brazil, Cape Verde, Guinea-Bissau, Mozambique, and of course Portugal to name a few."

Alex just stared at her. "To name a few," he repeated. He was a worldly and well-traveled man, but this was pretty much news to him.

"The woman mentioned the Front for the Liberation of the Enclave of Cabinda, FLEC. Cabinda is a small tract of land separated from Angola by a section of the Congo. There's been a small, armed insurrection against the government for the independence of the Cabinda Province for years and since Angola's independence from Portugal in 1975 it's gotten worse. Terrorists are usually very big on symbolism. Therefore, I say we'll find the bomb under the Angolan dolls. This is all speculation, of course." All the time she'd been talking, her eyes swept the interior.

Speculation, thought Alex. More likely right on target. Everyone who had ever worked with Skye would take one of her speculations over a two-day computer search any day. Her mind was like a computer. Filled with facts, data, information, statistics, little details, and extensive experience. When she cranked up and made the connections, out came valuable conclusions and ideas. He loved to watch her brain work. It might not be as sexy as the packaging, but it was alluring even so.

"Okay, makes sense, but how do you know which one is the Angolan doll?" He looked around. They all looked the same to him.

"By the costume, of course," she said over her shoulder as she raced into another room of the building.

Barclay let them know he was recording everything and had FLEC up on his computer in case they needed any additional information.

Alex followed her, checking his watch. "Less than an hour now."

"Fine. We'll search for half that. If we find nothing we evacuate."

"Agreed."

They walked quickly through the building. Tourists were everywhere, getting off the floating people movers and walking through the exits in an orderly, calm manner.

Skye looked around. "Over there," she said, running over to the dolls from the African continent.

"Have I permission to look under the skirts?" asked Alex, as he joined Skye's search of the area.

Skye just snorted her response. Bent over, searching among the props and set, with her shapely butt in the air, she no longer sounded like, nor looked like Snow White. Alex had to look away and move to a different country in order to stay on task.

"Voila, my little genius. Here it is," called Alex and then he was all business. No more fooling around. This was dangerous. This was real. What he uncovered was a big chunk of plastic explosives and it had a timer. He conveyed this fact to Barclay, who forwarded it to the Paris bomb squad and the others standing ready in the command center.

Skye talked to the people in charge of the ride to heighten the sense of urgency and accelerate the pace of the evacuation. Alex took the time to study the mechanism.

"Very simple, very amateurish. But sometimes they're the most dangerous. More unstable, less predictable. Barclay, send someone down here with your computer repair kit, stat!" he said as he knelt down to take a closer look.

"Time on the bomb?" asked Skye, wanting to know how much she should push the timetable for evacuation.

He looked at the clock counting down. "43 minutes."

They had plenty of time. When Barclay himself came running in, the clock had 39 minutes left and Alex had outlined in his mind how he was going to neutralize the bomb.

"You going to try to disarm the thing?" puffed an apprehensive Barclay. Alex was his ideal man, but this seemed like something beyond his typical day in the crime fighting gig. Alex laid out the familiar tools like a surgeon preparing his instruments for a delicate operation.

"Yes. In the meantime, I want you and the rest of the team to go out with the evacuated guests."

"Guests?" Barclay looked around, clueless. He hadn't recalled inviting anyone.

"That's Disney talk for the tourists," explained Skye, her eyes on the bomb. She had complete confidence in Alex and didn't even question his decision to work on it. "I think the entire park should be emptied, but most particularly…Alex…radius?"

"At least 500 yards from ground zero," relied Alex after he got a better look at the size and dimensions of the explosive. Barclay lost all of his color, not easy to do for someone who was naturally pale as a ghost.

"I'll start packing things up. We'll move the crew out, but I'll stay with the communications equipment. You may need a consult." He'd run like a hound dog when he saw Skye and Alex running and not before.

"Okay. You can start by getting me patched into what ever bomb squad team they have here. I may need some advice."

Barclay nodded and was off.

"Linda. Have you been monitoring?"

"Yes," came Linda's calm voice. "Everything is proceeding here. We're taking the prisoners out. The woman has some very interesting ideas on what she'd like to do you and all of your offspring. She didn't take kindly to having her plans spoiled by a Disney cartoon character. I'll be working with park security on the evacuation. You just concentrate on what you have in there."

"Will do."

Skye knelt beside Alex. He'd already taken off the front panel of the bomb and was studying all the components. His hands were steady as a surgeon's and just as delicate. He worked efficiently, but didn't hurry.

"What can I do?" she asked him.

"Four things. Get me some light so I can look into the guts of this thing, keep the sweat out of my eyes, give me a countdown by minutes and promise me you'll run when I tell you to."

Looking around, she grabbed one of the hundreds of muted spotlights in the display. She freed the apparatus, removed the colored cover, and trained the bright light on Alex's hands. The illumination didn't waiver. Her hands were as steady as his. She called the time at 30-second intervals and periodically wiped his forehead.

"I feel like a nurse," she said.

"That's good, because I feel like a surgeon," Alex responded as he gently turned the screws to another layer of the detonator.

"Is this a terminal case, doctor?"

"Let's hope so." He continued his delicate operation. "Oh shit."

"Please don't say 'oh shit' when you're up to wrists in a bomb."

"Sorry…didn't mean to set you off."

"It's not me I'm worried about setting off."

"Got that. It's just that these morons decided that if one wire was good, five must be better."

"Are you still on it?"

"Absolutely. But as a backup plan, we'll take it down to 8 minutes, then run the 4-minute mile out of here. Agreed?"

"Agreed."

At 12 minutes Linda's voice came over the earpiece. "Skye, we have a malfunction on the Dumbo ride. There are about 15 people stranded in the air at various heights. They're bringing in a crane, but I don't think we'll make the 10-minute window. Barclay is saying that the bomb squad is on its way with a blast blanket and other containment equipment, but they're about 8 minutes from the entrance and it will be another 2 or 3 back to your location. This is getting very close."

"Understood. We'll stay until the last few seconds."

Alex glanced up. "I'll stay until the last few seconds, you'll still run at 8 minutes." She didn't respond.

"Skye…" His hands were still nimbly taking apart the timing mechanism but his voice was sharp and angry.

"Just keep working." Skye didn't intend to go anywhere. If he blew up, she wanted to be right beside him, not at some safe distance.

"Skye. You listen to me." He glanced over at her and she could see the anger in his flashing blue eyes.

"You die, I die," she said. "Simple. Now keep working." She looked at the timer. "10 minutes."

He didn't have the time to argue. The man in him wanted to grab her hand and run. But he was a Special Agent and there were still 15 people in the danger zone…17 counting the two of them. He went back to work, certain of his ability to disarm within the time frame. It really was an uncomplicated bomb. It was just that there were so many wires, so many layers.

He worked another five minutes and had all the wires exposed. Skye watched in silence, fascinated and confident. Continuing to hold the light steady, she saw at least a dozen wires that Alex had uncovered, stripped, and stretched.

"Okay, this is where the hero looks at the wires and agonizes over which one to cut," she said.

Alex smiled. "No agony here." He took a cutting instrument from Barclay's little kit and cut them all. Then he wiggled his fingers, stood up, and stretched out the aches in his legs. The timer stopped its relentless drive to zero. The danger was over.

Skye communicated the end of the crisis to everyone and could hear cheering over her earpiece.

"My hero," she said, standing up herself, feeling the stiffness in her knees and back, not to mention the sore shoulder from her flight into Beta. She hadn't realized she'd tensed up so badly until she started shaking out her fatigued muscles. She looked at the clock. "Two minutes and 45 seconds. Hot damn, Alex, you're good. In the movies, the timer goes down to the last few seconds."

"This is real life, darling." He blew a stray fake black hair off his forehead. "And as fast as those long, lovely legs are, two minutes would barely get you out of the blast zone."

"True, but I knew I wouldn't have to run." She was shaking out a cramp in one of those long lovely legs and missed the look of rage that materialized on Alex's face.

He looked down at her with snapping eyes. Now that the danger was over, and the bomb posed no threat, he was going to blow himself. While he was working on the bomb, he held himself in check but his fuse had now hit the TNT. His voice was low, but the tone was very, very angry. "And, since this is real life, Skyler, could you please tell me what the hell you're still doing here?"

Skyler. What the hell? He never called her that. She looked up at him and shone the light in his eyes, then smiled, choosing to ignore the dangerous sparks shooting through his furious glare. "I'm here to provide light. You needed an assistant," she said in a reasonable tone.

"I could have rigged up something non human. And what the hell was that 'I die, you die' bullshit," he growled between clenched teeth. He was trying not to shout, but his jaw hurt from the tension of staying reasonably calm. She could see the fury start in his eyes then flood onto his face.

Her eyes narrowed and she crossed her arms. "That's the deal." Now that the threat was neutralized, she realized that she was perfectly serious about that. She wouldn't want to live in a world without him in it.

The music filled the silence as they stared each other down. *"It's a small world after all…"*

The dolls were still spinning around them, merrily unaware of their near miss with oblivion. Their painted smiles mocked Alex as his temper simmered, then flared.

He thought about calming down and venting his anger later in the gym…maybe taking down a few punching bags or jogging about a thousand miles. Then he looked at the spinning dolls and decided not to. He cracked instead. Turning, he kicked one of the little dolls clear over the water. Reminded him of his football days when he and some of the other guys took turns practicing as the backup place kicker. There was enough velocity on the doll's head to clear the goal posts at 50 yards. Field goal, three points. The rest of the dolls spun around in apparent delight.

"Will someone cut that goddamn music? I can't believe it hasn't driven someone insane," Alex shouted to the ceiling at no one in particular.

"I think it just has," laughed Skye, her hands on her hips.

"No darling, it's you. You. You're driving me insane. What the hell did you think you were doing? I told you to run. Goddamn it, I wanted you out of here!" He kicked another doll and this one shot through three countries before landing on a twirling gypsy.

"And I told you no."

"My concern for your safety distracted me. What if that would have cost me an extra 30 seconds?"

"You'd still have two minutes and five seconds to spare." Skye's temper was beginning to bubble to the surface as well.

"That's not the point." He was in her face now, but she didn't back up.

"Then what *is* your point, Special Agent?" she shot back.

"When I told you to run, you should have cleared the building." He kicked another hapless doll to punctuate his point.

"You wasted your breath on that one," she shouted. "We're partners. You're not in charge of my actions. Now quit kicking the goddamn dolls."

"It's either these dolls or your ass," he sniped and deliberately, never taking his eyes from hers, kicked another doll and heard a splash as this one fell short of the shore on the other side of the small, small world.

Throughout their relationship, there were certain looks he should have recognized as the prelude to his own ass being kicked, but he was looking at her through a red haze and didn't see the quickening of her breath and the lethal glare she shot him. It turned even more toxic when he punctuated what he thought of her point of view with a slow calculated kick to the head of a hapless tyke spinning close by.

"I said stop kicking the goddamn dolls." And he didn't hear the low, clear snarl of forced control.

Gripping her arms, he pulled her toward him. "When I say run, Special Agent. You run."

Would he ever learn? It was a simple rule, but his mind wasn't on *How to Handle Skye 101*. First rule. Don't grab. Her automatic response was swift and deadly accurate. She pivoted and because he didn't have a grip on her designed to restrain, she slipped from his hands easily. Her foot was aimed perfectly to land in his abdomen. She knew it was as tight as a drum and she'd inflict no damage, leave no bruise. Besides, she decided on a shove rather than a kick. The force of her powerful shove, however, sent him backward into about a dozen gaily spinning cherubs in oriental garb.

"And I say you shouldn't have wasted valuable seconds calling me off, you self appointed, all mighty guardian of good over evil. Next time, Aladdin, *you* run." Snow White stood in high temper above him, shooting brown eyed sparks, while he was sitting in a debris field of smiling heads and crushed bodies. Around him, apparently completely oblivious and unconcerned were at least a hundred other turning, happy children of the world. The music was still being piped in, the sweet voices of global youth singing in perfect harmony. *"It's a small, small world."*

Alex jumped up and circled the love of his life. Rarely could she take him down twice. He lunged, she turned away from him, he compensated, she tripped him and he grabbed her waist, taking her down with him, as together they took out another whole country.

"A piece of that ass belongs to me, Cindrella and I mean to keep it safe." His grip on her wasn't firm enough to contain her as she elbowed him in the wind pipe and spun out of his reach. She was on her feet again in a breath looking down at him.

"We're partners, you son-of-a-bitching, psychotic doll kicker. We have equal status on this case. I'm not your fiancée in here. This ass should be no more important to you than the 15 guest asses riding around on Dumbo, the goddamn flying elephant. And I'm not Cinderella, you moron, I'm Snow White." When Skye was on a tear, there was no one who was in her league. "The one who picked up after seven, count them, seven slovenly miners, then slept with all of them including Dopey before riding off with her witless prince with a smile on her face and seven little notches on her broom."

Her hands were on her slim hips, her eyes were flashing. Alex's anger began to dissolve under the sudden rush of lust. Damn, did she have to be so magnificent when she was pissed? So hot? So desirable? How perverse was it that he wanted to take her around the world right now, right here on the smashed bodies of grinning mini-robots.

"All at the same time?" he asked instead. "She slept with them all at the same time?"

"Yes." When Skye's temper flared fast, it always faded fast. "Grumpy needed an attitude adjustment; she gave Happy something to be happy about; she got Bashful out of his shell and Doc needed a ladder, but size doesn't matter. Plus she found two more while she was cleaning and had them before breakfast."

"And they would be."

"Horny and Lucky." Her ruby red lips twitched.

Alex's anger fell away. She was just so beautiful…and…well…quirky. Besides, he knew she was right. If they were going to make this partnership work, he couldn't be distracted by his feelings for her. He worked to get himself under control then let out a quick ironic laugh. "Christ, I can't believe we're having this conversation in the middle of the ride from hell, dressed in these stupid costumes from some twisted ten year old's imagination and you just said size doesn't matter." He looked around, then back to Skye. "Damn it, never mind. Give me a hand, here," he said reaching up.

Sighing, Skye automatically extended her hand, but he wasn't through with her yet. *Alexander Springfield 101.* Grabbing her hand, he pulled her down. She landed on top of him with a whoosh, followed closely by an oath and a deep, throaty laugh. When Barclay, Linda, and the security forces of Disney came rushing in a few moments later, they found Aladdin making time with the virginal Snow White. Or at least her top half was the recognizable and beloved Disney character. The skintight leotard she'd stripped down to revealed a very non-virginal butt planted between the legs of Aladdin.

"Now there's a picture to put on a postcard," laughed Linda.

"Jeez. Did the bomb go off?" asked Barclay as he turned in a circle and noticed the destruction.

"No," said Linda with a chuckle. "I think Skye did."

"Jeez, what did he say to her? You have it on tape?"

"I think he was taking her to task for not running."

"Well then, I'm with him this time," said Barclay seriously nodding.

"You say that over here where Skye can't get you."

The head of security was a middle-aged man with an interested gleam in his eye as he looked at the part of Skye he could see. "The Snow White, she has a short fuse, yes?" he asked. He was admiring the beautiful butt and he liked emotional, volatile women.

"Always has," responded Linda with a laugh and looked at Barclay. "I think this tape will be one we should consider for the 'Best of Skye' album."

"I beg your pardon?" asked the confused and aroused security chief.

"Never mind."

"Why does that doll look like Elvis?" asked Barclay pointing to a little guy spinning with an Aladdin wig.

"I think Alex wigged out, too," said Linda still laughing.

"Huh?" Barclay was clueless, but was saved from another moment of confusion. Suddenly there was a beep from the bomb and a light went on near the face of the timer.

"Shit," said Alex, instantly alert and looking over at his dissected patient. It appeared as though it had come back to life.

Skye rolled off Alex and as one, they jumped up and immediately ran to the bomb, all business again. A team, running toward the danger.

"Evacuate, evacuate," Skye shouted. She snatched up the light as Alex bent over the device. People moved quickly out of the building. Linda worked on getting everyone clear, while Barclay went back to the communication center.

"Something is heating up again," said Alex as he studied the exposed mechanism. He gently turned it over to reveal another mechanical apparatus. "Barclay, patch me into the bomb squad."

"Right away," said the familiar voice. "Here they are."

"*Bonjour. Nous entendons vous mettez a l'amende.*" A deep, French voice came through their earpieces.

"*Faire vous parlez anglais, s'il vous plaît?*" Skye asked them to please speak in English. She didn't want to waste time translating for Alex.

"Yes, of course. I will speak English. This is Chief Couverture"

"Where are you?"

"Turning into the parking area. About 5 minutes from your location. There are many people out here trying to leave."

Alex came into the conversation. "I'm holding something here. Looks like a backup detonator."

"What was the first detonator?"

"Simple timer."

"The explosive?"

"Third grade plastic explosives."

"Second detonator?"

"Looks electronic. Activated by the failure of the primary detonator."

"Pull it out, monsieur."

"Repeat please."

"Pull out the detonator. But be very careful. The detonator is its own explosive device. It can take your hand off."

Alex shrugged. The guy was the expert and it made sense to him. He took hold of the detonator and carefully but quickly pulled it out.

"Now what."

"Is there water in the vicinity?"

Alex looked down at the river running through the attraction. "Plenty of it."

"Submerge it. Quickly. Get it away from the plastic."

Alex would rather have stuck the detonator up the butt of one of the spinning dolls, but he tossed the device into the water. It made a small, satisfying plopping noise.

"I noticed you did that with your right hand," smiled Skye as she sat back on her heels.

"Well, since I'm left handed, I rather people call me lefty if the thing went off."

She leaned over and gave him a kiss. "I've never made love to a one-handed man before."

"I could give you a hand," said Barclay over the earpiece. Skye and Alex looked at each other stunned. Was that a joke? They decided to find out.

"Was that a joke?" asked Alex, grinning broadly.

"I'm not sure. Linda told me to say it. But really. I'd be glad to give you a hand."

Skye shook her head and mouthed 'not a joke.' "I think we can go off line now Barclay. I hear the bomb squad coming in."

Alex wiped his hands over his face and ran his fingers through his hair, now restored to his own thick, wavy brown. As the bomb squad burst into the room, he mumbled. "Just in the nick of time. They can take care of the really bad stuff…like dealing with the media and the government officials. Let's fade, Snow White."

"As soon as you show them the bomb, we can get dressed and move on to the interrogation."

Alex stood up, pulling Skye with him. He kept her hand in his.

"Well done, Agent Madison."

"Why thank you, Agent Springfield. Same to you. It was a pleasure working with you."

Skye and Alex worked as Special Agents for the Intelligence Division of the United States Department of Justice. They'd been working the case in cooperation with French officials because the guidance system had been stolen in the United States. Their team worked in the shadows and behind the scenes, always in cooperation with local law enforcement but never officially connected. The final act of all their operations was to fade.

Skye took off her wig and shook out her curly, wheat colored hair. It transformed her back into the stunning, contemporary beauty she was. Alex was trying to show the chief of the bomb squad the explosives, but the man's eyes kept going to Skye's shapely legs. Some other members of his team were equally fascinated. When Skye stretched and her costume strained over her generous breasts, Alex gave up. They'd take it all in for analysis anyway.

"*Mécanisme* simple," said the chief, wanting to minimize the American's heroism in front of this stunning beauty. He inflated his singular charisma and turned to Skye. "So, Snow White. I think I'd like to take you through your part in this adventure. Perhaps over dinner?"

"Monsieur Couverture." Skye smiled noncommittally at the explosives expert. She recognized the type. Cocky, brash, bold, and confident. Skye supposed one had to be if a man made his living sticking his hands into explosives. This one was youthful and very handsome.

She said something in French. It better be a refusal, thought Alex. A scathing one. And how did that French pervert know she was Snow White? She only had on half the costume and he seemed to be obsessing over what was under it ever since he entered the building.

It was obvious to Alex that the man was lusting after Skye. He felt his hands fist and forced himself to relax. He'd only known Skye for several months and still wasn't quite reconciled to how other men looked at her. He doubted if he ever would be. This Frenchman had no way of knowing she was his fiancée, soon to be his wife. He wondered as he crossed his arms over his chest if she'd go for moving up the date of the wedding. Rolling his shoulders to release some of the tension, he tried to think like an agent instead of a lover.

It was almost working, but he could feel his blood boiling again when Monsieur Couverture threw his arm over Skye's shoulder and moved in closer. Goddamn it. Did the asshole have to be so free with his hands? And why was she so friendly with him, for Christ's sake. It was a professional relationship, after all. He knew what was contributing to the heat he was feeling in his chest. She was speaking in French. Casually flinging it around in general conversation. Distracting him. That was the language she usually reserved for love. For making love to him. To his ear it sounded so sensual…so intimate. He liked it when she whispered words to him when she was pliant and sexually aroused…when she was naked in his arms. The heat in his body was now being fueled by another source entirely. He cleared his throat.

"Sorry, Aladdin," smiled Skye, completely unaware of his jealous reaction and attributing the strain she was detecting to post op tension. He had, after all, just disarmed a bomb. Twice.

She still felt very jittery inside and hadn't yet had time to process the anxiety in her heart. God, he just went right at it. No hesitation, no thought. She had every confidence in him and his abilities, but he wasn't a munitions expert. What if there had been something about the bomb that was far more sophisticated than the simple apparatus he thought it was. Well, at least in this instance if he made a mistake, she'd be beyond caring right now. Her body bits would have mingled with his. She'd think about that later, right now she had an egotistical Frenchman to deal with. And to scrape off her side.

She smiled at Monsieur Couverture and said, "we'll speak English so our bomb expert here will be able to understand."

"As it should be. Monsieur…"

"Shultis. Richard Shultis," said Alex keeping his arms folded.

"Yes, as I was saying to Ms. Sharpee you did a competent job. It was a very simple device, but you saved many lives. And imagine a world without this attraction."

"It would be a small, small world," snorted Alex.

Skye, Linda, and the rest of his squad chuckled, but not Monsieur Couverture. He clearly wanted to be the alpha male, particularly with the luscious mademoiselle watching. He recognized another alpha dog on his turf and he was ready to bare his teeth. Being French, however, he'd do it with finesse and grace.

"Indeed, Monsieur Shultis." He looked at Alex's costume with disdain. It showed some very impressive muscle definition, but it was a silly sight. He thought he could score some points there. "You look like a belly dancer. Be careful or my men will start putting francs in your belt."

Alex glared at Skye who swallowed her smile and just widened her eyes.

"How long will you be in Paris, chéri?" He wanted her attention back on him.

"Not very long. Our work is nearly complete." She wasn't going to share with this local bomb jockey what their mission was.

"You will have dinner with me?" He gave her his irresistible, seductive smile. It worked on nearly every woman he tried it on and there had been legions.

"I'm sorry, Monsieur Couverture…"

"Claude."

"Claude. First of all, I have a lot of work to do. Secondly," she pulled out the diamond ring on a chain around her neck. It hadn't been an appropriate part of her Snow White costume so she'd stashed it under her blouse. "I'm to be married in October."

Alex smiled. He liked how the diamond flashed and sparkled. Impressive. He noticed the oh-so-macho Monsieur Couverture's eyes pop and was glad he'd moved the caret weight up a few notches. Take that you fop.

Claude hardly skipped a beat. Giving a distinctly French chuckle, he took up Skye's hand and kissed the palm. "That only means we'll have more in common chéri." He flashed a ring on the fourth finger of his left hand. "I have a very intimate restaurant I'd like to show you and afterward…well. You're in Paris. What the colonial doesn't know won't hurt him."

"No. But what he knows may hurt *you*," snapped Alex, fire in his eye. He usually let Skye handle her own brush-offs, and he would have this time as well, but it was the intimate gesture of kissing her palm that pushed all of his buttons. He was already on edge from his argument with Skye and his date with the bomb. French or not, kissing her palm was far too suggestive. That was his palm. And his pilot. There was a palm pilot joke in there somewhere, but he was too distracted to put it together.

"You would tell the fiancé, monsieur?" His eyes flashed back with challenge. He looked at Alex with contempt. "How indiscreet." And boorish, he thought. How American. He didn't notice that Skye had pulled her hand out of his.

"I *am* the fiancé, monsieur." It was hard to pull off superior in pantaloons and a little gold vest, but Alex tried his best.

Claude didn't appear in the least impressed. He just gave Alex his most incredulous stare. "I see. And in what fairy tale do you live that fantasy? Beauty and the Beast?"

Skye put up her hands. "Gentlemen. We have work to do. Claude, thank you so much for your offer. It's nearly irresistible. But I must decline. Monsieur Shultis, I suggest we change out of the costumes. They're no longer regulation and we wouldn't want to damage the reputation of the park, or disillusion any of the guests." With that, she spun around and walked out of the room.

Alex nearly punched Claude for the drooling look he gave her retreating butt, but he didn't want to deal with the paper work. "She's mine, asshole," he smirked with satisfaction. "*Le mien*" And followed her out.

Catching up to her, he could tell he was going to have to do some making up.

"That was more information than Claude needed to know, Dumbo," she said through clenched teeth.

"Hey you're the one who popped your rock out from between your breasts, Snow Flake. Maybe you should have let him go diving for it himself. His eyeballs were already making the journey."

"What the hell are you so steamed about? I was handling it."

"You let him kiss your palm."

"He's French for God's sake!"

"That entitles him to a body part?"

She just glared up at him, refusing to answer.

"Shit," he said, looking at her ridiculous costume combination. Virgin and vixen. Irresistible. How could he blame any man with eyes for staring? Appreciating. And she *had* pulled out her diamond. His claim on her. Suddenly the pissed off attitude faded and fell off him. What the hell. Monsieur la Clod may have tasted her palm, but he got the whole entire banquet. And he was getting in the mood to feast.

"So. What do the Italians get?" he asked. Turning her back, she wiggled her butt. He laughed and shook his head. "Then what do I get?"

"You're not a country."

"No, but I got a snazzy vest and some pretty fru-fru pants." Taking her arm, he turned her into him. He braced himself just in case she wasn't through with her mad. She surprised him though, and threw her arms around his neck.

"Then you're entitled to the entire package." Pressing her body to his she kissed him with entirely too much heat for a woman named Snow. His response, in turn, would have melted a glacier.

"Are you sure Snow White never got it on with Aladdin?"

"I'm positive."

"Maybe we can live a fantasy and write a sequel."

She gave him another kiss and pulled away. They really did have work to do. "Tonight," she said. "Tonight we'll channel all this excess adrenalin into a fractured fairy tale."

She looked up at Cinderella's castle as they made their way through the now deserted park. It was a little surreal.

"I've always had a fantasy of my own."

"Hey, now you're talking," said Alex with enthusiasm.

"I've always wanted to go to one of those old castles in Scotland. Not the modern day mansions or places that have been built to look like a castle, but something old and authentic. With huge fireplaces and drafts and suits of armor in the entryways. And ghosts. Genuine ghosts." She smiled up at him. "Maybe I was some kind of duchess or something in another life." Standing there with her hands on her hips, half Snow White, half Italian goddess, she couldn't have looked less like a duchess or something.

"Duchess, hell. You were a queen. Although right now you look like the vision from a deeply conflicted schizophrenic's dream of the perfect woman," he added.

She looked down at herself and laughed. "Shall we get back into civilian garb and do some blending?"

"Another costume change?"

"Exactly," Skye nodded. "We need to transition from Disney to tourist. Then once we're out of here, we can transform into our public roles."

"Damn. Three costume changes in one day."

"Four if you count naked."

"Oh I'll count that, all right." He took her in his arms and smiled into her eyes. *"Maintenant que c'est par-dessus, je veux recueillir ma récompense. Votre costume a fait vous paraissez chaud comme l'enfer,"* she said in a sultry, soft voice that had Alex's pulse racing.

"Translation?"

"Now that this is over, I want to collect my reward. Your costume makes you look as hot as hell. *Je veux éteindre le feu que vous avez allumé dans moi.* I want to extinguish the fire that you lit in me."

"Think you can transition from Disney purity to triple-X delight?"

"What's my incentive?"

"I'll let you borrow my cute little pants."

"Think I'm woman enough to get into your pants?"

"We'll find out soon enough," he said bumping her then taking her hand in a comfortable gesture of companionship. "Good job today, by the way."

She smiled, warmed by his praise. "You, too." Stopping near the employee entrance, she gave him a very non-virginal kiss. "That will have to do until we get into that naked thing."

"You doing okay?" he asked when he noticed her stretching her shoulders and wincing.

"Fine. Feeling fine." Now that it was all over, she noticed her shoulder had taken a beating in her flight through the air and subsequent landing. Her quarry had broken her fall, but the velocity of the hit gave her some stiffness and probably a nasty bruise.

Alex looked at her with concern, but decided to wait and take inventory of her body later. Her whole body.

They emerged after a few minutes from their respective dressing rooms, still tall and attractive, but dressed casually with cameras, caps, sunglasses, and bags of merchandise. Together they left the theme park. No one would have recognized them as Aladdin and Snow White. They melted into the crowded parking lot and blended with the tourists who were still standing around gossiping in groups about the evacuation. It was interesting to hear all the various versions of the event from different points of view.

"Darling, keep that up and I'm going to have to kill you," said Alex as he opened the door to the car they'd rented.

"What?" asked Skye innocently as she slid into the passenger seat.

"You were humming *It's a Small World.*"

"Damn, I can't seem to get the tune out of my head."

"It's insidious."

"A diabolical Disney plot," she laughed as they sped away.

They reappeared at a secure location in downtown Paris. They checked on their prisoners, arranged for the interviews, and began some of the mountains of paperwork that would explode from this incident. When they emerged from the nondescript building, daylight had dissolved into a beautiful dusk, highlighted by hundreds of lights. They drove to the hotel in relative silence, Skye enjoying the sights and sounds of Paris. Alex enjoying Skye enjoying the sights and sounds of Paris.

Tired from a good day's work, residual tension, and little jet lag they decided to stay in for dinner. Ordering room service, they ate on the terrace of their suite at the Hôtel de Crillon. Alex watched her against the backdrop of the lights of Paris and the rising moon. With its 18th century décor of Louis XV furnishings, Italian marble and Baccarat crystal chandeliers, the hotel was a perfect setting for Skye's timeless beauty, thought Alex. He smiled. Damn, she made him fanciful.

"Want to go out?" he asked when they'd finished the last of the champagne and strawberries.

"No. I want to take a bath and soak out some of these kinks."

"You sure you're okay?" he asked again, this time with more concern. She'd just come back to duty after an extended medical leave and the run and physical take down today were not a walk in the park. He noticed a few times while they were eating she absentmindedly rubbed her torso. One of their recent disagreements had been over her health and her ability to handle the physical rigor of this operation. She thought he worried too much. He thought she was head strong and stubborn and would push right through her limit in order to get back into the field.

"I'm fine. I just feel a little achy. That bastard got in a few shots. I'm looking forward to interrogating him when he gets extradited back to the States." She stood and stretched. Alex watched her intently for any signs she might have reinjured herself. Because he was watching, she didn't allow herself to give in to the throbbing in her shoulder. He'd see the bruise soon enough...she intended to get into the Jacuzzi and lure him in with her.

"And you can quit looking at me like I'm a lab specimen."

Alex laughed. "That wasn't a lab specimen look. I was just trying to assess my chances of getting a little tonight."

"You would settle for only a little, my love?" Leaning over she lightly brushed his lips with hers, then used her tongue to trace the line between them.

"One could hope for more, of course."

"Frotter mon dos, mon Aladdin chéri et je frotterai votre lampe magique." French always got his motor running and she knew it.

"Translation, please," he asked as he stood and folded her in his arms.

"Scrub my back, my darling Aladdin and I'll rub your magic lamp."

"Ah. Well, that's a fantasy I can live with." He carried her into the bathroom, prepared to share her bath.

CHAPTER 2

The bomb started ticking again. This time she was observing from a safe distance. They were in a familiar piazza. In Rome. She was standing outside a bakery and watching him. Tension gripped her entire body. She could hear the bomb ticking off the seconds. Hurry. Hurry. The timer was going down to less than 20 seconds. Her heart was beating fast, throbbing in her ears. She could see Alex working on the wires. His fingers moving quickly, but the bomb was a hungry beast. It wanted him. As soon as he cut one wire, another would appear under it.

He was working under the hood of a car. A large black car. Like the one her parents used to drive around Rome. Oh God! No! Oh my God, he wasn't going to make it! The timer seemed to accelerate.

10. 9. 8. Damn it. Run! Alex.

7. 6. 5. She could see the numbers on the timer. She had perfect vision. She couldn't breathe. Run! She screamed. She wanted to go to him. Pull him to safety, but she couldn't move. Someone was holding her back. Let me go. Let me go.

4. 3. 2. 1. Run Alex, you have time! But he didn't run and this time the bomb went off. She felt the flash and heard the horrible rumble. Alex was thrown. Alex was burning. She could see him burning. Smell it. Feel the heat of the blast and the fire. He was melting...dying. Was he dead? No one could have survived that fire. Alex!

Her eyes flew open. Had she screamed?

"Skye," she heard Alex's concerned voice, low in her ear. It came through the haze surrounding her brain. "Darling, wake up. I'm right here."

She was shaking and breathing heavily. There was a fine layer of sweat on her naked skin. "Alex? Alex?" Turning to him, into him, she touched his chest, feeling for his heart. It was beating, strong and true. He wasn't burning. His body wasn't on fire. His heart was beating. He was alive. But which was the dream? The explosion and fire or the beating heart? Her own heart was still racing as she tried to control the shivers that racked her body.

Alex could feel the trembling and gathered her close. He nudged her into full wakefulness with his soothing voice, his hands rubbing her back. He pulled her away from the edge of the dreadful nightmare.

"Alex?" she said as her breathing came back to normal. Putting her arms around him she held onto him. Tightly. "Oh God…I'm sorry."

"Skye, sweetheart. It's okay."

"You're okay?"

"I'm fine." He kissed her forehead, now abnormally cold. When he felt her breathing even out, he loosened his grip and he turned on the bedside light. "You haven't had one this bad in weeks."

Sighing, she rubbed the tears off her face. She was awake now and knew it had just been a dream…really terrifying, but only a dream. "Just when I thought these bitching nightmares were going to take a holiday, they're cranking up again," she said in a shaky, apologetic voice.

"Tell me."

"No. It's over now. Go back to sleep."

"Tell me," he said more firmly, taking her back into his arms.

Sighing again, she settled more comfortably against his chest. "You were taking apart a bomb. Under the hood of a long black car." She sniffed and sighed, then went on in a soft, low voice. "We were in the piazza…in Rome."

"Oh, hell. I'm sorry darling." He understood right away and it made his heart ache for her.

Skye looked over at the mantle and the elegant hand carved wooden Florentine clock ticking out the passing seconds. She used to think a ticking clock was a comforting sound, like the heartbeat of the room. Now it reminded her of her nightmare. She shuddered again.

"What is it?"

She gave a little laugh. A pretty pitiful attempt, but one that made her feel a bit more in control. "The clock…the ticking clock. It must have penetrated my dream. Shit. That's pathetic."

"Here. Let me…" He started to get out of bed.

"No, not right now. I just want to lay here and listen to your heart for awhile." Kissing his chest she laid her head on it as she wrapped her arms around him. "I love you, Alex."

He held her tighter as he felt her relax again into sleep. There was a time when she tried to fight the dark demons of her dreams alone, never telling a soul about them. She worked her iron will until she fought them back and made them fade. When they started again last summer, he'd get up in the middle of the night and find her pacing, or wrapped up in her private thoughts, silently taking a beating every night. For someone who never feared anything while she was awake, these paralyzing images caused a dreadful disquiet that would rob her of her sleep and shatter her peace of mind.

After some time, she finally told him about her vivid nightmares and it helped define their relationship. Not only did she love him madly, by confiding in him she proved she trusted him completely. She never before revealed their existence…to anyone. She was always determined to battle, then conquer them solo. Lately, her approaching marriage and her love for Alex caused their vicious return to her nighttime world.

Skye had episodes of terrible nightmares twice before. First as a teenager after she'd seen her parents die horribly in a piazza in Rome. Perry and Angelina Madison perished when a bomb exploded and a fire ripped through their car…within full view of their horrified and traumatized daughter. The combined efforts of national and international law enforcement agencies never found out which one was the target and the case remained open. Her father had been a Special Agent for the department that now employed them and her mother had been the United States Ambassador to Italy. It was assumed that it must have been mistaken identity since the governments of two countries worked the clues for years and never found the people responsible.

Skye should have been in the car with them. She'd escaped the same fate because she'd begged her father to stop at a bakery for pastries. It was from the doorway of that bakery that Skye saw her beautiful, laughing parents burn to death and it changed her. She was only 15 years old but on that day she closed up, placing her heart out of harm's way.

Years later, she opened her heart again, putting her love and trust into a warm, wonderful relationship. This time to a life long friend. Her first love, her first lover. Jeff. He was a Washington DC police officer. Funny, open, true. He nudged her until she decided to risk living and loving again. They set the wedding date. She had the ring, a beautiful white dress and was going over the last minute details of the reception with her bridesmaids when his captain and the chaplain came up the sidewalk to tell her he'd been killed in the line of duty. She buried him one week before she was to marry him. Nightmares plagued her again until she beat them down and built a steel wall around her broken heart. Never again. Never would she place herself in a position where she could hurt that badly again.

Then Alex came into her life. When she met him, she thought he was a lawyer and successful businessman. Safe. No risk. She fell in love with him before she knew there was another man beneath the surface and that man played a dangerous game. When she discovered he was an agent for the Justice Department, she fought the attraction, his love, her own heart. He was a man with a gun. How could she set herself up for the possibility of paralyzing heartbreak yet again? Eventually, she could no longer fight her love for him…her basic and powerful need for him. They became engaged and she thought she had her fears successfully caged.

With her heart now exposed and vulnerable, she saw him go down in a shootout earlier that summer. She hadn't known he was wearing Kevlar and only saw him thrown back against a building, the blood from a shoulder wound splattering the wall. She thought he'd been killed. The emotional pain had been unbearable.

It was the catalyst for the horrible dreams to make an encore appearance and start plaguing her again. The nightmares that had disappeared for years, came back with a vengeance…her fears roared out of their confinement and were relentless. While she was sleeping, her guard came down and her mind would create a vivid picture of her life as it could be. Her heart begged her to back away from such excruciating pain. There were always two wedding dresses hanging in her closet now…both drenched in blood. She'd walk down the aisle and Alex wasn't there. Suddenly, his blood was everywhere and she'd stand alone at the altar in her dress streaked with his blood. So completely, excruciatingly alone. The next moment the pain would actually intensify. She was in the morgue. Her mom and dad and Jeff were there…horribly burned, mutilated and decomposed. Sometimes already skeletal. She'd stand there for a while in her blood soaked wedding dress…then slowly approach the fourth table…an almost endless walk. A sheet covered the face of the body, but she knew who was under there.

Dead. Cold. Gray. Gone. Alex. And her heart would bleed. When she woke up screaming or just moan in agony in her sleep, he'd be the one she searched for. His heart was the sound she needed to bring her down from the heartbreaking terror and paralyzing dread. Sometimes it took a long time before the images would fade and always some of the residual horror would shake through her.

She fought the nightmares valiantly. She fought for her happiness. For him. And she suffered. The toll it took on her peace of mind was agonizing for Alex to witness, but he pushed her. He wouldn't let her go. Couldn't let her go.

The nightmares had backed off for while, but as the wedding date drew closer, her subconscious was playing out her fears, mercilessly punching through her resolve when her defenses came down. Her mind would insidiously whisper that she'd come this close to happiness before…and that to count on it was to court disaster. They both thought that after they were married, after the wedding went off without incident, after her subconscious knew that the two grotesque wedding dresses hanging drenched with blood in her closet were not a prophesy, but a dream, the nightmares would diminish, then stop.

Tonight, there was a new player. A bomb. Hell, Alex thought. He'd had his hands all over a bomb as she watched. She was as steady as granite when they were working, when she was awake and alert. But the picture of it must have merged with the memory of her parent's horrible death and invaded her subconscious. She hurt. She ached. He knew because of the life he chose to lead, for her to love him took incredible courage. For her to marry him…well it was an act of valor, not just love.

Tonight, he'd watch over her as he did every night. It seemed to help her and she usually could find a few hours of restful sleep after she purged the horror. Alex could feel her steady breathing and knew that for this night, the battle was over. Gently disengaging himself, he walked over to the mantle, and took the clock out of the room. A ticking clock. Representing the dark memories of her parents dying in a bomb blast. Expanding on the memories, modifying them to play on her fear for him. Opening the clock, he stopped the mechanism. He didn't want that sound anywhere in the suite.

When he climbed back in bed, she came to him in her sleep, finding comfort in his presence.

"Alex?"

"I'm here," he whispered, gathering her close. A place he intended to stay. A place he'd always be.

But in the dark and shadowy night, her body needed more than just the words, the beat of his heart. She needed to connect to the life inside him...inside her. Her hands moved over him and he rolled on top of her, kissing, caressing, and using the heat of his desire to convince her subconscious that he was alive. His pulse, his blood's journey through his body throbbed with a concentrated and basic obsession to take her away from reality...to drown the horror with wave after wave of sexual tension...to release the pleasure and find the joy.

As she opened her heart, she opened her body and their primal need to mate overwhelmed them both. She needed him to fight for her...to go into her, merge with her and bring her strength. When he drove himself into her, he felt her let go of the rest of the dread. He felt the intensity of her passion, and knew there was no room for fear. Only him. Tonight she needed heat, not tender words, or a gentle touch. And when she rolled over him, devoured him, he realized he needed it, too.

Alex shifted in bed. He knew he was alone before he opened his eyes. Concerned, he got up and found Skye sitting on the terrace. The predawn light caught her in its diffused blush and she looked like one of the renaissance paintings in the Louvre. He just stared at her as he drank in her beauty. She was in profile, watching the city starting to wake up. Breathtaking. His. A Mona Lisa smile touched her lips when she felt his presence. How many times a day could he fall in love.

"You okay, darling?" he asked. "It's only 5:00 a.m. You're usually groveling for another few minutes of sleep at this time."

"It isn't even midnight at home. My groveling meter is all screwed up." When she turned and looked at him, her eyes clear and unguarded, he knew she was all right. She never let her nightmares rob her of her days. She saw the look of concern on his face.

"I'm okay and ready for the day. Really. Life is good." Her smile broadened. Then she ticked off her blessings. "My thighs are still vibrating from that incredible love machine I slept with last night. I'm having pancakes for breakfast. I'm looking over one of the most beautiful cities in the world. We successfully thwarted a money for weapons deal."

"Thwarted?" he asked laughing, taking her cup from her and drinking a huge swallow. He couldn't control his look of distaste when he discovered it wasn't coffee, but some kind of tea that tasted more like flowers than Earl Gray.

"Thwarted is a perfectly good word. I like it." She smirked at the expression of revulsion he tried to hide.

"Be sure to use it in your report, then. It will electrify the bureaucrats. Is there any coffee? I swear that stuff you drink is made from the potpourri you keep in the bathroom."

"That's exactly what it is. You know I'm passionate about recycling. I carry it in little bags in my luggage."

"I'm surprised it gets through customs."

"In the silver pot, by the way."

"What?"

"Your coffee. It's in the silver pot."

He poured a cup and gratefully washed the taste of lilies out of his mouth with the potent, high-octane brew they perked in France. Coming back, he claimed another kiss and discovered an even higher octane rush.

"You're right. Life is good. The coffee is hot and strong, we saved the planet once again, and I'm marrying the most beautiful woman on that planet."

"Anyone I know?"

"Na. I keep her in a tower in Fantasyland." He was going to suggest they go back to bed so she could turn the love machine back on when he saw her unconsciously rub her torso. "Things got a little enthusiastic last night...did I hurt you, sweetheart?"

She immediately stopped rubbing. "No." Her eyes filled with his reflection. "Darling...I needed you last night...I needed to feel you deeply."

"It was a bad one."

"I'm sorry..." Her words were cut off by his fierce, almost angry, kiss. She felt his powerful reaction and when he pulled back, she saw it in his stormy eyes.

"Don't ever apologize." Kneeling down in front of her chair, he cupped her lovely face in his palm. She looked a little pale and it pulled at him. "Your nightly battles are mine, too. Because we both know that if I didn't push...if I didn't want you so damn badly, you wouldn't be facing those monstrous images night after night."

She stared at him, then nodded. "All right." Then she smiled and waved her teacup at the clock, sitting mute on the mantle. "It's a little 'ticked off' this morning I noticed."

"Yeah. Well I just gave it a 'time out' for disturbing Cinderella's beauty sleep."

A warm, tender feeling washed over Skye as she looked at her Prince Charming kneeling at her feet. "How about we go into the bedroom and..."

A knock on the door announced their breakfast.

"Damn. You said you ordered room service?" She nodded and he gave her a quick peck as he stood up. Ever security conscious, Alex walked over to the door, looked through the peek hole, confirmed the presence of a room service waiter, and opened the door. He could smell pancakes...just the right prescription to blow away the shadow in his true love's eyes.

"So where are you taking me on our honeymoon?" Skye asked as she ate her pancakes. It was her favorite breakfast and she felt like pampering herself this morning. The nightmare was fading fast, but there was still a lingering trace of gray to mark its passing. She liked the distraction of talking about other, lighter things. Wonderful things. Honeymoons. *Her* honeymoon. Ten days with Alex all to herself.

"Top secret."

"You haven't decided yet." She could read the signs.

"I'm determined to surprise you."

"You haven't even started." Skye laughed. She could translate man speak almost as well as French. Alex had told her he was taking care of the honeymoon plans and she knew he'd come through. He was just more spontaneous and less of a planner than she. Skye had no idea what he had in mind, but she loved the feeling of mystery. Of not knowing. This was totally uncharacteristic of her. She must be in love.

"I've thought about it," shrugged Alex, nabbing a bite of pancake off her plate. It showed the depth of her love that she didn't seem to mind sharing her coveted French pancakes drowning in sweet, thick maple syrup.

"It won't matter where we are. I expect we'll only see four walls," smiled Skye.

"And the ceiling," he added. They finished eating in companionable silence, each absorbed in their own thoughts.

"Alex?"

"Hmm?"

"If I can get a hold of Bill, do you want to fly home this morning? The prisoners will be transported by the end of the week. Linda is here to coordinate everything. We can do all the paper work in D.C. If we leave by noon, we'll be sleeping in our own bed tonight."

"Are you up for it?" He'd been checking his email on his palm computer and looked up.

"Yes. I want to get home. As beautiful as this is, there's no place like home."

"Okay, Dorothy. Let's do it." He pulled out his cell phone and handed it to her, then finished his correspondence while she made all the arrangements. When she smiled and nodded, they got up to slip into the roles they showed to the public.

Alexander Springfield, CEO and Chairman of the Board. An attorney and self made millionaire…one of the world's most influential real estate developers. And Captain Skyler Madison, pilot for the corporation's private jet. Once the youngest captain flying for an international airline and now piloting her own craft for her future husband's corporation. Excellent cover and it made working their covert operations very convenient. Neither of them had a boss who would question their absences or need for flexibility. It was an ideal professional relationship.

Skye disappeared into the dressing room off the bedroom and emerged in a beautiful berry colored uniform. It had bright brass buttons with the corporate logo on them…the logo of Alex's huge multi-national company. The Skyward Corporation. He'd reorganized his assets and formed the new corporation after she'd agreed to resign from International Airlines and fly the corporate Gulfstream.

Alex had set it up with Jim Stryker, their director at the Justice Department, when he realized the benefits of teaming up with the woman who would become his wife. He could watch her back on one level while maintaining a professional relationship on another. And on the third level, his personal favorite, he could share his heart and home with her while making love to her all over the world. Life really was good.

Skye checked herself in the mirror. The uniforms had been tailored to fit her trim, toned figure, and the short skirt revealed her long, shapely legs. She'd pulled her mass of unruly curls into a tight braided knot at the back of her neck and projected the image of the competent, experienced professional she was. With her flight bag slung over her shoulder, she looked ready to fly. She was a breathtaking picture and greatly appreciated by her fiancé, who liked watching the transformation from the tousled morning nymph to the ideal renaissance painting sitting on the terrace to the smooth, polished captain he saw putting on her lipstick.

The fact she also looked like a sleek French high fashion model wasn't lost on him either. Paris loved her and it wasn't unusual to have people looking around for the ubiquitous cameras of professional photographers whenever she strolled along a city street.

Alex was equally impressive dressed in an impeccable Armani suit, his brown, wavy hair now conservatively combed, his accessories tasteful and expensive. He had the jackets cut to his exacting specifications and they fit his broad shoulders to perfection. It wasn't just his physical size and chiseled features that impressed, his posture and demeanor radiated success and power. He even smelled like power, Skye thought as he came over and kissed her exposed neck.

"Mmm. You smell yummy," she said, smiling into his reflection.

"Yummy? Are you forgetting your role and your place in the pecking order here?"

"Sorry, sir." Her tone went formal, but her eyes sparkled with humor and warmth. She turned and saluted. "May I have permission to tell you that you smell better than a well prepared French meal and that you look good enough to eat?"

"You have my permission." He gave Skye's lips a quick touch. "Too bad you're working today or I'd let you feast."

"Ah yes. My boss is very demanding," she sighed.

"And since I own the plane, the schedule is mine to command. You want to go back to bed?"

Skye laughed. "Don't tempt me. It's now 5:00 am Eastern time…my groveling time." Her eyes were dancing and Alex was relieved to see no residual affects of the nightmare.

He kissed her neck again and accompanied it by bringing his hands up along her long, lean torso. "Your call. You own the sky."

"Then let's go home." She looked into his eyes. His dazzling, beautiful blue eyes, now the color of the sky. "But hold the thought. I expect to make two landings tonight."

Smiling Alex picked up his brief case and followed his pilot out the door. She said home so automatically now. It warmed his heart that she meant the house they shared.

They arrived at Orly an hour later. As they walked through the executive terminal, Alex smiled at the heads that swiveled off their necks as his fiancée walked over to make preparations for flight. She was completely oblivious to what she was doing to the appreciative French men walking through on their way to and from their destinations. But her head did come up and track a beautiful Learjet taking off. She watched it until it disappeared through the clouds. Alex smiled. His future wife. He'd never have to worry about her fidelity. As some of the finest French male stock were trying to get her attention, she only had eyes for bodies with wings and a tail.

Alex let her do her job and sat in the executive waiting room going through corporate reports and making calls. He went on line and responded to his e-mail. A master of delegation, he managed to lead a multi million-dollar corporation while simultaneously working for the Justice Department. He'd started his career as a very successful corporate attorney. Then he parleyed an incredible propensity to take risks and began to work deals for himself. It quickly transformed into an empire. His buildings were in major cities around the world. His success came fast and early. He thought he was a happy man. He thought he had everything he wanted.

Then his sister Rita, a New York City police officer, had been tragically shot and killed in the line of duty leaving behind a husband and two little boys. She'd been his twin, his other half. It broke Alex's heart and left him alone and beyond grief. It had been the catalyst for him to do something more with his life. From the tragedy and his profound sorrow, he found what he'd always been looking for. Purpose. He took up the fight against crime and criminals. He honored her by taking up the mantle of law enforcement and it helped him heal.

Director Jim Stryker had been in the process of recruiting agents who were already successful in their professions. Skye was an airline pilot when she became involved. Other agents were doctors, professors, and accountants. It made them practically invisible. They blended because they were real and established in their professions. Jim mentored Alex from the time he walked into his office with his sad eyes and his passionate appeal. Alex took to covert operations like a natural. Actually he probably was a natural. Practically everyone in his family for three generations was engaged in law enforcement.

The son of a cop, the grandson of a cop, he'd developed the aptitude by proximity. Even his younger brother Tank was a beat cop in Chicago. It was in their blood. He'd been in denial for a short time, his passion lying dormant. His sister's death had been the catalyst, but it only ignited the passion that had already been there. Alex thought he'd wanted his life to take a different course, but the road lead back to his fate. And now he was not only successful, he was fulfilled.

Skye watched him concurrently dialing his cell phone and typing in e-mail messages. He'd taken off his jacket and rolled up his sleeves. His muscular forearms hinted at an active life. Her eyes went down to the strong and skillful hands as they flew over his keyboard. His fingers. The same fingers that explored her body last night. She had to look away before her knees gave out. Concentrating on the weather reports coming in, she made a few adjustments in her flight plan to skirt some bad weather over the Atlantic.

When she was ready to board, she turned her attention back to the man. Her man. He was still working, his intelligent eyes scanning the screen in front of him. He was as gorgeous as a film star, but no one would mistake him for an empty page. More like power and control. Then she thought of him in the Aladdin costume and a warm feeling in her heart intensified into a huge flame of pure affection. If she weren't in uniform and on duty, she'd be tempted to jump him. Actually, she had a great deal of pride in her self-control, but sometimes it annoyed her natural, more primordial side. Like now. Better get moving, she thought, or the animal inside her would start ripping at his custom-made shirt.

"Whenever you're ready, passenger Springfield, you can board," she said smiling her captain's smile. Regal, respectful, and practiced. The panting flutter of lust was confined for the moment in a compartment by her heart. She'd let it have its way when they were home. The flutter rattled the cage as Alex gave her a particularly enticing version of his sensual smile. Maybe, she thought revising her initial plan, maybe in the limo on the way home. Why have privacy windows if you don't intend to use them? She had a great deal of pride in her flexibility as well and her ability to make in-the-field strategic adjustments.

"Is Bill here?" asked Alex as he packed up his briefcase, rolled down his sleeves and shrugged into his jacket.

"He's already on the tarmac doing the preflight inspection." Bill was her copilot. He'd been flying with Skye since she first made captain for International Airlines several years before. When she moved over to join Alex's newly formed corporation, she offered Bill the right seat in the corporate jet and he jumped at the chance. The corporate jet was a sleek new Gulfstream G550, modified to Skye's specifications. It had been one of her lifelong dreams to fly one and now she got to regularly. It was another item in her 'life-was-perfect' inventory.

Skye put on her aviator shades and captain's hat, then turned to her boss, her fiancé, her partner. "Are you ready to fly, sweetheart sir?"

"Ready Captain darling."

"Hi, Bill," said Skye as she spotted him standing over the tires and inspecting the wheel well.

"Captain," said Bill formally as he turned and grinned at her. They were best of friends off duty, but in the airport it was all business. He both respected and admired Skye's abilities and gave proper respect to her position as first officer in the cockpit. Skye's copilot looked handsome and polished in his matching uniform. They made an impressive pair as they walked around the plane.

"Is Connie on her way?" Skye asked as they continued their visual check of the aircraft. Connie was another of Skye's best friends and the flight crew for Skyward Aviation, the division of Skyward International that owned and operated the Gulfstream. In a few weeks she'd be standing next to Skye as one of her attendants.

"Yes. She wanted one more look at the sights, so she decided on a long cab ride."

"Next time we should arrange for Carter and Duncan to come along. Paris is for lovers."

"Very convenient then that you're sleeping with the boss."

"Listening to corporate gossip?"

"No, mostly spreading it." He looked over every inch of the fuselage. "Is the boss settled in up there?"

"Yes, he's in the communications center making deals so we can afford the jet fuel for this baby."

Skye loved the flight over the Atlantic, chasing the sun. It gave her uninterrupted time to think. She had wedding details to mull over in her bride role and an ongoing investigation to wrap up in her special agent role. She also wanted the time to purge the last of the nightmare from her system. Nothing comforted her soul like being in the air. She turned when she heard Connie's voice.

Connie Monroe was a splendid sight in her uniform and huge smile. Flamboyant and fun loving, she was carrying armloads of shopping bags, evidence of her last pass through Paris. Her job was to take care of the cabin and made sure everything was well stocked and running smoothly. She also came over from International Airlines, where she'd been a head flight attendant before Skyward Corporation made her an offer she couldn't refuse. A cushy schedule, a variety of locations, her friend, not to mention the best darn pilot on the face of the earth, in the cockpit. Her life was perfect. To add icing to an already incredible edible cake, she was seeing Alex's driver and friend Duncan on a regular basis.

"Good morning, Captain," she said cheerfully. "Beautiful day for a flight."

"You have fun in Paris?" Skye knew she'd only have to ask one question to launch Connie. She listened as Connie raved about the restaurants, the shopping, and the hotel room Skyward Corporation arranged for her, all the while continuing her preflight check. One only needed a single ear when Connie got going. She was as outgoing and extroverted as Skye was reserved and controlled.

"There was some excitement at Euro Disney yesterday," Connie said, shifting her packages.

"I heard. Were you there?" For a strange minute she thought of running into Connie while she was dressed as Snow White. That would have been a difficult one to explain.

"No, but the story was all over the news. No pictures, though. Several of the eyewitnesses thought they had some exclusive footage, but no one seemed to be able to come through with any pictures or tape. Strange. Like the CIA came in and zapped all of their cameras or something," Connie giggled at the absurd thought.

Wrong agency, Connie, my friend. But close, Skye thought as she glanced over at Connie's face, glad that her sunglasses covered her expressive eyes. She was a master at disguising her feelings and emotions, but Connie knew her very, very well. Was she suspicious or just her usual gabby self? Sometimes she thought Connie suspected. Hard not to when coincidence piled on coincidence over the years. Trouble, Skye. Skye, trouble. Like peanut butter and jelly.

When Connie moved on to describe the leather pants she bought, Skye shook her head. No, Connie didn't suspect.

"Hey Captain...are you listening? If you keep shacking up with the boss and coming to work with that 'I got lucky last night' smile I'm going to have to find a job on this big bad plane for Duncan so I can do something with this heat you keep packing in here. By the way, is hunkin' Duncan going to meet us at the airport? I love riding home in the limo. It gives Chantal across the hall such fits of green-eyed envy, she looks like a shamrock. Actually, come to think of it, she's shaped like one too. Thinks she's so chi-chi. She worked at the White House once, you know." As they walked up the stairs into the cockpit, she put a little snot into her voice. Connie was great at voices. "'What's it like to be a stewardess? I always thought it was no more than being a glorified bartender and waitress. And you don't even get any tips.' I'll give her a tip. Your rear end is beginning to look like a couple of pumpkins, witch."

When they crossed the threshold into the cabin, Connie transformed. She stowed her bags, went immediately to the galley, checked her immaculately arranged supplies, fixed coffee, and made sure their passenger was comfortable. Even though there was only one passenger and he was a friend, she nonetheless performed her tasks with pride and efficiency. As Skye started the engines and prepared for take-off, Connie made sure Alex was safely buckled in and his chair was in its upright position. She sat in her own seat near the galley. Taking out a book she'd started in her suite...a suite bigger than Chantal's apartment and in a hotel that was five stars and counting. Looking out the window saying goodbye to Paris, she grinned broadly. Glorified waitress indeed. More like a privileged rock star. She couldn't wait to show off her new outfit. She'd change in the terminal at Dulles. Chantal would be coming home from her job right about the time Duncan dropped her off. She was going to make sure of it.

Skye got on the intercom. "The tower has given us the green light. Unless there are any last minute objections, let's go home."

As Alex felt the gravity pull him back into his seat, he felt the familiar pull of pride in the woman who would soon become his wife. Unique, skilled, brilliant, and beautiful. The takeoff was flawless and soon they were shooting through the clouds. His Skye sure knew how to fly.

CHAPTER 3

The following day, Skye and Alex drove into the city and parked under the Justice building. They went through the highly secured building and entered Director James Stryker's impressive office. He was an imposing man. Large, well muscled, with quick, intelligent eyes and a commanding demeanor, he filled the spacious office when he stood to greet them.

Jim was a highly respected, incredibly connected department director. He'd been an agent with the Intelligence Division and served with distinction before he came in from the field and worked his way to the head of the department. He'd trained with Skye's father and they'd been best friends until Perry Madison had been killed.

Jim was also Skye's godfather and as such had tried to talk her out of the life. He wanted to keep her safe. She was fearless, like her dad, and thrived on taking risks. Flying planes was as perilous as he wanted her life to get. But she was determined and when Skyler Madison put her considerably capable mind and iron will to something, it would have been easier to stop the tide or put out the light of the moon. He knew she'd have selected another agency if he hadn't consented, so he reversed his position and worked as her mentor. He figured at least he could keep an eye on her and minimize her danger.

Jim originally thought he'd be able to convince her to work inside with administrative details. Not a chance. She trained like a demon and quickly became indispensable as a field agent in the big cases. Now when people in the department passed on stories of Agent Madison's daring exploits, it was Skye, not Perry they talked about. His old friend would have been proud of his daughter and as terrified with every assignment as Jim was.

Alex Springfield was a different kind of agent, but equally as effective. Skye was a brilliant strategist who these days usually worked as Special Agent in Charge when on assignment. Her talent was in building teams and recognizing the talents of other people. Alex was his lone wolf and up until now he never even worked with a partner. He'd go in under deep cover and liked dirty, dangerous work. Intelligent, bold, and driven, Alex was his ace when he needed to play his high card.

Earlier that year, Jim had put them together on assignment, and it only took one. The attraction had been hot, fast, and irreversible. He could either try to pull them apart, something both his heart and his head found abhorrent, or agree with Alex's plan to put them together as a team. It was the merging of his two best agents and so far, it seemed like an excellent blend.

They were now in his office to report on their operation. He had the full report, but he preferred to hear it all first hand. Maybe it was the field agent in him, but he liked being occupied by the details. Preferring a more comfortable setting when engaging in a lengthy debriefing, he directed them to a leather sofa and chairs surrounding a large coffee table.

"First of all, let me say again how proud I am of the job you did in France. I just got off the phone with the Prime Minister himself. I've read over all the transcripts and I'm truly impressed with your resourcefulness. Skye, your simultaneous translation, and quick deductions saved both lives and property. If we would have waited to have the tapes analyzed, we would never have been in time. That and the astounding fact that you found the bomb in one of the most visually…ah…intense attractions in the park.

"And Alex, it appears you didn't sleep through any of your training on munitions. Well done. There were over a thousand men, women, and children in the blast area alone. Not to mention the residual horror and psychological damage to a country something like that can cause. The operation was textbook and the execution was bold and successful. You work very well as a team. The partnership appears to be working."

Skye beamed. Jim was never effusive with his praise. He was unfailing in his support, but 'good job' was about it. This little speech was both welcome and inspiring. The French Prime Minister must have set the stage and prompted all the words, Skye thought. The French never stop.

"Thank you," said Alex, smiling over at Skye. The partnership had been his idea, formulated by his need to be near her. Jim had concurred and Skye had been converted afterward. Smiling back, Skye crossed her long legs. She'd been away from the field for a while. This felt so good. She touched the soft burgundy leather…back in the saddle again.

"I just have one question for Skye," said Jim in his voice of command.

Skye looked into his familiar face expectantly. "What's that?"

"What the hell were you thinking?" She heard the bite in his tone, but just raised her eyebrows and gave him a blank look. He hadn't intimidated her since she was four years old.

"Referring to…"

"Referring to your presence at the bomb disposal." Jim's voice was steady and authoritative. He saw this as a breach of procedure and he wanted an answer.

"First of all," she said, uncrossing her legs, completely undisturbed with what sounded like a rebuke. "Alex wipe that smirk off your face. Secondly, I was lending assistance to my partner."

"It seemed as though your partner wanted to go solo," responded Jim.

"But his solo act needed a spotlight and I was the one who provided it." Skye kept her voice low and reasonable.

"You have both been trained in hands-free illumination. Alex could have handled the issue of adequate light alone," countered Jim. "You should have evacuated with the rest of the team."

Skye knew she was busted, so she just shrugged. "I had every confidence in my partner and calculated the risk as negligible. As it turned out, I was right. Twice."

Jim opened his mouth to counter the argument, couldn't think of one, then settled on a weak admonition.

"I'd ask you in the future to take better care of one of my top agents."

"I intend to. I'm marrying him aren't I?" asked Skye with a grin, deliberately misunderstanding Jim's meaning.

"You know what I mean." Jim had been playing Skye's game her whole life. Hell, he'd taught her some of the moves himself. His tone got stricter. "You are a very valuable asset and you needlessly put yourself in harm's way. In the future, I expect you to move if your partner says move and there are reasonable grounds for him to do so."

Alex wasn't about to let the opportunity pass. "Could you make that an order, sir?"

"Do you think that would help?" asked Jim with just a hint of irony in his voice.

"It would give me something to quote to her when she's being single minded. She's a nut about orders."

"She also knows I highly encourage discretion in the field."

"Throw me a lifeline here. She won't listen to reason and there may be instances when I won't have time to build a case anyway. If you make it an order, then I can just pull rank."

"Think that will help?" Jim asked again, his voice teasing, fondness in every word.

"I can see how she cowers before your immense power and vaulted position."

Skye made a dismissive sound deep in her throat. "Are you two through talking about me like I am sitting in a bar in Barbados instead of here in this room?"

They were saved from further discussion by Pearl, Jim's secretary. Efficient, gray haired and fiercely loyal, she'd been with Jim so long she could read his mind. She served coffee but not before she fussed over Skye and smiled endless smiles at Alex. She so loved a happy ending.

"I swear when the two of you come in, that woman transforms into some kind of romance junkie," griped Jim, shaking his head as Pearl closed the doors behind her. "She melts all over the carpet."

"Really?" grinned Alex. "I hadn't noticed."

"Then I seriously think you need more training. Damn, everything used to be so predictable. When did I lose control?"

Just then the intercom bleeped. "Director?"

"Yes Pearl?"

"The other Ms. Madison is out here and looking like she's been taste testing canaries."

Jim closed his eyes for a minute, shook his head as if to clear it, then smiled. "I rest my case. Send her in."

"I cracked it!" Skye's sister Sloane came bursting into the office, a beautiful, slender young woman who had, to her adolescent relief, finally begun to develop…in the body, not just the mind. She'd been born with a fully developed mind. Her I.Q. was off the charts.

Jim had suggested an internship for the little lawbreaker so he could keep an eye on her, but she was proving to be an incredible asset. Her genius was something he'd always taken for granted. Not any longer. He'd been feeding her impossible tasks to keep her out of mischief, and she was chewing them up and spitting them out with such frequency she was creating her own legend within the department.

"Hey you two, what's shakin'? When did you bounce back from where I'm not suppose to know where you've been and did you bring me a radical French souvenir? Better be something sleazier than a Mickey Mouse t-shirt. Ooh la la." She wiggled her butt. Obviously she had her fingers in secret files again. She gave them both a quick hug and kiss before she stood to deliver her report. "Anyway, Uncle Jim…"

"Sir," corrected Skye. In this office he was the director and not her Uncle Jim.

"Yeah, right. Sorry. Anyway, I cracked it Sir Jim."

Jim checked his watch, choosing to ignore the fact that Sloane must have hacked into Skye's reports…again. If he acknowledged the fact, he'd have to arrest her. "What took you so long? We gave you those disks this morning." His tech staff had already tried for nearly a week before handing the job over to the girl genius.

"Yeah, but today is Tuesday. I had to crunch my classes in there." Jim took the disk. It was fairly close to clearance level five and Sloane only had a level seven.

"Teaching or taking?" asked Alex, enjoying the fresh air that always seemed to follow in Sloane's wake.

"Taking. I'm never, ever teaching another graduate seminar. I don't care what the requirements are for the PhD. I'll just wait until I have fully functioning breasts and can wear two-inch heels without looking like I'm playing dress up in my big sister's clothes. Cripes, you'd think they never saw a 14 year old professor before." She started imitating voices. "You're so cuuuuute. So sweeeeeeeet. My little brother needs a date to the prom. Want to go to the movies? Whoops. Nope. It's rated 'R'. Hardy har har. You know, like the textbook for my class in anatomy and physiology isn't 'R' rated? And my all time favorite: 'What's it feel like to be a genius?' When what they really mean is: 'What's it feel like to be a freak?' It's a hard row of stumps to get people to take me seriously. I'm totally baked. No more."

"People here take you seriously," said Skye.

"That's because I fill the bill in the Tower and everyone there was delivered into the world serious and focused. Besides that, they all know my name and who I am, but I bet none of them could even tell you the color of my eyes."

"Blue," said Jim.

"Green," said Alex. And made Sloane's beautiful golden hazel eyes shine.

"The point is they don't ride the physical package, just the upper story. I'm a juvie and that's iced. They don't care about mileage."

"Or fashion, current events, cuisine, vacations or even eating most of the time," said Skye, her heart always sensitive to her sister's singular journey. Skye and their great aunt Hazel had raised Sloane. She'd been a baby when their parents had been killed and had grown into an amazing combination of brilliant intellect and teenage exuberance. She could slide from a conversation of computer jargon that only a handful of people could understand to teen speak that only people under sixteen could translate.

"Anyway, it's the best place for a freakazoid like me to hang. Other than the mall, that is. Can you two dump me there later? Libby wants me to check out a really wicked schlock joint. We're going to hang for awhile, then go to her house to measure, eat pizza and practice my spontaneous and unrehearsed put downs." She went over to the little refrigerator and grabbed a Dr. Pepper. Pearl kept it stocked just for her. Jim considered it part of the compensation package. Little enough to pay for Sloane's valuable services. "I want to be ready for that gross grouper you conned into escorting me to the wedding."

"Fisher isn't gross. He's a very handsome young man," countered Skye.

"What's this?" asked Jim.

"You know Fisher Mitchell," said Skye.

"Amanda's grandson? Yes." Fisher had been a passenger on a plane piloted by Skye that had been hijacked a few months before. He and Skye had worked together and had become fast friends and allies. Fisher's grandmother, Amanda Mitchell, was a former CIA agent who worked with Alex and Sloane behind the scenes. Amanda, Skye, and Sloane had developed a strong bond in the events that followed and both Amanda and Skye had hoped that Sloane and Fisher would hit it off. They hadn't.

"Whatever. Anyway, he thought he was all that on *Firewalkers*, that's an awesome vid game, you know. So when Alex challenged him to a duel…" explained Sloane between slurps.

"A duel?" Jim looked over at Alex who shrugged and smiled. He'd let Sloane explain, although he hadn't known that she was privy to the method he'd employed to snag her a date of Skye's choosing for the wedding. Fisher was quite remarkable and both he and Skye thought he was a kid whose ego could handle Sloane's superior second story.

"Yeah, that's when you go head to head on the slab. Anyway, he thought he was the way and Alex told him that if he lost he'd have to be my tug at the wedding," Sloane went on. Jim, as usual, was both fascinated and entertained by the prodigy. He wasn't quite sure what a tug was but put into this context, he assumed it meant escort. Thank God for context or he'd need an interpreter.

"What would have happened if Alex lost the bet?" he asked.

"Fisher got Skye."

"Oh, I see." Jim's lips twitched. What that told him was his man was absolutely sure of his victory in this duel.

"Anyway, this geezer here proved that finesse and middle aged brain cells can beat pure reflex any day. Fisher was a maniac, but he got licked, ripped and put away."

"Ah. Well. I take it this geezer won." Christ, Jim thought. If Alex was a geezer, what did that make him?

"Nudged him out and there you go. I have a side piece."

"I didn't know you were looking for one. I have a nephew you could have borrowed."

"Please. One schatchen within ten miles of me is enough."

"So Fisher lost to Alex and he has to escort you."

"Yeah, and he lost the wager fair and square. I bet he's still burning." Sloane snorted. "According to my sources, the cocky little bird bait thought he had it in the bag. Guaranteed. But Skye's guy orbited him. Completely burned his conceited, pompous, swaggering, over-bearing, supercilious, bigheaded, arrogant, egomaniacal butt. Don't know what he'd have done with Skye anyway." She looked at Skye and winked. "I can't wait to play him myself. His hand-eye coordination may be better, but the game also requires strategy. That's my milieu."

"Hmm. And you're going to spend the evening with this guy?" Sometimes when Sloane got wound up she could sound like her older sister...like a thesaurus on speed.

"It's an option." She'd die before she told anyone but Libby that he was a real dream. Libby took one look at this picture Sloane snapped when they'd met last summer and melted into a puddle. "So anyway I got a date. Big deal. Let's get to the important stuff." She indicated the disks in Jim's hand.

"Let's," agreed Jim checking his watch again. They all knew he only did that for show. If he really wanted them to stay on task, he had about a thousand ways of making it happen. Truth be told, he loved both watching and listening to Sloane. And with what she was delivering day after day, he could give her a share of his time and attention.

"So, here's the scoop on the disks. The author of this correspondence is a hacker. He used basic iterated applications, something we call disassociated press. It was a letter-based application of the algorithm that transforms text into garbage. First I had to figure the formula using a customizable, programmable, self-documenting text editor. I've been playing with one of my own design. Anyway..." Sloane stopped for a breath and saw the identical look on all three faces in the room. "You really don't want to know the recipe of this cake or how it was baked, do you, Sir Jim." Jim shook his head, smiling. He hoped he'd reach retirement age before the vocabulary around there became completely unrecognizable. Nothing made him feel more like an old dinosaur than a fourteen year old. And this little genius made him feel like a petrified fossil.

"Go find Barclay," said her smiling sister. "You two can binge on formula all afternoon."

"Okay. That's cool. I'll demo my new stuff. Say, has he asked Harriet, yet? I heard him mumbling in the elevator this morning and I think I caught her name in the rattle. I sure hope it's soon. She was wearing that red sweater you gave her today, so I think she's primed."

"Alex wrote down three alternative methods he guaranteed would be irresistible. That's probably what you heard him practicing."

"Oh, yeah? Did you see them?"

"No. Man stuff," Skye said smiling at the two men in the room.

"Well what did he say to you that made you fall in love with him?" she asked, winking at her future brother-in-law. Personally she'd have dropped at his feet as soon as he smiled. And she was just a tweener without a fully charged load of hormones.

"Let me see…" Skye looked over at Alex and found him grinning. "I think it was 'Hi'."

Jim cleared his throat and they all knew that tune. Recess over children.

Sloane grabbed some of the cookies Pearl had put on the coffee tray and pointed to the disks she'd brought in. "But back to business. You'll want to check out what's on those disks, Sir Jim. I kept my eyes closed while I was reading the information I harvested. Hot stuff. I'm not cleared for level five yet so I didn't see a thing. Gotta run. Page me when you guys are ready to skate." And in a flurry of teen scent, laughter, and cookie crumbs, she was gone. The room always seemed empty after she left.

"Damn, Skye. That girl is exhausting," laughed Jim. "I only understand half of what she tells me. She's either talking way over my head or way below my generational capacity to interpret. What 14 year old uses milieu in a sentence and what the hell is a schatchen anyway?"

"A matchmaker," said Skye distractedly, smiling after her sister. "I'm not sure how I feel about her being privy to level five data."

"You're talking about the young woman who hacked into Langley a few months ago, for Christ's sake. Thank God Amanda didn't press it."

"I also noticed she got out of here before we got to question her about how she knew we were in France," said Skye.

"Lucky guess?" asked Alex.

"Yeah, right. Do you want me to talk with her, Jim?"

Jim shook his head. "No. Let's just consider ourselves lucky that she's on our side. I think where the two of you are concerned she just wants to stay informed and close. She has legitimate reason to be concerned. I can't and won't tell her anything, but I won't stop her from finding out on her own. Probably couldn't, even if I wanted to."

"I take it the *Erase Skye* project is complete?"

Jim liked to have his agents keep a relatively low profile. Most of the time his two top agents could simply be themselves and take care of operations, but he'd used both Alex and Skye on several covert cases. This meant that there were people out there who knew their faces, but not their real names. Most of them were in custody or dead, but a few may have pushed through the net. That summer, Skye's profile had been raised by her heroic actions when her plane had been hijacked. Her picture had been all over both the print and visual media. It was Sloane's job to hunt out stories and expunge them. Neither Skye nor Alex ever gave interviews or consented to having stories written about them, but when unauthorized pieces were placed on Internet sites, they were removed quietly and discreetly.

"What about all those magazines?"

"Magazines have an average life of no more than 4 months, longer in some offices such as doctors and dentists. There are approximately ten thousand copies in public library archives. We have a small team out there now replacing the version with your picture on the cover with our version with the plane on the cover."

"Good God, Jim, how would someone pull that duty?" laughed Skye, unable to imagine a more mundane, mind numbing assignment.

"I have to have something for people to do who have displeased the Director."

"But going to every dot on the map and replacing a magazine?"

"Not every dot. The edition that went west of the Mississippi already had the plane on the cover." Jim knew many people in the media and found them to be both patriotic and cooperative.

"International Airlines put out my official picture with my hat and my hair pulled back, so that helped a little. I mean it was almost as bad as a passport snapshot." Both Jim and Alex looked at her and smiled indulgently. She had no idea how striking the rest of her features were. It helped, perhaps, but it couldn't diminish her beauty or her distinctive characteristics. On the other hand, memories of faces fade quickly and Alex and Skye had no unknown shadows or strange encounters since the incident. Even the media lost interest as soon as they were faced with the stone wall of Alex's privacy. Security at all their residences was state of the art. Phones were checked regularly for taps and Sloane set up their computer security so that it was airtight.

Jim sat back in his chair. "Okay, where were we before hurricane Sloane hit our shores? How about a full verbal account of the operation."

Alex summarized everything clearly and concisely. He looked over at his partner/ fiancée proudly. "She really did a job on this one."

"I couldn't have disarmed the bomb, though. I wouldn't have had the confidence to even begin," she frowned. "I'd like to take some training in that."

Jim laughed at her serious tone. "Maybe after the wedding we can plug up that huge hole in your training. For heaven's sake Skye, you can utilize experts on your team."

"As a matter of fact," added Alex speculatively. "She probably would have gone right to it, training or no training."

"I think Claude may have been able to talk me through it," agreed Skye with a smirk.

"He'd do anything to be able to whisper in your ear," said Alex sarcastically.

"Who's Claude?" Jim felt an unsettled current and was curious.

"He's in the report. He was the chief of the Paris bomb squad. A charming man," smiled Skye.

"A self absorbed narcissistic letch," added Alex, frowning over at his fiancée.

"Is that in the report?" asked Jim, accurately interrupting the vibrations.

"Just his name," said Skye, still smiling benignly.

"Good thing," said Jim. He smiled at Alex. "I take it he threw a pass at your partner?"

"He did."

"Learn to live with the reality, boy. You're partnered with what we used to call a looker, and there will be times when you won't be in a position to stand with her. She may have to swing those attributes to her advantage and you're going to have to put a lid on your possessive reaction. Don't make me regret putting the two of you in the field together."

He caught Skye's smirk. "The same goes for you, young lady. I don't want to hear you kicked the crap out of some mark because she was making eyes at Special Agent Springfield."

Alex actually laughed out loud, earning him an elbow in the ribs.

"So what do you have for us now?" asked Skye preferring to change the subject. It gave her a charge. The 'us' rang true, like a natural state of affairs. They were a team now.

"Interrogation of the people you have in custody, of course. I'd like you to stay with them for a while. There's a network hovering behind them and I want you to uncover what you can. Then we want to continue to trace all of the contacts the seller made to see who was in the game. The people making contact and sending offers are as much a part of this case as the group who were the highest bidder." Jim rubbed some of the fatigue out of his eyes. "This is a very dangerous time. Ten years ago, the worst we had to deal with were drug runners, counterfeiters, and extortionists. Now it's weapons of mass destruction. Frightening."

"Look, Jim. This is mostly tying up loose ends. Everything critical has been managed." Skye was always ready to jump to a new field assignment and hated to be tied to routine research. She sang this song after each major bust. And his response was always the same.

"Skye, I realize you would rather unravel the tapestry than tie up loose ends, but that work is still important." He smiled at Alex. "You're going to have to help me control her need for action."

"Any suggestions on how to accomplish that?"

"If I had any ideas, I'd have employed them before now. I guess you just have to prepare for a rough ride."

"Excuse me, Director Stryker," said Skye testily. "But I am not an amusement park ride. We have plenty of time before the wedding to engage in something more exciting than interrogating terrorists and writing reports."

"Skye, you came off medical leave and went right into the French operation," began Jim. "I want you to take it easy for awhile."

"Look, you imposed that medical leave on me, Jim. I felt great all during the operation." Damn, she thought she was hiding her aches fairly well.

Jim raised his eyebrows. "You look a little stiff to me."

Skye snorted. "A few bruises. I got more color on me at the world championship meets when I was thirteen."

Alex remained quiet, but he looked at Jim and nodded slightly. He'd noticed the winces when she thought he wasn't watching. She wasn't yet 100% and they all knew it. Skye caught the look that passed between Jim and Alex.

"Don't you two think you can gang up on me and restrict my activities. I will accept this namby pamby, routine, baby assignment and will take the little breather right now so I can put together the wedding, but when we get back from the honeymoon, I want some action."

Jim smiled when he looked at the expression on her face…determined, controlled and indomitable…and thought of her father. They had trained together and worked in the same cell until his death and sometimes she talked and acted just like him. It was both fascinating and a little terrifying. Perry had been a real danger junkie too. After his marriage and fatherhood, he mellowed a little, but would still take incredible risks. He'd also been extremely successful and a legend at the department. Skye was following in his mythical footsteps.

"Agreed," he said, knowing that was the only answer she'd gracefully accept. "Now what about the wedding."

"As far as Operation Matrimony is concerned, my team has been contacted and is ready for the initial phase of execution. We have a meeting scheduled so everyone will know their role, understand their responsibilities and be prepared to implement their part of the op. I expect our new marital status will commence without a hitch. I can, without any difficulty, divert time and energy to a simultaneous assignment." She used a voice she saved for reporting and managed to keep a straight face. If they were going to treat her like an administrative drone, she'd just start acting the part.

Alex grinned. He couldn't explain why hearing her talk about the wedding in that cultured, professional reporting voice turned him on, but it did. He had to suppress the urge to do a very unprofessional act on Jim's couch and used his incredible self-control to cool his jets.

Jim's eyes slid over to Alex. "Has she been talking like that throughout the entire engagement?"

"You raised her."

Jim smiled back. "You got me there."

"So let's review our schedule for the next month or so," she said. She wanted to meet with the Angolan ambassador and there were hundreds of pages of field reports to summarize. Basically the action was over and now came the tedious work of wrapping things up. By the time she left for her honeymoon, Skye wanted this case closed up tight.

"Well, that's all for the business portion of the meeting," said Jim after the schedules and assignments had been reviewed and agreed upon. "Tell me more about Operation Matrimony." Skye had asked him to escort her down the aisle. He had no daughters, so this was his first time. He was both deeply touched and thrilled. Glancing at Alex he had to admit that part of the reason he was so pleased was because he'd be walking her toward a man he liked and admired. "Anything at this point I should be doing?"

"Let me check my file," she said and as she reached for it Alex and Jim made man eyes at each other. Alex communicated, 'you trained her, too.' Jim communicated, 'she's your partner now. Your partner…your problem.' They finished up with identical *maybe we should make a run for it* looks. Then they both did a satisfying eye roll, before pasting matching *tell me more, I'm interested* looks on their faces. By the time she retrieved her materials, they were sitting attentively.

As Skye looked at her folder and consulted her *men of the wedding* checklist, she said sweetly. "If the two of you are finished with the telepathy thing, I want to remind you that it's too late for either one of you. There is no escape. You're both caught in the powerful, unassailable vortex of a woman's Big Day and you are doomed."

CHAPTER 4

A handsome, well dressed man paced around his office and stared down at the picture of the polished and professional woman on the cover. His heart pounded in his ears, his breath quickened and he could taste his lust…lust focused not on the woman, but on the possibilities that might reopen to him now. Possibilities he long considered beyond his reach.

His hands shook as he drew another line of cocaine through the tiny straw and up his nostril. It felt wonderful. He felt wonderful.

Was this her? There was a resemblance. Maybe his mind was dulled by being forced to live this mundane existence in this tedious city surrounded by people who could never appreciate what he once was. Was this really Virginia? Was this the woman who ruined his life? If it was…oh, if it was! She'd now be his salvation. Maybe his time in purgatory was over!

He absentmindedly kneaded the side of his nose. His drug use was up, but he knew that was only because of his deep, dark, unrelenting misery. It could soon be over. His pulse quickened at the thought. He took another hit. This time to celebrate, not just to inebriate.

"What to do," he mumbled as he continued to pace. "What to do." It became a mantra as he repeated it over and over.

First things first. He needed to find out more about the woman in the picture. If this were Virginia, he'd set a plan in motion that would use that knowledge as leverage. Freedom! Rebirth! Back to the life he deserved! A life he longed for.

Before his stint here in purgatory surrounded by the pale, prosaic population of this cultural and climactic desert, he'd always thought of his life as charmed…blessed by the fates. Then the darkness hit him and he'd been leading this…this half-life, abandoned by his beloved fate. He took another hit of cocaine, feeling fully justified to use the sacred powder to get through his days with some enthusiasm for living. He was in his own personal dark ages.

The magazine in his hand shook slightly from the rush of the drug and from the shock of seeing the face that had haunted him for so many years. This was such an unplanned twist of fortune…like it was preordained or something. Could it be the birth of his personal renaissance? Oh, he loved the thought of that…the sound of that. He'd be another renaissance man.

And this new dawn began with…*Newsweek*. Gads. He shuddered. He only read *GQ*, *InStyle*, *Cigar Aficionado*, *Bon Appetit*, *Wine Country Living* and *Esquire*. The magazines of quality, tradition, wit, and style. But today he visited his dentist to fix a chip in his bonding and an old *Newsweek* magazine had been sitting there on the table in the waiting room. What were the odds? He never looked inside those news publications, or the tabloids, or, heaven forbid, those sports magazines the Neanderthals of his species seemed to continuously growl over. But the cover was just in his line of vision as he sat down and he all but pounced on it. Snatching it up, he read the entire article. He almost left right then and there to start his search, but that chip was on a tooth that showed and he simply couldn't abide a crooked smile.

Pavel Ivanov, a.k.a. Paul Ivan, a.k.a. Peter Evans was at the same time a sociopathic genius, a polished entrepreneur, and a spoiled monster. He absorbed information like a sponge, but he tended to ignore everything that didn't directly impact on him, his life style, or his comfort. The world revolved around him and in his whole life there had only been one grotesque injustice. And the she-bitch on the cover of that magazine was the curator of this misery. The reason he was now living in…God forbid…the Midwest.

Pavel had come over to the United States as a boy. His wealthy, aristocratic parents emigrated from Russia, bringing their family and business with them. In addition to being highly successful importers and near royalty in Miami Beach society, they were something else…they were the liaisons between the organized crime families in southeastern United States and the Russian families operating in and around St. Petersburg. Organized crime was a young and growing business in Russia and his father and mother had seized the opportunity to become part of the profitable enterprise. Business thrived.

Little Pavel took to the decadence of the western way of life immediately and with a vengeance. He loved everything American, from its restaurants to its cars to its TV. He was educated at private schools and became used to the good life in and around Miami Beach. Because of his family's wealth and position, he carelessly consumed all the finer things money and ruthless privilege could buy. Life was wonderful.

Then suddenly, his parents were called back to Russia. His father was ecstatic because it meant prestige as well as money. Being called to a key position in the national syndicate was his dream. Pavel was horrified. Go back to Russia? He spoke the language, of course, but he hated the thought of living the Russian lifestyle. He refused to go back with them. His addiction for fine clothes, fine wine, fine food, and the Playboy channel needed to be fed. He couldn't imagine a life more horrific than one in northern Russia. Ice belonged in a margarita, not underfoot. And he despised vodka.

When they insisted that Pavel return with them, he did what any dutiful sociopath would do…he killed them. They were shocked, but they shouldn't have been. Not really. It was his family's legacy. It was in his very DNA! First he shot his delusional mother, then his ridiculously inflexible father. Fast, bloody and without remorse. It was their fault, after all. He was the son of criminals so he acted like one. In his own twisted mind he was convinced that deep down they would be proud of his treachery and his love of blood and larceny…and his ability to recognize opportunity.

He needed a plausible cover story and he had one ready. Not so much for the Miami authorities, who accepted without much investigation the murder/suicide angle. After all…who would not be suicidal to be forced back to Russia by the parent 'company.' No. He needed a story for the Russian crime family. And he improvised beautifully. Two dead parents shot and killed by a rival family. It could work.

It did work. Grief stricken and furious, he convinced his uncles in Russia he needed to stay to seek vengeance. By the time he meted out the retribution, a very convenient way of eliminating the competition…thank you very much, take a bow…he'd developed a whole new product line. Several of them, as a matter of fact. He was a natural and tireless in his need to be the best. Because of this, he was allowed, even encouraged, to stay in the U.S. by the Russian family.

His parents dealt drugs…a completely straight shot and one that was very unimaginative, in Pavel's never humble opinion. They did all right, but Pavel would have won a gold medal if crime were an Olympic sport. Sin for him was like a religion. If it was illegal, depraved, immoral or just plain corrupt; he considered it his mission to test its limits. He was truly gifted. When it came to drugs, murder, and depravity he thrived in its application. And he was proud that he did it with style.

His business had boomed when he went into the lucrative drugs for weapons market. No one had more weapons to sell than Russia and the Russian people were developing an appetite for cocaine. He grew up with a young Columbian who kept the white blow coming. It was a boom time.

When weapons became too hot to handle from the United States, he fell into the best sideline he'd ever developed. Women. Hardly any risk, easy to transport, always a steady supply. He frequented South Beach, a magnet for beautiful women, models and party girls. Harvesting them off the streets, from the restaurants, out of the parties, he sent them abroad. He chuckled. He'd send broads abroad. Clever. He could always entertain himself the best.

The Chinese mafia, who did a lot of business with the Russian families, had a huge craving for western women. And they had almost an unlimited amount of cash. Drugs they could grow or manufacture, weapons were of no interest to them, they could produce everything domestically cheaper than any Russian or Columbian. But what they couldn't make locally were tall, slender, beautiful Caucasian women. They were particularly partial to natural blondes. So young Pavel fed their addiction and became extraordinarily wealthy, and more importantly, incredibly powerful and connected.

He had a great business, a huge mansion in the middle of an ocean side complex, a yacht filled with beautiful women, a fabulous life, a wonderful circle of familiar friends and associates…then it all collapsed. Practically overnight. He'd been forced to stage his own death, change his name, start over in a new town. He even had to get plastic surgery to change his look…and he loved his old nose and face. And it all began with this…this lowlife peasant bitch! Virginia!

Pacing and slapping the rolled up *Newsweek* against his palm, he replayed the pain. Because of her he had to arrange for his own death and run for his life. Run to a place they wouldn't find him. Here. Where it snowed in the winter and people dressed in off-the-rack similitude.

The article inside was about this heroic pilot who'd been hijacked. Ha! She probably staged the entire thing. She was a consummate actress, a pathological liar, and an unscrupulous con artist. She'd told him her name was Virginia Montgomery from Minnesota or Wisconsin or one of those states that considers cheddar an acceptable cheese and domestic beer a tolerable alcoholic beverage.

She deceived him, ruined him, forced him to flee for his life…and oh God! An excited breath exploded out of his chest. He got hard just thinking about her. He never thought he'd ever meet his match. But Virginia. What a woman! He had no idea how talented she really was. Unfurling the magazine he lifted from the dentist's office, he stared at the beautiful face…changed from what he remembered…more stunning. That naïve girl she played when she was in his stable was perfectly performed…now she was on the cover of this magazine. What a daring and elaborate con. Somehow she'd worked to have this plane hijacked, then made it appear as though she saved the day! There was something about millions of dollars, as well. How much had she skimmed for herself?

If he believed in a supreme being, he might have thought she was made for him. Someone like her would have been worthy. His brilliant criminal mind melded with her lack of conscience. They would be perfectly matched if he didn't want her for another purpose altogether. Ruthlessly he set aside his frustration. His lust was going to have to be unrequited. She was far too valuable to him as his ticket back to his former life. A life he craved and missed beyond measure. She was going to make it possible for him to return to civilization. And that was more important than any match made in hell or any primal bodily function. He longed for his former life…the culture, the style, the personal power, the sunshine, the bikini clad goddesses.

His mission clear in his mind, he needed Rosalie on it right away. She was an unscrupulous computer geek he often used to uncover information by any means available. She'd do a thorough search…digging as far below the surface as she could get.

A part of him was afraid. What if this was just his imagination? Or what if the resemblance was simply a coincidence. Everyone had a twin, right? And there were significant differences in the features…still. Instinct was high on his hit parade and his instincts were telling him this wasn't wishful thinking or a delusional hallucination. He'd wait until he got more information before he took any action, but his well-honed gut embraced the miracle of seeing her picture as a sign he was going to be back in sunshine soon. He absentmindedly tapped the sculptured tip of his nose. Maybe he could reverse the facial surgery and get everything back. But that was a minor detail. First things first. He threw the magazine with Skye's picture on his desk and picked up his phone.

CHAPTER 5

Skye was working in her home office, a beautiful bright room with French doors opening onto a wide terrace overlooking breathtaking gardens and a large pool. It was the gardens that had sold her on the place. She smiled remembering Alex showing her all the properties in the area, leaving it for her to decide which one they would purchase as their first home together. He'd stacked the deck by planting hundreds of white gardenias along the driveway onto this estate and in the grounds out back. Clever, but obvious. White gardenias were her favorite and she knew freshly turned earth when she saw it. Adding it all up, she saw the fix. She was a Special Agent, after all.

He wouldn't have had to take such covert measures to get her to favor this property, however. She fell in love with the place the minute he rounded the curve in the road and she saw the house. A dream house. Spacious, elegant, and bright. There were stables for the horse Alex had promised Sloane and room for an airstrip and hangar for Skye's Cessna. Construction on that would start after the wedding.

They'd only been living here, Destiny Ranch Alex had dubbed it, for a few weeks, but it seemed like home in her heart. They would keep up his townhouse in Alexandria, a penthouse apartment in Chicago for when they visited family and an estate on Amelia Island in Florida, but this was where they planned to spend most of their time when not flying around the world. It was in these gardens that they were to be married…six weeks from today.

Skye smiled as she sipped her coffee and walked out onto the terrace. In a few short weeks, the lawns would be filled with people…noisy laughter, loud conversations and continuous celebrations…and that was just when the Coopers and Springfields arrived. Thinking of Alex's family, her family now, she felt warmth spread through her. She never realized how hungry she was for family until they came sweeping into her life. She loved Sloane and adored her great aunt Hazel, but she'd been the responsible adult since she was 15. The three of them had formed a unit. An elderly woman younger than her years, a young woman older than her years and a growing genius. Sounded like a situation comedy. Alex's family made her feel…well, surrounded by love and support. They were a unique combination of chaos, hilarity, passion, grit, and love.

Skye turned as Linda came out on the terrace.

"Where's Alex?" she asked as she came over and kissed Skye on the cheek.

"The last I saw him, he was taking off toward the stables," said Skye smiling.

"Smart man. Do you have everything ready?"

"That's an affirmative. The initial strategic planning phase of Operation Matrimony is well under way and today we'll discuss everyone's assignment." She indicated the neat stack of files on the desk inside. Linda hid her grin behind her teacup. She and Skye had trained together in Colorado. Everyone knew, even back then, that Skye was going to be a star. She was very physical and ate up the rigorous conditioning and combat training, but she was also organized and a born leader. Linda had worked several cases where Skye was SAC, and she was the best. The fact that they were also great friends was just a side benefit. Today she was Skye's friend, not her colleague, so she'd relax and enjoy the moment.

"Loosen up, Skye, will you? This is a wedding, not the investigation of an international drug cartel."

Turning to her, Skye blinked. Then she gave a little laugh. "I guess I've approached it a little like a major op. Jim always said the devil is in the details." Skye looked back out over the gardens. "A part of me can't believe this is happening, Linda."

"Well, if it's a dream, don't wake me up."

They both turned as they heard Connie, Sloane, and Hazel come into the room, all talking at once.

"Forget it, Hazel. I'm not going to do it," said Sloane.

"Do what?" asked Linda.

"Hazel has a scheme," said Connie, joining Linda by the food tray, always unerringly finding the goodies in any room regardless of its size and level of illumination.

"There's news," said Skye laughing.

A tiny woman wearing lime green capri length pants, moccasins and a faded tiger print polyester shirt swirled into the room behind Sloane. She had orange hair artfully arranged in some unique style only she could identify and held together by several butterfly clips. Skye leaned over and kissed the leathery cheek of her richly eccentric aunt.

"Look. You know those game shows?" Hazel asked in hopes of capturing allies.

"You mean like *Price is Right?*"

"Ohhh. That sexy Bob Barker. He's a hottie. He can eat crackers in my bed any day. But no, not like *Price is Right*. You have to know prices of things and I don't know when Sloane last bought a refrigerator."

"How about like never?" snorted Sloane, rolling her eyes.

"I mean like *Jeopardy* or the *Millionaire* show. No one could beat her. She knows every goddamn thing," explained Hazel.

"I don't know what color your hair really is."

"That was never a question on *Jeopardy*."

"Could be a whole category...*Colors of Crazy Hazel's Hair Since Puberty* for $500, Alex."

"Darling girl, I couldn't even answer that question. But Skye, really. Can't you see Sloane with those weenies on *Jeopardy* who think they know everything? They wouldn't be able to wedge in an answer." Hazel's hands were flying like an evangelistic preacher reaching out for converts.

"Alex, I'll take *Complete Indifference* for $100," said Sloane and tried to distract her aunt with little cinnamon buns from the food tray. Hazel didn't even skip a beat as she grabbed one with her flying right hand and used it to accentuate her point.

"Shouldn't be eating," she said as she took one in her flying left hand as well. "I want to look svelte for the wedding. But what the hell. When you get to be eighty just how many days have you got left to enjoy the simple pleasures? Not many, let me tell you." Then she turned back to Sloane. She might take a side road, but she always had her main quarry in sight. "Sloane, really. You're a natural."

"What's a 10 letter word for disinterested."

Hazel made a sound like a buzzer. "What?"

"Phlegmatic."

Hazel stuffed another bun in her mouth and threw up her hands. Her rightness in this obvious. "I knew she had potential when she was doing the *New York Times* crossword puzzle at the age of 5...in ink. Look out little girl, 'cause I'm going to shift into relentless on this one."

"Where have you been this whole week, for God's sake?" Sloane looked at Skye with mock exasperation. "This guy on *Jeopardy* won $12,000 in one day and the next day he didn't know that the mitral valve controls the blood flow between the left atrium and left ventricle of the heart."

Connie looked at Skye and said with round eyes. "What a dunce. I was just telling Duncan the other day, better slow it down a little, sugar, or you might pop your mitral valve."

Hazel slapped her knee and laughed. She really liked that one. "Well, the guy lost it all! But it wasn't that. There might be ten or so people in the whole viewing public who know that valve thing. It was what this girl said after that. Stay with me on this now. I told Sloane I knew someone with valve problems. At my age I know someone with every damn kind of problem really, so I was just making conversation during the Depends commercial. I get real squeezy during that commercial knowing it's just a matter of time before they appear on my regular shopping list so I can have that independent life style they say comes with every bag. Which I intend to have. Not going to stay home like Lydia just because I squirt when I sneeze." Sometimes following Hazel's digressions could make the listener dizzy, but somehow she always came back to where she started. She had a point and it was best to let her find it for herself. "Anyway, Sloane took her nose out of her book on some advanced form of nuclear engineering. You know, that big fat one I stand on when I need to get the green bowl off the top of the hutch. And she said to me 'they can fix that.' I said one word, just one freaking word. I said 'oh?' and she said, 'Yeah. Three possibilities, commentary, commissary…

"Commissurotomy, valvuloplasty, or a valve replacement," interrupted Sloane before she could stop herself.

"See? Then she went back to her book. That's her idea of conversation. I say a one-syllable word that I learned in kindergarten and she rattles off a medical dictionary like it was a list of common spices. You know like salt, pepper, paprika." Hazel laughed loudly and moved right along taking everyone on the terrace with her. "So I was talking to Livingston on that new cell phone you got me for emergencies. Anytime I'm getting hungry to talk to my honeypot, well, I think that pretty much defines emergency. Hot. Hot. Hot." Livingston was Dr. Livingston Lacy, retired, whom she zeroed in on while he was treating Skye and was Hazel's new steady beau. Dr. Lacy was a lifelong bachelor and even though Hazel scared the hell out of him, she fascinated him at the same time. They were getting to be quite an item. "Anyway, I get on the phone and ask him what he'd do if someone came in with a valve problem. And he said…now come with me on this one boys and girls…he said he'd have to look it up. Look it up! Can you believe it? And he hasn't lost any of his marbles like poor Dr. Gannon down at the senior center. Only surgery they let him perform now is cutting our toenails. Seems to enjoy it though. Especially Frida's. She still wears short skirts and sometimes forgets her underwear. So anyway if an excellent doctor like my sweetie pie has to look the damn thing up and Sloane has it just filed up there in her gray matter…well. I rest my case on a Serta!" Hazel laughed with delight again. "I figure I'll take care of the research into how we get her on the show and she can take care of the easy part…making us the big bucks."

There was complete silence in the room for about four seconds, then Hazel's distinctive high laugh filled the space. "My million dollar baby!"

Sloane just covered her face with her hands. "Alex, I'll *take Crazy Women with Orange Hair* for $100."

Bill came into the room and smiled. "Is Alex here? I wanted to tell him we brought our clubs if he wanted to do 18 later."

"No, they were talking to Alex Trabek," grinned Connie.

"Who?"

Hazel launched herself at Bill to pitch her idea on how to finance the rest of her retirement. He actually thought the idea had merit.

"Why not?" shrugged Bill. He'd always been fascinated with Sloane's genius. And the fact that she had a fresh, extroverted, age appropriate personality to go with it made her all the more remarkable. It was Skye and Hazel who could take the credit for her well adjusted mix of incredible academic accomplishments and her teenage quirkiness. "You certainly have the talent. And you're as photogenic as hell."

"Sure. Just what I need to fit in. The freakazoid on national television. Alex, I'll take *Why I Will Never Get a Date for the Prom* for $1,000."

"Is Alex here?" asked Carter coming into the room and making Sloane groan. "Did you tell him we brought our clubs, Bill?"

"We were taking about Alex Trabek."

"Of *Jeopardy?*"

"Yes."

"Did someone finally talk Sloane into setting the record?"

"I'm not going on the show," said Sloane emphatically.

Carter winked at her. "Not without a good haircut, anyway. Are you going to let Ida do something with all of this?" He took a handful of her hair and let it fall through his fingers.

"What. Now that Skye has found her dream man and your work there's complete, you think you can turn your manic attention on me?" asked Sloane, backing away from him.

"Of course," chuckled Carter and went to rescue a cinnamon bun from Hazel's growing appetite.

"Oh. Okay. As long as we understand each other."

Carter was Bill's partner and they'd been together for years. They'd both been working for International Airlines when Skye introduced them at a party. Carter was now the Vice President of Marketing, but he'd been a captain before moving into the corporate office. He was also the public spokesperson for the company, reaching celebrity status as the star of all their commercials. He was the picture of a handsome captain and he looked terrific in a uniform.

Carter and Bill considered Skye their pet project over the years and now their friend was fulfilling all of their dreams. She was going to be a bride. Parties, flowers, fabulous clothes, the best champagne. They each had a fat folder and were ready with swatches, samples, web sites, and a palm pilot full of caterers. Life was a dream.

"Oh, by the way, Skye," said Bill opening his stuffed briefcase. "We brought someone else who was in the neighborhood. Alex, your Alex, not Alex Trabeck, thought she might like to join the party." He looked out the door. "Stopped to talk with Duncan a minute. Here she is."

In walked a beautiful, auburn haired woman with sparking green eyes and an irresistible smile. When you have access to a jet, anywhere in the world is 'in the neighborhood'…even Chicago. Bill and Carter beamed at each other, knowing they'd scored a big one.

"Wyatt!" Skye's voice rose in absolute delight. She jumped up and enthusiastically hugged the woman who would soon become her mother-in-law. "Is Blake with you?"

"Of course, the last I saw him, he was running for the hills along with my son and Duncan."

"Can you stay for the entire weekend?"

"That's the plan."

"What about Tank?" Tank was Alex's little brother, although he hadn't been little since he hit puberty. He was a Chicago police officer and a beautiful combination of hard muscle and soft personality. Skye loved him madly.

"He's on duty and couldn't come. You'll have to count on me to make sure he's properly briefed." Alex's mom talked her language and they grinned at each other.

Captain Wyatt Earp Cooper, Alex's mother, was a legend in the Chicago police department. She was third generation cop. Her dad was a captain before retiring to Arizona and her grandfather was a marshal in the old west. Her brothers, Bat Masterson Cooper and Elliot Ness Cooper, were also in law enforcement. Bat with the State Highway Patrol and Elliot, of course, with the FBI.

Alex's dad, Blake Springfield, was an older version of Alex…tall, gorgeous, and commanding. He was also one of the leading prosecuting attorneys in the country. Wyatt arrested the criminals and Blake put them away. They were a real law and order duet.

When everyone had greeted everyone else and the volume of chatter in the room was reaching the noise level of the stadium on Super Bowl Sunday, Skye called the meeting to order. She brought out her folders and briefed everyone on their duties. She listened to their ideas, admired everything Bill and Carter had put together and began to make decisions.

"I'm thinking of a carved pumpkin décor," said Hazel as Skye started talking about decorations. "You have a wedding this close to Halloween and you have an automatic theme."

"I like it. We could have Dracula wait staff serving Bloody Marys and Tombstone Pizza hors d'oeuvres," added Sloane helpfully.

"Yes and the bridesmaids could wear orange dresses with black accessories. The guests can be encouraged to come in costume," agreed Bill, his eyes sparkling.

"Just so it doesn't clash with Hazel's hair," added Carter.

"That goes without saying."

"Wait," said Skye holding up her hand and laughing.

"Hey *ghoul* friend," said Connie. "Get into the *spirit* of the thing."

"I can *dig* it," said Bill.

"I think Skye would like to *bury* it," added Wyatt.

"Consider it a *dead* issue," shrugged Linda.

"But I heard that business elite are all *dying* to get an invitation," said Carter.

"But don't you think a Halloween theme is much too *grave* for the occasion," asked Wyatt.

"Enough!" Skye said, laughing. Then waited a few beats. "As if the idea had a *ghost* of a chance in the first place."

That started them all going again. Finally, Skye turned to her beloved aunt. "Hazel, I think I'd like to go a bit more traditional." Skye's voice became soft, almost dreamy. Certainly persuasive. "Try to visualize this. I was thinking of a complete sensory experience. We'll engage all the senses and create an unforgettable environment of lovely hospitality. First, acres of flowers. White Gardenias in particular. They aren't in season, so we'll have to plant them from the hothouse just for the day. They'll delight both the sense of smell and the sense of sight. I think it will enhance the day if our friends and family are sitting in a garden of visually pleasing color and fragrance. When we blend in soft rhythmic music from a small string orchestra and serve chilled champagne, we'll stimulate their sense of taste and hearing.

"At the same time we'll introduce drama though our vows. We'll weave in desire and passion with the stunning beauty of the women standing next to me. And as a final sensory treat, we'll spice it up with a heavy portion of sensuality because there is nothing hotter than a man in a tux. Put four impressively handsome men in front of a beautifully appointed altar and it will be like Shangri-La."

There was complete silence. How do you improve on perfection? Finally, Hazel gave it a shot.

"Been there. Except they called it *Shag-a-lot*. It was a tacky bar just off the strip. Good God, Skye. Where did all that sappy stuff come from? You sound like an infomercial for aromatherapy and happy, happy, joy, joy spas." Hazel's eyes narrowed until her artificial eyelashes nearly merged with her cheeks. She was fooling no one. Everyone had seen the tears that threatened to spill over. She sucked them in, not wanting to dissolve the glue keeping her eyelashes in place. "So are you saying there's no room in all that for the pumpkin carving contest and the bride of Frankenstein mannequins?"

"Yes, Hazel. That's what I am saying." She saw Hazel's teasing grin and knew no feelings were being crushed.

"All right then, I'll just have to take my ideas to the Senior Center. They like holiday themes. Reminds everybody what month it is. And that's a good thing if you're in a room with no windows."

Bill and Carter's final folder concerned showers. Skye stared at it, not knowing just how to put the brakes on their ideas. The thought of attending showers made her shudder...like she was tempting fate. She flashed on the last time she was to be a bride and the excruciating task of returning all the lovely gifts the weeks after Jeff was killed. There was a growing constriction in her chest.

Hazel's eyes narrowed as she glanced at her niece.

"One of the great advantages of being gay," said Bill. "Is that you get to attend both the bridal showers and the bachelor parties."

"Yes," agreed Carter. "We get to make table favors and open gifts with the girls, then get dressed in leather and drink a half keg of beer with the boys."

"Who's planning the bachelor party?" asked Sloane.

"That would be the best man. Says he's been planning it for almost ten years," laughed Bill.

"What do you know, Wyatt?" asked Carter.

Wyatt shook her head. "All I know is that Tank's been rummaging around old boxes, laughing like a maniac and snorting like a bull. Blake will be there to be sure he doesn't do anything to jeopardize his future in law enforcement."

"I think we should have a bachelorette party. Forget the showers," suggested Hazel. "Sorry boys, but pastel umbrellas are out." On this Hazel intended to be firm. Skye had been through all of the traditional showers once before and Hazel didn't want to bring her niece any heartache. Not even a second of it this time. "I think we should try the *Cock a Diddly Do* Club."

Carter looked at the fat folder neatly labeled 'shower'...in it he had color schemes, possible locations from the L'essence d'Excellence to Nells, menus, party games. "You mean go to a male strip joint, drink over-priced, watered down drinks, eat stale fish shaped cheese cracker doodle things and watch nearly naked, well built men strip down to g-strings and romp across a stage?"

"Yeah," said Hazel bobbing her highly penciled eyebrows up and down on her forehead.

Carter looked at his folder, looked at Hazel and threw it over his shoulder. "Works for me," he said.

"What about me?" asked Sloane. "You know...kid on board."

"I think someone with a biology degree can handle a live demonstration of Anatomy and Physiology. We'll give you a special dispensation for one night," said Skye. She looked at her aunt and nodded slightly...communicating her gratitude and her love.

"I'm sure your brain cells are as ancient as the corns on my feet, girl. Time you see what all the fuss is about," agreed Hazel.

Sloane beamed. Libby's circuits were going to fry this time for sure. Primo. Ten, ten. Maybe she could take some pictures. Libby had brothers, but still, that wasn't the same. She was going to see nearly naked male bodies. Live. In person. Wicked.

"Now on to transportation. Since I'm going to be sliding into my role as bride and as such I'll have the power and position of an Empress, I'll be temporarily grounded. That means Bill and Carter, you're in charge of picking everyone up." They grinned at each other. In this case picking everyone up meant flying the Gulfstream across the continent. This was going to be their pleasure.

"You may have to include some counseling prior to the assignment, Skye," said Carter.

"Yes. The only problem we've ever had in our relationship is who gets the left seat," added Bill.

"We're both captains. Two captains in a cockpit are like two grizzlies in a cage with just one leg of lamb."

"I'm an employee of Skyward Air," said Bill reasonably. "I'm officially captain when Skye's not in the seat."

"But I have seniority. I was a captain five years before you. And this isn't officially a Skyward Air flight."

"The only reason you made captain before me is because you're eight years older, daddy."

"That only means I have seniority in life, too. More experience."

"Experience flashing your captain's wings in front of a camera for the last four years. Besides, I have the uniform and hat of Skyward Air. The plane is owned by Skyward Air. You're a bit too broad to fit into my uniforms and you certainly can't wear Skye's."

"Not in public, anyway."

"No uniform…no cockpit privileges. It's the law."

"What law?"

"The unbreakable, unassailable law of fashion."

"Well, I designed them and I could get Antoine to make me one in less than 36 hours."

"Boys, boys." Skye was laughing and, like the rest of them, enjoying the Carter and Bill show. "How about this. Carter, go ahead and get the uniform made. I think it's a good idea to have one in the closet for whenever we need a third pilot. Bill, how about you sit in the left seat going west, and Carter, you sit in it going east."

They looked at each other and shrugged. Problem solved. Almost. "Well, who gets the captain's hat," asked Carter.

"You share," said Skye.

"His head's too big and getting bigger with every autograph he signs, I might add," snorted Bill. "Mine won't fit him." And off they went into another match.

Good God, thought Skye, smiling as she looked into the faces of her friends and family, all talking, laughing at once. How did her well-organized special op turn into a circus? Oh well, what the hell. It was exactly what she wanted.

"Let's move onto the real challenge," said Sloane. "How to find a tux to fit Duncan,"

"That's on Alex's check list," laughed Skye, waving a relatively small piece of paper.

"Someone mention my name?" Duncan himself walked into the room, nearly filling half of it. He was Alex's driver, mechanic, and friend and would be standing with Alex at the wedding. Over six feet six inches and muscled up from years of pumping iron, he was, in a word, huge. He winked at Connie and she sent him some air kisses. They were seeing each other regularly now. "I just wanted to remind Brainchild that it was time for her to be tracking."

Duncan was shuttling Sloane back to the university where she'd be completing her doctorate in Computer Science in December. He often drove her around when Alex was out of town or didn't need him. It wasn't easy for Sloane to coordinate classes at two universities and an internship at Justice when she didn't even have a driver's license. Duncan loved the extra duty. Not only had he been taken with Sloane from the first moment they met, Skye thought it had something to do with the fact that Sloane was teaching Duncan to read. It was supposed to be a secret, but it didn't take a trained investigator to work the clues.

Duncan wasn't unintelligent, just uneducated. He'd grown up in the streets of Miami, completely out of the system after he ran away at the age of 10. He and Alex had met when Alex caught him borrowing one of his vintage cars. Although he'd finished most of his growing, he was just a kid at the time. Couldn't believe the Bossman just stared him down. Duncan was used to people giving him a wide berth and did a real good look of mean at him, too. Bossman didn't even blink.

Alex was so impressed that someone had circumvented his security system; he threw Duncan the keys to the car and told him that if he brought it back, he'd give him a job.

It took Duncan the better part of a week to decide to trust the Bossman and test his word. When he brought the car back, Alex put him immediately on the payroll. His job was to maintain the fleet of cars and drive them when Alex needed a lift. Duncan figured he must have died along the way and gone straight to heaven. He'd give his life for the boss.

"What about your dress?" asked Connie, coming back in after seeing Duncan off. "You haven't even begun to shop. My sister had her dress before she had her man. Are you waiting for a white sale at JC Penney?"

Skye shuddered at the thought of even looking for a wedding dress. It was something she needed to do; she just didn't want her collapsing stomach to intrude on this beautiful day. She was having too much fun. Later. When she was alone and could fully deal with her anxiety, she'd think about it.

"I have that covered," she said quickly, then guaranteed a change of topic by mentioning the possibility of raw oysters over crab puffs at the reception. Carter loathed oysters. Bill loved them.

The little niggling fear at the back of her brain, the doomsayer always there but silent during the day, whispered she'd been here before. The planning, the laughter, the attendants. Flowers, food, and guest lists. And the dress. She'd donated the dress she was supposed to wear to her wedding with Jeff to Aunt Hazel's senior center for a benefit auction. It was the dress she saw in her nightmares. It was the dress that symbolized her fear that this could all go bad.

In her nightmares, where one dress used to hang, there were now two. She'd vowed she'd never buy another wedding dress. It would be like temping fate. Would something happen? If she bought another dress would that set off the chain of events what would leave her with a broken heart and another wedding dress hanging unused in the closet? She'd always thought she could get married in a nice suit. A nice aqua suit. She looked around the room and scolded herself. Coward. There was nothing sinister about a lovely long white dress.

Well, she sighed, she also vowed she'd never fall in love with, much less marry, another man in law enforcement. So much for promises made to yourself when the heart was involved. She loved Alex madly and wouldn't consider a life without him now. But there was that dark shadow and it was brutal.

CHAPTER 6

Alex always knew when another one was coming on, even though they didn't have a pattern. Sometimes she'd start dreaming almost immediately and sometimes it wouldn't ambush her until almost dawn. She'd start moving, trying to fight off the demons. Then came the horrible battle with the images of fire, blood, and bodies. She'd either wake up screaming or weeping uncontrollably. There didn't seem to be anything he could do but hold her tightly until the storm passed. Cradled in his arms, she'd eventually go back to sleep and could usually finish out the night in peace.

Nothing stopped them. When Alex suggested medication, she absolutely refused. She tried meditation, visualization, relaxation, chamomile tea, and aromatherapy. She cut out meat and cheese, then doubled her intake of meat and cheese.

During the day, she could deal with it. She talked about the dreams and was determined not to let them have any impact on getting married, being happy, and making a life together with Alex.

The nightmares had been relentless since their return from Paris. Tonight it had been particularly vicious. It must have been all the wedding planning that day. This was one of the screaming nights. He was instantly awake the minute the first one ripped through him. He could feel his own heart galloping and couldn't imagine what it was like for her. Before the second scream, he had her gathered in his arms.

"Shhh. Darling wake up. Sweetheart. Shhh." She clung to him and wept. This time it was her old dream joining forces with the bomb. Pieces of bloody wedding dresses and smoke and fire. And she was watching it all. Standing at the empty altar once again.

As he calmed her down, the nightmare faded, but the terror didn't completely dissolve. She could smell the smoke, taste the blood, feel the heat.

"Darling. Please," she sobbed. "Let me go sleep in another room. You don't need this. You need your rest, you need peace." But she clung to him, her hand seeking his heart. Alex knew what she needed. When she felt the steady beat, she could rest, go back to sleep.

"No," said Alex and held her tighter. It made him angry that there was a part of her that still wanted to flee from him. He rubbed her back, trying to relax her until she fell asleep again. "I can't be without you anymore. I need you here where I can watch you, hold you."

Tonight Skye needed more than just the soothing sound of his voice and the touch of his hands, because she'd come to a decision…one she was determined to carry through. In the morning she was going to leave, go back to her old home in Virginia to stay until the wedding. They could see each other during the day, but in the night she'd fight her own battles…alone. Alex deserved to have a restful night. Other couples did it. It wasn't like it was forever. When she thought of being away from him during the long nights, her heart ached.

But she was determined, so tonight she needed more. Her lips sought his and she kissed him with her whole aching heart behind it. Rolling him back onto the pillows, she put heat and power into her kiss, moving her hands over him, around him.

"Let me," she whispered as she trailed her lips and tongue down his body. She felt the sharp intake of his breath as her vigor increased and the residual relief of hearing his strong heart beat turned into a powerful need to mate. She took him into the madness with her and for a time, neither of them had a coherent thought. If she was going crazy, let that be the fuel to please him, to surprise him, to arouse him, she thought. If she was going over the edge, she was determined to give him this night to feel only her strength, her desire, her love.

"I love you," she whispered over and over again.

Alex felt wave after wave of pleasure and mindless need. From the depths of his consciousness, he knew she was touching more than his body. She was going as deep as she could go to find his essence, his soul. Diving in she continued to move and shift and ride until his release was complete and he was no longer grounded. It was wild and primal and natural and yet, because there was heart, it was uniquely human.

When they finally cooled down, just before dawn, they were both exhausted. He gently smoothed the hair back from her sweaty face. She was sound asleep in a dreamless state, her head resting on his chest, just over his heart. That was good. It would heal her. He kissed her and before he joined her in sleep, he whispered.

"You're my life. And you're not going anywhere." He knew she was planning something. He saw into her heart when she was making love to him…and he could guess that it had to do with her leaving. There was a slight smile on his lips. The beast inside him sure did like her method of saying goodbye. Maybe he should let her go just to see what that primitive side of her would do when they said hello again.

Skye came up from her deep sleep slowly. The wild session of lovemaking came back to her as soon as she moved her legs. Her thighs were well muscled and firm as granite, but there were some muscles in there that begged her pardon and wanted to register an opinion on how they'd been used and abused the night before. She shifted to get in a more comfortable position and a few more spots joined the protest. Toughen up, she smiled. I like it hot sometimes. I need it hot sometimes. She fell back to sleep with a contented smile on her face.

Later, she felt the sun through her closed lids. Slowly her lips turned up...she knew she'd be fine now. In the light of day, her nightmares were without power. She made that so. They robbed her of her nights when her defenses were down, but she'd be damned if they were going to take the joy from her days. She managed to push the images back and refused to let them intrude on her happiness and excitement. She knew from experience they would eventually go away. They would become less frequent, then fade.

She reached for Alex and found the bed empty. Sighing, she swung her legs over the side. When she smelled coffee, she smiled. It wasn't until she felt Alex kiss her cheek and put a cup in her hands that she realized her eyes were still closed.

"Thanks," she said and sipped the rich, black coffee. The caffeine helped give strength to her eyelids and she opened them. She blinked a couple of times and heard Alex chuckle.

"What are you doing?"

"Deep thinking and cautious sipping. I think maybe my eyes will open for business soon. What are you doing?"

"Making millions so you can replant the gardens for the wedding."

"Okay. But I think you can stop at three or four."

He came over and knelt down in front of her. She looked pale and tired.

"How about you roll back over and sleep for a few more hours."

"I will if you join me," she reached over and pulled at his tie.

"I wish I could, but I have a lot to clear off my desk before the wedding. Barclay and I are going to meet this afternoon to go over backgrounds we've uncovered. He's a wiz at getting the data, but he has no idea what to do with it. There might even be a Russian connection."

"Russian? Not some old cold war stuff."

"No. Some everyday criminal stuff. The Russian mafia. We were going over some of the contacts our thief made before settling on the highest bidder. Some of the bids came from St. Petersburg and Murmansk. If they have a few of the warheads of the old Soviet Union, this new guidance system would have been a very nifty accessory."

Skye nodded thoughtfully. "The Russian mafia. I know some of them."

Alex looked into her eyes. "Care to elaborate?"

"Not really. Closed case. Maybe someday when we're rocking out on the front porch. we can share old war stories."

He smiled at the thought of their rocking on the front porch. They both had a lot of living to do first. What she was really saying was she preferred not to go there. He understood that. They rarely talked about their old cases and that was all right with him. Some things were best not revisited.

"Alex?" With that one word, he knew what was coming.

"No," he said decisively, kissed her lightly, and straightened.

That opened her eyes wide. "What do you mean 'no.'"

"I think 'no' is a perfectly understandable word."

Her eyes narrowed and she put aside her cup. "How did you know I wasn't going to ask you if you wanted a five finger quickie before you left for the office."

He laughed. "Because I know you."

She actually did fall back on the bed. "Alex. I want to go to back home until the wedding."

"Let's see…I think I already answered that. No. You are home."

"It wasn't a question, Alex."

He sat down next to her, grabbed her hand, and levered her back up to a sitting position. He took her chin in his strong fingers and turned her face around to his.

"Look at me. I'm not going to let you go. Not even for the few weeks we have before the wedding. I don't want you sleeping alone. Please, Skye. I love you and I want you in my bed."

"But Alex." Her eyes teared up. "I wake you up nearly every night now. I think they're getting worse. My idiotic subconscious is nervous about the wedding, even though I'm not. At night that part of me gets around my usual defenses. Alex, I'm a raving lunatic, and I can't keep robbing you of your peace."

"I'd be less at peace not having you here with me. I'd be pacing all night like a caged animal. You may wake me for a few minutes, but I think that's better than having me go crazy."

"We can get together for sex and such."

"Sex and such?" He laughed again. "Go back to sleep, my love. I'm not talking about sex and such. I'm talking about having the woman I love near me while I sleep." He kissed her cheek.

"But…"

"Of knowing where she is," he kissed her neck.

"But…" She was losing her train of thought.

"Of knowing she's safe," he kissed her ear.

"Alex, please." The train jumped the track.

"Do you love me?" His eyes compelled hers to look deeply into them.

"Of course, but…"

"Then please." He kissed her lips. "Don't leave me."

She deepened the kiss and felt his resolve. Finally, she whispered, "I surrender."

"Now about that quickie," he said, changing his mind about the morning meetings and removing his tie.

Later, he got redressed and covered his exhausted fiancée. She was sleeping and he knew it would be a restful, dreamless sleep now. She'd already fought the demons that night. She needed a distraction, he thought, then smiled. And he had just the thing that would do it.

Pavel read Rosalie's report. There wasn't much on her…this Skyler Madison. Fabulous alias! A bark of laughter escaped him as he read on. Skyler. Right. Sounded like the name of a comic book heroine or something. The world was so gullible. But then, he couldn't complain. He'd made a fortune off that fact…and it appeared as though this Skyler person was on her way to doing the same. She was engaged to one of the richest men in the country. Great con! Fabulous con! The Mt. Everest of cons! He truly appreciated immoral genius.

The file was thin, the background information sketchy. Rosalie said the lack of concrete data was unusual, considering she'd been an Ambassador's daughter. And there were several extremely sophisticated blocks on all of her personal records…indeed if there were any at all. She couldn't get the bitch's social security number, government documents, school credentials…nothing. Like she'd already worked hard to expunge her earlier life. Pavel smiled and nodded his approval. What a pro! She was in his league for sure. He got some perverse pleasure from that. For years, it had been a mortifying memory…bested by some farm girl. Brought down by a provincial milkmaid. Now he found he'd been in a battle with the goddess of deceit, the empress of larceny.

And here was another fascinating tidbit! Perfect. What a prodigy! There had been an explosion when she was still in her teens and her parents had been killed while she watched from a piazza in Rome. He almost had an orgasmic reaction to that bit of news. So she killed her parents, too! Bravo! If he had a country, she could be its queen. He was momentarily torn between taking her as a life partner and having his life back. But then, he was a narcissist, so it really wasn't much of a skirmish.

There was one other important detail that was so coincidental; it was like it was pre-ordained. The anti-god trying to right the wrong. Not that he could ever get the last six years back, but this was sure to bring balance into the dark side of the universe! Fate herself not only placed that *Newsweek* in his line of vision, but she connected one Skyler Madison to the place of his self-imposed exile.

The gullible mark's parents lived right here in Chicago! Alexander Springfield…son of Captain Wyatt Cooper. Pavel wasn't much for national or world news, but he did like to keep up with the local press coverage. Especially the police beat. An occupational necessity since he was back running drugs, guns, and women.

Captain Wyatt Cooper was very well known to law enforcement. God. Poetic justice defined! The indomitable Captain Wyatt Cooper. The really thick Captain Wyatt Cooper. The queen of con was engaged to her son and she couldn't even see it. See through it. It would almost be worth it to let this Virginia/Skyler, or whoever she was, play it to the end. Just stand back and enjoy the show! What was her ultimate game? Take the sap for a bundle? Or maybe go for the whole enchilada. Arrange for widowhood.

Pavel sighed. What a woman. What a fine con. Too bad he had other plans for her. Plans he had six years to dream about, but never thought he'd ever be able to implement. She was the key to his prison, his ticket home, his bridge out of exile.

He turned to the three men standing guard in the corner of his home office. A strategy came to him clear and well formed in an instant. That was his genius, he thought.

First he needed to personally confirm her identity. He had to be sure before he put his life on the line. Nothing was more precious to him than his life!

"Call in all the troops, I want to brief them."

CHAPTER 7

Alex wanted to be alone with Skye, so he took his truck out of the garage and drove around to the front entrance. They hadn't had a lot of time together, just the two of them. Between Operation Matrimony, working on the case and before that, the final outfitting of the corporate Gulfstream and the implementation of the strategic initiatives for the Skyward Corporation, they had very separate and intensely time consuming responsibilities. He looked at Skye as she skipped down the front steps and threw open the passenger door. She seemed to thrive under all the details and duties. She was still far too thin, but she was getting her color back and was filling out some of the curves she'd lost.

When they'd compared their calendars last week, this afternoon was the only significant opening until the wedding. He wanted to give her the wedding present he'd been working on for the last few months. Ever since he finally wore her down and got her to commit, he'd been keeping a secret from her. Today was the day he unveiled it.

Most of the time he didn't think much about his wealth one way or the other. He liked the thrill of acquisition, negotiation, and exercising his intelligence, but the actual money was just a side effect of his actions. In the past, it sometimes interfered with his relationships. People would befriend him and then hit him for a loan; women would respond to him and then seem to be more interested in his credit line than in his wit.

Skye never paid any attention to it. She was well off in her own right, but Alex was consistently listed as one of *Fortune Magazine's* wealthiest men in America. In a word, he was loaded. But it wasn't something that consumed him. His passions these days were Skye and his work for the Justice Department. Money wasn't something he thought much about anymore…on the other hand, there were days like today when he just loved being stinking, filthy rich.

They drove to the general aviation airport near their new home where she hangared her little Cessna 182. He'd asked her to fly him to a meeting this afternoon…to a small corporate facility that wouldn't accommodate the Gulfstream. She saw it as a great opportunity to combine her love of flying with her love of being with Alex and was really looking forward to the afternoon. Just the two of them for a change.

Skye was feeling as light as air. Everything was going great with the wedding plans, the corporate Gulfstream was a dream to fly, the case was coming to complete closure, and she was nearly 100 percent physically. The day was one of those sky-blue days, her father used to say. Alex didn't often go up with her in the Cessna, so this was going to be fun.

Resting her feet on the dashboard, she tapped time to Jimmy Buffet's *It's A Rag Top Day*. Her sneakers left little prints in the accumulated dust and pealing paint. The truck was Alex's first investment. He was fifteen and a half and he paid $450 for the then14 year old Ford pickup. It was money he made mowing lawns and running errands for neighbors. He polished it every day…back when it had paint. When he got his driver's license on his 16th birthday, he drove it proudly around the neighborhood and later on many teenage adventures…some sanctioned, some not.

Nearly two decades later, with a lot of tender loving care from Duncan, there was still magic under the rusty, dusty hood. It ran like a dream. It only looked like a nightmare. Alex had leather seats installed about 10 years before when the old vinyl couldn't take any more duct tape. He loved driving it, even though he owned several foreign and domestic cars, SUVs, and motorcycles.

Before he met Skye, he usually left his beloved truck in the garage, more symbolic than functional, only taking it out when he wanted to drown himself in nostalgia. He remembered one particularly painful incident when he playfully brought it around to pick up a woman he'd been seeing and she refused to get into it…was insulted by the offer. That was their last date. He figured they just weren't compatible. Like me, like my truck.

On his first trip to visit Skye's family, he went on a hunch and picked her up in it. She took one look at it and grinned at him. She didn't get the attraction, but she seemed to like riding around in it. From that first day there was a very healthy love/hate relationship going with Skye and his pickup. She loved him though, truck and all. He knew the moment she hopped in that their relationship was solid and going to work.

Alex parked near the entrance to the small terminal.

"Wow," said Skye looking out on the tarmac. "Get a load of that beauty."

"What?" asked Alex opening her door and giving her a hand out.

"Someone brought in a Lear. Looks new. God, Alex…it's the 60 model. She has a rate of climb of 4,500 feet per minute and engine thrust of 4,600 pounds. Just a second while I get my pulse back on track."

"And I thought I was the only thing that could get your heart beat racing." This was going to be better than he thought.

She laughed. "You're the only one who can get it racing, then do something about it," she said. "A beautiful aircraft like that can just get me all hot and bothered, then fly away from me into the sunset." She gave him a quick kiss. "Not that I don't love my little Cessna and my magnificent Gulfstream."

"But the Cessna is a toy and the Gulfstream is a job…exciting and pleasant, but your work."

She glanced at him strangely. "Yeah. Exactly. You really get it."

"I do. It's like my truck and me. My other vehicles have a purpose. My truck's only job is to make me happy."

"If you say so. I think it only proves you need therapy." Her eyes were planted on the beautiful plane.

"Shall we go over and take a look."

"No. Why torture myself?" she grinned. "Let's go for a ride in my toy."

He took her arm and they went through the terminal and out onto the runway. She noticed everyone staring at her. She looked down at her blouse and jeans.

"What?" he asked.

"I just wanted to check and make sure nothing was falling out or undone. People are staring at me in there."

"That's a bit paranoid." He looked at her beautiful face. "Or self absorbed."

"Yeah. My imagination." She looked around. "I thought you said you called ahead and the plane was ready."

"I did."

"Well?" she asked, sweeping her arm out and raising her eyebrows in an 'I don't see the plane out and ready, idiot' look.

God, he was enjoying himself. Alex couldn't remember a more fantastically executed and beautifully orchestrated mission he'd ever staged than this one. It had everything. Drama. Suspense. A pretty woman. A benevolent benefactor. A titanic surprise ending. All it needed was a symphony playing music that would culminate it an enormous crescendo…right about…now. Man, he wished he'd have thought of that. Well, too late now.

He cupped her face in his hand, gave her lips a light tap with his own, then turned her in the direction of the jet. "It *is* ready, my love. I present you with your wedding gift."

She looked at the gorgeous jet, then back at him. Putting her arms around his neck she gave him a big smooch on the lips, then looking back at the hangar, she laughed with delight. A group of mechanics were watching them.

"Shall we go ask them to bring out the Cessna? Obviously they didn't get the message."

Alex laughed, too. This was just getting better and better. "No, darling. It's you who isn't getting the message." He taped her temple with his finger, took her by the shoulders, and pointed her toward the Lear again. "Your plane is out and ready to be given its pre-flight check. You're certified as a qualified pilot in this model. I confirmed it a few months ago."

"Well, certainly I can…" She looked at the plane, then back at him. Grinning, she turned to all the people gawking at her from the windows and doorways in the terminal. She waved. They waved back.

"So everyone here was in on this?"

"They found out yesterday when it arrived."

"Wow. Alex. This is going to be fun." She looked at the sleek, well-designed jet. The stairway had been lowered, inviting them in. "How long can we have it? Did you rent it?"

"No," he said slowly. Now for the big payoff. "I bought it. It's yours."

"Mine. Yeah. Right," she said, snorting at the joke. It was a good one. "As in honey, I just bought you a nice chair to go with the sofa. Or darling, I bought you that set of glassware you were admiring in Macy's window?"

"No," he grinned. "As in honey, I love you. As in darling, I wanted to buy you something that wasn't even on your list, but has been in your good dreams. As in darling, every time you see one of these taxiing down a runway, you nearly suffer whiplash watching it take off. As in darling, there are times when being really, really rich can be fun."

"So you went out and bought me one at the local Plane-mart." She snickered. "You really crack me up. Whoops. Shouldn't say crack up when taking my future husband for an air spin."

"And you shouldn't act like an ungrateful wench, or I'm going to send it back." Grinning even more broadly, he pointed at the name on the plane. Destiny. She'd been so busy looking at the lines of the plane, she hadn't noticed. Something was starting to creep in to her consciousness. Something more wonderful that just about anything she could imagine.

Reaching inside his pocket, he pulled out a set of shiny new keys. A gold key ring with the word Destiny written on it gave her a clue to where they'd fit. She was a seasoned investigator after all. She could put the clues together…they just took a moment to compute. She had to move to a whole new frame of reference.

He saw the play of emotions cross her face. Shock, disbelief, incredulity, then his favorites…delight, enchantment, excitement. He'd seen some of the same emotions that morning when they decided to start their day in the shower and wound up rolling around on the floor of the bedroom, gathering a few rug burns along the way. Watching this show was almost as good as an afternoon of sex. Well, not really. But better than a movie or an afternoon on the golf course. Well, maybe not the golf course.

She looked at Alex, then back at the lovely, graceful jet. It was sleek and beautiful in the afternoon sun. As if the weather decided to lend its grace to Alex's wedding gift, the sky couldn't have been bluer; the air couldn't have been fresher. She looked back at Alex's smiling face. He watched her every expression. Yeah…much better than golf.

She tried to laugh, but it got hung up in her throat. "Mine? You're serious? You aren't doing something really, really dirty here are you?"

He shook his head. "Shall we go take a look at the interior?"

"Have you already kicked the tires and checked under the hood?" she asked, the sparkle in her eyes and the sheer joy on her face were pictures he'd hold in his heart forever.

"I'd have no idea what I was looking at, but the ground crew has done just that, if you would like to take it for a test drive."

"I think I'd like to christen it first." She winked at him, grabbed the keys and ran toward the plane, turning half way there to face him and making little backward skipping movements, crooking her finger at him and wiggling her eyebrows. He smiled. He hadn't yet moved. Sometimes she was just so damned cute, he only wanted to watch…to take her in.

So she wanted to inaugurate the jet first. That brought his temperature up. He was also secretly thrilled. It was the little things she did that surprised and delighted him. Flying had always been the most important thing in her life, besides her family and friends. The fact that she'd postpone the excitement of flying her own jet even for a short time, gave him a jolt of pleasure. In his mind it was further proof that she loved him. He caught up with her by the time she reached the stairway to the plane. Grabbing her by the waist, he swept her off her feet and carried her up through the doorway like a modern day pirate.

He was kissing her deeply when she pressed the button to bring up the stairs and shut the door. She had her shirt off and was unbuttoning his by the time the door closed and engaged. She barely registered the beautiful interior designed by her future husband. All she was interested in was the answer to one question.

"Bed?" she gasped as she pulled at Alex's belt and worked his zipper down.

When her hand found the buried treasure, her pirate groaned, and whispered. "Rear."

His mouth was plundering its own treasure, his hands seeking more.

"Rear?" she asked in a teasing voice, planting hot little kisses along his jaw line and down his neck. Sliding her hands around to the back of his jeans, she moved below the waistline to his well-muscled butt.

"No, Captain…" He groaned again. He thought her hands were doing fine right where they'd been. His butt didn't agree but to hell with it. She moved her hands back to the front and nearly drove him to a climax standing barely two feet from the doorway. Exercising some control, he put his arms around her waist and lifted her. Completely molded to his body, panting his name and working her magic, they somehow made their way to the plane's rear. Alex pushed another button hoping he remembered the schematics and nothing would fall off or open up to the outside. The long leather sofa in the back flattened into a bed and they tumbled onto it as they finished undressing each other.

"I christen this plane Destiny," she whispered, as she felt the wonderful release wash over her. "Our Destiny."

They decided to christen it again before Skye got up to look at the cabin. She had his shirt on and was walking around barefoot. There was a basket of fruit on the table between the large, leather chairs so she snagged an apple and started munching between exclamations of pleasure. Alex just stood there, engaged in his favorite pastime. Watching Skye.

Feeling his eyes on her, she turned and held out the apple. "Wanna bite?" she asked and raised an eyebrow.

He looked down her entire torso. "It's a tempting offer, Eve."

"Try and resist, Adam." She took another bite, adding a little slurpy noise and some exaggerated tongue movement.

"We should have christened the plane The Garden of Eden," he said, feeling hot again.

"But then after one bite, you would have fallen out of it." Turning, she started forward to see the most important part. The cockpit. "And as I recall, you would have fallen out of it several times."

He shook his head; sometimes she took a conversation to points that left him dead-ended.

He decided to watch her some more rather than comment. Her long legs were extenuated by the fact that his shirt did little to cover more than her torso and butt. Following her, he leaned against the doorway, his arms folded over his bare chest.

"Can I have my shirt back?" he asked, suddenly inspired.

"Pardon?" She'd been inspecting the electronics and the radios while he'd been inspecting her.

"It's mine and I want it," he said tugging at it.

Smiling, she cocked her head. "But then I'd be completely naked."

"Exactly." When she only raised her eyebrows at him, he tugged again. "Well?"

"Take it up with the captain," she said wiggling her butt and turning to walk back to where her clothes were scattered. When she passed him, he reached under his shirt and cupped the moving butt, then squeezed and turned it into him. She didn't resist.

They stood in the doorway and played for a while, having fun and letting their hands and fingers enjoy recess. Finally, Skye let out an exaggerated breath. "Either you let me get dressed and take this baby up for a spin, or you finish the job here and take me for a spin."

"Both," he said and laughed when she jumped up in his arms and wrapped her strong, muscular legs around his waist.

"Fly me," she whispered in his ear before she started kissing and nibbling it. And he found both the take off and landing were very, very satisfying.

Later, after quite a bit of time in the small lavatory, she was all cleaned up and ready to take the plane up. Alex watched another complete transformation. She was all captain now. Safety and the responsibility for flight were very serious business for Skye. The sanctity of the cockpit and the protocol for take off dictated her actions and occupied her mind. She wouldn't endanger herself, her passengers, or other aircraft by acting unprofessionally. Even alone and unobserved, she conducted herself with solemn conscientiousness and professional precision. Alex respected that and stayed back while she went through her pre-flight routine. He admired her meticulous preparation and her scrupulous code of behavior and conduct.

She lowered the stairs again and went out to walk around the aircraft. She literally did kick the tires. She also took a powerful flashlight and checked all around the fuselage and the engines. Her inspection wasn't just a superficial peek. She had a degree in Aeronautical Engineering and really knew what she was looking at. And what she was looking at thrilled her in both its beauty and function. Satisfied, she climbed back in and closed up the door. She double checked the lock and secured the safety release.

"Are you ready, passenger Springfield?"

He nodded, knowing his role.

"Then buckle in, because we're going for a ride." She smiled when he went to a seat by the window and sat down. She didn't invite him up into the cockpit and he didn't ask. She appreciated that. He'd be a distraction. He respected people's positions and expertise and was never threatened by her superior knowledge and skill in certain areas. Just as she'd never expect to sit next to him in his boardroom or in negotiations with his business associates. They merged on most levels of their lives, but not all. And that was okay.

While Alex didn't intrude into the cockpit, he did take the chair that would afford him the best view of her working the controls. He was dressed now in his reclaimed shirt and wasn't sure whether it was such a good idea if he wanted to keep his mind off her wonderful warm, naked body for the rest of the afternoon. He could smell her distinctive perfume wafting up from it. Like an animal, he sniffed the scent of his mate on the collar. He sniffed again. Damn, she made him goofy. Time to move his mind to other things.

Watching her precise movements he listened to her no-nonsense tone when she communicated with the tower. She laughed at something one of the tower people said and responded with all the necessary jargon.

Then she flipped several switches firing up the engines and the scream of their duet drowned out any further opportunity to hear her voice.

Grabbing the intercom to the cabin she turned to him, winked and said, "Passenger Springfield, please buckle up. We've been cleared for take off."

She expertly taxied to the end of the runway where she completed all of her preflight routine. Then she strapped and harnessed herself in, shifted a bit in her seat to get her feet and arms planted and pulled the throttle to full power. The jet shot forward and was off the ground a few seconds later. They circled into the flight pattern and flew off to the west.

Skye tested every nuance, instrument, and radio; she banked the jet left and right in random patterns. Skye was in her element. She was a bird. Fast, lighter than air and free. She knew only happiness in the air. How could she ever thank Alex, she thought, for not just the gift of an aircraft, but for the gift of exhilaration? Of joy. She'd find a way. She glanced back at him. He was looking out the window and periodically paging through a file. Patient…wanting to participate in her favorite past time. Then an idea hit her. Calling in for a flight plan, she did some calculations. No problem. She made a few phone calls and everything was set.

An hour later, she went back on the intercom. Alex had been working on his laptop and looked up and out. He'd fixed her some coffee and checked on her a few times, asking if she was enjoying the test ride, assuming they were going in wide circles or something. They were over a layer of clouds. Perfect, Skye thought. He wouldn't see where they were until they were nearly on the ground.

"Passenger, darling, fiancé. We've been cleared for landing. Please turn off all electronic devices and secure all movable objects."

He grinned at her, turned off his computer, and raised his coffee cup. She smiled back and began her descent.

Alex recognized City Airport in Chicago the minute they popped through the clouds. He could see the familiar landscape of his youth, the Hancock building, the Sears Tower, and the new Soldiers Field. His grin got broader. These days he didn't go home often enough. He had no idea she intended to actually go somewhere. He wondered if his family was all on duty or if he should give them a call.

When they taxied to the smaller executive terminal, she pulled around at the direction of the ground crew and methodically turned everything off. She touched the instruments, the leather arms of her seat. A wonderful shiver went up her spine. Mine, she thought.

Turning, she smiled at Alex who was watching her from the doorway.

"So. You like it? Shall we keep it?"

Standing, she kissed him with both passion and infinite tenderness. "You're a wonder to me. I love the gift but the man who gave it even more. Thank you."

He licked her taste off his lips. "My pleasure."

"Shall we catch some dinner while we're here?" she asked.

"Sure. Maybe we can give Mom, Dad and Tank a call."

"Maybe," she said noncommittally as they opened the door and descended onto the tarmac. They crossed arm and arm toward the terminal. Alex was home. He rarely came back here. It wasn't that he didn't like Chicago. He loved it. It was just that the opportunities had been so limited over the last 10 years or so.

When they walked into the light and the bustle of the terminal, Alex and Skye were immediately greeted by shouts of welcome. Alex had only a second to look down at Skye's pleased face before he was embraced by a uniformed police officer bigger than a bear and a happy, handsome couple. Wyatt and Blake and baby brother Tank. Alex stood among his family and returned greetings and pleased family noises. They were all talking, laughing, hugging, and generally radiating love and affection. Skye watched Alex. He always looked and acted younger when he was around them. Years fell away and it was good for him. He grabbed her as they crossed the parking lot to the car and gave her a quick kiss.

"More of that later," he said softly. "For now, thanks."

"So how's life in the jet lane?" asked Tank and he and Skye kept up a steady flow of adrenalin induced chatter. Skye hadn't come out of the clouds yet, and Tank was always revved.

Tank was driving a late model SUV, racing through the back streets, not worrying overly much about the speed laws. Just coming off his shift, he hadn't had time to change. He looked different in his neatly pressed regulation uniform. He had them made special so that they would fit his large muscular body. He favored the Cooper side of the family with dark coppery hair and a stockier frame. Removing his hat, he pulled his fingers through his long wavy hair. It framed an extraordinarily handsome and expressive face with a smile that would stop a woman's heart. Shorter than Alex by 3 inches, he out weighed him and could bench-press an ox. He was far more outgoing than his older brother and was a constant source of both delight and consternation within the family. He was the perfect little brother.

His undergraduate degree was in criminal science and he was working toward a Masters Degree in forensic pathology. He graduated from the police academy nearly top in his class and was waiting to hear if he was accepted into the fast track special investigative division. He was making his mark all on his own in the law enforcement community. The fact that his mother was a well-respected captain on the Chicago police force and his father was the most successful District Attorney in recent history had nothing to do with his success. There was no arguing, however, that he came by his interest in the law early and often.

Tank had wanted to be a police officer since he could walk and talk. Alex chose the law and pretty much stayed away from the enforcement of it, going with corporate instead of criminal. Their sister Rita went to the academy right after college and then went on to New York to pursue her career away from familiar territory. It was where she met David Delton, a fellow officer, married, had two babies, and died. When Rita Cooper Springfield Delton had been killed in the line of duty, it was their family's lowest and saddest time. A dark time, when everyone reexamined their lives and choices. It was when Alex decided to join the fight.

As Tank rolled through another stop sign, his mother had to comment.

"Stop isn't just a suggestion, Tank," she admonished.

"Is that Captain Cooper talking, or my Mom?"

"Captain Cooper is off duty. That was your mother speaking."

"It that case…" Tank deliberately and with great showmanship stopped dead at the next stop sign he came to. "Captain Cooper's a wuss compared to…The Mother."

"Let's go to Carlo's, shall we?" said Wyatt preferring to ignore her son.

"Yeah, Mom didn't have time to thaw anything out."

"Very funny, and who said it was my turn?"

"It's Tuesday. You always make half frozen pot roast on Tuesdays."

"I forgot how deductive you are, Sherlock," teased The Mother.

"Only about food. Anyway, Carlos will have mushroom linguini on special tonight."

"Tank knows all the specials in Chicago," explained Blake laughing.

"It's a gift," they all said in unison.

The five of them went into the loud and lively pub and ordered gallons of beer and tons of linguini. Skye drank iced tea and filled them in on Operation Matrimony as Alex and Tank staged a manly eating contest. Alex was completely outclassed and conceded early. It was a wonderful evening as people stopped by the table to share greetings and gossip and to meet Skye. She watched years fall off of Alex's face as he drank too much beer and discussed critically important issues like the Bears chances to reach the playoffs. Not this year.

It was like having a four-hour vacation. When they returned to City Airport, Skye and Alex felt refreshed, happy, and re-energized.

"Now that you have your Lear jet, we can ditch the old guy and run off like we planned," asked Tank giving her a peck and a hug.

"I thought the plan was to wait until after the wedding so we get the house, too," whispered Skye loudly.

Tank slapped his forehead. "Damn. It's not too late. He could never hold his beer. He won't remember a thing in the morning."

"See you in a little over a month," said Wyatt as she kissed her future daughter-in-law. Then she took her youngest by the ear and off they went in a wave of laughter.

"Shall we shake on back to our time zone?" Skye asked.

"Thanks for the fantastic surprise," said Alex, taking her hand and going back into the terminal. "I feel like a battery-operated appliance that has just been recharged."

"Oh really. Hmm. Any part of you do vibrating?"

"Darling, you're killing me."

Skye laughed. "What a way to go."

"Save some for the honeymoon."

"Oh, there will be plenty of honey in this moon. So where are you taking me?"

"It's a secret."

"Still haven't started yet, huh?" Alex just shrugged. He and his mother had a few private moments while Tank had pulled Skye up to the Karaoke stage to sing a favorite Jimmy Buffet song.

As they walked through the terminal, Skye stopped, turned, and looked over her shoulder. She glanced around and frowned.

"What is it?" asked Alex; alert in spite of the buzz the beer gave him.

"Nothing," said Skye. "I guess it's nothing. I just had one of those creepy feelings that someone was looking at me."

"Darling, whenever you walk through a terminal, people stare at you. You're a beautiful woman."

"Why, thank you." She gave him a dazzling smile just as a man turned to take another look at her. He ran right into a concrete post, bounced off, rubbed his nose, and continued to follow Skye's progress with his eyes. Then he turned and greeted a young woman just coming off a flight.

"I rest my case," said Alex laughing.

"All right counselor." Skye laughed with him. "Knuckle dragger. Must have spent the last month in a monastery. I didn't even crank that smile above a five." She looked around as they exited the building through a door reserved for pilots and passengers boarding private aircraft.

Stopping on the tarmac, she glanced over her shoulder again. "No. This isn't like being looked at. It is more a feeling of being watched. It's different."

Alex respected her instincts. "Do you want to take another swing through the building? I can watch you from here. The doors are glass and it's dark enough out here to be unobserved myself."

Skye thought about it for a minute, scanning the faces in the crowd. Charging up her radar and comparing faces to those she'd stored away. Nothing.

"No," she said slowly, thoughtfully. "There's no need. We're leaving now anyway."

"Who was that?" asked an incredibly handsome man with a Russian accent pointing at Skye as she crossed the terminal with Alex. He was impeccably dressed and his voice was cultured and friendly, but his eyes were blazing. "I am sure I know her."

The young man behind the counter smiled back pleasantly. Something about the man made him uneasy, but he couldn't put his finger on what it was. He seemed polite enough…and the suit was definitely not off the rack.

"She's a knock out, isn't she? I'm sorry, sir, but I don't know her name." This was actually quite true. He knew the plane she flew and the call numbers on the plane, but it was the man she was with who signed for the landing fees and the fuel. Besides, it was against policy to reveal any information about their customers.

"Never mind. She just looked familiar to me." The well dressed man smiled, nodded and walked away, but he followed the stunning blonde with his eyes until she left the building, then stood at the window staring out onto the runway. As people rushed by behind him, a look of malevolence and pure hatred replaced the mask of friendly curiosity.

Watching, waiting, his eyes tracked the goddess of cons as she walked out to a jet with her mark, Alexander Springfield. Rosalie had furnished him with a picture of this Springfield and it was him. Pavel could care less about the mark, however. He only had eyes for the woman.

Seeing her again after all of these years made him itch. In the relative shelter of the hooded window he could stare at her retreating back and watch as she playfully talked with the man at her side. She'd picked up some tricks since he saw her last. She certainly did something with her hair that gave her more style. And she'd obviously been to a dentist about that unfortunate overbite.

But it was her. He was now absolutely sure of it. His prayers to the epicurean gods had been answered. Life would soon be returning to a state of balance. He could feel it. Taste it. Yes! The idiot kid at the counter wouldn't confirm her name, but he was sure. Standing in the terminal, staring at the jet they got into…insane jealousy pounded through him and removed the last of the lingering lust. She was flying around in luxury…free…on top of the world…able to live in the open. While he had to stand at the window to watch like a goddamn beggar in the streets of Rio.

"Well, my dear. Enjoy the ride. You have a date with fate. And fate is my mistress tonight!"

"You go on board, I'll do my external inspection and be in soon," said Skye.

Alex gave her a quick peck and walked up the stairs. He made himself comfortable and watched his fiancée walk carefully around the plane using a flashlight to inspect every vital part of the craft. His eyes drifted around the airport, not wanting to make business calls yet. He frowned when his eyes landed on a tall, dark man standing in the reflected light of the terminal. He was just standing there and he was definitely watching Skye. Her intuition had been accurate. Alex couldn't get a good look at the man since he was standing with the bright lights behind him, but he had a distinctly negative feeling about the unmoving figure. He was too stiff, too rigid. He was getting to be an expert in men looking at his future wife, but this guy felt like someone who was angry or antagonistic. There was interest, but more than that. Much more.

"Ready?" Skye asked as she came through the doorway.

"No." He wanted a closer look at the man. Skye was in a risky business and she'd played the game and won with some dangerous people.

"No?" Skye looked at him confused.

"I think you were right on about being watched. There's a man standing at the window there and I think I'd like to talk with him. Do your pre-flight check. I'll be right back."

"I'm going with you."

"No. I don't want it to look like we're charging him. I'll just pretend I left something in the terminal and check him out visually first. If bells go off, I'll see if I can convince him to have a chat."

"Okay. I'll be in the cockpit."

"Watching the watcher?"

"You got it."

"Fine." But as Alex disembarked, he saw the man turn and merge into the crowd of people getting off a commercial flight. Still anxious for a closer look, Alex walked in after him. He hadn't been able to get a clear enough look at the man's features or what he was wearing and there were too many people rushing around. He searched, but gave up when he couldn't pick anyone in the crowd who felt or looked suspicious.

When he re-boarded the plane, he informed Skye that the man dematerialized. She didn't seem at all concerned and that was its own brand of worry. She was always alert, but never fearful.

Alex stared out the window on their flight home, trying to sort out the nagging feeling of danger. He wished he could get the man's rigid, angry posture out of his mind.

Skye negotiated the plane into a flawless landing and taxied up to the general aviation terminal. She'd talked to the ground crew and they were going to tow the jet to the corporate hangar. Sitting for a few more moments in the pilot's seat she stared at the instruments and enjoyed the feel of ownership. It was an amazing day. It had been an amazing year. This time last year, she thought she was happy and fulfilled. How could she have been so clueless as to what real happiness was? She looked back over her shoulder. Alex was still on the phone making some deal or other. He winked at her...happy, too. It looked like this thing was going to work.

CHAPTER 8

Skye couldn't put it off any longer. This was the step that she dreaded…looking for and purchasing a wedding dress. She'd tried to convince the special team of Operation Matrimony that it was because she really preferred a tailored suit to any kind of dress, but they wore her down. This was her first marriage. It was going to be huge. She was going to wear a wedding dress. One that she'd wrap in tissue after the big day and show to her children. She thought the chatter about children was far too premature and she didn't even want to closely examine the part of her that warmed with pleasure at the thought. So she relented and now regretted it mightily. The white wedding dresses, drenched in blood had visited her that morning in a rocking nightmare she was still trying to bury.

Walking through the elaborately etched cut glass doors into a large foyer with something close to terror in her heart, she pasted a smile on her face. Let's see, she thought. Today I play the role of excited bride. Fine. I can do this. She put some more metal in her spine. There was no way her nightmare was going to control her choices or her movements during the day. Her jittery stomach and the feeling of walking toward her doom could be ignored. She knew how to play a role.

The store was a fashionable high-end warehouse with thousands of wedding dresses in all sizes. They guaranteed delivery in less than 10 days…which was a strategic necessity because they were down to four weeks and counting. Think of this an as op, Skye told herself. She really wanted to do this alone, but Sloane and Hazel insisted it was a family event. Hazel wanted to be with her to make sure she wouldn't back out and Sloane said it was her privilege as Maid of Honor. Libby had told her about this place and said it was really awesome. Her sister had been married twice and got both dresses here.

A woman approached them smiling. "Which of you is the bride," she asked looking from Sloane to Hazel to Skye and Skye liked her immediately. It helped calm her and she stepped the rest of the way into the dazzling showroom.

"She is," said Sloane. She looked up at Skye, who had opted for full height today, wearing very high heels. "You have dresses for skyscrapers?"

Skye looked down at Sloane and smiled. It was what her father called her after her incredible growth spurt the year before he died. A Skye-scraper. She hadn't heard that in years and it further warmed her heart.

"Indeed we do," beamed the woman. "Would you like me to assist, or would you like to look around for a while."

"I'd like to browse for a while," said Skye. The woman was very pleasant, but she wanted to do this in stages and not be pushed. Damn. She could actually feel her palms sweating.

Sloane and Hazel were in heaven. They went from one rack to another, scanning the selections in search of what Hazel called "possibles." Sloane swooped in and wickedly pulled out a long, ultra fluffy creation with about 14 layers of lace and a full puffy skirt.

"What about this one?" she asked, laughter in her eyes.

"No. I was thinking of something a bit less elaborate." Under her breath, Skye said. "Actually that one reminds me of the crocheted toilet paper cover that Hazel has in the guest bathroom, except that one is in three shades of green."

Skye was getting more and more tense as Sloane and Hazel pulled out dresses they liked. She hadn't seen anything she wanted to try on yet and was beginning to wonder if she was suffering some kind of neurotic block. Maybe she should just order something from a catalog or have a designer come in as Alex had suggested. He knew this was going to be difficult. But she wanted to face it. Her knees were telling her it was a pretty stupid idea. Save the courage for the really big things, like running down a devil with a briefcase full of top government secrets or something.

"How about this one?" asked Sloane turning around holding up a beautifully tailored dress with a low neckline and long sleeves. "It's so radically you."

"Not everyone could go that simple," said the salesperson beaming. She'd joined them on their journey a few minutes before. "But with your length and slender waist, it would be…"

Skye turned from a particularly interesting dress Hazel was showing her with a smile on her face and just stared at the dress in Sloane's outstretched hand…the smile freezing, then fading. It was the dress. Not just any dress, but *the* dress. The very same dress that had haunted her night after night. She'd seen it so often, she knew every line. She was sure of it. The dress she was to wear when walking toward Alex. Alex, who wouldn't be there when she reached the end of the aisle. Her eyes widened with shock and horror. Terror clutched her heart and she couldn't breathe. It had to be her imagination.

"No," she whispered in a ragged voice. "No, I don't…" *No, no, no, no,* echoed in her head. She put her hand to her throat; feeling the room spin, then start to fade. It was like an omen. No. It *was* an omen. A horrible, cruel sign. Disaster. Death. Oh God. Alex. Putting her hands to her face, she closed her eyes. Then she opened them and saw the blood. The dress was drenched in it. "Please," she said in a strangled voice. "Please take it away."

The salesperson thought she'd seen every reaction conceivable to different styles of dresses. From delight to tears to exhausted eye rolling to ridicule. Never, ever had she seen anything like this. Skye went completely white and her eyes were starting to lose focus. The seasoned salesperson *had* seen several faints in this store, though and she recognized the symptoms. Moving quickly, she secured a chair and brought it over to Skye.

Sloane's voice seemed far, far away. "Skye? Skye? Hazel. Call Alex. Something is wrong with Skye." She gently lowered the shaking and nearly catatonic Skye to the chair.

"Get her some water, please," said Sloane, rubbing her sister's ice-cold hands. "Skye, what is it. Talk to me. Is it your ribs? Are your lungs hurting?" They thought she was healed, but Skye always pushed herself and a relapse was possible.

"Could she be pregnant?" asked the salesperson as she handed Sloane the water. She realized the question wasn't too delicate, but it would explain the symptoms.

"No. I don't think so. Skye. Here drink this." Tears were sliding down Skye's cheeks as she shook her head. "Please. Can you tell me?" She looked up at the salesperson again. "She's had a rough year."

Hazel came rushing back over to Skye's side. "Jesus, Joseph, and Mary. What the hell is this? Did she get some bad clams at lunch or something? Alex is on his way." She looked into Skye's tortured face. "You have a baby in there, girl. I saw it on *Days of Our Lives*. That sassy blonde girl that turned out to be a lesbian…well, she got pregnant before she knew she really would rather swing the other way and she fainted twice. Boom. Right smack dab on her face. Stay sitting my girl. If you went down here, you'd wipe out 30 yards of lace and silk. A baby would be fine, though. May actually put some weight back on you."

Skye was still trying to push the terror out of her mind…out of the room. Nothing was working. She knew she was freaking out, getting weird, and acting like a lunatic. She actually saw herself as if she was out of her body. But she couldn't stop it. She was showered with dread. Drowning in it. Her breath was coming in gasps.

"Should we call the paramedics?"

"No. I don't think it's a heart attack, or anything," said Sloane.

"I saw a woman who suffered from panic attacks once. They had her breathe into a paper bag," suggested the saleswoman.

"You got one?"

"Only plastic."

"Well let's not try that," responded Sloane and looked up as she spotted the cavalry coming.

Duncan and Alex burst into the shop. There were little screams of fright and petite squeals of delight when the flurry of women saw the men. Alex and Duncan looked around and scanned for Skye. This was very scary territory for them, but they faced it bravely. It was the ultimate girl place. There wasn't one male hormone in the whole store…not one ounce of testosterone in the entire block. They were, however, far too concerned to be intimidated by it.

Seeing her, Alex rushed over and knelt down beside her chair. "Skye? Can you talk to me?"

He could see it in her eyes, feel it in his heart. This wasn't a physical relapse. It was an emotional one. Maybe it hit her hard that she was about to be a bride and the old doubts turned on again. Looking around, he focused on his surroundings. The place screamed wedding. Most particularly wedding dresses. He thought of her nightmares.

"Duncan. Get the door." As he picked up Skye, she buried her head in his shoulder putting her arms around his neck. It was a sign of how far gone she was that she didn't even object to being carried out of the store.

Sloane and Hazel followed, apologizing and promising to return. Skye vowed never to set foot in the store again. She wasn't going to look for a wedding dress, try on a wedding dress, or buy a wedding dress from this shop or any other shop. She was an idiot to think she could turn off her own strong aversions. Her arms tightened their grip around Alex. Alex. Safe. Here. Always here.

Alex carried her into the back of the limo, Sloane, and Hazel getting in with them. Duncan ran around to the driver's side. "Hospital or home?"

"Home. Please. I'm better. I'm all right," Skye gasped weakly, still pale as death and holding onto Alex's hand like a drowning woman. That was actually a pretty accurate description of how she felt. Her chest was tight and breathing felt like a blessed privilege rather that an automatic bodily function. "I just needed some air. To get out of there."

"What happened?" asked Alex. Skye looked at Hazel and Sloane. She'd never told them about her nightmares and didn't intend to now. The only reason Alex knew about them was, well, he slept with them nearly every night.

"It was my ribs," she lied. She was trained to lie and knew she could pull it off. "I was reaching for a dress and I suddenly couldn't get my breath. The doctor said I might get a catch in my side if I move the wrong way. I think I'll just go home and lie down."

Sloane looked at Alex as Skye rested her head against his shoulder and closed her eyes. Lie down? When had she ever done that voluntarily?

"No baby, huh? Well there's time for that," said Hazel.

"Baby?" asked Alex, feeling something turn in his stomach. Something not unpleasant. Not at all.

Skye opened her eyes and smiled weakly. "Like on *Days of Our Lives.*"

"*Days of Our Lives?* Is this some kind of girl code?"

"No…no, boy. It's just that she was a little shaky and that can happen when you plant one in her. Not that I'd know about that first hand. I had my babies when they were already born…one a teenager." She explained the whole *Days of Our Lives* thing to Alex, who pulled Skye in close. No baby. Not yet. Alex allowed himself a smile.

"So, it's the ribs, honey?" Hazel kept up the chatter. "Well just rest then. We can get a dress tomorrow. I remember when that idiot Warren Goldbloom fell off the ladder painting the steeple at the Baptist church, he couldn't dance for a year after he broke a rib. Every time he'd raise an arm, he'd moan and groan like an old accordion. Mercy. Not that anyone would ever want him to raise an arm much anyway. Didn't believe a good deal in personal hygiene."

Skye was glad for Hazel's babble as she went on to describe all of Warren's other faults. He must have rebuffed her advances somewhere along the way.

Sloane looked at Skye and bought none of it. She knew it was something deeper and she knew it was very personal. Sloane was a snoop and she didn't think much of boundaries, but she did respect her sister's need for privacy on this issue. This was a phobia and it had to do with the dress. Skye had purchased a dress once before and it ended in horrible trauma. Sloane could figure out the rest.

"I have an idea," said Sloane suddenly.

"Oh. Oh," giggled Hazel. "Head for the hills."

"Could I borrow Duncan after he drops you guys off?"

"What do you say, Duncan?" asked Alex. "You have any plans today?"

"What will you need me for, Bossman?" he asked. Alex looked at Skye's pale face. He'd been in the middle of a meeting, but he couldn't remember right now if anything had been decided. When Hazel called him, he just left. She sometimes had trouble formulating sentences when she was excited and all he heard was Skye and ill and hurry.

"I'm going to cancel all my afternoon meetings. You're free."

"Okay, Miss Brainchild," said Duncan, relieved to see the captain breathing easier now. "It's you and me."

"Wicked."

They dropped Hazel at the Senior Center where her Red Hat Mammas were organizing a book sale. Sloane and Duncan sped off and Alex helped Skye up the front stairs. Alex's long time housekeeper, Cynthia, greeted them, beaming. Her smile faded quickly when she saw Skye's face and Alex's concern.

"Oh my, don't you feel well, dear?" she asked.

"It was all that lace," said Skye with a very small smile. "It made me faint."

"You're pushing yourself, again." She shook her head and started for the kitchen for her universal cure for all human ills. "Mr. Springfield, you take her on upstairs. I'll make some tea and serve up some of her favorite cookies. So help me, child, if you start loosing weight again, I'm going to lock you in your room."

Skye looked at Alex, already feeling better. "How come you're Mr. Springfield and I'm dear and child and she threatens to lock me in my room."

"Must be your petite frame and gentle childlike manner."

Skye snorted and stretched. "I really am feeling much better, Alex. Why don't you go back to work and I'll take a nap."

"Now why won't that work?" Alex asked, and then answered his own question. "Because you'll wait until I'm out the door, then you'll either go to the gym, take the Mustang for a drive, get on the computer, read a report, write a report, go flying or all of the above. I want you to rest and you won't do that without a sentry."

"Well, I guess that didn't work."

"Not hardly. You haven't had a good night's sleep in months. Now, am I going to have to carry you up to your room, child, or are you going to walk."

"Can I sit in the atrium on one of the lounges, instead?"

"Acceptable. You go on in, I'll fetch the tea and cookies."

Alex found her lying with her eyes closed, a frown fixed between her eyes. As silently as he entered, she knew he was there. She could always sense his presence.

"Oh Alex," she sighed. "Sometimes I wonder why you don't just chuck me off the roof. I think I have really, truly jumped the track this time. I'm as loony as old Mr. Larken"

"He the guy who carries the rattle and barks like a dog?"

"Yeah."

"I don't think you're there yet."

"Is there a name for a wedding dress phobia?"

"Not that I know of. Tell me about it," he said as he placed a cup of tea in her hand.

"It's never happened as a waking nightmare before. I mean I can sometimes have the memory of the dreams sneak up on me during the day like any other memory. But this was different. Way different." She opened her eyes and he nearly stopped breathing when he saw the haunted look in them. How much pain would she absorb, how much fear would she swallow, before she decided it was too big a price to pay. They never talked about it, but they both knew the nightmares would stop if she decided to forget their wedding, find a nice safe accountant to marry and just fly planes for a living. Simple, safe, secure and out there somewhere as an option. The idea of it would sneak in and concern him at times like these.

"Tell me," he said again. She shifted, making room for him on the lounge. A good sign, he thought as he sat down beside her and tucked her into the protective circle of his arms. This was how she communicated best her deepest fears and darkest thoughts.

Sighing, she allowed herself a moment to just enjoy the feel of him. "I was at the bridal shop," she began. He felt her shudder. He hadn't realized how reluctant she was to actually go pick out a dress. Uneasiness about that crept into his gut, but he froze it out. She wasn't going to back out of the wedding. Operation Matrimony was on schedule and she'd just have to find a dress some other way. Or he'd marry her naked. He didn't give a damn.

"Sloane was doing her Sloane thing, presenting me with outrageous selections." She actually smiled and it warmed Alex's tender heart. "I should have just picked one of them, then brought it home and shown it to you. We would have eloped for sure."

"It isn't too late, you know. You can fly us anywhere and we can get married tomorrow."

"No. I want this wedding and I'm not going to let something as weenie as dreams, even daytime nightmares, prevent this from coming off. I mean it, darling. Al and Jason in little tuxedoes? Can you picture it? And Sloane has been developing nicely these last few months. I think finally some of the growth hormones have stopped multiplying in her brain and are finally going to give Sloane enough of a chest to work with. There are some incredible foundation enhancements on the market…"

"Darling," interrupted Alex. "First of all, you're stalling and it won't work on me. I'm a patient man. Secondly, I really don't think you want to be telling me about Sloane's foundation enhancements."

Skye chuckled. It felt good.

"You're right. I just feel so…well like this afternoon was scripted by a really bad screenwriter. Now that I'm here with you in this sunny place, it doesn't even seem all that frightening and the effects feel like a gross over reaction."

"Go on." Alex could be relentless when after the core of a situation.

"I was looking at the dresses and Sloane picked up a simple, very pretty selection and…and…" Skye swallowed and glanced up at Alex. "It looked like the dress in my dreams. Exactly. The same dress." She felt his arms tighten. "And in my mind…oh Lord, this is so foolish." Alex noticed she unconsciously crumbled the cookie she held. It disintegrated into tiny pieces and fell on the plate in her lap. Her mind was saying foolish, but her subconscious was still very shaken.

"It was covered with blood. It looked so real. Then my damn body just reacted…violently. I couldn't breathe, my knees gave out. It was so strange. So strange." She looked down at the destroyed cookie, brushed off her fingers, and set the plate aside. "Alex, I know you probably think I need professional intervention."

"Do you think it would help?"

"My first inclination is no. No, it won't." After her parents had been killed, she'd been sent to well meaning grief counselors and psychologists. She told them what they needed to hear and they declared her well adjusted. She was having these horrible nightmares back then too, but never shared them. In addition she blocked the entire memory of the day her parents died from her conscious mind. The blocks she built were still there and only came down at night…in her sleep. The professionals never suspected. She was a consummate role player even back then.

Alex knew this…having uncovered it a few months before. "I want you to have peace of mind. I'll support whatever you have to do to get it." He took a deep breath. "Darling, we can cancel the plans for the wedding."

She sat up, a look of shocked dismay on her face. "What?"

He smiled. "I said cancel the wedding…not the marriage. We could just go downtown, ask Judge McNeary if she has time in her schedule and get married. I want you, Skye. I want you to be my wife. I don't care how we make that happen."

Skye thought about it, then shook her head emphatically. "Well, I do. No. I'm making myself angry. I'll not allow *me* to get in the way of what I really want. I'm stronger than these dreams. I just have to adjust some of my defenses." She looked at him and tilted her head. "If you're willing to put up with these incredibly idiotic fits, then I say Operation Matrimony is still fully operational."

"It's not me, darling. I hate to see what they do to you." He took her hand and brought it to his lips. Skye's fingers were still as cold as glacial ice. "Those incredibly idiotic fits take their toll."

Sighing, she drew her arms around him. "I just won't go near that store again. I suspect the poor salesperson would lock the doors if I tried. I just may have to walk down the aisle naked." That made him smile.

"I could handle that, but I'm seriously afraid we would never get to the 'I do' part." He kissed her and was relieved to feel the tension melt from her body. He decided to discover if all of her body had relaxed. They parted only when they heard the front door slam and the sound of Sloane's voice fill the hallway. A few seconds later, she came bouncing into the room.

"Hey, brother. Out with you. Do your business thing. Duncan is outside to take you back to your money factory. We women have wedding work to do."

With Sloane was a very tiny woman wrapped in what looked like layers of drapery material.

"Scram, Sam," said Sloane, cocking her thumb toward the door.

Alex looked at Skye. She shrugged. "Why don't you go back to the office and I'll see what the little schemer wants."

"You sure?" Alex asked, looking into her eyes. They looked clear and untroubled.

"I'm sure." He kissed her tenderly while the little woman stared with wide eyes and Sloane smiled indulgently.

"Is that the groom?" she whispered.

"It is."

"Oh *il mio dio*, he's gorgeous."

"He is? I never noticed."

"Hey, professor," said Alex as he released Skye, stood up and approached Sloane and her companion. "What's being professed today?"

"I have here the answer to the imperial question...what's a woman to wear to her wedding. Muffin La Rocca, meet Alex Springfield. He's the reason we're saying money is no object."

Alex took her offered hand and Muffin nearly crumbled under the weight of a thousand sexual fantasies.

"And this is my sister, Skyler Madison."

Smiling, Skye unfolded her legs. Then she stood up and up and up as Muffin stared...her eyes getting wider. They fairly popped out of her head when she saw the vision in front of her. "This is who I get to design a dress for? Please, please tell me this is who I get to design the dress for."

"Yup, and as soon as I call in the other two attendants, you can see the whole package."

Muffin just stared at Skye, her eyes flashing with passion and anticipation. Her brain was already measuring the bride and rejecting styles at a tremendous rate. This woman was unique, one of a kind. And a dress would have to be as well to be able to stand up to the charisma flowing from her.

Skye laughed as she shook Muffin's hand. "You're looking at me like an archeologist uncovering an undisturbed tomb."

"*Lei sono il magnificent!!*" Muffin looked up at Skye and beamed. "*Il suo corpo, il suo colorante, i suoi occhi, superbi.*"

"*Lei sono l'intalian?*" asked Skye with delight. "You're Italian?"

"*Sì.*"

"Well, then, I'm in your hands. What the hell." If Sloane knew her and could recommend her, that was enough of an endorsement. If the dress was too hideous for public viewing, she and Alex could always elope.

Alex smiled. He'd been studying Italian and had to agree with the little woman. His fiancée was indeed magnificent…her body, her coloring and her eyes were superb and were soon going to be all his. Feeling superfluous and knowing from the look in Skye's eyes that she was completely in control now, he left the ladies to their work.

Muffin studied Skye's face when she watched Alex leave the room and smiled. Such love. Such light. It became part of the formula for her design.

The rest of the day, Muffin sat on the floor, asking Skye about her vision for her wedding day and listening to her describe the man who had won her heart.

"So, the wedding will be outside."

"Yes, weather permitting."

"Do you know why the moon is so bright, even in the night sky?"

"Because it reflects the light of the sun?"

"Exactly. Your man is bright because he reflects your light and vise versa. We're going to design a dress that will knock Mr. Springfield into orbit. Let me draw some things and talk to a fabric person I know."

When Linda and Connie joined them, the wedding party was complete and Muffin's excitement turned to ecstasy. To design for Skye was a dream come true, but to be able to dress the combination of beauty, contrasts, and textures of the three women Skye had chosen to stand with her was indescribable glory.

Linda was petite, slender with creamy skin and thick black hair. Her almond shaped eyes were a gift from her Vietnamese mother and her wonderful bone structure was passed to her from her father's European ancestry. More reserved than the other two, but strong and serene.

Sloane was just budding into the lush curves she'd eventually develop. Young, robust, and brash. A bit awkward with her beauty yet, but with enough confidence to carry herself well. Olive skin, dark hair, golden eyes, beautiful.

And Connie, all curves and sass. Dark mahogany skin, a broad, sexy smile, and a figure that would make a grown man suck his thumb.

"Definitely strapless," she said as she looked at the three of them. All three had wonderful shoulders and excellent muscle definition so she wanted there to be as much skin showing as was proper for a wedding.

"Think I have enough to keep it up?" asked Sloane, although she was pretty psyched on the direction her chest was taking over the last few months.

"Plenty, and we'll take what you do have and enhance it."

"Hey! Hot dog! Optical illusion? Magic? Foam rubber? Rolled up gym sox?" That was what Libby did before she got the real thing.

"More like under-wire and push-up. You won't be able to compete with Connie, but you'll have enough to make your date drool."

Sloane laughed. "Please, don't mention date. And I think he already drools. The boy is a knuckle dragging Neanderthal. The only way I'd make him drool is if I coated my body in licorice, wore a hard drive on my head and came in on a skateboard. Besides, I'm almost totally sure if I had a set like Connie's I'd tip over and fall on my face."

Connie laughed, took a deep breath, and stuck out her chest. "Something to aspire to, little girl. These are all mine."

"You mean they're real. Seems to me you share them regularly with a certain driver we don't have to mention."

That made Connie laugh even harder. "My mama told me to share and believe me, I listen to my mama."

Sloane turned to Muffin. "I think you have an idea what you're up against. The wedding is only four weeks away. Do you think you can put something together by then?"

"Oh, *assolutamente!* I have the next few weekends off and my class schedule is very light this semester. I'll line up the seamstresses from my class. This is a once in a lifetime project and I know I'll be overwhelmed with offers of assistance. *Nessuno problema!* No problem."

Smiling, Skye took Muffin's hand. "Welcome to the team."

When she saw Muffin's sketches and a sample of fabric the next day, she knew that Sloane's intuition was right on the mark, as usual. For the first time in months, her stomach didn't roll when she thought of her wedding dress. There were flutters, but she was sure it was anticipation, not fear. The dress design was perfect and captured her fantasy. She smiled. And it would do a number on Alex, all right.

Pavel called in his staff and his army of bodyguards. Looking at them, he laughed maniacally in triumph, sipping champagne and pacing the office like a caged tiger. It sounded to them like he went a little mad. Not that this alarmed them, for they all knew he was insane. It was just that now he sounded like it. But he paid top dollar and there were always large bonuses for a job well done. His insanity was, therefore, immaterial.

His trusted aide was busy reading a report put together by a series of top investigators…investigators that didn't exactly work the right side of the law. She was also trying to decipher and digest the disjointed ravings of her boss.

"I was right. It was her. I almost couldn't believe it. She's changed her hair and her face looks different. Clever girl. But that walk, that voice, those eyes. Damn. It was her. I know it. I'm going to work some magic now. Yes sir. Magic with a capital 'M'. My days in this God-awful town are coming to an end. I thought it was her when I saw that face on the cover of *Newsweek*. The face that has haunted me for six dreadful, despicable years. This is my year. I knew it! This is proof that fate is back on my team!"

Pavel sipped a glass of 1997 Sauzet Montrachet and made a mental note to order a case of it to celebrate his sighting. He looked at his team. His organization had been downsized considerably since the golden years. He had to keep a low profile, after all. But he still had a nice business. There was always plenty of opportunity for a man with ambition and balls. He was a very wealthy man, but he wasn't a happy one. Things were about to change.

A week of heavy surveillance at every airport had paid off. He'd enlisted an army and put out a $25,000 reward for whoever spotted her first. He'd figured she would eventually come into town since this was where her mark's family was from. She'd want to play them, too. Random watch squads were a crude, rather primitive method of getting a line on his prey, but fate was still favoring him with her sweet disposition. He preferred the Internet to find people these days…but Rosalie simply couldn't get a line on this Skyler's schedule. Maybe she was slipping. No matter…he got what he wanted…what he needed.

When an excited Denise had called him and told him that the woman in the picture had met Wyatt Cooper at City Airport, he raced right out personally to get a first hand look. There'd been a few false alarms, but this one sounded promising. He didn't like what spurious sightings did to his appetite, so this time he told Denise it better be the bitch.

He'd spotted her right away when she came back into the airport accompanied by the famous Captain Cooper herself. There was a really large uniform with them, but it didn't make him too nervous. He had pretty much kept a low profile in this city. Keeping a low profile wasn't his style, certainly, but necessary under the circumstances. It was an excruciating paradox. He craved notoriety, but that would be fatal for him right now. He wasn't concerned with the authorities…it was the others, the family, the Chinese, who would make his life more than miserable. They would hurt him. Big time. He shuddered. He was a coward and very, very pain adverse.

"She changed her hair," he said for about the twentieth time. "But I know it was her. I know it. It was how she moved. Her walk. And that voice. Like silk. At first when I saw that picture on the cover I thought I was hallucinating. Wishful thinking." He continued to pace and rant as his associates stared at him and waited for him to blow out. They would get their assignments in time but for right now, they would be his audience.

"She's going to go for the billions…billions! I know it! You should have seen her with this guy…all but glued to him. He'd do a pre-nup. Still. Maybe not. Billions! Rosalie told me he's one of the richest men in the country…in the top five for years. And now it's within her grasp. It's just not fair! That bitch. She has no idea what she cost me."

Six years! That he could never get back. And the hiding! He'd lost his identity, his former life. And he'd loved that life. Rich, successful, accepted by the wealthy and beautiful people of Miami Beach. Spending his mornings eating brunch on South Beach, his days lounging in his luxury condo overlooking the ocean and his evenings partying with the hundreds of available women looking for some easy sex and free blow. The fact that he made millions selling young women to wealthy Asian men was to him just a business. He had no moral compass. Money was his god and pleasure was his measure of goodness.

He made a good living here, but he wanted his life back. There was, after all, a difference between making a good living and living well. He read that there were some fabulous new condos being built right on the Beach. He wondered if he'd be getting ahead of himself if he popped on down there for a look at the schematics. Oh, the fates were with him, all right. His bitch of a mother always told him he was born under a lucky star.

"You." Pavel punched his finger at one of the men. "Tell Rosalie to get in here…maybe we can track this opportunist another way. You two go bring up my photos of models. Any agency."

"All of them?"

"No, actually. Just those who are about 5 feet 11 inches and currently between jobs." He was brilliant. A plan was fulminating in his brain. And he could almost taste the clams at Yosts on the shore of South Beach.

"George, I want you to see if Bianca is in Miami. Don't make contact yet, just find out if she's out of jail and still in business."

"Denise!" he shouted. "Call Saucy and tell her I want an extra hour massage. The rest of you, scatter…I have to think!" He grabbed his Gourmet Magazine and went into the bathroom. No time like the present to start his plotting and planning. He had his quarry in his sights.

CHAPTER 9

The next four weeks flew by. Skye and Alex completed the reports, interrogated all the suspects, unraveled every thread, and neatly closed the case. Operation Matrimony was on schedule and like most of Skye's well-planned operations, went along without a major glitch. Any minor problem was dealt with through contingency modifications and decisive adjustments.

The Cooper/Springfields arrived five days before the big day. The whole loud, fun loving group filled the house with noise and laughter. Carter and Bill flew around the country collecting them in the Gulfstream and they'd just returned from the Arizona run with Wyatt's parents, Nels Cooper, a retired Chicago police captain and his sainted wife Anne. The two of them were keeping the entire group thoroughly entertained with stories of Wyatt's early days with her brothers, Bat and Elliot.

Three days before the wedding, everyone was in a festive mood and sitting around the pool. It was a warm day for October and they were enjoying the sunshine and iced tea. Life was so good, Skye was really beginning to relax despite the bad dreams by night and the hundreds of details by day.

David, Rita's husband and Alex's best friend, came out of the house, a young boy under each arm. They'd just been to the tailor for their final fitting. Jason was 10 and was slender and fair-haired like his father. Al was 7 and had the curly auburn hair and stocky build of the Cooper side.

"Would someone like to buy two tunas to grill for dinner," asked David. That made Al giggle. He was just young enough so that everything his dad said was funny. Jason was just old enough to roll his eyes. His dad may be a hero, but sometimes he was too goofy.

Linda was spending the week with Skye, doing attendant things. She was sitting with Wyatt and enjoying a conversation on a new search engine the Chicago Police Department was adopting. Linda's cover was as an information tech for the Department of the Interior. Not that anyone in Alex's immediate family got sucked into that fantasy, but it wasn't considered an important issue. David's eyes tracked right to her and made Skye smile. This was great. Matchmaking Made Easy.

"Linda!" the boys shouted in unison. Ever since they met that summer at a party in Skye's honor, David and Linda had been seeing each other whenever they could. She'd become quite the favorite with his children. Smiling, Skye looked over at Wyatt who returned the look and nodded slightly. Approval. More than that. Support.

"Hey. We've got a new girl in school," said Jason, excited to have something to tell.

"Yeah," echoed Al.

"And she's from Viet Nam."

"Yeah!" Al wasn't sure if that was in New York or not, but he liked the sound of it.

"Dad said your mom was from there."

"Yeah!" shouted Al, feeling in an agreeable mood.

"Your dad is right," said Linda smiling.

That went without saying as far as the boys were concerned. "Anyway. Her name is Ling Son. Do you know her?"

"Hmm. Let's see. Is she small for her age with eyes that look a little like mine? And does she have straight black hair?"

"Yeah," breathed Al in an awed voice.

"She doesn't know me, but she's a very special little girl," said Linda.

"Wow!" Jason was impressed. He thought Ling was cool, now he was sure of it.

"Hey Linda," shouted Al remembering a question he'd been thinking of for a while and deciding this was a perfect time to ask it. Jason was getting a little too much attention. "Do you know karate?"

"Why do you ask?"

"Because you look like Jackie Chan."

"Do you think that all people who look like Jackie Chan know karate?"

"Ah. Yeah. I'm pretty sure."

Jason looked from Al to Linda. "I think it's something you all can do."

"*We* all?" asked Linda gently.

"Yeah…all people with kung foo eyes," nodded Al.

"Boys," said David, a warning his voice. Stereotyping was abhorrent to him and he tried to teach his children to be sensitive to differences. But Linda gave him a 'let me handle this…I'm used to it' look and as the rest of the family watched approvingly, Linda taught her lesson.

"Ah," nodded Linda turning her attention to a confused Al. He could feel the disapproval but wasn't quite sure what he did. "Well then. What's your favorite food?"

"Pizza."

"And because that's your favorite, does that mean all handsome seven year old boys would say pizza is their favorite food?"

"Heck no. Teddy isn't so handsome, I think, but his favorite is French Fries…if you don't count boogers."

"No, I don't think we'll count that as a food group. Go on."

"Well, Randy's favorite is hamburgers. Sam likes spaghetti best. And Yamean's is something I can't pronounce. His grandma makes it and it smells like cinnamon. It's good. But it isn't pizza."

"So that means that even though they're all seven and handsome little boys, they're all very different."

"Yeah…we're all different." Al nodded.

Jason got it. Al was working on it. But both would remember it. David just smiled and fell more deeply under Linda's spell. Skye was ecstatic.

Al suddenly thought of something that confirmed Linda's lesson. "Larry Low sure doesn't know karate. When we wrestle, he mostly just sits on me."

Linda laughed her approval. "Now that we have that lesson learned and filed away, why don't you get Tank to help you bring that rock over here." There were several large boulders in the garden that the crews set aside to carry out the next day. The one she indicated was about the size of a small television.

Tank was glad to oblige and even though his nephews were more in the way than assisting, they managed to carry it over near the side of the deck where everyone was sitting. Tank dropped it with a grunt. Confused but game, he stepped back. Al and Jason did the same. Skye sat back to watch the show. This was one of her favorites.

Getting up from her chair, Linda went over to the rock. She circled it once, building her concentration, but looking relaxed and loose. With speed that the eye could barely register, she hit the top of the rock with the palm of her hand. A little "ha" was the only sound she made.

Then she straightened and brushed the palms of her hands together. The rock just sat there, looking exactly like it had when Tank set it down. Jason and Al, expecting it to be pulverized or something, tried to keep the disappointment from their faces. Linda looked at them and greatly admired the effort. Everyone else but Skye waited to hear her lesson. Something wise, they were sure. Something about having a mother of Asian descent didn't mean you were schooled in the martial arts.

Linda just took a deep breath and went back to her chair. Picking up her glass, she was about to take a sip, then said, as if it was an after thought. "Oh. You better take the rock back to the pile, boys." When Tank moved to help, Linda held up her hand. "No, Tank. I don't think they'll need any help. It may take them a while, but they'll get it done."

Jason and Al looked at each other, totally confused. Was Linda mad at them? They didn't mean to make her mad. How were they going to move that big rock all by themselves? Maybe if they just shoved at it awhile. Jason moved first, then Al followed right behind. They put their hands on the side of the rock, prepared to start the pushing. The minute they applied pressure, the entire rock crumbled into hundreds of tiny pieces. Stunned into statues, they just stared at the rubble.

Startled, Tank actually jumped back. "Whoa!"

Skye laughed, but it was the only sound on the deck. Even David sat stunned.

"Eat your heart out Jackie Chan," said Linda as she took a drink of her iced tea.

Suddenly the entire group exploded in excited conversation and exclamations of amazement and admiration. They were used to exceptional displays, they were, after all, an exceptional family, but this was a real show. Tank came over, took her hand, and blew on the palm.

"Better watch yourself, David. This has got to be one of those lethal weapons they talk about in the old martial arts movies."

"Can you imagine what that would do to a man's chest? Remind me to stay on her good side," said Blake grinning, strangely proud of this petite woman. He liked her heart and how she talked to his grandchildren. And now, it appeared, there was even more there to admire. David, my boy, he thought. Go get her. Looking over at Wyatt, he saw the same message in her eyes.

Skye laughed. "She only has one side, Blake, and it's always good."

"Thank the Lord," said Tank patting his chest and going over to grab another beer.

"Maybe we could have her do something about your fat butt," said Anne to Nels. "Ever since you retired, it's been growing. She could smack it and make half of it dissolve."

Nels bent down and gave his wife a noisy kiss. "Now, darling. I thought you said last night there was just more of me to love." His butt, though slightly larger that it had been when he was an active cop, was still in excellent shape.

"Don't 'now darling' me. You have to get into your tux on Saturday. The seat isn't made out of elastic, you know."

That launched the rest of the Coopers and Springfields into a brainstorming session on the practical applications of Linda's unique gift.

The boys were still in shock. They had yet to move.

David went over and sat next to Linda. He smiled at her and she smiled back. "Pretty impressive."

Linda flushed with pleasure, surprised she could still flush. She wasn't, after all, a young ingénue. "Thanks."

"And it looks like it has the side benefit of sucking the kinetic energy right out of my boys."

Laughing, Tank went over to unfreeze his nephews. Together, they carried the pieces of the rock back to the pile. By the time they were finished, the boys rediscovered their voices and started plying Linda with questions…then asking, begging her to teach them.

Later that afternoon, Tank came out carrying a large box with a bow. The family hadn't moved far from the pool and looked up expectantly. This should be good. Tank's surprises never disappointed.

"I thought I'd take this opportunity to present you with your wedding gift," he said with a grin as he placed the box on the table in front of Skye.

Al and Jason could hardly sit still. They'd provided an honor guard for Tank and obviously were in on some awesome secret. They were fairly popping with anticipation.

"Something to decorate your house. It'll go in any room." Tank stepped back and crossed his arms.

"I don't know if I'd open it, honey," said Wyatt. "Tank's taste in sculpture runs to sailboats made out of beer cans."

"Mom...now you spoiled the surprise."

That made Al and Jason squeal with laughter. Little boy laughter. Loud and slightly hysterical.

"Ah...Skye," observed David. "I think your gift is leaking." There was a wet spot in the corner of the box.

"Whoops, one of the beer cans must have had some left in it," laughed Tank. This was going to be good.

"A plant?" guessed Skye, reaching for the cover. That would be a very nice gesture. She smiled in anticipation.

When the box suddenly shifted she jumped and let out a little squeak. Tank laughed uproariously and Al and Jason jumped up and down.

"Open it. Open it." They shouted in a sibling duet.

A trick present, she thought. Just like Tank to have something mechanical in there. She looked at the boys. With their presence she could at least assume it wasn't X-rated. Very gingerly, she reached for the corner of the lid and carefully, slowly, lifted it.

Her eyes went wide and she didn't know who was more startled, she, or the adorable little puppy with paper bells hanging around its neck. She just stood there staring into the box. He just sat there staring at her. Never in her life had she had a pet. Her family moved around too much when she was growing up and after her parent's death she wasn't willing to invest her heart into something that would die. She never even had a gold fish. A puppy. A living breathing puppy. Suddenly it jumped and wiggled and Skye could swear it was...well, grinning.

"Skye?" said Alex. "Say something." Tank had asked his permission before he bought the puppy and he'd given his brother the go ahead, with the stipulation that Tank would take the dog during their honeymoon, and forever if she didn't like it.

"Oh my God," she whispered, dropping the lid to the ground. Her fingers went numb. "Oh my God." She looked up at Tank, her eyes swimming. "It's a puppy." She reached up and ran her fingers through her hair, not knowing exactly what to do. "Oh my God." The tears were actually threatening to spill now. She kept staring into the adoring brown eyes of the sweet little dog.

Tank looked at her stricken face. "Gosh. I didn't mean to make you cry, honey." He put his arm around her. "I thought it would be something that could sit with you when my brother abandons you for the office. He's sometimes a 16-hour-a-day guy when he cranks up and...well..." He trailed off when Skye started to sniff. He looked over at Alex who made a face and shrugged. She'd been opening gifts all afternoon and only displayed interest and gratitude...nothing like this.

Wyatt came to the rescue seeing that both men were about ready to crumble. She handed Skye a tissue. "We'll take him home with us, dear. This was kind of a shock. Dillion can use a companion."

Skye barely registered what Wyatt was saying. Dillion was the family police dog. He'd been a drug sniffer until he got acid thrown at him by a dealer. He'd lost most of his eyesight along with his sense of smell and his ability to find drugs. He wasn't pretty, but he was a wonderful dog. Skye loved him and played with him when they visited Chicago. She secretly wanted a dog just like him. She just never acted on it…never really occurred to her to do so. Puppies were…well, living creatures. She was getting all soft and gooey inside just looking at his fat little body. How could Tank see into her heart like that? He was just like his brother. God. A puppy.

"We'll find him a good home. You don't have to…" apologized Tank, his heart flipping around in his chest. He'd been so excited…thought he'd read the signs when he watched Skye with Dillion.

"Oh no," Skye said and picked up the puppy with such love on her face, that Tank beamed with relief. "I want him. I want him." She buried her face in his furry neck, then laughed out loud when he decided to wash her chin with his rough, wet tongue. "I love him."

Al and Jason crowded in, each putting a hand up to pet him. Tank let them play with the puppy before boxing him, so they were old friends. But the puppy only had eyes for Skye.

"He's wonderful," she said with the pride of a parent, then looked over at Tank. "Is it a him?"

Tank took the squirming puppy and rolled him over. "Yup. It's a him all right." That had Jason closing his eyes and Al squealing with laughter. Al was still young enough to love pee pee jokes in public. Jason was just old enough to be grossed out.

"I can see why you might have been a bit confused," Tank said as he handed the puppy back. "You probably haven't seen one that big before." That made Al clutch his side and giggle louder. Jason jumped him to cover his embarrassment and the two of them collected a pretty impressive bunch of grass stains before David broke it up.

"What's his name?" she asked giggling as the puppy went after her ear with its tongue.

"Lucky dog," said Tank and got a slap across the back of his head from his mother.

"That's for you to decide," said Alex.

"Oh my." She looked at the dog right in the eye. "This is a huge responsibility. What if he doesn't like his name? What if he won't come or if other puppies make fun of him." Skye was making incoherent baby noises and laughing when the dog wiggled in her arms.

Tank gaped at her. Skye was going kind of wacky on him here. But because it was his gift and she was obviously delighted and the puppy seemed to already think of her as his goddess…well, he couldn't have been happier.

"I didn't think to buy you a book of puppy names."

"I don't need a book. I only need one name. Let's see. What kind of dog is it?" She looked over at Tank, who just stared at her and raised an eyebrow. The look said 'you're suppose to be a smart lady, figure it out.' She was acting kind of stupid, but he was sure there was still a sharp deductive mind in there somewhere.

"Tank? What kind of dog?" She looked at him and the puppy took that opportunity to try a bit of her hair. Tank continued to stare at her.

Then the day dawned and she beamed. "Oh. Right." She said, laughing again as her puppy tried to give her clues directly in her other ear. "A German Shepard?"

Smiling, Tank confirmed it with a nod. A police dog for Skye.

"Well, let's see." She sat down and put him on her lap. "What do I call you?" The puppy looked up at her, lovingly, leaving the issue entirely up to her. She thought there was a look of anticipation on his face, but she didn't know that much about puppy expressions yet. "Hmm."

Al and Jason shouted out dozens of possibilities from Fartmaster to Bob. Skye oohed and ahhed over each one, but didn't commit to any of them. Then she smiled, looking from Alex to Tank. What a relief. It just came to her, like a psychic nudge.

"I know the perfect name. I'm going to call him Kevlar. Do you like that puppy?" She made little kissing noises and Kevlar went into a fit of delirious puppy quivering. "You're bullet proof...a handy condition for a big, brave police dog." She hugged him and Kevlar licked her cheeks in wild approval.

"Oh thank you, Tank. This is the perfect gift." She went over and kissed Tank on the cheek. The puppy wanted in on that action and took the other cheek.

Then Tank jumped back and looked down at the huge wet spot on his T-shirt. "Holy shit, Skye, control yourself."

"Whoops," said David laughing. "I think your gift is leaking again, Skye."

"Oh my," she said, laughing hysterically. "Should I hit him with a paper, or something?"

"Worked for Tank when we were training him," commented Blake.

She went and put the puppy on the grass, laughing when he decided he was done peeing and just wanted to roll around for a while.

"Just wait until he finds her shoe collection," grumped Tank as he took off his shirt, sniffed it and made an ugly face. "You better lock up her Glock for the next few days, Alex, or we could be eating puppy steaks for dinner."

Later, during a lull in the family action, Wyatt turned to see David coming toward her. For once, he was alone. "Hi sweetheart. Enjoying a reprieve?"

"Yeah, Linda asked the boys if they wanted to learn some karate moves. Anything to channel some of that energy into the air instead of jumping on the furniture, chasing the puppy, pounding on each other and spilling everything in sight. They've been a little hyper since they got here."

"A combination of nerves and all the Mountain Dew they can sneak by volunteering to pick up cans."

"And the donut holes they found under Tank's bed."

Laughing, Wyatt hooked her arm through his. They walked leisurely out the French doors and onto the back terrace.

"I...ah...have something for you, Wyatt. Something I thought you might want to give to Skye." He handed her a small box, then went to lean against the railing. He wanted to give her a few moments alone to process the contents.

Wyatt knew what it was immediately. Her eyes teared up and her heart ached. She opened the precious box. Her grandmother's diamond earrings. She'd given them to her daughter Rita the day she married David. It all came back to her in a rush of pictures and moving images. Rita smiling, laughing. So much in love. Rita walking down the aisle on Blake's arm. David waiting for her, Alex by his side. So young. Now, forever young. The diamonds shimmered and blurred through her clouded vision. Until Skye came into her life, the hole left by Rita's death was almost too much for her to bear sometimes. She closed the box slowly and tenderly held them against her heart.

"I'd very much like to give these to Skye," she said softly, her voice thick with emotion. "Thank you David." She went over to him, reached up and lightly kissed his cheek.

"Good. Good." David was having trouble with the constriction in his own throat. He remembered the day that was so vividly replaying in Wyatt's mind, too. A day that would live in his heart forever. It was only recently that he felt his heart had started beating again.

"Ah. Wyatt. Um. Maybe this isn't the time, but..." He looked down at the face that was so like Rita's. How Rita's would have looked had she lived. "Ah..."

"What, David." She knew how to coax and prod, be it a suspect or one of her sons. "What are you trying to say?"

"I was wondering what you would think of me, well...um." He stuffed his hands in his pockets and glanced over at Linda who was in the yard carefully instructing his boys.

"Oh David," Wyatt smiled as she brushed the tears from her cheeks and looked up at her precious son-in-law, the father of her grandchildren. "You're as much my boy as those two I gave birth to. I want you to be happy and I know Rita would want the same thing. You weren't meant to travel alone, sweetheart, and I think the boys need a steady female presence in their lives." She looked over to where Linda was showing Jason a simple karate exercise. Al was shifting from foot to foot waiting his turn. They could hear Linda's gentle laugh as they both forgot the discipline lesson and begged to go straight to the kicking and punching. Patiently she got them back under control. "Maybe, if you're very lucky, a woman who can also be a good mother."

Just then Linda looked over smiled and waved. David and Wyatt waved back. David put his arm around Wyatt. "I'd never entrust Rita's boys to just anyone. She'd have to be very, very special."

"Yes. Special." Wyatt patted the back of the hand that rested lightly on her shoulder. "Well. We know one comforting fact. She's already passed the Skye test. And Skye is very, very insightful."

"And it looks like the little beasts may have found someone to tame them." David laughed as Linda lined the boys up and made them stand still. Very still. Al's knees vibrated a bit, but he stayed steady.

"You mean the two little angels have found someone to love?" asked the grandmother.

"They obviously are crazy about her. There was only one other test for her to pass." David smiled down at Wyatt and looked into her dancing eyes. "The most important test of all."

"That would be a pass." Wyatt's eyes misted again for a second, then cleared.

David took a deep breath and blew it out. "Okay. So now I have to ask you."

"What?"

"How does a New York cop, a responsible father of two go about courting a beautiful professional woman with her own life and goals?"

"How did you attract Rita?"

"Rita and I were a couple of horny kids. We met and simply couldn't keep our hands off each other. We had to get married." Suddenly he realized whom he was talking to. "I mean we didn't *have* to get married. Oh, man…um…excuse me."

"Excused." Wyatt laughed. She remembered them together, very well. And Jason came a proper year after they were married. "Have you and Linda…"

"Linda and I have talked about everything but relationships. Our only physical contact has been on the dance floor and a few fast friendly kisses. She seems to like me. There's definitely something there. And most importantly there's a mutual attraction between her and those two little bodies attached to the fastest mouths this side of an evangelistic prayer meeting."

"Why don't you ask her how she feels?" She'd seen how Linda looked at David and knew what the answer would be.

"I'm nervous as hell."

"What do you do when you answer a 911 call?"

"Take a deep breath, bury the nerves, and just do it."

"There you go."

CHAPTER 10

"So who is this man driving my automobile, Duncan?" asked Alex as he, Tank, David, and Blake got into the back of the limo with him.

"A psychotic NASCAR burnout, Bossman. He drives fine as long as there's no right turns."

"All right, then. He should be able to handle all the horses under the hood."

"I still say you should have let me do the driving." Duncan looked around. He couldn't remember if he'd ever actually ridden in the back before.

"I want you to be able to enjoy yourself tonight."

"But I don't drink, Bossman. I'll be sober."

"But you're not working, either. You're a member of the wedding party and ride back here with us." Duncan nodded, his long dread locks bouncing. He still couldn't believe the Bossman had asked him to stand up front with him. Didn't even ask him to cut his hair. He did have to get a tuxedo and Skye had vetoed the black leather idea, but all in all, he was really looking forward to the day. Honored beyond words and ready to behave himself. He worked the cork out of the first bottle of champagne someone had placed on ice in the back. Noticing the little bottle of apple juice sitting next to it, he grinned with appreciation. Touched again. The Captain. She thought of everything. He poured the champagne for the others and the juice for himself, then raised the glass. Time to get this show on the road, man.

The driver let them off at a local strip club. Very dark and seedy. Overpriced drinks, greasy, practically inedible food, gaudy, nearly naked women, blaring music. Perfect.

"Who arranged all of this?" asked Alex as they entered the dark, smoky interior. To the left was a large room with a sign in front that said Private Party.

"Why I did, big brother. I am, after all, the best man. And since I'm the best man for this job, be prepared to be entertained."

114

They went in and were immediately joined by about 100 other men of Alex's acquaintance.

"How did you get all the names?"

"Skye snatched your personal data unit and copied your address book, then cross referenced them against the wedding list."

"That's coded, with three layers of passwords," he frowned.

"Well then...never think of cheating on her, my man. She gave me a disk with names addresses, e-mail addresses, and phone numbers. Damn, she's like a computer on speed sometimes. David contacted them all and Duncan made sure they all have transportation. He lined up enough taxis and limos to be sure everyone got safely home. Carter and Bill were in charge of the food."

"Ah. I see. Well, that explains the impeccable presentation of the little hot dogs, stunning canapés, and man sized meatballs next to a tray of mini-creampuffs, perfectly aligned bowls of salty snacks and the color coordinated napkins and paper plates."

"Hey...they came through with the kegs," laughed Blake.

"Yeah, of imported beer," grumbled Tank.

"So maybe the place was out of Bud or Blatz," shrugged David.

"Then pack your bags, Alex...you need to move to a new town."

Soon after the guest of honor arrived, videos of Alex flashed on a large screen over the bar. Alex running naked through a sprinkler when he was about six, jumping up and down in a tub naked when he was about four, going down a slide naked when he was about two. Damn. He'd forgotten about his mother's obsession for capturing every moment of his childhood. Through some kind of editing, Tank had isolated certain anatomical parts and enlarged them.

"That was taken a few days ago," howled Tank as the screen showed a very small penis bobbing wildly as its owner was obviously running toward the camera sans diaper.

"Hey! How did they get your picture?" laughed Alex, shaking his head. Paybacks were hell and he was hoping to be his brother's best man some day. Because nearly ten years separated them, Tank's videos would be in living color.

"That's not me. There was no screen big enough to contain my manliness, big brother."

When women Tank hired came out on the dance floor, they were luscious and very talented. Smiling, seeing nothing that even came close to the woman he had in his bed every night, he shook the hands of his friends, relatives, and associates. His uncles Bat and Elliot were there along with their sons and sons-in-law. They were given the responsibility of keeping an eye on their father, Nels, who kept up nicely in the drain the keg operation and soon was supporting his sons when they could no longer walk a straight line. As the night progressed, the entire entourage got drunker and louder. Around midnight a balladeer, a woman with just a g-string and a smile, belted out a few specially penned verses.

There was a rich man from Chicago
No pilot in his collection
He looked to the sky
And opened his fly
As she flew in she saw his erection.

So the hot sexy pilot from Virginia
Laughed as she took off her clothes
It's not too firm
It looks like a worm
But it could be a dick if it grows!

So said the young man from Chicago
Why don't you give it a stroke.
It made his cock
As hard as a rock
And the pilot flew in for a poke!

Not all the verses held together as everyone in the room added their own spin to the song and soon they made less and less sense. The men all thought every word was hilarious.

The women heard the guys coming and were at the door to greet them. Their evening at the Cock a Diddly Do was fun, but none of them had sunk into inebriation. When they heard singing, Skye figured she'd have to open the door. She wasn't sure they'd be able to put the key in the lock. She was right. Five grinning faces, some of whom didn't realize they'd reached the front door appeared as she opened it.

"There was a hot pilot from Vagina…" sang Blake when he saw Skye's face.

"I think that's Virginia, Dad," corrected Alex as they helped each other into the foyer.

"Oops. Didn't mean to offend," snorted Blake and sent Tank off into a fit. That was all the encouragement he needed, so he decided to start again. "There was a virginal pilot from…oh hell…somewhere…" Suddenly, the rest of the ditty escaped him as he refocused on Skye's smiling face. "And there she is…the hot pilot herself. Where's my own sweet bride?" He had no volume control anymore and his voice echoed off the walls.

"Right beside you, you idiot," said Wyatt, putting her arms around his waist and trying to propel him toward the stairs.

"Hey, didya know our son's gettin' married on Saturday?"

"Oh my. Is that what all the gifts are for?"

Blake frowned. That was definitely a question. Her voice went up at the end of the sentence, but what was the answer? Hmm. Too late. Lost the thought. He looked down at Wyatt's smiling face instead. She still did it for him.

"Mmm. Beautiful as the day we were married." His words slurred and his eyes blurred.

"You're piss faced," laughed Wyatt, trying to keep Blake's hands from sliding down her butt.

"You're goin' to have to stop hangin' 'round with the criminal element…" he said trying to focus on his wife's face. "Your vocabulary tends to de…deter…deteriorate…I'm slightly inibr…inibria…intibri…oh hell, I'm piss faced."

"I think I said that," grinned Wyatt.

"Am I goin' to get lucky tonight?" he asked making sexy eyes at her.

"Will it get you up the stairs?"

"Sure thing."

"Okay, then consider yourself lucky."

"Score," he shouted with delight. "You boys are on your own. Carry on." He wrapped his arms around his wife and from years of experience, unerringly hit her mouth with his. His hands started pulling her blouse out of her slacks.

"Not here, up there." She pointed to the top of the stairs. They started up together, Blake walking and Wyatt steering.

Tank shivered as he leaned against the balustrade watching them. "Anyone else think that's really, really creepy?"

"Why do they do that?" asked Alex, leaning against the other side of the balustrade. They looked like a couple of Springfield bookends, with the stairway in between them.

"Damn…like they want us to know they do it."

"Darling," said Skye laughing. "If they didn't do 'it,' the two of you wouldn't be here."

"Thought you came from Sears," said Tank looking at his brother.

"Told me you hatched from an egg."

"At least your story was closer to the truth."

"Yeah, well I could read by then."

"Bright kid."

"I'll take Alex, Linda, you have David. Duncan, do what you can with Tank. You're the only one big enough to assure a successful trip up the stairs and into bed."

Blake and Wyatt had reached the top. "Which way, my love," shouted Blake in his famous summation voice. "Nirvana awaits."

"Good God, that's really gross." Tank closed his eyes. Then opened them up immediately as his head started spinning.

Duncan had his arm. "Ready to go up, Little Bro?"

"Nope. Gotta date." He held up a piece of paper with the names and addresses of the strippers. He'd been holding it in his fist all the way home. "Just trying to figure which one to call." It was upside down, but no one felt compelled to enlighten him.

"How about alphabetical order," said Duncan as he put his weight into propelling Tank up the stairs.

"If I find a phone, Dunc, old pal, you dial it for me?"

"Sure enough. But if you can find a phone, I'll stick it up my ass and sing Dixie."

"Whoa, no need to do that." Tank tripped at the thought, but Duncan had a firm grip and kept them moving up.

"I think I'm safe. Couldn't even find your pecker during the outdoor wizzing contest."

"Yup, but once I found it I won both distance and duration."

"That was only because you drank a whole keg. Had to go somewhere. Too bad you didn't go for accuracy. Going to have to toss your shoes."

"Talk about piss faced. Tank got piss footed…piss feet," mumbled David. "Could someone give me a hand here?"

Linda, laughing, willing, and able, turned to David. He hadn't even made it across the entrance hall yet. He was still leaning against the doorway, thinking the room was far too big for him to negotiate without the benefit of a wall or railing. He was contemplating his options when Linda came over to him.

"An interesting accessory you have there, David," she commented as she slid her arm around his waist and snapped a bright red garter he'd wrapped around his wrist. He looked down at it and then into Linda's lovely face. Something warmed him all over and he didn't think it was the gin. Or whiskey. Or bourbon. Or beer. He grinned. "Damn did I lose one? I was wearing both of them when I left tonight."

Blake roared from the top of the stairs and Tank stopped, losing momentum in a wave of giggles. Duncan had him moving again after he stopped erupting.

"I'm not sure it was all that funny," said Wyatt.

"Reminds me of a joke," blared Blake, turning and using his prosecutor's voice. At a volume suitable for the capital rotunda. "There were these men participating in a pissing contest at a bachelor party." Blake always prided himself in customizing his stories to fit the situation. "One man was wearing women's black lace panties. So the other guys asked him how long he'd been wearing women's underwear. And you know what he said?"

Tank actually stopped again to give it some thought. David knew he'd recognize the punch line when he heard it, but it didn't immediately come to mind.

"He told the guys, 'Ever since my girlfriend found black lace panties in the glove compartment of my car.'" That set all the men off like a launch at Cape Canaveral.

"Your luck is beginning to run out," warned Wyatt, giving her beloved a push down the hallway.

"Ah, sweetheart…don't make me beg," he responded as they went through the doors of their bedroom.

Duncan took Tank to his room and poured him into his bed. Since he wasn't singing Dixie, Tank must not have wanted to even look for a phone.

Linda was stronger than she looked and managed to get David to his room. He fell into bed and as she started to leave, he took her hand and pulled her down until their lips met. The kiss was sweet and wonderful.

"My boys are in Virginia with Saint Sloane, right?"

"Right."

He looked up at her blinked and smiled. "If my sons ever, ever come home in this condition, I hope you'll deal with them."

"I will."

He smiled even broader. "Does that mean I can count on you for the next, say 50 years or so?"

"David. We'll talk about it when you're sober."

"Right. Sober." His eyes closed, then opened again. Beautiful. Expressive. "Only when I'm sober, my heart beats so fast, I can't get the words out. I feel myself pulling back, trying to find the perfect words, the perfect time." He grinned. "I guess this is the perfect time. I think I love you Linda. Will you stay here, with me? Tonight? Let me…" He closed his eyes again and this time he was out.

Linda stood there, then leaned over, and kissed his sweet face. He was a handsome man, but she saw beyond that to the wonderful father, the man who stayed with his wife's family, who honored Rita's memory and who was courageous and resourceful. She admired his mind and loved…loved? Yes, it was love. She loved his calm, sensitive manner. She knew he was a tough cop and a brave man, but it was his heart she admired most.

Letting his words melt through her, she tenderly smoothed back his hair and smiled. She'd miss field assignments, but she was sure with her computer and research skills she could find something in New York. She knew she was jumping the gun a little, but what the hell. He'd just told her he loved her. They would build on that. Build something strong.

She undressed him, undressed herself, and climbed in beside him. His mind was fuzzy, but his body responded automatically to its longing. Sometime in the early morning hours, he rolled over to find her in his bed and they made love. Slowly and with building passion. They spent the rest of the night uncovering each other's needs, measuring their own release, then surrendering to each other and daring to open up their hearts again. It was love and it was breathtaking.

Alex wasn't nearly as blind as the rest of them. He felt a buzz, but didn't want to be fuzzy the next day so he quit around 10:00 and stuck with soft drinks. He did, however, let his future bride help him up the stairs and into their room.

When they got inside the door, he spun her around and covered her mouth with his. He wanted her and started to pull her robe open. His hands went automatically to her breasts and her response fueled the fire he felt building inside him. "I need to feed," he moaned as his mouth followed his hands. "Tomorrow night you'll be in Virginia. Can't you talk Hazel out of that?"

"No, Alex. She's very firm on this issue and I have pretty much gotten around all of her other ideas."

"You mean the wait staff dressed as Dracula?"

"Yes, and the menu for the dinner, and the band, and the flowers, and…" Skye moaned as his hands moved slowly up her thighs.

Alex chuckled. "I understand. Okay. This one thing for Hazel…but I'll miss you. I don't know if I'll be able to sleep without your warm body curled up next to mine. Maybe if I sneak up to your room?"

"Hazel has the radar of a bat. You set one foot over the threshold and something goes off in her head. Then she'll chase you off with a wrench, a ping pong paddle and pepper spray."

His head came up and he grinned. "Hmm, sounds like you're speaking from actual experience. How many boys trying to sneak in your room did she have to chase off?"

"Hundreds," she moaned. "Oh Alex. Don't stop. I miss you already."

"How about we make this night one that will last us until we come back here married."

"Married," she sighed and a warm, wonderful shiver went through her. "As in husband and wife. Alex, it's really happening. In two days I'll be back in this bedroom as your wife. Do you think it will make a difference? Will you want me as much?"

"Well, I don't know," smiled Alex. "I've never been married before. Are you going to morph into something unrecognizable? Like a cold, nagging, hag who's been casting a spell these last few months?"

"Have you been watching Disney movies with the boys again?"

"No, darling. All I know is that every day I love you more and I think that knowing you're my wife will only make what we have more compelling." His lips found her mouth. "More powerful." He kissed her again, deeper, hotter, his hands moving over then into her body. "More perfect." He didn't get any further as she melted against him.

"Right answer," she whispered in between gasps of pleasure. "You get the grand prize."

CHAPTER 11

The next day, the ladies ate pancakes and enjoyed coffee and tea on the veranda. Duncan sat in the middle of them with about a ton of granola in a bowl. He looked like a boulder jutting out of a garden of flowers.

"Any of the men stirring this morning?" asked Linda, helping herself to another cup of coffee. She hadn't gotten much sleep, but she felt great. She'd left David's room a few hours before so he could catch some rest before his boys returned.

"No. What is it about bachelor parties that makes everyone's IQ slip about 50 points," asked Wyatt. She'd left her man in bed, still sleeping.

"Provided it was 50 in the first place," said Connie. She'd spent the night in the little guesthouse out back. Since her and Duncan had appeared at the same time, Skye assumed they'd spent the last half of the night together. Love was in the air. Love was everywhere.

"True," laughed Wyatt.

"Times like these I bless my little red wagon," said Duncan, thoroughly enjoying his morning with the ladies. He didn't think it at all strange that there wasn't another man in sight.

"How long have you been on that little red wagon, Duncan?" asked Wyatt.

"About 10 years I guess. Right after I got really big." He looked at his hand and made a fist the size of a small asteroid. "I woke up one morning after I got hammered and stoned and they were bloody. I had no idea what I'd done. Thought maybe I might have killed someone. When the cops came to the door, I was sure of it. Went to Juvie for almost a year. Didn't kill no one, but took out about a dozen bikers. I never forgot the feeling of panic that morning, though. So I decided someone blessed with my size had a responsibility. I needed to take care of it and use it well." He stuffed another shovel full of granola into his grinning mouth and sighed as he chewed. "Sometimes I miss the buzz, though."

Skye gave him a big kiss on the cheek. "Cynthia made peanut butter cookies yesterday. I put a dozen on the front seat. That should buzz you up just fine." It was a well-known secret that Duncan's will power couldn't withstand the onslaught of Cynthia's homemade peanut butter cookies. A man was certainly entitled to one addiction.

An hour later, David and Blake slowly made their way onto the veranda. "Coffee," croaked Blake.

"What happened to that incredible summation voice you were using in the hallway last night?" laughed an unsympathetic Wyatt.

"If I used that volume this morning it would crack my skull from the inside. You got any aspirin to go with that coffee?" Blake looked around as if a bowlful of painkiller would be part of the morning buffet.

"Where are the boys?" asked David pouring coffee. "I thought Sloane was bringing them back this morning."

"We figured it might be difficult for you to face their ah…enthusiasm this morning," said a smiling Linda. "So Sloane took them to the stables. And Kevlar went with them. They should be good until noon."

"When can we nominate Sloane for sainthood?" asked David, sighing as he took a sip of coffee. He'd swallowed some aspirin earlier, when the pounding in his head had popped open his lids and sent his eyeballs sailing around the room. He looked at Linda and smiled. Last night he was hammered, but not unconscious, so he remembered everything he said to her. Everything he did to her. Everything they did to each other. As soon as they were alone, he intended to elaborate and to uncover what she thought. The fact she was giving him direct eye contact and soft, sweet smiles was a very good sign.

"So David, did you confess to Linda that you danced nude on the bar sandwiched between the naked Buxom twins?" asked Blake.

"Sure did," responded David nonchalantly. "Said you were providing encouragement from the top of the tables with the pom pom triplets."

Alex came in, hair damp from his shower, his eyes tracking for Skye.

"Hey, I turn my back and I find one of my groomsmen making time with my bride?" demanded Alex as he came out the French doors and poked Duncan in the shoulder.

"You mean that's not one of my duties?" asked Duncan in an astonished voice. "Bummer."

"Get your business taken care of?" asked Skye. When she'd left him, he'd been on the cell phone, the Internet, and the land phone on the desk. He looked like an orchestra conductor performing the 1812 overture.

"Yes. Couple of mergers, couple of contracts. Although there's only one merger I'm interested in now." He bent down and kissed Skye.

"Aw," said Tank walking gingerly into the room. "How cute is that?"

"About as cute as you wearing a thong on your head," Alex said, smiling wickedly.

"Too bad you couldn't get it past those ears," snorted David.

"Yeah? Well what makes you think I didn't have them exactly where I wanted them?" retorted Tank, frowning. He really needed coffee and about two more gallons of water. He was as thirsty as a camel and just as likely to spit this morning.

"I remember when thongs came in pairs and you wore them on your feet," cackled Hazel as she brought in a blob of brown on a platter with what looked like malted milk balls around it. Hazel was notorious for her creativity in the kitchen and her unique and mysterious food combinations. Since it looked like something that needed either watering or planting, everyone quickly professed their lack of appetite or their profound fullness.

Rising, Skye took Alex's hand. "How about a walk through the gardens. The florists have been hard at work since Wednesday."

"Sure." They hadn't had a great deal of time alone and a walk sounded perfect. Besides, he wanted to get as far away from the brown stuff as possible.

The day was sunny, warm, and perfect. The gardenias had been kept alive in the green house and were being planted all over the grounds. Their perfume added texture to the atmosphere and pleasure to the moment.

"I have another gift for you," said Skye as they walked hand in hand through the vast back yard. "It came last night after you left. Since tomorrow is also your birthday, I thought you should have a special, more personal gift." She reached inside the large pocket of her jacket and handed him a box wrapped in silver paper with a big blue bow. "Happy birthday darling."

"Didn't I tell you all I wanted was to unwrap you tomorrow?" Smiling, he took it from her and ripped off the paper. He frowned in confusion as he stared at the cover of a disk. His eyes tracked the picture and title, then his face lit up like a sunrise. The younger, more lighthearted Alex emerged. His blue eyes almost glowed with delight.

"Good God, Skye. How the hell did you get this? *Firewalkers: Outer Dominion.* This can't be on the shelves yet. I thought it was still in production."

"It is."

"How did you get a copy of it?" Alex looked up. Confused, but not really caring if she'd engaged in corporate espionage to cop a prototype. It was his now. He was a consummate video game player and his fingers itched to try it.

"I know the president of the company," explained Skye, thrilled with his obvious pleasure. She didn't really get the attraction to blowing up animated two headed monsters, but that didn't matter. She got his reaction and that was enough. "She was on a flight of mine and we talked and shopped during a delayed layover in Paris one day. I showed her the best places to shop and she owed me one so she sent me the first copy of the trial product. By the time it comes out for the general public next year, you should have the thing completely mastered."

"Wow…wow. Darling, this is great." He kissed her enthusiastically, although Skye detected a level of distraction that hadn't been there before he opened his gift. "Thank you. I can't believe she let this out of R and D."

"I had to sign a waiver that you wouldn't duplicate it in any way."

"Hmm. Sure. Fine." He was reading the back of the box, no longer attending to the flowers...or to her. He looked up with anticipation. "Ah...is there anything for me to do? I mean right now?"

"As a Special Agent, a corporate CEO, or a groom?"

"All of the above."

"No, not until tomorrow."

"All right, I think I'll call a meeting of my groomsmen. We should...well...coordinate all those groomsmen things."

"Ah ha. You do that," smiled Skye.

Alex took the steps of the veranda two at a time and headed for the den, shouting the names of the entire male population of the house. From their reaction as they assembled and studied the gift, she was some kind of hero. They were in awe of her power to make a dream come true. She shrugged. It was just a game. She got it for him on a whim. He'd given her a jet, for God's sake. Shaking her head she headed back to sit with the women. It had to be a boy thing.

They were all chatting and discussing last minute details when Cynthia came out.

"Telephone for you, Captain. It's the caterer."

"Thanks, Cynthia." She looked at her watch. "You're officially off now until after the wedding. Come join us."

"Thank you, but Hazel and I are going to go get our nails done." She grinned girlishly. "And if we're feeling really frisky, we might even get pedicures."

"Well then have a great time and we'll see you back here tomorrow. I should be here by about 10:00. We'll be headquartered in the master suite."

Since she was declared off the clock, Cynthia gave her a big hug. "I never thought this day would come. But it's here. We'll see you tomorrow. Your wedding day." And Mr. Springfield's salvation, she thought as she watched Skye go into the parlor to take the phone call.

She came back out on the porch and gave Linda the eye. Linda nodded and they went into the home office. It hadn't been the caterer.

"Good news. The weapons supplier finally cracked. Kept screaming that the Russians turned on him. I want to go back and see if we can find a connection. Sloane's software picked up several of his communications, but I seem to remember that it was the Russian response and bid that came to our attention first. Something must have flagged it. I'm wondering if it could have been deliberate. Someone over there working with us for some reason."

"Oh for crying out loud, Skye. Turn it off. You're getting married tomorrow." Linda laughed, then sighed. "I'll check it out as soon as you leave on your honeymoon."

Skye grinned. "That would be good. And if it is important..."

"I know where to reach you."

"No. I was going to say, if it's important, take care of it yourself. I don't plan on coming up for air for ten glorious days."

Linda laughed. "Damn. You're making me hot."

"I don't think it's me, Linda. Spill it. How about you and David? He did a little reach and grab last night. His eyes weren't really tracking all that well, but they landed on you. You two becoming more than friends?"

"Oh, Skye. You know me and my heart better than anyone. He…he told me last night he was in love with me. And we. Well. We…"

"Oh Linda. That's wonderful." Skye was ecstatic. For both of them. But the serious look on her friend's face concerned her. "Isn't it?"

"Yes, of course. Love is always wonderful. But…you know…well…he was in a drunken stupor."

"But he hasn't been drunk these last few months and he's been showing interest almost since the moment you showed up on his radar. How do you feel about that?"

"A part of me is so happy, I can't even describe it. But…"

"Is it the boys? Because you know they worship you."

"Skye," she said with a soft, loving smile. "They worship you. They're fascinated with me and I know I can build on that. I hope that it will be love someday. I know it's already love inside me."

"It isn't the boys. It isn't the fact that David is one of the most special people I know. Is it Max? Are you thinking of Max?" She saw the expression on Linda's face and knew she hit the mark. Linda's expressive eyes reflected love lost, and a melancholy that stirred Skye's own memories. Max was a man Linda loved and who, like Rita, had been killed in the line of duty.

"Oh, Linda," she said softly as Max's grinning face flashed through her own mind. The three of them had been friends since they trained together.

"Yes, I am…I have," Linda swallowed and nodded. She was so glad that Skye was her friend. So relieved she could say this out loud. "In a strange way it gives David and I something in common. Oh Skye, I don't know if I'm ready to love again. To give my heart again. It's so frightening. I watch you, but I don't know if I have the same kind of courage. Then there's my job. Fieldwork isn't without risk. I don't mix it up like you, but if I stay with Justice…"

Skye didn't speak right away. What could she say? Did she have the right to say anything? Sure. What the hell. Max had been her friend, too and she knew what he'd say, what he'd want her to say. To do.

"Love just happens, Linda. You know I fought it with Alex, but the heart rules." She took both of Linda's hands and looked into her eyes. Some of this was going to hurt, but she knew it had to be said. "Remember what you said when Max died. You said you thought you had time. Do you remember how you felt? There wasn't only profound grief; there was that horrible piercing regret. Whatever comes from this, don't let that happen again. God, Linda. Seize the moment. Seize the man. You'll never have guarantees. You've fallen for another man with a gun and a dangerous job. You can't control that, but it will be easier to live with the potential for loss than the overwhelming regret you'll feel if you don't let your heart lead. Max loved you. He'd want this for you. Just like I'm sure Rita would want David to be happy and her boys to be loved."

E. K. BARBER

Linda looked at her friend, her eyes swimming with tears. Then she hugged Skye tightly. It was exactly what she needed to hear. Skye saw the light return to Linda's face and could feel her friend's release. "I think maybe my heart is giving me no choice. I love him, Skye."

Suddenly, Skye realized her words were apt in her own situation. She meant what she said and it settled something inside her, too. Seize the moment. Seize the man. Well tomorrow, she was going to do just that.

CHAPTER 12

Skye looked up at the house that would now be Hazel's. When Skye and her Mom and Dad traveled all over the world, they retained ownership of this big, beautiful Victorian home. They would come back to it when they needed a taste of stability and a feeling of place. Hazel had put in her unique touches over the years, so the place was also interesting, eclectic and comfortable. Sloane grew up in the house and had decided to stay. She had a room and a horse at Destiny Ranch, but she split most of her time between college campuses anyway. Her friends were all in the neighborhood and Skye didn't want to disrupt her teenage social life. It kept her grounded with an environment as normal as it could be for her.

Alex and Skye sat out in front, in his ratty old truck, reluctant to say goodbye and necking like a couple of teenagers with nowhere else to go.

"I have something I want to give you," said Skye finally. She was nearly breathless and considered forgetting her aunt's sensibilities and superstitions. No. She'd promised Hazel. What was one night against an entire lifetime of nights? The answer came as a thrumming vibration from deep inside her. One whole lonely solitary night.

Blowing out her breath, she reached inside her large purse. A small box wrapped in the familiar silver paper and blue bow rested in the palm of her hand.

"You already gave me more than any man could imagine," said Alex, looking at the box. Curious, but not greedy.

"Are you referring to my undying love, my generous sexual appetite or *Firewalkers: Outer Dominion.*" The men had been playing non-stop all day. Alex suspended the game for the moment, wanting to take his girl home one last time.

Smiling, Alex tugged at a curl. "*Firewalker*, of course. As a matter of fact, if you would hurry up and hop out, I could get back before Tank has the sixth level figured out."

She looked around the threadbare cab, still holding the box. "I was going to get you a new truck."

"Hey, it took me almost 20 years to get it looking like this. That's a long time to invest in the creation of a masterpiece."

"Yeah…a master piece of scrap."

"Scrap," protested Alex. "It's a classic. What's wrong with my truck?"

"Other than the fact that the birds won't even shit on it anymore, and momma and poppa rust spot just had twins…I can't imagine," laughed Skye. The mystery of men and their appetites continued.

"You like this truck plenty when we go parking." He smiled wickedly knowing he scored a direct hit on that one. They had experienced some pretty hot moments in the front seat of his beloved truck.

"Which only goes to show you that you're irresistible." Leaning over, she nibbled on his neck.

"Ever consider the fact that after we're married, you own half of it?" he asked with a little groan of pleasure, returning the favor and bringing up her heart rate.

She shuddered. "Can I have my half painted?"

"Sure and how about putting up some cute curtains in the window." His hands went under her sweater and found a few favorite spots.

"That was sexist. Would you care to rephrase before I call Wyatt?" sighed Skye, floating in a sea of heat.

"Not that. I take it back," he said, his breathing becoming more labored as her hands decided to join the exploration.

"Okay then. No curtains. But a door handle would be nice."

"You don't like the piece of rope?" Alex's head came up and he actually looked as though he wanted her to like the damn rope he put on the remains of the handle on the passenger side. She gave in and put the kidding aside. Taking his face in her hands, she kissed him. Hard.

"Darling, when you pulled up in this truck, the very first time, I fell in love with you all over again. It proved to me you weren't a shallow, self-involved millionaire tycoon. It showed me your humanity." She smiled at him, a tender look on her face. Her voice had gone lovely and low. Reaching up she smoothed his hair off his forehead in a gentle gesture of pure affection.

Alex was touched and actually had no answer to that. He thought they were in the teasing, lusty mode. How did she get to the serious mode so fast? Her words were loving, her touch so warm and light.

Deciding to say nothing, he pulled her toward him. They kissed one of their exquisite, gentle kisses reserved for contained moments of deep affection rather than the prelude to intimacy. It's what they used to build the critical connection for a lasting relationship…the connection that would sustain them through the challenges that were bound to be on the horizon. She felt the pull of his heart and surrendered another portion of hers to him. When he pulled away, he continued to look into her rich brown eyes. It was these moments that made him sure she was his. It was more than a physical and emotional attraction. It was far more basic, far more vital. It was fate.

Skye felt it…no…more fundamental than that. She knew it. She thought of the name on the ranch and on the jet. The name stamped on her heart. Destiny. Hers and his. Constant. Steady. Permanent. It didn't require a lot of thought or reflection. It just felt so good.

"Can I open that now?" Alex asked finally, pushing her out of her thoughtful reverie. She nodded and he took the small box off her lap.

Alex smiled while he ripped off the paper and took the top from the box. The smile faded when a look of surprise took its place. His heart seized and he stopped breathing for a moment. He knew what this meant to her. Knew what this meant for him.

"Your father's compass," he whispered, gently taking it from the nest of tissue paper. There was nothing more precious to her than this beat up old compass. It had been her father's and she cherished it above all her possessions. She took it on every flight and believed it had a special karma that kept her safe. Really believed it. Tomorrow she'd put a ring on his finger symbolizing her commitment but this simple gift symbolized her love. He looked up at her and she knew she'd chosen just the right thing. He cleared the lump from his throat, finding it difficult to put what he felt into words. Finally, he just admitted. "I don't know what to say."

"For nearly my entire life, I've never been without it. Now I want you to have it. It's the talisman that will protect you from harm. It's always worked for me. Keep it with you. It will forever point to me when we're apart and I know it will always bring you home safe."

"Thank you," he said simply, this love glowing in his eyes. The compass felt warm in his palm. He stared at it and swore the needle pointed right to Skye's heart. Smiling, he put it in his pocket. Safe.

"Dad would have liked you, Alex," she said, warming his heart even more. "I think he'd have chosen you for me."

"Maybe he did. Maybe he was up there making the moves."

"Oh no. If there was anyone up there pushing you, it was Mom. She was the romantic. The matchmaker. She'd have loved everything about you."

"Yeah?" Her words pleased him. The Madison stamp of approval. What could be better on the night before he was to marry their daughter?

"Yeah," Skye grinned. "Especially your butt."

"My butt?"

"She was Italian." Skye shrugged in a uniquely Italian way.

"Ah." Alex could feel her reluctance to leave.

"Well…time to go. See you tomorrow," she sighed and tried the handle. It usually worked one out of three or four tries. This time it was four. Perhaps the truck was alive like in a Stephen King novel and it detected her lack of enthusiasm to get out. She opened the door and it gave its usual loud creaky protest. "Maybe I'll get some oil for my half."

"Hey, this baby hasn't burned a drop of oil since Duncan started tuning it up."

"For the door," she laughed when he frowned at her. "For *my* door," she corrected.

Her face turned reflective and she looked into the strong, handsome face of her future husband. "I figured a man who would stick with a truck like this would just plain stick…and I'm afraid I need a man with staying power."

She could see he was touched by her words. Enough philosophy, she thought as she jumped out. Her expression turned playful. "And then there was the fact," she added grinning, leaning back into the cab, "that the owner of a truck like this was sure to have some animal in him."

Skye looked around the truck's interior and back into Alex's blue, blue eyes. A hot blast of desire shot through her. Come to think of it, this truck elicited some of her more primal instincts. The limo never made her feel quite this, well, horny. She was feeling more than a little frisky and Alex must have seen it in her eyes.

Alex snatched her wrist and pulled her slowly back into the truck looking hungry and giving off some pretty potent vibes. His voice was low, hypnotic. His smile irresistible.

"How about we start the honeymooning right now? Climb back in here, Snow White, and we can get a room somewhere on the highway." His grin turned boyish and carefree. They'd been through a lot together. She'd put him through about ten acres of hell. But today, now, in the sunshine, he looked like a boy with a toy. A very hot boy. She looked a little further south. Revise that. He looked like a man with an appetite.

Her gaze returned to his flashing eyes and she saw he was more than half serious. The suggestion was silly, really. They'd been living together for months. They would be married forever starting tomorrow. Skye waited for a heartbeat, then slowly climbed in and closed the door. Sliding over, she wrapped her arms around his neck and pushed her generous breasts against his shoulder. The glowing coals ignited and the fire roared.

"Put the pedal to the medal on this magic carpet, Aladdin," she whispered in his ear, deliberately adding a puff of sweet, hot breath to her request. "'Cause Snow White is melting and ready to ride."

CHAPTER 13

Skye jerked awake, a moan on her lips. Automatically she reached out and realized she was alone. The bloody wedding dresses from her old, too familiar nightmare were fading from her mind. A shudder went through her. She looked around, disoriented. Her room in the Virginia house came into focus. She knew the nightmare would be bad tonight. Alex wasn't there to hold her. She missed him, warm and real next to her. How could she miss him so much when she'd just seen him a few short hours ago? *Mio Dio.* She could still feel his hands on her, gentle, but demanding. But she could also see in her dissolving imagination his lifeless body on a slab and feel the horror of waiting for him at the altar in a blood soaked dress.

It was still and dark in the old house. She was sure it was after midnight. A sigh escaped her lips. That made it her wedding day. The next time she saw Alex, it would be as she walked down the aisle to make him a promise. A promise to be with him and only him for all of her life. She felt the little flutter in her stomach when she thought about getting married. It was something she wanted so badly. The sigh turned into a moan as she turned and buried her face in her pillow. At times like these, she felt like he was getting no bargain.

As she swallowed the last of the horrible dread that accompanied her nightmare, she thought of her cell phone sitting on the bedside table. Should she call him? Her eyes went to the clock. It was 2:13. In less than 12 hours she'd be with him. 4:00. They wanted to get married in the sunlight and then share a sunset as they dined and danced. Could she stand the wait? Of course she could. She was coming more awake now. Her mature adult self was coming on strong. Even as she thought about getting up and driving to the house and climbing in bed with Alex, back where she belonged, the adult Skye kept her planted where she was.

Sighing again, she tried to close her eyes, really wanting to get a few more hours of sleep. It was going to be a long day tomorrow…today…and probably very emotional. She'd need all her energy. She brushed the tears from her cheeks. Hell and damnation if her eyes were puffy in the morning, Hazel would have home remedies all over her face. She wasn't sure if she could stomach a cucumber, yogurt, and cracker crumb facial on the morning of her wedding.

Her eyes popped back open and a shudder racked her. The bloody dresses were still there. Oh, God. She'd have to get up to get out of this place her mind put her in.

Just then she heard the nearly silent tweet of her cell phone. She'd turned it way down when she went to bed so it wouldn't disturb anyone in the house, most particularly Hazel, who was determined to keep anyone from disturbing Skye. She just stared at it. Had it really rung or was it her imagination, made more vivid by her dreams? Was wishful thinking playing games with her mind? It tweeted again before she moved.

Looking at the caller ID, she nearly wept with the release she felt. The release of all residual dread.

"Oh Alex. How did you know?" she whispered as she snuggled back into her pillow with the phone at her ear. She was going to be just fine now. It may only be his voice, but that was plenty powerful enough to chase the monsters from her bedroom.

"Darling." His voice was warm and deep and soothing. "I woke up at 2:13. It was either the burrito supreme from Taco Bell that Tank insisted I eat at midnight, or it was your heart sending me a mayday." He'd known when he came fully awake that it had nothing to do with Mexican food. The fact that she sounded very much awake and a bit congested meant that she had another of her really bad ones. "Are you all right, my love? Do you want me to come over? I can be there in a half hour."

"Oh Alex." Tears rolled down her face now. "You *are* here. Your voice is all I need."

"How bad was it?" he asked gently.

"Like a freight train, I guess. It doesn't matter."

"Darling, are you sure you don't want me to drive over?"

"No…really. I'm fine now. Just another episode of psycho woman. Sometimes, darling, I don't know why you don't just throw me over for a less wacko model."

"I thought about it, but I'm not sure I could find another pilot."

"There's Bill."

"Yes, but he doesn't body slam me, snarl at me in the morning, get into trouble every other damn month or have a crazy aunt."

"True. I guess you really should marry me tomorrow. You're never going to find another package like that."

"Today."

"Yeah…happy wedding day."

"Happy wedding day, my love."

"Is this a Hallmark moment?"

"I'm sure it is," said Alex chuckling.

"And Happy Birthday."

"Thank you, I can safely say this will the best birthday I've ever had."

"Having a party?"

"Later today…with cake and a few friends. Stop that."

"Stop what?" she asked, confused.

"I wasn't talking to you, sweetheart."

"You're not alone? I thought you said you were in bed."

"No, I'm not alone. And yes, I'm in bed."

"Kevlar?"

"Who else?"

"The three strippers Tank invited back to the house."

"Please. Give me a little credit. They left an hour ago."

"Ah. So how's my baby?"

"Your baby," said Alex in an aggrieved voice. "Is laying on top of your pillow, and has been whining all night."

"Aw. Poor baby."

"Excuse me. I've had to listen to it."

"It sounds like he isn't the only one in the room who's whining."

"I'm tossing him in with Tank after I hang up. At least he'll be able to sleep through it. He decided to drink toasts to all of your attributes and he didn't stop until the bottom of the bottle forced the issue. Stop that."

"What?"

"He's licking in my ear."

"But you love that."

"Not with all that puppy slobber attached to it."

"I'll remember that next time. Let me talk to him."

"Talk to whom?"

"My baby."

"The dog?"

"Shhh. Don't make him feel unloved."

"Not a chance of that happening," muttered Alex under his breath.

"Put the phone by his ear," insisted Skye.

Alex grumbled, but he did it. Kevlar started licking the phone furiously when he heard his mistress make kissing noises on it and saying his name. He wagged his tail until it pounded a dent in Skye's pillow. Alex wasn't inclined to tell her that he'd been hugging it before the dog demanded equal time.

Alex held the phone away from his face when he brought it back to his own ear. He looked over at the puppy. Kevlar circled the pillow three times, settled into just the right spot, and fell contentedly to sleep.

"What the hell did you say to that mutt?" asked Alex, astonished.

"Why?"

"He's sleeping like a senior citizen at a lecture on dental floss."

"Alex. I think you need a few more hours sleep."

"But what did you say?" persisted Alex as Kevlar shifted in his sleep and let out a long happy puppy sigh.

"I told him I'd be home soon and your ears are mine. Then I sent him a hundred kisses and told him to go to puppy dreamland." Her voice was perfectly serious and reasonable.

"God, Skye," chuckled Alex. "Sometimes I wish your team of fellow agents could see this side of you."

"Darling. We can't have them questioning the astuteness and good sense of the Special Agent in Charge. You must hold these moments in the strictest confidence."

"Or…" prompted Alex teasingly.

"Or I'll tell all of your business associates who think you're a hard bitten, ruthless negotiator that you bob for cheerios with your hands behind your back and beat your nephews because you've learned to hold your breath under milk."

"I did that once," complained Alex.

"Once is enough. Do you really want to be known as the great Cheerio Bobber? I mean everyone has to have a special talent, but that wouldn't even get through pageant promoters of the Miss Airhead USA contest."

He chuckled again. Where did she get these things? And at almost 3:00 in the morning. She sounded like she was doing okay at the moment, though. He could hear her coming back to full Skye. If she were true to pattern, she'd be able to sleep now.

"Are you okay now, darling?" he asked, just to be sure.

"Yes. I am…now." He'd worked his magic and she knew she'd be able to sleep without dreams. "Alex?"

"Hmmm."

"I love you more than I can put into words. More than I can describe. I needed you tonight. My heart longed for you. Do you know what it meant to me that you called?"

"I'll always be here, darling. You should have called me."

"No. I mean what it really meant," persisted Skye.

"Tell me," Alex knew, but he wanted to hear Skye say it, to hear it in her words, her voice.

"It means that tomorrow…I mean later today…while important for us…is not what's going to unite us. We're connected. By love and by something deeper. I love you, Alex. But more than that I'm a part of you. You're an extraordinary man with some kind of special empathy. I want you to know I'll do everything I can for the rest of my life to respect that gift and bring happiness to that exceptional part of you. I'm in your debt and I won't consider it paid in full until I've brought you a lifetime of love." She was beginning to feel drowsy again, her eyes were getting heavy. It occurred to her that maybe she should send some of that peaceful heaviness his way next time instead of the insanity of her nightmares.

"Alex?" He hadn't responded. Maybe the sleepiness did travel over the miles. "Did you fall asleep?"

"No," came the low, soft response. "I'm just processing what you said. If you only knew what you've already given me, you wouldn't consider the debt to be yours."

"I guess maybe that's a good thing," sighed Skye, yawning. "It's probably okay that I have something in the bank for the times I'm going to drive you nuts."

"There's something to be said about saving for a rainy day," said Alex coming back from the orbit her words had put him in.

"Is that how you inspired your clients to invest millions in your ventures?" asked Skye, adding a stretch to her yawn. She could hear the smile back in his voice. That was good.

"Of course, and also telling them a penny saved is a penny earned."

"Such wit," she said, closing her eyes.

"You're okay?"

"I'm okay. More than okay."

"Goodnight then, sweetheart. I'll see you at the end of the aisle."

"Good night, my love. I'll be the one in the white dress."

Two cell phones clicked off, but the connection between them was constant, steady, unbroken, and timeless.

CHAPTER 14

Skye awoke to the smell of a beautiful day. She took a deep breath of the fresh cool air coming through the open window of her bedroom. Her eyes were still closed as she stretched and rolled over. Hugging the pillow, she opened one eye. 7:30. Great. She could sleep for another half hour before she had to get up and start the day. Her wedding day. The rush of pure pleasure she felt had her smiling into the pillow against her cheek. She wished she could cuddle up to Alex, but when Hazel had insisted on the traditional separation of bride and groom the morning of the ceremony, she'd agreed and now she had to live with it.

Skye took another deep breath of the smell of late October and her hand started for the cell phone, still next to her on the bed where she'd left it in the early morning hours. She'd slept without dreams after she talked with Alex. Her miracle. Soon to be her husband. There was no rule in the traditional bride's book that said she couldn't speed dial her trusty cell phone and hear the voice of the man who was her reason for breathing.

Skye's fingers found the phone and she was just about to dial when she heard her aunt's distinctive voice in the doorway.

"Just who do you think you're calling?" Hazel demanded.

Skye opened her eyes and frowned at her aunt who was standing in the doorway wearing a long red silk kimono with huge fuzzy yellow Tweetie Bird slippers. She was carrying a tray with coffee and a plate of what looked like large lumps of lasagna noodles.

"I was about to call the Hot Males of Do Me dot com and have some intense morning phone sex," grumped Skye, quickly putting down the phone. She'd call as soon as she was alone.

"Don't waste your money, they're all toothless senior citizens on the other end of the line trying to supplement their Social Security. Makes me hot as hell, but you're going to get plenty of the real thing soon enough. I know you were trying to call that Hot Male of Done You dot come. Don't jinx your whole future by talking to the groom on your wedding day. Some hocus pocus is just too powerful to mess with. Now eat something so you can build up the stamina you're going to need to get through the day…and," she giggled, "the night."

"Okay." Skye figured she could indulge the woman who'd made a home for her for the last fourteen years. Then she looked at the tray and almost reconsidered her obligation. "Hmmm. What's this?"

"I found some lasagna noodles in the pantry, so I boiled them up, put cinnamon on them with a little margarine and peanut butter between the layers. Try it. Nothing like a tummy full of carbs to bulk up your reserves of quick energy." Hazel's culinary creativity knew no bounds. No bounds, no recipes, no logic. No way.

Skye looked at the plate working on her avoidance strategy. "So much of it, too."

Hazel's cooking had always tested the limits of Skye and Sloane's courage and moral fiber. Most meals were a mystery and an adventure in bizarre flavor combinations. Skye gamely picked up a fork wondering where to start. She was saved by her dear, wonderful sister and dutiful Maid of Honor who picked just the right time to come bouncing into the room.

"Hey…breakfast lasagna. Wow, my favorite." Hazel beamed as Sloane snatched up Skye's fork and cut into the noodles. "And plenty for both of us. Got any toast to go with it?"

"What a wonderful idea," clapped Hazel. "I'll go pop up some. We have plenty of time before we have to leave for the ranch. Ida isn't going to be there with her portable beauty and miracle maker until 11:00." Ida was Hazel's best friend and an absolute artist with hair. She cheerfully left the room to fetch the toast.

"Wow…you're a freaking genius," said Skye softly, throwing back the covers and jumping into action. Special Agent Madison on assignment.

"That I am," she said as they both scrambled to find a plastic bag to scrape the noodles into. When they were younger they used to try to flush this kind of food experiment down the toilet, but after about the hundredth call to the plumber, they saved plastic bags from the grocery store for just this eventuality. They were back, sitting on the bed, smacking their lips and putting down the fork on an empty plate when Hazel brought in the toast. The noodles were safely hidden beneath the bed where Skye would take care of them later. This was excellent covert operation training for her she thought as she picked up the piece of toast.

"I think I have room for a few more carbs," she smiled and winked at her sister.

"By the way, Hot Male just called," said Hazel fanning herself with her hand. "Told him you were up and having breakfast in bed. Told me to remind you that you have a date later."

"I didn't hear the phone," frowned Skye, disappointed, but too happy to have it affect her mood.

"Got them turned off except for the one in the kitchen. We're taking no calls today. This is a special day and I'll have no distractions. Criminitly, the last wedding in this family was your Mom and Dad's, and was that a day to remember. Your Italian grandma and grandpa over here weeping about how their darling Angelina, their only child, was throwing away her beauty and her education on a heathen. Your dad getting all red in the face trying not to lose his considerable temper. Your mama all serene and happy. Just like a beautiful dark angel, she was." Hazel's eyes slid to Sloane's not quite developed features. "You look just like her, or at least you will when you finish your growing. Absolutely gorgeous."

Sloane snorted and touched her cheeks. "Were her eyes too big, her feet too long, her boobs practically non existent, her hair too curly, her teeth in a retainer at night, her dimples too, too cute…"

"They were when she was 14, I'm sure. By the time she was 24 and wearing her wedding dress, she was absolutely stunning." She patted Sloane's hands and squeezed the end of her nose. "You didn't mention your too, too perky nose."

"Yeah, well thanks for mentioning it. I'll put it on the inventory next time."

Hazel looked at her beloved nieces. After today, one would be forever gone from this house. Back only for visits. She looked at her Skye. The light of her life and smiled. That was just fine with her.

They were all showered and dressed for transport to the ranch when the big black limo pulled up to the house, much to the delight of all the neighborhood kids. They jumped off their bikes, skateboards and other rolling transports and whistled and waved as Duncan got out and held open the door for Skye, Sloane, and Hazel. Some of them would be joining their parents at the wedding later and they lorded it over the less fortunate. Skye made their day by giving them all a smile, then turned to the huge man.

"Duncan!" she exclaimed, pleased to see his broad, smiling face. "You weren't supposed to be driving today. You're supposed to be in a tux and standing by Alex. I'm counting on you to make sure he shows up."

"I volunteered," he grinned. "Insisted, really. Didn't want anyone else to drive the Captain to the Bossman. Not unless you've come to your senses and decided to elope with me."

Skye laughed with pure delight. "I'm not enough woman for you, Duncan." She reached up and affectionately patted his rich, mahogany colored cheek. "Not by a long shot."

He roared with laughter. She was more woman than he'd ever seen in his short, but seasoned life. His boss, and his friend, had found him a mate. And she was as noble and good and just as worthy of his loyalty as the boss.

Another reason he wanted to do the driving was to get an early look at Connie. He was quite undone over her and wanted to get a quick start on watching her.

"Let's be off, then," said Skye looking back at her childhood home. Good memories and bad ones. When she returned now, it would be as a guest. Her home would be with Alex. She took a deep breath. She was ready. Joining Sloane and Hazel in the back seat, they were off to pick up Connie and Linda.

"You want privacy?" asked Duncan from the front seat.

"No way. We want Buffet," Skye said. "Crank it up and let's start the party." Duncan popped in a Jimmy Buffet CD and they were bopping to the music as the sleek, long limousine moved through traffic.

Connie was all ready and gave Duncan a big hug and kiss when she saw him by the opened door. "Hi Bear."

"Hi Brown Sugar. You look rockin'."

"I feel rockin'. My friend's getting married today."

"Hey. News flash."

Connie turned to be sure Chantal was watching from behind the curtains. She was. Excellent. She gave Duncan another whopping kiss. Eat your heart out, bubble butt. The man's mine, the ride's fine.

"Stay tuned." Connie jumped into the back and Duncan slammed the door with a flourish. It was a ripe day filled with the best juju.

When they picked up Linda, the party was complete and they continued singing, laughing, and going over lists until they drove through the gates of Destiny Ranch. There were catering trucks and florists vans everywhere. Skye could see Wyatt in the middle of it directing the activities with the finesse and expertise of a New York traffic cop.

She was sure Wyatt would be able to bring order to all the chaos. She was, after all, a highly decorated police captain used to giving orders and facing fanatics. The caterer looked a little hyper and the florist seemed seriously psychotic. She grinned when she saw Carter and Bill shoot out the front door. Reinforcements. Those two were serious party animals. They would be able to take care of all the last minute details. Skye wanted Wyatt with her.

"Let me go out and make sure the coast is clear. Can't have the groom getting a gander at the bride," Hazel said as they pulled up to the front of the house. Tank was leaning against the open door as she climbed the stairs to the front porch.

"Hey big boy, where's your brother."

"He took off to Mexico with one of the strippers. He asked me to take his place."

"Well then. I'm sure one man is as good as any other. We wouldn't want all that fresh shrimp Skye had flown in here to go to waste."

"Unless it's my waist it goes to," laughed Tank patting his rock-hard waistline. "So, who's going to break it to her?"

"She won't mind, she just wanted an excuse to plant more gardenias and buy a new pair of shoes."

He came over and gave her rough wrinkled cheek a kiss. "She in the car?"

"Sure is, son. We deliver."

"Didn't change her mind?"

"Nope. Stubborn as a corn between your toes. Is the groom about?"

"The coast is clear. He went into town to pick up Amanda and Fisher."

"Great." She motioned to the car and the women emerged, laughing and jiving to Jimmy Buffet. No nerves there.

Tank laughed at them looking at his watch when they shimmied up the steps. "It's only 10:00. What the hell do you have to do to yourselves that's going to take six hours?"

"Let's see, there's the hair," said Wyatt as she came over to give her future daughter-in-law a hug.

"And the nails," said Connie.

"And the makeup," said Sloane.

"And the weeping," said Linda.

"And the repair after," said Wyatt.

"And then we'll need to weed the gardens."

"Measure the chlorine in the pool."

"Count the canapés."

"Vacuum the corridors."

"Make sure there is TP in the powder rooms."

"Paint the house."

"Change the sheets."

"Clean the air-conditioning ducts."

They all laughed hysterically as Hazel led them in a chorus of *I'm a Woman.*

"You open up the champagne early?" asked Tank as Duncan came up beside him.

"No. They got in the car that way."

"When Amanda gets here, send her up, will you?" Skye called from the porch. "Or you can bring her up and see first hand the secret rituals."

"Are you kidding? I can feel the estrogen bombs from here. It gets any more girly around here and I'll need a bra under my tux."

Normally his mother would have given him her famous "mother look" but today, she just laughed louder. Go figure.

"Maybe we should arrange for someone to get married every day. Sure seems to pick up the mood of the women folk," laughed Duncan.

"How about we go do something manly."

"Penn State on yet?"

"I think so. We could snag some chips, pop a couple of brewskies. Or lemonade and radishes, for you. Then sit with our feet up until this thing starts heating up."

"Hmm." Duncan waited a few beats. "So in other words, we can do that or all the things on the lists that the captain gave us."

"Exactly."

"All right then, I guess Penn State will have to win without us."

"Right."

"Let's start with the chairs."

"I'm right behind you."

CHAPTER 15

Tank stared at himself in the mirror. Freshly showered, shaved, combed and otherwise groomed, he felt human. His stomach was still a bit jittery, but his eyes were clear. His brother's wedding day. He smiled. He always wondered if he'd see this day. His heart was full of love for both his brother and his future sister-in-law. Al and Jason were in his room. David brought them in a few minutes before. He had to go meet the people in charge of parking the cars and asked Tank to ride herd on the two zoo animals.

"Hey, what's those?" shouted Al, as Tank picked up small black onyx studs.

"These are called studs."

Jason squealed with laughter. "No really. Aunt Connie said that Uncle Duncan is a stud. What are they called, really?"

"Okay. They're stud seeds. You put them on your chest, and they grow into studs."

"Are you a stud?" asked Jason, pulling Kevlar out from under the bed.

"Oh, yeah," said Tank, smiling at his reflection. "I'm the king of all studs."

"Then why don't you have a date?"

"I'm just too much man for one woman."

"Yeah. You're kind of large." Kevlar was barking in rhythm with Al's bouncing and the whole thing was really making Tank's ears ring. He thought about locking them all in a closet until 4:00, but knew that wouldn't set well with his mom. He really respected his mom and her potential wrath.

"Knock knock," shouted Jason.

"Who's there?" answered Tank dutifully.

"Amos."

"Amos who?"

"A mosquito bit me."

"Knock knock."

"Who's there?"

"Andy."

"Andy who?"

"Andy bit me again." Tank laughed like he hadn't heard it a hundred times before. They'd discovered knock knock jokes that fall, but could only remember a few at a time. Thank the Lord.

Al bounced and dropped a bit of information every time he went back into the air. "Sloane has…a date…Fisher has…to dance with her…and everything. We had lunch…and he said…said…he is…is not…not…not going to kiss Sloane and if she kisses him he's going to barf all over…but I think…I think…Sloane is really great…and if…and if I had to…I mean *had* to have a date…I'd pick Sloane 'cause…she can get to the same levels as Fisher can anyway." Al stopped for a breath and Tank took the opportunity to grab him by the waist and set him on the floor. That didn't stop Al from bouncing though. He was just too excited and besides Fisher had copped a whole bag of those mints that look like little miniature pillows and they'd sucked on them until they were gone. Pure sugar. Pure energy. Pure torture for Tank.

Tank grabbed his bow tie and made several passes at tying it. Finally, he gave up trying to get the tie even. He'd let his mom deal with the puzzle of just precisely how much of the silk material to wrap around the knot. It was a mystery to him. He looked longingly down at Jason's little clip-on tie. The kid only weighed about 85 pounds. He could take him down and the tie would be his. Too bad it was this teeny weeny version. He looked over at Al who was expending some of his nervous energy by jumping on the bed, again.

"Hey Uncle Tank," Al shouted. "Did you know that Aunt Skye is having…is having special mac and cheese dinners for us and that…and that she's going to have chicken nuggets for the…for the whore's drawers?" Al was having a little trouble with his sentences. Tank hoped the kid wouldn't hyperventilate and pass out before the wedding.

"Yeah!" yelled Jason. He wasn't sure what whore's drawers were, but the chicken nuggets were going to be the best.

"I don't think you should call them whore's drawers, kid," said Tank, making an ugly face and sending Jason into a fit of the giggles. Kevlar took that as an invitation to have his own fit of puppy giggles and started snorting and sniffing.

"That's what Miss Cynthia calls them," shouted Al at the top of his lungs, testing the limits of his volume control.

"I think she calls then hors d'oeuvres," corrected Tank, wondering if he was too young to commit to a vasectomy.

"Oh yeah. Whore's doors, not whore's drawers."

Kevlar barked with delight. He discovered the trash basket and was preparing for an archeological dig. Layer by layer he uncovered treasures until he found a wrapper from Delaney's Deli. The scents were enough to make a puppy lose control. And he did, but just a little puddle and he felt bad about it after. Then he ate the wrapper and decided to get a drink from Tank's toilet. Tank never put the seat down so it was a lot easier for a puppy to catch a slurp and swallow. Of course Al had trouble with the flushing, so there was always some risk involved.

Al was playing with the Velcro fastening on his tuxedo pants. They didn't have a zipper and that made him a bit nervous. He liked the sound of the Velcro opening and closing better than a quiet old zipper, but he wanted to be sure it was closed up tight so he didn't get embarrassed like that time at the school pageant when Sally Jensinger told him his zipper was down in front of everybody. He didn't think she saw any of what Hazel called 'his equipment' but he couldn't be sure. He danced on his toes. There were going to be hundreds of people and he was going to have the most important job. The magnificent Skye told him.

"Hey Al, you got to pee?" asked Tank. He could identify with Al's nerves. If he'd been 7, he'd have been dancing around, too. Now that he was older, only his stomach was jumping.

"Nope...just went." Kevlar came out of the bathroom. He thought he'd get his drink from his bowl in the corner. "I just want to make sure my equipment is all inside. The Velcro feels funny, like it might not be strong enough or something."

"I think it'll hold," laughed Tank, then discreetly checked his own equipment. "You ready to rock?"

"No, that isn't allowed. I have to be very, very still. Dad said. And Aunt Skye told me my job is so important, she can't get married without me."

"You have to carry Uncle Alex's ring."

"Yeah, but I'm talking about my secret mission."

"You have a secret mission?"

"Yeah. It's a secret."

"Yeah. Aunt Skye gave us both a very most important secret mission that we have to do or the wedding can't go on." Al was actually whispering. Whispering very loud, but whispering nonetheless.

Tank looked left. Al and Jason looked left. Tank looked right. Al and Jason looked right. Tank looked at Al and Jason. They looked at him. "You can tell me. I'm the keeper of the secrets. I'm the depository of all knowledge."

"Huh?" they said in unison.

"You're a suppository?" yelled Jason. He knew what that was. Tony Burke told him. Tony had to have one and he knew it went up the butt. Ouch.

"No...depository...never mind. You can tell me."

"Okay," said Al. He looked at Jason and nodded, like they were at a strategy meeting at the Pentagon. They leaned forward. Tank leaned forward. Kevlar put his wet nose forward.

"Aunt Skye said the most important thing we have to do is to be sure to hold Uncle Tank's hand when the music starts so he doesn't get scared," said Jason in a stage whisper.

"And so you can count on us." Because their faces were close and the sentence ended in an 's' Tank got a little wet from the spit flying through the gap where Al lost a tooth.

But when they each took one of Tank's hands he decided it was a small price to pay for the close-up look at the love he saw in their eyes.

They were so cute in their miniature tuxedoes, all eyes and ears, their hair in desperate need of repair. He looked at their hands, tiny in his big ones. To hell with the vasectomy. He'd risk it some day.

He looked at his watch. They had almost an hour. "Shall we go down and see if there are any whore's doors in the kitchen?"

"Yeah," they screamed together, and the three boys and their faithful puppy headed down to forage for vittles.

CHAPTER 16

Fisher pulled at his tie. Amanda tightened it. He glared at her and pulled it loose again. "Where is Grandpa? I feel like I've been bathed in estrogen."

"Don't get fresh," said Amanda, tightening it again.

"Grandma, cut the old lady routine. 'Don't get fresh.' Geesh, who scripted that? The Golden Girls?"

"Okay, then chill, kid, or I'll kick your ass back to Denver."

Fisher stopped struggling, then jumped when he heard his grandfather's deep chuckle right behind him.

"And believe me son, she can still do it." He leaned over and kissed his wife. "Hi, Mandy. Is Charles Lindbergh here giving you a hard time?"

Fisher had completed his ground school and was already flying solo. On his 16th birthday he intended to get his pilot's license, just like Skye. "I think we've come to an understanding," smiled Amanda. "He's having a little problem with the concept of formal wear."

"I thought there were laws protecting kids against abuse. I'm being grannie whipped and brow beat. I have to wear a tie. I have to dance with that unbalanced brainiac. The day is perfect for flying and I'm stuck going to a stupid wedding."

"Well, I just saw your date. She was greeting guests downstairs. I think she might be worth a day on terra firma."

"She's not my date. I lost a freaking bet. She's my penalty, my retribution, my sentence, my…"

"I get the point. I hope you haven't communicated this opinion to her."

"Why keep the pain a secret? She doesn't care. Al told me she has a thing for some creepy band member."

"Go on down and make yourself useful. I want to talk with your grandmother."

"Oh, yeah. Disappear, kid. Like I don't know you're going to talk spook."

"How do you know I don't just want to have a few moments alone with your grandmother." He raised his eyebrows as his eyes slid over to the bed.

"Oh God, Grandpa. Don't go there. You're totally creeping me out." He gave a huge shudder. "I'm going downstairs and see if I can con someone into giving me some champagne. Maybe if I have something to anesthetize me, I can make it through the day."

"No champagne, young man. You can have one glass at the toast. That's it."

"Cripes. Tell me I'm going to wake up." He strode out of the room, his lanky body already beginning to lose some of its adolescent loopiness.

Cameron stared after him, grinning. "He sure is a full bucket at the deep end of the gene pool."

"Where did you hear that expression?"

"Fisher Taylor Stanaslov Mitchell tried that one out last week."

"I knew our son shouldn't have named him after three former spies."

"Four, if you count me."

"I said former, now fill me in on what you've been doing."

"Oh no. No spook talk." He gathered his precious wife of over 40 years in his arms. He'd just come from Langley, but that could wait. "I really did want to get you alone."

"Ooooh. You're creeping me out."

Fisher went downstairs. Everything was awash in white smelly flowers and silver bows. Shuddering, he loosened his tie. He figured he could get it back up in a flash when he had to. He had very quick hands. He thought maybe he'd go into the den and try to snag a few more minutes on *Firewalkers: Planet of Light*, maybe catch a game on ESPN. Anything to counteract all these girly flowers.

Well, hello. An eye-catching young woman in a silver dress was competently directing the caterers and early guests. She must be the wedding planner or something. She was walking away from him, but he caught a glimpse of her stunning profile when she turned and laughed at something an elderly man was saying. He liked the curves and wow, those moves. Her dress shifted and shimmered as she walked. The strapless gown accentuated her long graceful neck and what looked like handfuls of dark brown curls were artfully piled on top of her well turned head.

Look out sweet thing. Fish is in the pool. He decided maybe he'd tighten his tie and do exactly as his grandfather had requested. Make himself useful. He stopped at the hallway mirror and checked his hair. It was doing its job today, all right. Plus his voice had changed nicely into a deep baritone. It mostly stayed down these days and he thought it could convince nearly anyone he was old enough for a glass of champagne.

Walking over to where she'd disappeared through the French doors, he spotted her near the pool where the florist was placing floating bouquets. Cripes, what a way to muck up a perfectly cool pool. Had to be a girl thing. He hoped the chlorine turned them all blue. As his long legs took him quickly over to where she was standing, he formulated his plan. He figured he'd ask her where the bar was going to be set up…acting real glacial and putting on a few years. Maybe he'd imply that he was an associate of Alex's, or that he was a pilot working with Skye.

"Excuse me a minute, I was wondering…" the woman turned and looked up at him with a smile. A beautiful, dazzling smile that knocked him stupid before it faded.

"Brainiac?" Was all Fisher could get through his astonishment.

"Hey guppy!" She saw the look in his eye before he realized who she was. He was a hip and hungry shark looking for a bite. And he looked fabulous. Cleaned up real nice. Of course she was never going to let him know she thought so.

"That's Fisher, or Shark, if you prefer."

"Yeah?" She looked up at him. He was gorgeous. The suit fit perfectly, unusual for a growing boy. And those eyes. They were a brilliant green, just like his grandmother's, and sharp too.

"Someone with an IQ of ten thousand should be able to remember a name." He glared down at her, putting his hands in his pockets to keep them from touching a stray curl that had popped out of her intricate hairdo. Her face was made up and her eyes looked even more dramatic lined like that. And her lashes were a mile long. Her luscious lips were moving. Pay attention Fish, my man, or you're going to come out of this looking like a fool.

"You going to get cleaned up? The wedding is this afternoon," Sloane said.

"Ha Ha. Don't remind me." He dragged his eyes away from her face and looked up at the beautiful blue sky. "I could be flying if I hadn't lost that stupid bet."

She knew he was trying to insult her again. And she had an intuition that it was to cover for his earlier interest. He'd intended to flirt with her and had cranked up the charm. She was sure it was still in there somewhere. It gave her a feeling of power, the budding knowledge of the kind of influence a woman could exercise over a man who was interested. Besides, she wasn't naturally surly and rude. It was her sister's wedding day and she wanted everything to be perfect. She decided to disarm him with a preemptive attack.

"I know something that might make up for it." She put her dazzling smile on again.

Made Fisher feel like reaching for his shades. Should have thought about that earlier. He looked damn near irresistible in his shades.

"What?" Shark eyed her suspiciously. He was completely baffled by her change of moods. What was that all about? Must be something women do. He was a kid. Girls had only just started looking like more than something to pinch and torment.

"Do you know what Skye gave Alex for a birthday present?"

"God give me a clue. The guy owns nearly everything in the known universe."

"But not in the future universe. Skye knows the CEO of Androcate. She got him a copy of *Firewalkers: Outer Dominion*."

"No way." He knew from the buzz in cyberspace it was only at the in-house testing stage.

"Way." She leaned in and grinned. "I'll give you until the wedding to practice. It's in the den. Tank is in charge of the boys, so you should have the place to yourself. Then after the festivities, I'll let you take me on."

"Got the cheats?" Now they were grinning at each other.

"No. They aren't out yet. The game won't even be distributed until next year."

"Just the way I like it. Boy against machine."

"Girl against machine."

"Boy against girl. Be prepared to lose, girl."

She narrowed her beautiful eyes and gave him a challenging grin. "It would be a waste of my time, boy. I don't believe in preparing for something that will never happen."

He checked his watch. "I'm supposed to escort you to this thing. Grandma told me that meant I should generally make myself available to you after the ceremony. To dance and stuff. I know it means the painful reality of pictures. See you after the 'I do's'"

Smiling, she gave him the 'whatever' sign, hoping it looked blasé and nonchalant. She watched him as he disappeared into the house, smiling and laughing with people along the way. Completely at ease. Confident, cocky and sure of himself. Why did she suddenly find that so appealing. She shrugged. Go figure. Put on makeup, get your hair all done up, slink into an elegant dress, and the heart gets all caught up in romance. She checked her watch. No time to give it any thought now. She was Maid of Honor at this gig and she had maidly duties to perform.

CHAPTER 17

Wyatt, Connie, Linda, Amanda, Cynthia, Anne, Hazel, Bill and Carter were all sipping herbal tea and nibbling on little sandwiches in the master suite with Skye when Sloane came in. They'd claimed the room and relegated the men to the downstairs guest rooms in the time honored tradition of the bride's needs rule. The room smelled of woman. A wonderful combination of bathroom powders and crystals, perfumes, flowers and hot tea.

"Flowers are all delivered and placed in their proper places," Sloane reported. "They're really bitchin' Skye."

"I have to stop eating these or I won't be able to zip my dress," said Connie laughing and popping another tiny sandwich into her mouth.

"Muffin is here with her needles and thread. So eat away," said Carter. He and Muffin had become fast friends. He was as sure as she was that the dress she designed for Skye would launch her career. Carter had several friends in the trade and was proving very helpful in the business end of building a clientele.

Time flew by and soon it was 3:00. One hour and she'd be taking a vow. Skye looked out onto the lawn. She touched her heart and knew he was nearby looking at the same sight. Alex. Closing her eyes, she saw him in a hundred different slides in her mind. There were no nerves, no doubts. Her heart was filled with her love. Excusing herself, she went into the bathroom with her cell phone. It was the only time Hazel left her side.

The sky was blue and the day was warm. A perfect fall day. It was a good sign. Alex stood very still, looking out the window. Was there a part of him that still didn't believe this was happening? His hand was poised at the ends of his tie. Flashes of Skye were playing in his mind and he was enjoying the show. He looked at his watch. 3:00. One hour and she'd be his forever. He studied his bare left hand. By the end of the day a ring would be on his finger. Her ring.

His cell phone chirped. Surprised, he picked it up, looking at the caller ID. A warm, rich feeling flowed through him. Skye.

"Hello, darling. You haven't changed your mind, have you?" he asked, pleased she'd call him.

"Are you alone?" asked Skye, trying to picture him. She always loved him in a tux.

"For now. I gave everyone duties."

"I love you," she said simply.

"Darling, as redundant as this sounds, I love you too."

"Are you nervous?"

"No, are you?"

"No. Just very, very happy." And she sounded like it.

"Where are you?" he asked, suddenly curious how she pulled off a covert phone call.

"Hiding in the bathroom. It's a good thing I've had special training. Aunt Hazel would have a fit if she knew I was calling you."

"Did you talk her out of the orange hat?"

"No, she had her shoes dyed to match especially for the occasion. Said since I decided to get married so close to Halloween, I was going to have to live with her black and orange theme. Ida toned down the orange in her hair though. Told her it clashed with the hat. It's now a luscious, soft brown."

"How will I recognize her?"

"Think Las Vegas Showgirl."

"Went with the false eyelashes and blue eye shadow, did she?"

Skye laughed. "I have to go. They'll start wondering what I'm doing in here so long. I love you Alex."

"I love you Skye"

Anne and Amanda left, giving Skye both their hugs and best wishes. Carter and Bill escorted them out. The minutes were ticking away and Skye found herself daydreaming. God. This was it. Her wedding day. Her wedding. They made it. She made it. Alex would be waiting for her in less than an hour to marry her. She felt every fiber of her being sing with anticipation and…what was it? Joy. It was joy. Ever since the death of her parents, she didn't think she ever truly felt a carefree moment. But that was melting into her as well. Could the day be more perfect? Smiling, she turned to make the final preparations to meet her destiny.

"Okay, time for the last ritual," said Connie, taking Skye's hand and leading her into the circle of women.

"Do I have to tell her about what to expect on her wedding night now" asked Hazel swishing in from the dressing room. She was decked out in a long black sequenced dress that would have made her look like Morticia Adams if it weren't for the brilliant makeup, and the orange hat and shoes. Somehow, the whole look worked.

"I think we can skip that part," laughed Skye.

"I don't know, I wouldn't want you to go in unprepared," Hazel said with a mock frown and an exaggerated wink.

"I'll call you if I have any questions."

"And what makes you think I'll be available? Livingston is in town and we might just find something better to do tonight than sit by the phone. As a matter of fact, he told me he's been working on the machines to bring up his stamina."

"They have drugs for that now," laughed Connie.

"I'll take my chances," responded Skye. "I don't think I'll need to call."

"Now on to the something old, something new, something borrowed and something blue," said Linda.

Wyatt came forward. "Something old. These were my grandmother's. They went to my mother on her wedding day, to me on mine and then to Rita on hers. David gave them back to me a few days ago. We want you to have them."

Skye opened the box and tears started flowing. "They're beautiful. Thank you." She hugged her future mother-in-law. Mother in her heart already. Skye went to the mirror and removed the earrings she bought and replaced them with Rita's diamonds. They felt warm on her ears. To her fanciful heart it felt like a part of Rita, the part that wished her joy and happiness, was with her now. "I'll love her brother and honor this gift," she said softly. "Forever."

Tissues were passed around. Muffin came out of the dressing room carrying her creation. "Something new." She laid the dress on the bed. "All ready to be draped on the most fabulous body in the state."

"Something borrowed." Hazel opened an old cardboard box and pulled out a white lace garter. "Dean Martin pulled this off my leg with his teeth when I was dancing at the Desert Inn in Vegas."

"That old geezer?" snorted Sloane. "He had teeth?"

"Sweetheart, that old geezer was a real looker in his day. He's been dead many years now."

"That would explain the sunken eyes and sallow skin," she said, recalling a picture she'd seen of him on the front of one of the tabloids.

Hazel leaned over and Skye obediently let her pull it up her leg to her thigh.

"Of course my legs didn't go on forever. He probably wouldn't have made it if he had to cover that distance."

"And now something blue," announced Sloane reaching up and placing a necklace around Skye's throat. She and Muffin had worked with a jeweler to craft a stunning necklace, more aptly neck art. It was all hammered silver work in an intricate design running around Skye's long exposed neck and over her shoulder to the center of her throat. And in the core of a complex swirl was a brilliant blue gem.

"Is that a blue diamond?" asked Connie, stunned.

"Gorgeous. I've never seen one," breathed Wyatt.

"The jeweler who worked with this one said he'd only seen a dozen naturally colored diamonds in his lifetime. They're extremely rare," said Muffin. "This one is priceless."

Skye let Muffin fix the clasp and arrange the necklace. It was breathtaking. Suddenly, Skye's eyes filled again. "Oh my God, I recognize the stone. Oh, Hazel," she said softly. She couldn't get any volume behind her voice as her throat closed again with overwhelming emotion.

"It's been in the safe collecting a layer of dust...so thick I had to shovel it off." Hazel's eyes were bright with tears. She used waterproof glue on her lashes, so she let them come. "I know your mom would want you to have it on your wedding day."

Skye brought tissues to her eyes and explained. "My mother's. The diamond was my mother's."

"She wore it on her wedding day. It was a gift from your father. We had it reset for your day." Only Hazel and Skye knew the real reason why it had to be reset. Angelina Madison had been wearing it on the day she'd been killed. The original setting had been burnt, bent, and destroyed in the blast and the fire. Skye thought she never wanted to see again, but she was wrong. It was a perfect accessory and all the good memories came flooding in. It was a wonderful feeling.

"It represents the love your mother and father shared on their wedding day. You're the result of that love, honey," said Hazel softly, relieved to see the joy in Skye's eyes.

"Good God," sighed Skye as she refocused and looked around the room. Everyone was weeping and trying to dab at their eyes to salvage some of the makeup they'd applied. "Let's just give it up and start over again." They all looked at each other, wiped their eyes, and dove into the boxes, bags, and shelves of makeup for complete makeovers. Laughing, crying, and generally making the day unforgettable.

Finally, the time had come. There was nothing left to do but to get married.

"Are you ready to suit up for the big game?" asked Hazel, rubbing her hands and grinning.

Skye stood and nodded, sure she had all the tears damned up for now. Her makeup was safe.

"I don't know if anyone will pay much attention to you after they get a load of Hazel, but let's put this on anyway," grinned Muffin. This wedding was going to make her career and she couldn't have been more delighted. But mostly her satisfaction was in contributing to the magic.

"Can't go out naked," laughed Skye as Muffin helped her with the dress, smoothed it out and stood back.

They all gasped. No one said a word. The room was silent, filled with awe.

Hazel was the first to break the spell, and only because she felt the tug of time. "That'll work. Now I'm going down and see if my love boat is on the grounds." She hugged Skye tightly, holding her until her heart came back to her chest. "I love you, Skyler. I couldn't have loved you more if you were my own. Be happy."

"I *am* yours," said Skye simply, touching Hazel's cheek. "See you after the wedding. I'll be the one with the blue eyed God in a tux."

"Hey, that was what I was going to say."

"My daughter, by heart, soon by law," said Wyatt kissing Skye's cheek. Tears gathered in her eyes. "Thank you for making my son so happy. Enjoy your day."

"See you downstairs."

Connie, Linda, and Sloane stood for a minute longer with Skye. They were all gorgeous in their silver dresses. Different, yet the same in their harmony with Skye's song. They could feel her joy and it grew as it was shared.

"Shall we get married?" asked Skye, smiling.

Linda grinned. "I'm not doing anything better, sure."

Connie nodded. "My date's at the end of the aisle...so follow me everybody."

Sloane couldn't say anything. She was too happy, too thrilled, too touched. Her eyes met Skye's and she found she didn't have to say anything. They shared the moment, took simultaneous deep breaths, then moved out of the room and into position.

"You doing okay?" asked David. He, Tank, Duncan, Nels and Blake were all struggling with their ties. Al and Jason were left in Cynthia's capable hands. She was giving them snacks and keeping them away from the cake.

Alex smiled. He sure felt okay. Not nervous. Ready. He wanted Skye to be his wife so badly; there was an ache in his stomach. By the end of the day it would be official. Finally. He had no idea why that should make so much difference, but it did. "I'm doing fine."

He reached into his pocket and felt the compass. Then put on his jacket, shot his cuffs and stood ready to get married.

"Never thought this day would happen," said Blake. "I thought I might have raised a confirmed bachelor."

"I was just saving myself for someone who could hold a candle to your wife. She set the bar pretty high."

"That she did."

There was a soft knock on the door.

Tank went over and called out through the door. "What's the password?"

"Peanut butter cookies."

"Our salvation. It's the tie-er of ties."

Wyatt swept in with a plate of cookies and a broad smile.

"Wow, Mom. You look awesome." Tank grinned and grabbed a handful, popping one in his mouth whole.

"Why thank you Tank. Be sure you brush the crumbs before you go downstairs. Now, assume the position, boys." Wyatt looked at the line of handsome, well build, nicely turned out men and beamed. Duncan, huge and strangely gentle. Tank, her baby, a constant delight. David, gorgeous, steady, and the father of her grandchildren. Blake, the love of her life. Nels, her father and the man who infected her with the love of the law. Her family. With the precision and constancy of a General Motors assembly line, she tied each man's tie perfectly and effortlessly, kissing each cheek as she completed the task.

Then she stopped in front of the groom and looked up into his shining eyes. His tie was impeccable already, of course. No need for any adjustments. Her son. When did that adorable little boy turn into such a complete and happy adult? Tears threatened when she realized the complete and happy part was a recent development.

"She's one in a million, darling," she said, homing in on the reason for his state of contentment. "So are you. Happy Birthday, sweetheart. This is a day I've been dreaming about since the morning you were born. You weren't alone then. Rita was there waiting for you. Skye will make sure you won't ever be alone again." Wyatt's eyes stung with tears and her beautiful eyes showed profound delight tinged with a bit of melancholy.

"Don't get sloppy on me, Mom," warned Alex, feeling a lump in his own throat.

"Okay," sniffed Wyatt, smiling through a veil of sudden tears. "Let me put it this way. I already consider Skye my daughter. Today is only a formality. You do anything to jeopardize her happiness and I'll shoot out your kneecaps."

"Yeouch," said Tank laughing.

Alex took his mother in his arms, lifted her up, kissed her cheek, turned, and set her down next to Blake.

"If I ever do anything to jeopardize Skye's happiness, I won't stop you," promised Alex.

Blake took his son in a man hug. Not too long, not too intimate. Absolutely filled with love. "Enjoy your day, son. Be happy." Then he offered his arm to Wyatt.

"Need a date to this shindig?"

"Know where I can find one?"

They left the room laughing, prepared to completely enjoy the day themselves.

CHAPTER 18

The time had come.

Tank, David and Duncan had escorted everyone to their seats. When the music began, Jason and Al offered their arms to their great grandparents and with grand ceremony, took them to their seats in the front. Then they went over to where David was waiting for them next to Alex. Al had Alex's ring securely tucked in a special pocket in his jacket. Jason had Skye's ring. Skye had left it up to the boys to decide who was carrying which ring. David thought it might be too much to ask his sons to agree on anything, but they came to a conclusion quickly. Jason secretly wanted to carry Skye's ring, so he told Al that since his true long name was Alexander and he was named after Uncle Alex, he should carry the groom's ring. Al had absolutely no reason to question this logic and agreed immediately. He'd always liked being named after his uncle. It made him special. And now he was carrying the big shiny ring that didn't even fit on his thumb. He'd tried. It was cool.

Right on cue, Duncan offered his arm to Hazel and seated her next to Dr. Lacy, who took her hand. He must have been inspired by the beauty of her lashes because he couldn't remember ever being so publicly demonstrative. There was a reason he was still a bachelor and it mostly had to do with his inability to relate to the opposite sex. He wasn't even sure how he got here as Hazel's escort, but he guessed he'd asked her. Anyway, she was looking like quite a dish today.

Then Tank offered his arm to Wyatt and winked at Blake. Wyatt gently laid her hand on his arm and hoped she'd be able to hold it together for the next hour and knowing she probably wouldn't be able to hold it for the next minute. She could already feel the tears tickling the back of her throat. A picture of Tank as a young man performing the same function at Rita's wedding flashed through her mind. Blake hadn't been with her then. He'd been back with Rita, ready to take her down the aisle to David. Over a decade ago.

Tank had worn his first tux. He was full of fun and youthful exuberance back then. She looked into his face and smiled. Exactly the same. Older, handsomer, but the same grin, the same look of mischief. He was a Cooper, through and through.

"How many in your party?" he asked.

"Just two," said Bake, knowing his wife was having trouble with her breathing right at the moment.

"Smoking or non smoking?"

Then she laughed. She was going to be all right. Tank was making sure of it. How could she love this boy more, she thought.

"Let me tell you about our specials," he said and chatted softly all the way up the aisle. Then he gave her a little peck on the cheek as she took Blake's hand and they sat in the front row. Tank took his own deep breath and went over to join the men.

Al and Jason walked solemnly out in front of everyone, stood by the altar, and turned perfectly. Exactly how they practiced it. David's heart swelled with love mixed with a touch of sadness. Rita's boys. They were his pride and joy. His reason for living after Rita had died. They kept him alive. If it hadn't been for them and, he looked up at Alex, his brother-in-law, he'd have swallowed a bullet and joined her in death. Rita would have loved this day. Her boys standing with her brother. He missed her terribly, more on days like this. Lately, a melancholy feeling of loneliness his boys couldn't fill would come over him. He knew he was ready to find someone to fill his days, and more importantly, his nights. His eyes turned to the aisle as he stepped forward with Duncan and Tank.

Connie moved up the aisle first. She was beautiful and she made Duncan's huge heart skip a beat. As a matter of fact he put his hand to his heart and patted his chest as she walked toward him, making her laugh and the guests laugh with her. Her eyes sparkled and her grin seemed to dominate her entire face. She was irrepressible and she looked like someone poised to party. Let the celebration begin! It was a perfect prelude to the afternoon.

"You look good enough to eat, Brown Sugar," Duncan said softly, presenting his arm and escorting her the rest of the way to the altar.

"I thought you were a vegetarian," she whispered, then went left as Duncan turned right. He was beaming when he turned back to the guests. He looked at the faces of all the people at this event and again wondered what you called the kind of luck he had to be considered not only the Bossman's trusted driver, but also his friend. Duncan had seen women come and he'd seen women go, and he didn't think this day would ever come for the man he loved and admired more than any person on the planet. The fact that Bossman had found a mate and that she was someone as fabulous as the Captain. Well, it filled him with joy. And because the vessel was so large, the joy spread throughout the assembled group of guests and filled the back yard as well.

Linda was next. She walked down the aisle, graceful and self-assured. She was delicate and beautiful. Jason waved and she gave him a special smile. He was over the moon about her. Al bumped him, but not before she turned her smile to take him in as well. They responded to her warm regard by standing a little taller and completely keeping their hands away from each other. Just a little demonstration of Linda magic. Then she looked over to their father. Something passed between them and David could have sworn he felt a nudge from behind. He resisted the urge to look over his shoulder. Rita. He smiled. He twisted his wedding ring. The ring Rita had placed on his finger the day they were married. It was time. Time for the ring to be nestled in with Jason's first tooth and the medal Al won for spelling. Time for the ring to be placed with the sweet memories of his past. Time for him to take a step forward. He walked the short distance to Linda and she took his arm, then he escorted her to the altar where they separated, David to stand with his friend, Linda to stand with hers.

Wyatt watched it all through a watery haze of tears, her throat aching as she held back the sobs that were near the surface on special days like this. Her heart ached for her daughter, but she saw David's face and knew this was right. Right for her beloved son-in-law. Right for Linda, and of course, right for Rita's precious boys. Blake instinctively put his arm around his wife and held her as she allowed some of the grief and happiness to mingle and spill out.

Sloane was next. The dress accentuated her olive skin and transformed the pretty girl into a beautiful woman. She looked shapely and exotic and completely, wonderfully happy. Hazel took out a lace handkerchief and dabbed at the tears forming in the corners of her eyes. She didn't dare wipe them. Her makeup was on thick enough to fill in the cracks and she didn't want there to be crevices left by a stream of tears.

Amanda watched Fisher out of the corner of her eye. He was staring at Sloane like he used to stare at a new bike. A Trek T30 bike with a tough Cro-Moly mainframe, tall wall alloy wheels, and Wellgo alloy platform pedals. There was awe, admiration, and a whole basket full of wishes. Her little boy was growing up. She smiled at Sloane when she looked over in her direction, a bit too obviously avoiding Fisher's gaze. This was the young woman who would by the end of the year earn a doctorate in computer science. A genius. But not today. Today she looked youthful, excited, and absolutely stunning. Amanda winked. Sloane grinned and winked back. Fisher completely forgot that he could be in the air because he felt like he was already flying.

"I think you just hit the jackpot," said Cameron softly to his grandson.

Fisher came back to his fifteen year old senses, snorted, and whispered back. "I'd rather be flying." His grandfather's comment shook him out of the trance he'd been in. Thank goodness, he thought. He hadn't realized he'd been staring until Cameron spoke to him. But he just couldn't help it. She was just so…so ultra frigid. He tried, not too successfully, to find his bored, put-upon expression and get it back on.

His grandfather smiled. His grandmother smiled and to Fisher's horror they held hands and made those eyes at each other.

Then the music swelled and the people stood. Alex stepped forward. He was incredibly handsome, every woman's dream of what a groom should look like. His tux was impeccably cut, accentuating his broad shoulders and narrow waist. His demeanor was commanding and sure. There was both anticipation and relaxed certainty. But it was his face. His expressive eyes. His lovely smile that drew everyone's attention and captured their imagination. The slight turn of his lips, the flashing blue eyes. The sky behind him wasn't as blue. Or as bright.

All eyes went from him to look back at what would be his first glimpse of his bride. Alex could feel his pulse pounding against the stiff collar of his shirt. For an awful moment, he wondered if she'd show up. They'd been through so much…a roller coaster of emotions and sensations. Her reservations, his complete lack of them. Her fears, his need to fight them off. Her reluctance, his absolute certainty. And in the end, her unconditional surrender, made all the sweeter by its high price.

Tank, standing just where a best man should, said under his breath. "Think she'll show? Maybe she came to her senses."

David nudged him and said. "She'll show. Who'd get custody of the puppy?"

Duncan said, "I don't know, it looks like a fine day for flying."

"We'll give her ten minutes, then I'm hitting the buffet," whispered David.

"Buffet, hell. I'm going straight for the bar. Did you see the fox unpacking the glassware?"

Tank made kissing noises and David laughed.

Good God, they were worse than Al and Jason, Alex thought. His two nephews were standing tall and serious, perfect little gentlemen.

Then Alex heard Tank made an unrecognizable sound in his throat. Like a little strangle.

"Whoa," was all David could get out.

"Good God, almighty," whispered Duncan in his deep voice.

Alex stared at the vision at the end of the aisle. As long as he lived, and he hoped it would be a long and happy life, he'd never forget how she looked when she came out of the doors and walked toward him.

She was made for this moment. This one single moment in time. Her head high, her intricately woven hair interlaced with flowers and glittery jeweled highlights. No veil. Her eyes steady and clear, her hand resting lightly on Jim's arm. She saw only him as their eyes met and locked. Her full generous lips smiling a secret seductive smile just for him. Skyler Madison was making it clear to everyone on the lawn that she wasn't just walking down the aisle; she was walking toward her destiny.

It was Alex who drew her; Alex who possessed her; Alex who sustained her. She was walking toward the source of her happiness, the foundation of her joy. She was walking toward her new life. There was no doubt, or fear, or hesitation. Blue eyes locked onto brown, both bright with passion and promise.

She was flawlessly elegant and exquisitely ethereal. No lace, or frills. A long white dress made of a fabric that looked lighter than air hugged her curves and flowed around her like a cloud. It had long sleeves, pointed at the wrists and a low simple neckline that revealed the top of her full, beautiful breasts. It was perfection. But the most stunning and unexpected feature was the light that came from her. While most brides will shine with an inner glow, hers was punctuated by a dazzling flash of reflected light.

There were silver threads running through the material of her gown and when the sun caught them, Skye looked like a sparkling, glowing vision. A shine of illumination surrounded her; a celestial light seemed to be emanating from her. Her dress shimmered when she walked and glistened like newly fallen snow in an untouched field on a sunny day. She was breathtaking. The brilliance of the dress, the radiance of her smile, the vivacity of her eyes dazzled everyone and nearly blinded Alex.

She was carrying white gardenias with silver threads and ribbons running nearly down to the ground. The simplicity of the dress and the flowers drew the eye to the flash of the stunning diamond around her neck then up to her face. That unforgettable face.

She was moving toward him in slow motion, at least that was how it seemed to Alex. He swallowed hard and took another deep breath. Even his heart seemed to be beating in slow motion. He was riveted, filled with wonder. His bride. He'd seen her in his dreams. His imagination had created pictures. Nothing prepared him for this…this vision. She didn't even look mortal. And she was his; this magnificent woman was coming to him. The intensity of his love, his feeling of destiny was atmospheric. She literally took his breath away and he had to remind himself to fill his lungs. Her scent, the scent of gardenias came with it and he was lost in her essence.

Skye looked down the long aisle and saw him waiting for her. Beside her was Jim, the man who had helped her, loved her and now accompanied her on the path to her future. Alex, her heart whispered. Alex. She looked into his face and hoped her own mirrored what she saw there. The love. The passion. The timeless fidelity. The quiet affection. The infinite desire. She saw nothing but him. Her hand was steady; her stride was graceful and sure. Inside there was serenity that she was sure she'd never felt before. Was it peace at last?

She fell into his blue, blue eyes, the color of her favorite sky. All they had been through. All they had been to each other flowed between them. There was no one else in the garden but the two of them.

Jim stopped in front of Alex, he had something precious to turn over to a man he trusted. Jim turned to the woman who had been such an important part of his life and gave her cheek a light kiss then placed her hand into Alex's.

"Be happy, Skyler," he said simply. It was all he could get through his constricted throat. When he'd seen her descend the stairs a few moments earlier, he didn't know if his legs would move him toward her. The daughter of his best friend. It hit him hard that he was standing in Perry's place. The flashes of memory…of Skye as a toddler, Skye as a teen, Skye as a young woman. He imagined this was what happened to every father on his daughter's wedding day.

When he found his legs could move, he went to her, offered his arm and realized that for him, she was as much a daughter as if she'd been born to him. He loved his two sons passionately. They were good men. But this woman. This stunning, confident, remarkable woman had his heart in her hand. Did all fathers have these mixed feelings? Wanting her to be happy, but at the same time wanting her to remain young and dependent and his little girl?

He liked Alex. Admired him and thought the match was made in heaven. That was what his head told him. In his heart he wanted to take Skye to the zoo, buy her ice cream and beg her not to love another man as much as she loved him. Then she smiled and he saw a flash of uncharacteristic uncertainty in her eyes…just a momentary flicker, but there all the same. Was she doing the right thing? Was she going to be happy? She needed him to be certain and strong and assured. And he found that he was. As they moved together toward the doors, his certainty extinguished any doubt that might have visited her heart as she moved to wait next to him with nothing but love there.

Jim stood next to her now. A place he'd always been. There was a sparkle of tears in Skye's glorious brown eyes when Jim placed her hand into Alex's. Alex would now be the man beside her.

"Thank you," was all she could manage as she rubbed his kiss into her cheek. Since childhood she'd always done that with his kisses. He accused her of rubbing them off, she insisted she was rubbing them in. She kissed him back. He was her past. She looked up into the face of her future. The electricity that passed between Skye and Alex as he accepted her hand nearly knocked out the whole front row.

Alex's hand was steady and warm. For a moment, they just looked at each other with such love and devotion that everyone held their breath. Then Alex smiled and raised her hand slowly to his lips, never taking his eyes off of hers. Skye smiled back. It was magic. Everyone let out their breath and sighed. Several thought to dab at the tears flowing down their cheeks.

Alex gradually returned to his senses and the rest of the world came into focus. There was ritual to attend to. They were to be married. This was a wedding. He smiled. Time to make it official.

"You look more like a pagan goddess than a virginal bride," he whispered under his breath as he slipped her arm through his and turned with her toward the altar.

"I could hardly play the virginal bride," she whispered back.

"You didn't find that dress in any bride's magazine. Have a fairy godmother, Snow?"

"Of course." She didn't feel like reminding him that it was Cinderella who had the godmother. "And now comes the happily ever after part."

"You have on anything beneath that?" asked Alex just before they came within earshot of the judge.

"You have to marry me to find out," said Skye giving him a mischievous look. Alex thought she really did look like something out of a fairy tale.

"Oh, all right. If you insist," he said, his blue eyes sparkling.

"I do," said Skye.

"Not yet, darling. That comes later."

As they reached the judge, they were both chuckling. Their laughter defined their relationship nearly as much as their love. It was a perfect moment.

The judge said the words that would make their union legal and official. Then she turned to Al and Jason and nodded. They'd been holding Tank's hands, fulfilling their solemn promise to Skye. With the help of the best man, Al dug into his pocket and produced a ring and handed it to Skye. It was a good thing Tank had a few of his wits still about him, because Al was totally dazzled and completely missed his cue. He hadn't taken his eyes off of her since she started up the aisle. It appeared as though he didn't even intend to blink.

Skye placed a ring on Alex's finger, then held his hand in hers as she looked up at him. Her smile was warm and sure, her voice soft and strong. "Alex, you've changed my life. You've changed me. With my mind, I will forever count my blessings. With my heart, I will forever love you. With my soul, I will forever cherish you. You've given me flight. With you beside me, I soar. I will adore you, treasure you and try every day to show you how much I love you."

Alex took his ring from the slightly more aware Jason. Her ring was identical to his. He could feel it on his finger. It felt warm. It felt right. Now it was his turn.

"I love you Skye. Before you, I was alone. For a long time my heart was dormant, my soul asleep. When I laughed, I thought I was happy. When I worked, I thought I was fulfilled. When I saw beauty, I thought I was moved. Only now when I look at you do I realize that nothing ran deep. I was none of these things. Your love has made me. I'll love you every day of my life because it will be what defines my life." He slid the ring on her finger as she smiled into his eyes. Perfect, she thought. Perfect.

Her husband. She loved him with her whole heart and trusted him to bring her more happiness than heartache. More joy than pain. More life and love and pleasure. Because their lives were complicated and they flew into danger frequently, he could give her no guarantees. Instead he gave her himself. All of him. She'd live with the potential for loss, because without him, she couldn't live at all.

All of her thoughts were expressed in her dark brown eyes and Alex could read them perfectly. When she was unguarded, like she was right now, he could see right into her soul. It hadn't been easy for her to love him, to trust him with her heart. He had to fight her and fight for her, but it made the victory even sweeter. He was touched by the courage it took for her to give into his persistent assault. Her nightmares still brought her heartache. He was sorry about that, but vowed he'd make sure her waking hours were full of his love, that she'd have a shield against the fear and misery.

The judge nearly missed her cue. She was entranced by the look that passed between Skye and Alex, by the words they spoke, and by the passion that flowed from them like waves.

She cleared her throat and did her duty. "I now pronounce you one."

There were floods of tears, acres of tissues, and a chorus of sighs. Hundreds of cameras clicked, flashed, and whirred. The wedding party and guests were witness to the merging of two souls. It was a moment that registered in the minds of everyone there and went straight to their collective hearts.

Alex slowly moved Skye toward him, prolonging the moment. She let him guide her, every sense alive and firing. The smell of flowers, the feel of the silky material of his tux, the sounds of music and fountains, and finally, the taste of his lips on hers. Nearly a sensory overload. Her entire body was now against his. The light reflecting off her dress appeared to encompass him in its luminosity. Rapture surrounded them as the music swelled and everyone watched their first married kiss. His lips gently touched hers…familiar, warm, infinitely sweet.

The guests applauded, but Alex and Skye were alone in their world. Time stood still as she slowly drew back and looked into his eyes. Her husband's eyes. Finally, he smiled. She smiled.

"Let's party," she laughed and took his hand as they walked down the aisle as one.

CHAPTER 19

It was a wonderful party. Alex and Skye continuously tracked each other in the crowd, exchanging looks as they greeted their guests. When their eyes met, everyone around them felt the blast. She'd smile and raise her glass, he'd return the salute and they would go back to talking and laughing with whoever was with them at the moment. She was a spectacular bride who never wilted, never stopped radiating absolute joy. Never nervous, almost serene. Her face, smiles, eyes, and body language all projected the fact that this was the most wonderful day of her life.

Those who knew the intrepid Alexander Springfield as a rational man completely in control at all times, would smile knowingly when he stopped talking in mid-sentence and looked around the room. His eyes would go to her like a magnet. She was wearing very high heels, as was her preference at parties, and stood out physically among the crowd. But he swore he could see an aura, a shine of light around her. So no matter where she was, he could find her immediately by just moving his eyes over the crush of people.

When the need to touch got irresistible, he'd just leave the conversation hanging and walk to his bride. People around the room would watch him and smile wistfully. Skye could always feel his presence and would be facing him by the time he reached her. Guests would sigh, then go back to their conversations, their champagne or their plate of food.

Alex would walk to her light, enjoying the surge of pleasure all over again. She'd just promised before everyone she loved that she'd be his and only his forever. He wanted to just put his hands on her. Touch her. Feel her. When he'd seek her out through the lovely afternoon and evening, no one who had her at the moment would begrudge him his fix. He'd claim his mate and she'd come into his arms. Then he'd take her to the dance floor or hold her for a few minutes, gazing into her eyes or gently touching her lips. They knew they had a lifetime together, but this was the gateway to that life.

"Hello wife," he'd say, just to hear the word.

"Hello husband," would be her response.

They were stealing a kiss behind one of the rented potted palms when the music suddenly stopped playing. They looked to the stage and found Tank at the mike. He wasn't quite steady, but he was plenty sober enough to know his place in history. He was the best man and he had to make a toast.

"Oh no," said Alex.

"Maybe if we just stay behind here, he'll lose the urge," she whispered, smiling at the cockeyed grin on Tank's handsome face.

"Okay, kids." They heard Tank's wonderful, powerful voice booming out of the speakers. "Come out from behind that palm tree and plant yourself where people can see you. This isn't prom night at R. U. High."

Skye and Alex stepped out and the smiling crowd parted.

"It's my function at this bash to make sure the groom shows up. Check. Make sure the ring is securely placed in his hand so he can slide it on the bride's finger. Check. Keep the kids from swiping too much frosting off the top of the cake. So what's wrong with that? Forget that check. And to make a toast to the happy couple." Reaching in his pocket, he pulled out a piece of paper and held it up. "Please meet me at midnight behind the pool house. Oops."

As people laughed and whooped in appreciation, he threw the paper aside and pulled out another one from his jacket pocket. He looked at the paper, then at Skye and Alex and then slowly let that paper drop, too.

Skye felt her heart in her chest. Most of the time it just worked in there without her noticing, but now she was conscious of every beat. She so loved him, the man who was now officially her little brother. He was gorgeous in his tuxedo. His long rust colored hair was waving despite his efforts with a comb. His flashing green eyes and ridiculously long eye lashes were fixed on his brother and his sister, not just by law, but by affection. More than one unmarried lady in the audience decided they wouldn't mind meeting him behind anywhere, any time. Tank cleared his throat. His smile was genuine and loving. Only Alex could see the hint of melancholy.

"The universe is a vast place. Cold and dark as space." Tank began in a voice Skye had never heard before. This was coming right from his heart and Skye could already feel herself choke up. "Sometimes two people are cast out in it who are meant to be together. Who fit. Who are perfectly suited to each other. They're out there, but they have to find each other."

Tank's eyes went from Alex to Skye's flushed and splendidly happy face. "I know my brother…known him my whole life. He never really came alive until he met Skye. I always thought of him as a lone wolf, someone who, while noble and decent and good, was solitary…perhaps destined to travel alone. I thought that fate was cheating him." He paused. There was so much more he could say. "But fate wrote the script and sometimes she's a generous and insightful creator of time and place. She had Skye in the wings."

There were chuckles, appreciating his words and his reference to her love of flying.

"Skye flew right into her destiny, into his life. She crossed his path, turned, came to him and he became complete. Her flight into fate was his making. Skye and Alex are now one heart, one soul. Alex can now travel in peace. Travel in harmony. Travel in grace."

Tank looked at Skye with such love and tenderness, Alex could hardly breathe. "To my sister, the holder of the light. The keeper of the key to happiness. She is everything, so she should have everything. She deserves my brother. He was made for her to love. She was created for him. They found each other in this universe and it's no longer cold and dark."

He raised his glass to the two of them while nearly everyone else in the room raised a handkerchief or tissue. "To the two of them…to the one." Tank brought his glass to his lips and drank. He was surprised he could still swallow, but he did. Everyone in the room did the same except for Skye and Alex. They were just too moved to move.

Skye's eyes filled, and the tears spilled out. She turned to Alex. "Oh, Alex. How did we get so lucky. That was so poetic, so completely perfect." There was a time when Skye would never let a tear fall. She could turn off her emotions at will. Since she met Alex, something opened up in her. A switch had turned on. And with it her propensity to shed tears.

Alex was still staring at Tank. He'd never heard his brother utter such beautiful words; he was completely undone by them. He automatically reached into his pocket and handed Skye his handkerchief, never taking his eyes off his younger brother. Green eyes met blue eyes. So dear to him…so much more so now. Then Tank's eyes slid over to Skye then back to his big brother, Alex saw the emotion. Recognized it. Another lone wolf…hoping to someday find his own mate. Alex raised his glass. Something more to share with the unbelievably amazing man the annoying little brother had become. Tank smiled, the wistfulness left his eyes, dissolved as they flashed in amusement.

"And now," he said in a master of ceremonies voice. "A song dedicated to them and their upcoming week. My wedding present to them."

He turned and Jimmy Buffet came out of the wings to the gasps and screams of the guests. The famous balladeer bowed to the bride and groom and grinned. Skye and Alex's all time favorite musical artist. He turned to the orchestra. They were ready for him. He started his set with *Honey, Why Don't We Get Drunk And Screw*.

Skye squealed with delight and actually clapped her hands together. She turned her bright eyes to Alex. Their favorite singer…their favorite song. They'd come together again after a painful disconnection listening to Jimmy Buffet on Alex's boat. And that particular song. Well, they took Jimmy's advice and ended a pretty long dry spell with an afternoon of drinking and screwing. Skye threw her arms around Alex and bopped to the music then joined the appreciative audience in applauding the wonderful singer.

"Well, that answers the question, where's my little brother," laughed Alex. "He just got dressed up and decided to act like an adult for a minute. Scared me. He's back now, though." He looked over at the laughing man dancing like an idiot, surrounded by lovely young women who he twirled around in quick succession.

"Let's slow it down," said Jimmy, his speaking voice as melodious and hypnotic as his singing voice. "To Alex and Skye…*Ever After, Now and Then.*"

Jimmy Buffet stayed for several more songs, chatted with Skye and Alex awhile, then flew off to Margaritaville.

The party continued to blow long into the night. No one wanted to go home. The weather remained absolutely perfect and the stars were an endless backdrop to their night of magic. Skye and Alex danced, chatted and stole more kisses behind the palm tree.

Skye finally grabbed her brother-in-law and danced with him. He held her gently against his broad chest, she was now a married woman, after all. Married to his brother, who he'd worshiped his whole life. He was more than a little tipsy, but still incredibly light on his feet.

"Thank you for the toast." She sighed. "And Jimmy and my puppy. You're the most wonderful man."

Tank stared at her. She still hadn't wilted and he felt like he'd been hammered for days. He made a silent vow to cut back on the drinking.

"How do you do it?" he asked, not realizing he'd just said out loud what was on his mind.

"Do what?"

"Stay so fresh. Christ, even those petunias know enough to wilt. Are you some kind of alien life form or something?"

"You did say the universe was a vast place." She looked around. "What petunias?" She hadn't recalled ordering any.

He pointed to the flowers in the pots. She giggled. "Those are gardenias."

"If you say so."

Skye pulled away and grinned. Fanning herself, she decided he was just too yummy to go home alone. Waiving one of his several admirers over, she left them on the dance floor to go find the other Springfield man. She was ready for another toe curling kiss from her husband.

Wyatt watched and smiled. Tank was her baby and she knew his heart. She remembered a few months before when they stood on a terrace watching Skye being particularly Skye-like. There had been the typical Tank smile on his face, but a wistful look in his eye. He'd told her in a moment of true Mother-Son confidence, knowing she'd understand, "I've never in my life ever envied my brother anything. Until now."

She did understand. Tank's capacity for loving was without boundaries. He completely and utterly loved every new girl, every new puppy, every new bike that came into his life. What he really wanted was what Skye and Alex had together. Love, unconditional devotion, and passion for the one and only.

The Springfield men fell instantly, completely, and enduringly in love. Blake did, now Alex and someday her precious baby. He'd find his one. His destiny. And the lucky woman would forever be captivated by his love. Like being run over by a Tank. She sighed and looked around for her one and only.

He was over by the bar and from the velocity of his hands moving around, he was arguing a case before the Supreme Court again. Several of Alex's law school buddies where standing around providing a rapt audience. She thought she better tag a dance before the closing arguments. They sometimes went on for hours.

Fisher wasn't sure how he was going to stay cool and still get the luscious Sloane in his arms for a dance. They suffered together through all the pictures. He thought his grandmother was over the top with the camera. It was like she was afraid there might be a single moment in the entire day that wouldn't be recorded. Cripes. But at least it kept Sloane close and he didn't need an excuse to stand with her. Then she went to the head table for the dinner and was having far too much fun with that old guy, Tank. Maybe with her brain she went for older guys. Made sense. But she was jailbait for him and any of the other older guys hanging around her. Her mind might be fully mature, but she was still a tweener.

He wanted to do the escort thing but the problem was how to keep his nonchalance, his on-the-edge cool 'tude, and still get her to notice him. More than that, to want to be with him. He'd asked all the teen girls to swing with him, hoping she'd feel neglected and maybe even a little jealous, but she never seemed to be without a dance partner herself. He even danced with her best friend Libby, but all Brainiac did was raise her glass and give him a thumbs up. What was that all about?

He tried the proximity caper. Placing himself in her path or at least in her general vicinity. Didn't work. She froze him out. Didn't even see him. So now he was setting his strategy for a more direct attack. He'd just go up to her and tell her it was time to perform the duties of an escort. He could look over at his grandma when he said it…like it was her idea.

Then his eyes narrowed. She was dancing with an old guy who looked like he had too much of the champagne. His hand kept slipping up her torso to touch the side of her breast and she kept moving to minimize the contact. She was clearly trying to keep herself at arm's length just as this perv kept trying to pull her in.

Sloane was really getting annoyed. She figured she'd shown Fisher enough disinterest and wanted to hang with him awhile. Then this old guy grabbed her and almost dragged her onto the dance floor. What was with him anyway? He was the husband of a business associate of Alex's and being drunk was no excuse for his groping. She didn't want to make a scene, but if this asshole didn't leave her alone, she was going to stomp his instep. The man twirled her in what the idiot thought was a graceful move…and halleluiah…her heart fluttered in her chest…there was Fisher, standing behind him and taping him on the shoulder.

"Excuse me, sir. You're dancing with my date and she promised she'd dance this one with me." The man ignored him and pulled Sloane to his chest hard enough to cause her to stumble. Fisher's eyes narrowed and with surprising agility, he stepped aside, then right back at the man's shoulder.

"Sorry gramps, but I have to insist." A shocked Sloane watched as Fisher took the man's shoulder in his fist, squeezed hard, then spun him around. At the same time he grabbed Sloane's hand, placed himself between them and put his arm around her waist. He did it with such speed and natural grace that it left Sloane breathless and the man standing alone in the middle of the dance floor completely befuddled. Fisher quickly moved away, with Sloane firmly in his arms.

Amanda and Cameron were dancing nearby and nearly applauded. "Now that was nicely done," said Amanda, proudly grinning.

"And I think he'll find that little bit of gallantry completely worth the time and effort. Seems it has sealed the truce."

"Wow that was a great move," laughed Sloane as she let Fisher lead her to the other side of the dance floor. "That man was a letch. Geesh. It took me all this time to get a pair and now they seem to be a hand magnet."

"Excuse me?" Fisher could feel his cheeks heat up. She was referring to her...well...her chest. Cripes. Then he realized it wasn't a kid-to-kid remark. It was like an adult chat. Wicked. He continued to lead her like his grandpa taught him. He hoped he looked as smooth as Cameron as he watched his grandparents glide by.

"Thanks...Shark," said Sloane sincerely. She decided not to elaborate on the chest remark. Sometimes her mouth really was on automatic pilot.

"Don't mention it," he responded with as much *savior faire* as he could manage, given that she was making him feel particularly heroic. He liked it.

"Okay. I won't," she said breezily, although she'd mention it to Libby, all right. Libby would just faint. "Want some cake?" She was really, really beginning to be aware of his arm around her waist and it was making her feel a little self-conscious...excited, but hoping she wasn't sweating too much and her makeup was still intact and nothing was lodged in her teeth.

"Maybe later," replied Fisher. Now that he had her and he didn't have to give up any of his cool to get her in his arms, he was going to take full advantage of the situation. For the first time in his life a young woman took precedence over his stomach. It was a momentous step toward his eventual surrender. He was infatuated and his heart was ready to throw in the towel. He risked a tighter hold and nearly stumbled when she moved into him and placed her cheek against his neck. This was more than wicked...it was...was...hell...when his brain got into gear again, he'd find the word he was looking for.

Linda and David had dropped any pretense of being duty bound to dance together and only separated when other friends and relatives cut in. She'd periodically check on the boys, but they were having a blast with the rest of the children in the special area provided for them. There was a shiny wooden floor they could slide on, snacks and fruit juice and music that sounded more like Disney classics than dance music.

Wyatt and Blake waltzed by them as Linda gave her latest report on his children. Their heads were together and David was chuckling over what she was saying.

"I think there may be a candidate in the running for stepmother to our grandchildren," smiled Wyatt.

"They seem to respond to her," said Blake smiling into his wife's shining eyes.

"Children respond to love and interest," she agreed, searching her heart for any sadness and finding none.

"Jason actually kept his napkin in his lap for more than a minute and a half."

"A new record," laughed Wyatt. "And Al kept his finger out of his nose all evening."

"That's my boy," laughed Blake with mock pride. He looked over at his son-in-law and noticed the look on his face as he held Linda after the music stopped. "David responds to her as well."

Wyatt nodded. "She's a wonderful woman."

"See a match?" asked Blake squeezing Wyatt's hand.

"I think it's time," responded Wyatt squeezing back.

"Indeed." Blake took his wife over to talk with the younger couple.

Sloane and Fisher danced, ate cake and danced some more. When the music stopped and they'd fulfilled all of their duties, they looked at each other and nodded.

"Ready?" asked Fisher.

Sloane nodded conspiratorially. "See you in ten. I have to get comfortable."

"Wear something that looks good with severed limbs and headless torsos, 'cause there's going to be serious blood letting," grinned Fisher, rubbing his hands in anticipation. He watched her lift her skirts and walk swiftly into the house. Sweet.

They met in the den and immediately engaged in noisy, enthusiastic combat. *Firewalkers*. Gallant beings from the planet Xantar. Sloane and Fisher were both tireless and they very quickly ascended into levels not yet explored by anyone outside of corporate testing.

Hours later, Sloane sat cross-legged, blowing watermelon Bubblicious bubbles and looking at Fisher out of the corner of her eye. Ever since she took an advanced anatomy and physiology class, she knew she was going to save herself for just the right man. She told Skye once that she was going to give it up for Terry Pickford, lead guitarist for the Restless Pretzels, but that was a little girl fantasy. Besides, as cool as Terry was, he didn't have beautiful green eyes and that ultra cool attitude. And with Fisher, it wasn't just a big mouth and counterfeit bravado. He'd proven himself both resourceful and brave on a real life proving ground when he helped Skye escape from terrorists the summer before. *You turn a man out of that boy, Fisher, and then look out*, she thought as she methodically blasted every marauding megabeast coming at her from behind the rugged terrain. *I'm going to save myself for you.* As she waited for the game to load level eight, she peeked at him again. He had a magnificent profile and a kick-ass smile. *And I think you're going to be worth the wait*, she thought as she took out a dozen more beasts.

Fisher could feel her eyes as she waited for him to catch up with her. He was completely irritated, but captivated at the same time. He felt schizophrenic. She was an overbearing brainiac who drove him crazy. On the other hand, she was incredibly bright and funny and that drove him even crazier. He wasn't sure when she got so pretty. Pretty, hell. That was too little a word for what she was. She was drop dead gorgeous. He knew that he was no match for her right now. She was a freaking genius. But if he worked hard, he could get a lot smarter. Also there were things he knew he could do in his life he'd be uniquely better at. Give him time, maybe ten years, and he'd be able to stand with her, be her equal. Not in mind things, but in life things. He knew he was clever and resourceful and, well, according to his grandma, he was going to be as good looking as his grandpa. He'd work hard to get his body as buff as Alex. *Yeah. You just wait, Miss Brainiac*, he thought as she was beating his butt. *The Shark is going to swim in your pond.*

They continued to play throughout the night, drinking oceans of Mountain Dew, pounding down acres of chips, unwrapping and shoveling in tons of peanut butter cups, chewing mega wads of Bubblicious and whooping it up, powered on adrenalin, competition, chocolate, and caffeine. Amanda checked in on them at 4:00 a.m. and decided to leave them alone. She watched them for a while until Cameron came silently up behind her. He saw what she saw and chuckled in her ear.

"Cute couple."

Amanda smiled and nodded. "Right now, Sloane is more woman than girl; Fisher is more boy than man. Give them a decade. The moons will align and they will be perfectly matched."

"Hmm. Let's see. I'll be 85 and you'll be only a spry 80. Maybe we'd better do something aerobic. Keep our hearts healthy so we'll be here to see it." He held her around her slim waist and kissed her ear. Even after all their years together, it lit her fire.

"What a nice idea."

"You know what Stanaslov says…it may take me all night to do what I used to do all night, but it beats the hell out of not being able to do it at all."

"Darling. How indiscreet to be quoting that old bear when you're seducing your wife."

"And his former lover?"

"That was before I knew you existed."

"Well, it's what's kept me alive all these years. I knew that if anything happened to me, that old bear would make a move. You're mine."

"Body and soul."

"Heart and mind."

"What's left of it."

"I'd say there's plenty," smiled Cameron, holding her closer.

"Well, if it's going to take all night, maybe we'd better get started," chuckled Amanda squeezing Cameron's still well muscled butt.

He chuckled, "Already starting, my love. Just get me horizontal." He kissed her deeply. "I think my days of holding you up against a wall are behind me."

"No great loss," she said, her eyes bright and her body responding to his, as it had for over four decades.

CHAPTER 20

The sun was coming up. Alex and Skye watched the eastern sky from their bedroom terrace, wrapped in each other's arms. Alex had taken off his tie and his shirt stood open at the neck. She kissed him there and all the way up to his jaw line. He was getting just a bit scratchy. His arms went around her a little tighter and he kissed the top of her head. Her shoes had come off the minute she hit the room and she was back to her actual 5'11"

He'd carried her in a few minutes before. Over the threshold, into her new life. She looked down at her shiny new wedding ring. It was on her finger now. She was his. Taking his left hand in hers, she brought it up into the light. His matching ring winked at her. He was hers.

"Tired?" he whispered.

"No. I know I should be, but I'm not."

He turned her around in his arms and cupped her chin. Bringing her head up, he gently, tenderly kissed his bride on their first morning together as husband and wife.

"I love you, Skye. I couldn't believe I could love you more when I woke up this morning. Our wedding day. But I do. I love you more. I know it shouldn't make a difference…the words…the promises. We made a commitment to each other months ago. But it does make a difference. I wanted you since the moment I saw you. Tank was right. I was so alone. I need you, Skye. I need you beside me."

She looked into his eyes. "My darling husband." She smiled at the tightening of his arms around her. "We've been moving to this day since the moment our paths crossed. Our fate was sealed. My love for you has never faltered. I have…I did. But not my love. I don't know if I deserve you or not. I don't know what tomorrow will bring. But if today…this one wonderful, magical day was all I was allowed…all I was given…I have more than I ever thought possible. If tomorrow comes, that's our miracle. Everything after today is a bonus. You were right. You were always right. You're my heart. You're my life. I love you." Her lips came up to meet his and the kiss was as timeless as the air around them. The world outside the circle of their arms wasn't important…not even there.

He scooped her off her feet and carried her inside to their bed. Now their marriage bed. They sat, facing each other, their lips in constant contact. Kissing lightly, then deeply, then coming back up. She worked the studs off his shirt, for once taking her time and not sending them flying around the room in her eagerness. She spread his shirt open bringing her hands along his chest.

His hand went behind her and brought the zipper of her dress down slowly, tracing his fingers along the flesh of her back.

"You took my breath away today," he whispered.

Bringing her head back she smiled at him, removing his cufflinks as he pulled her gown off her shoulders. Leaning over he trailed kisses down her long, soft throat and running his hands over her shoulders and down her torso, his desire growing as he felt her tremble.

She pushed his shirt off, so she could feel his skin against hers. He held her then and went back to her lips, drinking in as much of her as he could. Her fingers curled through his hair as her body responded and her nerves jumped and danced to his skillful strokes.

She moaned, deep in her throat and it enflamed him. Lowering her onto her back, she wiggled out of her dress. Her hands went to his waistband and his joined hers, removing all the barriers to his desire. She touched him and he lost his control in the waves of longing and need that flowed through him. His hand came up between them and he pulled off her one piece undergarment, freeing her breasts and the rest of her at the same time. He could feel her heat. He could sense her craving…hear her ragged breathing and his name on her lips.

"Alex," she whispered. "Alex. I love you. Show me. Love me."

He touched every part of her until she felt shattered with need. She touched every part of him until he couldn't stand the agony of holding himself back any longer. Finally, with their last bit of energy, they came together, their bodies following their hearts. Becoming one.

She lay under him, completely exhausted. Completely satisfied. Completely, blissfully happy. He rolled over, bringing her with him, so she could fall asleep in his arms. He held her, kissed her good morning and covered them with a sheet…watching as his new wife fell into a deep, restful, contented, married sleep. Making love as husband and wife was better. That was his last coherent thought before he joined her and drifted into sleep himself.

They woke up to full sunlight. Skye was still lying on his chest. She opened her eyes, then let them close again. Her eyes felt heavy and she decided she didn't need to move yet. All their guests were family and would make themselves at home…if they were up. Opening her eyes again, she decided to take just one peek at her husband before she slipped back into a few more days of sleep. She moved her head slowly, not wanting to wake him up. Neither of them had much rest this last week…hell, neither of them had much rest since they met.

His breathing was still slow and regular. Gently she moved her head back…and frowned. He was awake and smiling at her. She swore he came instantly awake whenever he felt her eyes open. She thought she might catch him this time, but she should have known better.

"How do you do that?" she grumped. His eyes were way too awake and alert for him to be human. "You're a robot."

When she put her head back down, she felt the rumble deep in his chest.

"I just like watching you come awake."

"Hasn't happened yet today." She heard the chuckle again. "Shhhh. I'm still sleeping." She yawned hugely and closed her eyes. "What time is it?"

"You have a better angle on the clock."

"But your eyes focus in the morning."

"You have a point." She felt him shift. "It's a little before 9:00."

She settled back in and nuzzled against his neck. Contented, relaxed, married.

"Comfortable?" he asked.

"Mmmmm. Wake me up before you put me on the plane, then kick it down the runway."

"That didn't even make sense," said an amused Alex. He ran his hand down the tangle of hair that was flowing over his chest. His wife. He looked at her rings glistening in the reflected morning sun. The diamond had been on and off her finger, but now it had a partner to keep it in place. Her wedding ring was on her hand and was going to be there for the next century or so. Permanent. Enduring. Like his love for her.

She wiggled a little to get into a more comfortable position. She loved his chest, but it was rock solid and sometimes she had to find just the right spot. Her shifting put him into ready mode. It didn't take much and he lay there wondering if he should let her sleep a bit longer, or if he should initiate Operation Seduction. He ran his hand up her naked back, barely skimming her skin. Maybe if she thought it was her idea, she'd shake her usual morning quirkiness and throw him a bone.

"I know what you're doing, darling," she murmured, her eyes still closed and drifting back into sleep. "It won't work. I hid my 'on' button last night. If you give me 5 more minutes, I'll turn over so you can locate it." She'd hardly finished the sentence when she was back asleep.

He gave her 30. It took him nearly that long to replay the entire afternoon and evening of the day before. Looking at her dress that was now a puddle of shimmering white on the floor, he saw her again coming toward him. He didn't want to lose a minute of it. He rewound her walk down the aisle several times. Every time, his body would respond the same way, with appreciation and wonder, blended with incredible heat. He was finding it difficult, hard, he thought, shifting, to keep his desire in check. He wanted her. He wondered if there would ever be a time he'd wake up not wanting her. No. He could answer that one without reservation. There would never be a time as long as he was alive and breathing, that he wouldn't want her morning, afternoon and night. She could exasperate him, terrify him, confuse him, drive him to the brink of madness, but he'd always want her. He always did.

After a half hour had elapsed, he nudged her and tried to slide out from under her. Her arm tightened around him, then lowered, bringing her hand into contact with the source of his discomfort. He heard her snicker and squeezed her butt.

"You better let go for a minute, darling," he said kissing her ear. "If you're still here when I get back, consider yourself fair game for the hunter's gun."

Letting go, she watched him walk naked to the bathroom. Her spouse. She decided not to wait for him to come back. She got out of bed and went in after him...the hunter just became the prey.

Everything was quiet when they came down the front stairs an hour later. Remnants of a big party were everywhere, from the wilting garlands to the champagne glasses decorating the bookshelves. They found Amanda and Cameron in the hallway talking in low tones...confidentially sharing a few thoughts.

"Hey you two. Despite all the cake crumbs around here, I can guarantee there are no bugs," said Alex, teasingly.

They both turned and smiled. Two old warriors facing the new generation of defenders of the light. A lot of power. A lot of talent. A lot of respect.

"So how is marriage so far?" asked Cameron taking Alex's extended hand and kissing Skye on the cheek.

"I think it'll work," said Skye looking at how easily Cameron's arm went around his wife's shoulders. "It appears as though you two have found the formula. How many years?"

"Forty-three. Of course, if we count it in number of actual days spent together it's probably no more than a year and a half," laughed Amanda.

"Darling, I never count the days," said Cameron smiling into his wife's amused face. "Just the nights."

That made all four of them smile.

"Where are you off to?" asked Alex pointing to Cameron's luggage.

"Akron, of course," said Cameron noncommittally. "I thought I'd hunt down Fisher to say goodbye, before I left." He nodded toward the den.

"Is he still in the den with Sloane?" asked Skye in surprise and she didn't even try to hide her delight.

"As the husband of Sloane's legal guardian, should I know what they're doing in the den?" asked Alex, smiling as well. He loved his sister-in-law and liked Fisher. They were young, but a nice dose of puppy love would make this event complete.

"I'd think it was obvious. Sloane and Fisher in the den. *Firewalkers* in the den..." shrugged Skye. "Combat."

"Ah yes. You are truly an excellent agent," said Alex. Since both Cameron and Amanda worked inside the CIA and held the highest national clearance, they were privy to all of Skye and Alex's secrets. "We're going to have to leave for the airport soon, too. Do you want a ride, Cameron?"

"No, thank you. I'm leaving for Des Moines from Andrews."

"I thought you said Akron," said Alex his eyebrows lifting.

"So I did," smiled Cameron and left it at that.

The four of them went into the den. Fisher was still working the controls and the oversized screen was exploding in color. He had the sound muted and kept his body still as he efficiently wiped out hordes of attacking space monsters. His eyes were tearing from a full night of playing and very little blinking, but he was smiling. He was almost at the end of the line and was going to be light years ahead of his friends in Denver.

As they came around the sofa, they saw why things were so quiet. Sloane was fast asleep, her head resting on a pillow in Fisher's lap. Fisher pressed the pause button and looked up at them.

"Hey, man. What time is it?" he whispered. His fingers were cramped and he had to pee for the last hour, but he kind of liked playing the game in this big, pleasant room as the sun was coming up. And mostly he liked it when Sloane gave up and decided to rest her eyes for a few minutes. That was three hours ago. He looked down at her. She slept real cute.

"About 11:00. Were the two of you here all night?" asked Alex, feigning a frown and sounding altogether parental.

"Ah. Yeah. We were," said Fisher putting down the controls more loudly than was necessary and moving his knees under Sloane's head. It was kind of embarrassing to have her fast asleep on his lap.

"Unchaperoned?" asked Cameron, thinking the whole situation was pretty well orchestrated and congratulating his grandson. Nonverbally, of course.

"Well, there was Sloane's brain, doesn't that count?" asked Fisher, relieved that Sloane's eyes came open.

Skye gave that some thought. "Yes, I think that would count. What do you think Amanda?"

"Chronologically, I think her brain is a product of some kind of ancient gene. I'd say it counts," smiled Amanda.

"Sounds lame to me," said Alex, folding his arms across his chest.

Yup, thought Fisher. He was going to pump some serious iron. He had to get arms and an awesome chest like that.

"Jeez, Alex. I'm 15. Think about it. I could put my hands on a girl with an IQ higher than the final bill for this wedding or on the controls of *Firewalkers: Outer Dominion.* Try to think back…way back."

Sloane stirred and sat up. The first thing Fisher thought as his eyes went back to her was that she woke up cute, too. He'd never spent the night with a girl before. He'd rather have his tongue torn out and stuffed up his nose than admit he liked it, but he really did like it. When he knew she was asleep, he touched those curls he'd been wanting to run through his fingers all night. And when her hand had rested on his thigh, well. Fruit loops and lucky charms. He actually had to move it before the little dicky came to attention. For the last hour he was making stupid mistakes because he kept looking down at her pretty face. He was fairly sure that some of the warmth in the room wasn't due to the fire in the fireplace and some of the tingle, well, down there, wasn't entirely due to his need to go to the bathroom. He was glad Sloane couldn't read his mind. His grandma could, though, so he avoided her eyes, and looked at Sloane.

"Rested your eyes enough Brainiac?" he asked, with enough sarcasm, he thought, to appease his adult audience and convince them there'd been no crunching or grabbing.

Sloane snorted and sat up. "Caught up yet, guppy?"

"Did you know you snore and drool when you sleep," retorted Fisher standing up, stretching out his long legs and throwing the pillow in her face.

"Yeah?" She smiled and stretched. "Well, I was dreaming of beating you up all the way to the end of the line. Every time. No. Wait. It wasn't a dream. It really happened." Using the pillow as a weapon, she caught him on the back of the head.

Amanda and Skye looked at each other and smiled. This was good. They were obviously crazy about each other.

Cameron and Alex looked at each other wondering why the kids couldn't get along. They obviously rubbed each other the wrong way.

"I came to say goodbye." Cameron went up to his grandson, who was nearly as tall as he was. He was sure the kid would rather have a handshake, but he was feeling like a hug, so he gathered the boy in his arms for a quick squeeze. To his surprise, Fisher squeezed back and held it for a few seconds.

"Bye, Grandpa. Take care and we'll see you in a couple of weeks."

"It's a date. Be sure your grandma gets home safe. Don't let anyone hit on her."

"Someone hits on her, you can put a hit on him," Fisher said softly so only Cameron could hear. He was a very smart and intuitive boy. He knew there was more to his grandfather than the supposed executive he tried to make himself out to be.

"Sounds fair." He held his hand out to his wife. "See me to the door, Mandy?"

"Don't I always?" She took his hand and they walked out of the den together. She knew he was going straight to Langley and she was quite sure he'd never been to Akron. There were some very sensitive transmissions from Russia he needed to translate and analyze. He was supposed to be retired, but being a spook was a life sentence. And she loved him for it, even as her heart longed to have him all to herself.

"You came from an incredible gene pool," sighed Sloane as she watched Cameron and Amanda leave the room hand in hand. She was a real sucker for true love and romance. Then she shook herself and looked at Fisher. "What the heck happened to you?"

"Well I'm sure you could explain it so no one could understand," responded Fisher quickly.

"You mean the fact that your deoxyribonucleic acid, or DNA is made up of a chain of nucleotides that are, in turn, made up of deoxyribose, phosphoric acid and nitrogenous bases and these are either purines, which are adenine and guanine, or pyrimidines which are cytosine and thymine. And, in your case, any one of these components may be defective."

"Do you ever put yourself to sleep," snorted Fisher, impressed, but not letting it show. "Because you sure can clear a room."

Amanda came back in, smiling. "Fisher, maybe you should get cleaned up and catch a few hours of sleep."

"Nah. I'm fresh." He turned to Sloane. "Want to snare some eggs, then come back in for a rematch?"

Sloane rubbed her hands together. "Sure. When are you two leaving?" she asked Skye and Alex.

"We should be off in an hour. One of the advantages of both owning and piloting the plane is that our itinerary has some flexibility. We'll join you and whoever is up for breakfast."

"Sweet." She turned back to Fisher. "You ready for some advice?"

"Sure, you know anyone who can give me some?" They walked out together, talking a language unique to teens, laughing and bickering.

Skye put her arm around Amanda's waist. "Shall I save my notes from Operation Matrimony?"

Amanda laughed with obvious delight. "I'd say that young lady will write her own script."

They had a lively, relaxed breakfast. When the plates were empty and the coffee cups were refilled, Skye turned to Fisher. "I wanted to give you these before I left. Amanda told me you won't be leaving until tonight, so I thought you might have some time this afternoon for a little solo work." She threw a set of keys at Fisher who caught them on the fly. He really did have great reflexes, she thought. He didn't realize it, but her toss was a little test. She wanted to be sure his all-nighter didn't blunt his reaction time. It didn't.

He looked down and then up at her, his eyes dancing. "The keys to your Cessna?"

"Help yourself. Duncan will take you to the airport when you're ready."

"Wow. Bitchin' This is great. Monstro rad."

He looked over at Sloane, his excitement and good nature overwhelming his need to keep digging at her. "I wish I could take you, but until I get licensed up I can't take passengers."

"I understand," grinned Sloane. "Consider your duties to escort me at an official end." She turned to Alex. "He may have lost the bet, Alex, but he comported himself with good grace. He kept his side of the bargain. He's a man of honor." Holding up her grapefruit juice she saluted her date. She already had hordes of souvenirs pressed in a big quantum physics book in her room upstairs. She'd have lots to tell Libby and she was happy.

Fisher gaped at her, then smiled his sexy smile. Or the smile he thought was a sexy smile. Sloane thought it looked kind of goofy. Cute, maybe. But goofy.

He looked at Sloane's pretty face and raised his own glass to her. He knew he did okay. He cranked up his smile a little more, moving it from what he thought was sexy to irresistible. He forgot that the people who called it irresistible were all related to him. But he had his grandpa's genes, or DNA or whatever Sloane was babbling about, and they had to be powerful stuff...no one could turn up the testosterone like his grandpa. He figured all he needed was a little more practice. Already, he had a lot to tell the guys back in Denver. And he had a picture of her in her sexy dress. She looked a lot older than 14. It would really impress the guys, he knew that for a fact. Plus he could truthfully tell them he spent the night with her on the couch. Wicked.

"How about we do one more pass at the *Firewalkers*, then call it a done date?" he said wolfing down another handful of donut holes.

"Excellent. I'll give you a last opportunity to humble yourself before greatness," responded Sloane flexing her fingers.

Fisher barked a derisive laugh. "Yeah right. While you were snoring, I was practicing."

"You needed it. While you were sweating through your finger exercises, I was in deep relaxation. I was visualizing myself on the back of Andromeda cruising through the valley of Char to the final level of the quest."

"Yeah? Well come on Brainiac. Time to test your technique." They walked back to the den exchanging insults and challenges.

They took their places on the sofa and set the game to advanced play. The first time through the advanced levels the night before, there was a great deal in the game to remember and figure out. That was Sloane's strength. She beat him most of the time. This morning, as they became more experienced, incredible eye-hand coordination was needed and that was Fisher's strength. He began to beat Sloane regularly. Each time she'd laugh and pound him on the back. Almost as proud as he was. She'd always been a good loser. Finally, she looked at her watch and sighed.

"Gotta skate, mate. It's been real, but I have to prepare for my class in genetics tomorrow. And I know you want to take to the air." Fisher got up reluctantly and offered her his hand. She took it and he hauled her up. He held onto her hand for a minute. It was small and finely boned. He liked watching it playing over the controls. They sure could move. Sloane looked up at him and they stared into each other's eyes for a few seconds, then youthful self-consciousness got the upper hand and they parted quickly. They packed away the equipment and straightened up the room.

At the door, Fisher took her hand again. "Ah. I just wanted to...ah. Well. It was a good weekend."

He was more than a head taller than she was and she looked up at him. Suddenly her knees were weak. Maybe it was fatigue, she thought. No. It was more likely clear green eyes. Beautiful expressive emerald colored eyes, bright and alert even after hours and hours of concentrated use. Was he going to kiss her goodbye? Her stomach felt like it just became a free-floating organ. For the life of her, she couldn't think of one clever thing to say. So she opted for simple and straight.

"I'm glad you lost the bet, Fisher. It was a special weekend, made more special because you were here." Her voice was soft and sincere; her smile was genuine.

Whoa, he thought. Where did that come from? His eyes lowered to her smiling lips. Flash forward. He wanted to kiss those lips. He frequently kissed his mom and grandma, but those were pecks and he wanted to linger on Sloane's luscious lips. The little kiddie kisses he gave to girls were no help at all. He'd practiced kissing on the back of his hand several times when he was a kid, well actually last summer, but that was nothing like coming in contact with the real thing. There was some soft sucking involved, he knew. He reached over, took one of her curls and brushed it behind her ear. Then decided to just do it. He lowered his head and gently tapped her lips with his. Cardiac dropkick. Her lips were soft. A velvet buzz. And when he straightened and looked down at her, they were still smiling.

"Well, that wasn't too gross," he commented smiling back. When did you close your eyes, he thought. He'd watched plenty of movies. And knew that people who did a real kiss closed their eyes. Cripes. Learning to fly a plane hadn't been this complicated. Then he stiffened as Sloane reached up, put her arms around his neck, stood on her toes and planted her lips on his. He found out that closing your eyes during a lovely, soft, sweet kiss was spontaneous. When she pulled away, he opened his eyes and grinned. This was good. This was very, very good. She tasted like peanut butter cups. His favorite.

She licked her lips. "Nope, I'd say definitely not gross."

"Sloane," he said, managing to keep his voice in the proper octave. It took some effort, but he was proud of the result. He was looking right into her bright golden eyes. What did Tiger Brewster and Berps Jenks say about the tongue. Tonsil hockey. Damn. When was that supposed to be introduced into the kissing thing? Not yet, he was pretty sure. And what the hell was he supposed to do with his hands.

"Hmm?" Her smile was just plain dreamy.

Fisher smiled back. She didn't sound like Einstein now. Apparently he knocked a few points off that whopping IQ with his lip lock. It gave him confidence.

"I just wanted you to know that I lost that bet on purpose." And when he went in to claim another kiss, he was amazed at how his words seemed to affect her. Her eyes went wide with pleasure, then she grinned and met his lips eagerly as her heart skipped a beat. He learned a valuable lesson on how to please a woman. It wasn't just his lips. It was his words. Go figure. She lengthened the kiss and he found he was actually holding her. His hands apparently needed no coaching or conscious direction on his part. They went around her tiny waist and brought her closer to him. Damn this was frosted. His first real necking, not just baby stuff. When he heard Skye and Alex outside the door, he reluctantly pulled away. And somehow, he didn't feel awkward or stupid. He felt, well. Manly.

"How about you ride with Duncan and me to the airport before you go," he said. "You can tell me more about DNA."

"Okay," agreed Sloane. She was more than a little breathless. She was sure her knees lost their meniscus and patella and there was definitely not a functioning anterior or posterior cruciate ligament or a medial or lateral collateral ligament either. She never in her life had ever been kissed like that. She swore she felt it all the way down to her toes. Yikes. She couldn't wait to call Libby. This was a day she'd never forget and she wanted to share every glorious minute with her best friend. She took a step back, but somehow her hand was locked in his.

"First we have to say goodbye to the happy couple. Then I'd like to change." She also wanted to take the opportunity to comb her hair, put on a little makeup and borrow that really happening chocolate brown sweater of Skye's that Alex told her complimented her coloring. They turned and walked out together, seeing Alex and Skye talking with the rest of the Coopers and Springfields. Joining the group, they were soon laughing and exchanging stories, but both of them still carried the feel of the kisses and the taste of things to come.

Skye and Alex spent the next half hour thanking everyone and saying goodbye. Blake and Wyatt volunteered to take them to the airport. Skye would be flying them to their honeymoon destination. Over the Atlantic to Scotland for a glorious ten days at a magnificent old castle on the North Sea. Bill and Carter had been to the airport earlier and prepared everything for flight. She was going to go solo in the cockpit this trip with the autopilot and computer system as backup. As delightful as her crew was, she wanted to be alone with Alex.

Skye looked out the rear window at the retreating house, the porch filled with the people she loved waving and smiling, the scene of the happiest day of her life. Her home, the place where she and Alex would begin to write their history. Not every day would be magical, but every day would be filled with her love for him. She weaved her long fingers through his and sighed. Perfect. Today, right now, life was perfect. She looked up into the face of her husband. Yesterday she woke up and she was still single. She looked at her wedding ring. Today she was legally, formally his wife. She felt so settled, so complete. Why should it feel so different? God. She was married.

Flight into Destiny

CHAPTER 1

Alex opened the door to their suite of rooms in the east wing of the old elegant castle, a smile of anticipation on his face. He was ready to start his honeymoon. More than ready. He'd been thinking of her out of her uniform all the way down the long dimly lit hallway.

"Darling," he called. "I'm here. Begin your assault."

He frowned. It was so quiet. So still. He couldn't feel her in the room.

"Skye?" Putting the flowers and bottle down on the table by the door he crossed over to the bedroom. The bed was made, the suitcases were sitting on the floor near the huge ornate dresser. No uniform hanging in the closet, no female debris in the room. No shoes in the corner. He didn't hear any bathroom noises but checked it anyway. Empty. He ran his hand over the sink. No moisture indicating use.

Confused, but not yet alarmed, he walked back into the sitting room and out the French doors to the terrace. He looked down and out over the dark water. The sun was now completely up, but the sea still appeared cold and ominous. He looked around. Nothing seemed disturbed. He could hear the surf crashing against the rocks below.

Frowning, he went over to the desk to see if she left a note. The pad of paper provided by the castle owners lay neatly by the phone. It was blank. Nothing. He felt like it was mocking him.

Could Skye have taken a phone call and gone out? He picked up the receiver and rang the reception desk.

"Good morning, Mr. Springfield how can I help you?" Came a pleasant voice, beautifully accented in the lilt of Scotland.

"Did you put a call through to my suite anytime this morning?" he asked.

"I haven't been here long, sir, but no calls have come into the castle from the outside since I've been here."

"If someone called from another suite, would that go through you?"

"Yes sir. We have only a few suites and they're all connected through the central switchboard. Rather like an intercom. No one has called and asked to be connected to your suite in the last hour. Would you like me to contact the overnight operator?"

"No. Thank you. No." It had been a long shot, but he had to start narrowing down the possibilities. So no one had called. That meant either someone came to the door, or she never got to the suite.

Alex had the strangest feeling. A little shiver ran up his spine. It wasn't her absence that disturbed him, there were hundreds of possible explanations for that, it was the complete lack of her presence. He shook himself. That didn't even make any sense. Except it did. She had a lingering scent, he reminded himself. A scent his subconscious, his primal instincts could detect. It convinced his subconscious that she'd never been here.

Where could she be? Making arrangements for a late dinner perhaps. Organizing a surprise? Did she remember something she needed to do back at the airport? None of these things felt right.

An unbidden and cold-blooded thought assaulted him. Was there such a thing as post-wedding jitters? Could she have realized the full impact of her promise to him and left him to be alone? To think? Maybe to escape? Had he pushed too hard? Could she have had some kind of emotional breakdown? Images of what happened at the bridal shop flashed in and out of his mind. And that was only about the dress. Maybe they should have sought professional help. Had she been harboring a deep seeded fear of her new life that now came to the surface and overwhelmed her? Did she feel trapped and did she wait until now when it was just the two of them to mount her escape?

No. That wasn't Skye. Leaving wasn't her style. She'd face it head on. Besides, she loved him. She wanted this marriage. She wanted him. It was something else. He knew it…he felt it.

He'd just have to wait for her return to get an explanation. He went to the small, well stocked bar and opened the refrigerator. He thought he wanted a beer, but he just stood looking at the shelves…then slowly shut the door without grabbing one. They'd taken off from Virginia, he looked at his watch, over 12 hours ago, at 1300, eastern time. Closing his eyes, he replayed their trip to Scotland, their ride to the castle, checking in. Nothing out of the ordinary.

He needed to get his thoughts together. Was there a sign he missed? He sat down on the forest green leather chair near the unlit fireplace. It was a beautiful room and exactly what Skye would have loved. Authenticity. A room rich and old and filled with ancient whispers. As Alex went inside his head, the surroundings faded into irrelevance.

For nearly a half hour, Alex saw nothing, heard nothing. He was replaying everything from the time they left home to this moment. There had to be an explanation somewhere, and this was where he'd start. He lost himself in the memories as he replayed the flight…

Alex had worked on some contracts while Skye flew the Gulfstream over the ocean but he'd periodically put aside his papers and go up to the cockpit to watch her.

She glanced over her shoulder and smiled. "Happy Anniversary, darling," she said in a honey coated sexy voice that put a few more logs on the fire.

"Anniversary?" he asked.

She tapped the cockpit clock. "We've been married exactly 24 hours."

"Permission to kiss the captain," he said.

She checked all the controls and instruments on the automatic pilot, then stood up. She went into his arms and wrapped hers around his firm waist. It was a lovely, married kiss.

"Permission to completely ravish the captain," he asked, his voice husky with desire.

Her full, sensuous lips turned up seductively. "Consider it an order."

He held back for a moment, prolonging the anticipation. He watched her mouth open in eager expectation. The bonfire was raging and he couldn't tell if the heat was inside him or radiating from her. He saw her pulse beating steady in her neck. Definitely his secondary target, but first.

His lips fit over hers perfectly. What started out as a light touch quickly developed into a scorching kiss, the contact sizzling and snapping. While his lips were busy, his tongue drawing hers into a hot, searing dance, his hands explored on their own. His wife of 24 hours. His wife. His.

They were both breathless when he drew back.

"Ever consider joining the mile high club?" he asked, his hands leaving a trail of shivers in their wake. He slowly moved them up her neck and captured her lovely face in his palms.

"Sorry, darling." Her voice was soft and sweet, the desire obvious in its breathy quality. "I'm on duty. You'll have to wait until we're on the ground."

"But I own the plane," he said, planting kisses along her cheek and jaw line, moving toward his secondary target. Actually his corporation owned it. But he owned the corporation. Same thing.

"Only half of it, sweetheart. I told you that you should have demanded a prenuptial agreement."

He sighed and kissed that inviting pulse on her neck. "Which side is mine?"

Skye couldn't respond right away, almost ready to chuck her responsibility and just rip his clothes off. The mile high club was looking better and better.

"The outside," she whispered and decided she needed one more kiss to sustain her.

Alex's arms went down around her and she stroked his back. Such a wonderful back. She could feel the muscles ripple and respond to her touch, even through the soft cotton of his shirt.

"Next time I bring a copilot," she murmured with regret. The automatic pilot in this craft could actually fly it, even land it with its pre-programmed flight plan, but she couldn't remove years of training like she could a jacket and hat. She needed to remain alert and diligent for the safely of her passengers. In this case her husband. Husband. Wow.

"Couldn't you just be a little less consciousness? We could do it right here." His hands were coming in to give his words some assistance. They moved down the front of her, his fingers running along her skin just inside the V of her blouse. She'd removed her jacket after take-off so all that separated him from her exposed skin was a thin blouse and a silk teddy. Her breasts had their own memory and they were willing to fall in with the enemy and vote for getting naked.

Skye's sense of duty and dedication to protocol were ruthless, however. She suppressed all her natural desire and smoldering needs and took his wrists in her hands. Her fingers felt like two iron cuffs. Sighing with regret, she gave him one more quick kiss.

"Sorry."

"How many more hours?" he asked as he took a deep breath into his lungs, held it, then blew it out.

"About 3 in the air and two on the ground," she said.

He groaned. "I don't know if I can make it. What if I beg?"

"Darling," she said laughing. "If you were less skilled, perhaps. This is a case of screwing up in reverse. You make me completely witless when you're inside me and that isn't a recommended condition for your pilot to be in."

He looked out the front of the cockpit and saw only ocean. "Where's Greenland?" he asked, hopefully. "Maybe we could stop there for a snack."

"Sweetheart. This isn't an afternoon ride in your truck. We can't just alter our course."

Looking out again, he shook his head. "It never ceases to amaze me how you can find your way out here without any landmarks."

She checked her global positioning unit and flashing transponder. She knew exactly where she was.

"What if we declared an emergency?" he asked. He was a problem solver, after all.

"We would get into a shitload of trouble. We have no emergency."

Looking down, he sighed a big one. "Speak for yourself. I've told you before a man could go blind if he has to cool off after coming to attention too often."

"Greenland is out of the question. Too much military airspace."

"Damn."

On the other hand, she thought. She let go of his wrists and he flexed his fingers. Such strong, talented fingers. Pulling out of his arms, she stepped back, readjusted her blouse and smoothed her hair. Giving him a little push, she went back to her seat.

"Please take your seat, civilian," she said with authority. "I have work up here." Sometimes a force was just irresistible and the man, far too tempting.

Alex thought it was a pretty abrupt brush off, but he never questioned her while they were in the air. This was her arena. Up here, she had the first and final word. All the words in between were up for grabs, of course, but there could only be one captain on every ship.

He went back to his seat, shaking out his muscles and grabbing a bottle of water from the bar. He chugged the whole thing and paced off some more tension before going to his seat.

Sitting down heavily, he closed his eyes and tried to slow his racing heart. About twenty minutes later, it started revving up all over again when he heard her sexy voice on the intercom. God. That voice. He felt the familiar tingle run through the lower portion of his body. Just when he thought he got things under control, she tossed in another stimulator.

"Please buckle in, Mr. Springfield. I'm expecting some turbulence soon. It could get very rocky." There was something more in her voice that just didn't sound like business as usual…like she was trying to suppress something. Bad weather? He looked out at the thousands of stars. They'd flown into sunset and darkness as they made their way across the Atlantic. But, it sure didn't look threatening.

A few moments later, she ended the suspense. "Passenger Springfield. This is your captain, speaking. Your own private, married, wife captain." She was using her phone sex voice. That sweet, low, slow tone that made him sweat.

Swallowing hard, he buckled in and gripped the arms of his chair. Damn. His body was reacting like a randy teenager watching his first porn flick. He almost groaned when he heard her next words.

"I've just contacted the tower in Reykjavik, Iceland. I'd like to spend a few hours on the ground to allow for a maintenance check on the internal structure of the main body. They will accommodate our request to land and will not have to send in customs if we guarantee no one will leave the plane. I've assured them that passenger and crew will not set foot outside the aircraft. I'm asking you for your complete cooperation in this. I'll see you when we're on the ground and have come to a complete stop."

Beaming in anticipation, Alex looked out the window as the plane banked to the left. How much more could he love this woman? She was always finding new ways to squeeze his heart and fan his passion. He'd have gone up and kissed the breath right out of her lungs, but he knew she'd be all business until she got them on the ground. She had an incredible amount of discipline when it came to her work. Another thing he loved about her.

Looking out the window, he saw a tiny speck in the horizon. At their air speed, it grew larger quickly. So did his desire. By the time his wife had expertly lined up the plane to the center of the runway, and gently landed it, he was as hot and ready as the bubbling, steamy natural springs Reykjavik was known for.

She came back on the intercom and purred. "Welcome to Iceland, husband passenger Springfield. We'll be staying in the plane, doors closed. Because the temperature inside the cabin is anticipated to raise to boiling levels very soon, we want to be good guests and not allow the heat to blow out the open doors and melt the beautiful ice fields on the northern part of the island."

Skye smiled wickedly and rechecked all her instruments. Everything was turned off…everything but her. She was ready to shed both her clothes and her responsibility as captain. She was just plain ready.

She took off her earphones, placed them neatly to the right of her seat and stood up. Turning to make her way to the back, she ran into a wall of chest. She looked up into the delighted and hungry face of her new husband.

"Ever do it Icelandic style?" she asked as he reached down and swept her off her feet.

"Not that I recall. Just what does it entail?"

"Lots and lots of friction. It's known to keep them warm through the long, cold nights."

"Show me?" He carried her through the cabin, kissing her and raising the temperature inside and out. He kicked open the door to the fully furnished bedroom in the rear of the plane and placed her gently on the center of the bed.

And she did. Several times.

Skye lay naked and tangled in the sheets, wrapped in his arms and completely satisfied. Her hair had come out of its confinement and spilled all over his chest. He loved the tangled, curly look of it. When it was in this kind of disarray, it usually meant they'd just engaged in some pretty enthusiastic physical contact. Pushing it back, she looked up at him. Her lips were puffy and her eyes were still dark with desire. She looked young and sexy and more like a naked picture on a Playboy calendar than a competent, professional woman…the captain of this craft.

"What have you done with the captain?" he asked as he kissed the end of her perfect, beautiful nose. "I know I carried her in here."

She had so many looks, so many faces. It was what made her an excellent special agent. He looked down at the diamond that flashed on her finger. It was a distinctive, one of a kind creation he'd selected just for her. A perfect princess cut diamond set in what looked like tiny gold wings. It reminded him of her. So many facets, all brilliant and shimmering.

"I don't know," she responded. "But we better find her, unless you think you can fly us across the ocean."

"Darling, I don't think I can walk across this room."

"Like the Icelandic position, then?"

"I'm completely sold on it." He kissed her again. "I can't wait to try the Scottish position."

Laughing, she ran kisses up his chest. "I guess I'd better go find the captain, in a hurry. I hear the Scots are partial to wild invasions and long sieges."

She gathered her clothes and went into the relatively spacious bathroom to get cleaned up and reassemble her parts. Alex just stayed in bed and watched, the advantages of being the passenger. It was so good to see her moving without any pain. It had been a long seven months since he first met her. Actually was assigned to watch her. She hadn't come out of that assignment unscathed. As a matter of fact, he'd almost lost her. Then a few months ago, her last fight for International Airlines had been hijacked. She brought everyone home, but she'd paid for that exploit with a beating and a few broken ribs. Now, she walked without protecting any part of her body from stiffness or pain. It made this time special and serene. Their honeymoon.

A year ago he was traveling a solitary course. He hadn't thought of himself as lonely, but looking back on it, he was unbearably alone. He was social, enjoyed the company of women, had many friends and a wonderful family, but no one was at his side. No one was home waiting for him so he had no home. No one had any part of his heart.

He smiled when he heard cussing coming from the bathroom.

"Goddamn hair. Ouch. I never had so much trouble with it before. It's all that rolling around. If you don't get more civilized." She poked her head through the doorway and aimed her hairbrush at him. "I'm going to cut it all off. I hate this mess. How would you feel about a short, practical cut?"

He loved her hair. Its texture, its ash blonde color, its curls, its smell. "If you cut it, can I have it? I'd keep it in my desk at the office."

She poked her head out again, and the incredulous look on her face made him laugh out loud. "You're sick," she said. "I really think you should consider some therapy."

"Physical therapy?"

She just snorted and went back to brushing. God she was cute, he thought.

"Want some coffee?" he asked, swinging his legs over the side of the bed and pulling on his underwear and pants.

"Now you're talking," she said. Twenty minutes later she came out of the bedroom completely transformed. Her hair was sleek and pulled back from her face. Her makeup was restored and she was clothed in her conservative uniform skirt and blouse. He handed her a mug of coffee.

She sipped. "Mmmm. Strong and steamy…just how I like my coffee." She looked up at him. "And my men."

"Men? How many of us are there?"

"Well, let's see. There's the lawyer." He nodded. "And the millionaire real estate tycoon. And then there's the protector and defender. The commando, he's one of my favorites. There's the special agent. Oh yes, Aladdin. He's hot. And of course," she reached up and kissed him. "Now, there's the husband."

His stomach clutched when he heard her say husband. It was so new and so powerful, he sometimes couldn't get his mind around it. She'd committed herself to him. Forever. She was his.

Skye smiled into his expressive blue eyes. They glowed from the inside. Her husband.

They looked at each other for a moment longer, communicating on a level that didn't need words. They were connected. They were one heart.

Finally, she shook herself. "Was I talking, saying something, in the middle of a sentence or anything?" she asked softly.

"I can't remember," he said. You said husband and it made time stand still for me, he thought.

"Well, we're on our honeymoon. We're entitled to be a little stupid."

"We are, indeed," he said and kissed his wife thoroughly.

She frowned and sighed. "What?" he asked.

"Nothing. I was just wondering how Kelvar was doing."

"You mean that goddamn, fucking shit maker?" He remembered her reaction just before they left to having one of her favorite shoes used as a puppy potty.

She remembered his frantic licking when she picked him up to hurl him out the window and how she thought the shoes weren't all that special anyway. "No, dear. Our little baby we abandoned to the questionable care of Tank."

"Oh, yeah. Well, Mom is near by in case he needs some parental advice."

"You're right. It's just that he was so sad when we left."

"Sad?" He laughed out loud. "Now, how could you tell? Was it the big smelly pile in your shoe or the slobber on my silk tie that indicated sorrow?"

She gave him her patented 'you're a moron' look. "It was his eyes. We just got him and then we left him."

"I think he'll be all right, darling." He kissed her concerned mouth. "He and Tank are so much alike."

"There's that," she agreed.

She set down her mug and moved toward the cockpit. "Back to work. Please sit down and prepare for take-off, civilian."

"You're the captain, Captain," he said, but he followed her instead.

She took her seat, put on her earphones, flipped the switch to the radios and contacted the tower.

"Tower, this is GS6520. Everything here checked out fine. We're fully operational and functioning within recommended parameters." She heard Alex's chuckle and turned from her mike, pressing the mute button. "Please, darling. Sometimes it's hard enough to convince the tower that I'm the legitimate voice of the captain. Your sound effects might undermine their already shaky chauvinistic attitudes."

"Consider me muted," he said, running his fingers over the sensitive side of her neck. She shivered. Muted maybe. Turned off, never.

She was listening to instructions from the tower.

"Roger, tower. Standing by."

She sat back. "There's a flight coming in. We have a few minutes." She looked up at him and smiled. "I thought I was the captain and I thought I asked you to take your seat."

"I just like watching you work. Turns me on."

"Tying my shoe turns you on."

Giving her a chaste kiss, he stepped back. He crossed his arms across his broad chest to keep them from grabbing her again.

Standing in the doorway, all hot and sexy, he was more handsome than any man she'd ever known. Any man she'd ever seen. Her eyes traveled over him. Lazily. Possessively. His gold watch gleamed and her eyes were drawn to his hands. They were incredible strong hands. Such sensitive, talented hands. Now banded with gold on the fourth finger of his left hand. A sigh escaped before she'd suppress it.

"What's our next stop?" he asked with a grin and a hopeful look on his face.

She laughed. "Darling. I have to fly this plane. We stop again and my entire body will be too liquid to push any of these buttons. Not that my mind would know what to do with them if I was capable of movement. Get out of my cockpit, civilian. I have to file my revised flight plan and get us off the ground. We have a honeymoon waiting for us."

She grabbed her preflight checklist and he reluctantly went back to his seat. Discipline, he thought. He didn't need to compress everything into a few hours. He had an entire ten days…and nights…with his bride…all to himself.

How much of the countryside they were actually going to see was probably what they could take in from the airport to the castle suite he'd booked. He smiled. It was going to be a long five hours. He picked up his contracts. Perhaps a little diversion. He didn't realize until they'd taken off and flown over 100 miles that he'd read the same paragraph twice before. He decided to give up and engage in his second favorite past time. Thinking about his first favorite pastime. He put his seat back and closed his eyes. And soon he was in a delightful dream that kept him happy for the duration of the flight.

CHAPTER 2

Now, back at the castle, Alex paced around the room. They hadn't touched each other…well not much…during the ride there. Skye was just too excited and wanted to look out the window at the lochs and glens. The sun was coming up and everything looked so dewy and fresh. Including, he thought, his wife. He couldn't believe she was still so animated after a long flight.

She never seemed to get tired when she was flying. Quite the opposite, actually. She was full of energy when she landed. Instead of jet lag, she always seemed to have jet drive. He was feeling good after his nap, as well. He was anticipating a great initiation into the rites of Scottish lovemaking.

The castle was magnificent. A perfect setting for a gothic romance. And how appropriate. Some of the ups and downs they'd suffered throughout their courtship felt gothic to him. A butler greeted them as they walked into the impressive front entrance.

That was when they'd parted company. In the cavernous foyer. The butler, his name was Giles, of course, had a message for Alex to see the concierge. Skye decided to go directly to their rooms. Giles was seeing to their luggage and assured her it would be in her suite right away. She'd kissed Alex and told him she wanted to get her uniform off and kick her shoes in a corner somewhere. He could join her in the shower. He almost went with her. To hell with the concierge. His jaw clenched. Damn it, why hadn't he? Instead, he'd clamped down on his desire and went to the small office off the foyer.

The concierge was as jovial and informal as the butler was stiff and proper.

"I've made the arrangements for the yacht you requested. You and your bonnie bride will be the only passengers. The waters around the Isle of Skye are beautiful and the island itself is a treasure," she said proudly. "It's more untamed than most of Great Britain. Absolutely gorgeous…breathtaking. There's a primitive nature about Skye that many find fascinating. It is an isle of extremes. Skye can be a wee bit temperamental, but well worth the journey."

"Perfect," smiled Alex as he signed the necessary papers to secure the boat for the following week. When he read the literature his mom had collected and saw the pictures and information on the Isle of Skye off the west coast of Scotland, he knew his Skye would love it. It was to be a surprise…something special for the second half of their honeymoon.

"Over here are the other things you ordered." She handed him a bouquet of perfect white gardenias. "There will be more sent to your room every morning. And, of course," she handed him a bottle of the best French champagne. "Compliments of the staff here. Enjoy, Mr. Springfield."

"Oh. We will."

That was it. He checked his cell phone again. No calls, no messages. Both the gardenias and the bottle of champagne now sat abandoned on the table by the door. Alex continued to pace as the minutes ticked away, hoping she'd impulsively decided to go for a walk. And if it was a surprise she was planning, it had better happen pretty soon. He was ready to jump out of his skin. He should just relax and wait, but something inside him was screaming that she wasn't just out…she was gone.

After another hour, he could no longer ignore the growing feeling of alarm. Should he bring Jim into this? What if it were some kind of emotional short circuit? It occurred to him that the concierge's description of the Isle of Skye seemed eerily close to how he would describe his wife. Had she gone extreme on him? What could have triggered it? Would she have waited until after the ceremony to leave him?

No…she was too happy. Too settled, somehow. That wasn't an act he saw the day before. He was sure of it. If it was, he knew nothing. And today? She stopped off in Iceland for God's sake…just to be with him. Something was terribly wrong and he needed to call in reinforcements. If Skye left him because of a psychological breakdown of some sort, she would have to deal with the humiliation of bringing her boss into her personal business.

He went to his briefcase and took out his secure cell phone. He checked his watch. Jim would be at home. Middle of the night calls rarely phased Jim. His agents were all over the world. Alex took a deep breath and dialed the familiar 17 digit number.

"What the hell are you calling me for?" asked Jim when he answered the phone, humor evident in his deep voice. "You need some advice, son?"

"Jim. Have you heard from Skye?" No preliminary chat. No trivial conversation.

"Heard from Skye?" Jim became more alert. It was the tone in Alex's voice, not the words that had concern creeping into his consciousness. "What's the matter. You two have a spat already?"

"No," said Alex impatiently, for the moment forgetting he was talking to his boss. Tough. He had no time for protocol. "Answer my question."

"Sorry, Alex. The answer is no. I haven't spoken with her since we said good night after the reception. What is it?"

"She isn't here, Jim. She's missing." After Alex told him about finding the suite abandoned, Jim really was concerned.

"This isn't like her. She'd know you would worry. Unless…ah…nothing happened to set her off or anything, did it?" Jim was familiar with her temper and knew it could be fearsome.

Alex snorted and made an ironic sound in his throat. "No, Jim. We're actually doing very well with this marriage thing, so far."

"Then I can only conclude this is serious."

"My impression is that it *is* serious. It's just a feeling right now, but it's powerful."

"Okay. I'll discreetly check with people here…you know, make a few calls and see if anyone has heard from her. Then I'm going to catch transport and come over." He already sounded like he knew he was going to find out nothing from her family and friends. He'd helped raise Skye. He knew her. And this wasn't like her at all.

"I'll work here, look for her. Set up Linda and Barclay if you can. We may need their help."

"I'll do that."

"Jim, do you have any idea…any idea at all who would take her?"

"Some, I suppose. There are several possibilities, but certainly none very likely." Jim's mind was racing, but he didn't like its direction.

"See you this evening sometime." Alex's hand shook slightly when he rang off. He didn't think she'd just leave him and call Jim, but he had to eliminate that before he began his search. Besides, he'd feel better having Jim here. Jim knew her better and longer and was privy to knowledge that may prove helpful. A burning fear was starting to form in the pit of his stomach as he walked out onto the terrace.

Alex closed his eyes and concentrated on the sounds of the surf, the fresh salty smell of the sea. He searched inside himself first. She was there. He felt her. When his twin sister Rita had been shot and killed, he'd known the second her heart stopped beating. The exact moment of her death. It had ripped a hole in his heart. Her presence had moved beside him for a few hours until he could get to her family, then it left him completely.

"Skye," he whispered. "Skye."

She was definitely still there in his heart. Hers was beating with his. It brought him some relief. He'd be able to function knowing she was out there. He'd find her. Reaching in his pocket, he took out the compass she gave him. He stared at it for a long time. The comfort he drew from it helped keep the panic at bay.

He was also certain of something else. She didn't leave him. Not of her own accord. Even if the idea of marriage distressed her to her soul and she wanted out, she would never do this to him. She would never do this to anyone.

Alex preferred action to waiting, but he weighed staying by the phone and in the room against going out in search of her. He looked at his watch and then at the phone. If she or anyone else called, they could leave a message. He had his cell phone and she'd call that number first if she were able. If she were able. The thought put ice in his veins.

Suddenly he shook his head. Idiot, he thought. He flipped open his cell phone and dialed her number. No. It wasn't going to be that simple. Disappointment shot through him as it rang unanswered. He left a simple message. "Call me." So either her phone was off or whoever had it wasn't taking calls.

He stalked purposefully out of the room and methodically began searching the castle while making several discreet inquiries. He decided on his walk down the corridor that he'd imply his new wife was a bit temperamental, just like the Isle of Skye, and that they had their first fight. His training dictated that there be a cover story that would explain a groom roaming around searching for his missing bride.

"Haven't seen her lad…not since the two of you came in. She must have quite a temper," the concierge said, her eyes amused in spite of herself. The Scots admired a good temper, for all that. But if she read the heat that had been pouring out of them when they walked it, the lass would be back soon. "You don't want to just wait until she comes to her senses and begs you to forgive her foolishness?"

He smiled in spite of himself. He just couldn't get a picture of Skye begging for forgiveness. "No. I prefer to do the begging," he said.

He'd do anything right now, he thought, to get her back. He wished it would be as simple as begging. With every passing minute, he was getting more and more concerned. He was caught up in the search right now, but if he stopped to consider the possibilities, there were few that wouldn't terrify him. And many that would scare him witless.

"I'll make some inquiries among the staff if you wish, Mr. Springfield. Unless you would prefer to keep this from spreading all through the castle and half the country."

Alex smiled again. "I guess I have no pride. I'd appreciate it if you would ask anyone you think may have seen her or anyone fitting her description. She knows people in Glasgow and may have decided to go with them."

He was improvising, but he wanted to add the possibility that she may not have left the castle alone.

"I'll get to it immediately. If she's in the area, we'll know it."

She was as good as her word. She must have eyes and ears throughout the countryside, Alex thought. Within a half hour, she caught up to him in the gardens.

"Mr. Springfield. Good news." She was smiling and hope sprung in his heart. It was dashed completely by her next statement. "It appears she left the castle with her friends from Glasgow, just like you thought. I'll bet you'll find a note somewhere in your room."

Alex knew better, but suppressed his anxiety and impatience. "That must be it," he said, planting a smile on his face. "Did someone see them leave?"

"Well sir, Colleen was cleaning in the corridor by your suite during the time between when you checked in and when you went into the rooms. She saw you, but Mrs. Springfield never passed her. Therefore, her friends met up with her somewhere in the grand foyer, the library, the staircase or the second floor corridor."

"Go on," said Alex, barely breathing now.

"Sean was delivering breakfast to one of our guests on the second floor and remembered seeing a couple in the library. It's located just to the right of the staircase to the third floor and your wife would have passed it to get to your suite. It was just a brief glance, but he had the impression of a man and a woman, both dressed for the outside. Coats, gloves, hats. I'm afraid he didn't see either of their faces, but it sounds like someone came in from the outside to wait for your wife. We're assuming she set up the meeting since none of our staff remember a couple asking for you or for directions to the library. In actuality, we usually send people to the drawing room who are meeting up with guests."

When Alex didn't comment, she continued. "I checked around and all the other guests were in their rooms, so it seems these people made two extra in the castle. No one saw your wife exit through the front doors, but that makes sense because you and I would have seen her had she left by the front door."

"How else could she have left the castle?"

"Many ways of course, but she most likely exited right out the doors in the library. They open onto a terrace in the rear and steps lead down to the gardens. We're assuming they left that way. The closest parking area would be near the service entrance. Donna noticed a dark late model car parked near the employee entrance when she came in at 4:00 a.m. It was too dark to get a color or a tag number."

Alex wondered if the woman ever considered investigation as a profession. She was thorough and meticulous. She also scared him more and more with each sentence of her report. His face remained interested and passive however.

"Anything else? Did anyone actually see her or the car when it left?" He'd want to talk with everyone again, but not until after he completed his initial pursuit.

"No. But the auto isn't there now and you saw your wife less than an hour ago, so she should be well on her way to Glasgow by now unless they stopped at an inn along the way. Maybe you should call her friends."

"Thanks, I will." he said with forced cheerfulness. "I'm off to find my bride and consummate this marriage."

She looked at his back with a frown. Then she shrugged. Americans. Such drama. She needed to think about the tours she was arranging for the group of seniors from Denmark. He'd find his bride soon enough.

Alex walked out to the car he'd rented and decided to drive toward Glasgow. He'd look for evidence in the castle later. Right now he wanted to be as close behind the people who had her as possible. While he was driving, he called to update Jim.

Jim's report was bleak. No one had heard from the happy couple and he'd taken a great deal of abuse from family and friends for thinking they would. Hazel was the only exception. Skye had called her from the airport to tell her they were safely on the ground and not to expect to hear from her for the entire ten days.

When he heard Alex's report, Jim was alarmed. He was already on his way to Dulles to catch a transport to Scotland.

"Who would take her like this, Jim?"

"Shit, where do I start?" he said. "She's made enemies along the way, Alex. We have most of the people she's really crossed incarcerated or under surveillance, and of course

Terrin and most of his surviving followers were executed last week in Soteras. It's a long list. I'm bringing her files with me and will work on them in the transport. In the meantime, start making a list of your own."

"Of my enemies?"

"She married you Saturday, Alex. Someone may be after you, your money, information you have…or all three. We can't eliminate anything right now."

Another wave of anxiety flowed through him. Faces from his past floated before him. Faces he'd hoped never to see again. "I'll start that list. It could be a fairly long one as well."

"Who knew you were going to be there? At that exact location?"

"That'll be a short list anyway. Damn it, though. No one who knew would have spilled it."

"Not intentionally, but it may help narrow things down."

"Okay, I can get that list together right now. Are Barclay and Linda in place?"

"Waiting for your call. Here is the number of the command center we're using for this." Jim recited the 17 digits and Alex memorized them. "Alex. We'll find her. Or trust her to find us."

Jim's words did little to dispel the fear as Alex drove through the countryside. Drove through it blind. He checked every side road for activity. Every time he passed a dark sedan, he slowed down and looked inside. He looked into cars, coming and going. Followed a few. Nothing.

He used the time to coordinate activities with his team, although he had little for them to do at the moment. His call to Linda and Barclay had been excruciating. After their initial shock and horror, they both swung into action. They were pursuing some leads Jim provided for them. Some cases with low-level clearance they could check immediately. Alex knew he'd have things for them to do; he just couldn't seem to get his brain into gear.

"How did they get Skye?" asked Linda. "She wouldn't have just gone willingly and quietly."

"In addition to the general fatigue she'd feel from a long flight…hell, a long week, I assured her we wouldn't have to worry about security. She probably wasn't on her usual high alert. I know she wasn't armed. Her Glock is still in her travel bag. Damn it. I wanted her to relax, to feel secure. It was one of the reasons I chose this remote place and kept the location to myself until a few days ago. She had no reason to think anyone would know she was here."

"That explains some if it, I guess. She still would have to be subdued in some way. Was there any sign of a struggle?"

"No, none. I'm going to check out the scene more thoroughly when I get back to the castle. I'm driving a perimeter right now."

"Could it have been mistaken identity?"

"Possible. I'll get you a list of the other guests and you can start checking. I'll want their backgrounds investigated anyway."

"I already have them, Alex," piped in Barclay, his voice strained with concern. "They have an on-line reservation system. The payment site is secure enough, but not the reservation page. I've started on background checks."

"Well done, Barclay. Thanks." Alex could hear him mumble but didn't take the time to ask him to repeat himself. He knew Barclay would work through stress, fatigue and every system he came across to help him…to help Skye.

"The question remains. If we assume Skye was the target, how did anyone know you were going there?" persisted Linda.

"That's what has been dogging me. Skye didn't even know until last week."

"Could someone have been following you?"

"No, I don't think so. Between the two of us, we're pretty good at intuiting a shadow."

"That's true enough."

"So who knew?" asked Barclay, going back to the original question.

"Our families, you, Connie, Duncan, Jim, Pearl and my administrative assistant. That's it. Skye didn't even file a flight plan until we were just about to leave."

"Alex," asked Barclay, his fingers still clicking along the computer keys. "When did you make reservations and under what name? If this wasn't random or mistaken identity, someone must have planned this out. Cased the place."

They were asking first-rate questions, Alex thought. That was good. They could focus. They were calming him.

"The reservations were made over a month ago. Mom did all the research and made the reservations in the name of Arthur Cordell. We wanted privacy and no media coverage. I called the concierge on the flight over here to let her know who we were and the fact we wanted no one to know our true identity."

"I can see why Skye didn't pick up on danger," breathed Linda. "Her radar wasn't even on."

And that, Alex thought, was his fault. He wasn't being rational, and knew he was playing hindsight, but his wife was missing and he was the one who put her in jeopardy. She wasn't thinking security, had her defenses tucked away and someone got by her. Alex shook off the feeling of blame and dread. It wouldn't help her now.

"Well, someone found out. If we assume for a minute no one leaked it, intentionally or unintentionally, then someone found out through the system. And that takes, time, talent and money," said Barclay. "A talented hacker can get anything that's out there on the internet. Alex, is your mother's computer secure?"

"Yes, Sloane put in the system. Her e-mail and personal files are tight."

"What about her phone?" asked Linda. "How often did you discuss it over the phone?"

"I don't think I ever talked about the location specifically. But she could have mentioned it to other family members over the phone. Can you run a bug check from there to all the numbers? We routinely do that from our place, but we may have missed it." He didn't think so, though. He and Skye were very careful.

Barclay wasn't ready to drop the computer angle. "How many computer units does your mom have in her home?"

"She has one in their office, one in Tank's old bedroom and one in the kitchen."

"Are they networked?"

"The office and bedroom units are. The one in the kitchen is a free standing computer."

"Are they turned on all the time?"

"Yes, they have Triband."

"Okay. Are they all connected to email?"

"I don't know. Why?"

"Well, suppose the security is attached to the email accounts and document files. That would prevent anyone from taking a look at her correspondence or breaking into her private files. If Sloane covered them, the blanket is impenetrable, although I could try from here to see if I can get in."

"Try that."

"All right. But the networked units are protected with Sloane's new software and it's so tight the CIA is looking into her system. On the other hand, your mom probably uses the unsecured non-networked kitchen unit to check stock prices, the news from the east coast, the weather report, stuff like that."

"I actually think she does," Alex knew where Barclay was going and it made him both angry and cold.

"Okay, now let's say she's sitting there with her first cup of coffee and decided to research all the castles in Scotland. She wouldn't have made the reservations on the unsecured line, but she may have checked availability."

"Oh, damn. That sounds right, Barclay."

"Anyway. Someone could have hacked into her computer and found the sites she was most interested in. I imagine your location came up frequently and in-depth. They could have hacked into the castle reservation system...took me all of five minutes...and found out a party of two was due to arrive on the day after your wedding."

"Why don't you try right now to get into mom's unit. See where she went. See if this location was obvious."

"Okay, sure. She won't get mad?" Barclay had a healthy respect for women in law enforcement and didn't want to make them mad, and most particularly didn't want to make them mad at him.

"I won't tell her."

"Okay. Sure. Fine, then." He turned to another computer and began his plunder.

"And Barclay?"

"Yeah?"

"If you find out my mom spends her mornings on the Hard Bodies dot Do Me site, I don't have to know about it."

"Huh?"

"Never mind, just try to get in. Assess how easy it would be for someone else to do so. See if someone could figure where we would be and when. If this is the possible leak, it will be a good start."

"Okay, Alex. I'll get right on it. Priority."

"Thanks."

"And Alex?"

"Yeah?"

"I've been working with Skye for a long time, and um…well, she lands on her feet, you know. She may have been snatched 'cause she wasn't looking, but she'll get to full alert. Then those kidnappers better watch out. She'll be really mad and those guys are toast!" Barclay's voice was as animated as it could get. Somehow his positive, intense trust in her talent, courage, and instincts had Alex's chest loosen a bit. He was grateful.

"Thanks, Barclay."

"Sure thing. Linda wants to talk to you again. I'll call you as soon as I have anything."

"Alex?" Linda's voice came back on line.

"I'm here."

"Alex, I was with David and the kids when I got the call. I lied to them and told them there was a computer glitch that was creating an emergency in my office." The first really big lie, she thought. And it didn't sit well on her heart. On multiple levels. She pushed the regret aside and went on. "But David isn't dense and neither is your family. They certainly have surmised that Skye and I and therefore you, work together. They aren't expecting to hear from you, but unless you want them to start speculating, you may want to run a quick e-mail home."

"Good advice, Linda." His family knew about his shadow life. He'd never told them outright and never shared details, but they were all in law enforcement and during the summer he and Skye had actually brought them into a case. For now, he'd cover things up. Maybe send an e-mail from Skye to Kevlar, checking in on him. Tank would spread the word.

"Unless you want me to tell them something…about what's happening." That would have been Linda's preference, but she knew even Skye would have opted for discretion.

"No. That I don't want to happen. Not unless it's completely necessary. If she was the target, it's most likely related to a case. We need to keep this contained."

"Understood. Alex…I heard what Barclay told you. It's true. She'll be working from her side as hard as we're working from out here. She's remarkably inventive. Even if we don't come up with anything, we have to trust that they won't be able to keep her once she's turned on."

"You're right. Thanks." They disconnected and Alex was alone.

He continued to drive through the countryside, his eyes scanning the roads, side streets, and parking lots. Looking for anything his instincts would tell him was off. Barclay and Linda's words of encouragement dissolved quickly in the reality of the fruitless search. Skye was snatched away from him. He was right there, why didn't he do more to secure her? He just let her walk up to the room alone, right into danger.

Alex drove a logical well-planned grid knowing he wasn't going to find anything but unable to stop. He just knew he had to move. Do something. Sometimes luck and persistence paid off.

But it wasn't to be this day. Alex drove around, making all of his calls from the car. He checked obsessively to make sure his phone was on…in case she tried to contact him.

The call from Barclay came within a few hours. He'd hacked into Wyatt's kitchen computer and there'd been a very detailed and well-organized trail right to the castle. There were no secure dates, reservations, credit numbers, or names but the research was there…and the correspondence. Even a reference to a honeymoon.

Alex had to pull over for a minute. His emotions were jumping and fatigue was beginning to make him fuzzy. There was no way of knowing if this was exactly how the kidnappers found out their location, but it became a possibility and knowing the carefulness of the people he told, he figured it was also the most logical conclusion.

Still, he had more information than he did before. What did that mean? Someone who wanted Skye knew about his family. This person or group of people may have tried other family computers and found Sloane's sophisticated security system. If it was a hacker, he, she or they could have done the deed from anywhere. It could have been anyone. Barclay was trying to determine if the hacker left a trail, but it was unlikely he'd find anything in time. In time. What a frightening thought. Barclay wondered if Sloane should be brought in, but Alex vetoed that for now. He knew Barclay was up to the task and Skye always preferred to keep her sister out of the business whenever possible.

Alex needed to get back to the castle. He had to search the premises more thoroughly. At the beginning it was a toss up on whether to concentrate his time in the castle or on the roads. He was hoping he'd get lucky. Now he needed to methodically check everything at the scene of the abduction. As he drove up the winding road to the impressive stone structure on the hill, his mind replayed the morning. Had it only been nine hours ago? It seemed like days. This was a nightmare. His new wife was missing. He had no clues and he was very much afraid for her safety.

The castle was magnificent in the late afternoon sun. He brought her here because she always wanted to go to a real castle. He felt paralyzed as his mind flashed back to the delighted look on her face when he told her where they were going on their honeymoon. He knew she kept a copy of the printouts his mother made off the website in the drawer on her side of the bed. On several occasions, he caught her reading through the information.

Damn it. Damn it. This should have been her dream, not his nightmare. Where was she?

Could it have been random? Skye was a beautiful woman. Maybe Sean had been mistaken about the couple in the library and she was abducted by a psychopath. He shook that one out of his head. That possibility felt darker and more dangerous than an abduction aimed directly at her.

Mistaken identity? No. That didn't feel right either. She was in uniform and very distinctive. Hardly a woman who would be mistaken for someone else.

Were these people out to get him and waited until she was his wife before taking her? A possibility. Hurt her, hurt him. It closed his throat and froze his blood. He rubbed his face. Too many questions. No answers.

Barclay was trying to track the invasion into his mother's computer. Linda was running the names of the guests. They were both running names from some of Skye's cases. Jim was less than a few hours away. He leaned his head back and closed his burning eyes. None of this mattered now. He needed to methodically gather information. Gather data. He simply didn't have enough facts to form a conclusion, much less develop a plan to find her. To get her back.

He needed to start at the beginning. He took the flashlight out of the car, went through the deserted foyer and up the wide stairs to the library. If she was going up and the couple came out of the library and were coming down, she was in a very vulnerable position. When going up stairs a person can more easily be forced off balance by someone from above. And if there were two of them…

He used the light to erase the dark corners of the corridor leading up to the stairs, then searched them one by one. On the landing there were several large potted plants. He searched in them and around them. Nothing.

Walking through the doorway into the library, Alex stared at the huge space with shelves running two stories. They were filled with books. Comfortable leather couches and chairs were placed around the room. He stood in the middle of the space and slowly turned, looking, thinking, feeling. Books that appeared ancient lined some of the shelves, while others contained videos and DVD's. From Dickens to Disney, he thought as he continued his appraisal.

In homage to the twenty-first century there was a large entertainment area with a TV, VCR and DVD. Videos were stacked neatly next to them. Double doors led out onto a stone terrace. He walked over to them and just as he was about to unlock the doors and check out the grounds again, his light flashed off something gold attached to the curtain framing the doors to the terrace. He went over and looked at it.

Wings. His heart lurched. Skye's wings. Yes. His hand fisted around them. Something tangible. Not much, but that didn't matter. He looked at the doors. She was in here and that was how they took her out. This wouldn't have just fallen off her uniform. They were pinned to the fabric. She must have removed them and hooked them here. Maybe she left something else.

With renewed energy, he went out onto the terrace and began a slow, methodical search. Even though he went over every inch of the ground, he found nothing more. She left no other clue, no additional sign. That told him something…she wasn't able to. She must have been sufficiently subdued that she couldn't give him any more. That meant she was probably unconscious.

After another thorough search revealed nothing, he went back to the room. It had the same quiet, unoccupied feel. He looked into the bedroom anyway. Maybe she'd returned. Nothing. No one. There were no messages. She was gone. Someone had taken her and the only thing she could do was leave him her pin. He un-fisted his hand and stared at it. Skye.

He knew he should be hungry, but his stomach felt too tight to put anything in it. He sat down on one of the sofas in the huge common room and put his head in his hands. He didn't even notice the beauty of the room. The sumptuous surroundings blurred as he stared. Think. Think.

He needed caffeine. Something to kick his brain into gear. There was a coffee maker in the sitting room and he brewed a pot. He poured himself a cup, gulped it down, then grabbed another. His stomach churned the minute it was assaulted by the strong, thick liquid, but Alex ignored it. He found crackers, cheese and fruit. He ate. He tasted nothing, but knew it was fuel and he'd need energy to make it through the night.

Going back to the library, he did another search. Nothing. The castle was so vast and there were so few people occupying it, he didn't have to deal with people or curiosity. When one of the maids asked him if he lost something, his heart wanted to scream. Yes. I lost my wife. But instead he told her he'd lost a valuable cuff link. When she offered to enlist help, he declined. He didn't want to trample the scene before Jim could get some experts in there. But he knew no one would be more thorough than he and there was nothing to see. Nothing to find.

The gardens held no clues. The parking lot was loose gravel and there were no tire tracks. Alex drove around for a few more hours, inquiring at petrol stations and pubs. As the sun was setting, he let himself back into his room, no closer to the answer. The few hours sleep he had on the plane were not enough to keep the fatigue at bay, but he ignored the pull of weariness. Linda had reported on several people who might have had a reason to hurt Skye, and Barclay was checking their whereabouts.

When his cell phone rang, he grabbed it, his heart racing from a combination of the caffeine and his own hope. But it was Jim. He'd be at the castle within the hour. Somehow it soothed Alex's jumping nerves. Jim was here. They would find her.

He walked out on the terrace. The sky was black…as black as his mood. The first day of his honeymoon was over.

"Skye," he whispered as he unconsciously spun his brand new wedding ring around with his thumb. "Skye, where are you?"

CHAPTER 3

Jim arrived armed only with his laptop, a large briefcase filled with files and an overnight bag. Inside the computer was enough confidential information to keep foreign analysts busy for years. A button on top of the case would melt it down in five seconds if pressed. Jim carried it with his finger constantly on the button. Alex let him into the room and led him to the space he'd set aside for the materials Jim brought.

"I should have been beside her, Jim," said Alex pacing as Jim put his bag down and arranged his briefcase on the large desk.

Jim was startled by the thought. "Why would you say that? Did you suspect there was someone here who may be after her?"

"No. As a matter of fact, just the opposite. I thought she'd be perfectly secure. The location was only known to a few people."

"Then why are you beating yourself up about this? It doesn't help, Alex. Remember, she's a remarkably resourceful and capable woman. You can't be with her every minute. She'd kick your ass if you tried."

Alex dragged his fingers through his hair. Every minute that ticked by increased the tension in his already stressed body. He rubbed his tired eyes. "I know, Jim. It's just that I feel, well, protective, I guess. I was her shield when I fell in love with her. How much more does she mean to me now? She's my wife, damn it. And someone took her while I was on the premises. She was no more than a hundred feet away." Alex had to vent this out of himself before he was going to settle into a rhythm.

"It was a very bold abduction," Jim concluded.

"It was." Alex sat down and put his head back. "There was no struggle. Nothing was disturbed in the library or the garden. She left this," he showed Jim the wings. "So at some point, she realized she was in trouble. There was nothing else I could see, so she didn't have time to leave us anything more or she was unable to."

"They wanted her alive," said Jim thoughtfully as he unpacked all of his materials. One of his top agents was missing and the other was dead on his feet. He needed to keep it together, but beneath his efficient movements were deep concern and nagging fear.

Alex swallowed hard on Jim's simple statement of fact. It was true, but it chilled him to think of what would have happened if this couple had wanted her dead. "Or they could have just killed her in the library."

"Exactly. You found no evidence of that."

"No. No, I didn't." He remembered sweeping the library, the terrace, the gardens and the pathway to the parking lot with his flashlight. Wanting to find a clue, something, anything. But dreading finding a clue that would indicate she was injured. Or worse. "Barclay is working on the list of all the guests in the castle. It's a long shot, but if it was a case of mistaken identity we have to know."

"Not likely."

"Agreed. You know Barclay got into mom's kitchen computer and went through her internet searches. He found it all. If he could do it, others could."

"Think that's how they got the location?"

"It certainly is one way. My assistant has been with me for ten years and no one in the family would tell anyone. They all knew it was a secret. All our e-mail correspondence is secured by Sloane's system and a routine check of everyone's phone lines revealed no bugs or other surveillance devices."

"What about Hazel?" asked Jim. There was no malice in his voice. It was just that everyone knew she couldn't keep a secret.

"We told her as we were leaving for the airport." That made them both attempt a smile.

Jim brought with him a team of forensic specialists to comb the library and the gardens. The cover story was that the owner was completing a thorough inspection for structural integrity and soil erosion. They'd blocked off all the relevant areas and everything would be done quickly and quietly.

"Unfortunately it's a very public place and one that's extremely old. There'll be a great deal of forensic debris, so we'll have to be extremely lucky to find anything relevant," said Jim.

Alex indicated Jim's budging briefcase. "Shall we get started on the case files, then?"

"Yes. First we have to determine the who. Then we can work on the how."

"All I'm interested in is the where."

"Let's begin. Have you eaten?" Jim wanted his agent as sharp as he could be given the circumstances.

"Yeah. I fueled up earlier." Alex frowned. At least he thought he had. Didn't matter. He was itching to get into the files. To find suspects. To find clues to Skye's location.

"Okay, then. Why don't you shower and get comfortable. We have here a ton of files to review. All of Skye's cases. The summaries are in hard copy and disks. We'll go through those first. We can determine the most likely suspects. The complete files are here." He raised his laptop. "My eyes only. When we need to dig further, I'll run the probe."

Alex felt better after a shower and a change into a loose sweat suit. Jim got comfortable by loosening his tie.

"At this point, we'll assume her abduction is due to her association with the Justice Department, although it could be a simple kidnapping."

Alex looked up from his own laptop. He'd fed the top disk into it and was downloading the information. "How so?"

"You're a very wealthy and influential man. Someone could be holding her for ransom."

"Don't you think I'd have heard from her kidnappers if that were the case?"

"Yes. I think we can assume so. There's also the possibility that someone is trying to hurt you or get to you in some way. You've built your success legitimately, but there may be someone out there who resents you or perceives that you caused them injury. Of course there's the slight possibility that this may be related to one of your cases."

Alex felt a sinking feeling…so many possibilities. They simply didn't have enough information. He stared at the confidential files on the computer screen, then started to read.

After a few hours of constant reading he noticed the pain leaking through his brain. He had a ripping headache. Brought on by stress, fatigue and anxiety. Jim saw the pain and put command in his voice. "Take something for that headache before it debilitates you and clouds your judgment."

Alex nodded and nearly moaned. His head was splitting…still, he couldn't stop to rest his eyes, or to take time to relax. Instead he popped a few pills, poured in some more caffeine and ordered food from room service.

Hours pasted as Jim and Alex continued to scan the files in silence. The pressure behind Alex's eyes was exacerbated by the endless words scrolling on the screen. He recognized Skye's precise, concise writing style, but there was still so much to review. He'd been taking an acre of notes. His head was still pounding. Not even the powerful painkillers made a dent in the hammering in his temples. It seemed every time he reviewed a file, he added a name to the list of people who would like to take Skye on for another round.

Alex looked up abruptly from one he was scanning. "Holy shit, Jim. What were you thinking? Sending her alone into this one?"

Jim was reviewing his own case and looked up. "Which one was that?"

"The Blanda case."

"Yeah. That one got her the Dover Citation and a meeting with the President."

"But she was without backup."

Jim looked up and put on his director's face. Alex's face was stormy with anger and that pushed Jim's own temper. "Look Alex. She had to go in alone and unwired. They would have found a wire and they would have detected a backup. Those people weren't fools. They had sophisticated equipment and brilliant minds. The only thing they couldn't protect themselves from was Skye's eyes, ears, and memory. Now get over it.

Your new wife is a special agent with a long and incredibly successful record. Danger is her business."

Alex slowly nodded, controlling his simmering antipathy by keeping his mind focused on the files in front of him. He got the message. He'd gone into this relationship knowing all of this…it was too late now to be pissed off about it.

He continued to work through the night, reading cases, sorting them and filling his mind with details. Later he'd give it all some thought, try to find patterns, see if his intuition pointed anywhere. He'd always admired Skye, from the very first moment Jim filled him in on her and assigned him to the covert surveillance of her movements. He realized the dossier Jim had given him on her background was incomplete and superficial. Her remarkable record astounded him. He was in awe of her. He was also terrified. His list of possible suspects was growing.

Once in a while, he'd get up and pace, or stand on the terrace and stare out over the water. Some of these cases were dangerous in the extreme, he told himself, and she came through all of them. A small wicked voice whispered inside his head. Maybe she'd used up all of her luck. Maybe this time her luck hit empty…maybe this time fate was looking for balance…maybe this time…he shook his head. Not possible. He'd know.

Something was scratching at the edge of his mind. It was something Jim had said. Then he looked over at him. He was making his own list.

"What if she was abducted because of those eyes, ears and mind?" he asked. "What if someone wanted something in her remarkable brain." His hand swept the pile of files and disks. "You know she doesn't forget anything. The information she has filed away must be immense. She knows things not only about the people she's investigated, but about the department, her co-workers, the people in power who she's talked with and interviewed. Covert details and agents. She's met with high officials in the military, the judiciary, and the government. She knows names and places and faces. She'd be a fucking gold mine."

Jim looked up and frowned. Alex didn't like what he was thinking, but it was a possibility. "She'd reveal nothing under…" He took a deep breath. He tried to suppress the husband and bring up the special agent. "Under duress." He simply couldn't get the word torture out. "She's tough as hell. But what about drugs or other mind control methods. Would some group want her for what she knows?"

Jim was nodding. It was his worst nightmare. There were two people in his agency who could do real damage beside himself. One was standing in front of him, and one was missing.

Then Jim went very still. If he pursued this line of thinking, there was a standard protocol that chilled him. Alex could see it on his face. He knew it as well as everyone who took the oath. If captured for the purposes of interrogation or gathering inside intelligence and if revealing sensitive information was imminent due to torture, drugs or other forms of mind control and if rescue wasn't possible…then the agent was morally obligated to self terminate rather than risk revealing sealed information or deeply buried high clearance data. If rescue wasn't possible and if the abducted agent was unable to complete the self termination, other agents were directed to shoot to kill. It was putting an agent out in the cold. A sanction with extreme prejudice.

Alex's eyes were the color of high grade steel. "Have you ever had to sanction anyone?"

"Never," said Jim. "In all my years at Justice, I've not had to. Never even came close. But then," he looked at the stack of disks and files on the desk. "I've never had an asset like Skye."

Alex strode into the room and brought his arm across the table, sending disks and papers flying. "An asset!" he shouted, dread clouding his vision. "An asset! Skye isn't an asset, goddamn you. She's my wife. You'll not sanction her, Jim. You will not. You'll not put your signature on her death warrant."

Jim looked at the tortured, enraged man. "Skye's missing. Let's work hard to find her, or identify the reason for her abduction. We have time, but not a great deal of it. I can't have an agent missing for long without explanation…especially one with Level Three clearance." Jim was a brick wall, now. A brick wall with no heart. "If I detect at any time there are actions or movements that would indicate she's been cracked open, I'll sign the sanction. I have to." His throat was so tight, the last sentence was only a whisper. Her death sentence. "She'd insist on it."

Alex was breathing heavy now, he was in a rage. He was pacing like a caged animal. His fists clenched, wanting to surround Jim's throat and squeeze. He knew there was no physical punishment that would hurt Jim more than what he was going through, but he still wanted to hurt someone. Badly.

"Now, put that aside," said Jim firmly. "Don't court a possibility that's not yet necessary. I want you to channel all that fury into action. Let's find her, Alex. She's out there. Let's find her."

Alex rubbed his eyes and nodded. Picking up the files, he started again. The answer was somewhere. Skye was in the center of someone's plan and that individual had a name. Had a face.

Hours later, Alex was beyond fatigued. It wasn't just the lack of sleep that was dogging him now, it was the emotional drain. He'd close his eyes, but his mind couldn't rest. Wouldn't rest. Jim kept ordering food and he'd put it in his mouth knowing he had to. It was swallowing past the constriction in his throat that was becoming nearly impossible.

"Skye," he whispered. "Where are you?"

CHAPTER 4

Skye came slowly to consciousness. She was feeling incredibly muggy, more so than her usual morning blurs. Had she and Alex opened one too many bottles of champagne? No, that didn't feel right. She moved and felt a...a what. A floor? She was lying on a floor. Good God. Cold, too. And damp. And now that her other senses were checking in, she smelled a dank, musty odor. Shit. This most certainly wasn't the bed she'd seen in all the literature on the castle. The bed she intended to spend her honeymoon in. What the hell happened?

She was very uncomfortable, but felt no bruises or injuries. She opened her eyes slowly in case she was being observed, peeking first through partially opened lids. She saw no one. She actually felt no one, either. The only sound she heard was a steady dripping coming from nearby.

Deciding to risk being discovered awake, she sat up slowly. The room tilted and spun. Whoa. Drugs. Damn it. Someone drugged her. She hated that. Her hand went slowly to the side of her neck and she rubbed a sore spot. Double damn. The injection site. What the hell happened? Frowning, she accessed her incredibly organized memory files and found the ones she needed, the ones with the answers to her questions.

She'd left Alex in the lobby. She was happy and a little tired from the flight and a long wonderful week. Also, she was distracted by the beauty of the place and the anticipation of spending the next ten days there with her new husband. Her thoughts had floated to a nice warm bath and a huge comfortable bed and...and...what?

Hell. She sure made it easy for someone. Sleepy and horny. Sounded like two of those damn seven dwarfs Snow hung with. She looked around. Well, Snow White, you're in an avalanche of trouble now. That will teach you to let your hormones short circuit your security system.

She remembered walking up the broad staircase. There was a couple coming down, walking past her. She vaguely remembered a hand next to her coming up, like someone was going to scratch his head, then there was a pinch in her neck. Instant reaction. They walked her into a large room. Books. A library. Sinking fast. Nearly paralyzed. Had to get a message to Alex. Then…what? Nothing. Curtain down. Show over. No second act.

She'd rerun the whole thing again, but right now she'd settle for a bathroom. Why did she always wake up in these predicaments and the first thing she needed to do, even before she could begin to initiate an escape, was pee. She looked around. It looked like a cell, actually like her image of an old dungeon. That might mean she was still in Scotland. Good news. They had tons of castles and didn't all castles have dank, cold, unpleasant dungeons?

She took another whiff. Well, she found out where the bathroom was. The far corner of the room. She didn't have to go that badly yet. She could wait. She looked at her watch. It was 6:00, but she wasn't sure if that was a.m. or p.m. Had she set it to Scottish time? Yes. So at least it was 6:00 a.m. or p.m. here, not in Virginia.

There were no windows in her lovely accommodations. No room with a view, here. The only light came from a barred window on the very top of the iron door of her room with its stone and mortar décor. It was dim, but enough to give her some comfort. She'd have hated to be completely blind. She wasn't afraid of the dark, but the thought of absolute darkness was creepy.

Something was off. What was it? Her intuition was taking a quick inventory. Then she suddenly felt the absence of her ring. She'd only been wearing the engagement ring for a few months and the wedding ring for a day, but they were as much a part of her now as her skin. She held up her left hand to confirm it. She felt a cold, hard anger bubble up from her gut. Those son-of-a-bitches! They robbed her. Was that the motive? The reason for her predicament? Simple robbery? That seemed very unlikely, but that also would be really good news right now. Maybe someone had just dumped her here.

She got up slowly, sure that it wasn't the solid stone wall that was moving in nauseating waves in front of her eyes. She braced herself against the stones until her world, what there was of it, righted itself. Her trained eye looked around and assessed her situation. Not dire, but not entirely without its problems, either. Chief among them…it appeared as though she was being held in a locked cage. The iron door was shut and she had no doubt it was both sturdy and locked. She decided to test it, just to be sure and it was indeed both. Her status was now officially a prisoner of some sort.

Her mind immediately began to shift and sort data. Who, where and why were her major concerns. Also, getting free. She put her ear to the door. She couldn't hear anyone or anything moving. There was a skittering behind the wall to her right, but it was too high to be a rat of the two legged variety. She could have done without that bit of company. She shivered. The bastards had taken her jacket, too.

The 'why' question popped into her head again. Why? Were they specifically after her? It seemed too elaborate to be random. Did they know who she was…who she *really* was? How did anyone find out where she and Alex were honeymooning? Then she sighed. She'd lived with Sloane far too long to believe anything could remain confidential, even under layers of security. If someone was specifically after her, wanted to find out their location, they probably could.

It didn't matter right now. She'd leave that problem to Alex. He was on the outside. It was his job to figure this all out. She only had one job right now. To escape.

Why would someone take her jewelry? She reached up and felt the simple gold earrings. Correction. Not all of her jewelry. Her diamond may have been too tempting a prize for her abductors. Who? Who would want her imprisoned? Or was she just to be left here to die? Well that wasn't going to happen. She gave up trying to put things together. She simply didn't have enough information and to speculate at this point would be fruitless. First she'd get out of here, then she'd employ her resources to ferret out the answers. When she heard the skittering again, she decided sooner rather than later would be best.

She sighed, thinking of how she could begin her escape. She didn't think digging out would be a feasible alternative. The earlier inhabitants of this cell probably thought of that already. There was no weakness around the mortar that she could see. That left the door. Locked, solid and seemingly impregnable. No problem.

Just as she was about to assess the strength of the door and the sophistication of the lock, Skye heard voices. Great. Where there were voices, there might be a key. It was too much to hope for a cup of coffee and an omelet, she supposed. She didn't think this suite came with room service. A ridiculous copy of an unscrupulous travel brochure popped into her brain as she lay back down to play possum. Unique accommodations in the lower level of a magnificent sixteenth century castle, complete with original fixtures in an authentic old-world ambiance. She closed her eyes. Minimalist furniture and genuine, bona fide sixteenth century air. The fact that the air could gag a maggot was their little secret.

Clearing her mind she concentrated on the voices. Two, maybe three. A flash of a man and a woman standing on the stairs, smiling. Nicely dressed. Nothing suspicious. Did she smile back? Yes. And they said? What? Hello? She couldn't remember. Didn't matter.

English. They were speaking in English. More correctly, American English. They were not Scottish. Had they brought her back over the ocean? No. She didn't have the feeling of being out that long. It was 6:00. She was guessing p.m. not a.m. Most people would like to be sleeping at the a.m. There were three distinct voices. Two men, one woman. Some laughter. Good. They were relaxed. Confident. That meant complacent. Just how she liked her jailers. She relaxed her own body as she heard them come closer.

"I'm not sure. It depends on the dose I guess. That's not my thing."

"She was still out this afternoon."

"She should be coming around pretty soon."

"She was a lot taller than I expected. But not much weight."

"I'd like to get a piece of it."

"Hey, that would be a real bonus."

"Don't even think about it. The boss has definite plans for her."

Skye could feel them stop on the other side of the door. Their voices had a slight echo as they were coming down what must have been a long corridor.

Skye willed herself to stay still, even as she swore something danced a waltz across her wrist. Welcome to the honeymoon suite at the Walled Off Astoria.

She heard a bar slick back. Not good. It wasn't a lock she could pick or finesse, it was an old fashioned, hard to maneuver door bar. Maybe the brackets were old and rusted and she'd be able to put some muscle into it. It wasn't a very silent or secretive method, but it looked like it was the plan for now. At least she wasn't tied up or shackled and that gave her all the advantage she needed. If she couldn't get the door open herself, she'd have to wait until her captors came back and take them on when they came through. Right now she wasn't steady enough. She needed to get up and move to get her blood circulating and the drug completely out of her system.

The door scraped open.

"Still out."

"Are you sure?"

"You want to go over and kick her?"

"Not a bad idea."

"No bruises, remember?"

"I think maybe I'll just go over and use my own method," said Man One. Skye heard his shoes scraping across the floor. He stopped just over her and lightly poked her with what felt like a size sixteen shoe. This guy was big. She could feel it...sense his bulk. He must have hunkered down, because his voice was right over her head.

"She looks like she might be coming around." Skye's possum act was perfected over the years and she knew she shouldn't remain completely still. To remain motionless would indicate consciousness and a phony act. So she moaned a little and shifted. Man One patted her on the cheek but she just moaned a little more, and turned over on her side. She nearly jumped when she felt him grab her breast and squeeze. So that was his own personal method. Pig. Asshole.

Skye held on tightly to her natural inclination to plant her heel in his crotch and bring up her other leg to break his nose. It would've been very easy, but she didn't know if they were armed or where the other two were positioned. Too many variables. She needed some time yet. She only shifted slightly and continued to keep her eyes shut. She'd have her day and Man One was going to be a limping giant if she ran into him when she was standing.

"Come on George," said Man Two. "Quit playing with the merchandise. Let's go get something to eat and come back later. She should be up and about by then."

Yeah, George, Skye thought. Go get something to eat. When I'm through with you, they're going to have to wire your jaw shut. Enjoy your last meal with teeth, you moron. She visualized herself giving him a taste of her foot and she could almost smell the blood pouring out of his nose and mouth.

"Nice tits for someone so skinny."

"Can't be real," sniffed the woman. Skye could hear the door creak shut and opened her eyes.

"Felt real enough," said George.

Skye couldn't believe they were arguing about her breasts all the way down the corridor. If she weren't so pissed off and in rather a fix right now she'd have laughed.

"She has money. Rich broads buy tits," argued the woman.

"I tell you, they were real."

Enough about my boobs, already, Skye thought with incredible irritation. What she really needed was information on where they were, who they were and what she was doing here. What were they telling her other than they were idiots? Her information was minimal and not altogether bad news. There were three of them. They were American. They didn't intend just to leave her here. There was a boss. He wanted her relatively untouched. Now that was an interesting tidbit.

An hour later, she heard them come back. She'd used that time getting ready for an assault...her assault. She stretched and took deep cleansing breaths...moving oxygen into her muscles and purging the last remnants of the drug. She stood just beside the door, but they didn't open it this time.

"You stay here until she comes around," said George. "Bianca and I are going to get some sleep."

"Sleep," Skye thought. Good. She'd wait for another hour until they were good and under then maybe take on the one outside the door. Patience. A virtue...and an intelligent tactical plan when outnumbered.

An hour later she knocked on the door...softly...tentatively. She knew how to play it.

"Excuse me," she said in a weak little voice. "Excuse me. Is somebody out there?"
She heard a chair scrape back.

"Who are you?" she asked, trying to sound disoriented and afraid.
No answer.

"Why am I here?"
There was still no answer.

"Please. I have to go to the bathroom." This was true enough...the slight edge of desperation was real. She put some real nice whine into the voice to accentuate her helplessness.

"That's not my problem," said Man Two.

"Please don't make me go in the corner." Maybe he'd open the door to get another look at her chest, she thought viciously.

There was another long silence. Skye knew not to continue to beg. If her captor was a sadist, he'd keep her in here just to hear her plead with him. If he wasn't, her whining might annoy him, even anger him. She played her cards and waited for him to call, raise, or fold.

Then she heard the bar on the door lift. Excellent.

"Get to the back of the cell," he said before he opened the door. At this point, Skye was willing to comply with everything and did as he asked. She just wanted the door open and have the opportunity to assess the situation. She felt she wasn't in imminent danger so she had some time to gather information and appraise her chances for escape.

The door swung open and a small, middle aged man with reasonably intelligent eyes held a gun on her. A very large gun. She noticed the safety was off and he held it with confidence and competence. She was going to be a very good girl. At least for the time being.

"All right," he said. "Keep your hands where I can see them and move on out."

Skye held her hands out in front of her and slowly went out into the corridor. There was a long line of other iron doors. Most of them were closed. At the far end were stone steps leading up. Since this was the only direction to go, she led the way.

Behind her, she could hear the man make a call on his cell phone.

"Bianca? The prisoner is awake and appears to be fairly alert. I'm taking her to the bathroom. Meet me at the one just off the ballroom." He listened. Skye could hear a woman's voice on the other end. She couldn't make out the words but the woman sounded a little miffed.

They ascended the stairs in silence. It was a long flight of steps that seemed to be carved out of the original stone of the mountain. She was sure it was the foundation of whatever structure lay above these rooms of despair. At the top were two ornately carved double doors. They were startling in their elegance. But as soon as Skye opened one of them and let herself into the hallway beyond, she could see why. The door opened into a large room. Big, beautiful and gracefully furnished. Even though the doors led to the dungeons, they were a part of this room and needed to be appropriately opulent.

When she stepped into the corridor, it was like taking a step into another world. It looked like a movie set. A movie set of the perfect Scottish castle. If the Chamber of Commerce needed a picture to put on its website, this was the place to take it. A short corridor opened into a huge entry hall with twin staircases soaring three stories. Massive fireplaces with ornately carved mantels stood at each end of the room. Two distinct wings moved away from the central hall and she couldn't see to the end of their plushy carpeted hallways. This was a home suitable for a king. It confused her even more. What the hell was she doing in the dungeon of a king?

She didn't get to see any more of the castle, however. Not nearly as much as she'd hoped. A woman, beautiful but obviously angry, came striding toward them. She too was armed and, to Skye's disappointment, she also looked like she knew which end to hold and which end to point.

"What the hell do you think you're doing? You should never do this solo."

"I'm not. There's me and Smith and Wesson."

"Very funny." She held her gun up. Well trained, thought Skye. She's not getting into my space at all. Many people in this woman's position would have been tempted to touch the captive, move her along. She kept her distance and let the threat with the gun do her prodding.

"The door on your left," she said. When Skye opened the door, she followed her in.

"May I have some privacy?" Skye asked primly, hoping she sounded affronted with the woman's rudeness. She really wanted to check out everything, including the shelves, drawers, doors and window. But she wasn't to be left alone. She used the facilities, trying to be satisfied with the blissful feeling of taking care of business. She washed up under the hostile stare of her captor who said nothing to her since she entered the room. Skye kept asking questions, but no response. When she reached for a glass to pour herself some water, the woman finally moved.

"No. No water."

"What? I'm parched." And Skye realized she was. She felt terrifically dehydrated and was sure it was the result of both deprivation and the drugs they'd given her.

"You will not drink any water."

Skye frowned. "The water should be fine."

"Our orders are that you get nothing to eat or drink."

Skye's mind clicked along trying to find the reasons for this bit of cruelty. She decided to postpone her analysis until she returned to the cell. For she had no doubt that was where she was going to end the day. These two were not giving her an opportunity. Skye knew how to bide her time. In truth she was feeling a little light headed. Not a good time to stage a mutiny. Wanting to appear compliant and weak, she let her hand shake as she dutifully put the glass down.

Together Bianca and Man Two led her back to her cell. She noted the distances, the placement of the possible exits and when they reached the cell, the bar on the door. Bad news. It looked heavy and was most certainly a twentieth century addition. The brackets looked sound and well fitted. The door was old, but solid.

Hell, that changed things. The timing wasn't ideal, but this may be the only opportunity she'd have. She couldn't afford to bide her time. The easiest way to get out was to already *be* out. She took a deep breath to clear her head and collect whatever energy the added oxygen would carry.

Now or never. She might not be allowed out of her cage again. She was feeling the urge to check out of this hotel. Stumbling a little to convince her captors that she was no threat, she watched out of the corner of her eye. Seeing the woman lowering her gun, Skye knew the two who watched her were about as complacent as they were ever going to get.

Just as she was about to cross the threshold of her prison, she spun around, slammed the door against the man holding the gun, side kicked the woman in the gut and sprinted for the stairs. She knew they were both down and separated from their weapons. She hadn't stopped to assess their level of consciousness or grab one of the guns…stun and run. Speed was her weapon. If she could get to the top and through the doors, she was fairly certain she'd be able to lock them in. On her little excursion she'd noticed a key on the outside of the doors leading to these fine underground accommodations. The thick oak would absorb any gunshots from below as she searched for an exit.

She was also banking on the fact that 'the boss' didn't want her marked or injured. That should include getting shot in the back. Just as she neared the top of the stairs, she looked up. Oh bloody hell. A man was standing in the doorway. He raised his gun and without hesitation, fired. Skye staggered a few more steps, then sunk to her knees and collapsed unconscious on the top step, only a few feet from freedom.

CHAPTER 5

Alex gave in to Jim's suggestion to get some sleep, but couldn't bring himself to use the bed. He sent Jim in there and lay back on the huge sofa and closed his eyes. He needed to take a minute. To rest them and try to beat back the throbbing pain behind them. He didn't realize he'd fallen asleep until the phone rang. He jumped grabbing his cell phone.

"Yes?" he said, then realized it wasn't his cell ringing but the phone on the desk. He shook his head, clearing out the cobwebs. He needed to be alert. Jim came out of the bedroom and stood beside him. They'd already attached a recording device.

"Alex Springfield," he said into the receiver. His heart, beating wildly, sunk as he heard the pleasant voice of the concierge.

"Mr. Springfield," said the concierge. "I've a fax down here. It's from your office. Shall I have someone bring it up?"

"Yes. Thank you," mumbled Alex. He looked at his watch and calculated the time zones. 8:00 a.m. eastern time. He was surprised to find he'd slept for over three hours. The pounding in his head had retreated a few paces but he frowned as he read the message from his assistant.

Alex. I didn't want to call and disturb you since I can never figure out what time it is over there. I just got a call from an Inspector Brady from the Strathclyde constabulary. I thought it was a coincidence that you were in her district. She wanted to talk with you, but I told her you were out of the country. She was quite persistent and wouldn't let me help her. I told her I'd pass on her name to you. I called and talked with her Chief Constable. She's legitimate.

There was a name, address and phone number.

"Could this have something to do with Skye?" asked Jim. Neither of them liked the fact that the local police were looking for Alex.

"I'll find out." Just as Alex picked up the phone, there was a soft discreet knock on the door. Neither of them were expecting anyone nor had they ordered room service. Alex looked through the security hole. A uniformed constable and a very pretty woman in a stylish dark suit stood in the hallway. The uniform looked distressed, the other clearly in command. Alex threw open the door. He didn't like the expressions on their faces.

"Mr. Alexander Springfield?" asked the woman in a solicitous voice.

"I am."

"My name is Inspector Payton Brady." She presented her credentials. "This is Constable Anthony McGroon. May I come in for a moment, sir?" Her voice was soft, with the sound of Scotland accenting her words.

"Please," Alex nodded and stepped aside. "I was just about to call you."

The inspector's eye contact with the constable indicated that he was to wait outside the door. He took his post as she entered the room. Jim came up beside Alex.

"James Stryker," said Alex, adding no other explanation.

The inspector nodded. "Mr. Stryker." She was young, petite and beautiful. Her hair was the color of flame and she had a few freckles across her nose. She looked more like a barmaid than an investigator. But her eyes were cop's eyes. He recognized the power. He'd grown up with it. They were penetrating and intelligent. Suspicious, but compassionate.

"Your office contacted you then, sir?"

"They did."

Inspector Brady looked right into Alex's eyes. He was obviously exhausted, but still had a sharp edge. And he definitely was guarded. "I'd like to talk with you, please. Would you like to sit down?"

Her eyes revealed empathy and a slight wariness. She was sizing him up at the same time she was gently trying to prepare him for something.

"No. I'd like you to get quickly to the point," said Alex. He had his voice of command back and wanted to get to whatever she had to say quickly.

"All right," she said.

From her expression, it wasn't good. He had no idea.

"Mr. Springfield. You're here on your honeymoon?"

"I am. How did you locate me?" His respect for her badge fought with his impatience.

She'd answer his question in her own time, if she chose to. Her face revealed nothing. She was the interrogator here and intended to control the situation. She could tell this man wasn't used to being on the receiving end of an interview.

"Do you recognize this?" Ignoring his question, she handed him a button encased in a plastic evidence bag. Alex looked at it and felt the slam of shock. It was one of the customized buttons from Skye's jacket. It looked charred, but his corporate logo was clearly stamped on it.

"Maybe I will sit down," he said indicating a grouping of chairs in front of the fireplace. He kept the button firmly grasped in his fist as he and Jim sat down. Alex noticed the inspector remained standing, effectively placing herself above him.

"I believe this is a button from my wife's uniform," Alex said, running his finger over the surface and turning off all of his emotions. They were far too volatile for him to deal with right now. He'd put them away and handle them later. Handing the button to Jim, he looked up at the inspector with cool, blue eyes. "Why do you have it and why does it appear charred?"

Ignoring his attitude, she silently studied him. Assessing. He was a difficult one to read. Giving a direct answer, asking a direct question, she thought. He was used to getting answers quickly and efficiently.

Payton had a steady gaze too and wasn't intimidated by his stare. She was used to finding out what she wanted first. His wife, huh? This was very revealing and potentially very tragic. She'd assumed the woman had been a member of his staff. Her questioning would now have to move in a different direction. It was a good thing she was an experienced officer of the court. She decided to answer his original question.

"Your corporate logo was on the front of the button. I simply went on the internet, traced the image and got your corporate name, address, and phone number. A very efficient and pleasant administrative assistant named Frances told me that you were honeymooning. Since your corporate jet is parked in Glasgow and you went through customs there, I assumed you were here about. A few calls and I found your reservations." She then shifted gears. "Could you tell me why your wife would be wearing a uniform with these buttons?"

"Skye is a pilot, Inspector, and she flies our corporate jet. She prefers to wear a uniform when in the cockpit. Projects a more professional image. As the CEO of the Skyward Corporation, I approve of her decision."

He said *is* a pilot, not *was* a pilot. He doesn't know, or is a pretty good actor. She was hoping to trip him up, but no such luck. He was going to be a tough one. Good. She liked tough ones.

"So she's one of your employees?"

"She is my wife."

"Had she worked for you long before you married?"

"No."

"And you're here in Scotland on your honeymoon?" Her eyes went to Jim. They saw her implied question…who would bring a third party on a honeymoon…there was more here and she'd be getting to that before she left.

"We are…now will you tell me how you got this button?" Alex was about to jump out of his skin. He held himself in check because he recognized the methodical, professional way the inspector was conducting the interview and he liked the feeling of confidence it gave him.

"I'm very sorry, Mr. Springfield." She glanced over at Jim. Her eyes said, stick by him, this is going to be brutal. "Early this morning a couple of lads stumbled over the charred remains of a body." Now she was watching Alex's face. Every nuance, every expression. He was trained to hide, she thought. That was revealing in itself.

When she saw some of the color drain from his face, she went on quickly. She always felt fast, direct, and without prevarication was the best way to get bad news out. "That button was discovered on the body."

Alex was void of any feeling. Completely empty. Nothing there. He heard every word, however. Had to. Needed to. Information was important. Data was critical. He heard Jim's gasp and soft exclamation of horror but didn't let it in. He continued to stare at the inspector.

"These buttons survived the flames as well." She reached in her pocket and pulled out three more, each in a plastic evidence bag. Each one chipped more out of Alex's composure.

"How tall was your wife, Mr. Springfield."

He heard the past tense. He chose to ignore it. Had to ignore it.

"She is 5 feet 11 inches." Still the present tense, Payton thought.

"Very tall for a woman." He nodded.

"And her weight?"

"About 128 pounds."

"Quite thin."

"She's been ill."

"Your description fits the body type of the corpse, sir." She kept her eyes on his.

"What else. There's something else," said Alex softly. He knew he was breathing, but everything else was turned off. There was more. That got through. He felt it.

She felt a jolt of surprise, but didn't let it show on her face. There was indeed more. She had more in her pocket and was holding it as a second wave. She liked to interrogate in layers. It was how to get through people's defenses. He seemed to know it. How was he able to read her so well?

Payton took a deep breath. She was watching him…needed to shake something loose. He was too composed. Okay, Mr. Springfield, she thought, see if you can deal with this.

"We found these on her left hand." She reached into her jacket pocket and pulled out something. Then, never taking her eyes from Alex's face, she opened her fist. In the palm of her hand, encased in plastic were Skye's diamond and wedding ring. She'd only worn that wedding ring for a day.

Alex looked at the rings and felt a hole being punched right through him. His training kept his hold on the thin thread of control during the questioning, but this was too much. He stared at the rings and felt the room close in on him. He couldn't breathe. His heart stopped beating, then started again, thundering in his head. He vaguely heard Jim swear. But that was from a long, long way.

"Skye," he whispered, his voice so ragged and raw, not even he recognized it. "Skye." He held out his hand and took the rings. There was a tunnel of light around them as everything else in the room dimmed.

Payton didn't try to stop him. If he was innocent, it would have been cruel. She wasn't cruel. If he was guilty, it didn't matter. She'd nail him. She opened herself up, wanting to take a gut level reading. She was good at this. One of the best. That was why she was called in. Her reading said innocent. That was strange, because her head was firmly on the side of guilty.

Taking the rings he crushed them in his palm, then brought his fists to his eyes, leaned forward and rested his head on them. Still. His body went completely still. He felt the rings' heat…their fire. He kept his eyes closed. There was no one in the room. He was alone with the symbol of their love and their recent vows.

He swore to be there for her. To watch over her. To love her and cherish her. "Skye," he whispered again.

Abruptly, he got up out of the chair and walked toward the terrace. Standing, Jim reached out. He was in utter shock, not knowing what to do.

"No," said Alex looking fiercely at Jim, his voice raw with emotion and barely contained feelings of both panic and despair. Jim backed off slowly. Payton did follow, however. This man was her prime suspect now. There were several ways off the terrace and she figured he might even be suicidal. It was a long way down to the sea and the rocks below.

As Payton watched him, he walked over to the ledge and leaned forward against the low wall. Payton tensed. If he jumped, it would essentially end her investigation. Jim came up beside her. Neither said a word.

Alex looked down at the ocean below, then opened his tightly clenched fist. Her rings. He closed his eyes and said her name again in such a haunted, poignant tone that Payton shivered. At this moment, he wasn't concerned with her or evidence or the interview.

Payton looked over at Jim's horrified face. That expression she recognized…that she'd seen before. Shock, pain, sorrow, anger. She looked back at Alex. He was absolutely rigid. Intense waves of emotion poured out of him, but she couldn't recognize their nature. Love, certainly, there was that. Passion? Pain? Was it shock? Grief? Guilt? She shook herself. The terrace was suddenly filled with it. He looked like a heartrending figure in some Greek tragedy. Painfully handsome, powerful and heartbroken. There was an aching tenderness in his voice when he said her name. She felt her own throat clutch.

Swallowing hard, she cleared her throat. That never happened before, she thought. She was considered a little too hard-hitting sometimes. Cool, detached. Well she got sucked into the vortex on this one and had to hold herself in check. Her heart wanted to take his hand or hold him. To give him comfort and end his suffering. She had a job, however. And she could best serve the dead woman by doing it. She worked for the victims. They were the ones she cared about the most. It was yet to be determined if this man was a victim as well.

Alex stood very still. He was opening himself up to her. He was waiting for the explosion. The cold, hungry, angry blast of death that would hit him and slaughter his heart. He knew what it felt like. He knew what to expect. It was a hollowing out of everything inside him. Worse than death. He'd felt it once before when Rita had been killed…the exact second her heart had stopped beating. It had slammed into him. He waited to feel the loss. It wasn't there.

Waiting. Holding his breath. Nothing. He started to breathe again only when he felt himself get lightheaded. Skye. If she were dead…if that was her body and all that was left were these rings, he'd know. He'd feel it.

His heart would be dying, his soul fading, his life ending.

But it didn't come. There was shock and horror, of course, but no grief. He was stunned, but not empty. He gave it a few more moments. Moments to get through his denial. It wasn't coming. He was sure of it. Sure. Her heart was still beating.

Opening his eyes, he took a deep, free, wonderful breath of fresh sea air. She wasn't dead. No matter what the physical proof said, the metaphysical evidence didn't confirm it. He felt calm inside…deep inside. Something in him was certain she was alive. That meant it was very, very important that he stay focused. He couldn't let the panic in. Wouldn't let it in. He forced himself to come back to the present…to the terrace.

He wanted more time to think and feel. But not right now. Now he had to move. Quickly. He felt it. She wasn't dead, but she wasn't there in his head, either. He looked at the rings again. They didn't belong in his hand. They belonged on Skye's finger. He needed to work with this inspector and take the steps necessary to find her. He took another deep breath and straightened.

One more step, he thought. Take another moment to make one more attempt to connect. Alex reached inside his pocket and pulled out the compass…his gift from Skye. He held it and looked at it for a long time. Skye. He thought, Are you out there? Where are you?

Payton and Jim watched him stare at a round piece of metal in the palm of his hand, the same hand that held the rings.

"Inspector Brady," Alex said in a voice that was now calm and perfectly steady. "Could you tell me which way, in your opinion, is due north?"

The question confused her but she pointed directly to her right, out over the sea. She thought perhaps he'd gone from shock to denial. He could easily turn on her if he had anything to do with his wife's death. She felt her weapon at her hip and was ready to draw it at the least provocation.

Alex looked back down at the compass. North was reading inland, significantly more to the left than where the inspector indicated. It was off by over 30 degrees. He closed his eyes, closed his fist over the face of the compass and took a deep cleansing breath. Something drained from him…doubt. And something else replaced it…hope. Gradually, he blew the air from his lungs. She was out there.

Opening his fist, he looked back down at the compass. It was now registering north exactly where the inspector had indicated. While it might have been wishful thinking before, or an illusion of the mind, Alex didn't think so. He also didn't care. Where there had been hope was now absolute certainty.

He looked down at the rings and found he could feel again…breathe normally again. He sensed Jim's approach, then his hand on his shoulder.

"Jim," he said softly. "I'm okay. Skye's alive."

Turning slowly, Alex could see the suspicious eyes of the inspector concentrated on him. Clear, intelligent, probing green eyes. Assessing. Wary.

He'd journeyed out of himself, found the answer he needed and was now back to do what he was trained to do. Skye was alive. She was inland and he was going to use all of his ability and talent to find her. The burned body…the rings and buttons…they were a diversion. Clever. It might have worked had he not been so certain she was alive.

Payton saw determination where she thought she was going to see devastation. It confused her.

"We need to identify the body," he said. Payton looked at him. He wasn't processing the evidence, she thought. He was talking about the body as if it belonged to someone else.

"There wasn't enough flesh on her hand to do a finger print analysis. We can't get preliminary DNA from a charred corpse. Her dental records are necessary, although there was a great deal of damage to her face and mouth." Her mind had registered at the time she inspected the corpse that someone wanted it to be very difficult to confirm the identity of the body. As if someone hoped the rings and buttons would be enough to convince both the authorities and her husband. It didn't look like there was a chance of that happening. Fascinating. He was so sure.

"Mr. Springfield, may I take a look around?" asked Payton.

Alex thought of all the files and top-secret documents Jim brought with him.

"No, you may not." That surprised Payton and put her on alert.

"Sir, could you tell me where you were last night?"

"Here," he said. He wasn't going to lie to her. She deserved respect. But he wasn't going to involve the local authorities unless he was given a green light by Jim and his contacts at Scotland Yard.

"Here?" She raised her eyebrows and went on. "And you didn't notice your new bride was missing?"

"I noticed," Alex said, distracted now. He wanted time to think. To plan. Why wasn't his brain moving? Jim still had his hand on his shoulder. The slight tremble Alex felt in Jim's fingers must be causing some static in his ability to think.

"Sir, could you tell me why you didn't report your wife missing?"

"No," repeated Alex simply.

"All right…that's your privilege but I think we should have a go at the station house." Payton felt her temper building and she knew it was going to be a long night.

"May I make a phone call?" asked Jim.

"Go right ahead," said Payton with a tone of impatience. "Call anyone you wish." She had suspicions. Springfield wasn't acting like a normal, bereaved spouse. He wasn't acting like anything she'd ever seen before…more enraged than grief stricken. And who was this other man? What did that mean. Had there been a kidnapping? This was going to be messy. Good thing she loved messy, too.

"Don't say anything more," Jim instructed, although Alex had said practically nothing. Payton interpreted that to mean a barrister would be appearing soon to intercede on the husband's behalf. She didn't like that. But she knew and respected the law. She ceased asking questions and wouldn't continue until he was represented.

While Jim was talking in soft tones, Payton studied Alex. He'd lapsed into silence, staring at the victim's rings, running his fingers over the diamond and the beautiful design of the wedding band. Payton had read the inscription. *Le coeur parle au Coeur.* It was French. Heart speaks to heart. As she watched him, he held on to what she now saw was an old fashioned compass. Curious.

How could his honeymoon have gone so badly? He wouldn't tell her anything. At least not voluntarily. His wife was dead. Her body charred beyond recognition and he seemed to be in deep denial. She'd have to uncover his involvement through inspection, deduction and solid collection of evidence.

Payton was itching to secure a search warrant, but she didn't want to leave the premises to do it. She'd send the uniform back to the office to get the necessary paperwork started and stay with this man. Maybe he'd crack. She looked at his face. And then again, maybe not.

Alex stared down at the rings. They wouldn't have been able to get them from her easily. He hoped she was drugged unconscious when they tried, or he'd be tending a full set of bruises on her again. She'd have fought until she went down before she took them off.

He saw the charred residue on them. Was he being delusional? Was his shock and grief preventing him from facing reality? Was she dead? Was this body they found hers? He rubbed his chest. No. He'd have felt her death. That he was sure of. A dissenting opinion was stubbornly, rationally telling him he didn't know that for sure. Evidence. There was evidence to the contrary. The evidence said a woman of Skye's height and weight, wearing her rings and uniform was dead. Skye was missing. Why couldn't his brain connect with his heart?

"A call will be coming through," said Jim softly to Alex. Jim knew Alex was in shock. He could barely function himself. Just then the telephone rang on the desk. Jim answered it, then held it out to Payton.

"It's for you, Inspector."

She looked at him in shock. "For me?" She took the receiver and listened to the person on the other end of the line. She said very little. Her eyes went from Jim to Alex to Jim again.

"I understand," she said and hung up. Her eyes were flashing, her temper right on the edge. It made her voice sharp and artificially polite.

"Well, gentlemen. I have been instructed to give you all the assistance I can. Word came directly from the Lord Justice General. I'm not supposed to ask questions, but you can imagine I have them. A woman is dead. She's my responsibility. If either of you had anything to do with it, I don't give a flying fuck who you know." Her green eyes snapped with fury.

Silence hung in the room. Before Jim could respond, Alex grabbed his jacket and moved toward the door.

"Inspector Brady," said Alex with a little ironic smile. "There's someone I want you to meet. And I hope you will very soon." He stood in the open doorway and indicated his intention that she and Jim join him. "First we have to find her and to do that I need to convince you that the corpse is not my wife." Alex looked at Jim's stricken face. "To convince both of you."

"Who?" Payton snapped. "Who do you want me to meet?"

"The woman you still think is your victim."

"Your wife?"

"Exactly. You'll like her very much and I know she'll like you. First let's find out who this other woman is. I want to see the body."

"No. You don't, sir." It was hard enough for her to look at it. She'd never want someone who loved her to see the horrible burned out shell they found.

"You've been given a directive to assist Jim and me. I'm hoping you'll do so without rancor. I'm sure we'll need your assistance."

"Sir. I understand this man here is some big hooey. But you don't want to see this body. Please. Let's proceed under the assumption it's your wife. I'll send for her dental records and we'll begin the formal identification."

"This will be quicker and time is critical. I need to see the body," he repeated as he looked directly into her eyes. "She's not dead until I see her dead. She's not dead until I feel her dead."

Payton didn't know exactly what he meant by that, but she stared into his intense blue eyes and found herself nodding. Hell. Why was she doing that?

The uniformed officer drove them to the morgue. Jim and Payton kept at Alex, trying to get him to wait until tests revealed the identity of the body. Jim wasn't convinced Skye was alive and was numb to the core with the possibility. He knew that Alex thought so, but he also knew that Alex wanted to believe it too badly. Maybe it was the only thing keeping him sane.

"Jim. She's alive. We can't waste time waiting for tests when I can confirm this immediately. Someone has her and the quicker I convince the two of you of that, the faster you'll channel your energy to finding her, not her killer."

They parked in the street and Payton led them into an immaculate, state of the art facility.

"The people who did this may have thought they were dealing with a small town doctor and a backwater constable. They may have thought that the body would be identified based on the physical evidence."

Alex had to admit that if he didn't know she was alive, he'd have found all the evidence convincing. He may have believed and grieved. As it was he had this pounding hope and unrelenting resolve.

Payton looked at Alex with compassion when they went into the refrigerated section. No amount of disinfectant, no amount of cleaning could erase the smell of death.

Through the glass door, they could see the autopsy table with its sheet-draped body. The staff took a break on Payton's request.

"Please, Mr. Springfield. Perhaps the crime scene photos would be enough." He looked down at her. Something like gratitude flashed over his face.

"You're very kind," he said softly. "You try not to show it, but it's there in your eyes." He looked at Jim.

"I need to do this alone. If it's her, I'll know it and I'm not sure of my reaction. I'll want to move quickly, understand? I'll need to be able to find her executioners." He looked at the two of them. They nodded. If he went extreme on them, they would have to bring him back.

He removed the gun from his holster at the small of his back. Payton backed up and put her hand on her own weapon. Alex's lips actually turned up at her quick reflexes. She saw the safety was on and relaxed. He handed the gun to her. She understood. He wanted nothing lethal within his reach. "Even if it's not her, I'm not sure how I'll react."

Payton and Jim watched from the hallway as Alex approached the covered corpse. Alex saw the shape. Long. Thin. Slowly he moved his hand to the sheet covering her face. Twice he stopped. He shook himself, deciding against the face. He moved his hand to the torso. Jim and Payton were holding their breath.

"God. The guy's got guts," she whispered. "He's putting himself through hell in there."

Alex lifted the sheet. He saw a charred hand. Long fingers. They could be hers. His heart was pounding. His chilled blood was pulsing through his veins...freezing him. He couldn't take his eyes off the hand. In his mind, her beautiful, strong, capable fingers superimposed themselves over the hideous black flesh and exposed bone. Her rings were found on this hand. God. Blinking the image away, his eyes were pulled up to the sheet covering the place the face would be. If he continued, he could find these grotesque remains were his Skye. If he didn't go on, he could continue to fool himself. Continue to believe she was alive. His eyes slid back to the exposed hand. Did he really want to know? Was this monstrous, burned...thing...the lovely hand that stroked his chest, moved over him with such love?

He almost lost it then. Lost his mind. But something fueled his resolve and he continued, lifting the sheet higher. The body was dreadful, nothing really human remained. The odors assaulted him along with the horror. The grisly sight and ghastly smells stopped his hand. The gagging reflex was powerful and he had to swallow hard to keep from being sick. Even if this wasn't Skye, it had been a human being. If this vile evidence of inhumanity was a decoy, the people who did this hideous thing had her captive. Revulsion blended with fatigue and dread and nearly paralyzed him. Taking in a lungful of air through his teeth, he steeled himself and marshaled all of his considerable will. Reaching in under the sheet, he pulled back some of the charred skin on her chest. He knew what he was looking for. He closed his eyes...and he found it.

CHAPTER 6

Pavel rubbed his hands together. Everything was going perfectly. His team reported from Scotland that the abduction was executed without a hitch. Brilliant! As soon as he knew he had the prize, he'd made contact with his Russian uncles. They were shocked to hear that he'd survived the explosion on his boat. He built for them an elaborate cover story…one filled with his own heroics.

He told them he'd fought treachery, near assassination by the federal government, and personal tragedy to hunt for the woman who betrayed them all. He'd gone deep underground and sacrificed mightily to find her. It was the only thing that drove him through the danger and the personal peril.

He laughed manically remembering the call. They bit on the bait. And swallowed. Everything. All of it! Fools. Idiots. They were nothing when compared to his genius! His next phone call would be to a South Beach realtor. He could feel the hot sand sifting between his toes already.

"I should have contacted them sooner. I didn't realize they wanted Virginia so badly. What they'll get is an even better version of what they remember. She's spent considerable time the last few years investing in some polish. Apparently the old geezer who bought her originally will still pay top dollar."

He paced and smiled over at Rosalie. She'd served him well. The castle was indeed the destination of the newlyweds. He only wished he could poke the invincible Captain Cooper and her witless husband with the fact that they provided the perfect trail. In the end, they should actually thank him. He didn't think their clueless son would have had a very long marriage. The stupid man couldn't even keep track of his bride.

"What have you found in the police reports?" he asked. He was only mildly curious. He was sure they would be chasing their Scottish tails until the groom finally filed some kind of missing person's report. Then they'd turn over the body, and the case would be closed. "Have they put out any bulletins?"

"No, nothing yet."

"I bet Virginia made a habit of disappearing…it would be her style. It's only a matter of time before Springfield gets the bad news. I wish I could have given him the pleasure of a honeymoon…but alas, I had a greater need. Maybe he'll get a good deal on the cremation…such a head start!" Pavel laughed again. What wit!

Rosalie shuddered, but accepted the envelope he handed her. When she left the office, Pavel called in two of his bodyguards.

"Have Rosalie meet with an accident. No…suicide, I think. She's always been a little high strung." He waived his hand in a gesture of benevolence. "But allow her to finish her shopping spree and luncheon first."

Pavel smiled out his window. He may be evil, but he really was generous to a fault. Dying satisfied and happy was the least he could do for a loyal employee. It was unfortunate, but she was a junkie and could be tempted to go to the other side. He saw her eyes flash when she reported on this Springfield's assets. He looked again at the information Rosalie compiled.

"Well, Alexander Springfield. How's the honeymoon so far?"

Alex found what he was looking for, but forced himself to take another look just in case there was any chance he was mistaken…or that his vision was modified by his overcharged brain.

Jim saw Alex sway as he pulled his hand back. Bracing himself on the edge of the autopsy table, Alex let the sheet fall back over the pitiful remains. Then suddenly, he whirled around violently and kicked over a nearby tray sending the instruments on top flying around the room. The air was filled with a cacophony of ear shattering sound as they flew and hit the wall and floor. The lamp was next and the florescent bulbs popped as they smashed on the tile. His hand came down and cracked a solid oak side table holding the notes and files of several autopsies.

Yanking open the door Jim rushed over to Alex, grabbing him before he could do any more damage. Alex was breathing heavily, his face filled with unconcealed rage. The dam had burst and it made Payton shudder. Her hand went automatically to her weapon. This man was capable of killing, she was sure of that. Alexander Springfield was gone. In his place was a dangerous, terrifying machine…an instrument of destruction. He looked barely rational and very, very frightening.

"Someone is going to pay," vowed Alex, looking at Jim with eyes that had a flash of madness. Shaking off Jim's grip, he tried to get his breathing under control. He looked at the two of them with burning eyes, fury flooding out of him. "Someone who wanted us to think that was Skye, who made us go through this torture, who still has her, is going to pay."

"Alex," said Jim, his voice shaking. "Alex, what are you saying."

"Goddamn it," he looked around the room. "Goddamn them."

More of Alexander Springfield came back into focus and the deadly mask of the avenger was suppressed until Payton relaxed her gun hand and blew out the breath she'd been holding.

When Alex stared back at the corpse still trying to shake the shock, Jim used his director's voice and demeanor. "Alex. Report."

It worked. Alex rubbed his face with his hands, one of which was bleeding slightly from skinned knuckles. He looked around him as if he just woke up in a strange place.

"Sorry," he said. Some more of Alexander Springfield returned, but not all of the killer dissolved. "Sorry," he repeated. "Jim, this whole thing was a fucking, horrific diversion. We have work to do. The people who did this…this inhuman act…they have her. We have to hurry."

"It isn't her?" asked Jim, wanting Alex to get back to the central question…his heart had stopped, and now was beating painfully in his tight chest. Looking around at the instruments all over the floor, he'd assumed from Alex's reaction that it was her…his agent, his godchild…his child. That his worst fears had turned into reality. "That isn't Skye?"

Alex looked into the eyes of a man who desperately wanted to believe him.

"No," he said steadily.

"How sure are you?" Jim saw that Alex believed, but he couldn't just take his word.

"I'm positive. That poor woman never broke a rib, Jim. They did a good job, but they weren't perfect. They made one mistake, they'll make more."

"Your wife had a broken rib?" asked Payton, very interested.

"Several of them. They recently healed. We can forward that documentation to your office. In the meantime, we need to position all of our resources to locate my wife…pool all our information to find out who did this."

"Excuse me for a moment, Mr. Springfield." Payton went over to the shrouded body, steeled herself and checked the ribs. What would have the man done had he seen evidence of recently healed bones? She was immensely glad she didn't have to find out. To her untrained eye, the ribs looked intact, but she'd check with the medical examiner. She was a thorough investigator and even though her instincts told her Alex Springfield was telling the truth, she needed corroboration.

"As soon as I get the confirmation from your wife's doctors, I'll start looking for the identity of this body. We find out who she is and I can start the trail there."

"Agreed." Jim was still riding on the relief he felt.

"Mr. Springfield. Are you all right?" Payton could see the fatigue return and wondered how long the man could stay on his feet. This highly charged emotional experience must have drained whatever reserve he had left.

"Yes," he flexed his injured hand and looked around. "I almost lost it when I saw the hand and I thought it was…that it was her," he said, shaking off the last of the madness that had engulfed him. "I guess I wasn't as far back from the edge as I thought."

"That's all right, Mr. Springfield. Why don't you come back to the castle with me now. I want to look into the backgrounds of all the guests," said Payton.

"That's been done," said Alex. "Everything there checked out. Don't waste your resources."

Payton stared at him for a moment, then over at Jim. That really annoyed her. They were working a parallel investigation and she didn't like it. On the other hand, she could use help on this one. She guessed finding a killer was more important than her ego. Making her decision, she nodded. She was now on their team…on board and ready to give assistance. This was going to be a challenging and interesting assignment and she was geared up. Taking Alex's gun from her belt, she handed it back to him.

"Trust me with it now?" he asked, smiling grimly, then noticed its lighter weight. She waved the magazine of bullets at him.

"Not entirely," she said and raised her eyebrows. "I'll be keeping my eye on you, Yank."

"Skye is going to love you," Alex said softly, his throat raw and dry. "Let's go find her."

"I'm sorry sir," Payton held out her hand. "One more thing. I need to take possession of the evidence. I promise I'll try to get the rings released when we locate your wife."

Alex thought about fighting her, but he needed her cooperation. Nothing was more important than finding Skye. Reaching inside his pocket, he took out the rings…Skye's rings. Looking at them for another few seconds, feeling his heart hurt, he placed them in Payton's open hand.

"I'll take good care of them, Mr. Springfield," said Payton kindly. Then with a stronger, more determined air she said. "Now fill me in on what you know, and let's go find her."

Skye's mind swam around awhile before it came back to consciousness. Christ, she thought. Second verse, same as the first. This was either deja vous all over again or the same modus operandi. Opening one eye, she raised her watch. It read 12:20. So she wasn't caught in a time loop. Either it was a little over nine hours since she last woke up from a drug-induced sleep or it was 21 hours later. She stirred and opted for the former. She wasn't stiff enough for almost a day in this state. Damn, they got her with a tranquilizer gun.

She closed the eye again. Thirst and hunger were creeping in, as was a really ripping headache. At least she wasn't riddled with bullets. All in all, she guessed she was lucky. She decided to take a nap. That sounded ridiculous since she was sure she'd been in a state of unconsciousness for hours, but she felt tired. Shifting positions, her muscles screamed at her, begging her for some relief. She did a little stretching, promising herself some yoga in the morning. Or, if this was a little after noon the next day, in the evening. Deciding she was in no immediate danger, she rolled over on her side, tried to get more comfortable and fell asleep. One of her greatest talents, she thought, was being able to sleep anywhere, anytime.

A few hours later, Skye woke up and decided to see if her keepers were posted outside the door. She knocked and tried the bathroom routine, not too hopeful they would let her out for that task again soon. She rubbed her aching stomach. Damn, she was starving. Maybe that was part of the torture. Deprivation. The thought of fluffy pancakes, rare steak and fresh shrimp skittered through her mind and gave her extra incentive.

Knocking and calling to her captors, she put her ear to the door. If they were out there, they would react in some fashion. Nothing. She couldn't hear a thing. She looked at her watch. Close to 3:00. Must be a.m. and all the bad little piggies were in bed. Maybe they'd abandoned her. She pounded on the door, yelling, kicking, screaming, and pretending insanity. It felt great and helped clear her head. Nothing like a good tantrum to get the blood flowing. When she let up, she listened again. Either there was a guard out there who slept like a stone or the corridor was deserted.

She smiled. Closing her eyes, she pictured the long corridor devoid of a sentry. They must be pretty confident that she couldn't escape. Of course even dirty rotten honeymoon-crashing bastards needed their sleep…she didn't think they were gone for good. She figured her best chance of escape would be in the next hour or so.

To prepare for her assault on the door, Skye walked around the cell. She needed to get the kinks out and pump some adrenalin into her system. Her mind got into gear as well. She'd need shoes if she left the premises and ran to safety. The bastards took them, too. That meant a search of the castle. If there was a phone, she could call Alex immediately and hide. The problem with that was she had no way of knowing where she was. She preferred the run. First she would get her bearings and then find a phone on down the road somewhere. Good. She had a plan…now the execution.

Alert, her blood circulating nicely, she began to work on Operation Freedom. She experimented with a few powerful sidekicks near the location of the bar on the other side of the door hoping the brackets would pull out of the wall or the bar would break. There was absolutely no give. Damn. The bar must be solid iron. Bad break. Actually, no break. That was the problem. All right, that meant persistence. And she could be relentless.

After repeated kicks, she had to stop. Panting, her legs screaming in protest, she gave herself a few moments to rest. Hoping she had at least weakened the brackets, she gathered all of her strength for one last all-out assault. Walking to the opposite wall, she turned, and ran full tilt toward the door. The cell wasn't large enough to get too much speed, but a few feet from the door, she launched herself, pivoted and rammed both of her strong, athletic, well trained legs into the door. She heard a crack and a ping. Landing on the cold, hard floor, she was certain for a moment that the crack she heard was her femur. Maybe her femur and both ankles.

For a full minute she just lay there letting the pain in her legs subside. Damn that hurt. Then she realized more light was in the room. All right! Score! The human battering ram felt more battered than the door, but nothing cured an ache like success. There was light coming from a crack between the door and the wall next to it. She got up slowly, her moan being heartfelt and genuine now. Nothing was broken, however, nothing but something on the other side of the door.

Skye inspected her work. The crack between the door and the wall gave her a view of the corridor and the bar still holding on. It was now bent. That was good. It was also still holding the door shut. That was bad. If she had something she could work through the opening, she could lift the bar and be on her way. She looked around the cell and almost laughed. Like something would have materialized in the last few minutes. Perhaps a crowbar. She'd have to remember to pack one next time she stayed at the Hell-Hole Ratisson. Not that there was going to be a next time. Here was one customer who wasn't going to go after the frequent guest privileges.

There was absolutely nothing in the cell and nothing on her person she could use to work through the crack. All she had were her clothes and underwear…then she grinned. What was more powerful than a pair of pantyhose in the hands of a genius female Special Agent. This jailbreak was in the bag. She quickly stripped off her pantyhose. They were running from multiple holes, but they would be strong enough when pulled tight. She worked one leg through the crack above the bar, then she took off her watch and hit it against the wall to mangle the buckle on the leather band. It was a nice rough surface and every woman knew that a sure way to snag a pair of panty hose was to have a rough surface within a mile of your location.

Slowly, deliberately she slipped the watchband through the crack below the bar and like an angler trolling for fish, she worked at catching the dangling hose. It was frustrating work. Time after time she'd bring the material close to where her fingers could wiggle it through and time after time it would let loose or she'd lose her fragile grip on it. She was surprised when she started sweating with the effort.

"God damn, son-of-a-bitching. *Budiulo. Cogglione Lei figlio di buona donna.*" A sting of profanity sometimes helped. Not so much at completing the task at hand, but it fueled Skye's motivation. Finally, she got a thin piece of material through the crack. She continued to work it through until she felt the leg tugging from the other side. Smiling, she pulled it tight. Now she had the bar outside the door looped in what she imagined was the crotch of her pantyhose. God save her. If she escaped, she supposed she could leave that little detail out of her report.

Standing up she realized how cramped her legs had gotten and took a moment to work life back into her limbs. Her whole body had tensed up. Glancing at her ruined watch, she marked the time. Too much of it had passed. If they came back, she wouldn't be able to play possum. Not with the bent bar outside the door clothed in her pantyhose. Explain that one, Lucy.

Now for the test. Please, she thought. Score one for women's undergarments. Let this work. Taking both legs in her hands, she pulled up. When the bar came up easily, she almost couldn't believe it. She was afraid she might have jammed it in with her kick, but luck was her companion…her best friend. With the bar off, the door swung open easily…not even a scrape or a squeak. Halleluiah! She was free! Taking a few seconds for a little victory dance, she wrapped up the pantyhose, tossed them into the dark corner and took a last look around her cell.

Asta la vista, Baby…I won't be back.

Skye stepped out into the long dingy gray corridor, turned and closed the door.

Placing the bar back, she knew it wouldn't fool her captors on close inspection, but it might give her a few more minutes on the run.

Silently, she made her way down the hallway. Decades, maybe even centuries of screams and cries from prisoners seemed to echo off the walls. It was spooky, but it was the pathway to freedom. Nothing ever looked more inviting. Another hot shot of adrenalin poured into Skye's blood stream. It drowned out her need for food, water, rest, and was a powerful painkiller.

As she passed each cell, she looked in, not sure if she was looking for ghosts or other captives. There was nothing all the way down to the end but a subtle feeling of residual despair.

As she hurried along, she became concerned that there may be locked doors up ahead. Wouldn't that be a pisser. Well, she'd just have to deal with it when the time came. She was a one-woman idea machine...at this moment she was almost sure she could fly if she had to. When she reached the top of the flight of stairs, she was relieved she wasn't going to be tested again. The big wooden door at the top opened easily. Hot damn. It did creak on its hinges, however, and she held her breath as she slipped through the opening.

Free. Well at least free from the damn dungeons. There was light in the large room, but not much from the windows. Still a little time before sunrise. She had to push herself to keep from sinking into the incredibly beautiful overstuffed leather chairs sitting in front of one of the fireplaces and continued to walk rapidly to the massive double doors at the front of the castle. They were locked and bolted. No matter. There were probably hundreds of ways she could get out. She passed a window with beautiful mullioned windows. Then she stopped and stared.

The sun was just making its appearance. With it came light and with that Skye could see the landscape. Snow. Acres and acres of beautiful undisturbed snow. Where the hell was she, Iceland? Then she looked to the west, at least her instincts, finely tuned by years of flying, told her it was to the west. Good lord. And mountains. Really high mountains and judging from the location of this castle, she was right in the middle of them. She was probably in some isolated spot in the highlands of Scotland. Fine. She'd take the high road.

She stared at the shear beauty of the scene. Again she had the thought of perfection. Like someone painted it with a brush. She wished she could just appreciate the splendor, but right now, it wasn't a welcome sight. She really needed to find something more to wear than what she had on. And something substantial for her feet, completely bare now. She wasn't going to escape the Cell from Hell just to die of exposure.

She had to make a search of the castle before she'd go through a door or window. Did they have front closets where guests stowed their outerwear? She looked around. The answer to that was no. But the front door was for company. What about a back entrance? She needed to find one anyway. Stood to reason that people wouldn't traipse through the rooms carpeted with priceless rugs in snowy, wet boots. They would leave them by the back door. Maybe it was in the kitchen and she could snag a crust of bread on her way out. Just some standard prisoner fare.

Suddenly her stomach punched her from the inside again, reminding her she hadn't fed it in, what…hours? Days? Stow that one in the rear car, Skye, she thought. Her problem wasn't starvation but the lack of appropriate footwear. She thought of the dozens of pairs of boots back home. Kevlar had taken out a few, but she still had a number of pair left. Alex would have said enough to bring joy to the entire Chinese population, but he exaggerated. She felt another ping in the heart. Alex. What was he thinking? What was he doing? She ignored a little flutter of fear that perhaps he'd been taken, too.

The place seemed deserted, but it was so huge, there could be a hundred people in the castle and it would still feel uninhabited. It was elegantly furnished, however, and was definitely not an abandoned property. If she could find a phone, she might be able to hide until help arrived.

Running silently through a large reception hall, she opened a door. Glory halleluiah, a bathroom. First things first. Going in, she turned on the lights, took one look at herself and turned them off again. She'd deal with her appearance later. Right now, she just wanted to use the facilities, get something warm to wear, find transportation, if possible, and get back to her groom. This was her honeymoon, goddamn it.

When she finished, she walked soundlessly down the corridor of a long wing branching off the far side of the huge room. She wished she could have lingered over the wonderful paintings and tapestries on the walls. Someone spared no expense. It made her incredibly curious. Unfortunately she didn't see what would have delighted her beyond belief. She saw no telephones or other communications equipment. Whoever owned this place wanted to control all the outgoing connections. That indicated high security. She really didn't have time to search through the rooms in this place for a careless cell phone or the main communications station. As soon as her captors found the empty cage, they would set off the alarm.

As if she conjured up the event just by thinking about it, she heard shouts. They were muffled, but she knew the tone and tune. Now she really had to hustle. But she was a firm believer in suppressing any kind of premature flight. She needed warm clothes and something to protect her from the elements in case she was a long way from civilization. There could be a service station just down the road, or there could be hundreds of miles of desolate mountain terrain. She'd hope for the former and prepare for the latter.

Survival was her objective. She didn't intend to freeze to death. Then she hit the jackpot. The kitchen. A back door. No coats, but several pairs of boots standing beside it. She also found a couple of shirts and a turtleneck sweater. She put them all on, knowing she'd look incredibly foolish, but certainly beyond caring. The boots were all too big, but better too large than too small.

She felt good in her layers of warm clothes. Confident and ready to take off. As she looked out the window, she noticed that the pathways under the thick pine trees were relatively free of snow. Good. She'd be able to run without leaving tracks in the snow. Why make it easy for them.

Cautiously cracking open the door, she saw no one in the yard, but a hardy blast of cold air greeted her. She didn't have nearly enough on if she had to spend the night out there. Should she go back in and try to locate a phone? If she couldn't locate one, she might be able to hide in this castle a week without anyone finding her. Adult hide and seek. But she couldn't risk it without some kind of outside backup. And she was pretty confident no one knew where she was. She had to get out of here, wherever here was. She had to risk the elements.

There was a door just to the right of the one she had standing open to the outside. Maybe there was a coat in there. She peeked. Shit. Linens. Stacks and stacks of tablecloths and napkins. Well maybe she could fashion a pure Damask cape or something.

"And what do you think you're doing?" Came a voice from the doorway. It was one she recognized. Man One. George. The pervert. It was accompanied by the familiar click of a gun being taken off of safety. Hell. She looked out the door at the vast countryside, then turned to face her captor.

CHAPTER 7

Payton was in her small office at the constabulary. She had no idea what the hell she'd gotten in the middle of, but that couldn't concern her now. This morning she thought she had all the clues she needed, now it seemed they were all bogus. Okay, so she'd start from scratch.

She had one dead body to identify. If she could do that, she could find the killer or killers herself. She had a strong feeling that Alexander Springfield, CEO of Skyward Corporation, knew a whole lot more than he was saying. He'd gone from her chief suspect to her sort of partner in one afternoon. Her head was still spinning from that one.

She thought about the woman in the morgue. Someone had gone to a lot of trouble to make it look like Skyler Madison was dead. Compassion formed in her heart for the woman whose only crime was to have a resemblance to her. Anger was there, too. What a waste.

Where to start. She went local first. Missing persons. Female. Almost six feet tall. Extremely slender. Nothing. Then she went to Interpol. Nothing. She sat for a while, thinking. What if the dead woman had no family? No one to report her missing?

Then an idea came close to the surface, but didn't pop through. She practiced what she usually did when she knew something was there...just on the edges of conscious thought. She stopped all action. Sitting completely still, she leaned back and put herself into the mind of the killer. He needed a woman with a specific body shape to begin with. Where would he find such a woman? Was it random? No. Her impression was that this abduction and murder was well planned and executed.

Payton let her mind wander at will. Thinking. Opening all the doors in her mental file cabinet. Come on. Come on. It couldn't have been a random choice. How many six foot, slender women walk down the street? Suddenly, there it was. She pounced on it. Skye had the shape of a high fashion model.

Payton went on the internet and plugged in the search criteria. Model. Missing. She sometimes found that information published on line or in the tabloids gave her more complete data than police records…not always accurate, but certainly somewhere to look.

She hadn't completely eliminated the possibility that the corpse was Skyler Madison and that her husband was creating an elaborate ruse to cover up a murder. He did have powerful friends and the older guy, Jim Stryker, seemed incredibly connected. It wouldn't be the first time high government officials covered for prominent citizens. Still…she respected the people who called her and asked her to cooperate fully. And her gut told her this Springfield was innocent…of this crime anyway. But innocent in general? She remembered the murderous look in his eyes. No. Far from an innocent and unassuming corporate attorney.

The medical records for Skyler Madison had arrived via fax and indeed indicated the earlier injuries to her rib cage, but that could be easily doctored. Pun intended. Her own medical examiner had issued a preliminary report on the corpse…no suggestion at all of any rib damage. Drugs were in her system. Death was due to a blunt force wound to the back of the head. Thank goodness the woman had been dead before she'd been toasted.

Her computer beeped. Damn. Sometimes the internet was just too deep. She had over 2,000 hits of stories concerning missing models. They must be a temperamental sort, she thought. She narrowed it down by date and got over 800 hits over the last few weeks.

She sighed and slid on her reading glasses. As much as she loved the internet and the immediacy of her access to information, she found all this data to be fatiguing. She started opening the files, however, and reading them carefully one at a time.

About 2 hours later, her eyestrain faded when she found exactly what she was looking for. She cross referenced it several times to see if the missing woman may have surfaced in the last few days. Nothing.

According to the tabloid article, Emily Johansson, a high fashion model from Evanston, Illinois living in Paris, had checked herself out of a rehab center north of London and had disappeared. There was a great deal of speculation that she'd suffered a relapse. She was a media hound, always seeking publicity and yet no one had seen her in over a week. She was under contract with a U.S. modeling agency.

"So even though the media missed you, Emily, no one had filed a formal missing persons report," Payton said to herself. She tried again, this time expanding her official search to the United States. The Federal Bureau of Investigation, the major websites where missing persons were submitted, the missing persons postings from the police departments of the major cities throughout the world. Nothing. Not her name, her picture, her description. Nothing. If someone hadn't wanted to gossip about her dropping out of sight after she left a rehab center, Payton may never have uncovered the identity of the body in her morgue.

Payton made a note to check toxicology for the types of drugs in her system. If the body were Emily, there would be recreational drugs still in evidence. She went back to everything she could find about the model. Emily had been very popular at one time, but her star was apparently fading…a has-been at the age of 28.

A recent picture revealed a very beautiful, very slender woman. She wasn't nearly as stunning as Skyler Madison, but after being doused with gasoline and set on fire, it didn't matter. Nothing on her face, hands, or body was particularly distinguishing. None of the pictures showed a smile. She needed to see teeth. The corpse had a slight crook in her left incisor. The doctor had said it could have been the result of an apparent beating around the face or a shift after her death, but Payton would guess not.

She finally found a very old picture of the model caught in a candid shot. There it was. The slightly crooked incisor.

"Hello, Emily," she whispered. This wasn't a positive identification, but it was a place to start. She rolled some of the tension out of her shoulders and did more research on Emily Johansson's background. Then she got on the phone and made several calls.

Her last call was to Alex. She told him she'd be right over. It wasn't until she was on her way that she realized it was after midnight. She shrugged. The man answered the phone on the first ring and sounded alert enough. She flexed her own tired muscles. He must be exhausted, though. She didn't think he'd slept since he arrived and that was the day before yesterday. Well, she'd give him this information and they would have another trail to pursue.

When Payton entered the room, she found Alex looking beyond exhausted. He was dead on his feet, but still grim and determined. She was seeing less of the CEO and more of the steely, hard agent or whatever the hell he was. Still, he greeted Payton with respect and she appreciated that.

"Mr. Stryker?"

"He's asleep in the bedroom." But as Alex offered Payton some coffee, the door opened and Jim came out looking haggard but alert.

When Payton had finished her report, life seemed to return to Alex's blood shot eyes.

"Well done, Inspector," he said.

"Once we eliminated Ms. Madison, the rest was what I do."

"But in record time, I'd imagine," said Jim. Competence in any form always pleased him. This young inspector was living up to her reputation. He'd been in contact with her commander and she was considered the best they had.

"I'm going down to the rehab center tomorrow morning. Maybe she left behind information that will be helpful. The people who murdered this woman are the same people who have your wife. You pursue your case, let me pursue mine. No one but the three of us know about Emily or Ms. Madison. As far as anyone else knows, we have an unidentified woman in the morgue and I am pursuing leads. I'm assuming you want this to stay between us?"

"That's right."

"Do you think anyone has been watching the castle, watching you?"

"No. No one has been watching the castle." Alex made periodic checks hoping to catch someone on a stake out. Payton believed him. He looked more than capable of spotting a tail.

"What about the forensic evidence?"

"Scotland Yard has everything. In one way there is too much and in another, not enough. They have hundreds of fibers, grains of dirt, hair, fingerprints, and other interesting debris. They have nothing helpful so far."

"What about suspects? Have you narrowed down who would want to take your wife?"

"Only a little. We have a team in the States working on tracing possible leads." Alex didn't elaborate, Payton didn't ask him to.

Payton got up and looked at Alexander Springfield. He was worried. Sick with it. But it didn't dull his mind. She hoped he'd find his wife alive at the end of this ordeal...sincerely hoped it, but didn't expect it.

Skye tried not to jump and managed to successfully keep her feet on the floor. George. The breast tester. Excellent. If it were only he, she'd punch his ticket right away. She could still feel his filthy hand squeezing her breast. *Budiulo. Figlio di puttana.*

"I thought I'd get my own linens. None were provided in my room." Turning slowly Skye looked into the face of a man who must have been six two, 220. He was actually quite a handsome brute. Nothing in his face or demeanor indicated a sinister nature. She liked her criminals to be evil looking, but what the hell. She intended to kick his ass anyway. Devilishly good looking or not, this guy was going down.

George held his gun loosely. Good. His eyes went down to her chest. Even better. She turned to give him an enhanced view. Purposefully she arched her back a little so her chest would be more prominent in his field of vision.

"I told them you recovered more quickly than what you were letting on. Did you enjoy my attentions? Would you like some more, maybe something harder this time?" He grabbed his crotch with his left hand. God, Skye thought. This guy was a moron. Good looking but stupid. Fine with her. Really good looking scoundrels typically had one common flaw. They were very vain. Pitifully so. Skye could play with that...his ego was going to be his downfall.

Skye snorted and looked him up and down. "Please. I have had better pinches in the back streets of Rome," she said, then paused a beat. "From toothless old men wearing diapers." Bam. Take that.

It hit its mark. "Oh yeah? Well why don't we go up to one of the hundred or so bedrooms in this place and I'll show you what a real man can do."

She snorted again, assessing, calculating. Come a little closer, she thought. She knew the range of her incredibly accurate kick and even though her legs ached from the impact with the door, she was sure she had a few more in her today. "You couldn't keep it up long enough to satisfy me, asshole." That one, too, hit its mark. Her smile was mocking and disdainful in the extreme.

"Forget the bed, bitch. I'm going to show you right here."

He started to reach for her, confident in his size and strength. Standing her ground, she never moved from her spot. She'd positioned herself just where she wanted to be. She'd need room to deliver her one-two punch and he'd need room to fall.

Skye knew he'd come to her. Patience. Steady. She was the cheese; he was the rat, and…then…snap. He never saw it coming. Skye's legs came up, first her right to disarm him, then her left right in the groin. Bull's-eye. Then before he even had time to howl and drop, she spun, bringing her right leg solidly into his face and her left following through. The man was unconscious, on the floor, bleeding from the mouth and nose and Skye hadn't even broken a sweat.

"Not bad on an empty stomach," she said out loud, picking up the gun and searching her man for extra magazines. Finding two, she slipped them into a makeshift backpack she fashioned out of a linen tablecloth. No phone though…damn.

Turning quickly, she went out into the cold. As she ran to the relative safety of the woods, she thought of room service. Hand to hand always made her hungry for rare, red meat. As soon as she got back to the honeymoon castle, she wanted a cow. She smiled as she found her stride and ate up the ground. Soon. She'd be back with her new husband soon.

CHAPTER 8

As the sun came up on another day, Alex heard a phone ring through the fog clouding his brain. He shook his head and looked around. It was the cell phone he kept within arm's reach. His heart lurched and he grabbed at it. Checking the caller ID, he frowned. The number was completely blocked. That wasn't supposed to be possible on this phone. Jim looked over from his laptop, alerted by Alex's reaction.

"Alexander Springfield."

It didn't surprise him when Alex heard Amanda's voice. "Alex, I've been trying to reach Skye. Her phone must be turned off." Or malfunctioning, or destroyed, he thought. He'd been trying to call the number ever since she disappeared. "I knew you would probably be right beside her, so could you put her on. I'm sorry to interrupt your honeymoon, but this is urgent."

"Too late," said Alex softly, his stomach clutching and his heart beating painfully in his chest. Something told him that if Skye had taken this call a few days earlier, she'd not be missing now. "You're too late."

"Oh my God, Alex. Tell me you know where she is." Amanda's voice was controlled, but Alex could hear the apprehension. Loud and clear. Jim was watching Alex's face.

"We don't. She was snatched nearly the minute we arrived. You tell me who has her." Alex's voice was razor sharp and hard as titanium. If Amanda knew something, he was going to find out what it was. Now. "If you know, you tell me."

"We're on our way, Alex. I'm assuming Jim is there." Amanda knew how to handle powerful men.

"He is, but you tell me now. Don't blind-side me on this. I don't give a flying fuck about security right now. You tell me." Alex voice had risen, losing some of the tightly controlled edge.

"Alex," said Amanda firmly. "I'm going to let Jim do that. I'm not going to tell you over this phone."

"Jim knows?" Alex almost shouted the words, glaring at the man across the room. Jim stood up.

"He knows the case. Alex, you'll know soon. I promise. Now hand him the phone. Alex. Do this. I haven't got time to waste convincing you. Skye doesn't have the time." Alex did as she asked, more because of her tone than anything else. He jabbed the phone at Jim. "Amanda," was all he said in explanation.

Jim needed little else. Taking the phone, he listened…only a few minutes…only a few words, but Jim's reaction froze Alex's blood.

"Oh, holy hell," muttered Jim and sat down heavily on the arm of a nearby chair.

Alex watched him and paced like a wild animal. It was exactly how he felt. Wild and untamed. When Jim finished, he pounced.

"Which disk?" asked Alex fiercely. "Which case?"

"Sit down Alex," said Jim solemnly.

"I will not," Alex responded, his eyes narrowed, his stance fierce, nearly violent.

"All right." Jim took a steadying breath. Alex could tell that Amanda shook him up, but he was getting his legs back under him. "All right. The case won't be among those we've been reviewing since I arrived. This one is here." Jim tapped his head. "The records are not in my possession. I'll have to tell it."

"Did Amanda have to give you special dispensation to do so? How long has she known Skye was in jeopardy, for Christ's sake? God damn her! God damn her!" Alex was shouting and pacing. His hands were in fists.

"I'll make allowances because of your exhaustion, Alex. But you better ratchet it back, son. Amanda just found out minutes ago. Now sit down."

Jim's tone made it impossible to do anything but obey. Calming himself with the thought that they at least had something. Finally, something they could use. Taking a deep breath, Alex got his emotions under control and sat down.

"It was one of Skye's most sensitive cases," began Jim. "Pavel Ivanov. An incredibly gifted operator. A twisted sociopath. Completely without conscious, but a genius nonetheless. Very resourceful and bold as hell. He ran weapons, narcotics, women. He worked the southern United States for the Russian mafia. The fall of the USSR infrastructure and the rise of the Russian mob families were like the mother lode of opportunity for him…a very deep and rich one. One of his more insidious ventures was providing female slaves to the mobs to pass onto their Asian counterparts. Lost women from the United States. The Asian crime syndicates had a large appetite for tall, blonde, young, slender women. Sound familiar?"

Alex nodded, a pain shooting through his chest. "Oh Christ," was all he could get out.

"Pavel had a modeling agency as a front for this branch of his operation. He'd recruit women, runaways mostly with no family, promise them fame and fortune and then they would disappear. We were turned onto the whole racket by the sister of one of the women who vanished. The young woman had written her sister about the wonderful modeling job she was offered, then suddenly stopped writing. When the sister went in to make inquiries, she was told that the young woman had never worked for them. She might have believed them, believed that her sister was making up the story to cover for her failure to land a job in the industry but one of the photographers said 'Hi Georgia' when she passed him. Her sister's name was Georgia and they looked a great deal alike. We immediately gave Skye a cover and placed her in the path of Pavel. She was pure gold and he latched onto her so quickly, we couldn't even believe it."

"Did you ever find the sister?"

"Yes and that's what took Skye in deeper than we had initially intended. We were originally going to use her to gather information and trace the location of the illicit stable. Their term," said Jim apologetically as Alex's face got stormier. "Then go in and clean house. But Skye wanted to see if she could locate some of the women who had already been sold."

"So she pushed the limit," said Alex. It was a pattern he recognized from spending the night going through her cases.

Jim nodded. "She was perfect for the op. Credible in the extreme. She took a vacation from her job, she was flying copilot for United back then, and went in deep."

"How deep?" Alex got up and went over to the bar. He opened a bottle of water and tried to extinguish the fire in his burning throat.

"She allowed herself to be delivered." Jim didn't think Alex needed to know the details. "As a matter of fact, we had to extract her from Hong Kong." He smiled slightly. "When she went back to work, she told everyone she'd been vacationing in Thailand. Even had pictures."

"Tell me all of it, Jim," said Alex angrily. He wasn't going to be distracted. "This may be the monster who has my wife and I need to know everything."

Jim hesitated, thought about it, then nodded. "All right, you're right. You need to know everything. Alex…can you turn off the husband and listen as an agent?"

It was Alex's turn to hesitate, but he nodded back. He wasn't sure if he could, but he was sure he wanted to know everything.

"From the beginning, then. Skye applied for a job with Pavel's agency. She knew right away she'd hooked him. He nearly did a tap dance on his desk when she walked in. She was worth a fortune in the Asian market and he meant to use her as the centerpiece for his aggressive new plan to corner the demand for slaves in that corridor."

"Did she…did she have to…" Alex never pried into Skye's past cases. Never really cared to. But something perverse in him wanted to know. Needed to know.

"No. She wouldn't have gone that far. The good news was that they wanted women who had not been used. If not virgins than something close to it."

That surprised Alex. Something like amusement nudged his heart. "I never thought of Skye as virginal. How did she pull that off?"

"She can act, son. Don't forget that." Jim shrugged, smiling a little at the memory. He had the same question when he and Skye had discussed the case. "We gave her a wholesome look. You'd be surprised what she can do with clothes and a different hairdo. She and Linda spent hours in a salon getting it straightened, as I recall. A few freckles dyed into her skin, no makeup, some dental work that gave her a slight overbite and there you have it. A virginal small town homecoming queen. We knew what he was looking for and she played the part. She told him she was from Waterloo, Wisconsin. I'm positive he had to look it up on the map just to be sure there was such a place. She told him her parents were dead and her grandmother was in a nursing home. She was alone in the world and came to South Beach to seek her fortune. As it turned out, he only did a cursory investigation. We had her covered, of course, but she was so dazzling, he didn't really probe too deeply."

"How did he get the women to consent…or did he kidnap them?"

"Some he kidnapped, but that was risky, especially since they were exports and he had to get them out of the country. Mostly, he got them hooked on drugs, amphetamines and cocaine mostly since they did the least amount of damage to their looks…then promised them an unlimited supply."

There was a long, cold silence. "You allowed her to get hooked on drugs?" Alex said in a low, ominous voice.

"Superficially yes. She insisted on it. She faked a lot of it, but couldn't fake it all. We had confidence that when the time came, she'd go in clean."

Alex got up and started pacing. He'd asked for this, but it was killing him. He knew that agents periodically would addict themselves to bring authenticity to their covert work, but it was an extreme move. Too many couldn't kick it when they came out of the case. Not to mention the pain of withdrawal and the life long fight against the lure of getting high. For someone like Skye who hated to lose control for even an evening, this would have taken an emotional toll as well. And this last year she was obsessed with getting off pain medication whenever it was prescribed. Prematurely, in his opinion. This brought so much into focus for him. He ran his fingers through his hair and looked with unseeing eyes out into what promised to be a beautiful day.

Jim could see that Alex had no idea Skye went through any of this. A lick of pride shot through him. His girl, his pride and joy. She kept secrets. He wouldn't have really expected her to keep anything from Alex. He was, after all, a top agent with equal clearance to hers. But for her, the oath was important. Not to be too corny about it, it was sacred to her.

"She never told me any of this," Alex said in a tight voice. "Christ she keeps things close," he said echoing Jim's thoughts. "I knew none of it. Damn it, Jim. You couldn't stop her?"

"Never occurred to me. She used her best judgment and I've learned not to question it." He could see the set of Alex's jaw. "Look Alex. This man was very careful and suspicious. He was evil, but brilliant. Many people in law enforcement had been marked by him, then assassinated. If he even thought she was an agent, she'd have disappeared forever. Nearly did, as it turned out."

"Explain." One word. Alex was used to giving one word orders. Jim was his superior, but in this Alex wouldn't be denied. For his part, Jim felt obliged and knew that his explanations would help get Alex through the revulsion and anger. He accepted Alex's blunt and arbitrary command.

"She went in deep, as I said. We kept track of her through a pair of old, nearly worthless earrings she wore. He was always having surprise searches, making his women strip down. She knew that once she went in, she'd be pretty much on her own. We couldn't fix her with any reliable tracking device. She thought of the earrings. No one ever actually perceives them, she said, unless they're valuable or they sparkle. Plus they're always on the body, even a naked one. She was right."

"She went in with three other women. They went on a photo shoot throughout Scandinavia where four tall blonde women barely get a second glance and were taken from their rooms in the middle of the night. Two addicts went more or less willingly and one was kidnapped. It was an incredible journey. They actually went through Finland to St. Petersburg. According to the information we gathered during the debriefing, they weren't even stopped at the border. Must have been some heavy payoffs.

"Then they flew to Harbin in China. We lost track of her several times. Scared the shit out of me. I didn't sleep for a week. Only my confidence in her kept me hopeful and certain we would hear from her. Our side used the information she gathered along the way in analysis for years." Alex knew that 'our side' meant the CIA. "She found the main vein in the gold mine of the criminal circuit and committed everything to memory."

"How did she get back?" asked Alex, hoping her resourcefulness would once again do its magic and bring her back to him.

"As it turned out, we got a message from her on a plain old low tech telephone. I know you can appreciate this. I'm sitting in my office trying to get Langley to help me put a tracer on the earrings and Pearl comes in as calm as a summer breeze and announces that Skye is on the phone and if I'm not too busy, she'd like to have a chat. She'd bounced the call off a house we kept in Miami. Smart girl. She wanted a record of a call to Miami. They wouldn't be able to trace the number, but the town would be enough."

"How did she get near a phone?" asked Alex, getting caught up in the tale in spite of his horror.

"She'd played the game so well, they left her in an office with a working telephone." Jim told the story, hearing Skye's voice in his head, rushed and breathy, but solid and concise. 'Hey Patriot. They think I'm stoned unconscious. I'm in Harbin at a place called the Rising Sun. Good Grief. These people need another cultural revolution. I'm going to take my three friends out of here along with the records I've collected along the way. The sister is in Hong Kong so that's my next stop. And I have an idea on how to get Pavel. I really, really want this asshole. Most of the women he sent in here are dead. Used and abused and then murdered. We're going to find something to fly and get the hell out of here. Get someone to the Ritz.'

"Needless to say," Jim said with another sigh after giving Alex a word for word account. "That someone was me and a team of people with papers."

"And?" prompted Alex.

"She did just that. She and the three women she was with had been purchased by an old Chinese warlord. He took one look at Skye and decided she was to be his, but he'd been told she was a docile Midwesterner hooked on cocaine and hash. As far as I know, he still hasn't recovered his wits." Jim smiled with the memory of the vivid account delivered by Skye at the debriefing of the lusty elderly man, filled with his self-importance and a perverted wish to dominate the western woman. He came to her shoulder and was apparently looking forward to standing and licking her breasts.

"She herded the three victims to the airport, the warlord's guards in hot pursuit. I swear the woman can smell jet fuel a mile away because she had no map. And Mandarin is a language she doesn't speak. Of course, they had no idea she could fly. She forcefully requisitioned a small jet and flew them to Hong Kong. We were waiting for her at the Ritz, but only the three other women arrived in the taxi from the airport. They were in pretty bad shape, but we got them and the information they brought with them wrapped up. Skye had decided to go in after the sister. Well, some really pissed off Russians were there along with a number of the Chinese Mafioso. It was a pretty bad scene. The sister had been dead for about a month. Apparently the women didn't last long once they were purchased."

Alex had been pacing again, but now he sat down. His knees felt like they'd been rubberized. "And?"

"Skye improvised, of course. She decided somewhere along the way that she was going to deliver her own brand of justice, so she let the Russians convince her to confess her true purpose."

"Convince her?"

Jim just stared at Alex. Did he really want all of it? Alex nodded.

"She...she allowed herself to be tortured. Primitive stuff, thank God. Electrical shock."

"Oh sweet Christ," whispered Alex as he closed his eyes and rested his head back against the soft leather chair. This was just getting uglier and uglier.

"You know she's tough, Alex. She had to allow some of it to add to her credibility. She told them Pavel had arranged her escape and that he had leaked information for years. She knew they would trace her call to Miami...Pavel's home base. When the Russian government started acting on her intelligence over the next few weeks it pretty much guaranteed they'd go after Pavel."

"How the hell did you get her out of there?"

"We always had an ace in the hole. Langley had an asset in place. A man at the high command in the Chinese mafia. He orchestrated her escape and they made it look like a Pavel connection again. She flew into Miami and disappeared."

"What happened to Pavel?" Alex wanted a piece of him. Preferably his heart.

"We believed the Russians got to him off the coast of Miami. His cruiser exploded and sunk."

"His body was never found?"

"No. And from what Amanda told me, it appears he staged it himself." Jim looked directly into Alex's eyes. "She thinks he's back and he has Skye."

"So Pavel is the person who took her?" Maybe he could take the man's heart after all. The blood lust gave him a rush and he felt energy come back into his limbs.

"Amanda thinks he masterminded it, yes," Jim nodded. "She'll have more for us when she gets here. She and Cameron are on their way. I suggest you get some sleep. Linda and Barclay can concentrate their efforts on getting as much as we can on him."

"No. No sleep," said Alex, his jaw clenching and unclenching. "I want the details now. All of them. Everything you can remember."

CHAPTER 9

By early afternoon, Payton came to give Alex another report. There wasn't anything of apparent interest in Emily's room at the rehab center. She left nothing behind.

"She didn't make many calls. Only three that were recorded. One was to the former boyfriend in Paris. One was to a number no longer in service. We think that may have been her drug connection. They buy disposable cell phones and change their number frequently. And the third was to her agency." Payton looked at her notes. "The Grenger Modeling Agency on Michigan Avenue in Chicago, Illinois."

"Where?"

"Chicago."

Alex looked at Jim. A connection. "We've confirmed that the people who have Skye could have found out about our destination from a computer located in Chicago."

"I'll want to interview the person who owns the computer," she said. "Name?"

"No." He could imagine Payton interrogating his mother. That would be an interesting interview.

"No? Mr. Springfield. May I remind you I'm working a murder investigation. And that the perpetrators are probably the same people who have your wife. Now, I've backed off the kidnapping investigation at the request of some very powerful people, but Emily, if that's who she is, bloody well deserves to have someone working for her with equal diligence and passion."

Alex looked at the heightened color in her cheeks.

"All right. You're right. Okay. We think that they got the location from my mother's computer."

"Your mother?"

"Yes, she did all the research. We wanted to keep everything a secret from Skye. She worked on a relatively unsecured computer, although our resident compu-geek said it would take more than a casual hacker to get the information at that. I'll handle the contact and report."

"All right then, but I still want her name for my records." Payton persisted. What the hell, thought Alex.

"Wyatt Cooper."

Payton stared at him for a moment. "Your mother is Wyatt Cooper? Captain Wyatt Cooper of the Chicago police department?"

"You know her?"

"What woman in law enforcement doesn't? She's a bloody legend. I've never met her, but I heard her speak at an international summit. She was brilliant."

That made Alex smile. To him, she was Mom. He sometimes forgot she wasn't just the woman who raised him. She was the remarkable Captain Cooper.

"I could arrange for you to meet someday...I have an inside track."

"I would love that." Payton nodded, impressed. But all that would have to wait. "Now, is there anything more you can tell me about your wife, her disappearance?"

"No. Nothing at this point." Everything Jim told him was incredibly classified. He was being truthful to Payton. He couldn't tell her anything new. "The pieces are falling into place on the who, but we still don't know where. Or if she's even in the country."

Something had been bothering him all night. Something on the edge of his memory. "I keep thinking I'm missing something. Why don't you order some lunch from room service. I want to go back to the beginning. I want to think."

Payton nodded. It was something he needed to do. That and get a few hours sleep, she thought.

Alex left the room and walked out onto the terrace. He reached in his pocket and took out the compass. Did he imagine it pointing in the wrong direction the day before?

"Skye," he whispered. "I know I'm missing something." He tried to use her method of deduction and reasoning. First, she'd empty her mind, then methodically review all the clues, all the data. When she found the right combination it would open the safe in her mind. Behind the door would be the answer. The trouble was, he was sure he was missing a vital number in the combination. At least his conscious mind was missing it. Something was plaguing him. Something he saw? Something he heard? Something he should know?

He took a deep breath, closed his eyes and emptied his mind. He started with the drive up the road to the castle and conjured up every detail, every conversation, every feeling. Every wave of intuition. He stood completely motionless, only his mind moving.

Jim watched him from the doorway. Payton came up beside him. "Is he all right?"

"Yes. I was just standing here thinking he looks like Skye when she's on a hunt."

"A hunt?"

"A hunt through her mind. In search of the information she needs to close in on a conclusion. She's quite remarkable. People often see the incredible outer package first. She's a beauty, but it's her brain that I know she's most proud of."

When Alex got to the image of her being taken, of her leaving her wings before she lost consciousness, he stopped. Would she have had time to leave him something else? The wings were not out in the open, but partially hidden so the people who took her wouldn't see and remove the evidence. What if she had a few more seconds? Could she have left another clue? Could the wings have been meant to stop him? Could they have been pointing at something else?

Damn, he'd been so busy with the cases, establishing the identity of the kidnappers, and uncovering how they'd known, that he was sloppy on the observation and development of the actual scenario. Putting himself into her place, her space, her mind.

She was being taken…he was pretty much convinced she'd been drugged. She was fading fast, unable to fight. She'd unhooked her wings, maybe she was being held by one of the kidnappers, but a hand must have been free. A hand…Alex shifted his position so suddenly, that Payton nearly jumped. He turned and there was something on his face besides fatigue and determination. There was anticipation. There was optimism.

"What?" asked Jim as Alex walked with purpose back into the room.

"I need to go back to where she was taken. I have an idea."

"But we've searched the area. Quite thoroughly."

"Exactly. If she left me something it would be well hidden."

"But," started Payton, then she was talking to an empty room. Jim had followed Alex back down to the library.

"I remembered something," said Alex and he strode into the library. "I remember thinking when I went through here that this room had everything from Dickens to Disney." He stopped in front of the video section. It was near the place he'd found the wings pinned to the curtains. His fingers traced down the row of Disney productions and he almost couldn't believe his eyes when he saw the copy of Aladdin. He stared at it a minute. There were two copies. It appeared as though Aladdin had a sequel. What if he'd been wrong and there was nothing there? Could he handle the disappointment? The frustration? Yes.

He pulled out the first video case and opened it up. Nothing but the tape itself. His stomach tightened even more. He pulled out the sequel. He almost thought he imagined the card that popped out when he opened the plastic case. She must have wedged it in through the top slot.

"Damn it Skye," he said under his breath as something like elation flooded through him. "You know how to fly."

It was a card. A business card, with a number on the back. Not much but right now they were miles from where they'd been a minute ago. Turning, Alex grinned at Jim and Payton. "Snow White left us a clue."

"I beg your pardon?" asked Jim.

"It's a long story."

"And no doubt classified," frowned Payton.

"Afraid so."

"Something that isn't classified is the fact that my wife is a consummate pick pocket.

She apparently was able to nip this from one of her abductors, then put it where I'd find it. Damn. I almost missed it."

"But you didn't," said Payton before Alex could berate himself. She wanted him to stay on track, not concern himself with the timing. "And she knew you wouldn't. What is it and what does it mean?"

"It's a business card and it has a phone number on the back. Mean anything to you?" He showed the card to Payton, holding it along the sides so he wouldn't disturb the prints on it.

"Carlton Manor. It's a Bed and Breakfast about an hour from here. Up in the highlands. Very remote. But it's seasonal. There would be no one there..." She looked up at Alex, then over at Jim and nodded. She could see they were already there. "Perfect place to hold someone."

"Exactly," said Alex, already heading for the door.

"Can I call for backup?" she asked, suspecting she knew the answer to that one.

"You *are* the backup," responded Alex.

"I'm driving," insisted Payton. "Neither of you have reflexes left."

As they left the library, Alex nearly ran right into Amanda and Cameron. They were dressed in high fashion and looking like a nice British couple off in search of tea.

"The butler at the front door told us he saw you come in here." Amanda looked meaningfully at Payton. "May we speak with you in private, Mr. Springfield?"

"No. Sorry. We have reason to believe we've found where they're holding Skye. We have no time right now. Inspector Payton Brady, I'd like to introduce you to..." Alex looked at Amanda and Cameron and said the first thing that came to his mind. "Lord and Lady Hyde-Smith."

Payton nodded as they all rushed down the stairs. "Yeah. Sure. If you say so."

"Come, we have a limo right outside," said Amanda.

Payton turned to Jim and Alex. "I suggest you take a minute to fetch coats. Also change into boots. We'll want to hike in. We're going up and there'll be snow. The good news is that the house is nestled in among a forest of pine. We should be able to get fairly close without being detected."

Alex and Jim nodded and did as she suggested. Payton grabbed her jacket, maps, binoculars, and rifle from her squad car and met them in front of a sleek black limousine. Cameron held the front door open for her. "Inspector, you can ride in front and direct the driver to our destination."

Payton didn't miss the fact that as soon as they took their seats in the auto, the privacy screen went up and she was effectively blocked out of the conversation. Suppressing the irritation she felt for about the hundredth time on this investigation, she let the rush of following an excellent clue sustain her.

"Tell us everything," said Cameron and Jim filled them in while Alex called the number on the back of the card.

"Nothing," he said when they turned to him. "No message, just the click and buzz of an answering machine."

"Perhaps it's a report number or maybe a relay." A relay number was most likely. Several people with the same number, and an answering machine with a shared code to get the messages were an excellent method of communication when direct calls were either impossible or unwise. Alex nodded and looked out the window. He rubbed the compass in his pocket. Something inside him felt close. Close to Skye.

Cameron got on his phone. "I'll have it checked out." A few seconds later he got a response. "It's a new number. Chances are we'll find the machine there."

An hour later, they pulled up a half mile from the Carlton Manor. The screen came down.

"I suggest Lord and Lady Whatever that you stay here. Your attire may be fine for tea, but we're going to be walking through the woods. We can call you with what we find. This is going to be reconnaissance, right?"

"Right," said Alex, but Payton saw him chamber a round in his gun and place it in a handy pocket. She couldn't fault him for that as she had done the same.

"Ready?" she asked.

"Yes," said Jim and Alex together.

Jim, Alex, the driver, a young man who obviously was more than a driver, and Payton walked swiftly through the dense woods. Soon, they could see the roof of the centuries old manor house. Payton brought her binoculars to her eyes.

"I don't see anything moving. No sign of life. There are some tracks, but that could be from the owners checking on the place. Nothing looks very fresh…it snowed the day before last."

They all had their guns drawn and ready. "Let's take a closer look," said Alex. He was getting a sinking feeling in his stomach. Had someone else put the card there, maybe months ago? Even if she'd put the card there, it only meant she lifted it from one of her abductors. It didn't automatically follow that she'd be held here. Maybe it was only the phone number that was significant.

They got closer and soon it was apparent the place was deserted. There was no movement inside or outside the large refurbished farmhouse. None of the few tracks were made after the snowfall and snow pretty much surrounded the house.

"Unless they flew in there, I don't see how they could have gotten in without making footprints," said Payton.

"Let's go in," said Alex, hardly able to contain his disappointment. All of a sudden he was exhausted again. The adrenalin was draining out of him leaving a feeling of bitter frustration.

"The window or the door?" asked Jim, feeling Alex's distress and sharing it. Less than two hours ago, it seemed it all fit so well.

"I know where the owners keep the key. I called them from the limo and told them we wanted to check the place out," said Payton. Alex looked at her. She was sure handy to have around.

"Might as well use the key," he said heavily.

Payton nodded and went to the shed in the rear of the property. She came back a few minutes later. "Ready?" Alex and Jim nodded. "Right in the back door, then." She started toward the door, but Alex put his hand on her shoulder.

"No. I'm in first." Payton saw he needed to be the first one in. She handed him the key with no argument. "Jim take the front, Payton take your pick. Raymond," he said to the driver. "You stay here."

"I think I'll go in right behind you, Alex," said Payton softly, her heart was hurting for him.

Alex knew it could be worse. They could have found Skye injured or dead. Instead they found nothing. Someone had jimmied the lock in back and had placed an answering machine in one of the downstairs bedrooms. Jim, Payton and Alex searched every inch of the large old house and found nothing else. Raymond had gone back and brought the car up the drive.

Amanda and Cameron were sitting in the living room with Jim. Raymond was left outside to watch the driveway in case someone decided to check the machine in person. No one actually thought that was going to happen. Ever. They suspected that after the kidnappers got what they wanted, the messages would be erased as easily as the fingerprints.

They listened to the messages on the machine. At least the clue gave them something. It was indeed a relay between two factions. The man who arranged it, presumably Pavel, and the team who carried out the murder and kidnapping. Nothing really incriminating was on the tape until it was put into context.

"We've arrived. The package you suggested is perfect. She loves the candy you sent for her."

"That must be in reference to Emily. The candy is drugs. That was the hook," said Alex. They all nodded.

"Timing is everything. Be bold. Don't be stealthy."

"They know that Skye would be more inclined to detect surreptitious movement and be alerted," said Jim.

"Our guest is all fired up." Payton winced on that one. They were horrible people. They were obviously referring to the body they torched.

"We hear the prince has not been seen. We aren't sure he's well informed."

"Excellent. And how is our priceless princess?"

"The princess is iced. She took a walk, but we got her back where she belongs"

"Do not dent the merchandise. Our customer demands perfection."

"We're ready for the client."

Alex leaned heavily on the hands he'd planted on either side of the machine, relief pouring through him. "Sounds like she's alive," he said.

Amanda nodded and smiled grimly "And that she's giving them some trouble."

Thank you, God, Alex thought. Alive and well.

He nearly jumped out of his skin when the phone rang. It was all he could do to control his desire to pick it up and shout at the man on the phone. Demand the location of Skye. The answering machine clicked, a code was delivered and the last message was played. Then a voice, Pavel's voice, came on.

"The customers will be there at 18:00. Turn over the merchandise. If they want you to stay, do so, but they will be taking ownership. Contact me on our secondary number when you get to London. I'll check this number as usual every day at 8:00 my time in case you have anything more to report." Everyone automatically checked their watches. The man was in the central time zone. "Be sure you call with any instructions given to you by the customer. Check our secondary number for travel instructions on Sunday."

After he hung up, Cameron was the first to speak. "All right, what do we know?"

"She's alive but she's going to be turned over to someone in less than 6 hours," said Alex pacing and trying to think.

"Six hours to find her," said Payton, as they all began pouring over maps she brought in. They were going on the assumption that she was close to this location.

"What about this castle?" asked Alex pointing at a dot on the map. "How far?"

"About ten kilometers. It is very, very exclusive. The owners rent it out by the month for a bloody fortune."

Everyone was looking at all the local possibilities, each registering an opinion. They began circling abandoned farmhouses, castles, and remote cottages.

"Damn, six hours and at least a hundred potential targets."

"That's too many, let's try to narrow it down."

"Will you let me bring in a team now?" asked Payton.

"I've just called in our own people," said Cameron.

Payton suppressed her annoyance once again.

"Which ones would be the most likely?" asked Alex. "I want to move out."

"Let's create a grid," said Jim. "We have to do this systematically."

"We have to do this *now!*" shouted Alex, straightening.

"There are six of us. Each of us should lead a different team," suggested Amanda.

Alex slammed his hand on the maps. "Continue your planning. I'm going to try and find her. We only have six fucking hours!"

"Then perhaps you all should combine your incredible investigatory skills…" said a seventh voice from the doorway, "and turn around."

CHAPTER 10

They all spun around as one and for a heartbeat, no one could react. Alex actually thought he might have conjured her up from his fatigued brain or hallucinated a vision from the wishful part of his heart. He almost asked Jim, 'do you see what I see?' There leaning against the doorframe bathed in the bright sunlight was Skye. Dirty, disheveled and with a look of utter exhaustion etched on her face, but smiling in a cocky, self satisfied way that had them all grinning back. An automatic response. A spit second later, Alex unfroze and rushed to her. She met him halfway.

"Skye," said Alex softly. Then louder as he gathered her into his arms and took his first deep breath since he'd entered the empty suite. "Skye!"

He lifted her off her feet, closed his eyes and just allowed himself a moment to feel her body melt into his. He couldn't think, couldn't speak. He was pure, raw emotion. Skye could actually feel him tremble and decided to stay silent for a few more moments. What was with him? She'd only been missing, what? Two days?

"So Aladdin, you got my little message?" she grinned at him. "I saw the sign for this place up the road and knew it was my next stop. Good thing too. I'm just about done."

"Where did you come from?" asked Jim, beaming, wanting to hug Skye himself, but bowing to Alex's superior claim. Alex wasn't about to share. His arms were wrapped around her and he intended them to stay that way for about the next decade.

Skye turned in Alex's arms. "The back door. You left it unlocked. And that driver is adorable, but needs a little more seasoning. Got right by him." She said it so nonchalantly that Jim laughed.

She looked around at the assembled group. "Well, I see you brought out the big guns. Imagine my shock when I thought I'd break in for whatever was in the refrigerator and wait for you to come rescue me and I saw all of you standing here. I thought for a minute I was hallucinating."

Skye smiled at Payton, who could see she was fading fast. Now that she was safely in the arms of her husband, she appeared as though she was liquefying. "I'm guessing you're the local?"

Alex performed the dramatic introduction. "Well, Payton, here's the woman we've been looking for. Apparently she didn't need rescuing after all. Inspector Payton Brady, Skyler Madison. My wife."

"It's glad I am to see you, Ms. Madison," said Payton with a genuine smile. "And when you're feeling up to it, we would like to have a report on how you've spent your honeymoon so far."

Skye laughed. It was weak, but it was game.

"It sure did take a wrong turn." Skye took her hand. "Inspector. I'm sure it will be a pleasure when I've had the opportunity to bathe, eat and sleep for a week." She swayed and Alex's grip tightened on her waist. "Forgive me, but I think I'd like to sit down."

She smiled up at Alex who directed her to a couch. "You look like shit," she said touching his unshaven cheek.

"Been in front of a mirror lately?" he asked grinning. She was here. In his arms. And he knew he wasn't dreaming. He was awake and he could see the pulse beating in her throat. Alive. A little wrecked, but well.

"I was just on my way to the salon," she said as they sat down. They stared at each other, not speaking, but communicating nonetheless.

Alex looked at her odd assortment of shirts and tops and the oversized boots. "I see you went shopping."

"Yeah, the butler lost my luggage."

Smiling at this indomitable woman, Payton took out her cell phone.

"What are you doing?" asked Cameron.

"Calling for backup. The people who took her are going to try to get her back. They could track her here."

"No. Please don't do that. We need to debrief Skye and assess the situation," he replied steadily.

"I'm going to call for backup," said Payton, just as steadily. Cameron was both imposing and commanding. Payton didn't care. "Ms. Madison is involved in an open case I'm working on. This is a police matter, not a situation."

"Jim, may I use your phone? It's secure, I'm assuming?" asked Amanda.

"It is." Jim pulled it out and handed it to her.

Payton sighed and looked at Amanda. "You're going to give me a number to call, right?" She looked over at Jim who just smiled an enigmatic smile.

"I am."

"Lord Justice General again?"

"No, but I think you'll recognize the man's name."

"All right, give me the number." Because she was a good and thorough investigator, Payton called it and confirmed that she did indeed know the name. Everyone in law enforcement knew the name of the director of MI5, Great Britain's equivalent of the CIA.

Amanda watched as Payton dialed the number. Rather than be offended by it, she admired her greatly for her thoroughness and lack of complete trust. This inspector was taking nothing for granted. She observed as Payton asked questions and listened carefully to the answers.

On the trip up here, the man on the other end of the secure phone did a deep background check on Payton Brady and had given Amanda a verbal dossier. It was pretty impressive. That, combined with Amanda's intuition gave Payton field clearance. She wouldn't be in on everything, but enough to satisfy her. He'd also suggested at the end of his report that Amanda might want to do a little recruiting while she was on the island.

"All right," said Payton, a little testy, but game. She slapped the phone back into Jim's hand. "You're calling the shots."

Amanda nodded.

"But there will be a price."

Amanda raised her eyebrow. "And that would be?"

"You tell me as much as you can, include me in both the planning and execution and let me do my job when this is over. If you expect me to trust you, then trust me."

Amanda and Payton went glare for stare. Payton passed that test too. Amanda nodded. "Agreed." She then turned to Skye and smiled. "Are you up to filling us in? Nothing detailed." She checked her watch. "Just the highlights."

"That's all I have," admitted Skye. "I was out a lot of the time." She could feel Alex tense, so she explained quickly. "Drugs, darling. Nothing too painful." Her voice was reassuring, but Alex remained edgy.

Now that she was sitting, some of her energy was returning. She looked around at the familiar faces. "Let me start from the beginning. There were only three of them. Hell. They got me right on the fucking stairs. It's humiliating. My only excuse was my body was aching for…" she looked at Alex and grinned…she did a Skye eye dance and let the implication stretch, then finished her sentence. "A hot shower…and I was looking at everything in the castle all at once. Well, let's just say I was distracted by both anticipation of physical pleasure and my incredible surroundings. Damn, I guess I was gawking like a tourist and horny as a Derby winner. No excuse, though. I actually smiled at this couple as they were coming out of the library."

Skye was too tired to pace, but her voice moved around the room instead. "Good God. I should have smelled something but my internal nefarious villain meter must have been completely dormant. Anyway I felt a little pinch on my neck and the world started spinning immediately. They tranquilized me like an elephant on Wild fucking Kingdom. But I picked the guy's pocket and managed to shake off the effects for a few seconds. When they yanked me past Disney, I knew I could leave something without them seeing. I did a little weaving and heaving, left my clue, then everything went dark. I woke up in a goddamn dungeon. A real one. No prop." She quickly reported on her misadventure.

Payton listened with admiration and noted the woman's resilience, courage and resourcefulness. Everyone else was already familiar with these attributes.

"And Alex," to everyone's surprise, Skye's eyes teared up. Sniffing, she caught her breath, then found her self-control, and went on. "Alex, they took my rings. The bastards took my rings. Let's go run down those son-of-a-bitches and get them back."

She looked down at her bare hand and a tear escaped out of the corner of her eye. Everything else they did to her pissed her off and got her fired up. This act hurt her heart.

Alex immediately took her left hand and kissed it. He looked up at Payton then back to his wife. "Payton has them, darling."

"Payton?" Nothing could have surprised her more. Or confused her. She looked at everyone, then back at her husband. There was something more in his eyes and on his face than the reaction to the kidnapping. Something deeper and much more excruciating. Something raw. The tears died up immediately and she frowned. "What the hell's been going on out here?"

Alex told her the rings had been discovered on a corpse in an attempt at misdirection, leaving out many of the details for now. He'd fill her in later. Skye felt the disquiet in his heart, however, and saw some of the residual horror in his eyes. She thought she'd seen more than fatigue there right from the beginning and she felt more than his relief when he held her. He'd gone through a nightmare and she knew what a beating that could be to the soul.

"I'll return them to you as quickly as I can, Ms. Madison," said Payton.

"Skye, please." She could feel Alex's muscles tighten through the fabric of his shirt and decided they would leave the subject for now. She knew where her rings were and that was enough. Alex needed a break right now. "So, who took me?" she asked looking up at him. "I gave you…what…two days?"

"Over four," said Alex grimly, the shadows still in his eyes.

"Whoa. No wonder I'm so hungry. Anyway, I'm sure you have it all figured out. Right?" She looked around the room and said cheerfully. "So fill me in."

That made them all smile. She'd been kidnapped, drugged, imprisoned, escaped a dungeon, traveled several miles in near frigid weather, some of it through very treacherous terrain, and her natural inclination was still professional curiosity.

"We do indeed have a name. One I think you'll recognize," said Cameron. He turned to Payton apologetically. "I am sorry, but there are significant elements of this conversation we need to keep close."

"All right," said Payton, miffed, but ready to cooperate. She could still hear the voice of one of the most powerful men in the free world in her ear. According to him, Amanda and Cameron were running the show. She nodded. "Let me see what I can do to find Skye some coffee."

Skye grinned over at her. "Run for prime minister and I'll guarantee your victory. And if there's anything edible out there, I'll see what I can do about a coronation. And think of 'edible' in very broad terms. I'm starving. Those cretins who had me were not playing by the rules of the Geneva Convention, that's for sure."

Payton smiled at Skye and nodded. For this resilient woman, Payton would go out and shoot wild game if she had to. She left the room and closed the door. "She's good, isn't she?" asked Skye.

Alex nodded.

"So come on, tell me. I can see from all your faces that you know."

"Pavel," said Amanda simply.

"But that son-of-a-bitch is dead." She looked around. "Oh. So. That son-of-a-bitch is *not* dead. Well, hell."

"We have an asset in Russia, planted deeply in the mafia. When Cameron left your wedding he went to Langley," Amanda's eyes moved over to Cameron. "That's a suburb of Dayton."

"Akron."

"Yes, of course. Anyway, he went to translate some important communication from her. She apparently was the one who nudged in Sloane's direction the data you used in your guidance system case. But more importantly, one of the documents held a reference to you. We tried to call you, but you'd already been taken."

"Reference to me? Damn. I don't know whether to be shocked or flattered."

"Maybe a little of both. Anyway, the reference was not to Skyler Madison, of course, but to Virginia Montgomery."

"The role that keeps on giving."

"Indeed. Pavel had contacted people in the high command and offered to turn you over to them. Luckily, he didn't reveal your true identity. I'm sure that's his insurance. His confidence that he could bargain with you led us to believe he had a plan in place to abduct you at some point. We certainly didn't think it would be here, or this soon," said Amanda, reaching over and taking Skye's hand.

"He wants to come back into the fold and thinks you're his ticket in. He apparently staged his own death and now wants to come back to life. He must be tired of hiding," added Cameron.

"But why me? How did I get on their hit parade? Why am I so important to these people? I passed through their system what...six years ago? I was barely a blip."

Cameron looked at Amanda. Alex felt a storm brewing in his head.

"You've had a price on your head for the last six years."

"A price on my head? My head?" Skye couldn't have been more astonished. She looked over at Jim to see if he knew about this and from his expression, he didn't. That astonished her even more.

"Yes. The equivalent of one million dollars."

"Hey now," she said grinning. "That's impressive."

Alex had an opposite reaction. "Skye had a price on her head...a million dollar bounty...and no one at Langley thought to give her that little bit of critical data?" he asked in a cold, controlled voice. He was beyond furious. He could feel the muscles in his jaw tense from the effort to control his temper.

"Or her Director?" added Jim, his own fury obvious in his voice.

"It really wasn't considered that significant," explained Cameron. "No one knew her name, her true identity or the fact that she had U.S. government ties. As a matter of fact, it was noted, then practically forgotten."

Skye shook her head to clear it. "Chill, guys. Cameron is right. But one million…holy shit. That's a load of cabbage. And Pavel wants to collect?"

"No, actually the money is incidental. He wants to come back into the family. He wants to come out of hiding and he figures if he delivers you, all will be forgiven."

"The guy was always delusional. They aren't going to forgive and forget."

"No, probably not."

"Why a million dollars?" asked Jim going back to what he felt was the most essential detail. He was still very angry and wanted further explanation. "There's no way a drugged-out reluctant slave would command that kind of money." Jim smiled grimly at Skye. "Sorry honey. You're priceless to us, but let's be realistic."

"There are likely a couple of reasons for that," began Cameron. "You only know the story from the moment you began the operation until the time you escaped. Our asset in Hong Kong, the man who assisted you, Skye, updated us. Your absence caused a real furor…on a number of levels. First of all, we think the man who purchased you was someone of great importance and that he was quite set on having you. Apparently you met?"

Skye snorted at the remembered meeting. "Actually it was more like an inspection."

"Well it sounded like love at first sight," said Amanda, approval in her eyes for the young agent. No trauma here. Just clear thinking. Well, she was going to need it. It wasn't over.

"More like lust. He was this old guy, but I could tell he was used to getting his own way, getting what he wanted. He spoke in French and was quite taken with the fact that I could respond fluently. I really needed him to trust me, so I did what I could to build a rapport."

"Some of us old guys haven't lost our taste for the finer things," smiled Cameron charmingly, his eyes sliding to his wife.

"Plus he didn't seem in any hurry to…ah…" She looked at Alex. "To consummate the arrangement. So then it occurred to me that at his advanced age maybe he couldn't…well…perform, shall we say." Her voice turned teasing and she winked at Cameron.

"I guess it happens." Cameron's smile broadened as did his admiration for this young woman. He'd always seen the beauty and her record was impressive, but he was assessing her heart and her grit while telling the story. Determining if she had the fortitude to play the game he had in mind.

"Anyway," said Amanda continuing the briefing. For that was what this was, Jim thought, his stomach tightening. This was preparation, setting groundwork, not simply reporting. Alex was holding Skye, lost in his relief and missed the nuances Jim picked up. Amanda and Cameron were here for another reason, he was sure of it. "You didn't know this because the game you were playing was spontaneous and you improvised brilliantly as you went along, but the Chinese family that Pavel and his Russian contacts were dealing with is the most powerful underworld family in the region. The family, headed by a man named Sung Du, lost a great deal of face when he had to admit to this powerful warlord that you were no longer available."

"Oh, well. I guess I'm not sorry I inconvenienced the son-of-a-bitch."

Amanda looked at Cameron who nodded slightly. She went on. "There's more, of course. In addition to assisting in your breakout, our man fed the pipeline with rumors that you had been sent to assassinate several key people. To close down Pavel, we made sure the rumors included him in the plot. His reputation for ruthlessness and instability fed nicely into the scenario."

"Why would they believe I was sent to assassinate anyone?"

Amanda looked steadily at Skye, then said the words just as Skye herself figured it out.

"There were actually several assassinations. We took advantage of the situation and fed information to a rival faction. They took out three of the people who stood between our man and the executive level of the criminal cartel. It elevated him to the highest position in the pyramid we've ever been able to attain. There has been no greater operation in the scheme of things over there and it all happened spontaneously. We put it into play almost without any plan at all, certainly without a great deal of deliberation. Perhaps that's why it worked so flawlessly. When Jim called for assistance, to get an agent out of the very pit of vipers we hoped to shake up, well," she shrugged. "The opportunity was too good to pass up."

"You used Skye," said Alex, his voice as hard as steel. This time his sarcasm and resentment weren't contained in a sheath of civility.

"We rescued Skye," said Amanda in a tone that equaled Alex's in steel and ice. "We then used the situation."

"Well the situation doesn't have a price on its head, does it? The situation isn't flesh and blood. The situation didn't just go through the last six years vulnerable and unaware." Alex was shouting now, completely ignoring Jim's warning looks. "The situation isn't being hunted. Damn you. Skye isn't a situation."

Skye shook her head at Jim and he nodded. He'd let her handle it.

"Alex," she said, putting her hand on his vibrating arm, forcing him through her penetrating stare to look at her. "I think what they did was brilliant. Don't lose sight of the fact that without Amanda, I'd most certainly be dead. Dead and cold for the last six years. Or perhaps worse. Alive, enslaved, addicted, and living in hell. The man who helped me out did so at great personal risk. I'll forever be grateful to him. Alex, think about it. They didn't know who I was…not my name, my identity, not the fact that I worked for Justice. I disappeared. No way to trace me. Then Pavel disappeared." She could feel some of the tension leave his body. He went from absolutely rigid to merely stiff. Seeing the truth through her eyes, he nodded. He'd turn down the heat. "The mission was completely contained. It should have been over."

"And the cartel moved on to other things until a few weeks ago when Pavel contacted them through his former network."

"So somehow Pavel found out who I was," said Skye.

"Yes. My guess is that he saw the news coverage from last summer's hijacking. You were on the cover of *Newsweek*, for Christ's sake, before we could stop it. There are still hundreds of covers out there we haven't been able to replace."

"When did he contact the family in Russia?"

"September 28th."

"Alex. Do you remember that night in Chicago when I thought someone was following us? That was about a month ago. We were with Wyatt, Blake and Tank. Anyone from Chicago, especially someone with criminal tendencies would know your mother. She's forever on the news. You told me that Barclay thought someone could get our honeymoon location through your mom's computer. It all fits."

"And from what Payton has been able to uncover, the model who was killed to replace you was from Evanston and worked for a modeling agency in Chicago."

"I know what our next stop is going to be," said Skye with feeling. Then she frowned, trying to put some pieces together. "But why here? Why in Scotland?"

"I think partially because there is much less security. Our home and offices are very closed," said Alex. Then adding something else that had occurred to him while listening to all the details of the original case. "Also, look at the geography. They want you. A million dollars worth. We have already ascertained they want you alive. To get you from the U.S. over there would be problematic. In the extreme. From here, however, they could take you by small plane or helicopter. They could fly over water, get into Sweden and use the same route they took when they had you originally…through St. Petersburg. You reported in your debriefing you weren't even stopped going the northern route. They must have almost believed in a higher power when they discovered we were planning on being in Scotland."

"And they hoped to have me out of the country before you discovered the body they planted wasn't me…if ever."

"Exactly. And someone is coming in tonight at 18:00."

"Let me get cleaned up and get a cup of coffee and we can be up there to meet them."

Alex grinned at her with a mixture of pride and exasperation. He was going to insist that she rest, see a doctor, stand down, and let him lead the team back in to settle the score, but she gave him the 'don't even think about it' look and forced him to put aside the husband and bring forward the professional partner. He swore that her audacity and nonchalance about her ordeal was taking him one step closer to insanity, but what the hell. At this point he wasn't inclined to deny her anything. It felt so good just to sit and look at her face.

Cameron sat back and watched Skye and Alex exchange thoughts and ideas. He was completely relaxed and very impressed. Amanda and Jim were simply letting them go. Both had been exhausted and drained a few minutes before, but as their strategies took shape, their combined energy gained focus and their conclusions were sharp and in his opinion, accurate. He looked at Skye, knowing he hadn't seen anything like her since...well, since Mandy.

"The good news here is that they wanted me alive," said Skye.

"Thank God," said Alex.

"They needed what's in your brain," said Cameron. Jim nodded. That was his original thought. "They want the name or names of the people who helped you escape. And, from what we can gather from our Russian source, they want to return you to the man who made the original purchase. It's a matter of honor."

"Ah. That's why they didn't rough me up the first time I tried to check out of their room from hell."

"Right," said Alex and Skye could feel his hand tense up. "And since they wanted to get her out of the country undetected and run no chance of having someone pursuing her, they staged her death."

"Sounds like Pavel's style. After all, it worked for him. So when do we move in on the castle?" Skye was ready to kick some more ass.

Alex couldn't take his eyes off Skye or he'd have caught a very powerful look between Cameron and Amanda, along with her slight nod. Jim caught it and decided he needed to sit down. Whatever was coming next was going to be tough.

Cameron pulled up a chair and sat down in front of Skye. Amanda stood behind him and placed her hand on his shoulder. In the silence, they all could feel his intensity and finally Alex dragged his gaze from his wife to the enigmatic man. Alex didn't like the grieved cast in his eye or the solemn look on his face.

"Skye," Cameron's voice was steady and commanding. She immediately sat up straighter and was prepared to pay attention. He had something important to say and he had to say it to her. "We came to warn you, but we also came...to recruit you. I want you to listen to me...to hear me out."

Skye looked into his solemn gray eyes. She was sure no one ever said no to him, but she'd hear what he had to say first. She nodded. Alex froze.

"The individual who helped you out of Hong Kong is still in place. Instead of being a minor minion, he has risen to a seat near the top. The top man, his immediate superior is Sung Du himself and he's just been diagnosed with pancreatic cancer, advanced."

"Justice," Skye said with feeling.

"Agreed. He has maybe six months. We would like to have our man chosen as his successor."

"Of the whole western territory? My God. What a coup. Is that possible?" asked Skye, impressed.

"There's only one other viable contender. A man, who if he becomes the head of the west, will not be able to co-exist with our man. It is vital that he not be chosen. If he is, our only asset is invalidated and we are out. Probably through assassination. After nearly fourteen years of unbelievable service, our man's reward might very well be a bullet in the head. But more than that, this is a very dangerous time in our world and we need eyes and ears in the region. It's a pivotal moment and Skye," Cameron's eyes snapped. "It revolves around you."

Skye was startled. "Me? Explain."

"Wait a minute…" protested Alex, not caring for what he was seeing on Skye's face. The determination. The anticipation. The accord.

Amanda's eyes lit up with passion and she continued. "Skye. We're no longer talking about opium and women. You know from your work in France that it's armaments now flowing in the underground market. Organized crime will always sell contraband and illegal goods and in today's world that's weapons. The former Soviet Union has nuclear weapons. There are several terrorist groups, much better organized than the people you dealt with from Cabinda who are well financed. The potential for a devastating tragedy is horrific. We need our man in there. If he gets the top slot, he'll be on the elite high committee. He'll be privy to the locations of arsenals. If he can get in place and stay there for even a year, we'll be able to close down this cartel. We're working in cooperation with both Russian and Chinese intelligence and they all agree…this is an unprecedented opportunity."

"I know you want to bring Pavel down for what he did to you and what he put you through," continued Cameron looking at both Alex and Skye.

"And you're asking us not to?"

"Exactly. Not yet."

"Go on." Skye was pulled in…intrigued. Alex was getting colder by the minute. Jim was resigned and knew there was going to be a lot more.

"Six years ago, when Jim came to Amanda and requested her assistance in getting one of his agents out of there, we were able to do so without compromising our man." Cameron smiled. "I think this agent, you, may be in a position to pay us back…to pay him back."

Skye nodded without hesitation. Alex frowned. He'd just gotten her back and didn't relish the thought of having her thrust into another dangerous mission. "Just tell me how."

"We haven't created a strategic plan. This situation has been extremely fluid and we're making spontaneous field decisions. Improvising."

Skye smiled. "My favorite."

"So I've been told," Cameron smiled. This might work. Amanda had assured him it was worth a try and now he could see why. Skye's record was impressive, but it was only words. The young woman sitting in front of him was the embodiment of those descriptions and reports. She was extraordinary. In Amanda's league and that was saying something. That was saying everything. He went on. "Your abduction, while painful, was fortuitous. Your escape even more so. And very well timed to help us with our overall goal to put our man solidly on the high council."

"Go on."

"We need you to go back in."

"I intend to…"

"No, Skye…I mean go back in alone and undercover."

"No," snapped Alex. It was where he thought they were going and he'd have none of it. "Not a chance."

"Let's talk this over, Cameron," said Jim. He knew his agent and was trying to stand in front of her.

"We haven't time. The opportunity is here. Now," said Amanda, passion lighting up her face.

"There has to be another way," said Alex.

"Damn it, Alex, I attended your wedding a few days ago. You two are very dear to me, but we're not talking about the individual pain that drugs and prostitution cause. The stakes are much, much higher. The case you worked on a few months ago involved circuits that can be used in guidance systems. Guidance systems are no good without missiles. And the Russians and Chinese have nuclear warheads. We are barely staying ahead of the people who want to drop these weapons on our cities. Cities, Alex."

"Certainly the governments of these countries…"

"The Russians have lost track of many of the components in the breakup of the Soviet Union. And in China, these warlords *are* the government. And they both lust after incredible amounts of cash. And money is what many terrorist groups have plenty of. The cold war was waged between governments who worked under a set of semi-civilized rules. Deterrent, detente, diplomacy. Today there are no rules. Some of these groups are the antithesis of civilization," said Cameron forcing himself to remain cool. "We are in a position to take a giant step toward removing the fuse from the dynamite that has been laying dangerously dormant for the last four decades."

"*We?* I don't hear a *we* in this. I hear you asking my wife to go back into hell. Jim," Alex said turning to their director. "We work for you. The fucking CIA can't just recruit from your pool of agents without your input. Let's go up there and take these guys. You can't sanction sending Skye back in there. We already discussed the damage that could be done if Skye was taken by someone who wanted information from her."

"We're talking about a controlled collapse of information, then an extraction," said Cameron angrily, his temper pushing through. "We don't expect her to go back in to her execution."

"Well, that's comforting as hell," shouted Alex sarcastically. "Back off, you goddamn spook. She's not going to play." Alex surged to his feet. Cameron came to his and the men were faced off like two fighters in a ring.

"Excuse me," said Skye calmly. "I for one would like to hear your thoughts and since it involves me, I'll decide on my level of participation. We haven't time for debate. Jim, you've loaned me out to other agencies before and Alex, darling. Please." Her voice became soft. Personal "Please sit down and hold me. I need your arms around me for this, I think." That got through Alex's hot fury, and he slowly sat back down and gathered her close.

"Hmm," she said, feeling the current of Alex's rigid fury. "Not a huge improvement, but certainly tamer. Cameron, can you go on, or would you like to stick your head in the snow before you proceed."

Cameron actually laughed. He looked over at Alex and shook his head. "I have been exactly where you're sitting, young man, and believe me, I know what this is costing you. I'll try to remember that."

Skye could feel Alex lose some of the rigid resentment and was relieved. They moved out of the red zone and it was safe to proceed.

"So tell me the plan," said Skye simply.

"Again, we're running this op with spontaneous field decisions so our plans are, shall we say, fluid. Mandy and I have complete discretion on this and have discussed it briefly, but let me lay it out and see how it resonates with you."

Skye nodded, Alex fumed and Cameron proceeded. "We believe the people who will be coming at 18:00 will want to interrogate you. From our information it will probably be Sung Du himself. He wants to tie up loose ends before he dies and this one has particularly plagued him the last six years. It's an incredible opportunity. The other contender for the top spot hasn't left Sung Du's side in over a year, so we're sure he'll be there, too."

"Why not just take Sung Du and the rival out and leave your man standing?" asked Alex, preferring that angle to a plan that seemed to revolve around his wife. "Take them alive, sweat them, and get your information that way."

"We thought of that, but when we heard they had Skye, we started thinking in a different direction. We were working out how to get a message to her through our man, who's coming in with the entourage this evening by the way, but that just got modified. Skye escaped and is here. Another fortuitous chain of events. It simply couldn't be more ideal. We now have a chance to speak with Skye ourselves with no chance of being detected. May I say well done again, Agent Madison?"

"Sure...so we're really on a roll now."

Cameron smiled at her expression of anticipation. "I think so. We will risk one more communication with our guy.

"The plan?"

"Three things. You go back in. You allow them to grill you. You seal the other man's fate by naming him as your contact."

Jim and Alex exploded with questions, concerns, and dissent. Skye stared into Cameron's expressive, intense gray eyes and he had his answer. He was both thrilled and terrified. It was a familiar combination.

"Simple, direct, neat." Skye nodded calmly, ignoring the heated debate going on between Jim, Alex, and Amanda. "They'll never suspect because realistically, there's been no time to set this up...in their minds anyway. Go on,"

Cameron continued the briefing and Skye took it all in. Then she asked him to repeat it so she had everything firmly imprinted. She knew she was exhausted and wanted to be sure she had every detail. For there was one thing that was obvious to all of them in the room. She was going back up to the castle. She was going back into the cell from hell.

"So. I go back in there and then have them force me to tell them who released me…then I reveal the name of the man who we want to discredit. Brilliant." She made it sound simple. They all knew it would not be.

"I'm sure you've shocked Pavel's people with your escape. Remember, they don't know you're a special agent. They may or may not share with Sung Du and his entourage the fact that you disappeared for while. Either way, it's good for us. If they do, it will highlight your resourcefulness. That falls in with our planted story about you being a contract assassin. If they don't, then they won't have any reason at all to suspect we've set this up."

"And how will they go about convincing her to reveal the name of the person who got her out of Hong Kong?" asked Alex, going back to what he considered the most salient fact in the whole plan. At the same time, his mind assessed the possibility of kidnapping her himself and taking her out of there. She was in a weakened state and he didn't think anyone would stop him. It didn't look like she was going to take into consideration his preferences.

"Darling," Skye said, squeezing his hand. She'd been unconsciously playing with his wedding ring, something that wasn't lost on him. He liked it. It made him feel connected. Made her presence real to him. "You know the drill. I'll let them think they forced the information from me."

"Why don't you just say it, Skye? You're going to let them torture you again."

She shrugged. "It has to look forced. My credibility can't be questioned. Our man's life depends on them believing me and that means I have to appear to be broken."

"As for the torture," began Amanda.

"I can take it."

"No doubt. The good news here, in addition to the fact that they want you intact to be turned over to the Chinese warlord who originally purchased you, is that they're still KGB trained. They'll start with deprivation. No food, water, rest. Stand you at attention or put you on a stool until you pass out from fatigue. Sometimes you'll fake it, sometimes you won't need to. They'll throw water in your face and make you stand some more. If we thought it would take on more extreme physical manipulation, we would have dismissed this option from the beginning."

"That fits. They had orders not to allow food or water. I thought they were just being cruel, but they were already anticipating my collapse. Setting the stage." Skye patted her stomach. "Well, if that's the case, dig through the cupboards for any old thing. Maybe I can fortify myself before I go back. Consider it armor against sublime torture." She could feel Alex shift angrily. He didn't think that was a funny crack, but before he could voice his displeasure, Amanda went on.

"If deprivation doesn't seem to be working, they will move to the physical. That will probably be electrical."

"You seem to know a great deal about KGB interrogation methods. Speaking from personal experience?" asked Skye.

Amanda just smiled. Skye smiled back and nodded. Skye sure would like to have seen all of Amanda's files.

"I got the electrical on my last visit through their lovely system," said Skye. "I came home fully charged."

"Shocking," said Amanda and they both laughed. The men didn't see the humor. Cameron glanced at Alex and their eyes revealed identical looks of both consternation and pride in their women.

"They'll feel they have time. Remember, they set a very elaborate decoy. Nothing has been publicly revealed about the body…they have no idea that Inspector Brady already knows her identity…or that Alex has even been notified."

"Agreed. They'll think they've bought themselves plenty of time."

"I think they'll want to break you the old fashioned way. Complete deprivation. They'll also think they're four days into that strategy."

"You think? You fucking *think?*" raged Alex, no longer able to contain his temper as the women discussed various forms of torture like they were talking about accessorizing an outfit for a special event. "This is all complete speculation…fucking, goddamn conjecture."

They both turned and looked at him. Amanda held back, knowing her young counterpart was well up to the task of taking on Alex's objections.

"No, they're all very high probability assumptions," said Skye in a low, reasonable tone. "Darling, please. What Amanda is telling me is actually good news. Chances are they'll stay away from the face, not beat or rape me, and will do little permanent damage."

"Oh, that's really comforting. So there will be few outside scars to add to your fucking collection. What if Pavel's people are really pissed at your escape? I have a feeling you didn't just quietly slip away. Tell me. Did you leave anyone lying on the castle floor?"

"Well…" said Skye evasively.

"I thought so," snapped Alex tersely, letting go of her and throwing up his hands. He got up and started pacing, no longer able to contain his fury and increasing apprehension through will power alone. "What if this Pavel can't control the actions of the people you messed up? It sounds like he isn't even in the country. What if revenge is more satisfying to these fuckers than his approval? What if Amanda's source is wrong and Pavel doesn't give a flying fuck any more if the family takes him back? You said yourself that if he really believes that, he's delusional." Alex turned, placed an arm on either side of her and leaned in. Looming over her until they were practically nose-to-nose. Knowing she was the one who ultimately would make the decision, he needed to persuade her…to get through to her. "What if he only wants to kill you himself or what if these people only want you alive to kill you themselves? What if their methods of torture are bloody?"

"If you say 'what if' one more time, I swear I'm going to start whistling *It's a Small World,*" she said through clenched teeth, her voice was artificially calm, chilly, steady. She held her own considerable temper in check, knowing that Alex was experiencing extreme anxiety…and he probably hadn't slept in days.

Alex's blazing eyes narrowed. Skye looked steadily into them. Alex's lips twitched first. How could he forget so quickly that he vowed if she came back to him he'd never shout at her again. "You wouldn't dare," he said in a soft, menacing voice.

She started to pucker up. Closely watching her, he considered her pursed lips an invitation and covered her mouth with his. If that was rude and unprofessional, considering they were in the middle of a briefing, tough shit. He was on his honeymoon and for this moment, his boss and two top CIA operatives weren't invited.

He pulled away reluctantly. "What if," he started very deliberately, still having her trapped in the circle of his arms. "What if…he's after revenge. That makes you a target, not a commodity."

"That isn't his motivator, darling. Neither is the money," said Skye with conviction. "Amanda isn't wrong. If Pavel did stage his death, that means he had to give up his life style. Darling, I got to know this man. He loved his life. That's what he wants and that's why he'll naively accept assurances he'll get it back, even though we all know he won't. By coming back to life, he's sealed his certain death."

"I don't understand why he'd come out of hiding," persisted Alex.

"He craved the recognition, the power. The old Mafioso used to call it *il rispetto*, respect. When this man would walk down South Beach and people would call out to him, he swelled up. He was an ugly caricature. Pompous in the extreme, but thinking himself as *il padrone*. The literal translation is 'the master,' but it's much more than that. Damn it, Alex, didn't you ever watch the *Godfather*? They never hid behind the walls. They flaunted their invincibility publicly."

Alex pushed off and resumed his pacing. "Don't you make this into some movie version of organized crime. This is real life, damn it."

"If he's been in hiding for six years, he'll do anything it takes to go back to his former life. I'm sure of it."

"Or perhaps kill the woman responsible for taking it away?"

"Darling, he could have killed me as soon as he discovered who I was. He most certainly could have killed me the other night. Instead he wanted me alive."

"And chained. Maybe he's just toying with his prey before delivering the fatal blow."

"This man is no cat, Alex. He's a jackal. He'll howl and prance around and deliver his prize to the leader of the pack. He wants back in. I know it. I know him." Skye stared intently into his eyes, trying to reassure him with her conviction.

"You're talking about my wife," shouted Alex.

"No, not now. We're talking about Special Agent Skyler Madison. I took the same oath you did, Alex," seethed Skye, loosing her grip on her temper.

"The two can't be separated. Don't throw useless semantics at me."

Skye stood, ready to take the fight to a whole new level when a wave of lightheadedness caused her to regret her sudden move. Her knees buckled. Alex swore, then came to her and gathered her in his arms before she could fall. The minute they touched, both of them let go of their anger. Steadier, she took his face in her hands.

"Darling. Trust me. I know what I'm capable of. I know what I'm doing. I wish it didn't have to be here and now, but we didn't write the script. That choice wasn't ours to make."

Alex took a deep breath and saw the truth in her eyes. And the determination. It nearly broke him, but he nodded. They both sat down again, and focused their attention on the details. Alex turned off his emotions while they talked. She'd go back in. Then under duress, she'd give them information that would lead to misdirection.

"We can provide you with some powerful morphine if they choose to get creative, Skye," said Amanda. "It's secured in tooth caps."

"No, I can take the pain. It'll keep me sharp. Drugs make me stupid."

"Are you sure? It will be undetectable. We put it in tiny capsules and lay it right in the back of your teeth. You'll have access to it even if your hands are tied. Think about it."

Skye shook her head and for the first time, Alex understood her incredible stubbornness on this issue. His eyes slid to Jim's and there was fire there, too.

"We'll monitor you," added Amanda.

"How?"

"Your original method," smiled Amanda, reaching for a large purse.

"Tracers in the earrings."

"Why try to improve on a demonstrated winner? We can work out various signals."

They spent another hour working on details and contingency plans. Everyone knew a hundred things could go wrong. But they'd all been in the field and had succeeded and survived through inventiveness and improvisation. As weapons, these experiences were as valuable as cannons. These were in Skye's control and she was one of the best.

"What about Payton? How do we explain to her that Skye decided to go back?"

"She has no clearance, so she can't be privy to any of the reasons why. I think she'll go on faith. We checked her out and she's a remarkably effective police officer. She already has done an extraordinary job identifying the body. We'll ask her to proceed with her investigation of the death of Emily Johansson. We're fairly sure she can tie in Pavel independently. We'll use her and his involvement in this criminal case to nail him. He'll have no option but to come over to us," said Amanda.

"I'd rather nail him bodily," said Skye.

"He's mine," said Alex.

"No, actually, we would rather have him be ours," said Cameron.

"Explain," said Alex harshly.

"You want to drain his brain," speculated Skye.

Cameron nodded. "Phase two. We thought he was dead. Now that we know differently, it provides us another excellent opportunity. We'll let Inspector Brady go in through channels and run an investigation. It seems as though Pavel may be recruiting through a modeling agency again. In the Chicago area."

"My home town. Will that be our next stop?" asked Alex.

Amanda smiled at him. "Yes. Think you can get police cooperation?"

Alex actually smiled back. "Yes. Especially a certain captain who's going to be royally pissed when she finds out Skye was located through her computer."

"Damn. Pavel is gravel. He's going down hard," said Skye.

Suddenly they heard gunshots. Reacting quickly and automatically, they all ran to the front of the house, guns out.

Payton charged out of the kitchen, pistol drawn and was the closest to the door. Before the others had crossed the foyer, she went out low and careful.

Raymond was lying on the ground by the car. In his hand was a rifle, but he hadn't had a chance to use it. A growing pool of blood was spreading in the snow beneath him. He was still moving, trying to get up. A man riding a snowmobile was racing down the drive and turning into the woods.

"Damn, he's headed for the castle," shouted Skye.

"Can we cut him off if we take the road?" asked Cameron. They couldn't let him get back to the castle if they wanted to put their plan into action.

"No need," called Payton as she raced to the car and grabbed the rifle from the driver's hands. "Stay down," she said looking into his pale face. He was in pain, but he was alive.

"Dead or disabled," she shouted at Cameron, who was standing closest to her.

They all frowned at her. The man was on a snowmobile going 30 miles an hour through the woods. He'd be partially protected by the trees, and he was moving away fast.

Cameron never hesitated, however. If she asked the question, she wanted an answer. If she gave him a choice, she must expect to be able to deliver his preference.

"Disabled," he shouted back and stood with his arms folded, waiting for the show. That stopped the others and they watched as Payton drew the rifle to her shoulder, took aim and squeezed the trigger. She missed, compensated, then calmly squeezed off another shot. Cool, efficient, unhurried. She took the man in the shoulder as he passed between two trees. He flew off the snowmobile, landed in the snow and tumbled. The snowmobile hit a tree and crumpled.

"Careful, he may be conscious," called Amanda as Alex and Payton raced over to him. They lifted the man none too gently out of the snow. He appeared to be conscious, but dazed. His shoulder didn't even seem to be bleeding all that much. She must have just tagged him. Now she cuffed him.

Amanda and Cameron checked the driver and confirmed that he wasn't mortally wounded. Painful, but not life threatening. "Sorry," said Raymond through clenched teeth. "He came on so fast."

Cameron patted his good shoulder. The agent was young and he'd learn from this.

"Are you going to let me call this in?" asked Payton trudging back up the driveway, her prisoner in tow. "Or is this something more you'll handle." There was an edge to her voice.

The cuffed shooter was now moaning in pain and delayed reaction to his tumble.

"You bitch," he said, his teeth chattering. "You tried to kill me."

"That's Inspector Bitch," she said. "And if I'd wanted to kill you, you'd be bleeding out from the hole in your heart, you stupid git."

Alex threw him against the car. "Is this one of them?" He looked over at Skye.

"I don't know. He isn't someone I had the pleasure of meeting."

"Who are you?" Alex demanded.

"No questions," said Payton with command, even a bit of temper. "Not until I'm officially told this isn't my case."

Cameron was already on his phone. He glanced up at her. "Officially, then. This isn't your case. Would you like to call your commander?"

She glared at Cameron for a few seconds, then shrugged. "No need. Let me go down and make sure there are no others," she said hefting the rifle and stalking back down the driveway in long angry strides.

Alex threw the man into the back of the limo. The young driver, who was in reality a MI5 rookie, drew his pistol and worked toward redeeming himself by offering to keep him covered until the team Cameron was calling in arrived.

"Now that was nicely done," said Amanda looking after Payton. "Cool under pressure. Adaptable. Intelligent." She looked over at Cameron, who had grabbed her around the waist and was steering her back in the house. "Call recruitment."

"She was absolutely incredible," said Skye.

"Her dossier is very interesting," responded Jim. "That wasn't a lucky shot."

"I got that much," said Skye with admiration.

"She brought home Olympic Gold for Britain when she was barely 17 in both the 25 meter pistol and the 50 meter rifle. Needless to say the Scottish police force was very anxious to have her and she's proven she isn't just handy with a gun. Graduated top in her class at the Scottish Police College. She has a good mind and is very well respected."

"What else?"

"I think we should let you uncover your own information," said Jim cryptically.

"Hmm, I will." Skye's tired face took on a speculative look. "And there's someone I'd like her to meet someday."

Alex actually laughed. He didn't think it was possible, but it just came out. Going back into hell, maybe, but still wanting to find someone for his brother. Their brother. Shit. Their wedding seemed like a lifetime ago a world away from here.

Payton found an old tin of biscuits and Skye was eating them with gusto and making 'yum' noises when the phone rang. Payton noticed that despite the suddenness of the sound, not one of them jumped. Nerves of steel all around.

It was Man Two's voice. He was leaving a report, an update. "Everything is fine. We're expecting our guests at 18:00." Then he gave the time and rang off.

"Damn," Skye said. "They aren't going to tell him. They aren't going to confess they lost me."

"That's good. If they had, we would have had to erase the message."

"Will you be able to build some further messages from the tape? To keep everything sounding like it's working well, even after we leave the country?"

"We'll splice what we need from the messages and plant them periodically," said Jim. "Hopefully we can keep Pavel hooked and on the line until you locate him and make your pitch."

"Can't I just kill him?" asked Skye grumpily. "Asshole ruined my honeymoon."

She was enjoying her second cup of strong coffee and the zip was making her feel feisty.

"He'll be more valuable to us alive, if we can reel him in. If he doesn't want to come in...then you can kill him." Jim's lips twitched. He knew Skye would bring him in.

"He'd probably suffer more if you take away his Bruno Maglie shoes and winter truffles anyway."

It was time for Skye to go back in. "Can we have just a moment," asked Alex. "Alone?"

Cameron consulted his watch, then nodded. "Five minutes." He looked steadily into Alex's eyes. He too was in love with a fearless commando. He knew the feeling. Everything that was going through Alex's mind and piercing his heart was an echo of his past. Alex could see it in Cameron's eyes, but was too concerned for his wife to be moved by it.

Alex took Skye into the bedroom. He didn't even know what to say, what to do. His entire body was tense and tight. He'd pledged to care for her. To be her shield and her shelter. Long before the ceremony, he'd promised to be her guardian. He couldn't get any words out so he just swept her into his arms and held her as tightly as he could without crushing her. She was here. In his arms. After the days of uncertainty and agony, he let the feeling of relief flow through him, then ebb back out just as powerfully. In its place was both fear for her safety and distress bordering on sorrow. How was he going to let her go, knowing she was walking into certain agony and deadly danger?

"You don't have to do this," he whispered through a constricted throat.

She let his strength engulf her for a moment. "You know differently. It's what we do. It's our job."

"Don't talk like this is a goddamn courtroom or a cockpit," he said savagely. She could feel his muscles jump and wondered how she'd feel in his place. Damn, the pain charged through her system. She knew exactly how she'd feel.

"You're going back to be tortured, for God's sake," Alex went on. "What does that make me...that I will let this happen? That I'll stay back here and let this fucking happen?"

She pulled back and she could see rage mixed in with the exhaustion. She also saw self loathing and that was something she wouldn't accept. It fueled her temper. She straightened and glared into his agonized face.

"Look, Alex. I was doing this long before I met you. This was my life...this *is* my life. You came into it with your eyes open. You knew from the beginning this was what defines me."

"You think that helps? You think a few words can pacify me?" He was shouting now, holding her at arm's length. "Shouldn't things be different now? What about us? You're my wife, Skye. I don't know if I can let you go back in there."

When she saw he was about to explode, she softened. Ready to absorb the blast rather than deflect it.

"Darling. Listen. Listen to me, damn it. Knowing you're out here does change things. Knowing you're out here makes this more tolerable. I didn't have balance before. Now I do. It's the reason I'll fight to live. I have something to come back to. I'll see your face, feel your energy, imagine our reunion. It gives me a handle to hang on to. You're my lifeline, Alex. Please understand. Your love is my armor."

He just stared down into her passionate brown eyes. Spent and speechless.

"I'll be coming back. Darling, I'll be coming back because now I have something more precious to me than my life to come back to." Then she smiled and snaked her weary arms around his neck. "Now give me something to sustain me, because it's going to be a long night." She touched her lips to his. For both of us, she thought. "Send me in with something to protect me."

And he did. Although it nearly broke him, he gave her all he had in a long, lingering kiss.

"Whoa. That'll work," she said smiling weakly as she slowly drew away from him.

She studied his face and was satisfied that he seemed steadier. She brushed her hand over his rough cheek. "You look like you haven't slept in days."

"I haven't and I'm sure I'm not going to get any soon." How was it that while trying to give her something, she gave him more in return?

"Darling, I'll be monitored this time. Take a break."

He shook his head and drew her gently back into the circle of his arms. "It seems I can't sleep without you beside me anyway. I might as well stay up and watch you bleep on the screen."

She took a deep breath, enjoying the feel of his strong arms. A few more seconds. Was that too much for a bride to ask on her honeymoon? Closing her eyes, she breathed him in. He felt her love flow through him and surround his heart.

"Okay," she said softly. "Time to go. Time to break back into the castle. They'll be so anxious to cover up the momentary lapse, they won't even question their luck."

"Got a plan?"

"I think I'll let them find me fast asleep on one of the beds."

"Like Goldilocks?" He ran his fingers through her now tangled hair and kissed her forehead.

She laughed and knew she could leave now. Her new husband had caged the fear and put the dread in with it. For now.

In the back of the limo, Amanda tested the equipment and nodded at Skye. She didn't insult the younger woman's intelligence and preparation by asking her if she got it all and remembered everything, even though she was tempted. She knew Skye. She knew that she was the best and that she'd stand.

"We're going to take you as close as we think is practical. First of all, time is of the essence. Secondly, it will save just a little energy. And that will come in very handy later." Amanda put her hand over Skye's. They stared for awhile, both knowing. Both caring. Both ready. No more words were necessary. Amanda nodded. Skye did the same.

They could see the castle clearly in the distance now and Cameron ordered the limo to stop.

Jim gave Skye a quick hug and a kiss on the cheek. "Don't be a hero," he started, then realized what he'd just said. She was being a hero by going back in. "I mean don't be a martyr. You have the extraction code. Use it and we're in there in 20 seconds."

She smiled at him and rubbed her cheek. The gesture was automatic and nearly broke Jim's resolve. The last time she did that he'd just walked her down the aisle. It seemed like a lifetime ago.

"See you in a couple of days or so," she said. "I'll try not to prolong it, but we have to play it so that I'm credible."

Leaning over, Cameron kissed her on the other cheek. "Good luck," he said. Her eyes slid to Alex who had gotten out and was waiting for her by the front of the car. Making sure everything was clear. For the moment, he was an active agent on a case.

"I'll take care of everything up there. I'd appreciate it if you would take care of things down here. It will make it easier for me," she said softly to Cameron.

He nodded, admiration reflected in his normally unreadable eyes. He'd stand with her man.

Skye got out and went to Alex. She put a hand on his chest when he made to follow her.

"No. It won't be any easier five feet from here." She looked into his eyes, then embraced him and put all of her love into a deep, passionate kiss. "*Je vous aime, mon chéri. Je serai postérieur dans vos bras bientôt.*"

She gave him another long intense look, then turned and walked quickly and silently into the trees.

Taking a deep breath, Alex leaned back against the car. He wouldn't go out into the woods with her, but he'd wait until she disappeared. The feel of her lips burned into his.

"You better come back to me soon," he said softly to himself. "Or I will surely die."

"It doesn't get any easier," said Cameron, coming up beside him and watching Skye make her way into the dense forest. "I've been in love with and married to a woman who thought nothing of danger and laughed at death for over 40 years. I think women like them must have a special force field around them."

"Maybe that's what makes them so appealing."

Cameron's lips twitched. "It's our curse."

Alex nodded, rubbing his chest. He could feel his heart aching. "Some honeymoon."

"You'll have time for that." Then he turned his gray eyes fully to Alex. "You'll find that whenever you or your wife return from a mission and you're both still alive, it heightens all of the senses. It makes every homecoming a honeymoon."

Alex smiled back at the man who was probably living now what Alex's future would entail. "There has to be some reward." He looked at his wife's departing back. She turned, waved, winked and was absorbed into the fog. Alex felt like he was in an old black and white film, maybe a Bogart movie. His smile faded and was immediately replaced by a hard, cold stare. "Because nothing this damn hard should be experienced without getting something indescribable in return."

She was gone. And he was already aching for her.

"Compartmentalize, Alex. Put your heart in one box, your fear in another. Neither will help her right now. Keep your head clear."

"There's really little I can do right now except wait."

"That isn't true. We still have work to do. Trust her to do hers."

"It's not her that concerns me. It's circumstance. Fate. Things we don't control, things we can't put into the mix because we don't know what's coming. Things could go wrong. The plan is solid, but…" His voice trailed off. He was saying nothing that Cameron didn't know.

"I can only say again, trust her. She's a master at deception and improvisation. And this time we'll be right outside the gate."

"Safe, here. Outside the gate. While she goes into the lion's den," he said derisively. "Right now, I don't think too much of myself."

Cameron nodded. He knew exactly what Alex meant. He was feeling some of that himself. "Compartmentalize that too, Alex. That, I think, is the toughest one of all."

Cameron waited silently by his side. Alex had to fight the urge to run after Skye. What the hell were they doing? He was young and prosperous. He'd given of his time, his effort, hell even his blood to try to make the world better. To finish some of what his sister had tried to do. Hadn't he done enough? Hadn't Skye done enough? She was a talented and highly skilled pilot. They could have a good life, an exciting life without all of this risk. All of this pain.

As if reading his mind, Cameron said softly. "The hell of it is, someone has to do it. We don't pick this life Alex. It picks us."

Alex stood there a while longer staring at the place where Skye had dissolved. The picture of her smile and wink etched into his mind. He could still feel her in his arms; they throbbed from the emptiness now. Come back now, he thought and we will leave this life and go home. She didn't rematerialize, however, and eventually he turned and went back to the car to begin another long vigil.

CHAPTER 11

Damn, home sweet home, she thought as she was pushed back into the cell she'd escaped from less than six hours before. She must be insane. Nothing had changed other than she was now going to be tied up. She sighed. Whatever.

Her assignment was to remain here and play it to the end. She no longer needed to worry about escape. No pressure. No preoccupation. There was something oddly liberating about that. She puffed out a little laugh. Now that really was insane. How could being tied up and thrown in a cell be liberating? She would use her time in here to think about that one. In the meantime, she tapped out a message on her left earring. All was well.

Skye sat down and got as comfortable as she could. She rubbed her stomach with her bound hands. The micro-dicked asshole wasn't so glad to see her, especially when she looked down at his crotch and snorted. He'd gotten in a punch to her stomach before anyone could stop him. She saw it coming and tensed her muscles, but it still knocked the wind out of her. When the man's arm went back to deliver another blow, the woman barked at him.

"Stop it, you moron. Remember Pavel said no marks. He meant it. His merchandise is always flawless."

Well, thought Skye, something to thank the little prick for. His god-awful pride in his product. Pompous little *minchione. L'idiota stupido.*

They found her where she was sure they couldn't miss her…in the middle of the damn road. She heard another snowmobile in the distance and placed herself in a position where she could be spotted, then pretended to run. The man on the machine caught up with her and she 'fell' down, twisting her ankle. As she suspected, they were so relieved to have her back, they didn't question how she managed to get so lost that she circled back toward the castle. They also seemed not to be too alarmed by the absence of one of their comrades. Of course they would want to keep a lid on that detail to maintain the cover-up.

So far, so good. Now all she had to do was wait. And she didn't have to wait long. She knew when the big guns arrived. The echo of the helicopter could be heard even down in the dungeons. The corridor was a perfect sound tunnel. Her team on the outside would be monitoring their arrival and she liked the feeling of comfort and protection it gave her.

Skye hoped they would come soon and she wasn't disappointed. Obviously, they wanted to get right to work. Within the hour, Skye was receiving guests in her humble habitat. She heard the voices first. There was both Russian and Mandarin. She didn't speak the languages, but she recognized their sound. So both houses of the cartel were in on the fun. Christ, who would have thought a slavery ring busted up so many years before would have generated such interest. She'd been living for the last six years blissfully unaware that there was a price on her head and a web of people out looking for her. What would she have done had she known? Well the answer to that question wasn't important now.

She sat down in the dark, dank corner of her cell and put her head between her drawn up knees. Closing her eyes, she took in great lungsfull of air. Time to send some oxygen to the brain and release a few endorphins. Not only were they a potent natural painkiller, they would keep her sharp.

The door swung open and she felt a dozen eyes on her. Let them look. Keeping her head down, she tried to appear as wasted as she possibly could. A few hours before, she'd had coffee and biscuits. She could take anything.

Someone said something in Russian and she didn't respond. Didn't even move. Obviously the man didn't like being ignored because a few seconds later, a beefy guy grabbed her by the arm and yanked her to her feet.

"Hey," she said, trying unsuccessfully to pull her arm away from the man. "Can't a lady catch a nap without unannounced guests barging in?"

She saw some familiar faces among the seven men and women standing both inside and outside the door. The guy who had her arm was new, but there was Ekaterina Rustam, head of the eastern Russian family. She was a particularly malicious bitch. Skye seemed to remember she had a few issues with Western women and anything related to fashion. God she was one ugly female. And Ji Cheng, chief warlord of the Mandarin contingent, decided to come to the party. And of course the head man, Sung Du. It might have been her imagination, but she swore she could see the cancer eating away. Skye moved her eyes from him before he could see her sense of righteous satisfaction. Rot, you son-of-a-bitch. Ji Cheng was next in line for the head slot and by all accounts even worse than the horrid, cancer riddled Sung Du. He was her target.

Standing in the background, elderly but completely in command, was Lin Tu Meng. Her personal favorite. He looked like a kindly and wise grandfather, but she knew he was both ruthless and without mercy. At one time he'd owned her, or thought he had. And he'd wanted her. Skye threw her hair back off her face, looked him right in the eye and smiled. Then she bowed her head, kept her eyes down for a few seconds and looked back up at him. She saw the same thing on his face she'd seen the last time they met. Interest. Curiosity. Lust. Desire. But now there was also a burning, churning fury.

"I'm most sorry I was forced to stand you up," she said to him in perfect French. She didn't speak his native tongue, but he'd been educated at the Sorbonne. His French was nearly as good as hers. "Perhaps if you can secure me a room at the Ritz in Hong Kong, we can renegotiate our agreement."

But she could tell that his lust was now secondary to his fury. He'd suffered humiliation by her actions. Pavel had thought that the reward had been posted so the old warrior could have his way with her. Wrong. Although she was grateful, Pavel had kept her unmarked for nothing. He thought Lin Tu Meng wanted the tall blonde Caucasian slave girl, but it looked like he wanted information first, then retribution. He wanted some face back. Far more than taking her body, he wanted to be able to go down to the lodge and tell the guys he bagged the bitch. Okay, so there was no possible mercy there. She had plenty of other cards to play.

He responded to her in French. Obviously he was the only one in the room who spoke the language. "You gave up luxury and a life of pleasure for this. You threw away a kingdom."

"Yeah, well it came with an ancient, revolting king and that was too big a price to pay for a few soft pillows and second-rate wine."

Bull's-eye. His hands clenched into fists and he looked like he was going to have a stroke. She wanted to accelerate his timetable, make him anxious to get right to the pain. The Russians may have tried deprivation for days, but she didn't think this ancient piece of shit was going to wait. He wanted to hear her scream, to see her sweat, to have her beg. Well she was prepared to do all three, but not quite yet. She wanted this to be above suspicion. Authentic. Timing was important. She'd shown herself to be resourceful and aggressive. For her to fold now would be suspicious. They had to think they broke her.

"I'll have you when they are through. You will wish you were dead," said the old man, his voice dripping with malice.

"If you mean to have me, you're right. I'll fall on a sword, you repulsive, old piece of…" But she didn't get to finish. He barked something in Mandarin she didn't understand. The translation came swiftly, though and that she could understand. He came over to her and slapped her hard. Shit and she'd just started to crank up, she thought, shaking the ringing out of her ears. This seemed to humiliate him even more, however. She'd made him lose control and that was unacceptable. He spun around and strode out of the room, his seething anger leaving a palpable silence in his wake.

Tan Sha, her man, shouted to the Russian who had her arm. He dragged her into another small room off the corridor. There it was nothing in the room but a table and two chairs…and…hello…a piece of very vicious looking equipment. Maybe she was going straight to GO, no collecting $200.

"You will stand here. You will not eat. You will not sleep," said Sung Du in excellent

English. "These things you will earn through cooperation. You will tell us what we want to know."

"God, you're such a pitiful cliché." Her eyes remained steady. So they were going to try deprivation first. Well, she was prepared. When the man who had her arm let go, she swayed. She was supposed to be already weakened, after all. It wasn't much of a stretch. She wouldn't be nominated for the Golden Globe on this one, but she knew how to play a part.

They left her there with two men in the room for what seemed like hours. When she tested their purpose by letting her knees buckle and go to the floor, one of them jumped up immediately and placed her back on her feet. She was sure she'd seen this in a movie once. An old, very predictable movie. They really were a sick old cliché.

Skye's internal clock was completely compromised, so she had no way of knowing how long she'd been standing. When the perceived hours turned into perceived days, she could feel her legs tremble. Her back ached, her head ached, her healed but still sensitive ribs ached. She took inventory of her body in search of something that didn't ache. There were plenty of spots, she found. They were worth noting as well and she spent some time doing just that.

After her inventory of places that didn't ache, most likely because the nerve endings were asleep or nonexistent, she worked on other methods for keeping her mind occupied. At first her daydreams slid to her wedding, but she didn't want to contaminate that magical day with these surroundings, associate those wonderful memories with anything this dirty, so she decided to review the plots of every movie she'd ever seen. She closed her eyes, but that made her dizzy, so she concentrated her sight on a spot on the far wall. She knew she was fading when she couldn't remember if Robert Redford was Butch Cassidy or the Sundance Kid. And she knew she was obsessing because the answer seemed really important.

She didn't even realize she'd fallen to the floor until she was roughly picked up and set back on her feet. Damn she was feeling nasty. What she wouldn't give for fresh clothes and chance to take a long shower. No. Not a shower. A steamy hot bath with tubs of suds. Strawberry scented shampoo. She took in as much oxygen as her exhausted lungs could gather. No chance there. So back to the movies. Before she went down again, she managed to go through the entire *Godfather* trilogy. Never had a stone floor felt so wonderful, been so inviting. Just a few minutes on the floor would be a really nice break.

Suddenly a wash of frigid water hit her face. Her reaction was spontaneous and she came to full consciousness immediately. But it was too early to let her captors in on that fact. It took all of her will power to keep still and force herself to come awake slowly, dazed and confused. She had to suppress the shriek and sputtering and the string of Italian profanity that would have been her preference. Bastards. That wasn't only diabolical, that was rude. Her grievances were piling up. Someone was going to get hurt.

Hands were on her, pulling her up. She restrained herself again. She wanted to put a power lock on whoever had her. Now wasn't the time to show her strength, however. Although, strength was becoming a relative term. She really was flagging. Sung Du was there when she finally got to her feet and opened her eyes. How many days? Felt like hundreds. A century of days. And she knew she was slowly starving. Her body hadn't had anything to feed on in days.

The two men she was now calling Butch and Sundance were on either side of her. One was Russian, one was Chinese. Which was which? Hell. She forgot. Was it important? She didn't think so.

"What's your name?" Sung Du asked. She pictured the cancer eating his pancreas and smiled. At least she thought she was smiling. She was so exhausted she wasn't sure her brain was still sending signals to her facial muscles.

"Vito Corleone," she gasped. It was the first name that popped into her head. Sung Du didn't look like he believed her. He must have seen the *Godfather*.

"You need more time," he said and turned and left her to her endurance test. More time? Like she was a turkey being prepared for a Thanksgiving dinner. Dinner. Turkey. This really was torture. Complete deprivation. No food, water, rest. She was beyond hungry, but she decided a morale booster would be to go through all of her favorite foods. She realized when one was in this state of starvation, the palate wasn't too discriminating. Everything, absolutely everything sounded good to her. Liver with anchovies and a dandelion sauce would have tempted her right now. Still she checked into Fantasy Island and imagined her first meal. She licked her lips to catch the water running from her face and hair. What would it be? Steak? Pasta? No. Pancakes. A whole stack of Cynthia's pancakes. Syrup. Coffee.

More time passed and even Skye's muscular, well-conditioned legs could no longer stay rigid. She went down more often. Each time there was a face full of water. She thought of that as her silver lining. The dripping water could be harvested by her tongue. It wasn't much, but she was measuring relief in very tiny units right now.

Time was completely without meaning. She only knew she was totally in her mind now. There was no physical being holding up her brain. No legs, no spine, no arms. There was such a massive amount of throbbing and aches, they could no longer be individually registered. She felt disconnected. She was in totally new territory and only a part of her was present and accounted for.

She barely felt herself being picked up yet again and placed into a chair. She was drenched in water now and shivering. Instruments were being attached to her arms, legs and torso. Act one must be over. What? No intermission? Something was placed in her mouth. A mouthpiece. She spit it out and it was placed back in. She spit it out again a few more times, getting a perverse pleasure out of someone having to bend over and pick it up. Each time, someone shoved it back in more roughly. Okay, enough of that game, maybe it would be better in her mouth, she thought vaguely. Knowing what was coming, she didn't want to bite off her tongue. Seconds passed, then she got the first jab of electrical current. It raced through her body, a body she thought was numb and beyond feeling. Wrong. A scream went through her brain. It didn't yet pass her lips, however.

"What's your name?" She opened her eyes and tried to focus. It was Sung Du himself. He looked well rested and well fed. Bastard. One of the men at her side took the mouthpiece out.

"What?" she asked, trying to get her bearings. She looked around the room. Everything was blurry. Like an impressionist painting. An impressionist painting of the guardians of hell. They were all there. All except the ancient Lin Tu Meng. Maybe he was up in one of the bedrooms getting his beauty rest. Her kidnappers were there for the entertainment, too. All three of them stood in the background. From the growth on the face of Man One, it must be two or three days since she saw him last. No wonder it felt so good to sit down.

Everyone had gathered for the show. Wouldn't want to miss the *Taming of the Shrew*. Well, stay with me people, she thought, I'm prepared to take it to the grand finale and curtain call.

"What's your name?" Sung Du repeated. His voice was soft, controlled and confident. She'd been tough, he thought but now she was just a weak, moldable animal. It was time to break her and he knew how.

He'd been delivered a death sentence, not by any court of law, but by his doctors in Beijing. He'd die by his own hand before the evil cancer consumed him from the inside, and he had just enough time before he took his own life to select his successor. He'd leave his portion of the cartel in good hands. He needed a name from this woman to complete his task.

The fact she was delivered to him now, at the dawn of his last year, was fate. Delivered to him by the insane man Pavel. Stupid man. He didn't know that he should never have come back to life. He'd be dead for real before the new moon. Once the man had crossed the line and delivered an assassin to the door of the cartel, he'd forever be marked for death. Nothing could redeem him. Sung Du was just playing him, telling him through his representatives that all was forgiven. Nothing was ever forgiven. He'd get the location of Pavel from the three standing with him in this cell. He looked at them. They would be far easier to break, he thought. He'd find Pavel and dispose of him as well. He'd live to see it done.

"What is your name?" he asked for the third time.

"Clarice Starling." Wrong. Pain tore through her and her body jumped in reaction. Damn, he must have seen *The Silence of the Lambs*, too.

"You're not amusing."

"Neither are you, you fucking asshole." Another jolt. "Okay. Okay. No more swearing. I get it," she said breathing heavily.

"You'll tell us who gave you assistance."

"I can't remember. All you Japanese look alike." This time her teeth chattered from the duration of the jolt. God, those Mandarins hated being lumped in with the Japanese by ignorant Caucasians. She knew what would set him off and it was working. She needed to accelerate his cruelty, play her game, then get the hell out.

"Your name."

"Lo mein." A jolt. She tried sashimi, char siew, cha sui bao, mwei jiong, yoke and every dish she could think of off the menu at her favorite Chinese restaurant in D.C. It was an excellent trick to make her mind go elsewhere while her body was being brutalized. Her tormentors were not amused. She got a jolt after each selection. She was nearly unconscious now. Good thing. She couldn't remember another item on the menu. Would she ever be able to eat Chinese again? Damn, this was getting intense. She was beginning to identify with Pavlov's dogs. Wasn't he Russian?

"Jennifer Griffin," she said finally. It surprised her that he accepted that. Must think she's fried and ready to cooperate. "My name is Jennifer Griffin."

"Who sent you?" He believed her.

"Pavel Ivanov."

"He was only the pawn. You used him. Who were you working for? Who bought the assassinations?"

She said nothing and got a full dose of fire.

"Was it the United States CIA?"

She shook her head and was able to answer truthfully. She gave a little laugh, which surprised her and Sung Du. She didn't think she had one in her. It made her denial more believable.

"No."

"Who?"

Skye went through the entire cast of Saturday Night Live. She also managed a few breaks by faking unconsciousness. Then, knowing the time was right, she confessed.

"I'm independent," she said through dry lips. "Gun for hire. You interested?"

That he believed. It was her conditioning and her skills that reinforced that idea.

"Who hired you? Who helped you escape?"

She didn't answer. Sung Du didn't like that. He signaled for another hit.

His eyes flashed malevolently. "You will tell us, bitch. You can do it now and save yourself a great deal of pain. For some reason the honorable Lin Tu Meng still wants you in his bed. We will send you to him, but not even his wishes have precedence over our need to know the name of the traitor who helped you six years ago. How did you escape from Hong Kong?"

"I fucked every jailer…" she got another jolt. "Twice." And another. Yeow. That hurt. She could feel herself getting fuzzy. Her mouth was beyond dry, it was arid. She wasn't sure she'd be able to cave in even if she wanted to. Wasn't sure she could talk. Just to get some relief, a brief respite, she faked unconsciousness again. What she got was more cold water in her face.

It went on for what seemed like days. Then blessed darkness descended for real.

When she awakened, it was a very gradual ascent into a place she was completely trying to avoid. But she knew it was time to start the final act. She'd established her credibility and now the anticipation of pain was what would ordinarily break someone. Right after unconsciousness, when the pain was temporarily gone and the victim got a taste of a painless state, that anticipation was a mind bender. A ball buster. In her case, a will breaker. That's why this form of interrogation was so much more effective than constant pain. Give the victims some relief, then break them with the promise of more pain.

When she regained full consciousness, she kept her eyes closed and could feel them in the room. They, too, knew she'd be at her most vulnerable when she woke up and they intended to be there. Her tormentors were confident in their methods. She moaned to telegraph her state to her captors. She wanted them all there. Needed the players in place. By shifting slightly, she assessed her recovery. She wasn't quite ready to move, so she wasn't yet ready to spill her guts…needed a little more strength. She was prepared to perform a pretty effective role as the woman who was tested beyond her endurance, but she had to have more muscle in her legs and arms to play the rest of it.

A great deal of talking was taking place and she cursed her inability to pick up any of it. Russian and Chinese were Amanda's languages. The languages of the cold war. She made a mental note to expand her knowledge to include some Chinese and Russian. She moaned again. Always a good idea to have sound effects. Remain too silent and they know you're playing possum. When she got back, first the pancakes, then the language lessons. No. First a shower, then a toothbrush, then the pancakes, then a honeymoon…she stopped just as she was about to add more items to the list…she couldn't believe she was making mental 'to do' lists. Oh, what the hell, it was something to occupy her mind and the anticipation that it was almost over gave whatever adrenalin was still in her body a chance to slog into her system. Let's see, what more could she add to the list…clean underwear, red meat, a manicure…suddenly she got another face full of frigid water. Shit. That was a tough thing to ignore. Okay, she thought. Show time.

Skye opened her eyes, gradually, groggily. Bringing her shoulder up in what appeared to be a sluggish and random act, she brushed her right earring lightly. Three times. Assuming she'd been out for a while, they needed to know the last act was being played. Most importantly that she was alive and in control. Thinking of Alex, pacing and waiting through the silence…she sent a signal to him through her heart. "I love you, darling. It won't be long now."

Looking around the dank, dusky room, she didn't have to feign disorientation. Everything was out of focus. Damn. She hoped she hadn't taken the performance too far…timing was everything now and she needed to be able to see. Blinking several times, her vision slowly improved. Fine. She'd just have to trust her own instincts and assume she had enough energy in reserve to pull off the op. Get eye contact with the CIA man, then make her move.

She moved her gaze slowly from face to face. There were ten people in the room. The seven people in the high command, and three of her kidnappers. They were actually looking a little nervous. Skye thought they probably had good reason to be. Measuring her time back in the cell by the length of the stubble on the mens' faces, she knew she'd been here long enough. Her peripheral vision took in the door. Only one man stood sentry.

"We are losing our patience with you, Madam."

"And I'm losing my appetite for pain," she gasped surprised at how breathy her voice came out. Weak. Pitiful. Perfect. "Are you in the mood for a deal?"

Sung's hand went to the switch and she put just enough panic to sound authentic. "No. No. Okay. I'll take your word that you'll ship me off to Lin Tu Meng…and consider myself lucky." She shifted on the chair. Assessing both her general condition and the tightness of the restraints. She felt okay. Certainly not one hundred percent, hell not even twenty two percent, but well enough to pull off her assignment. She had to trust their man. She did six years ago with her life, and she would again.

"I was brought in…" she shifted again, putting herself into position. "I was brought in and assisted by the same person. I'm a contract assassin. Pavel and a man named Barestrova were plotting…plotting to take a sizable share of the Russian territory." According to Amanda, Barestrova was dead, and she could use his name without fear of being contradicted.

She, in effect, gave Amanda's man in the field more push. Barestrova had been a loyal mafia boss and a very dangerous man. He'd been killed in a sweep of international law enforcement officials orchestrated by Tan Sha. It had been his information that made the difference. By casting Barestrova in a shadow, she was providing more cover for the real leak. For Tan Sha. Giving him more protection. It was a nice touch. A good strategic move. And at this point very believable.

She could feel Tan Sha's eyes on her, his admiration and appreciation. He'd been told by Amanda that this woman would hold, but he'd put his life on the line by being in the same room with her. If she broke for real, he was a dead man before sunset.

"Pavel is currently in the witness protection program. The CIA arranged to have his death look like a hit and then brought him in. He gave them information in exchange for his life. You've had a lot of problems in the last few years with deliveries, raids? Right?" She knew they had. Now they had an explanation. She didn't look at Tan Sha, but she knew she'd just paid him back. Given him some more years of usefulness. "Apparently the government cut him loose and he wants out of the life they provided for him."

Sung Du nodded. That had been his impression as well.

"And where would he be now?"

"I…I don't know where he is." She got a few more jolts, but couldn't honestly change her answer.

"The bastard rolled over on me too. I would turn him over to you if I could," she gasped with enough feeling that Sung Du was satisfied.

"One final thing. One more answer and you will end the day upstairs. A simple question. The name of the man you worked with in Hong Kong…the traitor who assisted in your escape six years ago."

"I don't know…I don't know…he never gave me his name." A jolt, longer and stronger than any of the others ripped through her. She couldn't hold back the scream.

"Please," she panted, pleading, panicked. "He…he never revealed himself. Played it smart. Kept covered." She was nearly breathless, every nerve vibrating, her skin felt like it was on fire. She didn't have to act now, she was in real distress. She forced the darkness that threatened to overtake her back into the shadows.

"I only…only saw him briefly," she said through clenched teeth. She paused hoping to punctuate her confession with one more jolt. One more. It came and she braced herself. She swore she'd never look at a light bulb in quite the same way again. Now. Now was the time. She knew it. They would believe her now. Believe anything she said. She whimpered and retched. Tears were flowing from her eyes. "I remember. I remember. When he released me," she whispered. "He…he couldn't hide his hands. Two fingers. Two fingers missing."

There was a stunned silence. Ji Cheng, second in command, evil poised to spread his own horrific vision, standing to the right of Sung Du began talking in rapid Mandarin. Everyone in the room was looking at him. Perfect. Now was her chance. Praying she'd saved enough strength, she sat up, and still hooked to the machine with thin wires, grabbed the gun nearest to her. It was Sung Du's. She staggered out of the chair breaking the thin wires, swaying and leveling the gun at Sung Du's chest.

"Now he and I will back out of here and…and disappear," she said, nailing Ji Cheng's coffin. She looked right into his stunned and furious eyes. He was nearly insane with disbelief and malevolence. It was a righteous moment.

Suddenly Tan Sha raised his gun. She turned and pointed her weapon at him, but was far too slow. Her reflexes were completely dulled by the pain and fatigue. Before she could shoot, he calmly squeezed off six rounds. All six shots hit Skye squarely in the chest, side and back as she spun around, hit the wall and fell to the floor. Blood flew out of the wounds and immediately stained the tattered sweatshirt she'd taken from the castle. She went down and didn't move from where she landed.

Tan smiled down at her lifeless body. "That's how we deal with traitors, bitch." He knelt down beside her and felt her pulse, then squeezed her shoulder. He took Sung Du's gun from her limp hand and rose.

"She's dead." He walked over to Sung Du, presented him his gun with an evil, vicious smile. "I'm afraid Lin Tu Meng may not want her any longer. She appears damaged."

Sung Du smiled back, pleased with the swiftness of Tan Sha's protection and now his wit…his successor. Fate blessed him. Fate made the choice. He'd been leaning toward Ji Cheng, but his forefathers sent him good luck with his bad fortune. Taking back his weapon from Tan Sha, he pointed it in the direction of Ji Cheng and fired six rounds into the startled man's face. His head dissolved into fragments of bone, blood and brain.

"That's exactly how we deal with traitors," he said.

He then went over to the three people watching from the corner. Skye's kidnappers. Pavel's partners.

"Where's Pavel?"

George stammered out "I don't know." Before he got a bullet right between the eyes. Sung Du pointed to Man Two. "Same question."

He only shook his head and got out "I…"

As his body toppled on top of the first man, Sung Du pointed the gun at the woman.

Shock and fear were on her face. Shock because they'd never signed up for anything like this and fear because she honestly didn't know.

She thought about making something up. Then she remembered a detail. Maybe she could build on that. Help them. Spare herself. God. She'd taken this job to get out of Miami for a while. To get out of the heat. And to make some significant cash. She was tired of hooking and wanted to take a break. She wasn't going to die because she wanted to take a break.

"He called me in Miami. We knew each other from the old days. He said he had a job for me. When I said I was on board, he said great. That's the last time I talked with him directly. He never told us where he was…he is a very suspicious and cautious man."

Sung Du raised his gun to the center of her forehead.

"Wait. Wait. Please," she begged. "I remember. I remember he said something about going to a play at the Shubert Theater. I didn't think of it at the time, but I'm almost sure that's in Chicago. How about I help you? I can help you find him."

"How do you communicate?"

"I don't. That was his job." She pointed to the dead man bleeding out beside her.

"You haven't communicated with him since he hired you?"

She shook her head. "But I can talk to some people. People who knew him from the old days. They might know where he is. I thought he was dead."

"Names."

She rattled off several names. Then Sung Du rewarded her by shooting her in the heart. She died with a look of shocked betrayal on her face.

Sung Du's cell phone rang. He answered it, swore and turned toward the doors leading out of the corridor.

"Someone is coming up the road. It may be nothing, but we should get out of here," he said to the people in the cell. They were all used to violence. It wasn't particularly shocking, nor very entertaining. They would have a lot to talk about on the way back to Russia. They would be flying home, low and silent, with all their questions answered. They stepped over Ji Cheng's body. Now all they needed to do was find Pavel and the leaks would be silenced. It was a good week's work. They were satisfied.

"What about the bodies?" asked one of his guards.

"Leave them to the rats. We will not be returning to this site." He turned to the woman as they walked through the blood and gore.

"Ekaterina, you will find Pavel. He was one of yours."

The Russian woman smiled. It was going to be her pleasure. She loved killing and she was feeling rather slighted that none of the blood splattered over the walls and floor had been put there by her hand. Pavel was going to wish he really did die in that boating accident.

CHAPTER 12

Alex, Cameron, Jim, Amanda and several MI5 people waited outside the walls of the castle. They saw the helicopter fire up. Payton and some of her officers were driving up the road toward the manor house. No flashing lights. Just a routine check. Or so it appeared. Everything had gone down and it was necessary to nudge the evil entourage into action.

"Where's Skye?" demanded Alex. He'd been pacing incessantly and was the first to hear the helicopter's engines. One of the tech people had her signal the whole time she'd been captive.

"She's still in the castle. Still in the castle, Alex. She hasn't moved. Let them go." Cameron answered for the man. He'd been monitoring her signal closely as well. They had a contingency if there was evidence they were taking her out of the country.

The helicopter took off. When it had disappeared over the horizon, they all rushed toward the manor house.

Alex ran into the huge front hall. Skye had drawn a pretty accurate picture of the place and he knew his destination. Sprinting down the hallway to the rear of the castle, he plowed through the wooden doors near the back of the large reception room. Stone steps went down and he took them two at a time, unmindful of their slick surfaces and sharp edges. He had to get to her. He ran down the long dank corridor, seeing the location up close. What a horrible place. He shouldn't have let her go. What was he thinking?

Turning the corner, he saw the carnage and terror jumped into his throat. Four bodies, all of them with obvious mortal wounds. His eyes took in the entire scene at once. He smelled gunpowder and blood and death. His heart stopped, his brain froze. He couldn't process all the blood, but as his eyes scanned the bodies, he saw that none of them were Skye. That was what his brain was telling him and it was enough to keep him on his feet. The iron door to a cell stood open and he turned to it. It looked like a cave, felt like the end of the earth. He rushed into the small room. She was in there. He knew it.

He was right, she was there. His breath caught in his chest and he was sure his heart stopped beating. Skye was sitting up against the wall, her sweatshirt was covered with blood, her eyes were closed. He rushed over and knelt beside her. Gathering her in his arms, he whispered her name over and over. "Skye. Skye."

He felt her steady heart beat against his chest and it brought his own heart back to balanced rhythm. "Darling?" Gently he released his grip as she moved in his arms.

She opened her eyes slowly, blinked and tried to focus. He could see the cloud of pain still obvious in her eyes, even through the complete and utter fatigue.

"Sorry," she said in a low raspy voice. "I really wanted to be standing when you came through the door. But I don't have any legs." She smiled weakly up at him. "It worked, Alex. We pulled it off."

Alex smiled down at her, relief mixed with pride, and a lot of residual dread just under the surface. "That you did, Special Agent."

"Do something for me," she whispered, her eyes losing their focus and fading fast. "Anything."

"Take me to a bathroom, a restaurant and a bed," she sighed and passed out in her husband's arms.

Alex lifted her gently off the cold hard floor. She lost more weight. There were dark circles under her eyes. Her hair was loose and tangled, her face was dirty and she was a mess...not to mention covered with blood. As he shifted her body solidly into his arms, Alex looked down at her and thought she never looked more beautiful.

Jim came running down the stairs along with some members of the surveillance team.

"Oh my God!" he gasped, losing his footing and nearly falling on the slick floor.

"This isn't her blood," said Alex quickly. "It's from the blood pellet shots. She was conscious when I got to her. I'm going to take her down to the Carlton Manor and have that doctor Payton called look at her right away."

"Let me help," said one of the young robust men, holding out his arms. He thought the tall guy looked like he was going to drop any minute.

"No. I have her," said Alex roughly. When the young man slowly lowered his arms, Alex realized the kid only wanted to help. "Thanks. But I want to take her out myself."

Jim quickly found something for every member of the task force to do while Alex carried his bride out of the castle and into the limousine. Amanda and Cameron were in there waiting.

She flew through the clouds and landed...safe. Consciousness pulled at her and she finally gave in to its incessant thrust. She was in a strange bed. A nice one. Soft. She sniffed. Smelled good too. She sniffed again. She couldn't smell herself. God, that was a relief in itself. Someone, probably Alex, had cleaned her up. It made her cringe inside.

She supposed that shouldn't have bothered her, but she'd been so gross. She barely had a memory of him holding her up in the shower. Holy Hanna on a skateboard. Was there ever a honeymoon like this?

Shifting, she realized she was naked under a large, silky blanket. How nice. Testing her limbs one at a time, she found them to be working. Her head felt like it was two sizes too big for her body, though. Blinking her eyes to clear them, they tracked to where Alex had just hung up the phone. Seeing her eyes open, he came over and kissed her tenderly on her lips.

"You were supposed to wait for me to give you love's first kiss. Then you were supposed to let your eyelids flutter open, throw your arms around me and live with me happily ever after."

There was a smiling, teasing tone in Alex's voice. He looked tired as hell and a little haunted, but there was light there, too. His life was just beginning to right itself again.

"Hey, you got that whole scenario right," smiled Skye, a.k.a. Snow White.

He smiled back and sat down on the bed beside her. He just wanted to sit there and look at her all day.

"Sloane had a copy of Snow White in her extensive collection. So I watched it."

"You watched Snow White?" Skye's tone was incredulous, her eyes were smiling.

He smiled a little sheepishly. "Yeah. I didn't think it was something I should admit until after we were married. Actually Jason, Al and I watched it one night when you were out getting a fitting or something."

"They liked it?" She couldn't believe after all they'd been through, they were talking about Snow White.

"It's actually a very scary movie and tolerable to them as long as we fast forwarded through the sappy parts."

Skye's eyes felt heavy…felt them slowly close. It took all of her will power to snap them back open and keep them open. She was completely exhausted and that short conversation had tapped into her shallow reserve of energy.

"Tan Sha?"

"Alive and at the side of Sung Du. As far as we can tell."

"Ji Cheng?"

"We found him dead in the cell. Ballistics may determine who did the deed, but at this point, it isn't important."

"Everything went exactly as planned," she sighed, her eyelids defying her signals and slowly closing. "Call everyone in, I'll give a report."

Alex smiled at her when she forced her eyes back open. "You've already done that, Special Agent Madison. You may not remember, but you regained consciousness in the car, and in about two minutes told us everything. Then bam…the lights went out and I carried you in here."

"I can't believe anything went out with all that electricity in me."

She missed the pained look on Alex's face because her eyes slid shut again. This time, they stayed shut. Alex decided to move in with her and slept as she curled up next to him.

He was so exhausted, he didn't wake up when Jim came into the room a few moments later.

Jim stood just inside the door and looked at his agents. Brave. Both of them. And so dear to him, it hurt. Safe, for now, but how many more times would he be able to send them into danger? How many more times would he have to? He allowed himself a few moments to lament his choices…a few moments of doubt and self recrimination. It showed on his face as something like grief. He didn't get his mask back in place quickly enough, as Amanda silently came up beside him.

"If they didn't do it for you, James, they'd do it for someone else. You, at least, can give them the training, the resources, and all the support they'll need to succeed."

Jim gathered himself, suppressed his indulgence into self exploration and looked at his own mentor.

"What if your son would have wanted to follow in your footsteps?"

"I don't know," said Amanda, understanding completely what was in Jim's heart. "It was never an issue. Daniel always wanted to build things. He was an architect before he reached the third grade. What about your boys?"

"A lawyer and a professor of biology."

"Thank the lord."

"Every day." Jim nodded at the sleeping agents. "But then, Perry's daughter wanted in. And not just in the department, she wanted to get right into the field. And Alex. Well, he was born to it. I think they might be the death of me."

Amanda smiled and slid her arm through Jim's. "Before you go six feet under, come on downstairs and we'll go over all the data we have. It will balance the scales, Jim. It will justify the high price."

Jim took one last look and silently backed out of the room.

"Where am I?" Skye whispered, trying to sit up a few hours later. Her voice was so weak. That was really annoying. She cleared her throat and frowned. She looked over to the far side of the room and found Alex, who had risen a few minutes before. She smiled. He was carrying what looked like her travel case and a garment bag. Glory Halleluiah. She was saved. Shampoo, makeup, a brush and clothes…clean, fresh clothes. How did her whole world get down to an irresistible desire for clean underwear?

Putting down the cases, Alex walked over and sat on the edge of the bed. Gently, he smoothed her hair from her face and gave her a sweet, tender kiss.

"We're back at the Carlton Inn. We decided to take advantage of the facilities. Payton called the owners with a story of a couple whose vehicle had broken down and found shelter in their establishment. I'll leave a substantial check to cover expenses. Jim just arrived with these." He indicated her luggage. It touched Skye that Jim, the head of an entire department, would run errands for her.

"Is he here?"

"Not anymore. He looked in on you to make sure you were all right then went up to supervise the team at the castle. They're cleaning up the mess in the dungeons. Payton went back to Glasgow and will meet us at the terminal."

"Are we going to be leaving for the airport soon?"

"Yes, we have to get to Chicago for the next phase. I'm sorry darling, but we have to locate Pavel. As fun as it's been, the honeymoon is over." He took her hand. "How are you feeling?"

She shook her head. In her mind, she could still hear the buzz and feel the sizzle of the electricity. It would be awhile, she supposed, before that was completely extinguished.

"I'm a little fuzzy, but I feel like all my parts are still functioning within normal parameters."

Alex chuckled. "At least we know your brain is."

"Shouldn't all that electricity actually fire it up to a higher power?" When she saw Alex's expression change, from quiet amusement to something painful and hard, she asked. "What?"

Alex took her hand and rubbed at the finger still bare of her rings. The memories were flooding in, and with them, the feelings. "We were only a mile from the castle," he said in a voice that was flat and hard.

"I know," she said softly, watching his eyes fade to ice. "That's what kept me hanging in there. I knew you were just outside the castle gates."

"And every time they administered a...a dose...a jolt..." Alex couldn't finish. His mind was replaying the sight of the castle lights fading. At first there was some speculation on what was causing the irregular dimming. Amanda told them. She'd known from the beginning. The current they were running through Skye was being diverted from the castle generator.

"Oh my God..." Skye whispered and closed her eyes. She knew, too. He didn't have to finish the sentence. She could imagine him standing outside, the lights dimming slightly every time they gave her another jolt. As difficult as it was for her, she could only imagine what it would have been like to be on the outside knowing what was happening. Her senses had been dulled with every hit. His must have intensified.

"Oh, Alex." A tear leaked out of her closed eyes and ran down her cheek. "I had no idea."

She really didn't, he thought as he gently wiped the tear from her cheek and noticed she'd fallen back into a shallow sleep. So exhausted, so completely spent. He knew how that felt too.

The lights had dimmed every time. Every time. His fatigue and revulsion had lowered his resistance to stand there through her torture. Toward the end, he had to be physically restrained. He vaguely remembered punching out two really beefy guys. They must have been agents because they had martial arts training. It didn't matter. They were on the ground and Alex was through them like they were bowling pins. He almost got through their perimeter when Jim had stopped him. Not with a fist or force, but with words.

"You'll kill her if you take one more step," he'd said. "There's no way you'll get to her before they put a bullet in her head."

At that moment Alex hated Jim. Stopping, he turned to look into the eyes of his boss, his mentor, his friend and wanted to kill him.

"You let her go in there, you son-of-a-bitch. Your own godchild." He saw Jim's distress, but didn't let it in. He hated Jim, the Department, everything. Jim saw it on his face and absorbed the blow.

But Jim knew his man; he knew how to stop him. He spoke the truth.

"I sent in one of my best agent to do a job. Now I expect you to do yours."

The lights dimmed again and Alex winced.

"Fuck the job. And fuck you. That's my wife in there, you cold hearted bastard." He was getting physically ill, his body was beginning to shake and his stomach was lurching. His mind was pulling him in one direction. Let her get through this to the other side. She can take it. But his heart was exploding with the need to save her from pain. He didn't think he could take it. He felt like a snarling animal. Jim was approaching him slowly, but with confidence.

"Come with me, Alex." Some of the red haze of rage dissolved and for the first time Alex noticed he was surrounded. Three silenced pistols were pointing at him. He hadn't shaved in days, his eyes were sunken from lack of sleep and he knew he must look like a raving lunatic. He felt like he was on the brink of madness. Would they have fired? He'd never know. And right then, he didn't care.

Jim had pulled him back, something none of them could have done by force. With words and an edge of authority, Jim talked him back to the command center.

"Can you eat something?"

Alex just shook his head. His stomach was in such knots, he didn't think there would be room for food.

"All right, but you're going to have to get some sleep. And if you can't do that, then get some kind of rest. There's absolutely nothing you can do right now." Jim's voice was low, but there was still that edge. Swallowing his own heart, he pulled out the strength they both needed to see the mission through to the end.

"Alex. I just saw the husband come out during a critical moment in an important operation. I understand it. But, Alex." Alex turned his aching, bloodshot eyes to look directly into Jim's. "I put the two of you together because I thought you would be able to maintain your professional composure." The compassion was now completely gone from Jim's voice…it was pure steel and ice. He was all director now. If Alex hadn't seen the flash of empathy in his eyes, he'd have thought Jim incapable of human feeling. "If you can't do that, if you can't control yourself, I'll call in the militia if I have to in order to restrain you and take you away from here. Do you understand me, Agent Springfield?"

In the business world, no one ever talked to Alex like that. But this was as far removed from that world as anyone could get. And both he and Skye were there by choice. They chose this life. How could he now deny it? He nodded. That was all it took. Communication over.

Alex didn't rest. Couldn't. Jim decided to let that go. He'd gotten through to his agent and that was all he needed to do at that point. He meant what he said. If the two of them couldn't put away their feelings for each other when they were on the job, it could place them both in jeopardy. They were a professional team and he couldn't afford to have them mess up at a critical point in an investigation because one or the other of them was in danger. Alex had nearly crossed the line…but he'd taken the necessary step back. He'd hold now…Jim was sure of it.

Alex left the communication trailer, determined to fulfill his professional responsibilities. He checked on the men he'd slammed and found out they were bruised, but not broken. They didn't seem to be the type to hold a grudge, and accepted his apology with grace. Neither man wanted to dwell too much on it since they'd been flattened so fast and so effectively.

Alex beat back the fear far enough to allow himself to function. He watched the steady beep of Skye's tracking device and her periodic coded messages. She was doing all right. That last seemingly endless period of time she didn't signal…when they assumed she was unconscious, he felt himself fight the restraints of his duty. Her signal came just in time. He wasn't sure what he'd have done had she not signaled she was going to end it when she did.

"Alex?" Her voice brought him back to the present. She'd come awake again and saw him staring at her bare hand. "Earth to Alex," she repeated. He must be tired to the bone, she thought. Probably all the way to the cells of his bones.

"Sorry," he said, trying on his smile again.

"I said I think everything is working."

"I'm glad you think so, but doctor has been here to confirm it." Alex didn't want Skye to completely dismiss her physical ordeal. Everything may be working in her estimation, but he wanted a professional opinion on that.

"Really?"

"Yes. You're suffering from dehydration, malnutrition, exposure, and fatigue, probably a compromised immune system. You obviously need to be fed…she thought your stomach could tolerate oatmeal…" Alex grinned.

"That would be interesting since it never has before." Skye shuddered. "I promised myself a cow."

"Well, maybe we should start with something a little easier to digest. In addition, she recommended starting your recovery with at least a week in bed."

"Hmmm. Now that sounds strangely like our original plan. But unfortunately that has to be put on hold." She smiled and reached up to him. "Help me up and let's get this show on the road."

"So much for the week in bed."

"It's all a matter of interpretation. She didn't precisely say which week, did she?"

"No, not precisely. And since I told her the likelihood of that was the same as icicles blowing out Satan's ass, she said you should take it very slow and have a complete work up as soon as we get to a location that has a major medical facility."

When she snorted, his face turned serious.

"That you will do." When she opened her mouth to protest, he added. "For me."

When she saw the fatigue on his face, she nodded. Now wasn't the time to butt heads. She smiled, inwardly, of course. That could wait until he had a good night's sleep.

There was a soft knock on the door. Alex went to answer it and Skye heard Payton's voice. Excellent. Now that she made the world safer for human kind, on to the important stuff. Time to launch Operation Matchmaker.

"I don't want to disturb her," she heard Payton tell Alex.

"Please," Skye called out grabbing Alex's shirt from the end of the bed and putting it on. "Come on in and disturb me."

Payton came into the room, a smile on her face. She didn't know all of what happened in the castle, but she figured out enough of it and thought Skye must be the most incredibly courageous person she knew. She was also one of the nicest.

"Is that a box of biscuits in your hand?" asked Skye greedily.

"Aye. And fresh ones this time. I thought your stomach might be ready for a little filler."

"God yes."

"And was it Prime Minister or Royalty you were going to arrange?" asked Payton handing them to Skye and watching with laughing eyes as Skye composed herself and tried not to look like she wanted to chew through the tin box.

"I've changed my mind. I have something better in mind. A different kind of arrangement. You're coming with us to Chicago, I understand."

"Aye, that I am."

"Then there's someone I'd like you to meet."

"You do have a singular mind."

"Honed to a fine, sharp point and almost ready to be reactivated."

Payton laughed with delight. "Well then. Who am I to fight it? Considering the specimen you married, I can only hope your taste continues to be flawless." She looked at her watch. "I'll meet you at the airport. I want to check in at the castle."

Alex caught a look in Payton's eyes and walked with her to the door.

"And I have something for you, as well, Alex." She reached into her pocket and handed him a small box. He opened it. Skye's rings. Alex's eyes blurred for a moment, then came back to focus as the brilliance of the diamond penetrated his tired brain and bruised heart. Something dark inside him closed up and something light reopened.

"Thank you," he said softly looking into her kind eyes. He smiled. She smiled. "I thought maybe you would need to keep them for evidence."

"Ah, well. I guess I'd know where to find them if need be." He was surprised to see tears form in her eyes. She blinked them away. "We Scots are a sentimental lot. I had them cleaned yesterday. I didn't think you needed to ever see that evidence bag again. Mr. Culver says you have a wonderful eye for gems."

"Mr. Culver?"

"Mr. Culver, our local jeweler."

They heard a string of Italian cursing coming from the bed as Skye tried unsuccessfully to open the tin of biscuits. "Speaking of gems," laughed Alex.

"Hell and damnation," said Skye. "You'd think a week away from my normal routine would pump me up. Alex, darling, could you make like a jungle beast and force open this lid. I think it's welded on."

Payton smiled. "Makes a quick recovery."

Alex smiled back. "Thinks she's from the planet Krypton."

"Oh, I think she'll allow you to be Superman right now. I'll leave you to getting the box open and the rings back on her finger."

Alex laughed softly. "At this point I'm not sure which she'd rather have."

Alex closed the door and went to give his mate a hand. The lid came off easily and she frowned fiercely when he gave her a superior look.

"I loosened it."

"That's what they all say."

"That's because it's true." Skye helped herself to a handful of biscuits using most of her considerable will power not to plow them all into her mouth at once. "What else did Payton give you?"

"Just when I think all of your attention was focused on finding the secret to opening the biscuit box, you impress me with your peripheral vision."

"Well?"

Smiling, Alex sat down next to her. He went for the biscuits and she pulled them out of his reach.

"Payton gave them to me. Tell me."

Alex nodded at the tin. "Community property."

She put them a little closer. "Okay, you can have four."

"Four? What formula are you using?"

"Mine."

"Ah. Well I'll take my four and give you something you can keep all your own."

"Darling, at this point I have everything I want. Well, almost everything." She looked up at him and he saw a hint of sadness. He thought he'd be able to wipe that away and when he showed her the box, he was sure of it. It was like the breaking of dawn. She tossed the biscuits on the bed and took the box from him. "Oh, that darling Payton."

"Hey, I bought them for you in the first place," he protested, but smiled when he saw the look of pure joy on her face when she opened the box.

"Alex. Oh, Alex." Skye wasn't sure what it was that was emptying out of her, but it was wet, coming in powerful waves and couldn't be stopped. She handed him the box and he removed the rings as tears poured out of her eyes and tiny sobs bubbled out of her chest. Holding her in his arms, he steadied her left hand as he put the rings back on her finger. He wanted to say something loving, something she'd remember as he put them back where they belonged, but he couldn't talk. He had no voice. His heart was filling with her tears and he knew he didn't have to say anything. There were no words for this moment. He waited until he felt her go limp and gently laid her back down. Asleep on a pile of pillows.

He leaned over and tenderly kissed her. No prince had ever done it better. *"Le coeur parle au Coeur,"* he whispered as his Snow White sighed in her sleep.

For the fourth time that day, Skye came awake. Still hungry, still sore, still exhausted. But this time, she looked at her left hand...this time she was complete.

"Alex?" She saw movement in the chair next to the bed.

"Here love." He'd seen her eyes go immediately to her left hand and smiled. He hadn't taken his eyes off her for nearly two hours. It was his compensation for making it through the last few days. He stood up, ready to move ahead.

Skye took Alex's offered hand and let him ease her into a sitting position. "Is the room spinning and lurching?" She moaned, blinking and hoping she wouldn't blow the few biscuits she managed to eat.

Alex looked around. "There doesn't appear to be any seismic activity in the room."

"Climb in here with me and we can make it rock." She tugged a little at his hand.

"I'm tempted, darling, but I really think any energy there may be lurking in there should be used to walk across the room." He could feel her hand tremble a little and he didn't think it was from latent desire.

"I'll remember you said that, you cad. Your near naked bride is requesting conjugal privileges and you have denied her. Strike one."

He let go of her hand and she fell back onto the pillow with a swoosh. "Now this is humiliating," she said petulantly, staring at the ceiling. Damn she was weak. Then she closed her eyes and frowned in concentration.

"What are you doing?"

"Summoning up the Force, Chewbacca."

Alex chuckled. "Well just let me know when you have enough to get yourself to the bathroom."

She opened her eyes again and extended her hand. "Help me Obi-wan Kenobi. You're my only hope."

"I thought I was Chewbacca."

"It was the hair on your face. I momentarily mistook you for a wookie."

Alex ran his hand over his scratchy beard. "Maybe I'd better join you in there."

"Good idea."

He thought so too. Not only did he get to touch her, feel her flesh, he'd be able to support her. From what he saw, she was weaker than she thought.

He got her back into a sitting position and helped her swing her legs over the side of the bed. "Damn," she said as she ran her fingers through her tangled hair. "I'll have to find a pilot to fly us home. I can take the co-seat, but I can't trust my reflexes right now."

"That's been taken care of."

Turning, she stared at Alex. It was one thing for her to decide to give up her seat. That was momentous enough. It was quite another not to be involved in the selection of the person taking that seat.

"Anyone I know?" Her voice had a hint of peevishness and more than a hint of sarcasm. She was supposed to be in charge of Skyward Aviation, after all. That was her domain. Alex loved the light that flashed in her eyes. So he laughed and helped her to her feet. She rocked, steadied, then held.

"Darling, quit snarling. We'll go in and shower. Then we'll go right to the airport. Your spare uniform is in the bag. You'll want to check the plane, I'm sure…and take the right seat."

"You aren't going to give me a fight? Make me swallow some pills? Chain me to a seat? Make me relax? Force feed me?"

"I know you'll be more relaxed in the cockpit than you would be as a passenger. And I won't have to force feed you. Jim made sure the galley was stocked up on all of your favorites. Although the doctor thought your stomach might be too jittery for solid food for another few days."

Skye's stomach rumbled at the thought of food.

"A lot the doctor knows. It's not her stomach. I could eat all the fruit in California, all the cheese in Wisconsin, all the lobsters in Maine and all the ribs in Kansas. Then get down to some serious eating."

Skye shook off Alex's hand and walked across the room. Slowly. Very slowly. She could feel Alex's eyes follow her and worked hard to maintain a straight line and up-right posture. Her first few steps were tentative, but she managed to find her legs. She was glad, however, when he joined her in the shower and held onto her.

As Alex was drying her off, he looked at the small bruises where the blood bullets had hit her. The projectiles were made on the same design as the paint ball pellets people used when playing war games and even though they didn't have a lot of power, they still could sting. Tan Sha's bullets were actually capsules of real human blood. It gave a very authentic look to the simulated wounds. It wouldn't have held up under close inspection, but they factored in the general noise and confusion and the darkened cell. Also the predisposition of everyone in the room to witness an expert execution. They would see what they expected to see.

"Quit taking inventory of all the little bruises," said Skye when he stopped rubbing the towel and gently touched the bluish marks. "Darling, I have some weakness and I'm feeling tired and hungry, but everything still works fine. Really. If we had more time I'd prove it to you."

Everything was, in fact, sore beyond belief, but she sure wasn't going to tell Alex that.

Alex, however, was a fine observer and knew everything she was feeling. On the other hand, he was so glad to have her back he decided to let her play out the fairy tale.

"I hope you trashed those clothes I was wearing," she said as she felt his arm around her waist. Deciding to chuck the pride, she leaned on him.

"You already did a fine job of that." He had, in fact, ripped them off her and carried her into the shower the minute they arrived at B & B. It was Amanda who had disposed of them by the time he came back into the bedroom. Amanda who had coffee and a huge tray of food brought in for him as he sat next to the bed, watching Skye. He found he could eat. Was, as a matter of fact, starving.

"Everything went precisely as planned," said Skye, matter of factly. She sat down in front of the vanity mirror, prepared to use makeup to disguise her exhaustion. She rested her arms for a moment before getting to the project. Looking up at Alex, she smiled. "What an adventure."

Alex kissed the top of her head and went to dress. "What an understatement."

Amanda, Cameron, Jim, and a man and two women Skye didn't recognize met them at the terminal. They went into a private room where the strangers were introduced as members of the British intelligence community. Amanda threw professional protocol to the wind and put her arms around Skye. They held each other for a minute, then separated and grinned. Identical grins, thought the assembled team.

They sat around a table and Alex placed a phone in the middle. He punched a button and Linda and Barclay's voices came out in a rush. Skye grinned.

"Hey, team. Have you both been briefed?"

"Sure have," said Barclay. "Told Alex not to worry. You'd go through those kidnappers like a hot knife through a piece of cake." Barclay had little trouble with his metaphors.

"Are you all right?" asked Linda, the concern in her voice obvious.

"I am. We're going to see you in Chicago, right?"

"Yes. Barclay can't leave right now, so he's going to talk me through the new program for Wyatt's computer."

"Excellent."

"This will be your preliminary report," said Amanda, taking charge of the meeting. "From it, we'll formulate the questions for your formal debriefing. We'll be able to add our man's report from his perspective and combine it with yours. For now, just tell us. Start from the beginning." Names would be left out of the report for now.

Skye would go through an official debriefing when they arrived in Chicago where she'd word her report in more formal language, but for now, she enjoyed telling the story from her point of view. These were her friends and colleagues and they wanted to know the details so she obliged them, with vivid commentary and sound effects.

"So then, zap, they gave me another jolt. Damn. I swear that if you stick a light bulb up my ass right now, you'd be able to see the glare from the space station. At just the right moment, I caved. Screamed like a banshee and whimpered like a dog. You should have seen their faces. Son-of-a-bitching sadists. I gave them all an orgasm before I gave them the information. I swear if I'd have broken a minute before, they would have been disappointed, frustrated and unfulfilled." She leaned forward in her chair and grinned at them "I spilled my guts. Told them exactly what you wanted them to hear and they just took it in like a Hefty paper towel. Super absorbent." Skye's face became more animated with each detail. This was the point where she usually began pacing, but her general state of fatigue kept her seated. It didn't stop her eyes from flashing and her hands from flying, however.

"Finally, we had a real Hollywood shootout. Christ, your man is unbelievable, Amanda. He was brilliant. His timing was impeccable. His expression, his gestures. You never would have guessed he was one of the good guys. Scared the crap out of me a couple of times. Anyway, his moves were like a practiced ballet. I grabbed the head guy's gun and our man took me out. Cool as ice…his eyes completely detached. He raised his gun before anyone else could get any ideas and pumped six of those blood bullets into me. It was beautiful. Bam, Bam, Bam. I felt them slam into me. Shit. They really sting, and the blood that splattered out of them. Damn, it was real. I could smell it. Then I staggered and gasped and fell to the floor. And I died just like in an old western. I lay there, twitched just right, gurgled and stopped breathing." Alex felt his own chest hurt but sat without expression.

"Too bad I couldn't get up and take a bow. It wasn't easy holding my breath with my chest screaming from the impact of the pellets, but what the hell. I knew I was minutes from a hot shower and some fine British tea. Last act. No curtain call. I heard a shout and some shots, but obviously, I couldn't open my eyes to see what was happening. I had to trust that all the players had read the script."

Skye rested back in the chair and grinned at this. Alex could see she was running close to empty and was putting on a show of strength. Her performance was nearly flawless. It was her eyes…usually brightened by layers of light…now nearly flat and without depth. The three from British intelligence just stared. They were in awe. This was their first dose of Skye and it was pretty intense. Jim was used to her method of initial reporting and smiled indulgently at his protégé. Her adrenalin would always crank up her presentation style, and her colorful prose would put the listener in the action with her. But the rest registered amazement at her cavalier attitude and what seemed like genuine delight.

Alex tried to ignore the pain in his gut. He was worried about the lasting effects of her escapade and there was still the residual terror over her part of the operation that had come back to the surface as she gave her report. His pride in her quieted his concern…for the moment. Later, he'd go to the gym and punch a few inanimate objects to get the remaining anxiety out of his system. It was pretty ugly and too heavy to carry around.

"Bottom line, three fingers is history. The cancer will finish off the head guy and I think I can safely say, the bounty is off my head." Skye looked over at Amanda and Cameron. She could see the two were impressed and it warmed her. "Your man was fantastic. He's a very scary character. I don't think he'll have any trouble moving up and taking the chair at the table when cancer does its job." Her smile was almost affectionate. "He really played the part. He even pushed the button on the electrical connection a few times. To tell you the truth, I wasn't completely sure until I realized I was still breathing after taking six shots that he was on board. Damn, the man can act."

Alex was smiling, but it was frozen on his lips. Glancing around the room, he wondered if there was a way to let off some of the pressure he felt now…here…before he popped. He wasn't sure he could wait to get to the gym to kick the hell out of something.

There was a knock on the door and a young woman entered. "Captain Madison, your plane is fueled and ready for pre-flight."

Skye smiled and nodded. "Thank you."

When the young woman left, Skye rose and stretched. She felt lightheaded and very stiff. Suddenly, she swayed as she felt the floor move under her feet. Alex saw and forgot about kicking things. He was right beside her and she gratefully accepted his arm.

"So where's my pilot?" she asked, swallowing against the slight feeling of nausea and working hard to ignore the cold sweat that made her skin feel separated from her body. Keep moving, she told herself. "I'd like to do a little briefing before turning over control."

Cameron stood up. "Ready for your briefing, Captain."

Skye looked at him, first in shock, then in dawning delight. "You?"

He smiled and nodded. "I'm looking forward to sharing the cockpit with you, Captain." He looked at Amanda who was chatting with Jim and the three from British intelligence. "The only thing better than the feel of a beautiful woman is the feel of a beautiful aircraft."

Amanda turned and gave him a narrow look. "Better?"

"Let me revise that."

"I would," said Amanda and made both Alex and Skye laugh.

"How about the only thing close."

"I can live with that." Amanda reached up and straightened his already impeccably straight tie. "How about a private moment before you take off?"

"You read my mind," said Cameron.

"It's a gift," smiled Amanda, putting her arm through his. "You'll excuse us for just a minute?" Alex and Skye nodded. Alex subtly moved his arm more firmly around his wife's waist. The trembling he felt would remain between them…for now. She was going to get medical attention as soon as they reached Chicago.

Amanda and Cameron went into a corner where they exchanged a few words. Personal? Professional? They probably were so intertwined after all of these years it would be difficult to separate the two.

Skye looked up at Alex. "I wonder how many times and at how many airports they've played that tune?"

"It seems to work for them," said Alex smiling down at his own personal and professional partner.

Skye nodded, loving the feel of Alex's arm gently supporting her. Indulging herself in an unprofessional moment, she put her head on his shoulder. "We're just starting. It's nice to see it can work…that there can indeed be a happily ever after." She sighed as Amanda put her arms around Cameron and he kissed her with passion. Then it was goodbye.

Cameron came over to where they were standing. He stared at Skye for a moment, saw the deep and heavy signs of pain and fatigue as she straightened and smoothed her jacket. Since she wanted him to ignore them, he did. He knew how to read a strong willed woman.

"Lead the way, Captain."

They were joined by Payton when they reached the tarmac. She was trying not to resent being excluded from whatever transpired in the small room in the terminal. Actually, her excitement over going to the United States and working with Skye and Alex on the criminal side of the investigation was an excellent consolation prize, she thought. They all shook hands and boarded the plane for home.

After familiarizing himself with the aircraft, Cameron competently and confidently took the controls. He looked over at Skye who had placed herself in the copilot's seat and winked. "Ready?"

She nodded and put her hands in a position to take over if anything went wrong on his side. This was strange. She felt like a parent dropping a child off at day care. She was confident in his abilities and knew her plane was in excellent hands, but it was still her baby. Taking a deep breath, she turned on her trust. It wasn't as difficult as she thought.

Cameron was equal to the task and Skye's assistance wasn't needed. He lifted off smoothly while she handled all the communication with the tower. He climbed to 30,000 feet, aligned them with the assigned flight plan and flipped on automatic pilot.

"Wow," he said, running his hands over the yoke like a lover caressing his mistress. "That was fun." He turned to her and grinned a pilot's grin and she returned it with an identical one of her own. They liked and respected each other before. Now they were bonded like members of some sweet secret society.

Alex came forward and put his hand on Skye's shoulder. He wanted to get another look at her. She still looked exhausted, even with the carefully applied makeup, but she had a goofy grin on her face, so she must be all right. And she was sitting down, anyway.

"We have about eight hours of flying time here," she told Alex, looking up at him. "You and Payton should use the time to kick back and get some sleep."

Cameron snorted. "Now that's not something you hear every day."

Skye looked over at him and rolled her eyes. "Cute."

"Payton is working in the communication room," said Alex, his hands now rubbing her shoulders. "She's anxious to get reports from her team. I'm going to catch some sleep in the stateroom. Join me later?"

Skye squeezed his hand and said, "maybe" but her eyes said 'not a chance.' She was in the cockpit of her plane and even though she wasn't the primary pilot, it was her responsibility. Even her husband of a week wasn't going to lure her out of it.

He smiled at her. "Well, I guess second place is better than no place at all." Then his grin turned teasing, his voice low and hypnotic. "When you're in your fifth hour of staring at the empty Atlantic and your eyes start to burn, be sure you think of me on that nice soft bed, sleeping comfortably away the hours." He patted her on the head and turned to Cameron.

"Sometimes it just pays to be the passenger half of the team. Enjoy your night with my wife." He loved to say wife and wondered if his heart would always pound that extra beat when he did. Then he turned and walked back to get some much needed sleep.

After he left, Cameron looked at the shadows under Skye's eyes and the fatigue on her face. "Skye, why don't you close your eyes for awhile?" He knew better than to suggest she leave the cockpit and join her husband in the stateroom. He was a pilot; he understood.

"I might, later." She smiled over at him. The cockpit was illuminated, but they were surrounded by dark sky and even darker ocean. The stars were bright above them and the constant sound of the engines added to the feeling of isolation. The atmosphere was perfect for confidences and private conversations. And Skye was both curious and interested in the life Cameron and Amanda shared successfully. They seemed to have it so together. She and Alex were just starting their life as a team. Maybe there was a secret to their success.

"Tell me about you and Amanda," she asked sleepily, feeling the pull of exhaustion, in spite of her will to ignore it.

"Where do I start?" he smiled.

"If it isn't classified, tell me how you met," Skye suggested.

"It's classified, but you have just enough clearance to qualify. Mandy was, well," he looked at Skye. "A great deal like you actually. I was on an assignment in what was East Germany back then. The wall was still up, the iron curtain was more than just an historical cliché, and we were engaged in a cold war. Mandy was on an assignment in Moscow. We were working in separate cells and when we met, we didn't know about each other's…well…occupation."

Cameron went back and told his story so well, that Skye could feel herself go back with him. His voice was low and melodious, his love and admiration for the woman who would become his wife and the mother of his son were obvious. Skye listened as he moved from adventure to misadventure, absorbing the tone as well as the time.

Cameron weaved in not only the facts, but descriptions of the relationship between him and Amanda. Cleverly placed among the incredible exploits were bits of advice, insight and guidance. Skye listened, and absorbed. Had her own father lived, she could imagine them flying like this, him talking, her listening, learning, growing.

She closed her eyes, Cameron's voice in her head. Soon she was drifting. And then she did see her father. Young, as she always remembered him, and smiling at her from his seat in the cockpit. He was tall and fair with wild sandy hair and soft brown eyes. It was good to see him again. She talked to him and told him all about her wedding and her life with Alex. He wanted to hear everything, said he was going to remember it all so he could tell Angel. That was what he called her mom. Angelina to everyone else, but Angel to him.

He listened to her fears and her joys. Her heart opened and she told him how she felt…so completely happy. Peace flowed into her heart mingling with the love and seemed to crowd out all the darkness that lingered in the corners. The sleep was doing more than refreshing her body, it was renewing her soul and healing her heart. There would be no more nightmares, he said and before he left he assured her he'd come back. Whenever she needed him, he'd come back.

Cameron watched her face as she fell into sleep. She was smiling and obviously engaged in a lovely dream. He was glad. She'd been through hell and back and the fact that she was having a pleasant dream was remarkable. Reminded him of someone he knew. Knew well. Someone he'd loved for over 40 years.

He smiled as he continued to study the instruments, and watch over the sleeping woman at his side. He and Mandy had a wonderful son. He was a world-class architect, highly successful and from what he could see, happy. His wife was lovely and Fisher was a constant delight. But if they'd had a daughter…his hand went over and barely stroked the fading bruise on her cheek. This was what he could imagine they would have had. His enemies and even many of his colleagues would have been startled and disbelieving to see the tender expression on his face as they continued to race across the Atlantic.

They were flying over water. Skye was in the cockpit, confident, smiling and talking with the tower. He was in the back, working as usual on his laptop. He had several briefs to complete and needed to get them out before they arrived back in the states. Looking up and staring out the window, he frowned as the scene changed.

What the hell? He must have fallen asleep. They were driving through a piazza in Rome; he saw people, a number of elegant buildings and the familiar statuary so prevalent in this beautiful city. How did he get in a car? Was he on the way somewhere from the airport? The back seat was empty and he couldn't see the driver.

Where was Skye? Asking the driver to stop, he opened the door and jumped out. Across the street was a flower vendor. Gardenias. Perfect. Crossing over, he negotiated a sale in his pitiful Italian. Skye would have done a much better job. Where was she? Then he turned around and saw her. Skye. He was confused, but delighted. Excited. She was in the car. In the driver's seat, in her uniform. She must have just arrived from the airport. Smiling, she waved to him, then shifted to start the car and bring it around to pick him up. Something didn't feel right. A shiver ran up his spine and he opened his mouth to warn her, but no sound came out. Suddenly, there was a roar and a tower of flames shot out of the car. Skye! He couldn't get to her…his body went numb, his mind dissolved in the pillar of fire.

The next thing he knew he was standing in a morgue. How did he get there? He must be in shock. There was a body…female…tall, lean…covered with a sheet, but the hands were exposed…crossed over the chest…grasping perfect Gardenia blossoms. As if she was already in a coffin. Walking slowly over to the table, his eyes fastened on them and couldn't even blink. Her hands. Bones covered with chunks of burned flesh. Grotesque. Her face was covered with a red cloth. Who? Who was under there?

On the bone that had once been a finger was the diamond he'd given Skye. Shining against a bed of scarred, charred flesh. Hunks of mottled, blackened skin and tendons. He couldn't breathe. The flowers flashed, then disappeared and in the skeletal hands rested the compass. He stared at it, grief hitting him, leaking through the shock. He had to be sure.

Clearly, in his head, he heard her voice. "It's the talisman that will protect you from harm. It's always worked for me. Keep it with you. It will forever point to me when we're apart."

God, no. She'd given him her protection and without it, she perished. The needle pointed toward the face…he had to be sure. Reaching up, he pulled down the cloth. Skye. It was her…her eyes…her eyes in the sockets of a hideous face. Blackened flesh pealing off the stark white skull, teeth exposed. Skye's eyes. He felt himself falling, screaming. Sanity falling with him, madness opening up and swallowing him.

Alex woke up with a start, breathing heavily, his body shaking, his face covered with sweat. He didn't move…just laid still and tried to force the images out of his head. The pulse of engines told him they were still in the air. In the air…not in a morgue in Rome. God. His pulse was still racing and he couldn't get his breathing under control. Looking around to assure himself that he was in the bed in the stateroom, reality began to reassert itself. The sheets were a tangled, damp mess. Skye. Glancing over, he saw the bed was empty. He didn't think that would ever make him feel relieved, but it did. She wasn't beside him.

Sitting up, he felt disoriented and groggy. Sleep should have refreshed him, but he felt sluggish, exhausted, and completely unsettled. His body screamed for rest, but he couldn't stomach going back to sleep. Wondered if he could ever close his eyes again. The image of her in the morgue had faded, but not totally dissolved from his brain.

Was this what it was like for her every night? Damn it. It was so real. It was a dream, but his reactions were not bounded by it. His horror, grief, shock, and revulsion were still with him and horribly disturbing. The emotions seeped into his wakefulness.

He raked his fingers through his hair and rubbed his damp face. He must not have really screamed. No one came into the room to investigate. Christ, his whole body was reacting to the shock, fear and unbelievable grief. The emotions were real, even though the dream was not. Getting up he almost staggered to the lavatory. Washing up, he stared into the face in the mirror. His face. He'd have to get it under control before he went out there, but he was desperate to see and touch Skye. Taking a few deep breaths, he tried to smile. It was worse than the parodies on Mardi Gras masks. He decided not to try to smile. He didn't feel like it…didn't know when he'd feel like it again.

Maybe he could work up a smile if he found his wife and got a huge dose of looking at her. He guessed the antidote for this kind of out-of-body experience was to be grounded by Skye. The reality of her. All of a sudden, he had to see her, feel her, hold her. Urgently.

Skye was in the cockpit talking with Cameron. She woke up a half hour before feeling happy. Free. Content. The exhaustion was still there, but had backed off. After apologizing to Cameron for falling asleep during one of his escapades, she took over the communications. The feelings as well as the memories of the dream were still with her. It did a lot to refresh her, although she knew there was a heavy load of hurt just below the surface.

She smiled up at Alex when she felt him standing in the doorway.

"I was just going to wake you. We'll be landing in less than an hour."

He looked at her, his expression unreadable. She looked better, but sometimes cockpit adrenalin did that. His hands ached to touch her, so he came in and put them lightly on her shoulders.

"Are we coming in over Canada?"

"Just below," she said. She felt something coming through his fingertips. His eyes were shadowed, but there was something in them that disturbed her.

"How's he doing?" asked Alex nodding in Cameron's direction.

"I think we can safely take him off probation."

Cameron looked up and grinned. "I'm thinking about applying for a full time position. This baby is a dream. She practically flies herself."

"Now don't be telling him that," said Skye. "He'll cut my salary."

She was foolishly pleased with Cameron's approval. Looking more closely at Alex she saw that even though he was smiling slightly, there was something in is eyes. His pupils were very large, transforming the usual brilliant blue into something much darker. And he was just staring at her. Something about the look…then she recognized it. She'd seen it often enough in her own mirror. The nightmare.

"You want coffee before we take this baby off auto?" she asked Cameron.

"I'd love some. Shall we buzz the flight attendant?" he teased.

"I'm afraid I am your entire flight crew on this journey," returned Skye, unbuckling her seatbelt. She was accustomed to some stiffness when she got up after a long flight, but this time her legs felt almost unresponsive. She nearly fell back into her seat. Alex reached over automatically, and she gratefully took his hand. Cameron ignored her discomfort, even though his heart expanded a little.

She walked back into the cabin holding Alex's hand, accepting his support. When they were alone in the galley, she turned to him and reached up, taking his face in her hands.

"What's the matter, darling?"

He looked at her for a minute, then said. "Just tired. I didn't get a lot of sleep this week."

True, but not good enough, she thought. She knew there was more but would wait for him to tell her, if that was what he wanted to do. She continued to look up at him, love pouring from her eyes.

Gently, tenderly, he took her in his arms and just held her. Skye. Her feel, her scent, her heart beating steadily against his.

Skye felt the tension, sensed the strain. She decided that for now, he didn't need to put what he was feeling, thinking into words. Moving her arms around his waist she stepped in closer, felt herself melt into him, their hearts beating together. His lips found hers and his kiss was demanding. He wanted, his body needed, and his soul hungered for her. She gave him more than she would have thought possible with clothes between them. The kiss seemed timeless because time stopped for them. Instinct told her what was in his heart. The pain. The suffering. The love. What his love for her cost him.

"I love you, Alex," she murmured, when his lips finally let go and she rested her head on his shoulder. "Let's get through the next few days, then we'll work together to erase this...this horrific honeymoon from hell."

"Cameron told me to compartmentalize." Alex breathed her in until he drowned in her essence. He told Skye what the older man had said. "It helped with my short term reaction...when I would have run after you and dragged you away from what you were walking into...he's a very...insightful man." He took her arms in his hands and pushed her gently back until she could look into his eyes. "But the longer term fix is going to take some time."

"I understand," she said, then lost herself in his next, breathless kiss. "Darling, I understand perfectly. Was it bad? The nightmare?"

Staring at her, he saw she wouldn't have to know the details to know what his mind had done to him while he was sleeping.

"I can't even describe it."

"You don't have to. Just hold on to the reality. Hold on to me."

When she looked up into his face and he stared back at her, some of the life returned to his eyes and she was glad. The reversal of their roles was not lost on either of them. It forged a deeper understanding. "I need you Skye," he said simply then gathered her back to his chest. "Just give me a few more minutes here, okay?"

Nodding, she let him hold her. It felt so good. Smiling against his neck, she decided to do a little nibbling while she was there. His cure had definite positive side effects.

"Can I talk you into my bed?" he asked finally, feeling his body's reaction to her talented lips.

"No."

"Was that regret I heard in your voice?"

"That would be deep, profound, intense, extreme regret."

"Hmm. Well I guess that's something to hold on to." He gave her a last squeeze and a deep breath shook out most of the residual effects of the nightmare. "You go give the captain his brew, and I'll go nudge the inspector."

"Be sure she's unarmed. She sounds like someone with a low flash point."

"Then she sounds familiar." He looked down at her and kissed the end of her nose. She sniffed, nudged him with her hip and poured four cups of hot, fragrant coffee. "Maybe if you come bearing gifts."

"Good plan."

"Strategic planning is one of my strengths."

He grabbed another breath-stealing kiss. "And dosing the morning flashpoint is one of mine."

"Just see that you don't employ the same methods on her as you do on me."

"I have good reason not to."

"And that would be…"

"I want to live."

Chuckling, Skye took her two mugs and went back into the cockpit. She didn't think she'd ever come to this point as long as she was captain of this craft, but she was actually glad Cameron was the responsible pilot. She was feeling extremely sluggish, more than she cared to admit. She felt she needed a week of sleep and an entire buffet of nutrients, but took a sip of her coffee instead. Caffeine would have to do for now.

"He all right?" asked Cameron, taking the coffee gratefully.

"Better," said Skye, not surprised he'd read Alex so well.

"It isn't easy, Skye. The hardest job we have in this business is seeing our spouse in jeopardy."

"I know."

He glanced over at her. "That's right. You do."

"He told me you helped him. I'm grateful."

"It's like a support group. Men who love their daring, fearless, brilliant, uncompromising, hard nosed, strong willed, danger seeking, risk taking, audacious, sometimes foolhardy wives too much."

"Can I quote you?" laughed Skye.

"Hell no." Cameron smiled over at her. "Strap in and I'll get us on the ground."

They landed smoothly 25 minutes later and taxied to a stop outside the customs office at O'Hare Airport in Chicago.

When they completed their post flight checklist, they joined Alex and Payton in the cabin and exited the aircraft. Cameron talked with a woman in the custom's office and they were through the process and out of the terminal in less than five minutes. The air was brisk and the night sky was filled with stars. Home, thought Skye and she longed for a bath, a bed and a plate of pancakes.

"This is where I say goodbye," said Cameron. He gave them all a firm handshake. "I'll let Mandy keep you apprised of any developments."

"Thanks for everything," said Alex and smiled. "I hope next time we meet it'll be a social function."

Cameron nodded. That would be his hope as well. He turned back to Payton. "Payton, it was a pleasure. If you're interested in moving from law enforcement into intelligence, you have the number I gave you."

"Thank you, Cameron," Payton said, showing her dimples. "I'll keep it in mind. But I'm afraid I'm a cop through and through."

Cameron looked at Skye and nodded approvingly. "I only wish the average citizen could know the price some people pay to keep their way of life secure. We're in your debt, Skye."

Skye smiled and kissed him on the cheek. "I appreciated the opportunity to pay back my own debt. Give our love to Amanda when you see her."

Then Cameron nodded, turned and disappeared in the direction of the large international terminal.

"Who was that masked man, kemo sabe?" asked Payton as she watched his back.

"I haven't the faintest idea," said Skye shrugging.

"What man?" asked Alex.

"You're a canny fankle," said Payton, laughing.

"Was that an insult?" asked Skye leaning against Alex again.

"I don't know, sounded poetic to me," said Alex, smiling. "That's what I like about the Scottish tongue, so musical even when getting nasty."

"And what was that about a phone number?" inquired Skye.

"That would be classified," said Payton.

"You liked saying that far too much, Inspector," said Alex.

"Aye. It was a rush at that," winked Payton.

CHAPTER 13

Alex arranged for a driver and car to take them to a penthouse unit he owned in one of the residential apartments downtown. They'd decided to keep Payton officially at a distance so she'd be staying at the Intercontinental on Michigan Avenue. She'd be conducting her investigation through official channels, then reporting to Skye and Alex unofficially. They made arrangements to meet the next afternoon for phase two of the investigation.

By the time they'd dropped off Payton and let themselves into the beautifully decorated top floor apartment, Skye's fatigue came to collect. What was a general weariness was now close to total collapse. Her eyes were so blurry, she couldn't even see Chicago's skyline much less appreciate its beauty. An entire wall of windows gave them a panoramic view of the city but all Skye wanted to do was get horizontal and catch the view of the inside of her eyelids. She didn't even stop, as she usually did, to gaze at the magnificent mile. Walking out of her shoes, she just headed straight for the bedroom, shedding clothes along the way.

Alex wanted to stay in the street and go for a walk to work out some of the kinks in his limbs and the fuzz around the edges of his brain, but he couldn't let Skye go up and into the apartment alone. He wasn't sure when he'd let her out of his sight again. The feeling of walking into their castle suite and finding her missing hadn't faded. He didn't know when it would, but he was sure it hadn't yet. He wanted to stay close

Locking up, he checked everything, made some calls, then followed his wife's debris field into the bedroom. She was lying on top of the bed, sound asleep and completely naked.

"Well, so much for any hope of starting the honeymoon tonight," he said and went over to gently move his slumbering bride between the sheets. She didn't stir…even when he brushed the hair from her face and softly kissed her goodnight.

Straightening and flexing his tired muscles, he went out to the bar room and fixed himself a drink. Letting the scotch warm him on the inside, he walked over to the windows and stood for a long time staring out over the city where he grew up. There was comfort here. In the morning, they would have work to do, but for now he just wanted to stand still and let the arms of his hometown embrace him in familiar surroundings, whispering assurance. He finished his drink, confident now that he could attempt sleep.

Skye woke up once during the night, and Alex watched as she weaved to the bathroom. He got up when she came back out, because she only made it a few steps from the doorway before she stopped. Her eyes were closed and it looked like she was going to just curl up on the floor. Chuckling a little, he guided her back to bed.

She sighed and mumbled "I'm hungry."

"What would you like?" he asked, doubtful she'd be awake enough to eat anything. Her eyes never opened.

He didn't think she was going to answer him as he tucked her in for the second time. But she yawned hugely, stretched and said, "I don't think pink is a color in the rainbow."

"Darling, you aren't making any sense," he said in her ear, but she was out again.

Even though his own exhaustion had returned, Alex didn't sleep well. The nightmare didn't make an encore appearance, but he kept waking and reaching over to be sure Skye was beside him. A couple of times, he'd just lay there, listening to the muffled sounds of the city and allow himself to feel. Pure emotion would seize him, rob him of the comfort of sleep.

His body remembered the grief, the fear. The only way he was going to purge himself of it was to let it consume him, then squeeze it out. His heart raced and his body tensed when he relived the moment Payton handed him Skye's rings, the long walk between the door of the morgue and the body. And the hand. The hideous burned hand.

I'm sounding like a tortured hero from Edgar Allen Poe's imagination, he thought when he kept seeing the hand every time he closed his eyes. He needed a new visual. So he tried. He thought of Skye on their wedding day, then his mind would drift and he saw her lying on the floor of a filthy dungeon, blood soaking her sweatshirt. A few times he got up and paced, confident that not even an earthquake would wake his wife. But then he'd want her beside him, feel her warm and alive next to him so he'd return to her in their bed. Lying there, watching her breathe, he could rest.

As if she felt the emotions, Skye moaned and turned into him. He gathered her up, held her and stared at the ceiling. What if these people had decided revenge was what they wanted more than information? What if their plan had not been to kidnap her but to kill her? Tonight he'd be somewhere in the world, his arms empty; his heart hollow. He held her tighter. The heartache was fading as the light in the room began to reflect the dawn, but not completely. Was it a blessing to love this woman, or a curse? Her hand moved and rested across his chest. He stared at it. Would he ever be able to get that charred hand out his subconscious?

Kissing his new wife he decided to give up on the sleeping. Slipping out of bed, he quickly dressed. He'd work for a while. Get back to a routine. Think of other things.

Standing next to the bed, he stared down at Skye, twisting his wedding ring. He smiled. His wife.

Skye was scheduled to spend the next day at the Lakeview Medical Center getting all her systems checked. She put up a fight when she awoke feeling human and ravenous. But he used his 'no compromise, take no prisoners' voice on her. He didn't realize that it wasn't so much the tone of his voice as the still haunted look in his eyes that had her agreeing in the end.

"Only if you take me first to Charlie's for one of their cholesterol specials…you know, the eggs, bacon, sausage, biscuits, pancakes. Oh, man. Right now I'd consider trading my Cessna for a stack of pancakes."

Alex raised his eyebrows and gave her a skeptical look. She was glad to see light return to his eyes.

"Okay, so not the Cessna, but certainly my half of the truck," she shrugged.

"You can't do that."

"Community property, buster. You forgot to negotiate a prenuptial agreement. Ha! You fool!"

"I mean you can't trade away half a truck."

"Look, the only thing keeping that truck together is the dirt. So I'll have it washed, wait for it to collapse in a heap, put half of it in a bushel basket and trade it off."

Alex just stared at her. "Where did we start this conversation?"

"Not sure. Doesn't matter. Take me to breakfast and we'll figure it out."

He smiled as she made her way to the bathroom to get ready for the day. She didn't know that three lawyers in his office had suggested a prenuptial contract before he made it clear he wasn't even going to consider something so idiotic. His smile turned wicked. If she ever left him, she'd need every penny of half his estate just to run and in the end, he'd catch her. He'd buy one of those castles in Scotland to put her in…just like…hell…which one of those characters was locked in a castle? Was that Cinderella or Sleeping Beauty? Repunzel? Maybe it was Alice or Little Red Riding Hood. Didn't matter. She'd never leave him…he wouldn't let her.

He considered taking advantage of her in the shower, but when he saw her gingerly lower herself into the huge jacuzzi, he decided to go to their private gym instead. He'd pound something for a while, then take her to the doctor to be sure she was going to be all right.

Other than more weight loss, which she vowed to take care of by the end of the week and general fatigue and symptoms of prolonged exposure, a low blood count, and nutritional concerns, the doctors told her what she already knew. No permanent damage…if she followed instructions. They recommended a diet high in protein, a whole regimen of nutritional supplements and a week of solid bed rest. The latter was essential because of her compromised immune system. She neglected to tell Alex about that detail, vowing to herself that if she kept moving, no germ could catch up anyway. Alex drove through the city and marveled at her ability to bounce back.

"See, I told you and Jim that I was fine. I just need to bulk up some and take all these vitamins. Let's go to Tony's for a pizza, then to Razzamatazz for a big fat burger."

Alex laughed. "Think we might be able to squeeze in some ice cream from Sammy's? And let's not leave out the Captain's Crabhouse for a lobster with shrimp chasers." He looked her up and down. "And where the hell did you put that huge breakfast you packed in already today?"

"Don't laugh, you dog. These were the things I'd think about while I was down in that dungeon. Those bastards made me stand for hours and I retained a backbone by keeping my mind focused on food. Once, when my ribs started in with that goddamn throbbing, I imagined the ribs from the Charhouse in Kansas City. I kid you not, I could smell them. I imagined myself up to my elbows in ribs and sauce."

Skye's hands were flying and she was looking around, delighted to be in Chicago, completely oblivious to what her words were doing to Alex's own appetite. "Then I decided to work my way from coast to coast and could conjure a favorite dish from every restaurant I'd been in from San Francisco to New York. It kept me on my feet, I tell you. I should write a book. I was about to start on Europe when they decided to move from deprivation to electric shock. That kind of drained my brain. Every time…" Her voice wound down quickly when she saw the expression on Alex's face turn from delight to something dark and brooding.

"Alex," she said, touching his arm, cursing herself for being so stupid. She understood in her heart that as horrific as the experience had been for her, it was even worse for him. Her torture had been physical and her body was now recovering nicely. His was psychological and that, she knew from personal experience, took a great deal longer to heal. "Darling. It's over. We've been through worse."

"Yeah, I know." He laced his fingers through hers and turned over her hand so he could see the diamond in her ring catch the light. "Tell me something."

"Anything." His hand was warm, his voice deep and soft. She didn't think the flutter in her stomach was just a craving for ribs anymore.

He sighed and put the smile back on. It really was a beautiful day. Why spoil it? She was here. She got a good report from the doctor. Why relive the nightmare? He decided to put it away. "What do you want on your pizza?"

She knew he was about to ask something else. She'd give him space to bring it up in his own time.

"Lobster, shrimp and a scoop of Rocky Road," she said and squeezed his hand.

CHAPTER 14

Skye and Alex picked up Payton on their way back to the apartment. Payton was going to work out of their residence. Their equipment was better and there would be a great deal more privacy. They filled her in on the doctor's report and she was delighted. She'd interviewed friends and former lovers of Emily, secured the name of her dentist and would be meeting with him the next day. Emily had no family other than a few aunts, uncles and cousins. No one close, either geographically or emotionally. Another reason Pavel chose her, she thought. No one to be alarmed when she went missing…no one to take the initiative to issue a formal report. Maybe ever. Payton's liaison at the Evanston police department was going to get her a search warrant for Emily's apartment. Maybe there would be something linking her to Pavel.

"I'm nearly positive it's her, but we want to be sure. The modeling agency that originally sent her to Paris turned out to be legitimate…no obvious ties to Miami. A well-established firm with some really big names on its client list. Apparently they haven't worked with her in months. Pavel must have made a contact independently. Many models visit competing agencies before they sign a contract and some maintain relationships with several on a non-exclusive basis."

Barclay was working with Payton to narrow down the hundreds of agencies in northern Illinois based on corporate reputation, timing, and apparent legitimacy. They weren't sure Pavel would have set up another front, but it was a place to start.

"After we drop you off, Alex and I are heading downtown," Skye reported. "Alex has a meeting and I'm going to the Serenity Spa to spiff up. Slap on some extra makeup, put this hair in order and I think I might be presentable. Then tomorrow, I'm going to canvas the modeling agencies you all come up with."

"You going to be the bait?" asked Payton. The word had Alex's stomach seizing again.

314

"Yes. I'm guessing he's still looking for a particular type. Tall, thin, fair-haired. I figure I'm as emaciated as I'll ever be. I'm older than I was, but I don't think that will matter if he's still looking for women to sell overseas."

Alex looked over at his wife. "Darling. His people will take one look at you and know for a fact there is a god."

Payton smiled. That was so sweet.

When Payton was finished with her research and all her e-mails had been sent, she went into the combination barroom/den and began working on her report. At one end of the room was a magnificent oak bar with an old pub feel and on the opposite end of the large space was a stone fireplace. There were glass doors leading out onto a terrace and she could see the city beyond. It was a beautiful city. She liked its energy and its location on the shores of Lake Michigan. Sitting on one of the soft leather sofas in front of the fireplace, she poured over the papers from her briefcase. She sipped tea and was absorbed in the data, not realizing what a tantalizing picture she presented. She wore a slight frown, her reading glasses accentuating her green eyes, her short red hair shining in the reflected light. She'd removed her jacket and pushed up the sleeves of her thin cotton sweater. She looked more like a professor than a cop.

It was Tank's first glimpse of her and his reaction was powerful and interested. He'd let himself into the apartment with his spare key. His mom had told him Skye and Alex were in town, so he assumed they would be there. He'd come right off the street, so he was still in uniform.

This must be the guest from Scotland they brought with them, he thought. She was a beauty. He smiled. Time to turn on the Springfield charm.

Tank cleared his throat. Her reflexes where quick, but subtle. In one quick motion, she turned, removed her glasses, recognized his presence, saw the uniform, deemed him harmless, placed her papers back in her briefcase, secured them, and stood up.

"Hi," he said, looking into her big fabulous green eyes and getting stuck on the next words. "Ah…you must have come in with Skye and Alex."

"I did, yes." She didn't elaborate. She was smiling in a friendly, but professional manner. "And might you be from the Chicago Police Department, officer?" She was a bit confused. She knew that Skye and Alex had decided to pursue a few leads in the city, but she didn't think they would have sent a liaison with the Chicago Police Department without contacting her first. And how did he get in here? She decided to use her vast investigatory experience and find out. "How did you get in here?"

"I have a key." He held it up. Her accent captivated him. He wanted to ask her questions, just to get her to continue to talk. At her look of confusion, he laughed. "My brother owns the place."

Her face cleared and Tank felt the first shock wave of lust when she smiled broadly and held out her hand. "Sure, then. You must be Tank. I should have known. Skye told me about you." Actually Skye had told her she was anxious that they meet and strongly implied that they fall in love, get married and have several beautiful bouncing babies. "There was just no family resemblance."

He took her hand and wasn't inclined to let it go. It was firm and well muscled. Since the hand belonged to her, she reclaimed it, but not before she felt the energy surging through his fingers. She wasn't sure if it was the natural energy of a virile, incredibly handsome man, or if it was completely unique to him. She was intrigued enough and attracted enough to want to find out.

"Hey, I'll take that as a compliment. It's tough living in the shadow of such an ugly big brother."

"Actually your brother is what a young woman's imagination would conjure if she was engaged in an afternoon fantasy." She showed Tank her dimples, knowing full well that they were a favorite of the opposite sex. And she liked Tank's reaction. Absolutely no jealousy, rivalry or envy. Just sincere pride and affection.

"Okay. You're right, just don't tell him that. He's already impossibly conceited." Tank's grin and tone were teasing.

"I was referring to the coloring, anyway." She touched her own red hair. "You look like you have a touch of the Scot in your blood."

He laughed. "More than a touch. Grandma Colleen MacKnight emigrated from Edinburgh sometime in the late 1920's." Tank grinned. "When I popped out with red curls and dimples, she wrapped me in plaid and drank a fifth of Dunfife."

Payton added a delighted throaty laugh to the overall picture she presented, and another wave of lust hit Tank broadside. He reached up and loosed his tie. He was feeling a little warm.

"I didn't get your name."

"It's Payton. Payton Brady." Her own dimples came through again. She was finding it a bit warm in the apartment herself. This man was unbelievably attractive. His uniform fit his muscular frame perfectly and accentuated the wide shoulders and well developed chest. He had beautiful eyes and a killer smile. She noticed no ring and he had a flirty style. Since Skye had been anxious for them to meet, she assumed he was currently unattached.

Payton was used to men going flirty with her, particularly when she was out of uniform. She rarely encouraged them. Most of her relationships were intense and short. She knew she had issues with men that she needed to resolve, but she just wasn't inclined to do so yet. Never really felt the need. No man had held her interest for long.

"Well, Payton," said Tank, deciding to take the tie off completely. "Don't let me interrupt your work."

"My work?"

"Yes, whatever you were doing when I came in." He nodded toward the brief case.

It wasn't that she didn't trust Alex's brother, but the reports were very confidential at this point and she rather they stayed in her secured briefcase.

"I needed a break, anyway." She noticed his strong, capable hands as they loosened and removed the tie. She loved strong capable hands.

FLIGHT INTO FATE *and* FLIGHT INTO DESTINY

"Great, let me shuck some of the hardware and we can relax. Maybe I'll have you read the Chicago Sun Times to me."

"I beg your pardon?"

"Just so I can listen to the Scottish in your voice."

Tank's hand moved to his weapon. Payton felt a slight tension in her gut; she knew she was completely exposed. Her reaction to someone going for a weapon was instinctual and automatic. Her own weapon was in her briefcase. She managed to suppress most of the involuntary response, but apparently not all of it. Tank slowed his hand and turned to the long wall unit in the corner before he snapped his weapon off his belt, laid it on the shelf and took off his utility belt, radio, and other cop gear.

Tank saw the little movement when his hand went to his weapon. Stupid, he thought. He was so used to having guns in the house, he sometimes forgot that not all civilians were comfortable around them. She looked more alert than frightened or grossed out, though. That brought up his curiosity a notch.

"You, ah, work with Skye and Alex?" he asked. Maybe she was an agent, or something.

"Oh no," Payton said easily. "I just met them. Alex and I have business, that's all." She wasn't sure what Alex's brother knew or didn't know. It wasn't her place to reveal anything at this point.

"He buying a castle in Scotland, or a golf course," Tank asked as he made his way over to the bar.

She laughed again. "I'm sure I don't know about that. I'm collaborating with him on some legal work."

"Ah." Tank opened the small refrigerator and grabbed a beer. "Can I get you a drink?"

She nodded her head. "Aye."

She assessed again as she watched him casually open the bottle and drink half of it in one big swallow. He came in, still in uniform and grabbed a beer right away. Her stomach fell and her smile dimmed at notch. At least he didn't go for the scotch.

"Want a Scotch?" he asked, as he grabbed the bottle off the back shelf and placed it on the bar in front of him. "I could be persuaded to join you."

"Can't abide the stuff," she said easily, although her eye did fall on his hands around the scotch bottle. Bloody hell. Well, it wasn't like she was ever going to see him again after today. "I'll have a Perrier, please."

"Can't abide your national drink? Will they allow you back into the country?" Tank laughed easily and got her Perrier out of the refrigerator. Just then, he heard Skye and Alex in the foyer.

"Ah, the owners." Tank opened the bottled water and set it in front of her, smiling broadly. "I guess that means we have to postpone the drunken orgy I had planned."

Payton laughed in spite of herself and when Skye came through the doorway, she saw Payton and Tank in one momentary snapshot. The first thought that hit her was 'perfect.' She stopped in her tracks while the image sunk in. Alex nearly ran into her.

"What?" he asked, on alert.

"Oh, just something that caught my eye," she said in one of those sly little womanly voices that made brave men shudder and cowards dive for cover.

Something was up, he thought. What was it? Lord, give me a clue. He looked over at Tank and Payton. Big hint. Okay. So that question was answered before he needed to spend any time thinking about it. He patted Skye's butt and whispered in her ear.

"Move along, my darling cupid. Time to get out your little bow and arrow again."

"Oh, I think Tank can shoot his own arrows just fine. It looks like he's chugged a whole bottle of testosterone and topped it with a charm chaser."

Alex snorted. "It's just the uniform. God. Women are such suckers for a stuffed police issue."

"Yeah, but what stuffing." Skye batted her eyes. She'd just spent the last hour at the spa wiping some of the surface fatigue away with creams and treatments. The rest was hidden under expertly applied makeup. She looked good.

But not good enough to fool Tank. He turned and stared at the two of them. Damn, he thought. What the hell had they been up to now? Certainly a honeymoon, even one that was intensely physical wouldn't do that to her. She looked absolutely spent. And Alex was hovering, with his arm around her waist like she'd collapse if she didn't have his support.

"I think I might just have to get me one." Alex smiled, squeezing his wife and leading her over to a stool by the bar...not letting go until she sat.

"Get you one what, big brother? What could possibly be manufactured on this planet that you don't already have?" Tank grinned at his brother, not missing the lost pounds and the signs of sleeplessness written on his face, too. And it wasn't because of any damn honeymoon, he thought. But, as usual, he didn't ask. He kept his worry buried along with Alex's secrets.

"A little brother with brains." Alex walked over and grabbed Tank's offered hand over the bar and affectionately shook it.

"Got to talk to Mom about that. But judging from all the moaning around the house about how hot it is all the time, I'd guess her childbearing years are over. Sometimes she pushes enough heat out of one of her flashes to melt candle wax."

"Such a conversation to have about your mother," scolded Skye with a mock frown. She leaned over and gave Tank a kiss. So, Tank thought as he looked more closely at Skye's face. They were in it together and, whatever it was, it was scary. She went on, appreciating his discretion and knowing how difficult it was for him to curb his interest and curiosity. "Remind me never to leave the room. I can't imagine what you must say about me when my back is turned."

"You mean other than your table manners and your drinking problem?" snorted Tank.

Skye rolled her eyes at him and turned her attention to Payton. "I see you've met."

"He's a wee bit hard to miss," said Payton pleasantly.

Tank decided to take it as a compliment. It was his call and he thought anything delivered in that sexy voice was high praise. And he decided to return the favor.

"And hard to miss such a bodacious addition to your room décor." Tank winked at Payton and finished off the beer. "I used to be able to catch a few beauties as they bounced off Alex, but since he met Skye, there's been only one woman around here. And she seems to prefer my brother. Go figure."

Skye looked around the room hopefully. "Where's my baby? I thought you were going to bring him."

"Your baby?" asked Payton with some surprise. She looked from Skye to Tank.

"Mrs. Kramer upstairs watches him while I'm at work. I came right here at the end of my shift."

"Well, darn. When I heard your voice, I was all excited. I wanted to see him. I bet he's grown inches and inches."

"You've only been gone a little over a week. Let me assure you the little asshole has done nothing but cry all night and chew holes in my sox. I think he suffered severe separation anxiety. Mom took the beast a couple of times so I could get a good night's sleep."

"Your baby?" asked Payton again. "You have a baby?"

Skye looked at Payton and grinned sheepishly. "Kevlar, my puppy."

"Ah," laughed Payton, delighted that this tough, nearly invincible woman called a puppy her baby.

"I miss him," sighed Skye, unashamedly.

"What about me? If I lick your face and shit in your shoe, will you miss me, too?" asked Tank grinning.

"If you do that, I'm sure I'll find you irresistible," said Skye, patting him on the cheek.

"You ready for a brew, Alex?" asked Tank as he opened the refrigerator and grabbed two bottles.

Twice in less than ten minutes, thought Payton.

"Sure." Alex went and sat next to Payton at the bar.

"What about you, Skye."

"No, nothing right now." She was reluctant to put anything intoxicating in her system. She wasn't sure if alcohol would put her under in her weakened state.

"I know, my presence is intoxicating enough." He handed a beer to Alex.

Payton watched Tank drink heartily from his bottle. She looked down at the uniform and back at the bottle as he chatted with Alex about the Bears. Skye didn't miss the little flash of disapproval she saw in Payton's eyes. Not good, she thought. She was determined that they would make a glorious couple and even a little flash like that had to be evaluated, analyzed and defused. She could already see Tank was attracted. He was wearing his 'love me' smile. Skye tilted her head. It really did look like Kelvar's grin.

Payton didn't stay long. They were all jet lagged and she had several meetings the next day. Their implicit agreement was that nothing needed to be done that evening, and certainly not with Tank there. So they just enjoyed the conversation and Tank had them howling over Grandma McKnight stories.

"Where are you staying?" asked Tank as Payton got up to leave, thinking he'd like to see the inside of her hotel room. He'd already established she was unattached. In his opinion, that made them perfectly compatible.

"Intercontinental," replied Payton.

"Great. I live near there. How about we share a cab? I had a few too many beers, or I'd drive you."

"A deal. Good night Alex. Skye. I'll contact you in the morning." They were off in a wave of laughter and sexual tension.

Skye and Alex talked with Jim for a while. They had everything nearly wrapped up at the castle and were coming back to Washington. Amanda was stationed at the B&B near the relay phone. Pavel was still calling in instructions and his now dead accomplices were being dubbed into tape with fictitious reports. He called from a stolen satellite phone, so even though they had the number, they couldn't fix his location.

The news from China was mixed. Sung Du had selected Tan Sha, which was a triumph. On the other hand Sung Du was determined to find Pavel before he died. Ekaterina Rustam recruited an entire Russian team of ex-KGB to locate him. Only Sung Du knew whether it was to capture or kill.

"So it's a race," said Skye, smiling. Alex could imagine Jim smiling too at the excitement in her voice. She did love a challenge. "We've narrowed down the number of agencies. We'll be ready for direct surveillance tomorrow."

"Well done," said Jim. "How are you feeling?"

"Fine," said Skye as if one word was sufficient. Topic covered. Subject changed. On to more important things. "Do you have a team standing by to take Pavel to his final destination?" They spent another half hour talking about how they were going to handle the delivery to Langley.

Alex kept his eye on Skye, watching as she began to fade and drift. After they hung up, he talked her out of going over to Tank's to get the dog. It was a sign of her general fatigue that it didn't take much effort.

"Maybe he stayed with Payton," she said optimistically.

Alex laughed. "You really are hopeless."

"No, really darling. I think I'm quite the opposite. I think I'm hopeful."

"There was something going on between them."

"There definitely was something brewing there," said Skye, smiling slyly, resisting the urge to rub her hands together. She got up to get a bottle of water and nearly collapsed.

All of a sudden, it was like a switch turned off inside her and her generator quit. She felt clammy and weak. A ripple of extreme exhaustion started at her knees and worked up her spine. There was a dark shadow collecting along her peripheral vision and she was looking down a long tunnel at the wall behind the bar. She wanted to call for Alex, but she couldn't marshal enough energy to speak.

"Can we get our own brew perking?" Alex asked, hopefully. He wanted to get his bride naked and in his arms. His body ached to make love to her. When he turned, he saw her suddenly grab the side of the bar.

"What is it," he asked rushing over to her.

"Dizzy," she said in a weak voice, blinking until everything came back into focus. He picked her up and she laid her head against his shoulder.

"Darling, I think you pushed yourself over the top again."

"I won't stay in bed for a week," she mumbled against his neck.

"Is that what the doctor's told you to do?"

"I'm not talking."

"Tell me."

"No. You can't make me." She sighed and closed her eyes. Just before she fell asleep in his arms, she whispered, "zap me. I can take it."

Alex carried her to their bedroom, gently undressed her and laid her between the sheets. He stared at her for a moment then went out to the bar and drank until the twisting in his gut retreated. She could take it, all right. He went to the gym and beat the crap out of a very heavy leather punching bag. It worked to dissolve some of the superficial darkness from his soul, but there was still plenty there to deal with.

She could take it. He knew that. He'd been less than a mile from her and watched as she took it for nearly three days. Suddenly, everything came pouring out of him…all the fear, the self loathing, the pain. He was manic as he went from machine to machine, from punching leather to racing uphill on the treadmill.

When he was exhausted and felt more in control he went back to the bedroom. After showering, he slid in next to her, gathering her close. It was a long time before sleep came to him. Skye still hadn't moved, but he could feel her breathing. Maybe she could take it, but he wasn't sure he could.

"I'd like to see you again," Tank said when the cab arrived in front of her hotel. "Would you like to go out for dinner tomorrow night?"

"I…ah." Payton stumbled with the 'see you again' part. As if they'd just been on a date or something. His powerful masculine aura was floating all over in the dark back seat of a cab. She'd been working on keeping her hormones from declaring a sexual emergency on the short ride to her hotel. Not too successfully either. By the time they stopped in front of the Intercontinental Hotel, his presence filled the back seat and she felt she was drowning in sensations.

"Look. You have to eat. This is my town. And I'm sure my brother will vouch for me…well, the first two for sure…" said Tank, leaning closer and sending in another wave of testosterone.

Add charm to his sexuality, she thought. Her brain wasn't going to win this one with her body. What the hell. Payton surrendered in grace and smiled.

"I'm not sure if I will have anything on tomorrow evening," said Payton, giving herself an out in case she came to her senses later. "But if you give me a ring late in the afternoon, I should know my schedule."

Tank's mind stumbled on the 'having anything on' part, picturing her greeting him naked at the door and him with a ring…then the context kicked in and he decided not to call her on it. Obviously it had a wee bit of a different meaning in Scotland.

"Fair enough," he grinned, not completely able to force the look of a naked Payton Brady out of his mind's eye. "I have the early morning shift tomorrow, so I should be off around 2:00 unless there's trouble."

"Fine, ring me here. If I'm not in my room, I'm either at meetings or taking a run. I saw people jogging along the lake shore when I arrived this morning and have been keen to get out there."

"I'll leave you a message," he said and got out, asked the cab to wait and took her into the lobby. "Would you like me to escort you to your room?" he asked smiling.

"I think I can find my way without a police escort, thank you all the same." She smiled back.

He was thinking she had the prettiest smile he'd ever seen. He also noticed about fifteen male conventioneers with name tags and hair pieces were looking in her direction and probably thinking the same thing.

"You never know when you might need a man with a gun."

Her own gun was in her brief case, but she had to agree that you never knew when you might need a man. Looking into his animated face, she was feeling a powerful need right now. She couldn't believe how drawn she was by this handsome and appealing officer. If he went with her to her door, she was pretty sure she'd have let him go through it and she wanted time to think about it. She put her hand out. At least another day.

"Thank you for bringing me home, Tank."

"I'll call you tomorrow," he promised, taking her hand and holding it.

She nodded. "You do that." With that, she recaptured possession of her hand and went to the bank of elevators. In the mirror beside the doors she could see his reflection. He hadn't moved and was just looking at her. She decided not to turn around. Best not to encourage him. As hot and attractive as he was, she was pretty sure he wasn't what she needed right now.

CHAPTER 15

Skye opened her eyes. Was it morning? She could feel Alex moving around the room. "Time?" she whispered. She felt feverish and achy.

Alex came over and sat on the edge of the bed. "Go back to sleep, darling. I'll go make the coffee."

"Did I fall asleep on you last night?" she asked, yawning.

"Actually, yes you did. Right in my arms." He smoothed her tangled hair as her eyes slowly closed again. Frowning, his hand went back to her forehead. He was no expert on temperature, but hers seemed elevated.

"Skye?" He'd already made the call to the doctor and found that she had omitted a few of her instructions. The chief practitioner was surprised that Skye hadn't spent the entire day before in bed, since that had been her best medical advice. He covered his wife with another blanket as she fell back into a deep sleep. He looked at his watch. His New York office was opening. Maybe working on some contracts would keep his mind from sliding into dangerous territory.

He came back a few hours later, having purchased two new warehouses in St. Louis. She was staring at the ceiling.

"Skye?"

"Morning."

"What are you doing?"

"Was Paul Newman Butch Cassidy or the Sundance Kid."

Alex laughed. "He was Butch Cassidy. Why?"

"It was a loose end I needed to tie off."

Alex shook his head. Skye's morning wake-up routine was always an adventure in disconnected thoughts. He went over and studied her face, looked into her eyes. She seemed better. She smiled and sighed.

"I've been laying here for awhile thinking I'd better get up, but I'm wondering if the electrical impulses that send messages to my body have been fried. I can't seem to get the body to shake out."

He sat down on the side of the bed and took her hand. It was warm and soft. Not the hand of a warrior, although she could use it like a weapon if she had to.

"You didn't tell me the doctor recommended you stay right there for at least a week."

She looked at him steadily then decided to confess…her way. "I decided that sharing her overly conservative, conformist, textbook, up-tight medical opinion was on a need to know basis."

"You think being cute is going to get you out of trouble on this one?"

"Hmm. Guess not. How about you get naked and I convince you through hard core sex that I'm perfectly capable of walking around this city."

"I think if I did that, you may not be perfectly capable of crawling around this city."

"Hmm. You actually make it sound like it would be worth the risk."

"And last night. Do you remember hitting the wall?"

"So I got a little woozy. Jet lag."

"My ass."

Skye sighed and closed her eyes. "No it's my ass now." It actually did feel wonderful to just stretch out. "I married it…it's mine."

He looked at the rings on her finger. In his mind he saw them in a plastic evidence bag as Payton put them in the palm of his hand. His jaw tensed with the memory. Would he ever be able to get that moment of pain and horror out of his mind?

"What?" Skye's eyes snapped open and she looked over at him. "What's the matter?"

"Nothing. I was just thinking about the case."

"No, you weren't," she said blinking.

He breathed out. "Just when I think you're only half operational in the morning, you get aware on me."

"I am only half operational, but the half that's operating is all aware." Her eyes tracked to his and demanded an answer. "What is it, darling?"

He absentmindedly played with her rings as he held her hand. "I'm just grateful you're here, safe. And sometimes I get a flash of what might have been had something gone wrong."

She sat up, winced and nodded. "Our life together isn't going to be easy."

"Payton knocked on the door and when I opened it, it was fine that she was a police officer because there was something going on. I was doing okay…steady. When she handed me the buttons off your jacket, I was still fine. There could have been lots of possible reasons that they were evidence. But when she handed me your rings…"

Alex's voice faded. Skye didn't interrupt as he continued to play with the rings on her finger.

"These were in another evidence bag. God. I knew you would never have taken them off voluntarily." He looked up and she saw the haunted look in his eyes. "For an instant, my head ruled. It offered only one explanation. Christ, for an instant, I thought you were dead. Jim thought so, too. God, he was a mess. I remember his grasp on my shoulder was so filled with shock, horror and…I don't know…compassion, I guess. I couldn't stop the feeling. And I can't describe it. It was beyond words."

"I know darling. I know."

He nodded, then rubbed his chest above his heart. "It makes it better that you do. I'm sure it'll get better. The memory of the feeling of complete devastation will fade, but…"

"What can I do?"

"Stay close. Just stay close to me for a while. And indulge me. Let me know where you are, what you're doing. Allow me to be overprotective for a time."

"All right."

"For starters, stay in bed today. I called Barclay and Payton. They're going to work together to narrow down the field of agencies. Barclay will feed her names and she will do direct surveillance."

"All right." He looked at her suspiciously, but she just smiled. She'd do it. For him. "I think you need a day of rest yourself. Will you stay with me?"

Her arms slid around his neck and he held her close.

"I love you, Skye," he whispered in her ear. "I never thought anything could be more intense than what I felt on our wedding day, but having you here when for that moment I thought you were dead. Having you here in my arms feels like such a bonus, such a miracle…love isn't a powerful enough word to describe my feelings for you."

Skye kissed his neck, sensing the slight tremor running through him.

"Darling. I…" She never finished the sentence. His urgent need to feel her alive and warm overwhelmed his desire to be gentle and cautious. He ripped off his clothes as her hands moved over his body. The storm inside him broke free and he made love to her until they both lay exhausted and spent.

"About that week in bed," she said much later, as she tried to get her heartbeat down to double digits. "If this was what the doctor had in mind, I think I could manage to be a good little patient."

"Maybe you could," moaned Alex. "But I'm going to need some time in intensive care before I'll be able to get dressed again." He held her tightly. "You doing okay?"

"I feel wonderful," Skye stroked his back and was satisfied that the tightness she felt earlier had worked its way out. At least most of it. The rest would take time.

Tank called Payton while driving home from his shift. There was no answer, so he left her a message and his cell phone number. She said she was looking forward to a run on the lake shore so he took a chance and parked near the running path on the shore of Lake Michigan. It was unseasonably warm for the first week of November and there were a lot of walkers, in-line skaters, bikers and joggers taking advantage of the sunny day. Walking aimlessly, he observed the people for a while without any real destination in mind. He was focused on finding a petite red haired woman with deadly dimples. Just as he was about to give up and call her room again, he spotted her.

He watched her running down the path and smiled. Persistence and patience paid off. In police work and in the pursuit of a pretty woman. God she was a beautiful sight. More than one jogger's head spun off his shoulders when she went flying by. She didn't jog, she raced like lightning…like she was running from something. Or that something was chasing her. He saw the well-defined muscles in her arms and legs and imagined them wrapped around him. His pulse immediately climbed to dangerous levels and he had to clamp on the controls to keep from jumping her when she spotted him and gave a friendly little wave. She veered off and ran toward him.

Payton looked up and spotted Tank. Wow. He looked like a movie version of the he-man cop. He was an incredible sight, relaxed in his uniform, wearing the badge and gun as naturally as his broad smile. He could illuminate the inside of a deep, dark cave with that smile.

He'd stopped to watch her and was leaning against a building with his arms folded across his chest. His beautifully developed chest. He was a pretty impressive sight in his uniform. Something besides her pulse began to throb inside her. She was grateful she had an excuse for being breathless…it was the exertion of the run, not the pull of the man, that had her pulse racing.

"Good day to you, officer," she said flashing a smile of her own. She flexed her arms and shook out the muscles in her legs. "Walk with me while I cool down a bit?"

Nodding, he tried to keep his eyes off her chest, which was moving in and out as she caught her breath. He was mostly successful, but it was a compelling sight and he did appreciate it. And the sweat was making her shine. God what a sight. He swallowed before he spoke, sure his voice would crack if he didn't.

"Sure." Tank pushed off the building and fell into step beside her. "I was afraid you were going to ask me to run. I can jog pretty well, and can chase a perp if he's fairly sickly and has no stamina. But there's no way I could keep up with you." Tank laughed engagingly. "It would have been embarrassing…like an elephant trying to run with a cheetah."

Payton loved that he didn't have to be the best at everything. Certainly didn't fit the profile of the normal guy, and most certainly the normal, well built, deadly handsome, macho police guy.

As she looked him up and down, Tank was grateful to the love gods that her assessment seemed to have approval attached.

"You don't have the form of a runner, that's for bloody sure. I think you'd crack concrete. Let's see. I'd say that your best long distance sport would be swimming."

"Hey! Pretty good. You'd make a great detective," he said giving her his highest compliment.

"Is that right?" She smiled a secret smile. "Well, it doesn't take an ace detective to follow the clues. You're obviously athletic. You're in great shape." Her eyes drifted over to Lake Michigan. "You grew up near a huge body of water." She shrugged. "Easy."

He smiled, delighted that she thought he was athletic. And in great shape. That was approval he heard in her voice and saw on her face. He was sure of it. He thought he could hit the target if he took his shot now.

"So how about that dinner tonight?"

She looked at her watch. "Can we make it late? I have a few things to take care of yet this afternoon. I decided to run, because I get a little muggy about this time of day when I travel west."

"Sure, any time." They chatted until they reached the Intercontinental.

"Want to come up for something hot right now?" She said it casually. Friendly.

"Wow, now that's an invitation," said Tank pretending to take her question as a really hot come on.

She laughed, her dimples winking at him and making his heart race as if he'd run the miles with her. "I mean something hot to drink, bucko. It's nearly tea time."

"My, my. How civilized."

"We British do what we can to bring culture to the colonies," Payton switched from her melodious Scottish lilt to a more sophisticated English accent. Tank laughed.

"How about this colonial shows his gauche nature and requests a strong cup of coffee."

Payton sighed expansively and shook her head. "What would you colonials do without your coffee?"

"Nothing. We would do absolutely nothing and our entire way of life would crumble."

"Hmm. I do believe the drink of the bean just keeps the whole country over stimulated."

Tank laughed. "This from a country known for its haggis and centuries long clan feuds."

Payton laughed with him. "Come on up. We'll order up some coffee and a pot of tea, I can check my messages, maybe return some calls. Then I'll know when I'll be free this evening."

"That sounds great."

When they got to her suite, he took off his jacket and threw it on the sofa. He loved the smell of the room. Fresh and female. He took care of ordering coffee for himself and tea for her. She went into the bathroom and came out with a towel wrapped around her neck then checked her messages.

"Excuse me please. If you'll be kind enough to sign for the service, I'll be in the bedroom returning a few calls."

"Sure." While he was waiting for her and the coffee to arrive, he wandered around the small sitting room, looking at the desk. Everything was neatly arranged. It was obviously a workstation. Her laptop was there along with several folders.

His curiosity poked at him like the caricature of the little devil sitting on one shoulder. He would love to see what she was working on. But he also recognized that people had a way of knowing when their privacy had been invaded and he wanted to be very straight with this lady. So the good little angel on the other shoulder won. He was glad he hadn't given in to temptation and peeked in her folders, because when he turned around, she was staring at him.

It didn't take Payton's finely tuned detective skills to know that he'd turned away from temptation and she appreciated his discretion.

Their eyes locked and held. Before either of them realized they were moving, they met in the center of the room. His hand went up and through her thick, short hair down to the back of her neck. He drew her to him and there was no resistance.

"You're so beautiful. I've been wanting to do this since I first saw you sitting near the fire." His other hand went around her tiny waist and he drew her the rest of the way.

It was like hitting a brick wall when he held her against him. Her arms went around his neck and her body simply moved on its own. It was pure instinct.

Tank's kiss deepened and she felt a low moan form in her throat then escape. It fueled his already heated body.

"Please," he whispered in her hair. "God. Let me touch you."

She didn't stop him as his lips followed his fingers down her neck. She tasted salty from her run and he loved the flavor, all blended with the scents of lotions and soap. He made his way back and recaptured her lips.

His hands became bolder, and she could feel his physical response as her lower body molded to his. She knew he was ready and it was only a matter of time before he would discover so was she. Her hands slid over his chest and she could feel his heart beating faster. Such a good and steadfast heart, she thought. Then her fingers brushed against the badge. The badge. Something inside her froze. Damn, what was she thinking. She wasn't thinking, that was the problem.

Suddenly her reaction to his touch changed. He could feel it the moment she pulled back into herself. Instead of the tremble of desire he felt when his hands first started their exploration, she shuddered violently. He pulled back. It took all of his strength to move his hands from her breasts to her face.

"What? Did I hurt you?"

She opened her eyes, and he saw incredible confusion and the punch of conflicting emotions.

Not yet, she thought. You haven't hurt me yet. And maybe it isn't too late to keep it from happening. She put her hands around his wrists and pulled his hands from her.

He nearly broke with frustration as she slowly moved away. He was still breathing heavily from his body's reaction to her, for God's sake.

"I'm sorry, Tank. This isn't going to work. I should never have let it go this far." She put her hands flat on his broad chest and pushed. She realized the only reason there was any movement was because he chose to take a step back. Even with her considerable strength, she wouldn't have been able to budge him otherwise.

She ducked under his arm and ran a hand through her disheveled hair. She quickly tucked her t-shirt back into the waist of her sweatpants. What was she thinking? Good grief. She knew what a deep passionate kiss and all that petting could lead to.

"Okay," gasped Tank, trying to get his breathing under control and his body back to earth. "Let's slow this down, then. Sorry. Sometimes my hormones get a bit enthusiastic and want to lead the parade. I can step back." He took another deep breath and let it out slowly. "How about that dinner?"

"I don't…" How could she go out to dinner with him? Wouldn't it be like leading him on?

"Payton," said Tank, reading the unease on her face and wanting her to feel comfortable with him again. "Nothing will happen that you don't want to happen."

She looked at him and blew her bangs off her forehead. "That's what I'm afraid of. Damn, you're a pure gallis."

"Is that good?" He was relieved to see some of the humor return to her eyes.

"As good as it gets, bucko. Okay. How about you go home and change and we meet in the lobby at 7:00. Then you can show me your town. That should give me time to check with your brother about your character and wring out my body."

Tank was quite sure he didn't want her to wring out her body, but he was also reluctant to press her right now. He'd rather have her come to him slowly than not come to him at all. Besides, he needed to look up gallis on the internet. "If he tells you stories about my high school days, just remember…it wasn't the whole cheerleading squad."

Payton laughed. He really was nearly irresistible. It wasn't until after he left that she realized there would be coffee and tea coming and that the something hot had turned out to be her after all.

As Alex and Skye sat side by side in bed, eating muffins, making crumbs and drinking coffee, they planned out what was left of their day. Both were feeling better and restlessness was creeping into Skye's well-used body.

"I feel a sense of urgency, Alex. We have to get to Pavel before the Russian cartel can find him. I want to go over to Mom and Dad's to bring them up to date on some of what's been happening."

Alex turned to Skye…since when had Wyatt and Blake become Mom and Dad? It touched his heart and he was sure it would please them. They'd decided, and Jim, Amanda and Cameron had concurred, that they would tell Wyatt and Blake about the breach on their home computer and anything else that they deemed necessary.

"You're right," said Alex. "Linda should be arriving soon, as well."

Reluctantly, they got up. Alex experienced a moment of regret when he saw how stiff and sore Skye was, but it didn't last. She kept sending him little air kisses and, sighing in satisfaction, she told him how fabulous it felt to be back on track with the honeymoon thing. Alex guessed she needed to feel something besides pain rocketing through her body, as much as he needed to feel her warmth shoot through his.

When Skye and Alex arrived at the large house on Lake Shore Drive, they were both surprised and delighted when David opened the door.

He hugged Skye and shook Alex's hand. "How was the honeymoon?"

"Memorable," said Alex.

"Electrifying," said Skye.

David was looking at Skye and didn't see Alex wince. He did see Skye winking at her husband as she put her arm through David's and walked with him to the huge kitchen in the back of the house. She knew from the smells that was where she'd find Wyatt. David escorted her knowing he'd either get an explanation for their appearance…or he wouldn't.

They couldn't hear the sound of shouting and laughing echoing off the walls of the house. "Where are the offspring?" Skye asked.

"They're off with 20 other little campers to spend the weekend in the wild."

"Coney Island?" laughed Alex.

"No. Upstate, actually. It worked out great. It's my weekend off and Linda told me she was going to be in town, so I thought I'd take advantage of my freedom to come over and see if she wanted to have dinner."

"You flew in from New York to see if a woman from Washington DC would be available for dinner in Chicago?" asked Alex.

"That's the plan," grinned David boyishly. "Isn't modern air travel great?"

Alex shrugged. "Makes sense to me."

"I'm actually only after the frequent flyer miles," confessed David. "I'm addicted to seeing those numbers go up."

"Our little secret," said Skye as they crossed the threshold into the warm, inviting kitchen.

"More secrets?" asked Wyatt as she turned. She took one look at Skye and stopped what she was doing. "Don't even bother telling me whatever cover story you thought would explain why you look like you lost 10 more pounds and are feverish and you," she poked Alex in the chest. "You look like you haven't slept for a week. And while you're at it, I don't believe for a minute you're in Chicago nearly a week before we were expecting you to renegotiate a contract on a building."

David grinned. So much for subtle. He guessed they were going to get some explanation after all.

"Would you believe we screwed like a couple of rabbits, we never left the room, Skye wouldn't let me sleep and we forgot to eat? And I have to renegotiate the building to support her incredible shopping habit?" asked Alex.

David just stood back enjoying the show, letting his mother-in-law take the lead.

"No," Wyatt responded slowly, keeping her gaze on her son. "And it wouldn't explain that look."

"What look?" asked Alex frowning. He thought of himself as an excellent role player. It was a requirement of being a good, no great, agent. But then, he never had to go up against his mother.

Wyatt just kept staring at him. Through him, actually. Damn it. It was a powerful combination of x-ray vision and a truth ray. He felt like spilling his guts. It was eerie. She didn't often turn her cop's eyes on him anymore. At least not since he'd grown up with a lot of grown up secrets to cover.

He glanced over at Skye. She was just smiling at him. Throw me a rope, he was thinking. She's your mom, was her telepathic reply. But she took pity on him.

"Mom," she started. Wyatt turned her eyes away from her son and immediately softened under the wave of pleasure she felt hearing Skye call her Mom. She smiled broadly and seemed to have forgotten all about the interrogation of her son.

Alex wasn't sure if he was miffed, relieved or just completely impressed. One word. Just one word and his bride disarmed the unassailable Captain Wyatt Earp Cooper.

Skye made a quick field decision, looked over at Alex and nodded. Permission to reveal minimal information.

"Obviously something happened in Scotland other than a fine, well planned honeymoon. Why don't we go find Dad and we can fill you in at the same time with some of the unclassified details," said Alex.

"Me, too?" asked David.

"I assume that even though dinner with Linda is a bonus, you're here because Mom called you with the news we were in town and you wanted to check out the story yourself," said Skye.

"Busted," smiled David, for that was exactly what happened. "Linda left pretty abruptly a few hours into your honeymoon and her story was a little weak."

"Only because you couldn't believe she'd leave your side, you charismatic devil."

"True."

"What's true?" They all turned to see Blake enter the kitchen. He hugged Skye, felt her condition, took his son's hand, assessed his condition as well and turned to his wife. "Have you grilled them yet, darling?"

"Grilled, baked and fried," laughed Alex, feeling some more of the ugliness of the last week fall away. Family. Home. Sanctuary.

Cops and a prosecutor. It was more than a little difficult for Alex and Skye to sustain subterfuge and maintain a covert role without them suspecting. As a matter of fact, the entire family had been involved that summer in a single operation when it had been nearly impossible to leave them out if it. Since then, they'd developed selective and prearranged amnesia concerning the event and never talked about it…but they knew. And they worried.

"Well, first I'm going to feed your bride some of Tria's chicken pot pie. Eat. Then talk."

"Great I'm starving," said Skye with passion. Tria's cooking was legend. She'd been Blake and Wyatt's cook for over 25 years. Tank's serious love affair with food started in Tria's kitchen. "Did Linda call?"

"Yes, she said she'd be here at 8:00. Apparently she has some equipment that she's going to install on my computer and some software to put into it." Wyatt's eyes slid over to Alex. "Kind of a coincidence having her add some additional security at the same time you two come to Chicago looking like you were lost for a week in the Himalayas."

Around the kitchen table, the remains of a potpie sitting in the center, Alex briefed his family with as much of the story as they'd cleared. Skye had been kidnapped and held by a man who operated a modeling agency somewhere in Chicago. It had to do with an old case. He'd uncovered the location of their honeymoon through Wyatt's computer.

"Don't worry Mom," said Alex when she shot to her feet, the anger that had been simmering, spilling over in an avalanche of hot words. "Your e-mail was never breached. We just didn't think to put the same security codes on your internet search engines. Linda is going to bring the equipment we need to lock that door."

They got Wyatt calmed down, then continued. "Without going into details right now, Skye escaped, we took care of the people who did the actual kidnapping and we're here to cop the guy who gave the order."

"Who are you working with here?" asked Blake. The story shook him up, particularly since he knew there was more, maybe a great deal more, that his son wasn't telling them.

"No one, in any official capacity. There was a murder. A woman who the kidnappers wanted us to believe was Skye. That's the primary crime. We're working through Scottish authorities since it actually occurred over there. They're interfacing through authorized channels over here."

"What about your channels?" asked Wyatt, not inclined at the moment to ignore the fact that she knew her son worked for Jim Stryker and the Justice Department.

Alex looked at Skye, who nodded. "We'll be working our own operation."

"And that would be…" prompted Wyatt.

Alex shook his head.

"You'll allow me to be in on the take down?" she pursued.

Alex shook his head again. With his mom it was better to stay silent. She could glean too much out of any word…any expression.

"If I can't have the pie, then give me a damn piece of it." Wyatt's temper flared and she slammed a hand on the table. "This son-of-a-bitch takes Skye based on information from my computer. I'm part of this, son. You talk to Jim. You bring me in."

Just then the doorbell rang and Alex almost said 'saved by the bell.' It would give him a chance to talk with Skye and get her input on what to do with Wyatt. She was one formidable woman when charged up and they might be able to use her in some capacity.

Linda arrived with a case of items for the computer. She wouldn't have had to deliver and install it herself. Any number of technicians more competent than her could have done it, but she needed to see Skye. When she entered the kitchen, she went directly over and hugged her friend. She felt the loss of weight and the slight tremor of fatigue running through Skye's muscles. She was privy to everything, but mindful of the people in the room, she said nothing.

When they pulled apart, she smiled. "Looks like Alex finally wore you out."

Linda walked over and hugged Alex with both affection and compassion. Letting her eyes speak for her, she communicated her thoughts to him. She knew she was among family, but she didn't let on through word or action that she was anything but some kind of computer tech and a friend of Skye's.

Blake looked at Wyatt and David meaningfully. He knew it was all a game, but he wanted it to be easy for his son. The way Alex looked, he could use some easy. "David, didn't you say you had some pictures of the boys from the wedding that you wanted to show us? Why don't we exercise grandparent's privilege and see them first. Then Alex, Skye and Linda can join us in the family room later."

Wyatt was reluctant and David hadn't stopped staring at Linda since she arrived, but they both nodded and followed him out. Not before David could wink at Linda and she could give him a special smile, however.

Wyatt just glared at her son, communicating the discussion wasn't over. Not by a long shot.

As soon as they left the room, Linda took Skye's hand and demanded a full report on her state of health. That taken care of, she gave them a file of possible modeling agencies that Pavel could have created. There were thirteen that came to the top of the list. All thirteen had been opened within the last six years, specialized in sending models overseas and didn't seem to have any major clients. Actually, Linda thought they should be investigated whether they were owned by Pavel or not...something about all of them wasn't right. Alex agreed and grinned.

"After we pinpoint the one owned by Pavel, let's throw the rest of them at Mom...give her something to chew on."

"Can we include Wyatt in some way in this investigation?" asked Skye. "I mean, for crying out loud. The woman is a highly decorated police captain."

"In a way, she's already involved. Barclay is nearly certain it was her computer Pavel used to track the two of you. It's not like we're bringing her in out of the blue," added Linda.

"Tell me how?" asked Alex. In their work for Justice, they often worked with local liaisons.

"I have an idea," said Skye. "Tomorrow..."

"Or the day after..." said Alex, noticing Skye's hand tremble as she lifted a cup of tea to her lips.

"Tomorrow," repeated Skye, quickly putting down the cup, feeling her blood heat up.

"Perhaps in a couple of days..." said Alex, absorbing her glare. He was used to negotiations.

Linda looked at the two of them and remained silent. This was a familiar duet.

Skye continued with her original sentence, ignoring the time frame for now. "I'm going to go to these agencies and bait the hook. We're pretty sure he'll bite. When it comes time to reel him in, I think we would find a legendary Chicago police captain very useful for intimidation. If he hacked into her computer, he obviously knows who she is. Probably knows whom she's married to as well. I'd like to use this recognition and her clout to pound the point that he has no options, nowhere to go. When we locate him, she goes in with us. Local law. A hammer. He goes directly to jail or he goes with us."

"I like it," said Linda. Alex nodded and smiled. His wife wasn't only fearless, she was a master at weaving in loose ends and when personal needs were appropriate, making them a part of the plan.

"And I need to start right away...tomorrow," said Skye, standing to end the conversation. When her knees gave way, her advantage was lost. Alex was beside her and helped her back into her chair. When he didn't say anything, she stood up more slowly and blew out a breath. This time, her knees solidified and she was able to stand. "Or maybe the day after. Shall we join the rest of the family?"

Alex smiled over at Linda and took Skye's hand. He was about to say something, but Skye squeezed. "I wouldn't if I were you."

"Damn…married for less than two weeks and she can already read my mind."

"That's because you're so damn transparent."

When they joined Blake, David and Wyatt, Skye laid things out for them. "First of all, I have to find this man. This individual re-entered my life and wanted me to disappear. The reasons can never be revealed, but let's just say it's a very old grudge. Do you remember when we flew the Lear here the day Alex gave it to me?"

Blake and Wyatt nodded.

"I had a feeling I was being watched and I think the person recognized me and who I was hanging with." She smiled at her in-laws. "Comes from being a part of a very prominent local family. Anyway, we think he went right to work to find out my location through hacking into your computer system. He couldn't get into anything that was very revealing. Your system was too secure, but he did get the Scottish connection. I can tell you, it was an excellent opportunity for him. It put me closer to where he eventually wanted me to end up." She stopped going down that road, and that was accepted without comment. "Anyway, when we uncover his location, I need to drop in on him and make him a proposition."

"Not arrest him?" asked David and Wyatt at the same time. They looked at each other and they all laughed. It was such a cop moment.

Skye looked at them levelly. "No. At this time, we need him for other reasons. But believe me. He'll pay." Then she looked at Wyatt. "I'd like to bring you with me when we go in to talk with him. He'll recognize you and I may need to play that card. He probably knows your reputation and," she looked over at Blake. "He probably knows the reputation of the man you sleep with. It'll underline the fact that he has no options other than the one I'll be bringing to him from…from the federal government."

Wyatt had about a million questions, but she didn't need to ask them. She simply nodded. "Fair enough." That was settled. Her expression changed. Softened. She looked at Linda. "Will you be there, too?"

"I will."

"To program a computer or to make dinner reservations."

Linda laughed. "My job description is a little vague."

"Well, darling, I think you were just told none of your business," laughed Blake as he looked at his delighted wife.

"And very nicely, too. Linda, you'll stay here with us while you're in town?"

Linda smiled. "Thank you Wyatt. That would be very nice." Her eyes slid over to

David who smiled back. Wyatt smiled, too. She'd give them each a room, but she suspected there would be a path in the rug between them.

At 7:00 Payton walked off the elevator and saw him immediately. He was holding a map and directing a couple of tourists to their destination. She could tell they were completely charmed by him. Friendly. Helpful. Handsome. She felt herself melting. When he turned and looked at her, she was already lost.

They had a wonderful time. He showed her around the city he obviously loved. And when they ended the evening at a neighborhood pub, she could see the town loved him back. Everyone bought him a drink and had a story to tell Payton. She thoroughly enjoyed herself, even though there was that nagging discomfort every time he chugged another bottle or sipped another glass. She was both impressed and appalled at his capacity. She was used to men in pubs drinking their weight in beer and scotch, but this man was an Olympian. By the time he took her back to the hotel, he wasn't completely steady on his feet.

"Can I come up?" he asked, kissing her in the back of the cab.

"Not tonight," she said. "You should go home and get some sleep. You need to be sharp out on the streets."

"I'm in training tomorrow." He blinked his eyes so he could focus. "I only need half a brain for that. Good thing, 'cause I think I killed a few cells tonight. I'm sure...absolutely sure I'd sleep better if I could make love to you first." His mouth came down on hers and his body pressed her into the seat.

She could tell he was ready, but she wasn't sure she was. Until she was sure...

"No."

But he didn't appear to have heard her and when they got to the Intercontinental, he got out of the back seat before she could turn and push him back in. He paid the cabbie and walked with her as the doorman opened the door.

"Are you going to be all right?" she asked when he swayed a little as they crossed the lobby. He'd insisted he see her to her door and they both knew it was partially because he hoped to get lucky.

"Sure. But maybe I'd better spend the night. That would make me miles beyond all right." He leaned against the wall near the elevators and since the lobby was nearly deserted, started tasting her lips again. He scowled at the two conventioneers who joined them on the elevator and he thought about arresting them. But they managed to get to their floor without breaking any laws. And because Tank had another 10 floors to wage his campaign, he and Payton were both breathless by the time the doors slid open onto her floor.

Their lips were locked tightly as Payton tried to remember which pocket had her room key. Her brain was buzzing and her memory seemed to lack the capacity to narrow down the location.

"Let me conduct the search," said Tank huskily and his hands replaced hers in moving expertly from pocket to pocket. Some of them were so provocatively located, he decided to be extremely thorough and check them twice. He palmed the plastic card when he found it and searched again. They were both panting when Payton tumbled to the deception. Tank had decided to check her bra for a possible hidden compartment.

"Is this a bust?" she whispered against Tank's mouth.

"It most certainly is," said Tank, his hands going under her bra. "And a mighty fine one, I'd say."

Payton's laugh ended in a moan, fanning the already considerable flame inside Tank into a raging inferno. Payton's arms went around Tank's waist. Her hand brushed up against his gun and she could taste the beer on Tank's tongue when it joined the assault. The combination brought some of her senses back and she managed to pull away from him, twisting in his arms, grabbing the key and breaking off the kiss.

"Can't say no, now," he said smiling down at her. "The rockets are ready to fire."

She felt him sway again and her missing senses returned. She slipped the key into the lock, trying to block out the look of anticipation and pleasure on Tank's face. He was sure he felt a big 'yes' in her response to him.

"No," she said simply and slipped into the room. Tank stared at the door for a full minute, expecting her to open it wide and invite him in to spend the night.

"What was that all about?" he said softly, frowning, still panting. He looked down. "I guess she was only up for the foreplay, boy. No sense in staying up tonight. I don't think begging will work."

He didn't know she was on the other side of the door, battling with herself. Listening to him, she felt terrible. She didn't move until she heard the elevator doors open, then took herself to bed. The hollow feeling in her gut reminding her that she wouldn't have had to be alone.

Skye was sleeping by the time Alex drew up to the parking garage under their building. She hardly moved when he scooped her up and carried her into the private elevator to their apartment. He didn't even stop to turn on any lights, but walked through the dim hallway back to their bedroom.

Just as he was about to put her down on their bed, she jerked and came awake. Her brown eyes were unfocused and flat.

"Whoa," she said, looking into the eyes of her concerned husband. Grabbing him around the neck, she buried her face into his soft cashmere coat. "Don't let go, Alex. I think I just had a posttraumatic moment. I swear I could feel the current."

Alex sat down on the edge of the bed, cradling her shaking body in his arms.

"Are you okay?"

"Yeah…yeah," she said as life returned to her eyes and she worked up a smile. "How about we stay in bed tomorrow and you can take care of purging this feeling I have of being plugged into a wall socket."

Alex smiled, a slight edge of victory sneaking into his steady tone. "I'm not sure I can arrange that. My partner thought she should get right on it tomorrow. I don't know if I can spend the day in bed with my wife."

"If you're going to make it to our first anniversary, you may wish to rephrase that comment."

"All right. How about I want to be with you in this bed." He started to undress her, kissing the skin he exposed as he went. "All day. To recover…to make love to you. To feel you under me, around me when I slip into you. To know you're safe in my arms. When I hear you moan with pleasure, I'll know your brain has been drained and my desire for you…my need for you…is all that there is for you. I want my wife…my wife…in my arms to celebrate our life together. To celebrate life…Skye. I love you…" He kissed her neck. "I want you…" His lips traced a line along her jaw.

"Oh Alex…" She moaned in pleasure as a different kind of energy coursed through her. "Only you can really heal me."

"Tell me how, darling."

"By taking me away from the pain…filling me. I want to feel…to feel what only you can turn on in me…"

"Now that will be my pleasure." He smiled into her deep, rich brown eyes. "But no need to wait until tomorrow…we can fill that prescription right now."

His hands gently moved over her skin, her breasts, down her ribs. She was so thin…but he didn't let that in. Wouldn't let it in. There was no place for concern tonight. This one night. He was consumed by the feel and taste of her. His hungry mouth ravished her and he found her heightened need for him opened them up to even higher sensual arousal.

The tension rising in her lower body was exquisite and completely extinguished its memory of pain and suffering. She quivered with the rich and intense coil of pressure in her belly until she thought she would split into pieces of herself. She couldn't get her breath as all her remaining energy went into an exploding climax that was immediately followed by an even more intense feeling of hunger and desire. Her body was starving tonight…for him. She moaned his name.

Just when she thought she couldn't go another minute alone, she felt him push into her and they rode the waves of passion together. This time her flight into fate took her to a place she'd never been…they'd never been. To be alive when they'd skirted the edge of death yet again increased their passion, their gratitude, their love. They fell asleep in each other's arms. Completely spent, but safe and secure.

Pavel flipped through several prime South Beach properties he found on the internet. He had a few minutes before he needed to call the relay number. His team reported that they were still interrogating Virginia, Skye or whatever the hell her name was. Their messages were brief and cryptic, as per his orders, but their meaning were clear.

"Our guest isn't feeling well. She hasn't been able to eat in days."

"Several people dropped in and everything is nearly settled."

"Our guest was extremely surprised to see her friends from the past. You could say she was shocked."

Pavel barked with laughter at that one. That Bianca was a real comedian. He was sure that was a reference to the method of torture currently being used on Ms. Virginia Montgomery. Take that, you bitch. No one could reduce a human to a snarling dog like the Russians. It may have taken six years, but she was paying for it now.

Pavel had a wonderfully vivid imagination and he used it to give him a picture of a torn and tattered Virginia…the sublime pleasure pouring into him from the image was arousing as well as entertaining.

Her beauty would be gone…in his mind he could see the hideous mask her face would become. He wished there would be blood and severed limbs and broken bones and disfiguring and the carving of flesh, but he knew the experts in his family felt that opening the mind was more important than clouding it with horror and agony. Their victims needed to lose their will, not their sanity. Too bad…slicing off pieces of her flesh would have come closer to what she deserved than depriving her of a few meals and prodding her with a blast of electrical current. Never having experienced either, he didn't think their use sounded dreadful enough.

He sincerely wished he could be there, but he dared not travel out of the country. There was a forged passport in his safe, but he didn't feel like risking it. Heightened security was everywhere and there may be more sophisticated detection methods than what was being employed when he used to blow on over to Paris for dinner and to deliver a few lovely morsels of flesh. He felt his intense paranoia was both justified and healthy. He'd stay put like he was told.

Looking into the fire dancing through the logs in his fireplace, he decided to ceremoniously end this chapter of his life by tossing in the well abused *Newsweek*. As the cover carrying Skye's picture smoked, then popped into flame, he imagined that happening to her for real…maybe the master electrician slipped and delivered too much juice…melting the flesh on her face.

In his mind, he could hear her screams…the sound of her begging for mercy…then for death. While he stared at the magazine, it curled in on itself and became a layered stack of smoldering ash. His nightmare was over. He'd seen the last of her…Virginia Skyler Montgomery Madison would soon be ashes…for real. Lin Tu Meng would use her up…then dispose of her as he had all the others.

Aroused, he speed dialed a number and ordered up two of his favorite models. Time to party!

CHAPTER 16

Tank was at the hotel the next afternoon when Payton came in. He was in uniform and had obviously just come off shift. Her heart did a dance. His broad grin indicated that he didn't hold a grudge over her abrupt departure the night before. She was glad. She really liked him and didn't want to do any injury. These were her issues, not his.

"Hey Scottish," he said cheerfully. "How about that coffee? It occurred to me, I didn't get it yesterday." It wasn't the only thing he didn't get, but he was too much of a gentleman to mention it.

Payton checked her watch. "I was just going to order some tea and something to eat from room service. I want to kick off these shoes and get out of this suit first."

"Works for me," said Tank, his grin getting broader. He wasn't quite sure what happened the night before, but he was ready to make another play. Persistence was one of his stronger attributes.

Payton smiled back. "Look, it's after midnight in Scotland…"

"How about I rub your feet, we order some sandwiches and maybe find a good movie on pay for view."

"Well," said Payton feeling the pull of his incredible charm again. "All right, but I do have some work to complete this evening. I'm expecting a call."

She'd spent time with Emily's dentist, forwarding all the x-rays to Glasgow. She expected to hear from the coroner within the next few hours. Once she got the positive ID, she'd work with the people here to have the body transported back to the states.

The rest of the day had been spent working with Skye and Alex. Skye was running a slight temperature, so Alex was keeping a close eye on her and wouldn't let her out of the apartment. God, they were so in love. The looks they gave each other were so powerful, you could almost see the waves of passion. Skye and Alex were working with a list of agencies and checking things out from their home office. Payton drove by several of the businesses and reported back to them. She planned to scope out several more the next day.

Tank could see she was preoccupied. That was fine. He liked dedicated women. He took her arm, steering them toward the elevator before she changed her mind.

He kept his hands off her in the elevator, determined that the afternoon remain casual, but when they stepped through the door of her suite, he could feel the yearning rip through him. She walked out of her shoes before she reached the door to the bedroom. "I'll be right back. Why don't you order something."

"Burgers okay?"

"Perfect."

"Do you want some wine?"

She shook her head, "No thanks. There's mineral water and ice in the refrigerator."

They ate burgers, a passion they both shared. Tank drank an entire bottle of wine and they watched an old Sean Connery movie. Payton lay back on the cushions of the couch as Tank took one foot, then the next and massaged them. She was purring and drowsy by the time his hands decided to move to new territory. They moved up her legs and before she knew what she was doing, her legs went around his waist and she was enveloped in his arms.

They rolled off the couch with a great deal of groping and fondling accompanying their heavy breathing. They were nearly naked when the empty wine bottle rolled off the table as they bumped into it. It fell to the floor. Payton stared at the empty bottle and frowned. Then wiggled away from Tank, pulling the open ends of her blouse together.

"Oh no you don't," gasped Tank, pulling her back against him. "You're not going to leave me panting and confused again."

"I'm sorry," she said scrambling up and backing away from him. "I should have exercised more control." She smiled sadly. "I'm not a tease, Tank. I just can't let myself get involved with you."

"Why?" asked Tank, anger beginning to seep into his normally controlled voice. "You got someone back home?"

"No," she said sincerely.

"Got something against men?"

"No."

"Is it because I'm a cop?" He'd heard this before. The hours, the pressure, the stress, the potential for disaster. He took it all for granted, but more than one woman he'd been interested in over the years turned it off when they found out he wanted to be a cop.

She almost laughed. He wouldn't have to ask if he knew about the badge she carried in her purse.

"Of course not."

"Then what?" He got up and took her in his arms again. His kiss drew out her desire and she molded her lower body to his. She could feel his immediate, intense reaction and she pressed to him even harder. Their kiss deepened, intensified. Tank moved her toward the bedroom and she didn't resist at first, but when they reached the threshold, she dug in and twisted away.

She ran her shaking fingers through her short, thick hair. "I…I will admit to feeling something. You're a very attractive man." She backed away from him. "But I'll not be acting on it again. If you could see yourself out, I have some work to do." She knew it was lame, but it was all she could think of.

Tank tried to take her hand, and she backed away.

"I can't," she said in a voice that was harsher than she intended.

Tank was furious. He was usually such an affable, easy-going man that his considerable temper was a formidable, thunderous sight.

"What do you mean, you can't. If you're attracted to me, and you say you are. As a matter of fact, your body consistently communicates you are, when you let it happen. If you're unattached, which you assure me is the case, then why can't you give in to what you're feeling?"

When she just stood and stared at him, his thoughts went elsewhere. "Are you trying to fuck with my mind? Is this a test to see how far you can push me?" He swallowed hard and took another deep breath. "You're not a child. You know this isn't easy for me."

Her throat closed up. How could she be so nasty to this wonderful man? He'd pulled back. He'd suppressed his heated response and denied his body…proven his strength. She had no answer. Nothing to say.

"Don't just stand there. Answer me, damn it!" He came toward her and she cringed. She couldn't help it. It was an automatic response to an angry man in a uniform. Suddenly she was a girl again and took a step back.

"What?" Tank said. He saw the raw terror in her eyes and looked down. His hands were fisted, but he certainly didn't intend to use them on her. Did she think he'd hit her? That pissed him off, too. Damn, why was he losing his head like this. He barely knew her. Women didn't generally set him off. Love them and love them some more. When they left, it was usually mutual and amiable. When he looked up again, she'd successfully covered her initial reaction and was defiant and regretful. Had he imagined the fear?

She shook her head and ruthlessly curbed the fear, then buried it again. How could she explain it? Why should she try. Why should she care? Because she really liked this man? She could easily attach herself to a cop, what would be more natural. They would understand each other and the world they worked in. But she knew it was the amounts of alcohol she saw him consume. Her mind hurtled her back to when she was a child.

Payton's father had used his fists, and he wore nearly an identical uniform. He was a police officer. He'd get a few beers in him and look for a way to blow off the stress and pressure of the job. First it was just her mom, then, as she got weaker and Payton got bigger, he turned to her. She had her arm broken, her ribs cracked, her shoulder dislocated and her eyes blackened, all before she was 10. He took her to a different doctor or a different hospital each time. Always in his uniform and he was never questioned.

She remembered the day she realized she could run. It was like Independence Day.

When her dad would come home after he stopped off at a bar, she'd run away from him. He never caught her, not once. A few times he'd snatch her before she could start the chase, but once she started off the mark, he couldn't keep the pace. She still ran marathons when she could. It always gave her a sense of freedom and control.

She looked at Tank's angry face and down at his clenched fists. Well let him try and strike her. She wasn't a child any more.

When he was sober, her father was a genial, clever, funny man. Just like Tank. No, not just like Tank. This all flashed through her mind as she stood watching him deal with his frustration. Did she try to explain this all to him? It wasn't like they were in a committed relationship or anything. Far from it. A few dates, a few passionate kisses. She put up the wall, but not before she heard her heart whisper…a few wonderful dates and a few hot, fantastic, dreamy kisses.

What the hell, she thought suddenly. She'd be flying back to Scotland soon enough. Maybe she should explain. She could give him something to think about and it may help the next woman who fell under the spell of those fabulous eyes and his adorable dimples.

Shit. Why did that image of another woman sting so much? She frowned. Why should she be worried about some other woman? To hell with any other woman. She looked up at him. She wanted him. Oh God, she wanted him tonight.

Tank watched her face in fascination. She was obviously having an internal dialogue and since she was staring right at him, through him, actually, he assumed she was talking to herself about him. Fine, let her. He wasn't about to interrupt. As she stared at his hands, he deliberately relaxed them. Something told him to chill and show her less aggression.

He wasn't going to say another word. Wasn't going to ask her for explanations or for a chance. He ran his tongue over his lips. The feel of her lips were still a vivid memory, and that skin and her lovely, lush body. Not to mention those freckles. God, he loved those freckles. He wondered if she had a cluster anywhere else.

"Payton," he said, at the same time she said. "Tank."

His anger was gone and in its place was a sizable charge of lust.

Her fear was gone and in its place was an identical charge of desire.

His lust recognized her desire and pulled the two of them together. Fast, hot and urgent.

This time, nothing got in the way, including clothes, shoes, or the brevity of their acquaintance. She pulled off his uniform as his mouth plundered hers. His hands went under her blouse and pulled it off from behind. Then they went after belt buckles and zippers and waistbands. They kicked off pants and underwear on their way to the bedroom, and when they got to the doorway, he picked her up and her delighted giggle, yes it was definitely a giggle and definitely delighted, drove him into an even deeper state of desire. They fell on the bed and began their initial exploration of naked body and form.

They were both in magnificent shape, both warm and wet and ready for lovemaking.

She was a marathon runner and he was a champion swimmer. They both had lungs of steel and the stamina of youth. Both wanted to give as well as receive. It was a glorious coupling and a fantastic ending to their afternoon. Neither had any doubt this was more than sex. It wasn't simple. It was going to get complicated, but throughout the night, there was no thought about the future, no regret, no end to their pleasure.

Finally, just before dawn, they fell into an exhausted, but contented sleep. Tank located the sheets and blankets on the floor and covered them. He smiled at her naked body wrapping around his. Still hot and nearly boneless, she sighed in her sleep. There were freckles on other parts of her body. Tomorrow's project would be to count them. He kissed the top of her Scottish head and fell instantly asleep.

Tank woke to the smell of coffee. He blinked a few times, orienting himself to his surroundings. He was in Payton's hotel suite. He reached over to the other side of the bed. Damn. Empty. Well, at least she made coffee. That showed promise. Maybe she wasn't a 'love them and leave them' kind.

God, when was the last time he woke up this satisfied. Hmmm. He closed his eyes again. How about never. Christ, she really was a marathon runner. She was tireless and he'd been afraid he was going to get to the finish line before her. Didn't happen though. Didn't happen three times in a row. Man, she was a hottie. He shifted his position. He was getting all turned on thinking about it. Maybe if he found her, he could get started on that freckle inventory.

Sitting up, he shook his head. He was always a bit fuzzy in the morning. He peeked under the covers. Fuzzy, but not totally soft. It would be a shame to waste it. He grabbed his uniform pants off the floor and padded through the living room and into the small kitchen area. He looked around. No girl. Disappointment. Being an ace police officer, he decided to conduct a more thorough search. Since the suite wasn't all that large, it didn't take long. Missing girl. He couldn't believe she'd just get up and leave. He'd find her. He grinned, he was standing in her suite.

He grabbed a mug from the cupboard and poured a cup of coffee. His grin grew as his eyes caught a clue. Ace police officer would never make detective if he didn't start with the obvious. How about opening the little note propped up against Mr. Coffee…the note with his name on it, he thought.

Good morning. Actually it's nearly afternoon in Scotland. My body, while finely pleased and singing your praises, is still on Scottish time and begged for a run. You were so adorable snuggled into the blankets, I didn't have the heart to prod you into joining me.

She thought he was adorable. That was a start. He took the little note into the bedroom and put it in his shirt pocket. He'd place it in an inlaid box he kept on top of his dresser. It was like a treasure chest. He resisted the temptation to reread it…again.

He looked at the rumpled bed…her body was finely pleased and singing his praises, huh? He didn't need to reread the note, he had it memorized. Finely pleased and singing his praises. Talk about adorable. He checked his internal love indicator. Yup. He was in love, all right. He wondered how much of a hassle it would be to have a relationship with someone from Scotland. Time to think of that later. He had to shower and run home to change. Love or no love, he still had a job to get to.

CHAPTER 17

Payton stood in front of Skye and Alex's apartment later that day and rang the bell. She got a great deal accomplished and wanted to report to Alex. She eliminated a few more agencies in one of the outer suburbs. They were narrowing the field.

Tank was gone when she returned from her run and had left her a note to call him, but she wasn't sure exactly how she was going to handle their relationship.

Did she hope to see Tank here? Just as she was about to dig through her purse to get her cell phone to leave a message, her heart leapt when her thoughts, maybe even her desires, materialized into human form. Tank opened the door.

"Hey!" he said with a wide grin. He was still in uniform, sort of. His feet were bare and his shirt was unbuttoned. He was as sexy as an underwear ad. Then her eyes went up to the bottle he had in his hand. So he was already starting. Didn't surprise her, but after last night, she let some disappointment get by her defenses.

"Hi Tank. I'm here to see Alex."

"I told him he couldn't come out and play until he cleaned his room. You'll have to come back later."

"Bloody hell. And I was so looking forward to going to the park." She laughed and stepped through the threshold as he held the door open.

"Actually, he and Skye took Kevlar for a walk. I think she wanted the walk more than the dog and Alex won't let her out of his sight. Ah. Newlyweds." Tank knew it was more than that. He'd been filled in as much as the rest of the family, but still wasn't sure what part Payton was playing in the whole thing. Alex had an empire after all, so maybe she was just a dealmaker.

He looked at her with appreciation. I hope it's a long, long walk, he thought, already anticipating some lip locks and body squeezes. She looked all professional today…a briefcase and everything. Wow.

"Want to play with me, instead?" he asked, hopefully.

"Hmm." She looked him over. "How much do you know about English Common law?"

"Let's see, I know English…at least the Chicago brand of English. I know law," he tapped the badge on his chest. "And you can't get any more common than me…so, do you want to play with me instead?"

She laughed. "Sure, why not. Got a deck of cards? We can play poker or something." She walked into the living room, her heels clicking on the hard wood floor of the foyer. He loved that sound. Kind of coincided with the beat of his heart. "You play?"

"My favorite, but I'd rather poke you," he said, grabbing her arm and turning her into him. She tasted the beer on his lips when he kissed her. It wasn't horrid or anything. It just reminded her that he seemed to be very fond of drinking. By the time he drew back, she was pretty much drunk herself.

"Good one," she said and saluted.

"I thought so." He let go and took her hand. "Can I get you something?"

"Sure. I'd love a soft drink. A cola would be great."

"Nothing stronger?" he asked as he went behind the bar.

"No, thank you."

"Okay," he said grabbing a can of cola and getting another beer for himself. He poured her drink into a glass of ice and brought it around to her.

"Shall we sit down and neck, or would you like to get naked in front of the fire?"

She laughed. "Are those the only two alternatives?"

"The only two that come to mind right now," grinned Tank.

Payton resisted the nearly irresistible. "I think maybe I'd like to sit and just talk."

"Oh, oh," said Tank with mock seriousness. "Not the sit and talk stage." He shook his head, taking her hand again and leading her over to the sofa. He leaned over to kiss her, but she put her hand on his chest. He groaned. "Not this again. I thought we got beyond the blocking phase. You know you can't resist me."

She smiled at him. "Last night you got me at a weak moment."

"Define weak. I was scared to death you were going to want to go another round. I saw no weakness."

His lips were close to hers again. The current passed between them and it was powerful. Payton stood up and took her glass with her to the wall of windows overlooking the lake. Maybe if she put some distance between them, she could think. "When did Alex and Skye leave?"

"A few minutes before you got here," said Tank as he put his feet up on the coffee table. He'd let her back off if she wanted to. He was determined that they were going to spend the night together, had come over hoping she'd show up. He'd get through the barrier, whatever it was. "I'm sure Kevlar took them on his usual route and since there are quite a few trees and fire hydrants in the area, they'll be gone for awhile." He lifted the bottle of beer to his lips and chugged a few swallows. She turned and watched him, her smile frozen on her face.

He watched her eyes as she looked down at the badge on his chest. "I guess I could just leave these reports with you. You do, after all, wear a badge."

"You could do that." Then in a voice that was both conversational and steady, he asked her what was foremost on his mind. "Why the chill."

"Pardon?"

"We're alone in the apartment and you're over there by the window. I think I've indicated both in body language and in implication that I'd like to take advantage of our time alone to engage in something more intimate than small talk. If you're afraid Skye and Alex will walk in on us, we can keep our clothes on, you know."

"Look, Tank. I'm flattered, but last night was a casual physical coupling between two consenting adults. It was far from a commitment."

He just stared at her. "A casual physical coupling by two consenting adults? Is that English Common Law? My memory is of something much hotter and more meaningful than that."

Payton came back over and put her glass down on the coffee table next to his feet with a solid clunk. It sounded like a judge's gavel, and had a resonance of finality about it that Tank didn't like. "Look," she said. "You're a very nice guy…"

"But…" he said, his jaw clenching with frustration.

He saw her eyes move to his badge again.

"But…I'm just not looking for anything serious right now." She found she had to fight herself as well as him on this point. But she knew how to be hardnosed and she intended to be here. She felt her Scottish blood heat up. "One night doesn't entitle you to assume there will be any more."

"I'd normally agree with you, Payton," he said as he got up. He put his empty bottle down and went back behind the bar. "But I felt something last night coming from you. I don't think I imagined it." He opened the small refrigerator and got out another beer.

"Tell Alex to call me when he gets in. It doesn't matter what time." She took her briefcase from the floor near the sofa.

"You're a cold one, Payton Brady." Then he sighed. "Let me get my shoes back on and I'll see you safely home."

"No. Don't bother." She didn't like being called cold. She never thought of herself that way…in her personal relationships. When she was a cop, she could be plenty cold. Maybe that persona was leaking into her personal life. She looked over at him, prepared to argue when she saw his anger begin to bubble up. Okay, that did it. She was out of there. She turned toward the doorway.

Something popped into Tank's consciousness and he thought he'd test it. "You back away from me when I'm in uniform or when you realize I'm a cop."

That stopped her. He was in uniform tonight all right and it did distract her. Especially when he was angry and had a bottle in his hand. "Yes," she said without looking at him. "I guess you're right."

"So you *do* have trouble with cops," he said, tension making his voice edgy.

Disappointment was knifing through him because he knew that was something about him that would never change.

"No. I…" she started.

"The uniform, the badge or the gun." His voice was steady, but his eyes were hot. "You don't like the idea that you're attracted to a cop. You have trouble with that. Why not admit it?"

"That's not it, damn it." She found herself turning and looking him in the eye. Maybe he should know how she perceived him. What the hell. "I have trouble with cops who drink too much!" She said it in an equally controlled voice.

"Who drink too much?" Tank couldn't have been more astonished. He looked down at the bottle of beer in his hand. It was only a beer. But it was his third. He looked up at her. "You think I got a problem with alcohol?" He did remember his resolution at Skye and Alex's wedding that he was going to lay off the suds for a while. And he knew he did drink a lot. But he never thought of himself as a drunk.

"It doesn't matter. It's your business," Payton said quickly. She couldn't believe he made her say that. She never intended to share this bit of very personal information with him, or anyone else for that matter. She never had.

He looked at her again, then slowly tipped the bottle over and let the contents flow down the drain. She watched, completely unmoved. How often had her father done that?

"You think that impresses me?" She snorted and turned to leave. "Tell Alex I'll call him in the morning."

Tank vaulted over the bar and stood in front of her. She was so astonished, she just gaped at him. She looked at the height of the bar. How did he get all that weight over it so easily?

"Now, that impresses me," she said without thinking.

"Yeah? Well, how about this." He gathered her in his arms and put all his considerable talent into one, long toe-curling kiss. By the time he pulled away, she couldn't remember exactly why she was so hot to leave.

"Okay. So that was impressive, too." She smiled and took a deep breath. Then gently pulled away. "But I'm still leaving and I'll still thank you to give Alex the message."

Tank stepped aside, but retained her hand. He cupped her chin in his large hand and pulled up her face until their eyes met.

"Tell me about it. Please," he said softly. He could feel her body drawn to him; he knew she was fighting her preferences. There had to be a reason, a good one, he thought, for her to fight so hard with herself. "We spent the night together. It felt like a natural thing to me and I think it did to you. It doesn't entitle me to any expectations, but I think it entitles me to a few explanations. If you're going to walk out, I think you should tell me why, don't you?"

Payton sighed. He was right. He was such a fun-loving sort that she forgot there was a solid and sensitive man in there. Sweet.

"Let's sit down," she said. Her knees were still rubbery from the kiss. She led the way to the sofa in front of the fireplace. The location he first saw her.

"Want a beer?" he asked and when she turned her fiery gaze on him, she saw the teasing light in his eyes.

"Very funny."

"I thought so."

"Actually you can fetch me a glass of water. If I'm going to tell you the story of my life, I'll need to keep my throat open."

Tank came back and sat on the couch next to her, two glasses of water in his hand. She took one, then looked at the other with some chagrin.

He drank from his and smacked his lips. "Ah. Water. And a very good vintage."

She shook her head and laughed in spite of herself. He was trying to make this easy for her and she loved him for it. Loved him? Wait. Back up. Too late. Damn. This really complicated things. Well, then she'd just have to fight herself a little harder. She took a drink to cool her throat and sank back into the leather cushions.

Tank drained his glass, then put it down and took her hand. "Your accent kind of gives a man a powerful thirst and if I'm going to give up beer, I guess I'd better get used to the softer stuff."

"I haven't asked you to give up anything, Tank," she said softly. She set her glass next to his.

"No, you haven't. But I'm an excellent detective. Actually, I've just been accepted into a special branch of the department for investigatory science. So. Let's see. You haven't had a drink since I've known you, not a long time, but long enough. You have a very negative reaction to my attraction to the suds. For some reason the combination of this uniform and that aforesaid attraction is very upsetting to you. Your look of fear last night when I was really pissed was uncharacteristic of you. This indicates you may have, at some time in your past, been badly treated by a drunk man in uniform. Am I close?"

Payton just stared, then completely alarmed Tank by tearing up.

"Oh shit." He drew her into his arms and held her. "I'm sorry. I didn't mean to sound so cavalier about it. Talk to me, sweetheart."

She nodded. "First of all, you're a wonderful detective," she began. She took a deep breath and simply told him. "My father was a cop."

"Father?" That did surprise him. He thought maybe a boyfriend or ex-husband or something a bit less dramatic.

"And I guess if a broken arm, cracked ribs, a dislocated shoulder, black eyes, and other assorted bruises, cuts and contusions means I was badly treated, then I was…by a drunk man in uniform."

Tank didn't say anything…couldn't. His rage was too immense. He didn't want to scare her with it. Father or no father, the man was on borrowed time. He'd see to it. How could a father do that to a child…his own child? This was far more serious than he first imagined. He'd pictured a few shouting matches, like he witnessed with some of the couples he knew when liquor was a problem. Nothing like this even occurred to him. He felt the tension rocket through his arms.

Payton could feel the change in him...sense the anger. She was very, very good at feeling anger in the air. She felt herself pull away. Her mind screamed at her that Tank was a different sort of man, but her body's reaction to this kind of fury was conditioned by years of abuse. Putting her hand on his tense, hard chest, she tried to lever herself out of his arms.

"Don't," he whispered, trying to let her hear the sympathy and compassion that flowed from his heart. He felt her pulling away the moment she began to do so...and now he knew why. "Let me hold you. I can control the anger. It won't come out. And if it does, you'll never, ever be its target. I promise you."

"Words," she sighed wearily. "Just words. I can't tell you how often he'd say he was sorry. He'd pour the scotch down the drain, promise never to drink again. That was the worst...the very worst. He was a lovely man when he was sober and when he made those promises, I'd hope. Hope. Then he'd slide back into his old pattern. When I see a man in uniform taking a drink...it just hurts my heart. Does he have a little girl? Will he hurt her? Hit her? Worse?"

Tank turned her in his arms until he could look directly into her eyes. "Don't let that man rule your heart, honey. He already hurt you enough. Not everyone is like him. Not even close."

"I know. I know," she said, seeing the compassion as well as the anger. "My experience is unique to me. I try not to make judgments. But my heart isn't always in control. Look, I never share this with anyone. It makes me a bit woozy just talking about it. Let's just drop it. He's been dead for over 14 years and he really did very little damage to me after I learned to run."

"So you *were* running from something," said Tank, not yet ready to let it drop.

"What?"

"The other day...when I saw you running. My first impression was that you were running from something."

She smiled at him. "You really are a perceptive man. You'll make a wonderful detective." She continued to move away from him. Instinctively he knew he shouldn't hold her and let her move out of his arms. She had to see and feel she was in control. His anger was now settling into a very dark place in his gut. The man was dead and there was nothing he could do to him now. Nothing but prove to his daughter that a man in uniform didn't beat little girls.

She sat up and gave an involuntary shudder. "You could also turn your talent to counseling. I'm loath to share that bit of sordid family history with anyone."

"Does it help?" He was never sure if reliving a childhood trauma was good or not.

Payton looked at Tank's kind eyes and concerned face.

"I don't know." She looked inside herself. Did it help to tell someone? "My heart is still quite silent on this issue tonight. I know that I feel okay about telling you. You were right. After our...um..." she raised her eyebrows.

"Our night of passion and incredible body bonding."

She laughed. "Yes. That. Anyway, you did deserve an explanation. It wasn't fair to imply that you had a problem when it's me who has the problem. When a police officer raises a bottle, it makes me clutch up inside."

"What if I take off the uniform first?" he asked, taking her hands in his.

She shook her head, but didn't pull away. "Tank. Really. This has nothing to do with you. It's me."

"But I want everything to do with you to have something to do with me," countered Tank, not quite sure if he was making sense.

"Was that the common Chicago English?" She shook her head as if to clear it. "If it is, you'll have to translate for me."

"I want to continue to see you." He drew closer to her. "If I could just speak to your heart, now." He planted a tender little kiss on her lips. "I want you, darling Payton."

"Tank," she breathed. Not moving her face, inviting the next kiss. "You're really making this difficult."

"Great. That's good." He tasted her lips again. "Pure honey. You tell me the rules and I'll follow them. I'm really, really good with rules. Ask my mom."

"Tank," she said again, her breath starting to come in little gasps. "Really. You have very little invested in this relationship. Let's just say good night and…"

They both turned as they heard Kevlar barking and Skye and Alex laughing in the foyer.

"I'm taking you home tonight and we're finishing this conversation," said Tank as he gave her lips a last gentle peck and stood to greet his little four-legged nephew who had scented Uncle Tank and came bounding into the room.

"Hey guy!" The puppy took a leap and Tank caught him on the fly. He was delighted to hear Payton giggle and clap behind him and went to the jar on the bar to give Kevlar an extra doggie treat for making the lady laugh.

"Don't give him too many of those," warned Skye. "We don't want him to be a rolly, polly puppy."

"Jeez, Skye," snorted Tank. "Did you notice how your vocabulary goes south every time you get around this dog?"

She came over, planted a kiss on Tank's cheek and took the puppy from him. "Oh, golly gee."

"And the only time I get kisses from you any more is when I'm holding the damn mutt. I swear you're aiming for the dog and hit me by mistake."

"Exactly." She put Kevlar on the floor. "Hi Payton. I hope you haven't been waiting long. Our faithful butler here volunteered to open the door and be civil. Did he fulfill his function?"

"That he did."

Tank smiled at Payton and Skye noticed the little extra zing that went with the look. Damn. She told Alex they should have stayed away longer. She'd given into his overly protective directive to get off her feet when he saw that she was getting winded. She hated that, but she'd promised him she'd be a good girl.

"Do I get a treat?" asked Tank.

"Sure," said Alex as he went behind the bar and poured himself a glass of wine. "Budweiser or Corona."

"How about Root."

"Huh?"

"As in root beer?"

"Sure." He was used to his brother being strange, but Skye picked up on the non-alcoholic suggestion right away. It stirred something inside her. She knew there was some relief mixed in with the surprise. Her eyes slid to the two glasses on the coffee table…looked like water. That would imply a serious discussion. Skye was a good detective, too. All of the conclusions she drew were right on target. She couldn't wait to share her insights with Alex.

"I thought you said Kevlar learned to sit," said Alex handing Tank his root beer.

"He did…my guy, the puppy genius. He learned it in one night."

"Man. It took over a year for you to learn it," laughed Alex. "Skye can't get him to sit."

Skye looked down at her dog and said, "sit."

Kevlar jumped and rolled and panted and pawed, but his little butt never touched the carpet.

"Sit." Now his butt wiggled, because the sit word always meant a treat was coming.

"Did he forget?" asked Skye, looking at Tank.

"No. He needs an incentive." Tank walked over to the shelf where he stowed his weapon. He casually drew his gun, pointed it at the dog and said in his best cop voice, "Sit, you son-of-a-bitch!"

Kevlar's butt slammed onto the carpet and the dog grinned up at his God. His tail twitched, but everything else stayed absolutely still.

"Holy shit, Tank. You use that method in public and every living thing in a city block is going down on its ass," laughed Alex.

"Stop that, Alex…don't encourage him. Tank, how could you?" Skye could barely speak, her horror reflected in a gaping expression that made Alex laugh harder.

"I thought, hey, if it works on perps, how much smarter is this dog than an asshole who grabs an old lady's purse with what's left of her social security in it? Besides," he re-holstered the gun. "I never draw on the mutt in public. Isn't good for PR."

Alex roared and tossed Tank a pretzel. Tank caught it one handed and threw it in his mouth. He grinned and bowed. Suddenly Tank realized there was a civilian in the room and looked over at Payton. She wasn't laughing, either.

"Um. Sorry about that. We kind of grew up with guns all over the house. I guess that wasn't very funny."

"No. I guess it wasn't," said Skye, still completely horrified. "I can't believe you even showed him a gun. What if he got it into his mind to chew on it, or something."

"Damn it, Skye," chuckled Alex. He thought the trick was hilarious, especially since Kevlar was still sitting. "His name is Kevlar for God's sake. Lighten up."

"Lighten up? Lighten up? He's just a puppy." She frowned at Tank. "Do you draw on Jason and Al, too? Eat your cheerios or splat?"

"Splat? Christ, Skye. I'm quite sure I've never said splat in my whole life." Tank's lips twitched. "Kevlar is a German Shepard...you know...a police dog? Big, bad and ready to serve and protect. He should get used to guns if he's going to live around this family."

"He's a baby," Skye insisted, her hands on her hips. "And Al and Jason have to be protected, too."

"Skye," Alex tried to stop laughing, but her anger made the whole situation even funnier. "Their dad is a New York City cop. He wears his gun home every night. You know Tank locks up his weapons when Al and Jason are around."

"Well I'd thank you to do the same when Kevlar is in the house." She went over and picked up the still sitting dog. "Poor baby. Did Uncle Tank scare you?"

Payton couldn't help it. She tried to get on Skye's side, but it just wasn't working. She'd been exercising her will power to keep a straight face, but the whole scene really belonged on a situation comedy. This was better than American television. Alex was still laughing uncontrollably, a sight in itself considering who he was, and Tank looked like he was about ready to explode with the effort to remain contrite. He kept making faces at Alex behind Skye's back. It started as a giggle, then spilled over from there. Before she could take it back, she was laughing as hard as the men.

"Skye," she said, holding her side and gasping. "I really want to say that I agree with you 100 percent." Her eyes were watering. "I really, really want to say it."

Kevlar jumped out of Skye's arms and went straight for Tank who caught him on the fly.

"I think the only one traumatized in this room is you, sis." Tank went over and gave Skye a kiss on the cheek. "But in deference to your parental outrage, I'll continue Kevlar's training without the lethal weapon."

Just then, Kevlar decided to show off another talent and gave the room a clue to what he ate off the street on his walk that morning and he did it with a delicate little popping noise. He turned to Tank and grinned.

"Oh man," choked Tank, fanning the air. "Talk about lethal. Here, he's your dog."

Skye coughed. "Oh no, when he does stuff like that, he's all male. Take him out on the balcony. And Alex, you go out there with him. You need to get control of yourself." Alex was still chuckling when the men went to air out the dog.

"God, what a circus," said Skye. "Let's go into the library and you can fill me in on what you found out today. I'll pass it on to Alex." She also needed to sit down. The walk around the block tired her more than she wanted to admit or let anyone in the room see.

They spent the better part of an hour going through all of the information from both Interpol and the Chicago branch of the FBI. Emily had been positively identified and was on her way home.

"I think my usefulness is nearly at an end, here," said Payton.

"Does that mean you'll be going back to Scotland?" Skye felt a rush of disappointment.

"No, actually, I'm thinking about taking some vacation time and seeing this case through. I'll need your permission to do so. My commander supports me, but can't devote official time and resources to the project."

"I think your help will be very valuable. You have a good idea of what we're up against and I could use another woman on the case. As soon as we've located the agency, we can use you on the team. I'll need backup."

"I'm curious. Does Tank know about your shadow career? The man is incredibly perceptive."

Skye smiled. "Alex's family pretends they know nothing. They've worked out an arrangement whereby Alex lies, they know he lies, they figure out the truth, he knows they know the truth, and they all respect the secret. Nothing is overt, everything is cryptic and coded. It's an amazing dance, but it works. So to answer your question, he does know. However, we never talk about it."

"What should we tell him about me?"

"Oh, I think you can tell him everything." Skye looked at her and smiled the smile of a confidant. "You've been telling him some things all ready, haven't you? Personal things?"

"You're also a perceptive lady." Payton smiled back. She really could use a girl friend right now.

"Do you want to talk about it?"

"Yeah, I think I do. Do you want to hear it?"

"Yes. I admire you very much, Payton. And more than that, I think my dear little brother has already developed a thing for you."

"The feeling is mutual," sighed Payton giving in to the need to talk to someone about her feelings. "How can it happen so fast?"

"Because when you find someone to love, it's your heart and soul that recognizes him. All you have to do is not allow your mind to create static that will interfere with nature."

Payton told her everything. About her father, her early life, her budding relationship with Tank. And her concern over Tank's drinking.

"I wouldn't care so much, but I'm afraid he has a large portion of my heart already. I'm not my mother. I'd never just take it, but I don't want to risk the heartache either."

"Tank drinks a lot. But I think it's more habit than need, more environmental than an addiction. I could be wrong, but I don't think so. I know I've seen him crank up the consumption lately and frankly, it's had me thinking. Now, you come into his life and throw a spotlight on it. Time will tell, but I don't think he's going to consider curbing his drinking any great sacrifice if you come through the door to replace it."

Skye took Payton's hand and looked into her new friend's eyes. "I also know for a fact that he's the same man sober, buzzed or completely wasted. He's a man of honor." Skye was surprised at the tickle at the back of her throat. She was shouting at him less than an hour before and now she was getting all mushy talking about him. "He's open and fun loving, but never think that means he's superficial. And," she said before she turned all weepy. "He's a damn good cop, just like you."

Payton smiled gratefully. "You must think I'm neurotic or something. I mean coming from an abusive home…an alcoholic father. But I really think I've come to grips with it all. I don't drink because I'm scared shitless of becoming my father, and I can live very nicely without it. I also know that most people can enjoy a few drinks without being alcoholics and that not every drunk beats his kids. I know that up here." She tapped her head. "I just have to overcome my conditioning and feel it here." She tapped her chest. "And maybe that will only require a new period of conditioning…from an honorable man," Payton said softly in a reflective voice. Suddenly she felt a sense of freedom and her eyes cleared.

A very satisfied Skye knew she'd done all she could for Tank. It was now completely up to him. "I don't think you're neurotic, and someday over a glass of wine and a Perrier, I'll tell you about disturbed." She stood up and took a deep breath to clear out the ghosts. "Come on, let's go join the men. I'm sure the air has cleared out by now, that is unless the two guys have decided to take Kevlar on and turn the whole thing into a contest."

"Men."

"Amen."

The guys were neither drinking, nor trying to outdo Kevlar. They were engaged in mortal combat. The big screen exploded in little people and flying body parts. Skye went over to her husband and planted a long passionate kiss on his intense lips.

"Damn, Skye," said Tank. "You sure do have guts."

Alex smiled into the eyes of his bride and put the controls on the sofa.

"You can tell they're newlyweds," he said to Payton as he put down his set of controls. "She distracts him just as he's going where no man has gone before and he doesn't even body slam her."

"Her courage and bravery are well documented," said Payton.

"You three want to be alone for awhile?" asked Tank. He knew there was a reason Payton was here and didn't want to get in the way. "I can take Kevlar out again."

"No, I don't think so, thanks," said Payton. "I was just delivering some papers, I don't need to stay." She looked at Alex. "You can call me after you've reviewed all the documents." She looked at her watch.

"Why don't you stay for dinner, Payton," asked Skye. "Alex arranged to have some food brought up and it should be here any minute."

Payton smiled. "Hmm. Food served in elegant surroundings with three incredibly interesting people." Kevlar let out a whooping sound. "Sorry, four…or a take out and American TV alone in my room. Tough choice. Can I help set the table?"

"Great," said Tank, winking at Skye. He noticed the little connection that the ladies had developed while they were in the other room and hoped Skye had put in a good word for him. "That's usually my job."

"The only thing is, we can never convince him you don't need two forks for the main course," said Alex.

Just then the doorbell rang signaling the arrival of the food. The chef of Chicago's top Italian restaurant had prepared a feast and the four of them decided to forgo the formal dining room and eat around the smaller kitchen table. The Springfield boys entertained the ladies with tales of their childhood on the streets of Chicago.

"You ever use that stove, Skye?" asked Tank when every plate was empty. She noticed he stayed with water and iced tea rather than his usual bottle of wine with dinner.

"I'll pretend I didn't hear that chauvinistic remark," sniffed Skye. "I fly planes. Why not ask your brother?"

"You ever use that stove, Alex?"

"Good save," snorted Alex.

"I didn't want her calling Mom."

"I'm really looking forward to meeting her," said Payton.

Tank's heart skipped a beat. If she was planning on meeting his mother, she was planning on staying for a while. He knew it was just a simple, inadvertent statement, but he decided he'd put greater meaning into it. It warmed him. Something had to replace the buzz he usually got from a bottle of wine. He tested his reaction to total sobriety and found it was okay…as long as he got the girl.

"Mom's finishing up a big one right now," he said. "Very high profile. I'll bet if we turn on the news tonight we'll see her working the media."

"She must be a remarkable woman," smiled Payton.

"She raised us, didn't she," said Tank.

"Let's hope she isn't finished," said Skye. "How about coffee around the fire?"

They each carried their mugs into the living room as Alex turned on the lights and ignited the fire.

"So enough about us, I want to hear about your life in Scotland." Tank sat down next to Payton and put his arm around the back of the sofa behind her.

Suddenly the lights flickered and went out. The fire, on an independent propane line, kept the room from plunging into complete darkness. Remembering a time the summer before when the darkness was a prelude to armed men invading their home, Skye and Alex went immediately to their weapons. Skye's was in her purse and Alex had placed his behind the bar. Tank grabbed his pistol off the shelf where he'd placed it earlier.

"Who knows you're here?" asked Tank, his cop voice serious and commanding.

"Family, Jim, Barclay, Linda," said Skye.

"I'll check the balcony to see if it's just this building or the whole block," said Alex.

Payton cursed herself for being so complacent. Her gun was in her briefcase in the office. Moving swiftly, she found the door with little difficulty. When she had her gun in her hand, she felt better, more in control. Silently, she made her way back into the living room.

Tank noticed Payton move quickly to the shadows. *She* knew Skye and Alex were here, he thought. He wasn't ever sure what they were working on at any given time, but he knew there was always a potential for danger. Who was Payton? What did he actually know about this woman? Damn! She hadn't really revealed anything the last few days, always evading. He tried to focus his eyes on where she went. He didn't think she was hiding in fear in a corner somewhere. Somehow she didn't strike him as the timid type. Shit. Seduce the brother…get closer to the target. Was that her game? Sounded like the plot of a really bad spy flick.

"Looks like it might be the entire block," said Alex when he strode back into the room.

Skye had placed herself by the door. "No movement outside and the door to the stairs hasn't opened. The elevator will be inoperable. Security system is out." Just then, Skye's cell phone rang.

"Shit," hissed Alex as he ran his knee into a table. He located her phone on the bar.

"Alex Springfield." He listened. "Okay. Thanks. I appreciate the call."

"A transformer went out on Lakeshore. A semi took it out. I'm going to verify the call, then we can relax and enjoy the dark."

He called his security company, an internal organization contracted by Jim. He wanted to be sure the earlier call was legitimate, and it was.

Suddenly, he heard Tank shout. "Drop it and put your hands where I can see them."

He spun around and heard Skye racing across the foyer. Tank came out of the hallway holding a spitting mad Scottish Inspector by the waist. "God damn it. Settle down before I break my promise and deck you."

"You glaikit ass. Put me down. Take a scunner, you goddamn American cowboy." She was pissed as hell at Tank for taking her gun. He moved so quickly for such a big man, she didn't have time to react.

"Not until you tell me why you had a gun pointed at my brother." His arm tightened around her, making it difficult for her to take a deep breath, but she managed.

"Are you off the latch? I wasn't pointing it at anyone, you overstuffed, dimwitted yank."

"Ouch, good one, Payton," said Skye, laughing. She looked at Alex. "All clear?"

"Yes. Verified," said Alex, crossing his arms and enjoying the demonstration of intercontinental, interdepartmental cooperation.

"Tank, put her down," chuckled Skye.

Tank slowly put Payton on her feet. He had both her gun and his in his hand. He was beginning to feel like there was something going on under the surface, but his training demanded caution. He figured as long as she was disarmed, she wasn't a danger to him or his family. He was wrong.

As soon as she was on her feet, Payton spun and brought her knee up hard. When he doubled up, she used all of her strength and her superior balance to push him over. She took her first full breath and decided to put it to good use. "Sit, you son-of-a-bitch!"

Alex and Skye just stared. The lights flickered and went back on. Tank was still holding onto the two guns, but was sitting flat on the floor. Even though there were beads of sweat on his forehead and he couldn't take a deep breath, he had his gun on his quarry.

Payton wasn't at all intimidated by the gun. She was in high temper and considering giving him another swift kick. Only her understanding of his need to protect his family kept her foot from following through.

"Sit, you son-of-a-bitch?" snorted Skye. She looked from Tank to Kevlar, who was sitting at attention in front of the fire and hadn't moved since Payton's command, back to Tank. "I always thought they were related. It's the mouth."

"Does anyone other than me think this is hilarious," said Alex, feeling his brother's pain, but unable to control the amusement flooding from deep inside. He put the safety back on his gun, placed it on the bar and roared with laughter for the second time that evening.

Skye laughed along with Alex and soon tears were popping out from beneath her lashes. Alex threw a bone to Kevlar, who was still planted on the floor. The puppy grabbed the treat between his jaws with the precision of a major league catcher.

"This isn't funny," rasped Tank, as he grabbed the pretzel Alex threw at him. It was simple reflex, and was done with equal precision. And it reduced the temptation to grab himself.

"Oh yeah," said Payton, back in good humor now that the threat had proved non-existent. "Don't be a bloody Eejit. Tis bloomin' funny. Can I give you a hand?" She offered Tank her hand.

"Oh no. You're just after an opportunity to reclaim your gun." He lowered his own weapon. "I take it you're a friend with a gun."

Payton looked into Tank's furious eyes. "This is really one of those once in a lifetime moments," she said grinning, her green eyes dancing. "One you can wait for your entire life and never get to act out. One you can script and never get to play…" She couldn't suppress the giggle at Tank's glower.

"Okay, I get the picture, damn it. Cut the suspense, I'm dying here…"

Payton reached into her inside jacket pocket and opened up her credentials. Tank took a quick look and lay down on the carpet. "Shit," he moaned. "A cop."

"And let's see, I'm an Inspector, that would be the equivalent of a Detective over here, so," she got down on one knee, leaned over and kissed him lightly, "that would mean I outrank you, Officer Springfield."

She sat down on the floor beside him with a laugh and looked at Skye and Alex, still chuckling and enjoying the show. "You know some things in life are just so bloody perfect that you could just die and go straight to heaven with a smile."

She gave a little squeal when Tank's strong and sturdy arm snaked around her waist and he pulled her on top of him. She was still laughing and Tank was making growling sounds. Kevlar raced over to join the fun. Barking and licking as if the whole incident was staged for his amusement.

"Shall we leave the children alone to work out their differences?" asked Skye.

"Yes, I think so, darling. Be so kind as to turn out the lights when you're through wrestling," he said to his brother, although he seriously doubted if he'd remember.

Tank thought the best way to suppress Payton's laughing was to engage her in a lip lock.

Alex started toward the bedroom, turned and waited for his wife by the doorway. Skye scooped up Kevlar, who was trying to get his tongue in between Payton and Tank's lips.

"Some police dog, you are," she said, nuzzling his furry neck. Then she went to Alex, put her arm around him and they walked down the hallway with their little boy between them.

Tank had his arm securely around Payton's waist and wasn't going to let her go. Her face was only inches from his and he could see the humor in her eyes. At least she wasn't mad at him anymore.

"Inspector?" he asked, his lips twitching, in spite of the dull throb between his legs. She nodded, her eyes sparkling in the firelight.

"And I thought you had something against cops."

"Oh, right now I do."

Tank frowned.

"I have my whole body against one." She stretched out her body over his, placing her elbows on his chest and propping her chin on the palms of her hands. His arm was still around her waist, but it rested gently and she felt connected, not trapped.

"Um. Are you okay?" she asked. "I hadn't really intended to turn on you like that; it was an automatic reflex. You know, cop training. That and a wee bit of temper, I suppose. No one has ever taken my gun from me before. Do you think everything still works?"

"Well, now," Tank put his hand around her neck and brought her down for another kiss. "I guess you'll find out soon enough if all the equipment is still operational, Inspector."

He smiled, trying to absorb the fact that she was a cop. She must be a good one, too, if she reached the rank of Inspector already.

"A cop," he said, then gave her another quick kiss. He smoothed her hair behind her ear looking deeply into her eyes. "After what your father did to you, you still wanted to be in law enforcement?"

"More than anything." She put her head on his chest and he put his other arm around her. Now she felt more than connected; she felt whole. "I don't want to go too deeply to uncover the reasons I chose the profession. I'm sure there are whole textbooks written about why a child would choose to go into the den of her tormentor. But I do know it was all I ever wanted to be. Once I got into it, I found I was good at it." She brought her head up and looked at him. "Did you ever want to be anything else?"

"Well, there was that very brief time, after I saw Crocodile Dundee, that I wanted to be a crocodile hunter but that only lasted a few days. I've wanted to be a cop my whole life."

"Me too." She settled back onto his chest. Her eyes were getting heavy. The adrenalin pumped her for a little while, but it was already almost morning in Scotland.

"Stay with me tonight." he whispered when he noticed her blinking fatigue away.

"You're trying to take advantage of a weak moment," she said, stifling a yawn.

He reached down and brought her face up. Smiling, he gently touched her lips. "Please, darling Inspector. Let me make love to you tonight."

He rolled her over, placing his elbows on either side of her so his body wasn't resting on hers. He kissed her neck and found the place that seemed to make her unable to resist him. It worked. She moaned and reached up, burying her fingers in his long, copper colored hair.

"Here?"

"I have my own room and everything."

"How convenient."

"Times like these, it pays to be the family freeloader."

In one smooth motion, Tank stood up and pulled her up with him. They laughed when they both realized they still had their guns in their hands.

In identical movements, they flipped on the safeties and shoved them into their waistbands at the small of their backs. Then Tank lifted her and carried her off to his room at the rear of the apartment. She took the opportunity to explore his neck and had his bottoms undone by the time he gently laid her on the king sized bed. She looked around. "Beautiful." Tank grabbed a remote and started the fire in the small fireplace in the corner.

"Gotta go turn off all the lights. The bathroom is through there." He was still walking a little funny, but he was sure he'd be able to perform when called upon to do so.

Payton watched him stride back through the door. Responsible, she thought with a flush of pleasure. He remembered the lights. That added another mark in the plus column. Checking out the bathroom, she found it fully stocked, from toothbrushes to spare robes. She was going to strip down, but she remembered how it felt when he did that for her. Instead, she used the facilities, brushed her teeth and smiled at her reflection. When she came out into the bedroom, Tank was pulling down the comforter and sheets. He turned out the lights in here, too and lit candles on the mantle and the bedside table. They were scented and gave off a wonderful, masculine spicy smell. God. Did she just step into a romance novel? It made her stomach flutter.

Tank turned and stared at her for a minute. She was the same woman he'd made love to the night before, beautiful, sexy, bold. But there was something else. He saw trust. She was preparing to put more than her body into this night, she was going to put her heart into it. Because he knew his own heart, it didn't concern him. He'd never let her regret her faith in him.

They moved toward each other and met in the center of the room. She looked up at him and smiled. He reached around and nipped her gun out of her waist band. She did the same to his.

Tank chuckled as he took them and placed them on the bedside table. "This is like a double gun ceremony."

"Maybe I should pat you down." Her hands reached inside the front of his uniform pants. "Are you still armed?"

He enjoyed her touch for a moment. A long moment.

"Did you find the cannon?"

She laughed softly. "I think it's still hiding."

"Can't blame it. Recognizes the knee."

"I'm sorry. I know you were only protecting your family."

"For just a moment, I thought you might have seduced me to get to them."

"I think you watch too much TV."

"Do you think, Natasha?"

He looked down at her. Candlelight was creating shadows and movement along her beautiful features. He brought his hands up and framed her face.

Her lips parted as her eyes moved to his full smiling lips, coming down to claim, to conquer, to seek surrender. His hands undressed her slowly, rubbing her skin with his fingertips as soon as it was exposed.

When she was naked in the fire and candlelight, she slowly did the same for him. Her lips and tongue working with her finger tips to claim, to conquer, to seek surrender.

"Darling, trust me," he whispered. "I'll never hurt you."

For a moment she stared at him, her eyes serious and searching, then she smiled the sweetest, most poignant smile he'd ever seen and nodded.

"I do. I place my happiness in your hands." She turned her face and kissed the palm of the hand he'd placed on her cheek.

He embraced her, his heart filled with desire and commitment and felt the warm, sensual pleasure of her naked body molded to his. He picked her up again and laid her on the bed, moving his hands over her body, preparing her, loving her.

"I love you, Inspector," he said as he smiled into her lovely eyes, willing her to see the truth.

Her eyes widened even as her body arched under his gentle touch. "You don't have to..." but she didn't finish the thought, much less the sentence. She heard him whisper "I love you" and every time he did, she fell deeper and deeper into his heart.

When she finally slept, her arm across his waist, her head on his shoulder, Tank watched her face ease into complete relaxation. He looked at her strong, capable hands. When he'd seen her competently carrying a gun, he just reacted, disarming her and grabbing her. She'd seen him and hadn't reacted to him, knowing he was one of the good guys. What would have happened if she really had been on the other side? Would he have bested her so easily? I guess I'll never know, he thought. Remembering the delight on her face when she presented her credentials, he smiled in the dark. Except for the knee to the groin, now that he had time to think about it, he liked the memory of the evening. It would definitely become a family classic.

He covered her and kept his arms around her, stroking her soft, muscular back. She sighed in her sleep and he smiled. She wanted to be a cop her whole life, just like him. He still felt a shock to his system when he thought of her as a police officer. How perfect was that? He also felt that he'd been looking for her his whole life and hoped she felt the same way. Maybe part of that running was toward him. He drifted until he fell into the deep and dreamless sleep of a completely satisfied man.

Skye stretched and turned over in bed. Opening one eye, she saw that it was 5:37. She tried to translate what that was in real time, but couldn't decide what time zone she wanted to be in. Should she be in Scottish time since that was where she should have been or Eastern time since that was where she lived. No. She closed her eyes. Figure Pacific time, she thought, for no particular reason other than it would be 3:37 and way too early to get up.

Maybe she'd cuddle, though and reached her arm out to hunt down her husband. He wasn't there. Frowning, she thought he might be farther over on the bed, so she shifted. Her hand found his pillow, but no hard body. Sighing, she grabbed that. Yes, it was his, she could smell him. She hugged the pillow and was just about under again when she felt him get back in bed.

"Good morning, darling. Can I have my pillow back?" He tugged playfully at it.

"Mmm. Okay. But then I'll have to use your chest." She threw her arm around his waist and repositioned herself…and felt a tongue slap over her face.

"Either you've picked up some peculiar habits, or the dog is awake," she mumbled, not opening her eyes.

"He's not only awake, my love, but he took me outside so he could leave a manly puddle in the bushes."

"Is that why your nose is so cold and wet?"

"Exactly."

"What a good dog," mumbled Skye. Kevlar heard those magic words 'good dog' and perked right up.

"Only someone who hasn't left her nice warm bed would compliment the dog, not the sainted husband who accompanied him outside while his pillow snatching, blanket hogging bride slept on."

"I don't hog the blankets. I just take my share. Community property. Besides, it keeps you close to me." She could feel Kevlar's tail thumping the bed. "Give the dog a reward. There are some biscuits in the drawer."

It was only 3:40 in Los Angeles, she thought, good night. Sleep pulled her under immediately.

Alex got a biscuit out of the drawer and threw it on the far side of the bed. "How about you give me my reward while the dog is distracted, Skye?" He smiled. He kissed the top of her head, then went back to sleep himself, sandwiched between his warm bride and a grateful puppy. Life was good.

CHAPTER 18

When Tank woke up the next morning, he was alone again. He looked at the clock and saw the two guns lying side by side...like cop poetry or something. He had a few hours before he needed to report, so he rolled over to finish the dream he was having. There was a beach, a red head, and...coffee? He opened an eye. Coffee.

"Good morning. Are you still asleep?" The voice had the sound of Scotland in it.

"I am, yes."

"And would you dreaming?"

"That depends. Are you a beautiful red head with a badge?"

"I have a badge."

"Is your name Bambi and do you wear high heels and a garter belt?"

"How high is your tolerance for pain?"

"I'm a coward."

"Then you may want to rephrase that last question."

"Is your name Inspector Bambi?"

"Better. Would you like your coffee enema now?"

Turning, he sat up and making the enema an impossibility. He took the coffee gratefully and shook out the cobwebs.

"Skye and Alex up?"

"Just Alex. I take it you and Skye are not the cheerful early risers in the family."

He looked at her through bleary eyes. "Damn, and I thought you were perfect. Now I find you chirp in the morning."

She smiled and shrugged. "Depends on the time zone."

"At least I won't have any more hangovers."

Her coffee cup stopped halfway to her lips. A little shocked look passed over her face before she could stop it. Then she pursed her lips and blew out a little breath. She took another sip of coffee, put the cup on the table, and smoothed out the blankets. She also seemed very interested in putting the little pillows back on the bed. She was stalling and they both knew it.

"Look, Tank…"

He knew he'd zinged one in there and took pity on her. "Is this the place for the 'thanks for the great sex, but I don't want a commitment' speech?"

She sighed. "Stop being so cute." She couldn't control her reaction and reached over and smoothed some of the hair back from his forehead. Her hand rested in his hair for a moment, then she looked down at the pattern in the sheets and reached for her coffee again. He didn't think the damn pattern could have been that interesting and felt a little rock in his stomach begin to expand.

"Right. No cute. Consider it completely stopped" he said, still feeling the ghost of her touch on his hair.

"Tank." She sighed, again. This was so strange, so unexpected. "Let me do it this way." She looked up at him. "I have to ask you a few questions." Revert to her training, this would be better.

"Go ahead, Inspector." Tank's heart was beating vigorously. He leaned back against the pillows propped up against the headboard and tried to go for the casual look. He could feel the pulse in his jugular.

She nodded. She put on her cop's eyes. Tank raised his eyebrows. He was impressed. They bore into him and were like mini truth detectors.

"Your sister-in-law tells me you're an honorable man. Could you tell me why she'd characterize you in such a way?"

Tank blinked. "Wow, what a way to start the day. Let me settle in here." So Skye thought he was an honorable man. Now if he could get Payton to love him, his world would be perfect. "May I take your hand during this interrogation, Inspector?"

She nodded, but never took her eyes from him. She felt his warm touch and his fingers laced around hers.

"First of all, I want you to know that Skye is one of the most perceptive, intelligent woman I've ever known."

Payton smiled. "Is that because of her positive assessment of you?"

"Of course." Tank cocked his head and grinned.

"No cute."

"Right. Sorry." Tank erased the smile. "Actually my positive assessment of her isn't contingent on her positive assessment of me."

Payton blinked. "No need to overcompensate and sound like a high priced consultant. That would be solidly in the cute category."

"Right." Tank nodded solemnly trying to purge all the cute. "Now if you want a real testimonial, ask my mom."

"I may do that some day, but for now, I want you to answer my original question. Why do you suppose Skye considers you an honorable man?"

"Well. First, because I am a man. I know there's a lot of boy in me. There always will be. But I'm grown and know when to pull out the responsible adult. Honorable? I think I'm decent and good. I keep my word. You can believe me and trust me."

His voice had grown soft and to Payton's ears, seductive. She tried hard to keep a barrier up and intact. It was needed to prevent her from throwing caution to the wind and just going with the flow of her intense feelings. Flashes of Tank in uniform with a bottle of beer to his lips gave her the backbone she needed to continue.

"Tank, this is all happening so fast. I know these are my issues but if you want me to trust you, I have to feel a measure of control. If this develops into a relationship, I'm not going to ask you to give up drinking. But will you respect my opinion if I ever ask you to stop or to slow down?"

He looked at her for a heartbeat. "First of all, I don't want to scare you, but I think what we have is already a relationship. To honestly answer your question, I'll always respond to you on this matter with respect. I'll defer to your opinion but more importantly, I'll defer to your needs. Your need for my sobriety and control are far more important than my need for a cold tall one." Then he just couldn't help it…some cute popped through. He smiled and brought her hand to his lips. "Except maybe when the Bears play Green Bay. Then I might beg you for a special dispensation."

He saw her lips twitch and felt a powerful need to touch her.

"May I kiss the Inspector on the mouth?"

"No, the Inspector has a few more important questions." Tank's fingers trailed up her wrist and felt the throbbing of her pulse. There was stress there. He wanted her in his arms, they ached to hold her, but he'd play this out her way first.

"You said last night you loved me. While this was both tender and appropriate for the circumstances, we were making love after all, I need to know if this is your standard line. Do you say it casually to set the mood or do you save it for really special occasions?"

Tank stared. This was really different. Direct, straightforward, without equivocation. She'd be tough to bullshit. He'd dated police officers before, but never one like this and was really beginning to feel grilled. He smiled. He liked it. He felt himself getting kind of hot. He also decided to give her an honest, candid answer.

"It's not a standard line, darling. I mean, the words come easily to me, very easily. But last night they were just for you. How do I explain this?" He looked at the ceiling, then back at her…right at her. Right into her. His voice was almost hypnotic. "I say 'I love you' all the time. It's in my nature to love. I love pizza. I love strawberry ice cream. I've loved every single woman I've ever slept with and, before I knew what intimacy was, I loved every girl I took to a dance or walked home from school. I love my mother and I love Skye. I loved my sister, Rita. I've loved women. Many women. But until last night I've never said 'I love you,' like I'm saying 'I love you' to you. It's a different feeling. More powerful. It's like…like I could love you the rest of my life. Like the word love isn't big enough…strong enough. That's the difference. Does that make sense?"

She saw the truth in his eyes. She was very, very good at smelling a load of crap when someone was shoveling it her way. Her little internal lie detector pointed to truth.

"May I now hold the Inspector?" Tank asked. He really wanted her to feel as well as see his love.

She shook her head. She knew if he touched more than her hand right now, she'd melt and never get back to this place. "Tank…what do we have here?"

"What do you want it to be?"

"It's not fair to answer a question with a question."

"Why not?"

She just stared at him.

He shrugged and drained the rest of his coffee. "Okay then. How about this. As soon as I can arrange it, I want to follow you to Scotland. Then we can take the time to find out."

He set his cup next to hers. Two cups, two guns, now all they needed was two donuts and the picture would be complete.

Tank looked up at Payton's stunned face. He knew she hadn't expected this turn in the conversation. He grinned at her. She did ask, however, and he saw it as a great opportunity.

"I absolutely refuse to wear a kilt, however…that would be a deal breaker. I can assure you that I love bagpipe music…all cops do. Makes us all weepy and sentimental."

Payton didn't say a word. Couldn't say a word. She just sat staring at him. Was there ever a man like this? Suddenly, tears were forming in the corners of her eyes. Hell, where did they come from? There was no bagpipe music in the room. She felt weepy and semimetal anyway.

"Permission to hold the Inspector," he asked softly. She nodded and sniffed. He turned, opened the drawer in the table by the bed, grabbed a handful of tissue and opened his arms for his leaking Inspector.

She came into the circle of his arms, buried her face in his neck. Tank stroked her hair, her back and when she calmed down, he lifted her chin and kissed her.

"Okay. If you feel that strongly about it, I'll wear a kilt, but you're going to have to beat the ladies off me."

"Oh Tank. What are you thinking?"

"I'm thinking I want more time with you."

She sat up, dabbed at her eyes and sighed. "And how long are you planning on staying in Scotland?"

"As long as it takes."

"As long as it takes for what?"

"For you to live with me, love me, have my babies."

Payton emphatically shook her head.

"Tank. First of all, there's no way I'm going to let you come to Scotland."

He frowned. He hadn't expected this response.

"Why not. It's a free country. Scotland's a free country, right?"

"It is, but if you're only going there to be with me, it'll be a complete waste of your time and money."

"You mean sleeping with me...making love with me...this is just some flirtation? A little out-of-country fling?" He didn't even try to keep the anger out of his voice. "Look, I tried to play this as straight as I could...answer as truthfully as I could. I don't like games and I don't like women who play them."

Sighing, she absorbed his anger. Actually she was bolstered by it. "I understand that. But I want you to remain here. Don't come to Scotland, Tank. I have a few things to tell you."

"No. No more interrogation. I have to get ready for work." He pushed her back and tried to untangle himself from the blanket.

Smiling, she touched his scratchy cheek. "Your duty doesn't start for two hours. You have time."

He gave up on finding the end of the blanket and glared at her. "I may have the time, but right now I don't have the patience. I'm asking you to back off."

"No." She looked at his stormy face. "No I don't think I will."

"I mean it. I'm cranky in the morning, I didn't get enough caffeine, I've been drinking fucking root beer, a real manly drink, by the way, and I'm wrapped like a mummy in this fucking blanket. You're all perky and dressed and I'm skuzzy and naked. To top it off, you're playing flirty girly games with me. Now, move back."

He glared at her. She started to laugh.

"A true Scottish temper...now that completes the package."

"Let me tell you how much that really helps my mood," he said sarcastically. He added flashing eyes to his scowl and she laughed even harder. She dove into him and covered his pouting mouth with hers. When he fought her, not too hard, she just wrapped her arms around his neck and pressed her body to his. He rolled her over on her back and the blanket gave up its hold and fell away. By the time he realized he was free, he was more turned on than mad and she was pulling her t-shirt over her head and wiggling out of her running shorts.

"I need to bring up my heart rate," she said in a breathy voice. "I can either go running or you can make love to me. And since I'm now naked, I don't think a run in the park is the way to go."

She was completely irresistible, not that Tank was inclined to resist at this point. He channeled all his temper into enthusiastic sex and felt alive and invigorated by the time they lay sated in each other's arms on the other side of the bed.

He picked up her t-shirt from the headboard where it had landed. "So where did this come from? I know it isn't one of mine."

"I carry a bag in my car."

"And I imagine you've been up for hours." He sniffed her hair, all fresh and smelling like apples.

"Of course. The best part of the day."

Tank moaned and stretched. "Damn. If I could wake up to this every day, I might just become a morning person."

"Well, I guess that relates to what I have to say." Her hands stroked the broad chest and she felt him stiffen.

"Oh no, you had your fun." His voice, just moments before warm and soft, frosted up a little.

Turning, she looked at him. She put her cop's eyes back on.

"I'm sorry, darling. But, I think I have to insist."

"Okay. We may as well get everything out." He stroked her naked back absentmindedly. She called him darling. Wow. Maybe that meant she'd let him wear her down and change her mind.

"First I'm going to let that flirty, girly comment pass. I think you're entitled to one since you don't yet have all the facts. Second, I want to give you a few of those facts, Officer."

"You aren't going to tell me you have a fiancé and five kids back in Scotland, are you?"

"No," she smiled. "I'm going to tell you that I'm a United States citizen and I've been thinking about moving back here permanently."

A look of pure astonishment came over his face. This was the last thing he thought he'd hear. He'd been thinking about the difficulties of an intercontinental relationship. He couldn't just ask her to give up her position in Scotland and he was fairly sure he wouldn't be able to permanently leave his hometown. This changed everything.

He couldn't think of what to say, so he just stared at her. First he finds out she's a cop, now he finds out she's a U.S. citizen. He couldn't believe his good fortune. It was like fate's blessing.

"I hadn't thought of where I was going to settle," she continued when she saw the normally effusive Tank apparently had no words for this occasion. "It would have to be a large city. Chicago is large. I know I didn't want to go back to Cincinnati where I was raised."

"Wait, wait. I feel like I've just fallen into the rabbit hole," Tank said as he held up his hand. "Are you saying you were born in the United States?"

"Aye, I was. My dad was a Cincinnati cop and my mother was a Scottish immigrant. After dad died, I was 13, we moved to my Mom's hometown in Scotland. I spent a wonderful adolescence there. Healing and growing and going to school. After Mom died last year, I've been thinking about coming back here. Now," she kissed him. "I have increased incentive and, I think, a new hometown."

"Damn. I just can't get my mind around this."

"Well. Since I know you play poker, and so do I, let me put this into a context we both understand. If I settle in Chicago for a time and find you've been bluffing and playing loose with the foreign visitor, there will be no place for you to hide. The Scottish tradition of clan feuding is legendary and has started with less provocation."

His smile was slow and building heat by the second. "Then I'll lay my cards on the table and prove I'm not bluffing. And I'm going to raise the stakes. When you come to Chicago for a time, how about moving in with me?"

"Move in with you? No. I think not. It's too fast, too risky."

"No, it's not."

"Yes, it is."

"No…it's not."

Payton got out of bed and put her hands on her hips. Tank thought she couldn't be more adorable. "Yes…it is."

"Why? You're a cop. Cops are clue chasers. Living together would sure give us a clue as to whether or not we should take it to the next level."

"The next level?"

Tank laughed. He knew he was spinning her fast…keeping her dizzy so she just might break through her issues to her true feelings.

"You know…making it legal."

"You mean a contract, or something?" She looked at him with confusion. It seemed rather cold, but she guessed it would protect his assets.

"No. I mean a marriage or something."

She couldn't have been more shocked if he picked her up and chucked her out the window. The look on her face was enough to make Tank want to laugh out loud, but his smart genes kicked in and he just sat, serenely smiling at her while his proposal sunk in. He hadn't realized until he said it that he'd decided on this course of action during the night, when she lay securely in his arms. He just couldn't have envisioned that she'd make it so easy for him to negotiate her to this point.

Payton couldn't get a word past her throat. It felt completely closed. Was that a proposal? It sounded like a proposal. Was he serious? It sounded like he was serious. Oh God, she thought, sitting back on the edge of the bed. I'm mentally babbling.

"Well?" Tank insisted when she opened her mouth and closed it for the second time. "Don't do that."

"Do what?" He was really enjoying himself. She couldn't have looked less like an Inspector right now. She was flustered, incredulous and absolutely speechless.

"That…looking at me."

"You want me to look at something else?"

"Yes. No. Yes." She was starting to panic. And the more she felt she was losing it, the calmer he seemed to become.

"Okay. I'll look out the window. Now would you like to give me your opinion of m…" Payton clamped a hand over his mouth.

"Stop. Oh God. Please. Let's not deal with the 'm' word until we get used to the 'l' word." She slowly removed her hand. He took a deep breath and opened his mouth. She raised a finger. "I mean it."

He couldn't resist her anymore. He put his arms around her and drew her to him. "Fair enough. One step at a time. First, I'll have you in my bed." He kissed her. "Mission accomplished. Then I'll have you fall in love with me…"

Instead of her hand, this time, Payton planted her lips on his mouth. She had no idea how this happened, but her heart was exploding with love for this wonderful man. She'd take him at his word and trust him. Her eyes were shining when she came up for air.

"Mission accomplished," she whispered and enjoyed the surge of pleasure she saw in his magnificent eyes.

CHAPTER 19

Alex frowned. He worked on complicated legal documents all the time, wheeling and dealing. He should be able to figure this out. He knew his mom stocked the kitchen to please her new daughter and that this package of frozen pancakes was meant to be served to his wife. He took them out of the box. They looked like they were already cooked. Did he put them on the built-in griddle or in the toaster like those little waffles Al and Jason liked? He turned the box over. Ah. Microwave directions. Now that was more like it.

He put the hard, frozen circles of pre-made pancakes on a plate and placed them in the microwave. Selecting a time at random, he thought a couple of minutes should do it.

He got out the breakfast tray, grabbed a white gardenia out of the vase on the table and placed it with the syrup, flatware, napkin and a streaming mug of black coffee. When the microwave bell indicated fresh, hot pancakes up and ready, he put them on the tray and smiled. He was sure to get a nice reward for his effort.

When he entered the bedroom, Skye opened her eyes and blinked. "I smell something breakfast-like." She stretched out her long body and gave him a brilliant smile when she saw the tray. The smile was a great reward, but he wanted syrup kisses to go with it.

"Is this what married life is going to be like?" Skye wiggled and positioned herself into a sitting position against the pillows.

"Of course. Didn't you read the fine print on the contract?"

"Darling, I was far too dazzled by you to see any kind of fine print."

He sat the tray on the bed over her legs and kissed her forehead. It was cool. He smiled. "Well it was there, just under the part about not using my razor."

"Oops. Sorry."

"I thought we had established some of these rules before we made it legal."

"It's just that yours is so nice and sharp."

"It isn't any more."

"Well, that's what you get for hiding it in the back of the drawer. Like a super agent wasn't going to find it there."

"I'll buy you a razor factory, just leave mine alone."

"Yes dear," she said, but Alex heard no apology in her voice. She was placating him. Time to play dirty.

"Although I suppose when you take on a family, you have to learn to share."

"Yes. That's true."

"So next time Kevlar needs to have his teeth brushed it's all right if I use your toothbrush?"

The grossed out face she gave him indicated a direct hit.

"Sure. Go right ahead. And the next time he eats half a gopher that he will causally upchuck and rediscovers the joy of rolling in raccoon shit, I'll let him ride in your truck."

"Sounds fair, and after I give him a bath, I'll dry him off with one of your matching, designer fru fru towels."

Skye burst out laughing. "What the hell is a fru, fru towel."

"You know. The useless little ones that just hang there that match the shower curtain and all the little special soap dishes and tissue dispensers that you women have to have all over the damn bathroom."

"You mean the nicely coordinated, special towels that we don't allow our men folk to wash their ugly trucks with?"

"Yeah, those."

"Okay." She took a sip of coffee and frowned. "Damn. I can't even remember where we started this conversation. I'm not awake yet. Wait for the caffeine to kick in and we can discuss the other provisos in this contract I signed. Under duress, I might add."

"Duress?"

"Yes, I was so blindly, madly in love with you on that day, I'd have signed anything you put in front of me."

Alex smiled, thinking he was blindly, madly in love right now.

"Didn't you make yourself some?" she asked as she poured syrup over the perfectly round pancakes. She put her fork into them and didn't even make a dent. Using her incredible eye for details and her deductive mind, she concluded they were formerly frozen pancakes, converted into little round bricks suitable to be used as ammunition in an artillery barrage by too much time in the microwave. Because her lovely new husband was watching her with such pleasure, she demonstrated her undying love and unconditional devotion by pouring more syrup over them. Maybe if left for a few minutes, the syrup would soak in and soften them up.

"Payton and I already ate."

"She stayed over then." Skye beamed. She could feel her fork making headway into the first pancake and with some relief she managed to cut off a small piece with her knife. She put it in her mouth and tried to muffle the crunch.

"She sure did, and I think love is in the air." Alex was a perceptive and incredibly talented agent. He didn't miss a thing. He was enjoying watching his beautiful and sensitive new wife trying to protect his feelings by chewing the clearly inedible pancake. He must have guessed wrong on the time in the microwave. He was trying to decide how long he was going to let her suffer. Thinking of the razor caper, he thought another few bites.

"She's perfect for Tank. She's smart and tough and courageous…and she's a cop, too. They'll have a lot in common." Sawing another chip off the pancake, she scooped it into her mouth. Alex crossed his arms and grinned at her.

"Maybe if I get your gun, you can blast those pancakes into bite-sized pieces." He went over, took the plate off the tray and set it down on the floor for the eager Kevlar. "Darling, I love you for the brave attempt, but I can't let you risk your dental work by…"

"Don't!" exclaimed Skye with alarm. She snatched the plate off the floor before a disappointed Kevlar had time to snag the treat. "He only has puppy teeth. Those pancakes will hurt."

Alex laughed at her horrified expression. "There really is a part of your mind that's gone, darling. *You* were going to eat them."

"Yes, but that's different." She picked up Kevlar. "I'm your wife. I have duties. Kevlar is just a baby. I have to protect him."

Kevlar wasn't so sure he wanted protection. All he knew was he had a treat, then the one who smelled like the flower bushes took it away. He consoled himself by jumping up on the bed and licking her face. Yum, syrup.

Alex scooped up Kevlar and put him back on the floor, then setting aside the tray, he pulled Skye into his arms. "Well, since I removed your obligation to eat the breakfast, how about performing another of your wifely duties."

She smiled. "Now, which duty would that be?" she asked, stroking his cheek and running her fingers through his hair, still damp from his morning shower.

He kissed her thoroughly, then let her go and turned his back on her. "I was going through my reps this morning and I felt a little kink in my neck. I need you to massage it out."

She giggled and ran kisses all along the back of his neck. "As long as you consider it foreplay, I'd be glad to massage anything out."

Alex looked down. "We have a whole lot of body parts volunteering for that duty."

It was almost an hour later before they were showered, dressed and in the kitchen. Skye tried again with the frozen pancakes and found them to be pretty good.

Tank and Payton came in hand in hand. Skye saw right away that they'd shared more than just a night of sex. She was thrilled. She really liked Payton and couldn't wait to fill in Wyatt. Tank looked handsome and polished in his uniform, as usual, but there was something else. Like he'd settled somehow.

"Good morning," said Skye cheerfully.

"Been comparing arrest records?" asked Alex.

"No, actually…that never came up."

Alex was on the verge of asking him what did come up and did it stay up, but Skye gave him one of those 'don't even think about it' looks and he reigned in the question before it got out of the gate.

"Alex is making frozen panbricks for breakfast. Want some?"

"Ah, Mom's microwave specials. No, I'm running a little late. It takes me more time to get to the cop shop from here. I can grab some donuts there. I'll have another cup of coffee, though."

"Kelvar, sit," said Skye with a small dog biscuit in her hand. "Sit." The puppy just jumped and panted excitedly.

Tank got the dog's attention and brought his index finger down. The dog sat down obediently. Payton smiled at him and he winked.

"If you think I didn't see that and am fooled for a minute that I had anything to do with his behavior, then you must think I'm an idiot," said Skye.

"No, it's the dog that's a little mushy between the ears…not his mistress," laughed Tank.

Alex looked up from the financial page of the New York Times. "My son has a mistress already?"

"He's a Springfield, isn't he?" smirked Tank with a superior air.

"I'm curious," said Payton. "Why the name Kevlar?"

Both brothers looked at each other and rubbed their chests.

"Let's just say Skye was inspired," said Alex.

Payton looked at them. "Both of you?"

"Couldn't let big brother get ahead in points," said Tank easily.

Payton closed her eyes and shook her head. Then she looked at Skye. "This is the most unusual family."

"Tell me about it. And you haven't even met them all." But she would, thought Skye. She saw the look in Tank's eyes whenever he glanced in Payton's direction. She would.

"Alex and I would like to work with you this morning," said Skye to Payton, her eyes sliding subtly toward Tank.

"Hey," he said taking his cup to the sink. "I know when you need privacy. Her relationship with the two of you never came up. Too much of my charm going on. Better decide in your meeting just what the cover story will be." He grinned at the three of them. "I'm only interested in what happens under the covers." He went to Payton and gave her a peck on the lips. "Where are you going to be at lunchtime?"

"She'll be here," said Skye easily. "Mom just called. She and Dad are coming over for lunch. Mom used her cop voice, so I expect she has something to report."

"Great," he smiled down at Payton. "See you then."

"I'll walk you to the door."

"Wow. A morning send-off from the little woman." Tank wiggled his eyebrows at her. Alex rattled his newspaper like subliminal applause.

"Skye," said Payton, in a smooth voice, heavy on the Scottish accent. "Wouldn't you say it would take less time to reach the street if he were chucked off the balcony?"

"I'd say that would definitely save him time," agreed Skye. "Our problem is his size. His body could be squeezed through the balcony door, but I'm not sure about his head."

"Man, you two are cruel in the morning. I think we should definitely keep them separated, Alex," said a grinning Tank.

"Agreed. Which one shall we keep locked up?" asked Alex, eyeing his new wife.

"We'll alternate. Skye will take the even days and Payton will take the odd."

"How dare you call Payton odd," said Skye. "She's a little eccentric, but certainly not odd."

"I'm only eccentric in my choice of men. Talk about odd," snorted Payton.

"How did we lose control of this conversation?" asked Alex, frowning.

"I have no idea but I have to run. I have to go beat the streets." He grabbed Payton's hand and walked toward the doorway. "Oh, and Skye?"

"Yes?"

He took his index finger, got the dog's attention and moved it in a circle. Kevlar rolled over on his back and stuck all four legs straight in the air.

"Oh," said Skye with delight. "He's brilliant."

"The dog or my brother," asked Alex casually as he refolded the paper.

"The dog, of course. Your brother is a moron."

"This is true, but it appears as though he's won the fair Payton."

"And vice versa, I'd say." Skye threw a biscuit to her brilliant dog. "Have you noticed that he grows by the day. Pretty soon, I won't be able to pick him up." She sighed not knowing exactly how she felt about that.

"That'll be a day for tears and tissues," he said as he came over and took her in his arms. Time for his syrup kisses. The best part of living with a pancake addict was the sweet morning lips.

She frowned at him. "It's just that he's so cute."

"God made puppies cute so you don't kill them when they put a fragrant pile on the bathroom rug. By the time he's grown and more handsome than cute, he should be able to exercise more control." He decided to steal his kisses. By his third helping, she'd forgotten everything except the incredible feel of his lips on hers.

When Payton came back in, Alex excused himself. "I'll let the two of you set the strategy for today. I have a building to buy in Hong Kong."

"Was that a euphemism, or does he really have a building to buy in Hong Kong," asked Payton when she and Skye were alone.

Skye laughed. "It sure is a different world living with a billionaire. It makes casual conversation a bit skewed."

"Indeed. You're looking much better, mate" smiled Payton, pleased to see some color back in her new friend's cheeks.

"I am coming back strong," said Skye, then grinned and poured them both another cup of coffee. Time enough to talk strategy. She wanted the scoop. "You and Tank have a good time last night?"

"We did, yes," replied Payton. Then in a time-honored tradition, spilled everything.

"You're a U.S. citizen?" said Skye in astonishment. "Oh. This is perfect. I was a little concerned over the transcontinental issue."

Payton's eyes narrowed; her good nature made her look more amused than annoyed. "So when did you decide we were meant for each other?"

"She was planning a round of wedding showers a few moments after she met you," said Alex from the doorway.

Skye tried for an incredulous look, but it came off more smug than innocent. "And was I right? Huh?"

Alex looked over at Payton, who shrugged and beamed.

"Damn, it's scary."

When Blake and Wyatt arrived at lunchtime, Wyatt was relieved to see the pallor in Skye's face had been replaced with a pattern of lively color. Some of it had been from chasing Kevlar around the apartment, but mostly it was the result of good food, sleep, and her son's, well…influence.

Skye gave them both a big hug. "Excuse me a minute while I go butcher lunch. I hope you like hot dogs."

"Kevlar's been a nasty boy again, I take it," laughed Blake.

"He got the two toned beige and forest green Ferragamos."

"Not the t-strap wedge slides," asked Wyatt horrified. Skye nodded.

"Fry his liver and poach his brain. He's given up his right to live," declared Wyatt with feeling. Kevlar knew that tone and remained hidden under the sofa.

"But, not to a fair trial. Even a dog is entitled to a fair trial and to be judged by a jury of his peers," protested Blake holding up his hand to punctuate his words.

"That beast has no peers."

"There's Tank."

"Someone mention my name?" They all turned as Tank walked in holding the hand of a red haired beauty dressed in a conservative but lovely green silk suit.

Wyatt smiled at what she saw in her son's eyes. The look of love. She'd seen it before. Several times, as a matter of fact, but this time…there was something else.

"Hey, Dad. Making a summation?"

"No, just making a bid for trial by jury on the case of Kevlar vs. Ferragamo."

"Oh. Oh. I thought I taught him to go only for the rubber balls."

"I threw those slimy things away," shuddered Skye.

"See. Mitigating circumstances. Mom, Dad, meet Payton Brady. Skye and Alex brought her back for me from Scotland."

"And all I got was tartan scarf," said Blake. He was closest to Payton and took her hand. "Call me Blake." He could see she was laughing at everything Tank said. He liked that. He liked her.

"That I will and thank you, Blake. Captain Cooper," Payton said as she moved to Wyatt. "I've admired your work for years."

"Wyatt, please." Wyatt took her hand. It was a firm confident grip and she looked into the lovely face and laughing green eyes…eyes with a lot of power behind them. "Cop?"

Payton nodded and something passed between the two women. "Aye. 'Tis *Inspector* Payton Brady."

Wyatt raised her eyebrows, impressed. Approval sparkled in her eyes. Tank just stared at the two of them.

"Hey…I was around her for days and still didn't tumble…well I tumbled, but…I mean."

"You mean you didn't guess that she was a cop?" asked Wyatt helping him out.

"Yeah, that's exactly what I mean."

"Well, sweetheart. That's why I'm a captain, and you're still an officer. I suspect that you were concentrating on Payton, the woman, and the clues got lost in all those little love birds circling your head."

"Please, Mom, not in front of my girl." He casually slung his arm around Payton's shoulders.

Wyatt took another look at Payton. Well, well. On her second appraisal in less than five minutes, her heart filled with delight. Payton wasn't hiding her feelings as she looked up at Tank. If Wyatt was reading the signs correctly, and she was an ace detective before she was a captain, her youngest had found his mate. She couldn't wait to get Blake alone to fill him in.

With much laughter and teasing, they told Wyatt and Blake about Tank's introduction to Payton's occupation. Then Skye filled in Tank with the same information she delivered to the rest of the family. Tank knew there was more…there was always more, but he was satisfied.

Alex stood behind the bar and served drinks. Wyatt noticed Tank nonchalantly taking the root beer Alex offered. More to tell Blake, she thought and her mother's heart lifted even more. It was time Tank grew out of his partying ways. Somehow she always knew it would only take a good woman…and in her mind Payton was just the ticket.

"You're working with Alex and Skye?" asked Blake.

"I am, yes." She didn't elaborate and was fascinated by the switch in subjects. Obviously when someone associated with Skye and Alex gave a cryptic answer, there were no follow up questions. There was that implicit line they didn't cross. What a family, she thought. What a wonderful, caring, insightful family.

A few minutes later, Linda came in with David and there were more introductions. Then it was down to business…and in this family the business was serious law enforcement.

Wyatt pulled a folder out of her briefcase.

"After you filled us in the other night, I went over all the unsolved homicides in the city, the suburbs and the surrounding towns. If your man is in my neighborhood, he may have left some other bodies. Nothing popped. On a hunch, I refined the search and found this." She tapped the folder. "It's a suicide, but a strange one. A Rosalie Fowler was found hanging from a beam in her kitchen. The tox reports show a high level of several recreational drugs. From their levels, I doubt she could have tied a knot, much less maneuvered herself into a noose. There was no note, which is also unusual. And she'd just spent several thousand dollars on clothes from Saks and Nieman-Marcus...hardly the last act of a suicidal person."

"Not until she got the bill," commented Tank.

"She could more than cover it," said Wyatt. "She'd recently made several large cash deposits into her bank account. The reason this attracted my attention is that her neighbors told the investigating team she was a consultant in information technology and computer science."

Everyone sat up straighter.

"Good catch," said Skye.

"I was motivated." There was a steely look of cop in her eye. "I did a more thorough review of all the reports. The team did a nice job of documenting the scene. I think it's interesting that she didn't have a computer or laptop on the premises. She was a sole proprietor and worked from home."

"That is curious," agreed Alex. "Robbery?"

"No. There were extremely valuable pieces of jewelry and some very nice electronics untouched. The theft was a cover-up...not for profit."

"There is definitely something else," smiled Payton. She recognized a build up when she saw it.

Wyatt smiled back and nodded. "Indeed, Inspector. There was no cell phone on the premises either...another curious fact. What self-respecting consultant wouldn't have a cell phone. But I did trace several calls from her land line. There weren't many, but the last one was probably the motive for her murder." She recited a very familiar number.

"The Skyward Corporation World Headquarters," said Linda, impressed.

"And I don't think she was interested in applying for a job," nodded Wyatt. "While that's interesting and probably ties it into your case, here's the piece we go with. There was another number...several calls over the last six weeks. It's the number of a very exclusive modeling agency in Lakewood. I think you can call off the stakeouts and random reconnaissance, Skye. I'd put your team to work on this one. The woman definitely made her living on her brains, not her looks. I don't think she called to inquire about a modeling career."

Skye grinned and nodded. "Thanks for the boost, Mom. It sure pays to be connected. While I spent the day lazing around in bed, you came up with a target."

"I have enough here for a warrant. So when you find the bastard, I'll be able to back you up with paper."

"What's the plan?" asked Tank.

"You and Mom and Dad are going back to work." Skye looked at Payton. "Payton and I are going to see what's shaking in the modeling world. Linda will be on communications. Then we'll all meet back here for dinner and we can report what we find." She looked at Linda, who nodded. She'd be relaying the name of the agency to

Barclay and reporting to Jim. She'd also be putting together a fake dossier and background for Skye's cover.

"What about me?" asked David.

"You're in charge of ordering the food."

"Hot Damn," said Tank. "He knows all my favorites!"

"And me?" smiled Alex.

"I could say, go buy an island or something, but I imagine you'll want to be at my back."

"That'll work," Alex nodded.

Less than an hour later Alex, Skye and Payton sat in front of a large elegant building in the northern suburb of Lakewood. Payton was going to go in and provide backup for Skye and Alex would be monitoring them from the car. Skye tried to convince him to go do his CEO thing and leave the surveillance and contact to her and Payton, but he insisted on being near. He'd have gone in with her, but she won that disagreement by telling him he'd be a bit too obvious sitting in a waiting room filled with young women. Payton was beautiful enough and certainly female enough to be a plausible applicant for a modeling job.

From the patched-in messages Amanda was leaving for Pavel, the man thought Skye was long-gone to Russia. He was told to stand ready…that he would receive his million dollar reward soon. His people wouldn't be on the alert here in Chicago. As far as Skye was concerned, the coast was clear.

Payton went in first and watched the receptionist as Skye strode into the foyer of the agency. She took no offense as the woman fairly fell over herself to get Skye's name and set up an immediate meeting with one of the associates. Payton had been told to wait in the small, pleasant room just off the lobby. At least she wasn't sent on her way like the next dozen women who entered. Watching the face of the receptionist Payton saw no alarm or look of recognition. Skye was on target so far…no one recognized her…no one was even looking for her.

Skye was escorted directly through a large glass door in the rear. Payton could see Skye plainly as she entered a small office, so she sat and got comfortable. Surveillance in here was no hardship. Nothing to eat, of course. Flat stomachs and bony torsos were necessary, but the chairs were soft, the music was soothing and the herbal tea was hot and fresh.

A half hour later, looking excited, Skye emerged from the office and went out the front door. Payton thanked the receptionist and told her she was going out to get a burger and fries. The horrified woman didn't react right away, but found her voice as Payton walked toward the outside door.

"But Ms. Scott, Hannah is anxious to see you. Red heads are making a comeback…"

"It's not natural," shot Payton over her shoulder.

In the car, a pumped up Skye shared her information. "Hot damn. It's his. Pavel is the owner, I know it! Mom is a freaking genius. I swear I could smell him. His ass is ours now. Ms. Boneyard…"

"Boneyard?" asked Payton.

"Actually Barnard, but she weighed about 12 pounds, so she had this kind of picked-over look, anyway..."

Alex smiled. Payton was staring. She hadn't yet seen Skye in full command...in good health. She'd get used to it. His wife was...well...intense.

"Anyway, the freaky Ms. Boneyard invited me to this party on his estate. Private invitation only. They'll check it for sure, high security. It's his exact M.O. I got the impression it was like a cattle call...you know, line them up, pick them out. Set them up; send them out. Lots of drugs, get them hooked, lots of potential for getting lost in the shuffle."

"You going in alone?" asked Payton with concern.

"Not a chance," said Alex before Skye could respond. "I'll..."

"Get back behind the barrier, husband," smiled Skye. "Except for beefcake bodyguards and security people, it's always a women's only party. We don't have time to set you up and honey, you're far too built to put on a dress and pass as a high fashion model...so I'll take an all-female enforcement team."

"What's a few more women at a women's only party?" grinned Payton.

"Exactly. And, to make this whole caper absolutely perfect, the estate has a private airstrip. We can fly in."

"Feel up to it?" asked Payton.

"Oh, yeah. Nearly fully charged." She glanced over at Alex. "I got a transfusion of pure energy this morning."

"Pancakes?" Payton teased.

"Exactly, Inspector." Skye winked and made funny girl-eyes at her new friend.

"You seem very nicely animated. Must be you have a plan." Payton liked the light she saw in Skye's eyes. She'd yet to see her at 100 percent, but could now imagine the force of it.

"I do. The party is tomorrow and I think four snazzy ladies can go and blend nicely. I'll get Linda to alter the invitation and include you, her, and Wyatt. We'll find him, I'll talk to him, you and Wyatt will slap him with some official paper that will effectively box him in, and we'll make arrangements for him to be delivered to...well, to some friends of ours." She wasn't going to say Langley. "Linda will go in for backup. Then we fly back here and have lunch with four handsome hunks. I happen to know Tank's day off is tomorrow."

"Can't I just arrest him?" asked Payton, still wanting her shot.

"Can't I just kill him?" snarled Alex, and the look on his face gave both ladies the impression he was perfectly serious. Skye quickly changed the subject and they continued talking strategy until they were all satisfied. Or nearly so. Alex wanted to come along, of course, but Skye talked him out of it. A part of her wanted him far away from Pavel.

CHAPTER 20

Skye rented a beautiful Bonanza B36TC. In addition to the pilot and front passenger compartment, there was a nicely appointed cabin with four leather seats facing each other in the back. Linda climbed in front. She'd taken a second seat course and could fly the plane and land it in an emergency. She was secretly terrified that she'd someday have to.

Wyatt and Payton climbed into the rear and buckled in. Payton was thrilled. She hadn't flown in a small plane in years and this was a real bonus. They'd all dressed in daytime party attire. Payton had called it a "being a pro-on-the game" look. Lots of neck and breast, lots of leg. In Skye's case, that was really saying something.

Payton knew she had a lovely figure and worked hard to keep it in shape, but it was much more petite. She smiled. Tank seemed to like it just fine, though. Then her eyes slid to his mother and she blushed. She pulled down her skirt, hoping to distract Wyatt's telepathy. This woman had radar and Payton was pretty well convinced she could read minds. Tank was sure of it.

Wyatt smiled back. "You look lovely. Just right for the part. There isn't anyone there who'll question your presence as a top modeling candidate. I, on the other had, am there as an agent to future stars. That will be perfectly obvious." Wyatt had chosen an exquisitely tailored plum colored suit. She opted for no blouse, so the neckline revealed a luscious cleavage. Far too provocative for the station house, but for today, just right.

"Would you be thinking I was sucking up if I told you I see absolutely no visible flaw in your appearance either?"

Wyatt laughed with delight. She was already in love with this young woman and today was a day to seal the relationship. Smoothing her skirt, she winked at the woman who'd captured Tank's fancy. Skye had filled her in on all the details.

"We go in, find Pavel if he is in residence, make the deal, then fly out. Fast, easy and back with the men for lunch," said Skye from the front seat.

"Well, we're sure dressed for it," said Linda.

"In New York maybe, but I'd say we'll create a headline in Shy Town," smiled Wyatt.

They took off smoothly and before they could relax, Skye was already announcing their descent. They looked down and saw the huge estate. The landing strip was right beside it along with what looked like a nine hole golf course and a private lake.

"Who said crime doesn't pay?" mumbled Skye, banking in for her final approach. She was as careful and methodical with her little plane as she was with a Boeing 767 carrying 250 passengers.

"We are. And today we deliver the message," said Wyatt. "Look out, Pavel, the lady posse is in town."

The plane made a smooth landing and Skye lined it up with the small hangar at one end. There were several other aircraft including a personal jet. Golf carts were near the building with drivers standing by.

"Pretty beefy looking staff," commented Linda.

"Armed, too. Concealed. Pretty much confirms the presence of illegal activity," said Wyatt.

"If not Pavel, then certainly something requiring your attention," nodded Payton.

"And my daughter-in-law holds a gilded invitation...how convenient," smiled Wyatt, a gleam of conquest shooting out of her steady green glare.

Skye smiled. Her team wasn't impressed at all that the armed bodyguards might pose a barrier. All it represented was confirmation of a bad guy in residence. Lady Posse indeed. It was a great feeling.

"Let's go confirm or disallow our target's presence," said Linda. "The extraction team is standing by if the man takes the deal."

"If not, he's all yours, Wyatt," said Skye. "You and Blake should have a winter filled with a flurry of indictments."

"Sounds like my kind of weather forecast," said Wyatt.

Two men advanced on them and checked the invitation carefully.

"Where's your pilot?" one asked looking over at the small plane.

"I flew it in myself," replied Skye, annoyed at the man's skeptical look. "What. You think you have to have a penis to operate an aircraft?"

The other man took another long look at the invitation then up at Skye. The woman was definitely the boss's favorite recruit, but she wasn't one of his usual brainless bimbos.

"You know your boss likes to mix it up sometimes," said Skye, accurately reading the man's body language. "When he found out I had my license, he got a little extra charge out of it. Talked about getting high, then going higher...and seeing the advantage of working with a model who knew how to...shall we say, work a throttle?"

The man nodded, satisfied. "You were told no cell phones or other electronic devices?"

"We were."

"Gotta scan you."

"Fine."

The man ran a device carelessly over each of them. He longed for the old days when he used to be able to pat down all the guests.

Skye wondered what the man would think of the guns each of them had strategically placed on their person. If there were metal detectors near Pavel's headquarters, they would have to remove them. The wand the man had in his hand was just for electronics, however, and they went in fully armed. What a putz. Conscientious and careless to a fault. It showed both his paranoia and his arrogance.

They were taken directly into a large indoor pool and patio area, where dozens of beauties were lounging in various stages of undress. Groups of women stood around gossiping…glamorous, gorgeous, gullible. A few looked at the newcomers and measured the competition, but mostly they showed little interest. Drugs were everywhere and were being liberally shared. The food table filled with gourmet selections was largely ignored while the bar did a booming business. The game was obvious. The trap Pavel used to assure cooperation. Get them hooked, then control their will. Well, Skye and her righteous team of female enforcers were there to close him down.

Wyatt put on large sunglasses, having to suppress her natural inclination to start cuffing the pushers who were replenishing the small bowls of cocaine and pills. She didn't want to be recognized, but she needn't have worried. She was so out of context that no one gave her a second glance.

They merged quickly into the assembled human buffet and began to mix and mingle. Apparently, the armed and vigilant guards weren't programmed to watch for female infiltration. Their shaded faces moved over them and passed right on by.

Skye had a nose for determining the center of the action. She saw a steady stream of women coming in and out of a room at the south end of the long stone terrace. She figured she'd find her quarry in there holding court. That was his style.

Walking slowly, sharing whispered observations, pretending to participate in the party chatter, the posse followed Skye's lead.

"I'll go and ask for an audience."

"Agreed," nodded Wyatt, bringing her wine to her lips when one of the guards looked in their direction.

"It seems informal," said Payton, her cop's eyes watching as three stunning women came out of the room Skye indicated and were directed to a stretch limousine pulling up in front of the mansion. They didn't look too steady and were assisted into the back seat by two very serious looking men in dark suits. "I think we should call in the tag on that vehicle. I don't like the feel of it."

"EEB2811," said Linda. "Already noted and I know just who to contact as soon as we return."

"The room should be empty…no one's gone in since those ladies left. Shall we have a go?" asked Payton.

"Showtime," said Skye, rolling her thin shoulders with both anticipation and a profound sense of justice.

"Okay, headliner. Your supporting cast will back you up," breathed Linda.

"Remember...the man is dangerous. A first class schmuck and an egomaniacal marionette, but unpredictable and soon to be desperate. It also looks like he has considerable muscle."

"I counted an even dozen," confirmed Linda.

"Noted...now does anyone wish to use the ladies room before we go bust some balls?" asked Wyatt in such a gentile voice, they all laughed.

They created quite a picture of beauty and poise as they approached the men standing on either side of the French doors leading into the room. Skye and her entourage blended perfectly with the theme of the place and when she asked for entry, the doors were opened to her. A wand was passed over them to detect any electric or listening devices, but they weren't patted down and each of them was armed to the teeth. So much for high level security...good for them...justice delivered to the bad guys.

A man was on the phone, pacing in front of a huge fireplace. His suit was impeccably tailored, his shoes were new and well polished, his Rolex watch gleamed on his wrist, and the air about him was filled with self importance. He glanced over at them and waved his free hand.

"Changing room over there...clothes off. I need to see your tits and asses. Blow is on the bar...you will party for me and if I like what I see, you may get the ride."

When they didn't move, he ended his call and turned on them with annoyance.

"What?" he thundered, throwing up his hands. "You waste my time?"

Skye stepped forward, her gaze direct and lethal.

"Hello Pavel." The man was the same basic body shape she remembered, but his hair was lighter and his face had been significantly altered.

Pavel focused on her as she came further into the room, the shock on his face was almost comical. His stuttering response certainly was.

"What?...who?...where?...where?"

She looked into his eyes. They were the same. It was all the identification she needed. Even a skilled plastic surgeon couldn't change the eyes.

"Identification confirmed," she said calmly. "Remember me, you pathetic putz?"

"You! You! You!" Pavel's breath came out in gasps, his voice getting increasingly hysterical.

"Right the first time, asshole."

"You were taken to Russia! Lin Tu Meng took what was left of you after they got what they needed. I'm going to collect the million dollar bounty and...and..."

Both Payton and Wyatt listened to the exchange and knew there would probably be no further explanation. A bounty? A million dollars? What was left of her? They heard what they heard though and watched as Skye transformed into a seriously scary agent. Linda knew everything. She shook off the dread of what could have been and took her position as back up.

"Bianca is dead, so is your team of fuck-ups," said Skye when Pavel stopped to take a breath.

"No. Bianca's not dead...you're dead," Pavel shrieked. He was so shocked and disconnected that he didn't even realize what he was saying.

"Then think of me as an avenging angel," scoffed Skye menacingly.

"Well then, fine! If you're not dead, then you can just explain yourself to my head of security!"

He flipped open his phone, but Skye lashed out and slapped it away before he could make a call. It flew against the stone fireplace and shattered.

"The head of your security is about as effective as that phone right now."

"What do you think you're doing? That's a custom made Nokia Vertu, you bitch." For a moment he was more affronted by the destruction of his property than the implication of seeing Skye alive and in his library. "I demand to know why you aren't in China!"

"Must have missed my connections." Skye shrugged, enjoying Pavel's disintegration.

"Yes? Well, that's not what my people tell me," insisted Pavel. "I've just confirmed my reservations to Miami. The million dollars I get for delivering you will be the down payment for my South Beach condominium."

Linda, Payton and Wyatt looked at each other. Was this man for real?

"Pavel...I want this to sink in...your colleagues are all dead."

"Dead? That's ridiculous. I just received their last communication. They're in Paris and returning with my money tonight."

The spliced responses on the answering machine in Scotland appeared to have completely fooled him. Way to go Amanda. Chalk one up for the other female member of her posse.

"I assure you they're all dead." She shot several colored pictures onto this desk...pictures of his team as she last saw them. Dead and bloody. "And you soon will be."

Pavel looked at the pictures and gave a little scream as he jumped back.

"This isn't real...you staged this. You're the goddess of cons. I know all about you. I just heard from Bianca this morning."

"We know about the message relay. The voices you heard on the tapes have been spliced and dubbed. Bianca is in the morgue, Pavel. They all are. I was there when Sung Du killed them, but not before they provided him with information on where you are. Your family never intended to take you back Pavel. They used you to get me and now they want you dead. You've been placed on Sung's hit list. You should never have come back to life. Ekaterina Rustam has been told she must find you and execute you...and you know her reputation. She always gets her target."

Pavel went white. "Then...then why are you here?"

"The feds got me out. They sent me to convince you to take their offer. They knew you would need visual confirmation of my escape and your complete and utter failure.

I'm going into their witness protection program and they're willing to take you in as well."

"Don't be insulting. They send people to obscure places. Worse than this." His hands flew around the room. "I intend to be back in Miami by this time next week. I'll wait to hear from Sung Du."

"Oh you'll hear from him, all right. Just before he sends you to hell."

"He owes me a million dollars. I sent you to him. If he lost you, that's his problem." Pavel was pacing now, running his hands through his hair and trying to think. "I have a plan and it doesn't include talking to people from the United States government. What have they ever done for me?"

Skye was amazed at the depth of this man's delusion. Amanda better get his brain drained fast because he was self-destructing. For now, she had other cards to play.

"I think you'll find the offer of protection is the best you'll get under the circumstances."

"What circumstances?"

"If you don't want to work with the federal government, you may bunk in a local scum warehouse, or travel to Scotland and be the guest of the government there."

"You must be mad...what are you talking about?" Pavel looked toward the doors, but wasn't yet ready to muss his suit by pushing through the Amazon woman.

Skye raised her voice. "Ladies, would you like to present your alternatives?"

His eyes went wild when he recognized Captain Wyatt Cooper. She took off her sunglasses and stepped forward along with two other women. The small Asian woman locked the doors and pulled the drapes. He didn't like that at all. He had an open door policy with his staff. He was about to tell her so when the famous Chicago Police Captain took something out of her gorgeous purse. He recognized the lovely lines of an original Toni Baradani creation. She had taste. And she also had...

"I have here a warrant for your arrest."

"On what charge." He decided he wasn't going to compliment her on her bag after all.

"I wish it could be invasion of my privacy, but we'll keep it to conspiracy to commit murder. Give me five minutes and there will be numerous drug charges to make the package more interesting. Does the name Rosalie Fowler mean anything to you?"

"Don't be silly. The foolish woman had an accident...or did she commit suicide. Doesn't matter...leave your paper with the man outside."

"Your man outside will also be brought in for questioning, as will your entire staff." Wyatt stared at Pavel until she got the measure of his guilt. She really would have preferred to take him down herself, but she promised her daughter-in-law she could have him. Damn.

Payton came forward. "And I have here an order to begin extradition proceedings to take you to Scotland to answer questions related to the murder of Emily Johansson."

"Don't be ridiculous. I don't know anyone by that name." The name really didn't mean anything to him. He'd picked her picture out of a stack of possibles and left the details to his contact in Miami.

"And what are you here for," Pavel demanded as he looked at Linda. "A citation for letting my dog shit in a public park."

"No. I'm here as backup." Linda smiled at him sweetly.

Pavel looked at her and snorted. "You look more like fucking Miss May."

Before he could blink, Linda had him up against the wall, her elbow in his throat. "You want to rephrase that?" She twisted his arm, turned him and forced him into a chair.

"This is my home, you'll give me respect," whined Pavel petulantly, rubbing his arm.

"What I'll give you, is one chance to live," said Skye.

Skye laid out the proposition. Pavel saw his visions of South Beach, brunch and beautiful people fade, then pop out of existence.

"Run, and you'll be hunted by Sung Du, Ekaterina Rustam, the United States government, the state of Illinois and Scotland Yard. One will surely get you. Some will have orders to kill."

"They wouldn't…"

"I'd volunteer for that duty myself, you fucking bastard." It was all she could do to keep from drawing her gun and doing it there and he saw that temptation in her eyes. "Here's the number. Call it and someone will be here within the hour to take you in. Don't call it and the next time we meet, you won't see me coming." Skye's tone was steely, cold and perfectly believable. "It's just that simple. Call that number, Pavel…it's your only chance. It may not be caviar, but it beats certain death and dismemberment. Come on ladies, let's leave him to think it over…provided he still has the capacity for rational thought."

She gave him one last long stare, then turned and left the room. They could hear Pavel howling and ranting as they walked through the French doors back into the sunlight.

"I'd leave him alone for awhile," said Skye to the curious men standing on the terrace. "He couldn't get it up and he's having a personal crisis."

The man looked at the four beauties and nodded solemnly.

"You're one scary lady," said Wyatt as they walked back through the estate. And she meant it. "Ever thought of using that tone on Kevlar?"

Skye laughed off the tension she felt in her spine. "He'd know I was bluffing."

"But you weren't back there, were you?"

"No," said Skye with feeling. Wyatt nodded. Her daughter-in-law was a very complex woman and she just saw another facet. One she thought she admired very much. It touched her sense of justice even though it froze her mother's heart.

They commandeered a golf cart and got to the plane in less than five minutes. "Pile on in, ladies. I do believe this case is closed."

Laughing, they all got into the Beechcraft. Skye completed her preflight check, then fired up the engines and rolled to the end of the runway.

"All ready?" she asked and hearing affirmative calls, she pushed the throttle to full power. The plane left the ground, smoothly and gracefully. Skye felt more than the plane lifting. She felt her heart lift as well. Alex would be waiting for her. Her husband. They had a lot of debriefing on this case, but maybe they could carve out a few days to spend celebrating their marriage. She smiled thinking about the possibilities. Maybe Banff in the Canadian Rockies. Maybe Paris. She sighed. Maybe home.

Suddenly, all thoughts of a few days with her new husband evaporated. Her senses were sparking. What was it? Something down there, something on the road leading to the complex? That was it. Earlier, she'd seen carts roaming the grounds. Security, she thought. Now there was absolutely no movement.

"Something isn't right," she said and immediately everyone on board was on high alert. "Look around, do you see any of the security we saw when we flew in here?"

Wyatt looked out the side window. "It's too quiet, too still," she said.

"Do you suppose Ekaterina found him already?" asked Linda.

Skye looked over at her. They thought they would be way ahead of the Russians.

"Someone in Pavel's organization may have ratted him out. The ship was sinking, jump now and avoid the rush," Skye speculated.

"Damn, what's that?" asked Payton. A long black car was slowly approaching the main building. It stopped and three men got out. They began to move stealthily toward the house. "Bloody hell, three men. Armed with automatic rifles."

"Goddamn it. Now I have to save the prick? This just sucks." Skye turned the plane toward the airstrip, then calculating, shook her head. "We haven't got time to land and pick him up. Payton, if I fly by, can you take them out?"

Linda and Wyatt stared at Skye as if she'd lost her mind. But Payton took out her Glock. "May I have yours as well, Skye. I might need a few more rounds than I have in mine." Skye reached down and handed hers back.

"But Payton," Wyatt said in a stunned voice. "All you have is a handgun and we're moving. And they're moving."

"I'm assuming you can fly this craft straight and true," said Payton.

"You shoot straight and true and I'll stay steady."

"Right then." Payton opened the small side window. "I'd suggest you get behind the leather seats, Wyatt. It'll give you more protection."

Wyatt stayed right where she was. She appreciated the young woman's concern, but she was going to give them another pair of eyes.

Skye circled. The men below were very intent on their target and had yet to look up. Skye lined up her flight path, reduced her speed as much as she dared and brought it in low and slow.

As it turned out, Payton had no need for Skye's gun. With swift efficiency and deadly accuracy, she took out the three armed men. Wyatt and Linda watched in awe, thrilled with the unparalleled display of marksmanship as Payton lined up her shots, fired and hit her targets dead on. Whether or not she killed them was immaterial. Two men ran from the house when they heard the gunshots and would finish the job.

"Holy mother of God," said Linda. "That was incredible. Way to go Payton. I don't think even Alex could have done that and he's the best marksman I know."

"I've never seen anything like it," said Wyatt in a low appreciative voice. She didn't miss Linda's reference to her son. It reminded her that he was more than a real estate investor just as it seemed Linda was more than a just a bridesmaid. "I've been on the force for nearly 30 years and I've never…"

They heard a crack of automatic machine gun fire and a simultaneous pinging sound as bullets hit the fuselage.

"Where did that come from, did you see? I swear if it's Pavel's men I'm going to turn him over myself."

"Over there," called out Linda, pointing to a lone cart in the rear of the house. "And I doubt it's one of Pavel's men. It looks like two bodies next to the trees. He must have been the backup."

"Think you can get him, Payton?"

She smiled wickedly and nodded. "Bring me in again, Skye, but this time I think you should maintain speed. We've attracted too much attention. We don't want to become a target ourselves."

"You're the shooter," said Skye, banking, coming around, then increasing speed. "Linda, Wyatt, keep down. Payton, get ready."

"I see only one," said Payton, slapping a fresh magazine into her gun.

"No two," said Wyatt. "One by the tree."

"Affirmative," said Skye. "And they see us. This isn't going to be a free ride."

"Now I know how a duck feels during hunting season."

"Here we go."

Skye flew low, but this time she came at full speed. The man near the cart completely dismissed any danger from the plane baring down at him. He stood in the open and that was his mistake. He started shooting wildly and Skye could hear the pinging of bullets. Payton, on the other hand, got him in one shot. She took aim at the other man. As Skye swooped over the tree line, she saw the shooter go down. Whooping, she waggled her wings in triumph.

"You did it," she called back to Payton, grinning. "You…" Suddenly the congratulatory words caught in her throat. "Oh my God. Oh no. Oh shit."

CHAPTER 21

"There it is. I can see it coming through the clouds." Blake, Tank, and David joined Alex on the tarmac. They were supposed to be meeting their women at the restaurant, but to the man, they were anxious to see them sooner rather than later.

Just as they saw the flash of the fuselage in the reflective sunlight, an ambulance pulled onto the road leading to the general aviation terminal, its siren wailing, its lights flashing. It was coming hard and fast.

They all stared at it for a minute. Alex grabbed his cell phone, then realized the women hadn't taken any of theirs in with them.

"Let me go find out," said Alex. But when he started for the doors of the terminal, he felt them all right behind him. He went over to the young man standing by the window with binoculars. There was no control tower in this general aviation building. Only radios and visual confirmation.

"Excuse me," said Alex. The young man jumped and turned.

"Can I help you?"

Alex nodded at the ambulance that had now turned onto the short road leading to the left runway. "Did the Beechcraft coming in order that?"

"Yes sir. The lady asked that there be an ambulance ready to transport a passenger directly to the hospital."

"Nature of the injuries?"

"She didn't say."

"Can I call her on the radio?"

"I wouldn't recommend it, sir. She's on her final approach and you don't want to distract her. She said there may be something wrong with her left aileron and asked for the right runway."

All four men felt the cold wave of dread and all four men shook it off. It was a nightmare, but they would know soon enough. The young man watched as they turned as one and ran out of the building.

The plane came down and made a perfect landing. That would seem to indicate that Skye was in control. But they all knew Linda could land it in an emergency. The presence of the ambulance indicated an emergency. When the plane taxied toward them, they saw the bullet holes. None of them spoke.

It seemed to take forever for the engines to shut down and the propellers to stop spinning.

Skye was the first to jump out the door. She turned as Alex shouted her name and indicated that he should hurry. The paramedics were already running around toward the two doors located on the side of the craft. Skye opened them as Wyatt jumped out onto the black top. Her suit was covered with blood. Blake's own blood ran cold, but she was moving well and didn't seem injured. Then they all came to the same realization at once. It wasn't her blood. She directed the paramedics inside and turned as Linda climbed out of the passenger side door of the cockpit. Tank immediately knew what that meant. Unless they'd taken on another passenger, it was Payton. His heart stopped and he found it difficult to catch his breath.

He reached the plane just as the paramedics were gently taking Payton's inert body out of the plane. She was bleeding from a head wound and was unconscious. Tank had never been so afraid in all his life. He couldn't stop the uncontrollable beating of his heart and he definitely felt light headed. He didn't register his father's hand squeezing his shoulder.

"Take a deep breath, son." It was the first time that Tank realized he was holding it. "Let's find out how serious it is before you lose your cool here."

The paramedics laid Payton gently on a gurney. Skye was right next to them telling them all she knew. The men were able to hear most of what she was saying.

"Gunshot wound. She's been unconscious for about 5 minutes. We couldn't keep her awake." Skye's eyes were tearing and she could hardly speak past the lump in her throat. Payton was so pale.

Skye looked up with stricken eyes toward Tank as he came up beside her. "God. I'm sorry."

Tank took Payton's inert hand in his as they walked swiftly toward the ambulance. He let go so they could load her in, feeling like he was out of his body, everything focused on her. The medical team tried to block him from getting in the back with her, but one look at his face had them changing their minds and waving him in.

"Linda, Wyatt, stay with Payton." Skye motioned to Alex. "I have to go back in," said Skye in a low urgent voice. "Payton put bullets in all the men we saw, but there could be more. I had to get Payton back here…we couldn't take the time to land and extract Pavel."

"Why not just let them kill the bastard."

"We can't. What if they were sent to interrogate not assassinate."

Alex looked at her grimly. "Hell. He knows now you're alive."

"Exactly. He has no idea how important that information is."

"That would expose our man in China."

"Undo all that we went through to set him up." Suddenly Skye swayed and went pale as paper.

"Skye!"

Gabbing for Alex, she whispered, "Give me a minute here."

"What is it?"

"I think the adrenalin cocktail went to my head." She looked up at Alex's face, glad everyone else surrounded Payton. His features were going in and out of focus and she could feel herself floating away from consciousness.

"I'll call Jim…he'll have to do the extraction from the ground." Frowning, Alex slipped an arm around his trembling wife and reached for his phone.

"No," rasped Skye, blowing out another long breath, trying desperately to get more oxygen in her system and mitigate the feeling of weakness in her legs. She knew it wasn't a simple reaction to the shooting. It was her internal system shoving back at her. Giving her a warning. Alex knew it too. He started punching numbers, but Skye put her hand over his. "We don't have time. Help me into the cockpit. By the time I get to the site, I'll have my legs back. I'll go in, get Pavel and return in less than an hour. He shouldn't be a problem."

She found a reserve of backbone and stood up straighter, shrugging off his protective arm.

Alex stared at her, weighing the risks.

"Once I'm in the air, the automatic flight adrenalin will give me another shot. I'll be fine. We don't have time to debate this, Alex."

Alex had seen this happen before. Even on the edge of exhaustion and collapse, she transformed when there was a plane to fly. He figured he could leave her in the cockpit and go get Pavel himself once they got to the site. The idea had appeal. No one said Pavel had to be conscious. He rather hoped the man gave him considerable trouble.

"Okay, let's go."

"No, you go follow Payton," insisted Skye, putting the palm of her hand on his chest. "Call Jim and coordinate the ground operation. I want to do this solo."

"The hell you will."

"Darling, I don't have the time or energy to check out the aircraft. There may be something functionally wrong with it. I need to fly over the lake to cut off time."

"I have confidence in the pilot. Let's go."

"Alex, listen to me. If I have to ditch…well, they have a perfect record for getting people out of Lake Michigan."

"Well then."

"A perfect zero."

Alex looked her in the eye and smiled sardonically. "You die, I die."

"Shit." Skye stared at him for a second seeing the snap in his blue eyes. Turning toward the door, she started to climb in.

Alex helped Skye into the cockpit then ran around to the other side and climbed in himself. "Kind of bites, doesn't it?"

"To say the least." Relief flooded in when she felt the shot of energy flow into her reserves. Her hand no longer trembled when she started the engine. She saw Alex glance back at Payton's blood all over the back cabin. She had to block that out for now. The family was with her and they would report as soon as they could. She took three long deep breaths and shook her head. "Ready?"

"If you are, darling. We can still do this slower and drive in."

"No. It's just a feeling, but I think time is critical. All that pain…it can't be for nothing." Skye swallowed hard and glanced over at Alex's grim expression. "We have to get him out."

"Or silence him." Alex strapped in and nodded. Skye worked the radio, then lined up the plane and pushed the throttle to full.

Wyatt watched the plane leave the ground with her son and daughter-in-law on board, flying into danger once again. She glanced back toward the ambulance where her other son and his new young woman were speeding toward the medical center and felt her husband's arm go around her.

"It's times like this that I wish our family had gone into the grocery business," she said through the lump in her throat. She was worried about Payton and also her son. What would happen to him if she didn't make it?

Turning, she went to join her other child through marriage. She'd seen the look on David's face when the plane landed. He was back reliving the night Rita died. The haunted look was just beginning to fade from his face, but not from his eyes. He had his arm around Linda as she was filling him in. Together they went to the car to follow the ambulance.

Inside the ambulance, Tank produced his badge and told them Payton was also a police officer. The paramedics were intrigued, but were too busy to respond. They were assessing the wound and stabilizing her vital signs. They started an IV and began cross matching her blood.

"Looks like she has massive blood loss. Could have nicked the vertebral artery." They continued to talk in medical language. Tank didn't want to distract them with questions, but the sound of the machines and the paramedics' voices scared him. None of it sounded good. He looked down at her pale face, now covered with an oxygen mask. He wanted to hold her. They were trying to stop the flow, but some of her precious blood poured off the gurney and onto the floor.

"Excuse me, sir," said one of the paramedics. He hadn't realized they were talking with him. "Could you help us with any of her history? Her birth date? Is she allergic to anything? Does she take any medications?"

"No, I'm sorry. I really don't know that much about her yet." That hurt his heart. Please, oh please, he thought. Let her come out of this so I can find out all the answers to those questions. He watched her face. It looked like some of the color was coming back. They arrived at the hospital and the doors flew open.

"We heard there was an officer down," said one of the attendants. "Let's get her in here stat." The minute they hit the doors, doctors and nurses surrounded her.

Tank paced inside the small emergency room as specialists examined her. He refused to leave, and everyone was too busy to push the issue.

"We need a neurosurgeon in here now!" called the attending physician.

"Blood pressure dropping." The medical team was having problems stemming the flow of blood from the wound. They brought in EKG and EEG machines. Possible brain damage screamed through Tank's consciousness.

He felt his mom and dad's presence beside him. They stood listening to the action, smelling the antiseptic and the sweet odor of fresh blood. Tank knew he was on the edge of terror, but couldn't find the energy to pull back.

"Do you want to come out and sit down, son?" asked Blake softly.

Tank shook his head. He absolutely couldn't get any sound through his swollen throat. He just stood and stared at Payton. She never moved. The steady beeping of the monitor was a comfort, however. Her heart was steady and true.

It was nearly a half hour before the neurosurgeon came bustling in.

"I was in surgery. Let's take a look." She glanced over at the Springfield guard but she was all business and went straight to her patient.

As the rest of the team stepped back, she did a thorough exam. She looked closely into each eye, then felt the wound. The results of all the test were presented, studied, and discussed. She leaned over again and did a little sewing. Just when Tank was about to climb out of his skin, she straightened and snapped off her gloves.

"Are you the next of kin?" she asked Tank.

"Yes," he said softly. He didn't want to delay getting the information with formalities and his parents didn't contradict him.

"I'd say this young woman dodged a bullet, but she obviously didn't. We use that term when we want to impress upon the patient and her family how lucky she is. Let's just say she dodged disaster by the placement and depth of the wound. She'll have one hell of a headache and she'll need to take it easy for quite awhile, but I see no need for surgery. She isn't bleeding into the brain and there's no tissue damage to repair. A major artery to the brain was nipped, but we got that closed up real tight and it doesn't appear as though there's any brain damage. The paramedics did a heroic job. I believe enough oxygen still got to the major centers of the brain. The blood loss is of concern, but we're pumping that back in as fast as we can." She rolled her shoulders. "No guarantees. We'll know more when she wakes up and we can access her memory and motor functions. I'm not needed here. Dr. Janice Sprecker is our chief of staff and will be taking the case."

Tank still didn't hear the exact words his heart needed to hear. He was so scared he couldn't even verbalize the question, so he was grateful when he heard it from his mother.

"Dr. Terruchetti, are you saying she'll be all right? She'll make a full recovery?"

"Hello, Captain Cooper. She one of yours? Be sure to stop at admissions. All that tedious paperwork for a gunshot wound. Takes longer to complete than the recovery time." She took a pen out of her pocket and scribbled in the chart. Tank felt like grabbing the pen and creating an all new emergency. "Well, you heard me. That's precisely what I'm saying. She's a very lucky woman. A few centimeters to the left and I mean centimeters, she'd have been an organ donor. No hope." The doctor never won any awards for her bedside manner. She tossed the chart onto a table and bustled out of the room.

"Oh God," said Tank, swaying, pulling his fingers, still stained with her blood, through his hair. "Oh God." He went over to Payton and with the nod of the smiling nurse, he took her hand. Blake wisely placed a metal stool next to him and made him sit. No one wanted the Tank to topple. For sure, there was no one on the premises big enough to catch him.

CHAPTER 22

Skye filled Alex in as they flew back to the estate. He was on the phone with Jim and the extraction team from Special Operations was being dispatched to the scene. They were about 40 minutes out. Alex and Skye were less than ten.

"Now we're in the position of having to save his ass. Damn, that isn't even in the same universe as fair," frowned Skye. "And quit watching me like that."

"I'll quit watching you when you get more color in your cheeks than Aunt Gertie's pearls. Are you doing all right?"

"Yes. Not great, but good enough. I'll give you a two-minute warning if I'm going to put us nose first into the ground."

"Appreciated. So, what do we do if he doesn't take the deal?"

"He'll take it. He knows if he doesn't, he's a dead man."

"My privilege."

Skye looked at him and knew what he was saying.

"He's a coward, Alex. He'll take the deal. He'd prefer to live well, but in the end he'll prefer to live period. But if he doesn't, I get him. The man kidnapped me, ruined my honeymoon, was responsible for my near electrocution…"

"I thought for a moment you were dead," said Alex softly, his eyes blazing with suppressed rage and something else Skye had never seen before…something close to profound sorrow. It penetrated her own soul.

Skye looked at him, looked into his eyes and nodded. "Your privilege."

She turned her attention back to her instruments and the feel of the craft. She was an intuitive flyer, always had been. She'd been in the air her whole life, first as her father's passenger, then his student, and finally as a licensed pilot. The feel of the craft under her capable hands was as vital as what the instruments told her. As she took the most direct route over the lake, she could feel the pull on her left aileron. Damn. She looked down at the cold, deep water. Closing her eyes for a moment, she assessed the feel of her craft…let it move through her fingers. She was almost sure the sluggishness was from a small dent in the skin of the craft and not from anything internal. Still, she was relieved when they were over land again.

They circled the large house and saw three more bodies in front. Otherwise the place appeared deserted. Apparently all the guests found somewhere else to go for the rest of the day.

"We may be too late," said Alex checking to be sure he had a full clip in his Glock. "Looks like the Russians want their man badly. They must have sent their hit teams in waves. Got any spare clips?"

"In the flight bag." They'd decided when they formed their partnership to carry identical Glocks. Interchangeable clips, a nice touch for partners. Reaching over, he placed two spare clips precisely where she preferred them, in her left pocket. He took several himself. "Christ," he said. "What were you expecting, a military action?"

"Be prepared."

"Actually, it looks a little like a battlefield down there."

"Payton took out five of them." She glanced over at him grimly. "Did she look like she was going to be all right, Alex?" It was the fourth time she'd asked the same question.

"Yes. Really. But don't think about that right now. Let's get out of here with our package, then worry about Payton. She's in good hands. I'm sure that everything that can be done is being done. Mom knows every damn emergency doctor in the city."

"Okay. Okay. Clear the mind. We could be landing in the middle of a very dangerous situation. Maybe we should wait for backup."

"Your call. How do you feel?" asked Alex, but when he saw another van speeding up the long driveway, he knew the decision was made for them. It wasn't one of theirs.

"We're going in," she said and heard her husband chamber a round in both their guns.

The airstrip was on the opposite end of the property so they could land in relative safety. Skye put the plane down quickly and effortlessly. As soon as she shut off the engine, they jumped out and ran toward the house. It was silent and still. Pavel's body guards must have placed themselves at the front of the estate.

Skye led the way since she knew exactly where she wanted to go. She could hear gunshots, but knew Pavel wouldn't be engaged. He'd be huddled in some corner while his paid staff was out defending him. Bastard. At least it made it easier for her and Alex. If they assumed all assault came from the front, they would find Pavel in the back. They did.

Pavel was emptying a large safe, panic in every jerky motion. Skye smiled in satisfaction as she looked at what he was pulling out. A bonus for them. Good stuff was usually in a safe. Data, places, names. Great. She felt like pouring through some really good stuff. But that was for later. Frosting on the cake.

"Are you going to take the deal?" she asked in a soft low voice. For the second time that day, Pavel spun around and started sputtering.

"What? What the hell are you doing here?"

"I'm here to save your sorry ass…or not. Time's up. Tell me you want to go in, and my friend and I will get you safely out of here. Refuse and we'll tie you to that chair and draw a bull's-eye on your forehead."

Alex stepped beside her, looking fierce enough to do just that. The fact that he'd have preferred the latter choice was obvious. It made up Pavel's mind in record time.

"All right. All right. But I have to insist that they place me in the sunbelt. I won't go to some godforsaken town that doesn't warrant even a large dot on a world atlas. I'll need some kind of cosmetic surgery, but I get to pick the surgeon. Perhaps the genius who did this." He waved his hand in front of his face. "And I want to have access to all my accounts. And I have to bring Saucy. She knows just the right places to massage. Stress. What it does to my neck…well…"

Skye wanted to punch his lights out but restrained herself with the thought that Barclay had already cleaned out all of his accounts and that the delusional little piss-ant would be incarcerated in a federal facility, in isolation, for the rest of his life.

"Let's go," nodded Skye, agreeing to nothing.

"Look, you brainless bimbo from bumpkinland, don't rush me. I have to pack. There are a thousand things to do."

"How about we get a head start on modifying your facial features." Alex had reigned in his fury long enough. He buried his fist into Pavel's face, putting a huge portion of his pent-up anger into the punch. All it took was one. Pavel crumpled to the floor bleeding from his destroyed nose and mouth.

"Feel better?" asked Skye.

"Much, thanks."

"Your hand okay?"

"Yeah." Alex felt like shaking it out, but restrained himself.

"Well, you're carrying him."

"Maybe I can just drag him around awhile."

"Do we stay here or take him back to the plane?"

Alex glanced at his watch. "With our fire power, we can hold them for at least twenty more minutes if the Russian hit team breaks through. Our people are almost here. The route to the plane is vulnerable and the runway is nearly all exposed."

Skye nodded. Her preference would have been to take off, but she bowed to Alex's superior tactical knowledge. Alex got on the phone with the special ops team on the road. They were armed, ready and would be there in fifteen to twenty minutes.

"Do we stay here?" she asked, looking around.

"No. We go up. Easier to defend. Harder to find. Can you make the stairs?"

Even though her knees were a bit weak, she nodded. There was no choice, and when there was no choice, the answer was easy. She took both weapons as Alex hoisted Pavel onto his shoulder.

"The little creep could have done without a steady diet of pastries and imported wine," he grunted.

"At least you shut him up and took him out of the equation. I'd have hated to rely on his silence and discretion if Russian persistence wins over the hired guns' firepower."

They were halfway up the back stairs when that was exactly what happened. Gunshots stopped abruptly. That meant that all the Russians were dead, all of Pavel's men were dead, or they declared a cease-fire. When they heard shouting in Russian, they had their answer and knew they were going to stand and defend. It wasn't lost on them that they were now in a position of defending the man who had nearly cost one of them her life.

They chose a room on the far end of the third floor with two routes of escape should they be discovered. Alex heaved Pavel on a bed and checked the doors that lead to a balcony on the far side of the room. Skye stayed at the door to the hallway. They'd been careful not to let Pavel's gushing face leave a blood trail and she felt confident they could stay hidden until reinforcements arrived.

"I see two on the lawn," whispered Alex glancing over at Skye. "If we leave them there, our people will be engaged immediately. They're in a superior position, each with two automatic weapons." They both knew if he took them out, anyone nearby watching or listening would know their location. If he didn't, their colleagues could catch a volley of bullets as they drove into the perimeter.

Skye nodded at the question in his eyes. "Take them."

Alex looked down at Pavel. "That sorry pile of human garbage isn't worth this, Skye."

"No…but what he has stored in his brain might be. Be careful."

Alex nodded. He opened the French doors and silently stepped out onto the balcony. Taking a deep breath, he stood and took aim. Four quick, sharp pops. Two head shots each. Fast, efficient, deadly. Unfortunately, also revealing. Skye heard shouts from inside the house and feet pounding on the stairs. The hit team knew they were on the third floor now. She didn't turn as Alex came up beside her.

"Stay or run?" she asked again, tying her hair back with a scarf, preparing for either. Neither of them was dressed for a shootout…no Kevlar, no rifles, no large cache of ammunition. Still, they stood ready…stood together.

"Stay," he said and got back on the phone. The team was less than five miles out. Alex gave them their exact location. "I'll watch the yard and the perimeter," he told the commander in charge of the extraction team. "My partner has the hallway and the door."

Alex pulled a large dresser in front of her before taking his place at the balcony. Two men rushed out of the house and began returning his fire. Skye and Alex put their concern for each other aside. It would get in the way and they both knew it.

A few bullets smashed into the door and the dresser announcing the presence of the enemy in the hallway. Skye wisely stayed covered. Let them come to me, she thought. And two of them did, moving efficiently down the long corridor, taking shelter in the recessed doorways, firing to cover their progress. Skye timed it all, noticing their patterns, calculating the risks. She crawled over to the opposite side of the doorway. Then when she knew they were moving, not shooting, she exposed herself and got two of them. Legs and heads. She was sure they had vests. She heard screams of pain, but didn't keep her head up long enough to determine how much damage she did.

She recognized the sound of Alex's gun and the fact that he'd stopped, hopefully, to reload. She didn't take her eyes off the hallway to check him…she couldn't.

"I see them, they're coming up the road" shouted Alex over the sound of automatic gunfire, shattering glass and fracturing wood. It gave Skye's heart a lift. Not the fact that reinforcements had arrived, but that Alex was sound and safe.

More shouting from outside the room indicated that a lookout had spotted the special ops team, as well. Was the hit team going to fight, run, or surrender? The splintering of the wood next to where she'd been standing when she'd taken her shots answered that question. They were going to stand and fight. It was a foolish decision.

From Alex's strategically superior vantage point, he brought the team in safely. Russian gunmen unlucky enough to try to get a shot at the new arrivals were cut down by Alex's expert eye. Within minutes, their team had passed under him into the house and he spotted no more unfriendlies from his site.

The shooting outside the door accelerated and Skye kept her head down. Alex came up behind her to cover the door as she repositioned herself and reloaded. Together they defended their location, returning fire and laying cover for the new forces coming up the stairs.

After another ten minutes of fierce fighting, the shooting stopped.

"All clear!" came a shout and the sign was repeated several times down the long hallway. The air was cloudy with gun smoke and a few of the injured called out their surrender in heavily accented English.

"Standing down," shouted Skye, collapsing against the dresser.

"Skyler Madison? Is that you? Everyone in there all right?" A deep familiar voice came from the far end of the smoky hallway.

"Jack?" Skye forced herself to stand up straight, a delighted smile on her face. She shoved her gun into her waistband.

"Hey, fly girl, can't you stay out of trouble. I swear all I have to do is follow the smell of gun smoke to find you." A very handsome well-built man in the fatigues of Special Operations came striding toward her. "I'm getting tired pulling your sweet winged 36 C-cups out of the fire."

"Seems you have selective memory, ground slug. I remember hauling your sorry ass up a long steep hill in Columbia last year."

The man came around the dresser and grabbed Skye, giving her a hard, lustful kiss on the mouth. "Well, you know what they say, fly girl…once you've saved a man's life, you have to rub his back, fix his meals and make love to him every night."

Skye laughed. "Never heard that one."

"That's because you hang with the wrong people." He gave her another kiss. Then saw her pallor. "You hit?"

"No, just some residual fatigue," she said and when Jack raised his eyebrows questioningly. "It's classified."

"Well, hold on to me buttercup…I came with a full charge." After a closer look, he got more serious. "You need our medic?"

"Not unless she has a BLT, a diet Pepsi and a hair brush."

Jack laughed and shook his head. "Didn't know we'd see you this trip. Talk about a sandwich, you still look good enough to eat." He held her out for inspection, his affection obvious. "Lost weight though. Been pining away for me? When are you going to come to your senses, come back to me and have my babies?"

Frowning, Alex cut his conversation with Jim off in mid-sentence. It was time to mark his territory.

"Stand down, Colonel. I got married." She flashed her rings. "As a matter of fact, I'm on my honeymoon."

"Married?" Astonishment flashed on his face, then faded into a smile. "After you turned me down at least a hundred times? Time to get an annulment, buttercup, and come away with me. What kind of wussey lets his bride out of the bedroom to go on assignment?"

Skye saw Alex coming over fast and tried to pry herself out of the circle of Jack's arms. There was fire in her husband's eyes and he still had one full magazine.

"Jackson, I want you to meet my partner, Richard Shultis."

Still keeping an arm around Skye's waist, Jack shot out his hand. "Hey. Nice shooting, Richard. I appreciate the cover. From where those hired guns were located, we would have had our hands full trying to secure the perimeter. Taking them out before we got here made it easy for us. I appreciate it. You saved lives today."

Alex frowned, torn between wanting to smash his fist in the man's face and accepting the compliment and shaking his hand. Since his bride was gently extricating herself from Jack's too-intimate hold and a compliment from this obviously competent soldier was an ego booster, he opted for the latter.

"My pleasure. I didn't get the name."

"Lieutenant Colonel Jackson Larabee. I hear you have a package for me."

Alex nodded over to the bed where Pavel still lay prone and unconscious.

"Good God. Appears to be little damaged. Looks like your work." Jack smiled at Skye. Alex thought the smile was far too familiar for a professional occasion and was reassessing his first inclination to pound on Lieutenant Colonel Jackson Larabee's face. Skye caught the vibe and decided it was time to exit.

"Actually it's Richard's work. He was closer to the little prick. He's all yours with our compliments."

"How about we meet later for a drink and you can fill me in," asked Jack, his smile turning provocative and inviting. Alex frowned. Men were pigs. Didn't Skye just tell him she got married?

"I can't. A member of my team was injured in the initial response and I want to go check on her."

Jack didn't even argue, just nodded. She had her priorities just where they should be.

"We'll get to cleaning up the place," he said and seemed to be compelled to start with

Skye's hair. Reaching out, he flicked a chunk of wood out of one of her curls. Alex's eyes narrowed. He wanted to do that.

When Skye took one last look around, Jack's eyes changed. Alex caught the flash of longing before the bravado snapped back into place when she turned to him. He hid it well, but Alex's perception was supercharged by a surge of pure annoyance. There definitely was a story here.

"We'll leave you to it then."

"Need some help getting to your conveyance?" Jack didn't like the tremble he saw go through Skye. He knew from experience it wasn't residual post battle stress.

"I'll take it from here," said Alex, sliding his arm around Skye's waist.

Jack nodded reluctantly. "Well, it was great seeing you, fly girl. You got my number. Call me sometime."

"It was good seeing you too, Jack. Thanks for the backup." She extended her hand this time, blocking any possibility of another lip lock.

"Anytime. And I do mean anytime, buttercup."

Alex thought the Colonel held on to his wife's hand a little too long, but what the hell. She was going home with him. And she did look pretty impressive in her tight fitting dress, accessorized with a Glock in her rhinestone belt and plaster dust in her hair.

Jack turned to Alex and grinned. "Thanks again, Richard. If you ever want to transfer over to Special Ops, be sure to ask for me. We could use you."

Alex nodded and shook his hand. If the guy hadn't been lusting after his wife, they probably could have gotten along very well.

Skye and Alex walked swiftly down the hall. Jack's team was efficiently checking all the rooms, assisting the wounded, tagging the dead and preserving the scene.

"Well trained," observed Alex, not ready to say what was really on his mind until they got out of the house.

"Jack's the best," agreed Skye, then thought it prudent to change the subject. "I don't want to fly out of here until the entire fuselage and aileron connections have been checked out so we need transportation. I want to get to Payton."

Alex was far from ready to change the subject, however. He was just biding his time...and the time came when they walked out of the house into the sunshine. "How come you didn't tell that asshole who I was and what I was?"

"Pavel?"

"Don't pretend you don't know who I'm talking about. He had his hands all over you and what was with all the mashing?"

"Mashing?" Skye laughed, then went on with the reasonable tone that puts all women in a superior position in the battle of logic. "First of all, darling, we agreed after that incident with Claude in France, our true relationship was on a 'need-to-know' basis."

"Well I think that letch needed to know."

"Secondly, Jack is not a letch or an asshole. Do I have to remind you he just saved us from a whole lot of hurt?"

"Yeah, well. That's his job." Alex frowned, trying to focus. How did he lose his advantage? The man, Larabee, was all over his wife. In public. In front of her new husband. The fact he didn't know who Alex was didn't mitigate the facts. And how the hell did this cocky son-of-a-bitch know his wife's bra size? Didn't seem like a lucky guess. And the name. Something about it. Jackson Larabee.

"The name is really familiar. Jackson Larabee. Colonel Larabee." Then it dawned on him. "I remember. He volunteered to lead the incursion team last summer to rescue you and Flight 127. Turned out we didn't need them, but I remember the name. Amanda put out the request and he came forward. Drew an excellent plan and stood ready in Trinidad."

That made Skye smile. Alex chose not to like the smile. Not in the least. Far too pleased and sentimental.

"He likes to get in the middle of things," she said shrugging.

"I think he likes *who* is in the middle of things. So are you going to tell me who he is?"

"He's Lieutenant Colonel Jackson Larabee, special forces attached to the Central Intelligence Agency."

"You know what I mean, buttercup."

"We worked together on several occasions."

"Yeah. I'll bet he volunteered every time."

"Honestly, Alex. That's a chapter from my former life."

"Looked like a whole damn book from where I was standing."

"Another book, another time."

"And in what section would I find this book?" asked Alex, not ready to drop it.

"Excuse me?"

"Action adventure, romantic intrigue, chick lit, x-rated bedroom escapades of a hot and horny, sex starved, special operations, letch, asshole, commander?"

Skye smiled slyly. "You're jealous."

"You're damn fucking right. It seems like every time we walk away from an op, we leave some guy panting and drooling."

Stopping in mid-stride, Skye looked up at him.

"But it's you I'm going to sleep with tonight." Her voice was soft, sultry and suggestive. It snapped his mind into a completely different direction and drained his irritation. They may look, crave and dream, but the reality was his. All his. When the irritation faded, concern flooded in. Skye was no longer pale, she was flushed. He stopped under a large tree in the front yard and turned her toward him.

"Either you're blushing from the attention of one special forces colonel or your running a temperature." When he tried to touch her forehead, she brushed his hand aside.

"We've just been through a gun battle. I'm a little warm," she said, frowning at the headache she felt behind her eyes. When she saw the look in his eye, she added. "Don't even think of carrying me out of here."

"How about I commandeer one of these vehicles and we get on the road."

Skye nodded and didn't move away from the firm grip he had around her waist.
"I want to go right to the hospital," she said.
"You do? Without a fight?"
"To see Payton," she said firmly.
Alex nodded and helped his wife into the front seat of one of the cars abandoned on the lawn. Seeing Payton might be the primary reason, but she wasn't leaving until she got checked out as well.

Night was falling and Tank continued to stare into Payton's face. The doctor said she'd wake up when her body was finished taking care of the insult to her head. There was a concussion, but she wasn't in a coma. Simply unconscious. His mom had filled him in on the op, telling him about her incredible display of marksmanship. No surprise there. His mom was pretty impressed though. Not a bad start to their life together, impressing her future mother-in-law right out of the gate. Not that they'd settled on anything like marriage yet. But in the last few hours, he'd placed it in a number-one priority position.

Tank was able to study all of her beautifully sculpted features while she lay still and silent. He looked at her hand, so small in his. He had no idea she was an Olympic gold medalist. Linda told him. Payton hadn't brought it up. So much to learn. So much more to know. He kissed her inert hand and held it gently, stroking her fingers. No rings. Not yet. Looking at his watch, he wondered if he should bug the doctor again. Only ten minutes had passed since he last asked if she was still going to be fine.

Wyatt came in once in a while and stroked his hair, doing what only a mother could do. Chase away the monsters; banish the fears. He was grateful. Mostly because it worked. When she said Payton was going to be all right, he believed her. Even more than the doctor, actually.

Outside the door, Blake and Wyatt sat with Linda and David. David held Linda's hand loosely in his. Wyatt was on the phone with Alex.
"They got him. Skye and Alex are on their way here to fill us in."
Linda smiled and nodded. Another case closed. Maybe her last one. She glanced over at David. The look on his face when she saw him at the airport was staying with her. He shouldn't have to go through that fear day after day. She didn't do the dangerous stuff like Skye, but she was close enough to it at times that something could go wrong. Fieldwork was like that. She thought of the bomb Alex had dismantled and the fact she was in the blast zone.
"Want to take a walk?" he asked.
Linda looked at the door to Payton's room, worried, but not terrified like she'd been when she saw all the blood pouring from her head.
"They'll call us if there's any change," reassured David. He had to walk or he was going to jump out of his skin. When his wife had been shot, there'd been no vigil at a hospital. Just a knock on the door and the face of his captain and the departmental

chaplain. God. He wanted to get out of there for a while, but he needed to walk with Linda. He just wanted the assurance of her beside him.

"Sure." She got up and they walked down the corridor and out the front door. It was chilly, but beautiful. Neither of them spoke as they walked the grounds. Linda knew David needed to say something and she was going to give him the time to do so.

"Linda." He cleared his throat. Good beginning, she thought, smiling. At least he could remember her name. As if to confirm it, he said it again. "Linda. I, ah…"

"Do you need to get drunk again?"

He laughed. "It does seem to help to have a few in me, but I'm going to have to do this sober. I can't always be so tongue tied."

"Pretend I'm a criminal." He had a very talented tongue and she didn't want it to be tied either.

"Okay, hands against the wall and spread 'em."

She laughed. The sound of it sailed through his heart and gave him what he needed.

"I know it's a strange time to be saying this. With Payton in the hospital. But she's going to be all right. Skye and Alex are all right and on the way in. Well." He blew out a breath. "Ah. I just want you to know that I don't consider our relationship, what we have, casual. I love you, Linda."

He stopped walking and she looked up at him. She smiled. She thought the timing wasn't strange at all. It was perfect. "I love you too, David."

He smiled back at her. Such a sweet, poignant smile. "Today. Today when I saw that ambulance pull in, I wasn't sure if my heart was still beating." He pulled her into him and held her tight. "I know for a fact, I wasn't breathing. It could have been you. Damn. I knew you weren't a computer programmer for some nameless department of the federal government when I fell in love with you, but being forced to face the fact…"

"David. You know I can't tell you."

"I know, and I respect that. I know you work with Skye, and frankly, although I have amnesia where her shadow career is concerned, I know that her work is dangerous. That kind of jeopardy is something I'm familiar with. Oh, hell. I don't even know what I'm saying here. I guess I just want to hold you." He held her gently against him, completely enveloped, both in his arms and in his emotions. "Will you stay with me tonight? Reassure my weakened heart?"

"Of course," she said, her hand moving up his chest and resting over his heart. He bent her head back and kissed her. Some of the gentleness faded in the feeling of release as his need tore through him and into her. His passion fanned by his incredible relief.

"That would be good," he said as his world became balanced once again. "Want to go back in?"

"Just a few more minutes. Let's keep walking. You told me what was on your mind, now it's my turn." She kept his hand in hers. "David. I want you to know I've talked with my boss. And with Skye. I'd hoped that someday you'd tell me what I saw in your eyes and felt in your touch. I've already decided that we need to give this…this relationship a chance. That it's important to me. That you're important to me. You and the boys," she added so he knew that she loved them too. "And I think that it will collapse in on itself if you can't be reasonably certain of my safety. I've asked for an administrative position. A real one this time. No more travel. No more danger."

David was staggered by her. Staggered and grateful. He'd never have asked her to give up anything. But his soul sang with relief. "Will that be enough? Will you be happy?"

"David," she said in a voice that had the steel he knew was there. "I will not let this relationship go. *You* make me happy. And I'll still be doing important work. I just won't need to carry a gun anymore."

"God, I love you Linda." He bent down, picked her up until her toes left the ground and kissed her. Linda could attest to the fact that his tongue was no longer tied and she moaned with pleasure under his deep and penetrating kiss. She felt a difference. Like something had opened up inside him. She meant what she said to him. This was what would make her completely happy. This and the two little bonus cards waiting at home.

"I love you too, David." And she kissed him back.

Payton stirred. Tank could feel pressure on his fingers where they lay entwined with hers. Blinking, she opened her eyes and looked around the room. They were a little blurry from the painkiller, but they were alert enough to see his face. She smiled.

"Did I get them?"

Tank laughed and did that feel good. This would be another good one for the family folklore. No disorientation or trauma here.

"Yes, darling. You did."

"All of them?"

Obviously there was no brain damage either. The doctor wasn't sure she'd remember the events leading up to her injury.

"Yes, darling. Well done."

"Thanks." She moved her head and a pain tore through it. She frowned. "Whoa. That hurt. Did I bump my head?"

"No. You were shot." He tapped the bandage lightly.

"In the head?" she asked incredulously.

"Yup."

"I guess I should have ducked," she said in a voice that was gaining strength. Tank was greatly relieved to see some life dancing in her emerald green eyes. She flexed her fingers and moved her toes. "Everything seems to be working…everything but my right hand, that is."

Raising her right hand firmly held by his, he said, "And you aren't getting it back anytime soon." His eyes turned serious. "You were lucky."

When she smiled weakly, the dimples popped out. She didn't like the look of concern on his face. "The bullet probably ricocheted. Everyone in my constabulary says I have a hard head."

Tank chuckled, but he felt more like crying with relief. Leaning over, he gave her a long hard kiss.

"Thanks, Doctor Tank," she said licking her dry lips. "Good medicine."

"Unlimited supply. But I warn you. It could get addictive." His eyes flashed happy again and Payton was glad.

"Everyone else okay?"

"Yes."

"And Skye went back and got the bloody bastard?"

"She did."

"I'm not dying or anything, right?"

"Not even close."

"Good. I'd hate to go meet my maker just having said bloody bastard."

"That probably wouldn't be a good idea."

"I feel sleepy."

"You lost a lot of blood and you have a slight concussion." He looked at her closely to assure himself that she really was just sleepy, not slipping back into unconsciousness or a coma or something. Damn he was feeling wrecked himself.

"Oh. Well, that's fine, then. Would you like to climb in here with me?" She sighed and yawned. He looked like he could use a soft bed.

"I would, but we're not alone."

"Oh. Okay."

"Later."

"Deal. I love you, my fine Chicago cop." Her eyes closed and she fell asleep. He leaned over and kissed her.

"I love you my fine," he smiled. What the hell. She was sleeping. "My fine Scottish mate."

Payton smiled as Tank softly kissed her again. She wasn't that far under yet.

Wyatt and Blake continued to sit in the waiting room. Wyatt had talked with Alex and Skye, wanting to be sure all of her children were well and accounted for. Skye was running a fever and was currently fighting with both the attending physician who wanted to admit her and her new husband, who wanted her to get medical treatment. Wyatt was fairly sure that her daughter-in-law would be sleeping in her own bed tonight.

"I guess there's no chance any of these errant children will move into the grocery business," she sighed sipping her umpteenth cup of coffee.

"I don't think so, darling. The dye has been cast."

"We were lucky today."

"I know. And maybe we will be lucky again tomorrow."

Wyatt laid her head on his shoulder. "I actually was relieved when Alex decided to go into law. Especially when he decided on get-rich law instead of prosecution." She sighed again. "Now it seems he's in the thick of it, too."

"And it looks like they all chose partners who are part of the fight."

"A passion for justice is a good thing to share in a marriage."

"It's worked for us for over 30 years."

"Damn, that's a long time." He leaned down and gave his wife a long lingering kiss. She still had blood all over her beautiful suit. He suppressed a shudder. Not hers. Not this time. He'd work on the fear, as he had throughout his marriage.

"I love you, Blake."

"I love you too, Wyatt Earp Cooper."

Skye was indeed in her own bed. Alex fumed around the room, slamming doors and grabbing a bottle of water from a small refrigerator in her bathroom. He struggled with the cover of the more aggressive antibiotics prescribed by the doctor.

"I swear if you don't take these, I'm going to turn you over and let them dissolve up your ass."

"Yes, dear," said Skye, suppressing a giggle. It wouldn't do to push her husband any further.

Alex looked over at her and scowled.

"You're sure agreeable now that you've had your own way."

"Yes, dear," said Skye in a very agreeable voice, she thought.

Alex continued to work the cover of the prescription bottle, cursing as if it were some kind of magic incantation designed to open child-proof lids. Skye was tempted to prod him. Remind him that he had to get the bottle open before she could swallow the miracle cure. But even though her marriage was only a few weeks old, she knew how the game was played and kept her mouth shut. It was a struggle, but she was determined to make it to her one-month anniversary. Thank goodness when she could no longer suppress the laugh, it came out more like a wheezing cough.

Alex immediately looked up at her, eyes narrowed.

"And I suppose that cough is some kind of reaction to the exhaust fumes floating up from the street and not because of your aggravated immune system."

"Darling, please come to bed with me." If she could get him closer, maybe she could subtly get the bottle away from him and pop it open. She really was feeling lousy and wanted to get better so her honeymoon could get back on track. "I need something to help me sleep."

"Did the doctor give you another prescription?" Damn, he thought, not another bottle.

"No, husband," she said, patting the bed beside her. "I need Dr. Springfield's cure…hot hands, soft lips, hard body. I need to have my blood pump out the germs by turning up the heat. And, darling, only you can turn it up hot enough to burn out the invasion." Being horizontal and on her own soft king sized mattress, looking at her handsome love machine, having closed another complicated case, felt like heaven. A sudden surge of well being had her eyes flare up and her lips curve seductively.

Alex could actually feel the flame and his body's reaction was immediate and burning. The top of the bottle gave up its stubborn hold and sailed across the room.

Skye laughed. "A prescriptive orgasm…how about putting those fingers in me and doing the same?"

Alex grinned, his bad temper incinerated by her invitation. He handed her the tiny tablets and the water. She made a production of placing them on her tongue and watched as her husband swiftly stripped. Wyatt had the puppy, so there would be no distractions this night.

With nothing pressing for the next day, Alex figured this would be the night they'd celebrate their marriage. They'd make love throughout the night; just hold each other when they spent their reserves, sleep in late, drink coffee naked and stay in bed all day. They'd been lucky. Time to cash in on the fates that had placed her in his path, in his bed, in his life. He climbed in beside his precious wife, took her in his arms and began his assault.

EPILOGUE

Operation Turkey Day was in full swing. The entire extended family was flown down to Alex's estate on Amelia Island in Florida for the long holiday weekend. The women decided they would take over the planning and the men, the execution. The men, however, were currently in the kitchen looking at a raw bird and a mound of unpeeled potatoes.

"But I put it in over an hour ago," griped Tank as he took the turkey out of the oven and put it on the wooden cutting board in the center of the room. He poked at it with a fork while the men stood around it like doctors in an operating theater. To a micro-waver like Tank, an hour seemed about right.

"Did you turn it on?" asked David.

"You mean did I rub its breasts and spread its thighs?" asked Tank.

"Not the bird, you idiot. The oven."

"It feels hot in there," said Nels putting his hand in the oven.

"Then why is the bird still raw?" asked Alex drinking a Corona and poking at the turkey with his finger. "Duncan, you're the mechanical genius here."

"Hey, man. I'm a vegetarian. I don't cook birds," said Duncan taking a pull on his bottle of cranberry juice. "I'm perfectly satisfied without eating flesh."

A picture of Connie flashed into nearly everyone's mind, but no one said anything. They were in the middle of a real emergency. "Well, I'm not eating nuts and berries for Thanksgiving," said Tank irritably. "This was a hell of a time for Skye to tell Cynthia to go visit her sister."

"Yeah, going to visit your family on a holiday instead of working. What a bitch," laughed Blake.

"You passed the goddamn bar exam, Alex," said Tank, not willing to concede. "How hard can this be?"

"Last time I looked, cooking a turkey dinner wasn't one of the categories on the exam," responded Alex.

"Where's the bag the bird came in?" asked David. "Aren't there directions on that?"

Tank looked absolutely blank. "The bag had directions? What? Slap it in a pan, turn on the oven and stick it in? I got that part. Anyway, I threw it out. It's probably under a bunch of coffee grounds by now." He took another look at the turkey and poked at it accusingly. Then he saw a little white bag sticking out of its butt. "What the hell does this bird have up its ass?"

"Maybe it's the directions," said David hopefully.

Tank took a fork and tried to pry it out.

"Just grab it and yank it out," said Blake.

"You must have been a chuckle a minute in the delivery room with Mom," said Alex.

"It's gross," said Tank pulling it out with two fingers.

"This from a guy who used to pick his scabs and eat dog biscuits," said Alex.

"Well, now. That stimulated my appetite," said Duncan.

"This whole thing is making me lose mine," said Tank. "Who would have thought that raw food could be so unappetizing." He read the side of the dripping package. "Says it's a gravy packet. Hey. Score. We have gravy. Doesn't look like much, but maybe you add water to it or something."

"I think it's leaking, your fork must have poked through the bag," observed David.

"Quick, a pan. We can't lose our only real asset," said Alex.

Duncan grabbed a pan from the hooks over the cutting board and Tank dumped the little white packet into it.

"There's something else in there," said Blake.

"Twins?" laughed Alex.

"Oh God. You don't think they would have left a baby turkey in there," said Tank, getting a little pale.

"First of all, turkeys lay eggs," said Alex. "They don't have babies. Secondly, this is a tom."

"I don't care what its name is," shot back Tank, preparing to dig into the cavity for the second package.

"No, I mean a tom turkey, a guy."

They opened the second package to reveal the internal organs. They all looked at the gizzard, liver and heart with something akin to revulsion. "Just when you think you have been grossed out to the barf stage, in marches an encore. What do the women do with this shit?" asked Tank.

"Feed it to the dog?" asked David. They all looked at Kevlar. He was a guy. He was part of the team.

"I don't know. It's kind of a leap to go from kibbles and bits to a heart," said Blake.

"And you wonder why I'm a vegetarian," said Duncan, chuckling.

"Hey, there's something in the other end, too," said David. He took it out and held it up. There was a universal gagging response. "What the hell?" It was curved, cylindrical and to their horrified imaginations, it looked just like a penis.

"Is that what I think it is?" asked Tank.

"Alex said it was a tom," said David.

They stared at it for a minute. "What's it doing stuffed in the neck hole?"

"I guess once the turkey is dead, it doesn't matter which end gets stuffed."

"You don't think at some point in time we've unwittingly eaten one of these…you know like maybe Mom cut it up and put it in the stuffing or something?" asked Tank trying unsuccessfully to get the picture of his mom's homemade stuffing with little bits of meat in it out of his mind.

"God. Makes me feel like I have an olive lodged in my throat," said David.

"It's got a lot of bones in it. Do turkey peckers have bones?" asked Duncan.

"They're entitled to boners, too," said David. He held it up. "It's like they have a permanent erection."

"Not a lot of meat on it," said Blake.

"Probably saw the axe coming and pulled it in," said Tank. "Just put it down, okay?"

"Guys, I think maybe it's the neck," said Alex.

"I don't care what it is, we aren't cooking it," said Tank firmly.

They all stood back and looked at the bird, now fully open at both ends.

"Anyone got a brainstorm?" asked Blake. "Do we call in the women for a consult?"

The others all said "no" in unison.

"I know," said Alex. "Let's go get Carter and Bill. It's time they paid their manly dues. They're going to have to help the side they were born into."

"Agreed," said Tank.

"Who's going out there with all those women to admit we couldn't even cook a bird?" asked David.

"Not me,"

"Not me."

"This is your house, Alex," said Tank reasonably. "You're king of the castle. Go call a couple of your subjects."

"Right. How about I just go out there and casually ask Bill and Carter to come in here and help us select a wine."

"Sounds good."

"Like a plan."

Alex walked out to where the women, along with Bill and Carter, were sitting sipping wine and looking at the hundreds of wedding pictures each had taken. Their laughter and good spirits somehow irritated him. How could they sit around like that? They had to get this show on the road if they were going to be able to catch any of the Detroit game. Their games were normally a waste, but today they were playing the Bears. He looked in the dining room and saw that the women's part of Operation Turkey Day was complete. The tables were set, the sideboard held the serving dishes and the desserts lined the buffet. Everything was in order and ready for the feast. Except the feast was raw.

Alex went over to where Bill was giving Hazel advice on how to keep her VW bug from backfiring and scaring all the neighborhood dogs. Like Skye, he had a degree in engineering and he often fixed his own vehicles. Alex figured that qualified him to be a man today…on their team, so to speak.

"Hey, Bill. How about you and Carter come on out to the kitchen and help us with the wine."

"Sure thing, Alex." He looked over at Carter who was talking to Skye. Hazel had baked a cherry pie using cherry lifesavers and they were working out an avoidance strategy. Carter's radar picked up Bill's signal and he excused himself. "Just put it close enough to the edge so that either the dog or the boys will bump it off the server. Help it along if you have to."

When they left the room, the women looked up. Wyatt grinned. "Couldn't figure out how to roast the bird."

"We should have been able to smell it cooking by now."

"Should we go in and help?" asked Linda.

"Hang tough, girls. We do it now, we do it forever," said Hazel. Since they were all afraid of Hazel's cooking, even on a good day, they decided to heed her advice.

"Did you thaw those appetizers Cynthia made before she left?" asked Sloane. "I forgot Hazel's oyster and cranberry dip. Left in on the counter."

"Even after I reminded her. Some genius," smiled Hazel good-naturedly. She'd take the dip down to the senior center the next day during the leftover grab bag potluck.

"They're in heating trays on the sideboard," said Skye. "We can serve ourselves as soon as we sort through Jason's pictures." Jason had been given his own camera and was proudly showing them all the pictures he took. He was fascinated with under the table shots and they were working on identifying the feet and ankles of the guests.

When Carter and Bill arrived in the kitchen, it looked like a scene from Animal House.

"What the hell?" laughed Bill, looking at unopened bags of stuffing mix, cans of cranberry sauce, bunches of vegetables, bags of potatoes, bakery boxes and a huge raw turkey sitting in the center of the room like a bird sacrifice on a pagan altar. "Looks like Tank isn't the only big turkey in town."

"Oh, ha, ha. Like that one hasn't been used six times today," said Tank, rolling his eyes.

"Come on, guys," said Alex. "You're the closest thing we have to an x chromosome. I swear you have to have one to be able to coordinate something of this magnitude."

Carter looked at Bill and nodded. "We have the perfect solution. But Alex. This is going to cost you."

"Anything. I just want to watch football."

"Well then break out the beer and pretzels and make way for the genius." He reached into his pocket. They all thought he was going to whip out a wand or something, but nothing so dramatic. He opened his cell phone and dialed.

"Franny? Carter. You doing your thing today? Great. Can you handle an emergency?" He held the phone out as someone on the other end screamed at him.

"Darling. I know. I know what time it is. But, sweetheart, I'm here to deliver the magic words. Money is no object. That's right." He listened for a moment, then looked at Alex. "What was the final count?"

"Better make it 20. We have Duncan and Tank."

"Around twenty, chéri." He held the phone out again. "That would be fine. Just fine." Carter ended transmission and grinned. "Turkey dinner for 20 to be picked up at 5:00. Duncan, you're going to have to disappear for about an hour and take the limo. You'll need the room. And Alex, cash in your Disney stock, because this is going to cost you. David, you go out to the hutch in the dining room and secure every large bowl you can find. Tank, you make sure the ladies are occupied and then lock the doors. There's nothing that needs to be done until 4:00, when Duncan will leave. Operation Turkey Dinner has just been changed to Operation Deception."

"You mean we're free until then?" asked Tank.

"As a bird." He looked over at the raw turkey. "Well, maybe not *that* bird."

"You are Caesar," said Tank. "We bow before you. We worship at your feet."

"What are we going to do with all this stuff?" asked Duncan.

"Box it up and take it down to the food bank on your way to Franny's"

"Good idea," nodded Duncan and the men folk put their backs into piling the food in the car.

When they came back into the empty kitchen, Blake stood and stared at the door to the dining room. "I'm married to and you're the children of a crack detective. She'll know."

"She'll suspect. She won't know if we don't confess," responded Alex.

"Good point."

"Now lock the door, grab the beer and let's turn on the TV." They went into the family room that was attached to the kitchen and settled in to participate in their Thanksgiving ritual. Football followed by a little football, chased down with a little more football.

Thanksgiving dinner turned out to be a loud, chaotic affair and Skye loved it. Someone found a catering wrapper stuck to the bottom of the gravy bowl, but no one mentioned it again. It would be revisited, no doubt, but for this day, everyone concentrated on the eating, the laughing, and, it seemed, the loving.

Wyatt looked around the table. Tank and Payton were mining the carcass, trying to find the wishbone. Neither one of them was sure just where it would be located. Tank was still sticking to root beer and Payton was well on her way to a full recovery. David sat and watched Linda cut his kid's meat. He obviously thought that was just about the sexiest thing a woman could do. She looked at Skye at one end of the long table and Alex at the other. Pretty far apart, given the length of the table, but completely together. The looks they gave each other would have ignited the candles if they hadn't already been lit. A year ago, all three of her boys were alone. Unattached and unsettled, somehow. Now they all looked connected…contented and marvelously happy.

"So," said Duncan. "Does the Little Brother have a mate?" He was munching on the stuffing, homemade biscuits, squash, and mashed potatoes, leaving the rest of the family to chew the bird. Connie was thoroughly enjoying ripping through an entire leg and smacking her lips. Their culinary differences didn't seem to be a barrier to their obvious attraction.

"He does indeed," grinned Tank. "Payton has a lot of things to clear off her desk in Scotland when she's able to travel. But as soon as that's done, she'll be making a permanent move to Chicago." Tank kissed the palm of her hand. "Maybe she can travel after the first of the year."

"I think that's stretching a scratch like this a wee bit." She touched the side of her head. She'd combed her hair over the healing wound and contemplated the interesting hairdo Bill had suggested to blend in the growing hair to the rest of her cropped style. It was coming back in a silvery gray. It would probably never have pigmentation again. Carter said the exotic silver steak would give her an interesting and distinctive cachet.

"I'll have some vacation time by then and can go with you," he said. He intended to stay close; the image of her blood dripping off the gurney was fading, but not completely gone.

"Lovely. All my friends over there will see what lured me west."

"How about we get married before we go," said Tank around a mouthful of pumpkin pie.

She gaped at him and shook her head. "How about we talk about an engagement first."

"All right. But I already talked to the Santa on the corner of Michigan and Ohio and he promised me I'd get what I wanted under the tree if I was very, very good."

The fire in Payton's eye assured him that she'd give him everything he wanted under the tree and anywhere else. Especially since she could attest to the fact that he was very, very good…at least he had been in the shower that morning. A great combination of both naughty and nice.

"Darling, I have a great deal to do before Santa delivers. I have to close some cases. Pack my things. Sell my house. Then I have to find a new job over here. That could all take a while."

Tank looked at his mom and smiled.

"I guess now is the time I enter with the potential solution to one of the items on your list. I meant to talk with you privately, but in this family that means no less than a dozen people." She saw Payton's smile and decided to go on. "Every U.S. Attorney's office has established an LECC, a Law Enforcement Coordinating Committee, made up of federal, state and local law enforcement personnel. Its major function is to improve the coordination and cooperation of various agencies working in the same area and there are a few openings in the northern Illinois District. I think you would be ideally suited for the position. They're looking for people with solid police credentials who can coordinate big cases. If you're interested, a woman by the name of Dorothy Martinez would like to talk with you next week."

Payton didn't say anything for a few seconds. She was stunned. It was precisely the kind of thing she'd consider a dream job. She thought it would take her years to find something like this over here. On the other hand, there was the potential of perceived favoritism. Of unfair nepotism. Of using family connections. All kidding aside, she was going to be the daughter-in-law of Wyatt Cooper and Blake Springfield. Then she smiled. *Well, I guess that means I'll have to be especially good*, she thought. And she knew she'd be especially good.

She looked at Tank, who could barely contain his excitement. She could see it was tinged with a little apprehension as well.

Tank wasn't all together sure of her reaction. Would she think he was trying to control her life? He was the one who asked his mom to check it out. This was a job that would get her off the street, he thought. He wasn't sure he'd be able to handle seeing her bloody ever again. It still gave him the shakes to think about it. Payton was pretty head strong, though. Even if it was a great opportunity, she might turn it down because she was being a stubborn Scot. The seconds ticked by. Shit, he thought, she was pissed. She wanted to do everything herself. Well, damn it. That was nearly impossible in this family.

Then she looked back at Wyatt. "'Tis a risk to be recommending a woman who will be part of the family soon."

"No risk. I saw you operate under fire, remember," said Wyatt. "And there's no 'soon' about it. Whether or not you decide to put up with Tank for the rest of your life, consider yourself part of the family now."

Payton nodded and grinned. She had no family and never really had. She loved her mother and they'd repaired their relationship after her father had died, but it had just been the two of them. A family. A family *and* Tank. A family *and* Tank *and* a dream job. Perfect. Christmas had come early this year. "Then if it's all the same to you, Captain, I'll call Ms. Martinez. Then do you proud. And," she looked at the grinning Tank. "Take him off your hands in the bargain."

"Hey Uncle Tank, are you going to get married?" shouted Jason. He was listening to everything and it finally fell into place for him

"Yes." Tank grinned.

"To Payton?" Both he and Al loved Payton. She talked so different...like someone in the movies. Plus she got shot. Actually shot. For real.

"Sure am."

"Wow. How great is that?" shouted Al.

"I'd say it redefines great," said Tank.

"Huh?" said Jason and Al at the same time with the same wide-eyed look on their faces.

"Never mind," laughed Tank. Payton watched him with his nephews and liked what she saw. She wanted a family. Maybe not right away, but she wanted a few wee Tanks someday. That was for sure.

"Okay," nodded Jason, satisfied and ready to move on. "Hey! Dad and Linda are getting married too, you know."

Suddenly the people around the table got very silent. All eyes moved to David, who'd been chatting with Linda and Skye. He looked over at his oldest son with something that looked like horror.

"What's this?" asked Wyatt, ever the investigator.

Jason was grinning, although he was a little self-conscious now that everyone, including his Dad and Linda, were looking at him. And Al was poking at him, making it a little difficult to think. But he'd put it together, all right and he was going to show everyone Sloane wasn't the only genius in the family.

"Well I'm going to be a cop, like grandma, when I grow up. A detective."

"We all know that," said Tank.

"Okay. So I figured it out," he announced proudly.

"He figured it out," agreed Al hopping a little in his chair.

"Tell us," laughed Skye. They'd all come to the same conclusion, but she wanted to hear it from a child's perspective.

"Okay. First, he took Mom's ring off his finger and put it with her badge and my tooth."

"And my booties," added Al, wanting to be a part of the investigation and report.

"Yeah. And that means he's free now."

That brought a few tissues out, but he proceeded. David looked at Linda, just Linda.

"Then they're always making googly eyes at each other."

"Yeah! Great big fat googly eyes," shouted Al. He thought his bother was a genius and really liked his vocabulary most of all. He started making some googly eyes of his own to help make the point. David tore his eyes away from Linda and watched his youngest demonstrate the fine art of making googly eyes. He wasn't sure if he was appalled or amused. Linda was sure. She was definitely enjoying Jason's presentation of his case and Al's delightful rendition of David's googly eyes.

"And last night when Linda was reading to us, I asked her if she'd come live with us." Jason looked so much like his father as he was ticking off his case, they all had to smile.

"Yeah, he asked her if she'd come live with us," confirmed Al.

"And she said she'd even marry Dad if that's what she had to do to get us."

Linda put her face in her hands. She was laughing, but she wasn't sure she wanted to meet David's eyes right then. She'd also noticed David's bare ring finger. She was sure he meant to propose, but they barely had ten minutes alone together and David was a man who had to work up to things.

"So I figured it out," said Jason with a final nod, accepting the sounds of approval from around the table.

"He figured it out. He figured it out," punctuated Al in case anyone missed it.

David cleared his throat. He just stared at the two boys, not sure if he should laugh, give them a time out, or just lock them in a closet until they were 18. They were smiling up at him, proud and, he thought, a little hopeful.

"Ah. Okay. Maybe I should ask Linda to go for a walk with me," said David finally.

"Don't blow it, Dad," warned Jason gravely.

"Yeah, Dad. Don't blow it," said his little echo.

"Yeah, Dave. Don't blow it," said Tank, earning a swat from Wyatt.

Linda lowered her hands to reveal glowing eyes. They gave him his answer. It made asking the question far easier. David looked around at all the people in his life that meant the most to him, who were with him through all the joy and all the sorrow. What the hell. He reached into his pocket and pulled out a small box.

"Never mind the walk. Jason, do you and Al want to help me with this?"

They shot out of their chairs, Jason spilled his milk and Al tripped over Kevlar, but they got lined up real fast next to Linda. David reached out and took her hand in his.

"I always considered myself lucky to have found one woman I could love. I never thought I'd find another. But I have. I love you, Linda." He glanced at his sons, then back at Linda, love pouring out of his eyes.

"Dad!" Both the boys said simultaneously, moving nervously on their feet. They were pretty freaked out hearing the love thing. They wanted to get right to the big question.

"We come as a package deal," smiled David.

Jason started chanting "Ask her." Al, of course, took up the chorus. Tank kept his mouth shut. He was sitting way too close to his mother.

Linda and David were looking at each other, the message delivered and answered between them. Finally David said, "Knock knock."

"Who's there," asked Linda laughing. Both boys completely stopped their chanting. They were so impressed, they were speechless.

"Will."

"Will who?"

"Will you marry us?"

Linda looked down at Jason and Al, now laughing with delight. Their moment of speechlessness only a brief respite. They were yelling their approval. How cool was that proposal, anyway?

"Marry us, marry us." They chanted, jumping up and down. They decided to provide additional incentive. Something to get Linda to say yes for sure.

"We'll make our beds," said Jason. "Without being asked."

"And brush our teeth."

"And pick up our toys."

"And take our baths." That stopped Al's bouncing. He just stared at his brother, then shrugged. He'd get him back.

"And eat our broccoli," he said forgetting he hated broccoli, too.

Linda looked up at David, her eyes brimming with laughter. "When opportunity knocks…"

"Open the door," he said, knowing he'd get his answer, but was as curious as Linda on how far his children would go.

"And comb our hair," said Jason, now talking more to Al. Al's hair never looked combed.

"And quit eating our boogers," said Al.

"And hit the toilet every time," shouted Jason.

"And not pull Mikaela James's hair."

"And never spill my milk."

"Or my juice."

"Or cereal."

"And I won't forget to put my dirty underwear in the hamper."

"Me either."

"And never jump on the bed."

"Or the couch."

"Or the chair."

"Or the…the…" Al couldn't think of another thing they jumped on, and neither could Jason so they just started wriggling, twisting and shouting.

"Say yes! Say yes!" This time Tank didn't care. He started chanting, too.

Linda looked up at David. "I guess we got as much as we're going to get."

David nodded. He liked the sound of that 'we'. "And your answer would be…"

"I say…" she looked at the boys who stopped shouting at her dramatic pause. "Yes."

David pulled her to him and completely grossed out his two boys by giving his future wife a powerful, passionate kiss to the applause of everyone in the room.

"Oh phewy," choked Al, rolling around on the floor holding his stomach and making gagging noises until Kevlar jumped all over him, barking and licking the gravy off the underside of his chin, making him giggle.

"Jeez Dad, get a room," said Jason.

David tore his eyes from Linda and frowned at his oldest. "What?"

"Tank told me to say that," he said innocently, jumping on top of Al and Kevlar and, considering the married thing all settled, moved on to wrestling.

David opened the box and took out the ring that Skye helped him pick out the week before. He put it on her finger. "God, we need you," he said laughing.

She laughed too, admired the ring greatly, winked at Skye and turned to get hugged by the entire clan. She'd never in her life been happier.

Things started winding down as the sun set. Everyone was stuffed, happy, and ready for a nap. Alex grabbed Skye's hand and led her out the French doors to the terrace overlooking the beach. Skye leaned against the ledge and breathed deeply of the salt air then smiled up at her husband.

"Happy Anniversary, darling," said Alex bringing a single white gardenia from behind his back.

"One month," she took it from him and smelled deeply of the blossom. He sat down on the ledge next to her and put his arm around her. She rested her head against his chest and listened to her favorite tune…the steady beat of his heart. "Are you ready to try again on that honeymoon?"

"We leave on Monday," he said turning her in his arms. "I rented the entire castle this time. We'll have the place completely to ourselves."

"Oh Alex, how perfect. The same castle?" She looked up at him, delighted. Then saw a shadow pass quickly through his eyes. Her imagination? "No bad memories?"

"Some, but I figure we're both stronger than any bad memories. I really liked the place…for about the first ten minutes. And I want to build some new memories to drown out the old ones." He looked into her expressive brown eyes, filled with love and compassion and decided he didn't need to hide the shadow.

"The endless hours in that room, not knowing where you were…what happened to you. Then the knock on the door…Payton handing me what she thought was conclusive evidence of your death…in that damn evidence bag." He cleared his throat. "For a brief moment, I thought you were dead. I can't describe my feelings in words. We can't have anything that haunts us and this haunts me. I want to go back there. I want to put that awful moment to rest and I need to have you there with me to do that."

She nodded, going back to a night when she thought he'd been killed. There was such bone numbing grief and agonizing sadness that life no longer seemed worth living. A feeling so hollow that it had to be worse than death itself. She turned into his chest and held him tight. Finally, a way of paying him back for the nights of comfort he gave her during her nightmares. Hers were gone now…time to tackle his. "I understand completely."

"Yeah. I knew you would."

"We'll go back together." She looked up at him. "You said 'for a brief moment.' You knew, despite the evidence, that I was alive?"

"Yes. I was certain. Jim thought I was delusional and Payton thought I was a possible suspect. But when I held the compass and looked into my heart, I knew your heart was still beating. That you weren't the dead body they found with your rings and your uniform."

"You knew that body wasn't mine because you felt my heart still beating?"

"Yes. Yes, I did. As long as we live, our hearts are connected." He reached into his pocket and pulled out the compass. "It pointed the way to you, darling. I felt you in my heart, and I knew in my soul that you were still out there."

He lowered his head and put all his love into a kiss that had their two hearts beating faster. "Well, wife. Shall we call it a day and go upstairs to our marriage bed?"

"It's only 7:00."

"It has to be midnight somewhere."

"Good point." Laughing, hand in hand, they snuck up the stairs to celebrate their anniversary. Fate had put them together. Love made their hearts beat as one. Destiny assured their future.

Also by E. K. Barber:

Flight into Danger

Captain Skyler Madison is a seasoned pilot and the youngest person ever to make the rank of Captain for a major airline. Alexander Springfield is a multi-millionaire who made his fortune in real estate. They are both highly successful professionals...and they both have a secret. They spend a part of their lives in the shadows as highly trained Special Agents for the intelligence gathering division of the Justice Department. The irresistible pull of their physical attraction and the passion they share for justice move them toward a partnership, both as colleagues and as lovers, while they resolve a case involving drug deals, murder, betrayal and near tragedy. Get your ticket aboard the Flight into Danger. It is well worth the ride.

Flight into Terror

Alex waits in the terminal for Skyler, who is taking her last flight with International Airlines before she begins her new life as a private pilot for Alex's newly formed company, Skyward Corporation. He has white Gardenias in his hand, a diamond ring in his pocket and anticipation in his heart. A heart that is in danger of exploding in his chest when International Airlines must make the announcement all airlines dread and all friends and family fear. International Airlines flight 127 from London has disappeared from the radar screen. Skye's plane has been hijacked...and have the hijackers picked the flight to terrorize! In the cockpit is their greatest nightmare...not only a legendary pilot, but a one woman intelligence unit with incredible connections. Saving her plane and its passengers costs her both a physically and emotionally. In addition, Alex's bold assistance in the rescue brings into clearer focus the risk she is taking by loving him. She overcomes her personal demons, while facing real danger once again.